THE ENEMY

A step sounded in the corridor to Sten's left. He turned . . . And faced a figure that had likewise stopped still, one robed in black, the robes glittering with many small discs. Mri. Kel'en. The golden eyes above the veil were astonished. A slim bronze hand went to the knife at his belt and hesitated there.

The enemy. The destroyers of Kiluwa and Talos and Asgard. Sten had never seen one in the flesh at this range. Only the eyes, the hands were uncovered. The tall figure remained utterly still, wrapped in menace and in anger.

"I am Sten Duncan," he found courage to say. "I'm the assistant to the Federations envoy."

"We should not have met," said the other, and with that the mri turned on his heel and stalked off in the direction from which he had come, a black figure that vanished into shadows at the turning of the corridor. Duncan found himself trembling in every muscle. He had seen mri that close only in photographs, and all of those were dead.

We should not have met, the mri had said . . .

Someone was being deceived.

DAW TITLES BY C.J. CHERRYH

THE ALLIANCE-UNION UNIVERSE

The Company Wars
DOWNBELOW STATION

The Era of Rapprochement
SERPENT'S REACH
FORTY THOUSAND IN GEHENNA
MERCHANTER'S LUCK

The Chanur Novels
THE PRIDE OF CHANUR
CHANUR'S VENTURE
THE KIF STRIKE BACK
CHANUR'S HOMECOMING
CHANUR'S LEGACY

The Mri Wars
THE FADED SUN:KESRITH
THE FADED SUN: SHON'JIR
THE FADED SUN: KUTATH

Merovingen Nights (Mri Wars Period)
ANGEL WITH THE SWORD

The Age of Exploration
CUCKOO'S EGG
VOYAGER IN NIGHT
PORT ETERNITY

The Hanan Rebellion
BROTHERS OF EARTH
HUNTER OF WORLDS

*Forthcoming in hardcover from DAW Books

THE
FADED SUN

BOOK ONE
KESRITH

BOOK TWO
SHON'JIR

BOOK THREE
KUTATH

C.J. CHERRYH

DAW BOOKS, INC.
DONALD A. WOLLHEIM, FOUNDER
375 Hudson Street, New York, NY 10014

ELIZABETH R. WOLLHEIM
SHEILA E. GILBERT
PUBLISHERS
www.dawbooks.com

First Paperback Printing, January 2000
6   7   8   9

DAW TRADEMARK REGISTERED
U.S. PAT. OFF. AND FOREIGN COUNTRIES
—MARCA REGISTRADA
HECHO EN U.S.A..

PRINTED IN THE U.S.A.

KESRITH:
For Don Wollheim, with most especial appreciation

SHON'JIR:
To Elsie Wollheim . . . for being Elsie

KUTATH:
To Betsy Wollheim . . . for carrying it all forward

BOOK ONE

KESRITH

Chapter One

Wind-child, sun-child, what is Kath?
Child-bearers, laugh-bringers, that is Kath.

It was a game, *shon'ai,* the passing-game, Kel-style, in the dim
round hall of the Kel, the middle tower of the House—black-
robed men and a black-robed woman, a circle of ten. Warriors,
they played the round not like children, with a pair of stones,
but with the spinning blades of the *as'ei,* that could wound or
kill. On the name-beat, the snap of fingers, the *as'ei* flew across
the seated circle of players, and skilled hands seized the hilts in
mid-turn, to beat the time and hurl the blades on in the next
name-beat.

Fire-child, star-child, what is Kel?
Sword-bearers, song-weavers, that is Kel.

They played without words, with only the rhythm of their
hands and the weapons, flesh and steel. The rhythm was as old as
time and as familiar as childhood. The game had more meaning
than the act, more than the simplicity of the words. The Game of
the People, it was called.

Dawn-child, earth-child, what is Sen?
Rune-makers, home-leaders, that is Sen.

A kel'en who flinched, whose eye failed or whose wits wandered, had no value in the House. The boys and girls and women
of the Kath played with stones to learn their skill. Those who be-

came kel'ein played thereafter with edged steel. The Kel, like the mothers and children of the gentle Kath, laughed as they played. They of Kel-caste were brief and bright as moths. They enjoyed life, because they knew this.

> *Then-child, now-child, what are we?*
> *Dream-seekers, life-bearers, we are—*

A door opened, echoing, the sound rolling through the hollows and depths of the tower. Sen Sathell broke in upon them, suddenly and without warning or courtesies.

The rhythm ceased. The blades rested in the hands of Niun, the youngest kel'en. The Kel as a whole inclined their heads in respect to Sathell s'Delas, chief of Sen-caste, the scholars. Gold-robed he was, like light breaking into the dark hall of the martial Kel, and he was very old—the oldest man of all in the House.

"Kel'anth," he said quietly, addressing Eddan, his counterpart in the Kel, "—kel'ein—news has come. The rumor is the war has ended. The regul have asked the humans for peace."

There was utter silence.

An abrupt move. The *as'ei* whirred and buried points in the painted plaster of the far wall.

The youngest kel'en rose and veiled himself, and stalked from the gathering, leaving shock in his wake.

The sen'anth and the kel'anth looked at each other, old men and kinsmen, helpless in their distress.

And from the deepest shadows one of the dusei, a brown, slope-shouldered mass larger than a man, stirred and rose, ambling forth into the light in that mournful, abstracted manner of dusei. It pushed its way irreverently between the two elders, thrusting its massive head at the kel'anth, who was its master, seeking comfort.

Kel'anth Eddan patted the beast with age-smooth fingers and looked up at the old scholar who, outside the divisions of caste and duty, was his half-brother. "Is the news beyond any doubt?" he asked, the least trace of hope yet remaining in his voice.

"Yes. The source is regul official communications, no city rumor. It seems completely reliable." Sathell gathered his robes about him and, tucking them between his knees, settled on the carpeted floor among the kel'ein, who eased aside to make room for him in their circle.

They were, these ten, the elders of the House, save one.

They were mri.

In their tongue, when they made this statement, they were merely saying that they were of the People. Their word for other species was tsi'mri, which meant not-people, and summed up mri philosophy, religion, and the personal attitudes of the elders at once.

They were, as a species, golden-toned. Mri legends said that the People were born of the sun: skin, eyes, coarse shoulder-length manes, all were bronze or gold. Their hands and feet were narrow and long, and they were a tall, slender race. Their senses, even in great age, were very keen, their hearing in particular most sensitive. Their golden eyes were lid-folded, double-lidded as well, for a nictitating membrane acted on reflex to protect their vision against blowing dust.

They were, as outsiders believed, a species of warriors, of mer-cenaries—for outsiders saw the Kel, and rarely the Sen, and never the Kath. Mri served outsiders for hire—served the regul, the massive tsi'mri merchants native to Nurag of the star Mab. For many centuries, mri kel'ein had hired out to protect regul com-merce between-worlds, generally hired by one regul company as defense against the ambitions and ruthlessness of some business rival, and mri had therefore fought against mri. Those years and that service had been good for the People, this trying of one kel'en of a certain service against the kel'en of another, in proper and traditional combat, as it had always been. Such trials-at-arms refined the strength of the People, eliminating the weak and unfit and giving honor to the strong. In those days the tsi'mri regul had recognized themselves to be incapable of fighting and unskilled in planning strategies, and sensibly left all matters of conflict to the mri Kel to settle in the mri fashion.

But for the last forty years, mri had served all regul combined against all humans, a bitter and ugly conflict, lacking honor and lacking any satisfactions from the enemy. The mri elders were old enough to remember the life before, and knew therefore what changes had been wrought by the war; and they were not pleased with them. Humans were mass-fighters, animals of the herd, and simply understood no other way of war. Mri, who fought singly, had early suspected this, tested it with their lives, found it bitterly true. Humans rejected *a'ani*, honorable combat, would not respect challenge, understood nothing but their own way, which was widespread destruction.

Mri had bent themselves to learn humanity, the way of the enemy, and had begun to adjust their operations and their manner of service to the regul accordingly. Mri were professionals when it came to combat. Innovation in the yin'ein, the ancient weapons that were used in *a'ani*, was dishonorable and unthinkable; but innovation in the zahen'ein, in modern arms, was a simple matter of retooling and adjusting methods, a matter of competency in the profession they followed for a livelihood.

Regul, unfortunately, were not as capable of adapting to new tactics. Regul had vast and accurate memories. They could not forget what had always occurred, but conversely they could hardly conceive at all of what had not yet happened, and did not make plans against it happening. Hitherto the regul had depended on mri entirely in the matter of their personal safety, and mri foresight—for mri could imagine—had shielded them and compensated for that regul blindness to the unexpected; but in latter days, when the war began to take regul lives and threaten regul properties, regul took matters into their own unskilled hands. Regul issued orders, prudent in their own estimation, for actions which were militarily impossible.

The mri had attempted to obey, for honor's sake.

Mri had died in their thousands, for honor's sake.

In the House, on this world, there lived only thirteen mri. Two were young. The rest were the makers of policy, a council of the old, the veteran. Long centuries ago the House had numbered more than two thousand in the Kel alone. In this present age all but these few had gone their way to the war, to die.

And their war had been lost, by regul, who asked the humans for peace.

Sathell looked about him and considered these old ones, kel'ein who had lived beyond their own years of service, whose memories gave them in some matters the perspective of sen'ein. They were Husbands to the she'pan, masters-of-arms while there had been Kath children to teach; and there was Pasev, the only surviving kel'e'en of the House, she most skilled in the yin'ein next Eddan himself. There were Dahacha and Sirain of Nisren; Palazi and Quaras and Lieth of Guragen, itself a dead House, taking refuge with the Mother of this one and adopted by her as Husbands. And from yet another dead House were Liran and Debas, truebrothers. These were part of an age that had already vanished, a time the People would not see again. Sathell felt their sadness, sensed it reflected in the beasts that huddled together in the shadows. Eddan's dus, whose species was reputedly never friendly with any caste but the warrior Kel, sniffed critically at the scholar's gold robes and suffered himself to be touched, then heaved his great bulk a little closer, wrinkled rolls of down-furred flesh, shamelessly accepting affection where it was offered.

"Eddan," said Sathell, stroking the beast's warm shoulder, "I must tell you also: it is very likely that the masters will cede this world if the humans should demand it as part of the peace."

"That would be," said Eddan, "a very large settlement."

"Not according to what we have just heard. It is rumored that the humans have secured the whole front, that the regul lords are in complete withdrawal, that the humans are in such a position now that they can touch all the contested areas. They have taken Elag."

There was silence. Elsewhere in the tower a door closed. At last Eddan shrugged, a move of his slender fingers. "Then the humans will surely demand this world. There is very little that they will miss in their desire for revenge. And the regul have left us open to it."

"It is incredible," said Pasev. "Gods! there was no need, no need at all for the regul to have abandoned Elag. The People could have held there—could have turned the humans, if they had been given the equipment."

Sathell made a helpless gesture. "Perhaps. But held for whom? The regul withdrew, took everything that was needed there for the defense, pulled ships from under their control. Now we— Kesrith—have become the border. You are right. It is very likely that the regul will not resist here either; in fact, it is not reasonable for them to do so. So we have done all that we could do. We have advised, we have warned—and if our employers refused to take that advice, then there is little we can do but cover their retreat, since we cannot restrain them from it. They took the war into their own management against our advice. Now they have lost their war; we have not. The war ceased to be ours some years ago. Now you are guiltless, kel'ein. You may justly reckon so. There is simply nothing further that can be done."

"There was something once that might have been done," Pasev insisted.

"The Sen attempted many times to reason with the masters. We offered our services and our advice according to the ancient treaty. We could not—" Sathell heard the footsteps of the youth downstairs as he spoke, and the disturbance disrupted his train of thought. He glanced hallward involuntarily as the door downstairs slammed with great violence. The sound echoed throughout all the House. He cast the Kel a look of distress. "Should not one of you at least go speak with him?"

Eddan shrugged, embarrassed in his authority. Sathell knew it. He presumed on kinship and friendship and stepped far out of bounds with Eddan when he made that protest. He loved Niun; they all did. But the autonomy of the Kel, even misguided, was sacred regarding the discipline of its members. Only the Mother could interfere within Eddan's province.

"Niun has some small cause, do you not think?" asked Eddan quietly. "He has trained all his life toward this war. He is not a child of the old way, as we are; and now he cannot enter into the new either. You have taken something from him. What do you expect him to do, sen Sathell?"

Sathell bowed his head, unable to dispute with Eddan in the matter, recognizing the truth in it, trying to see things as a young kel'en might see them. One could not explain to the Kel, could not refute them in debate nor expect foresight of them: children of a day, the kel'ein, brief and passionate, without yesterday and without tomorrow. Their ignorance was the price they paid for their freedom to leave the House and go among tsi'mri; and they knew their place. If a sen'en challenged them to reason, they must simply bow the head in their turn and retreat into silence: they had nothing with which to answer. And to destroy their peace of mind was unconscionable; knowledge without power was the most bitter condition of all.

"I think I have told you," said Sathell at last, "all that I know to tell you at the moment. I will advise you immediately if there is any further news." He arose in that silence and smoothed his robes into order, gingerly avoiding the reflexive grasp of the dus. The beast reached at his ankle, harmless in intent, but not in potential. The dusei were not to be treated with familiarity by any but a kel'en. He stopped and looked at Eddan, who with a touch rebuked the beast and freed him.

He edged round the massive paw, cast a final look at Eddan; but Eddan looked away, affecting not to be interested any further in his departure. Sathell was not willing to press the matter publicly. He knew his half-brother, and knew that the hurt was precisely because there was affection between them. There was a careful line drawn between them in public. When caste divided kinsmen, there had to be that, to save the pride of the lesser.

He gave a formal courtesy to the others and withdrew, and was glad to be out of that grim hall, heavy as the air was with the angers of frustrated men, and of the dusei, whose rage was slower but more violent. He was relieved, nonetheless, that they had listened to all that he had said. There would be no violence, no irrational action, which was the worst thing that needed be feared from the Kel. They were old. The old might reason together in groups, might consult together. The kel'en was, in youth, a solitary warrior and reckless, and without perspective.

He thought of going after Niun, and did not know what to say to him if he should find him. His duty was to report elsewhere.

And when the door closed, aged Pasev, kel'e'en, veteran of Nisren and Elag's first taking, pulled the *as'ei* from the shattered plaster and merely shrugged off the sen'anth. She had seen more years and more of war than any living warrior but Eddan himself. She played the Game all the same, as did they all, including Eddan. It was a death as honorable as one in war.

"Let us play it out," she said.

"No," said Eddan firmly. "No. Not yet."

He caught her eyes as he spoke. She looked at him plainly, aged lover, aged rival, aged friend. Her slim fingers brushed the fine edge of the steel, but she understood the order.

"Aye," she said, and the *as'ei* spun past Eddan's shoulder to bury themselves in the painted map of Kesrith that decorated the east wall.

"The Kel bore the news," said sen Sathell, "with more restraint than I expected of them. But it was not welcome, all the same. They feel cheated. They conceive it as an affront against their honor. And Niun left. He would not even hear it out. I do not know where he went. I am concerned."

She'pan Intel, the Lady Mother of the House and of the People, leaned back on her many cushions, ignoring a twinge of pain. The pain was an old companion. She had had it forty-three years, since she lost her strength and her beauty at once in the fires of burning Nisren. Even then she had not been young. Even then she had been she'pan of homeworld, ruler over all three castes of the People. She was of the first rank of the Sen, passing Sathell himself; she was above other she'panei as well, the few that still lived. She knew the Mysteries that were closed to others; she knew the name and nature of the Holy, and of the Gods; and the Pana, the Revered Objects, were in her keeping. She knew her nation to its depth and its width, its birth and its destiny.

She was she'pan of a dying House, eldest Mother of a dying species. The Kath, the caste of child-bearers and children, was dead, its tower dark and closed twelve years ago: the last of the kath'ein was long buried in the cliffs of Sil'athen, and the last children, motherless save for herself, had gone to their destinies outside. Her Kel had declined to ten, and the Sen—

The Sen was before her: Sathell, the eldest, the sen'anth, whose weak heart poised him constantly a beat removed from the Dark; and the girl who sat presently at her feet. They were the gold-robes, the light-bearers, high-caste. Her own robes were white, untainted by the edgings of black and blue and gold worn by the she'panei of lesser degree. Their knowledge was almost complete, but her own was entire. If her own heart should stop beating this moment, so much, so incalculably much could be lost to the People. It was a fearful thing, to consider how much rested on her each pulse and breath amid such pain.

That the House and the People not die.

The girl Melein looked up at her—last of all the children, Melein s'Intel Zain-Abrin, who had once been kel'e'en. At times the kel-fierceness was still in Melein, although she had assumed outwardly the robes and the chaste serenity of the scholarly Sen— although the years had given her different skills, and her mind had advanced far beyond the simplicity of a kel'e'en. Intel brushed at Melein's shoulder, a caress. "Patience," she advised, seeing Melein's anxiety; and she knew that the advice would be discarded in all respects.

"Let me go find Niun and talk to him," she asked.

Brother and sister, Niun and Melein—and close, despite that they had been separated by law and she'pan's decree and caste and custom. Kel'en and sen'e'en, dark and bright, Hand and Mind; but the heart in them was the same and the blood was the same. She remembered the pair that had given them life, her youngest and most beloved Husband and a kel'e'en of Guragen, both lost now. *His* face, his eyes, that had made her regret a she'-pan's chastity, gazed back at her through Melein's and Niun's; and she remembered that he also had been strong-willed and hot-tempered and clever. Perhaps Melein hated her; she had not willingly received the command to leave the Kel and enter the Sen. But there was no defiance there now, though the she'pan searched for it. There was only anxiety, only a natural grief for her brother's pain.

"No," said Intel sharply. "I tell you to let him alone."

"He may harm himself, she'pan."

"He will not. You underestimate him. He does not need you now. You are no longer of the Kel, and I doubt that he wants to be faced by one of the Sen at this moment. What could you tell him? What could you answer if he asked you questions? Could you be silent?"

This struck home. "He wanted to leave Kesrith six years ago," said Melein, her eyes bright with unshed tears; and possibly it was not only her brother's case she pleaded now, but her own. "You would not let him go. Now it is too late, she'pan. It is for-ever too late for him, and what can he imagine for himself? What is there for him?"

"Meditate upon these things," said Intel, "and tell me your con-clusions, sen Melein s'Intel, after you have thought a day and a night on this matter. But do not intrude your advice into the private affairs of a kel'en. And do not regard him as your brother. A sen'e'en has no kin but the whole House, and the People."

Melein rose, and stared down at her, breast heaving with her struggle for breath. Beautiful, this daughter of hers: Intel saw her in this instant and was amazed how much Melein, who was not of her blood, had become the things her own youth had once promised—saw mirrored her own self, before Nisren's fall, before the ruin of the House and of her own hopes. The sight wounded her. In this moment she saw clearly, and knew the sen'e'en as she was, and feared her and loved her at once.

Melein who would hardly mourn her passing.

So she had created her, deliberately, event by event, choice by choice, her daughter-not-of-the-flesh, her child, her Chosen, formed in Kath and Kel and Sen, partaker of the Mysteries of all castes of the People.

Hating her.

"Learn restraint," she earnestly wished Melein, in a still, soft voice that thrust with difficulty into Melein's anger. "Learn to be sen'e'en, Melein, above all else that you desire to have."

The young sen'e'en let go a shuddering breath, and the tears in her eyes spilled over. Thwarted for now, the sen'e'en for a moment being child again: but this child was dangerous.

Intel shivered, foreknowing that Melein would outlive her and impose her own imprint on the world.

Chapter Two

There was a division in the world, marked by a causeway of white rock. On the one side, and at the lower end, lay the regul of Kesrith—city-folk, slow-moving, long-remembering. The lowland city was entirely theirs: flat, sprawling buildings, a port, commerce with the stars, mining that scarred the earth, a plant that extracted water from the Alkaline Sea. The land had been called the Dus plain before there were regul on Kesrith: the mri remembered. For this reason the mri had avoided the plain, in respect of the dusei; but the regul had insisted on setting their city there, and the dusei left it.

Uplands, in the rugged hills at the other end of the causeway, was the tower of the mri. It appeared as four truncated cones arising from the corners of a trapezoidal ground floor—slanted walls made of the pale earth of the lowlands, treated and hardened. This was the Edun Kesrithun, the House of Kesrith, the home of the mri of Kesrith, and, because of Intel, the home of all mri in the wide universe.

One could see most of Kesrithi civilization from the vantage point Niun occupied in his solitary anger. He came here often, to this highest part of the causeway, to this stubborn outcrop of rock that had defeated the regul road and made the regul think otherwise about their plans to extend it into the high hills, invading the sanctity of Sil'athen. He liked it for what it was as well as for the view. Below him lay the regul city and the mri edun, two very small scars on the body of the white earth. Above him, in the hills, and beyond and beyond, there were only regul automatons, that drew minerals from the earth and provided regul Kesrith its reason for existence; and wild things that had owned the world

before the coming of regul or of mri; and the slow-moving duse
that had once been Kesrith's highest form of life.

Niun sat, brooding, on the rock that overlooked the world, hating tsi'mri with more than the ordinary hatred of mri for aliens
which was considerable. He was twenty-six years old as the People reckoned years, which was not by Kesrith's orbit around
Arain, nor by the standard of Nisren, nor by that of either of the
two other worlds the People had designated homeworld in the
span of time remembered by Kel songs.

He was tall, even of his kind. His high cheekbones bore the *seta'al,* the triple scars of his caste, blue-stained and indelible; this
meant that he was a full-fledged member of the Kel, the hand of
the People. Being of the Kel, he went robed from collar to boot-
tops in unrelieved black; and black veil and tasseled headcloth,
mez and *zaidhe,* concealed all but his brow and his eyes from the
gaze of outsiders when he chose to meet them; and the *zaidhe* further had a dark transparent visor that could meet the veil when
dust blew or red Arain reached its unpleasant zenith. He was a
man: his face, like his thoughts, was considered a private identity
one indecent to reveal to strangers. The veils enveloped him as
did the robes, a distinguishing mark of the only caste of the People that might deal with outsiders. The black robes, the *siga,* were
held about the waist and chest with belts that bore his weapons
which were several; and also they should have held *j'tai,* medallions, honors won for his services to the People: they held none
and this lack of status would have been obvious to any mri that
beheld him.

Being of the Kel, he could neither read nor write, save that he
could use a numbered keyboard and knew mathematics, both
regul and mri. He knew by heart the complicated genealogies of
his House, which had been that of Nisren. The name-chants filled
him with melancholy when he sang them: it was difficult to do so
and then to look about the cracking walls of Edun Kesrithun and
behold only so few people as now lived, and not realize that decline was taking place, that it was real and threatening. He knew
all the songs. He could foresee begetting no child of his own who
would sing them, not on Kesrith. He learned the songs; he learned
languages, which were part of the Kel-lore. He spoke four languages fluently, two of which were his own, one of which was the

regul's, and the fourth of which was the enemy's. He was expert in weapons, both the yin'ein and the zahen'ein; he was taught of nine masters-of-arms; he knew that his skill was great in all these things.

And wasted, all wasted.

Regul

Tsi'mri.

Niun flung a rock downslope, which splashed into a hot pool and disturbed the vapors.

Peace.

Peace on human terms, it would be. Regul had disregarded mri strategists at every crucial moment of the war. Regul would spend mri lives without stinting and they would pay the bloodprice to edunei that lost sons and daughters of the Kel, all because some regul colonial official panicked and ordered suicidal attack by the handful of mri serving him personally to cover his retreat and that of his younglings; but far less willingly would that same regul risk regul lives or properties. To lose regul lives would mean loss of status; it would have brought that regul instant censure by regul authorities, recall to homeworld, sifting of his knowledge, death of himself and his young in all probability.

It was inevitable that humans should have realized this essential weakness of the regul-mri partnership, that humans should have learned that inflicting casualties on regul would have far more effect than inflicting those same casualties on mri.

It was predictable then that the regul should have panicked under that pressure, that they would have reacted by retreat, precipitous, against all mri counsel to the contrary, exposing world after world to attack in their haste to withdraw to absolute security. Consequently that absolute security could not exist.

And that regul would afterwards compound their stupidity by dealing directly with the humans—this too was credible, in the regul, to buy and sell war, and to sell out quickly when threatened rather than to risk losing overmuch of their necessary possessions.

The regul language contained no word for courage.

Neither had it one for imagination.

The war was ending and Niun remained worldbound, never having put to use the things that he had learned. The gods knew what manner of trading the merchants were doing, what disposition was being made of his life. He foresaw that things might revert to what they had been before the war, that mri might again serve individual regul—that mri would fight mri again, in combat where experience mattered.

And gods knew how long it would be possible to find a regul to serve, when the war was ending and things were entering a period of flux. Gods knew how likely a regul was to take on an inexperienced kel'en to guard his ship, when others, war-wise, were available.

He had trained all his life to fight humans, and the policies of three species conspired to keep him from it.

He rose up of a sudden, mind set on an idea that had been seething there for more than this day alone, and he leaped to the ground and started walking down the road. He did not look back when he had passed the edun, unchallenged, unnoticed. He owned nothing. He needed nothing. What he wore and what he carried as his weapons were his to take; he had this by law and custom, and he could ask nothing more of his edun even were he leaving with their blessing and help, which he was not.

In the edun, Melein would surely grieve at such a silent desertion, but she had been kel'e'en herself long enough to be glad for his sake too, that he went to a service. A kel'en in an edun was as impermanent as the wind itself, and ought to own no close ties past childhood, save to the she'pan and to the People and to him or her that hired him.

He did feel a certain guilt toward the she'pan too, to her who had mothered him with a closeness much beyond what a she'pan owed a son of her Husbands. He knew that she had particularly favored Zain his father, and still mourned his death; and she would neither approve nor allow the journey he made now.

It was, in fact, Intel's stubborn, possessive will that had held him this long on Kesrith, kept him at her side long past the years that he decently should have left her authority and that of his teachers. He had once loved Intel, deeply, reverently. Even that love, in the slow years since he should have followed the other kel'ein of the edun and left her, had begun to turn to bitterness.

Thanks to her, his skills were untried, his life unused and now perhaps altogether useless. Nine years had passed since the *se ta'al* of the Kel had been cut and stained into his face, nine year that he had sat in heart-pounding longing whenever a regul master would come up the road to the edun and seek a kel'en to guard a ship, be it for the war or even for commerce. Fewer and fewer of these requests came in the passing years, and now there came no more requests to the edun at all. He was the last of all his brothers and sisters of the Kel, last of all the children of the edun save Melein. The others had all found their service, and most were dead; but Niun s'Intel, nine years a kel'en, had yet to leave the she'pan's protective embrace.

Mother, let me go! he had begged of her six years ago, when his cousin Medai's ship had left—the ultimate, the crushing shame, that Medai, swaggering, boastful Medai, should be chosen for the greatest honor of all, and he be left behind in disgrace.

No, the she'pan had said in the absolute, invoking her authority, and to his repeated pleading for her understanding, for his freedom: *No. You are the last of all my sons, the last, the last I shall ever have. Zain's child. And if I will you to stay with me, that is my right, and that is my final decision. No. No.*

He had fled to the high hills that day, watching and not wishing to watch, as the ship of the regul high command, *Hazan,* that ruled the zone in which Kesrith lay, bore Medai s'Intel Sov-Nelan into manhood, into service, into the highest honor that had yet befallen a kel'en of Edun Kesrithun.

That day Niun had wept, though kel'ein could not weep. And then in shame at this weakness, he had scoured his face with the harsh powdery sand and stayed fasting in the hills another day and two nights, until he had to come down and face the other kel'ein and the Mother's anxious and possessive love.

Old, all of them. There was not a kel'en left now save himself that could even take a service if it were offered. They were all greatly skilled. He suspected that they were the greatest masters of the yin'ein in all the People, although they did not boast anything but considerable competency; but the years had done their subtle robbery and left them no strength to use their arts in war. It was a Kel of eight men and one woman past their reason for living, without strength to fight or—after him—children to teach: old ones whose dreams must now be all backward.

Nine years they had stolen from him, entombing him with them, living their vicarious lives through his youth.

He walked the road down to the lowlands, letting the causeway take him to regul, since regul would not come to the edun in these days. It was not the most direct route, but it was the easiest, and he walked it insolently secure, since the old ones of the Kel could not possibly overtake him on so long a walk. He did not mean to go to the port, which was directly crosslands, but to what lay at the causeway's end, the very center of regul authority, the Nom, that two-storied building that was the highest structure in Kesrith's only city.

He felt uneasy when his boots trod concrete and he found all about him the ugly flat buildings of regul. Here was a different world from the cleanliness of the high hills, even a different smell in the air, a blunting of the acrid flavor of Kesrith's chill winds, a subtle effluvium of oil and machinery and musky regul bodies.

Regul younglings watched him—the mobile ones, the young of regul. Their squat bodies would thicken further in adulthood, greyish-brown skin darken, loosen—fat accumulate until they found themselves enveloped in weight almost too great for their atrophying muscles to lift. Mri seldom saw elder regul; Niun himself had never seen an elder in the flesh, only heard them described by his teachers of the Kel. Adult regul kept to their city, surrounded by machines that carried them, that purified their air; they were attended by younglings that must wait on them constantly, who themselves lived precarious lives until they chanced to reach maturity. The only violence regul perpetrated was against their own young.

The younglings on the square looked at him now in sidelong glances and talked in secretive tones that carried to his sensitive hearing, more clearly surely than they realized it could. Ordinarily this spitefulness would not have troubled him in the least: he had been taught less liking for them, and despised them and all their breed. But here he was the petitioner, desperately anxious, and they held what he wanted and had the power to deny it to him. Their hate breathed about him like the tainted city atmosphere. He had veiled himself long before he entered the town; but with a little more encouragement he would have dropped the visor of the *zaidhe* also. He had done so on his last visit to this city, being a very young kel'en and uncertain of the proprieties of conduct be-

tween regul and mri. But now, older, a man in his own right, he
had the face to leave the visor up and glare back at the younglings
who stared too boldly; and most could not bear the direct contact
of his eyes and flinched from meeting them. A few older and
braver than the others, hissed soft displeasure, warning. He ignored them. He was not a regul youngling, to fear their violence.

He knew his way. He knew the Nom's proper entrance,
fronting the great square around which the city was built in concentric squares. It faced the rising sun, as main entrances of central regul buildings must. He remembered this. He had been here
as escort to his father, who was about to take his last service; but
he had not been inside. Now he came to the door before which he
had waited on that day, and at his presence the regul youngling on
duty in the vestibule arose in alarm.

"Go away," said the youngling flatly; but he paid no attention
to it, and walked into the main foyer of the echoing place, at once
stifled by the heat and the musky flavor of the air. He found himself in a great place surrounded by doors and windowed offices,
all with titles written on them; he was quickly sick and dizzy from
the air and he stood confused and ashamed in the middle of the
hall, for here it was a matter of reading to know where he must go
next, and he could not read.

It was the regul youngling from the vestibule desk that came to
him in his distress, stumping across the floor in short, scuffing
steps. The youngling was flushed dark with anger or with the
heat, and breathing heavily from the exertion of overtaking him.
"Go away," the youngling repeated. "By treaty and by law you
have no business coming here."

"I will speak to your elders," he told the youngling, which he
had been taught was the ultimate and unanswerable appeal among
regul: no youngling could make an ultimate decision. "Tell them
that a kel'en is here to speak with them."

The youngling blew air, fluttering, through its nostrils. "Come
with me, then," it said, and cast him a disapproving glance, a
flash of white, red-veined, from the corner of a rolling eye. It
was—it, for regul could not determine their own gender until maturity—like all regul, a squat figure, body almost touching the
floor even while it was standing. It was also a very young regul to
have been given the (among regul) considerable honor of tending

the Nom door. It still bore itself erect, bones showing through the skin, the brown, pebbly hide fine-grained yet and delicate with beige tones and a casting of metallic highlights. It walked beside him, a rolling gait that needed considerable leeway. "I am Hada Surag-gi," it said, "secretary, guardian to the door. You are doubtless one of Intel's lot."

Niun simply did not answer this rudeness on the part of the tsi'mri guard, naming the she'pan by her name with such insolent familiarity. Among regul, elders would be *the reverence,* or *the honorable,* or *the lord* . . . , and he reckoned the familiarity for calculated insult, marking it down for a later date, if so happened he found himself holding what Hada Surag-gi desired. The youngling at present was doing what he wanted it to do, and this, between mri and tsi'mri, was sufficient.

Steel tracks ran the bowed edges of the walls, and a vehicle whispered past them at a speed so great the presence was only an instant. The tracks went everywhere, on the wall opposite the doors, and another and another vehicle passed, missing one another by a hand's breadth. He did not let himself appear amazed at such things.

And neither did he thank the youngling when it had shown him through a door and into a waiting room where another, seeming adult, kept a metal desk; he simply turned his back on the youngling when it had ceased to be of use, and heard it leave.

The official leaned back from its desk, cradling its body in the mobile chair that—amazingly—moved under power: another such vehicle, a gleaming steel device such as he had heard the adult regul used to move about without rising.

"We know you," the regul said. "You are Niun, from the Hill. Your elders have contacted us. You are ordered to return to your people immediately."

Heat rushed to his face. Of course they would have done this, forestalling him. He had not even thought of it.

"That does not matter," he said, carefully formal. "I am asking service with your ships. I renounce my edun."

The regul, a brown mass, folded and over-folded, its face a surprising bony smoothness within this weight, sighed and regarded him with small, wrinkle-edged eyes. "We hear what you say," it said. "But our treaty with your folk does not permit us to accept

ou with your elders protesting. Please return to them at once. We
do not want to quarrel with your elders."

"Do you have a superior?" Niun asked harshly, out of patience
and fast losing hope as well. "Let me speak to someone of higher
authority."

"You ask to see the Director?"

"Yes."

The regul sighed again and made the request of an intercom: a
grating voice refused, flatly. The regul looked up, rolling its eyes
in an expression that was more satisfied and smug than apolo-
getic. "You see," it said.

Niun turned on his heel and strode out of the office and out of
the foyer, ignoring the amused eyes of the youngling Hada Surag-
i. He felt his face burning, his breath short as he exited the warm
interior of the Nom and walked onto the public square, where the
cold wind swept through the city.

He walked swiftly, as if he had a place to go and went there of
his own will. He imagined that every regul on the street knew his
name and was laughing secretly. This was not beyond all possibility, for regul tended to know everyone's business.

He did not slow his pace until he was walking the long causeway back from the city's edge to the edun, and then indeed he
walked slowly, and cared little for what passed his eyes or his
hearing on the road. The open land, even on the causeway, was
not a place where it was safe to go inattentive to surroundings, but
he did so, tempting the Gods and the she'pan's anger. He was
sorry that nothing did befall him and that, after all, he found himself walking the familiar earthen track to the entrance of the edun
and entering its shadows and its echoes. He was sullen still as he
walked to the stairs of the Kel tower and ascended, pushing open
the door of the hall, reporting to kel'anth Eddan, dutiful prisoner.

"I am back," he said, and did not unveil.

Eddan had the rank and the self-righteousness to turn a naked
face to his anger, and the self-possession to remain unstirred. *Old
man, old man,* Niun could not help thinking, *the seta'al are one
with the wrinkles on your face and your eyes are dimmed so that
they already look into the Dark. You will keep me here until I am
like you. Nine years, nine years, Eddan, and you have made me
lose my dignity. What can you take from me in nine more?*

"You are back," echoed Eddan, who had been his principal teacher-in-arms, and who adopted that master/student manner with him. "What of it?"

Niun carefully unveiled, settled crosslegged to the floor near the warmth of the dus that slept in the corner. It eased aside, murmured a rumbling complaint at the disturbance of its sleep. "I would have gone," he said.

"You distressed the she'pan," Eddan said. "You will not go down to the city again. She forbids it."

He looked up, outraged.

"You embarrassed the House," Eddan said. "Consider that."

"Consider *me*," Niun exclaimed, exhausted. He saw the shock his outburst created in Eddan and cast the words out in reckless satisfaction. "It is unnatural, what you have done, keeping me here, I am due something in my life—something of my own, at least."

"Are you?" Eddan's soft voice was edged. "Who taught you that? Some regul in the city?"

Eddan stood still, hands within his belt, old master of the yin'ein, in that posture that chilled a man who knew its meaning: *here is challenge, if you want it*. He loved Eddan. That Eddan looked at him this way frightened him, made him reckon his skill against Eddan's; made him remember that Eddan could still humble him. There was a difference between him and the old master that if Eddan's bluff were called, blood would flow for it.

And Eddan knew that difference in them. Heat rose to his face.

"I never asked to be treated differently from all the others," Niun declared, averting his face from Eddan's challenge.

"What do you think you are due?" Eddan asked him.

He could not answer.

"You have a soft spot in your defense," said Eddan. "A gaping hole. Go and consider that, Niun s'Intel, and when you have made up your mind what it is the People owe you, come and tell me and we will go to the Mother and present your case to her."

Eddan mocked him. The bitter thing was that he deserved it. He saw that this over-anxiousness was what had shamed him before the regul. He resumed the veil and gathered himself to his feet, to go outside.

"You have duties that are waiting," Eddan said sharply. "Dinner was held without you. Go and assist Liran at cleaning up. Tend to your own obligations before you consider what is owed to you."

"Sir," he said quietly, averted his face again and went his way below.

Chapter Three

The ship, a long voyage out from Elag/Haven, had shifted to the tedium that had possessed it before transition. Sten Duncan took a second look at the mainroom display and was disappointed to discover it had not yet noted the change. They had spent the longest normal-space passage he had ever endured getting out of Haven's militarily sensitive vicinity, blind and under tedious escort. That was suddenly gone. It was replaced likely by another passage as tedious. He shrugged and kept walking. The place smelled of regul. He held his breath as he passed the galley-automat, the door of which was open. He kept to the center of the corridor scarcely noticing as a sled whisked past him; the corridors were built wide, high in the center and low on the sides, with gleaming rails recessed into the flooring to guide the conveyance sleds that the regul used to get about the long corridors of their ship.

It was not possible to forget for an instant that this ship was regul. The corridors did not angle or bow as they would in a human-made vessel; they wound, spiraled, amenable to the gliding course of the sleds that hugged the walls, and only a few of them could be walked. In those designed for walking, there was headroom in their center for humans—or for mri, who were the ordinary tenants of regul ships, but tracks ran the sides, for regul.

And about the whole ship there were strange scents, strange aromas of unpalatable food and spices, strange sounds, the rumbling tones of regul language that neither humans nor probably even mri had ever pronounced as regul might.

He loathed it. He loathed the regul utterly, and knowing that that reaction was neither wise nor helpful in his position, he constantly fought against his instincts. It was clear enough that the re-

ction was mutual with the regul; they restricted their human
guests to six hours in which they were supposedly free to roam
the personnel areas to their hearts' content; and after that came a
twenty-two-hour period of confinement.

Sten Duncan, aide to the honorable George Stavros, governor-
to-be in the new territories and presently liaison between regul
and humanity, regularly availed himself of that six-hour liberty;
the Hon. Mr. Stavros did not—did not, in fact, venture from his
own room. Duncan walked the corridors and gathered the appropriate materials and releases from the library for the honorable
gentleman to read, and carried to the pneumatic dispatch whatever communications flowed from Stavros to Stavros'regul counterpart bai Hulagh Alagn-ni.

Regul protocol. No regul elder of dignity performed his own
errands. Only a condemned incompetent lacked youngling servitors. Therefore no human of Stavros' rank would do so; and therefore Stavros had chosen an aide of apparent youth and fairly
advanced rank, criteria that regul would use in selecting their own
personal attendants.

He was, in effect, a servant. He provided Stavros a certain prestige. He ran errands. Back in the action that had taken Haven, he
had held military rank. The regul knew this, which further en-
hanced Stavros' prestige.

Duncan gathered up the day's communications, laid others
from Stavros down on the appropriate table, and delivered the
food order to the slot that ultimately would find its way to the correct department, and bring an automated carrier to their door with
the requested meal, at least as regul construed it, out of human-
supplied foodstuffs that had come with them.

Like exotic pets, Duncan reflected with annoyance, with the
regul trying, as far as convenient, to maintain an authentic environment. As in most wild-animal displays, the staging was trans-
parently artificial.

He retraced his way down the hall, through the mainroom recreation area and library. He had never set eyes on any of the regul
save the younglings that frequented this central personnel relaxation area. Curiously enough, neither had Stavros encountered Hulagh. Protocol again. It was likely that, in all the time they had yet
to spend among regul, they would never meet the honorable, the

reverence bai Hulagh Alagn-ni, only the younglings that serve
him as crew and aides and messengers.

Regul elders were virtually immobile; this was certain; and He
lagh was said to be of very extreme age. Duncan privately su
mised that this helplessness was a source of embarrassment to th
elderly regul in dealing face-to-face with non-regul, and tha
therefore they arranged to keep themselves in such total seclusio
from outsiders.

Or perhaps they judged humans and mri unbearably ugly.
was certain that there was little that humans could find beautifi
in the regul.

He opened the unlocked door that let him into the double suit
he shared with Stavros. The anteroom was his, serving as sleepin
quarters and all else he was supposed to desire during the lon
passage: regul revenge, he thought sourly, for human insistenc
on the long, slow escort. The reception salon and proper bedroo
both belonged to Stavros. So did the sanitary facilities, whic
were in the adjoining bedroom and likewise not designed fc
human comfort: he wondered how Stavros, elderly as he wa
coped with that. But it had not been deemed wise to make a
issue of regul-human differences even in that detail. The theor
was that the regul were *honoring* their guests by treating the
precisely as if they were regul, down to the tradition of dealin
only through youngling intermediaries, and the tradition tha
placed Duncan's own quarters uncomfortably in the tiny ant
room, between Stavros and the outer corridor.

Precious encouragement for confidence in regul civilizatio
Duncan thought sourly, when he thought about it: he was to de
fend the honorable human gentleman from harm, from conta
with rude outsiders, from all unpleasantness. It seemed no insu
to regul hospitality to assume that such rudeness might be antic
pated.

And Stavros remained a virtual prisoner of his exalted ran
pent within one room, without any contact with the outside sav
himself.

Duncan sealed the outer door and knocked on the inner, a fo
mality preserved necessarily—first because listening regul (a
suming regul listened, which they firmly believed) would n
understand any informality between elder and youngling; and se

ond, because they had been at close quarters too long, and both of them cherished what privacy they could obtain from each other.

The door opened, controlled by Stavros' remote devices—incongruous to see a human, especially a frail and slight one, sitting in the massive chair-sled designed for regul elders. Desk, control center, mode of transportation: Stavros disdained to propel it across the room. Duncan went to him, presented the tapes and papers, and Stavros took them from him and began to deal with them at once, all without a smile or word of greeting or even a dismissal. Stavros had smiled a few times at the beginning of their association; he did not now. They lived under the continual witness of the regul. He was treated, he suspected, as if he were in truth a regul youngling, without courtesy and without consideration of himself as an individual: he hoped, at least, that this was the source of Stavros' coldness to him.

He knew that he was far from understanding such a man. He saw some qualities in Stavros that he respected: courage, for one. He thought that it must have taken a great deal of that to enter on such a mission at Stavros' age. An elderly human had been wanted, a diplomat who, aside from his duties as administrator of the new territories, could obtain greater respect from the regul that would be neighbors to humanity. Stavros had come out of retirement to take the assignment, not a strong man, or an imposing one physically. He was, Duncan had learned in their only intimate conversation, and that before boarding, a native of Kiluwa, one of the several casualties of the war in its earliest years; and that might explain something. Kiluwans were legendarily eccentric, of a fringe-area colony left too long on its own, peculiar in religion, in philosophy, in manners: like the regul, they had not believed in writing. For the years after Kiluwa's fall, Stavros had been in the XenBureau—retired to university life of late. He had children, had lost a grandson to the war at Elag/Haven. If Stavros hated regul either for Kiluwa or for the grandson's sake, he had never betrayed it. He seldom betrayed any emotion beyond a certain obsessive interest in the regul. Everything in Stavros was quiet; and there were depths and depths beneath that placidity.

The old man's pale eyes flashed up. "Good morning, Duncan," he said, and instantly returned to his studies. "Sit," he added. "Wait."

28   *C. J. Cherryh*

Duncan sat down, disappointed, and waited. He had nothing else to do. He would have gone mad already if he had not had the ability to bear long silence and inactivity. He watched Stavros work, wondering over again why the old man had been so determined to learn the regul tongue, which occupied his many hours. There were regul who spoke perfectly idiomatic Basic. There always would be. But Stavros had succeeded well enough on their voyage that now he could listen to the tape from the regul master of the ship, outlining the day's schedules and information, and needed to glance only occasionally at the supplied written translation—regul propaganda, praising the elders of homeworld, Nurag, praising the correct management of the director of the ship—Duncan found it all very dry, save for the small hints of the progress the ship was making.

But from such things Stavros learned, and became fluent at least in trivial courtesies—learned at a rate that began to amaze Duncan. He could actually understand that confusion of sound that remained only confusion to Duncan.

Such a man, a scholar, an intelligent man, with grandchildren and great-grandchildren, had left everything human and familiar, everything his long life had produced, and now took a voyage with the enemy, into unknown space. Although a governorship was a considerable inducement, the hazards for Stavros were more than considerable. Duncan did not know how old the man was: there had been rumors at Haven verging on the incredible. He did know that one of the great-grandchildren was entering the military.

If Duncan had enjoyed any intimacy with Stavros he would have been moved to ask him why he had come; he dared not. But every time he was tempted to give way to the pressures of their confinement, his own fear of the strangeness about them, he thought of the old man patiently at his lessons and resigned himself to last it out.

He did not think that he contributed anything to Stavros, be it companionship or service, only the necessary appearance of propriety in the regul's eyes. Stavros could have done without him for all the notice he paid him. Personnel had chosen half a dozen men for interview, and he, one of the Surface Tactical officers at Haven, had been the choice. He still did not know why. He had admitted to his lack of qualifications for such a post: *Then he'll know that he has to take orders,* Stavros had concluded in his presence. *Volunteer?* Stavros had asked him then, as if this were a point of suspected insanity. *No, sir,* he had answered, the truth: *they called in every SurTac in the Haven reach. —Pilot's rating?* Stavros had asked. *—Yes,* he had said. *—Hold any grudge against the regul?* Stavros asked. *No,* he had answered simply, which was again the truth: he did not like them, but it was not a grudge, it was war; it was all he knew. And Stavros had read his record a second time in his presence and accepted him.

It had sounded good at the time, fantastically desirable: from a war where life expectancy was rated in missions flown, and where he was reaching his statistical limit, to an easy berth on a diplomatic flight under escort, with guaranteed retirement home and discharge in five years; discharge at less than thirty on a pension larger than any SurTac could reasonably dream of, or—and this was the thing that Duncan pondered with most interest—permanent attachment to a new colonial directorate, permanent assignment to Stavros' territories, wealth and prominence on a developing world. It was a prize for which men would kill or die. He had only to endure regul company for a while in either case, and to win Stavros' approval by his service. He had five years to accomplish the latter. He meant to do it.

He had not been much frightened when he stepped aboard the regul ship: he had read the data known on the regul, knew them for noncombative, nonviolent by preference, a basically timid species. The warrior mri had done their fighting for them, and provoked further conflicts, and finally the regul had called the mri into retreat, gotten them under firm control. New regul were in power on their homeworld now, a pacifist party, which also controlled the ship on which they were travelling and the world to which they were bound.

But he had learned a different kind of fear over the long slow voyage, a sullen, biding sort of fear; and he began to suspect why they had wanted a SurTac as Stavros' companion: he was trained for alien environment, inured to solitude and uncertainties, and above all he was ignorant of higher policies. If something went wrong, and he began to appreciate ways in which it could, then Stavros was the only considerable expenditure; but Sten Duncan was nothing, military personnel, without kin to notify, a loss that could be written off without worry. His low classification number signified that he could spill everything he knew to an enemy without damage to any essential installations; and Stavros himself had been long secluded in the university community of New Kiluwa.

Perhaps—the thought occurred to him—Stavros himself was capable of expending him promptly if he proved inconvenient. Stavros was a diplomat, of that breed that Duncan instinctively mistrusted, that disposed of the likes of Sten Duncan by their hundreds and thousands in war. Perhaps it was that which had stolen away Stavros' inclination to talk to him as if he were anything more than the furnishings. Regul dealt with rebellious younglings, even with inconvenient younglings, instantly and without mercy, as if they were an easily replaceable commodity.

It was a nightborn fear, the kind that grew in the dark, in those too-long hours when he lay on his bed and considered that beyond the one door was an alien guard whose very life processes he did not understand; and beyond the other was a human whose mind he did not understand, an old man who was learning to think like the regul, whose elders were a terror to the young.

But when they were in day-cycle, together, when he considered Stavros face to face, he could not believe seriously such things as he thought and imagined at night. So long pent up, so long under stress, it was no strange thing that his mind should turn to nameless and irrational apprehensions.

He only wished that he knew what Stavros hoped he was doing, or what Stavros expected him to do.

The tape loop cycled its third time through. Duncan knew its salutation, at least, the few words in the regul language he knew. Stavros was listening and memorizing. Shortly he would be able to recite the whole thing from memory.

"Sir," he interrupted Stavros' thoughts cautiously, "sir, our—" the tape went off, "our allotted liberty is just about up if you want anything else from the library or the dispensary."

He wished Stavros would think of something he needed. He longed to enjoy that precious time outside their quarters, to walk, to move; but Stavros had forbidden him to loiter anywhere in regul view, or to attempt any exchange with any of the crew. Duncan understood the reasoning behind that prohibition, a sensible precaution, a preservation of human mystique as far as regul were concerned: *Let them wonder what we think,* Stavros would say to many a situation. But it was unbearable to sit here while the liberty ran out, with the ship newly arrived in regul space.

"No," said Stavros, dashing his hopes. Then, perhaps an afterthought, he handed him one of the tapes. "Here. An excuse. Look like you have important business and stay to it. Find me the next in sequence and bring both back. Enjoy your walk."

"Yes, sir." He rose, moved to thank the old man, to appreciate his understanding of his misery; but Stavros started the tape again, looked elsewhere, making it awkward. He hesitated, then left, through his own room, to the outside.

He drew a few deep breaths to accustom himself to the taint of the air, felt less confined at once, even faced with the narrow halls. Regul living spaces were small, barren places, accommodating only space for a sled's operation; most things were grouped within reach of someone sitting. He suppressed the desire to stretch, settled himself into a sedate walk, and headed for mainroom through a corridor that was utterly empty of regul.

Mainroom served all personnel for recreation and study; it was the library terminal also. Simpler, Duncan thought, to have included a library linkup to the console already in their quarters and obviate the need for them coming out at all, but he was desperately glad that they had not. It provided an excuse, as Stavros had said. And perhaps there were restrictions on some passengers who could read and understand more than they. He did not know. He studied the twisting regul numbers on the cartridge he carried and carefully punched the keys next in sequence.

Machinery clicked, the least delay, and the desired cartridge shot into position. He provided the library with their special code, which changed the alphabet module, and, notified that humans desired the cartridge in question, the library flurried through authorizations, probably went through another process to decide that printout was supposed to accompany the cartridge—actually three forms of printout, literal, transliterated and translated came with each—and finally from its microstorage it began to produce the printouts.

Duncan paced the room while the machine processed the print sheet by sheet and checked the time: close. He walked back to the machine and it was still working, slower than any human-made processing system he had used. It had reactions like those of the regul themselves, sluggish. To fill the seconds he counted the changes in the viewscreen mockup that was the center of the library wall. It showed their course through human space, curiously never once acknowledging the presence of the armed escort vessels that had been the source of so much controversy. It was out of date as of this morning. At every pulse it cycled through to other views, to landscapes fascinating in their alien character (carefully censored, he was sure, lest they learn too much of regul; there were no living things and no cities and structures in the views) to starfields, back to the progress mockup. It dominated the room. He had watched it change day by slow day during their approach to jump. He had ceased to think of the voyage as one with a particular destination. Their peculiar isolation had become an environment in itself that could not be mentally connected to the life he had lived before and from which it was impossible to imagine the life he would live after. They had only the regul's word for where they were going.

He watched through three such cyclings and turned back to the machine, which had stopped in the middle of its printing, flashing the Priority signal. Someone of authority had interrupted it to obtain something more important. His materials were frozen in the machine's grip. He pushed the cancel button to retrieve the cartridge, and nothing happened. The Priority was still flashing, while the library did what it was commanded to do from some other source.

He swore and looked again at the time. The printout was half in the tray, the tail of it still in the machine. He could go and keep scrupulously to the schedule or he could wait the little time it would take for the machine to clear. He decided to wait. Probably the stall was because of the printout, an unwieldy and awkward operation, printout surely a rare function of their library apparatus, inefficiently done. The rumor used to be that regul themselves did not write at all, which was not, as they had discovered, true. They had an elaborate and intricate written language. But the library was designed for audio replication. The majority of regul materials were oral-aural. It was said, and this seemed true according to their own observations, that the regul did not need to hear any tape more than once.

Instant and total recall. Eidetic memory. The word *lie* was, he remembered Stavros telling him, fraught with associate concepts of perversion and murder.

A species that could neither forget nor unlearn.

If this were so, it was possible that they could depend on the exact truth from the regul at all times.

It was also possible that a species that could not lie might have learned ways of deception without it.

He did not need to wonder how regul regarded humans, who placed great emphasis on the written word, who had to be provided special and separate materials to comprehend slowly what regul absorbed at a single hearing; who could not learn the regul language, while regul learned human speech as rapidly as they could be provided words, and never needed to be told twice.

When he thought of this, and of the regul younglings, so helplessly slow, so ponderous in their movements, and yet the piggish little eyes glittering with some emotion that wrinkled the corners when they beheld a human, he grew uneasy, remembering that these same younglings, unless murdered by their own parent, would live through several human lifetimes and remember every instant of it; and that bai Hulagh, who commanded them and the ship and the zone where they were bound, had done so.

He resented both their long lives and their exact memories. He resented the obstinacy of their ubiquitous machines, the bigotry and insolence that kept them confined and tightly scheduled as they were, surrounded by automation that made their regul hosts more than the physical equals of humans; and with all the accumulating frustration of long imprisonment, he resented most of all the petty irritations that were constantly placed in their way by their regul hosts, who clearly despised humans for their mental shortcomings.

Stavros was headed for failure if he sought accommodation with such neighbors. It was a mortal mistake to think that a human could become regul, that he won anything at all by slavishly imitating the manners of beings that despised them.

That was the worm that had eaten at his gut ever since the first days of this chromium-plated, silken-soft imprisonment. All about

them were regul and regul machines, hulking beasts helpless but
for that automation, like great shapeless parasites living attached
to appliances of steel and chromium; and Stavros was utterly,
dangerously wrong if he thought he became esteemed of regul by
giving up the few advantages that humans had. The regul looked
with contempt on the species whose minds forgot, whose knowledge was on film and paper.

He sought to say this to Stavros, but he could not come close
enough to the man to advise him. Stavros was an educated man;
he was not: he was only an experienced one, and experience cried
out that they were in a dangerous situation.

He struck the library panel a blow with his hand, for the time
was out and he was defeated by the monstrosity—incredible that
the thing could be so slow. It was as futile and thoughtless as
jostling any human-made machine; but he knew in the second
after that he should not have done it, and when the Priority signal
at once went off, he was for an instant terrified, believing that he
had caused it somehow, antagonizing some high-ranking regul.

But the machine started to feed out the rest of the paper and
shot the cartridge out in good order after, and he paused to gather
them up. And when, in turning to leave, he looked up at the panel,
he saw that the whole display had changed, and that they had before them the visual of a star system with seven planets, with their
ship plotted in toward the second.

Their final destination.

As he watched, he saw another ship indicated on the simula-
tion, moving outward on a nonintersecting course. They were in-
system, in inhabited, trafficked regions, nearing Kesrith. Time
began to move again. His heart quickened with the elating surety
that they had indeed arrived where they were supposed to, that
they were near their new world. Coming in to dock at Kesrith's
station would be a process of more than a week, by that diagram,
but they were coming in.

The imprisonment was almost over.

A step sounded in the corridor to his left. For an instant he ignored it, knowing that he was overtime and expecting a surly rebuke from a youngling; and the ominous character of it had not
registered. Then it struck him that it did not belong here, the measured tread of boots on the flooring, not the slow scuffing of the

regul nor even Stavros' fragile tread. He turned, frightened even before he looked, by a presence that was not of them nor of the regul.

And he faced a figure that had likewise stopped still, one robed in black, the robes glittering with many small discs. Mri. Kel'en. The golden eyes above the veil were astonished. A slim bronze hand went to the knife at his belt and hesitated there.

For a moment yet neither moved, and it was possible to hear only the slow changes of the projector.

The enemy. The destroyers of Kiluwa and Talos and Asgard. He had never seen one in the flesh at this range. Only the eyes, the hands were uncovered. The tall figure remained utterly still, wrapped in menace and in anger.

"I am Sten Duncan," he found courage to say, doubting that the mri could understand a word, but reckoning it time words intervened before weapons did. "I'm the assistant to the Federations envoy."

"I am kel Medai," said the other in excellent Basic, "and we should not have met."

And with that the mri turned on his heel and stalked off in the direction from which he had come, a black figure that vanished into shadows at the turning of the corridor. Duncan found himself trembling in every muscle. He had seen mri that close only in photographs, and all of those were dead.

Beautiful, was the strange descriptive that came to his mind. Seeing the mri warrior: he would have thought it of an animal, splendid of its kind, and deadly.

He turned, and the blood that had resumed somewhat its normal circulation drained a second time, for a regul youngling stood in the mainroom, its nostrils flaring and shutting in rapid agitation.

It shrilled a warning at him, anger, terror: he could not tell which. Its color went to livid pallor. "Go to quarters," it insisted. "Past time. Go to quarters. Now!"

He moved, edged past the regul and hurried, not looking back. When he reached the sanctuary of his own doorway his hands were shaking, and he thrust himself through even while it was opening, then shut it at once, anxious until the seal had hissed into function. Then he sank down on his cot, knowing that, all too quickly, he must face Stavros and give an account of what he had done. The library materials tumbled from his cold hands and some of the papers fell on the floor. He bent and gathered them up, feeling nothing with his fingers.

He had committed a great mistake, and knew that it was not to be the end of it.

They were going to the world that was said to be the mri home-world, to Kesrith of the star Arain.

Regul claimed title to it, all the same, and the right to cede it to humans. They claimed the authority to command the mri and to sign for them.

They betrayed the mri, and yet carried a kel'en on the ship that brought the orders that turned Kesrith over to humans.

We should not have met, the mri had said.

It was obvious that the regul at least, and possibly the mri, had not intended the meeting. Someone was being deceived.

He gathered himself up and expelled a long breath, rapped on Stavros' door and entered this time without permission.

Chapter Four

Another of the ships was leaving this evening, one of the several shuttles that ferried passengers and goods from the surface of Kesrith up to the station—and thence to starships: to freighters, liners, warships—anything that would remove panicked regul from the path of humans.

Niun watched, as he was accustomed to watch each evening, from that high rock that overlooked the sea and the flats and the city. It was true. He had accepted the fact of the war's end at last, although a sense of unreality still possessed him as he watched the ships go—never so frequent, not in his lifetime, nor, he thought, in that of his elders. The fact was that the regul city was dying, its life ebbing with every outbound ship. He obeyed the she'pan's order and did not go near the city or the port, but he thought if he were to go down now into the square, he would find many of the buildings empty and stripped of things of value; and day after day, by the road that wound along the seashore, the merest line visible from his vantage point, he could see traffic coming into the city, bringing regul from the outlying towns and stations; aircraft came to the city, and fewer and fewer left it again. He had a mental image of a vast heap of abandoned regul vehicles at the edge of town, of ships at the port. They would have to drag them into heaps and let them rust.

It was rumored—so Sathell had gleaned from regul communications—that the chief price of the peace the regul had bought had been the cession of every colony in the Kesrith reach.

Tsi'mri economics had finally proven more powerful than the weapons of the Kel, more important, surely, than the honor of the mri in the regul's estimation. Kesrith was a loss to the regul, to be sure, a mining and transport site, expensively automated; doubtless to lose such a colony was embarrassing to the regul elders; doubtless it was inconvenient for their business and commerce; doubtless for the regul in those fleeing ships the inconvenience ascended to tragedy. Regul valued many peculiar objects; variance in the quality and amount of these and their clothing and their comforts betokened personal worth in their eyes; and the loss of their homes and valued objects that could not be taken onto the ships would be grievous for them; but they had no Revered Objects, nothing that could afflict them to the degree that the loss of homeworld could affect the People; and the honors they coveted could be purchased anew if they were fortunate—unlike mri honors, that had to be won.

And therein Niun did not muster any great sympathy for any of them. His personal loss was great enough: all the life he had planned and desired for himself was departing from possibility with the violence and speed of those outbound ships. The migration had become a rout, night and day; and events gave clear proof that the personal plans of Niun s'Intel Zain-Abrin were nothing to the powers that moved the worlds. But the threat to the House: that was beyond his power to imagine; and that the powers that moved the worlds had no concern for the fate of the People—that was beyond all understanding.

He had tried to adjust his mind to this change in fortunes.

Where shall we make our defense? he had asked of Eddan and the kel'ein, assuming, as he assumed that sanity rested with his people, that there was to be a defense of homeworld, of the Edun of the People.

But Eddan had turned his face from his question, gesturing his refusal to answer it; and in the failure of the Kel, he had dared ask the she'pan herself. And Intel had looked at him with a strange sorrow, as if her last son were somehow lacking in essential understanding; but gently she had spoken to him in generalities of patience and courage, and carefully she had declined to give any direct answer to his question.

And day by day the regul ships departed, without mri kel'ein aboard. The she'pan forbade.

He was watching the end. He understood that now, at least that. Of what it was an end he was not yet sure; but he knew the taste of finality, and that of the things he had desired all his life there was left him nothing. The regul departed, and hereafter came humans.

He wished now desperately that he had applied himself with even more zeal to his study of human ways, so that he could understand what the humans were likely to do. Perhaps the elder kel'ein, who had such experience with them, knew; and perhaps therefore they thought that he should know, and would not reward ignorance with explanation. Or perhaps they were as helpless as he and refused to admit the obvious to him; he could not blame them for that. It was that he simply could not admit that there was nothing to be done, that there were no preparations to be made, while the regul so desperately, so anxiously sought safety. He knew, with what faith remained to him in his diminishing store of things trustworthy, that the Kel would resist in the end; but they were to die, if that were the case. Their skill was great, greater than that of any kel'ein living, he believed; but the nine were also very old and very few to stand for long against the mass attacks of humans.

The imagination came to him over and over again, as horrid and unreal as the departure of regul from his life—of humans arriving, of human language and human tread echoing in the sanctity of the edun shrine, of fire and blood and ten desperate kel'ein trying to defend the she'pan from a horde of defiling humans.

Brothers, sister, he longed to ask the kel'ein, *is it possible that there is some hope that I cannot see?* And then again he thought: *Or, o gods, is it possible that we have a she'pan who has gone mad? Brothers, sister, look, look, the ships!—our way off Kesrith. Make our she'pan see reason. She has forgotten that there are some here who want to live.* But he could not say such things to his elders, to Eddan; and he would ultimately have to account for those words to Intel's face, and he could not bear that. He could not reason with them, could not discuss anything as they did among themselves, in secret: they, she—all save Melein and himself—remembered Nisren's days, the life before the war. They had taken regul help once, escaping the ruin of Nisren, and refused it now, resolved together in councils from which he, not of the Husbands, was excluded. He insisted on believing that his elders were rational. They were too calm, too sure, to be mad.

Forty-three years ago, the like had come to Nisren. A regul ship, rescuing she'pan Intel, had carried the holy Pana and the survivors of the edun to Kesrith. The elders did not speak of that day, scarcely even in songs: it was a pain written in their visible scars and in the secrecies of their silence.

Shame? he wondered, heart-torn at thinking ill of them. *Shame at something they did or did not do on Nisren? Shame at living, and unwillingness to survive another fall of Homeworld?* Sometimes he suspected, with dread growing and gnawing in him like some alien parasite, that such was the case, that he belonged to a she'pan that had wearied of running, to an edun that had consciously made up its mind to die.

An edun which held the Pana, the Revered, the Objects of mri honor and mri history, to behold which was for the Sen alone, to touch which unbidden was to die; to lose which—

To lose the relics of the People—

It betokened the death, not alone of the edun, but of the People as a race. He held the thought a moment, turned it within his mind, then cast it aside in haste, and fearfully picked it up again.

O gods, he thought, mind numbed by the very concept, Another shuttle lifted. He saw it rise, up, up, a star that moved.

O gods, o gods.

It was *shon'ai,* the Passing-game. It was the flash of blades in the dark, the deadly game of rhythm and bluff and threat and reckless risk.

The Game of the People.

The blades were thrown. Existence was gambled on one's quickness and wit and nerve, for no other reason than to deserve survival.

He felt the blood drain from his face to his belly, understanding why they had looked through him when he asked his vain questions.

Join the rhythm, child of the People: be one with it; accept, accept, accept.

Shon'ai!

He cried aloud, and understood all at once. All over known space mri would react to the throw the she'pan of Kesrith had made. They would come, they would come, from all quarters of space, to fight, to resist.

The Pana was set in the keeping of Edun Kesrithun.

The circle was wide and the blades flew at seeming random, but each game tended to develop its unique pattern, and wisest the player who did not become hypnotized by it.

Intel had cast. It was for others to return the throw.

The first of Kesrith's twin moons had brightened to the point of visibility. The stars became a dusty belt across the sky. The air grew chill, but he felt no impulse to return to the edun, to resume the mundane routine of their existence. Not this evening. Not upon such thoughts as he carried. Eventually the kel'ein would miss him, and look out and see him in his favorite place, and let him be. He spent many evenings here. There was nothing to do in the edun of evenings, save to sleep, to eat, to study things no longer true. None of them had sung the songs since the day the news of the war's end came. They frequently sat and talked together, excluding him. Probably, he thought, it was a relief to them to have him gone.

The geyser named Sochau belched steam far across the flats, a tall plume, predictable as the hours of any regul clock. By such rhythms the world lived, and by such rhythms it measured the days until the humans should come.

But for the first time in all the days since he had heard of the war's ending, he felt a suspicion of gladness, a fierce sense that the People might have something yet to do, and that humans might find their victory not an accomplished fact.

A star grew in the sky as the other had departed, rapid and omen-filled. He looked up at it with quickening interest, enlivened by something, even a triviality, that was not part of the ordinary. The shuttles did not usually descend until morning.

He watched it grow, cherishing imaginings both dread and hopeful, a mere child's game, for he did not really believe that it would be anything but a variance in regul schedules for regul reasons, as ordinary as anything could be in the organized routine of Kesrith's dying.

He watched it descend and saw suddenly lights flare on at the port in the farthest area, realized suddenly that it was not coming down at the freighter or shuttle berths, but to the area given over to military landings, and it was no shuttle. It was a ship of size, such as the onworld port had not held in many years.

The ship was nothing in the dark and the distance but a shape of light, featureless, nameless. There was nothing to indicate what it was. Of a sudden he knew his people must have word of this—that doubtless they had already been alert to it and only he had not been.

He sprang down from his rock and began to run, swift feet changing course here and there at the outset where the fragile earth masked dangers of its own. He did not use the road, but ran crosslands, by an old mri trail, and came breathless to the door of the edun, chest aching.

There was silence in the halls. He paused only a moment, then took the stairs toward the she'pan's tower, almost running up the first turn.

And there a shadow met him—old Dahacha coming down, Dahacha with his great, surly dus lumbering downsteps after him. Everyone brought up short, and the dus edged down a step to rumble a warning.

"Niun," the old man said. "I was coming to look for you."

"There is a ship," Niun began.

"No news here," said Dahacha. "*Hazan* is back. Yai! Come on up, young one. You are missed."

Niun followed, a great joy in him: *Hazan*—command ship for the zone; and high time it came, among regul panicked and retreating in disorder. There was resolution in the regul after all, some authority to hold the disintegrating situation under control.

And *Hazan!* If *Hazan* came, then came Medai—cousin, fellow kel'en, home from human wars and bringing with him experience and all the common sense that belonged to the fighting Kel of the front.

He remembered other things of Medai too, things less beloved; but it made no difference after six years, with the world falling into chaos. He followed Dahacha up the winding stairs with an absolute elation flooding through him.

Another kel'en.

A man the others would listen to as they would never listen to him, who had never left the world.

Medai, who had served with the leaders of regul and knew their minds as few kel'ein had the opportunity to know them—kel'en to the ship of the bai of Kesrith zones.

Chapter Five

The door was locked, as it was at every unpermitted period. Sten Duncan tried it yet another time, knowing it was useless, pounded his fist against it and went back to the old man.

"They refused to answer," said Stavros. He sat in the desk-chair, with the console screen at his left elbow a monotone grey. He looked uneasy, unusual for Stavros, even at the worst of times.

They were down, onworld. That was unmistakable.

"We were to dock," said Duncan finally, voicing the merest part of the concern boiling in his mind.

Stavros did not react to that piece of observation, only stared at him dispassionately. Duncan read blame into it.

"If there's been a change in plans, something could be wrong either on the station or onworld," Duncan said, trying to draw the smallest reassurance from the old man, a denial of his apprehensions—even outright anger. He could deal with that.

And when Stavros gave him nothing at all in reply he sank down at the table, head bowed against his hands, exhausted with the strain of waiting. It was their night. It was halfway through that night.

"Perhaps they're sleeping," Stavros said unexpectedly, startling him with a tone that held nothing of rancor. "If they chose to keep ship-cycle after landing, or if we're in local night, bai Hulagh could be asleep and his orderlies unwilling to respond to us without his authority. The regul do not inconvenience an elder of his rank."

Duncan looked back at him not believing the explanation, but glad that Stavros had made the gesture, whether or not he had another in the back of his mind that he was not saying. It did not ease his feelings in the least that Stavros had never said anything to him in the matter of the encounter with the mri, had only asked quiet questions of what had happened there in the mainroom: no blame, no hint of what had passed in Stavros' mind. Nor had Stavros said anything when they were shortly afterward presented with another schedule, their hours of liberty cut in half, a regul youngling constantly watching their door and following at a distance when he left the room.

The retaliation fell most heavily on himself, of course, confining him more closely, while that did not much concern Stavros; but for their safety and for the future of regul/human cooperation it augured ill enough. The regul's official manner did not change toward them. There was still the formal manner, still the salutations in the day's messages. Characteristic of the regul, there had been no direct mention of the incident in the hall, only the notification, without explanation, that their hours had been changed.

"I'm sorry, sir," Duncan volunteered at last, out of his own frustration.

Stavros looked for once surprised, then frowned and shrugged. "Probably just regul procedure and some minor change in plans. Don't worry about it." And then with a second shrug, "Get some sleep, Duncan. There's little else to do at the moment."

"Yes, sir," he said, rose and went out to the anteroom, sat down on his own bunk and tucked his legs up. He set his elbows on his knees and head on his hands and massaged his aching temples.

Prisoners, thanks to him.

Stavros was worried. Stavros doubtless knew what there was to concern them and he was worried. Perhaps if the regul had accepted the offering, Stavros could have demonstrated the punishment of the human youngling who had created the difficulty. Perhaps he had not done so because, in the main, they were both human and Stavros felt an unvoiced attachment to him; or perhaps he had declined to do so because a regul elder would not have done so under the same circumstances.

But it was clear enough that they were under the heavy shadow of regul displeasure, and had been for many, many days; and that they were not now where they had been told at the outset they would land.

A sound reached him, a sound of someone passing in the corridor, one of the sleds whisking along the tracks outside. He looked up as it seemed to stop, hoping against hope that the thing had stopped to bring them news.

The door opened. He sprang up, instantly correct. The sled indeed had stopped before the doorway, and within it sat the oldest, most massive regul that he had ever seen. Roll upon roll of wrinkled flesh and crusting skin hid any hint of structure that lay within that grey-brown body, save the bony plating of the face, where eyes were sunk in circular wrinkles, black and glittering eyes; and flat nose and slit mouth gave a deceptive illusion of humanity.

It was the face of a man within the body of a beast, and that body was lapped in brown robes, silver-edged and shimmering, gossamer enfolding a gross and wrinkle-crossed skin. The nostrils were slanted, slits that could flare and close. He knew this movement for an indication of emotion in the younglings, one of the few expressions of which their bone-shielded faces were capable—a roll of the eyes, an opening or closing of the lips, a flutter of the nostrils. But had he not known that this being was of precisely the same species as the younglings, he would have doubted it.

Incredibly the elder arose, heaving his body upright, then standing, on bowed and almost invisible legs, within the sled.

"Stavros," it—he—said, a basso rumble.

Humans could not imitate regul expression: the regul perhaps could not read courtesy or lack of it among humans, but Duncan knew that courtesy was called for now. He made a bow. "Favor," he said in the regul tongue, "I am the youngling Sten Duncan."

"Call Stavros."

But the door was open. Duncan turned, about to comply with the order, and saw of a sudden Stavros in the doorway, standing, coming no farther.

There was a rumbling exchange of regul politenesses, and Duncan took himself to the side of the room against the wall, bewildered in the flow of language. He realized what he had suspected already, that this was the bai himself who had come to call on them, bai Hulagh Alagn-ni, high commander of the ship *Hazan,* successor to the Holn, and provisional governor of Kesrith's zones during the transfer of powers from regul to human.

He made himself unnoticed; he would not offend a second time against regul manners, complicating things which he could not understand.

The exchange was brief. It was concluded with a series of courtesies and gestures, and the bai subsided into his sled and vanished, and Stavros closed the door for himself, before Duncan could free himself of his confusion and do so.

"Sir?" Duncan ventured then.

Stavros took his time answering. He looked around finally, with a sober and uneasy expression. "We are grounded on Kesrith," he said. "The bai assures us this is quite a natural choice for a ship of this sort, landing directly at the port—that it was a last-moment decision and without reason for concern to us. But I also gather that there is some instability here, which I do not understand. The bai wants us to remain on the ship. Temporary, he says."

"Is it," Duncan asked, "trouble over that business with the mri?"

Stavros shook his head. "I don't know. I don't know. I think that the whole crew is expected to remain aboard until things sort themselves out. This, at least—" Stavros' eyes went to the ceiling, toward venting, toward lighting, toward installations they did not understand and did not trust. The glance warned, said nothing, carried some misgiving that perhaps he would have voiced if he were safe to do so. "The bai assures us that we will be taken to the central headquarters in the morning. It is planetary night at the moment; we are already on Kesrith main time, and he advises us that the weather is fair and the inconvenience minor and we are expected to enjoy our night's rest and rise late, with the anticipation of a pleasant advent to Kesrith."

The bai is being courteous and formal, Stavros' expression thrust through the words themselves. There was no credibility there. Duncan nodded understanding.

"Good night, then," said Stavros, as if the exchange had been aloud. "I think we may trust that we are delayed aboard for some considerable number of hours, and there is probably time to get a night's sleep."

"Good night, sir," said Duncan, and watched as the old man went back to his quarters and the door closed.

He wished, not for the first time, that he could ask the old man plainly what he thought of matters, and that he could reckon how much the honorable Stavros believed of what he had been told.

In the time that they had been on scant favor among regul, Duncan had begun to apply himself to learning the regul tongue with the same fervent, desperate application he had once applied to SurTac arms and survival skills. He had begun with rote phrases and proceeded to structure with a facility far above what he had ever imagined he could achieve. He was not a scholar; he was a frightened man. He began to think, with the nightmare concentration that fears acquired in their solitude, that Stavros was indeed very old, and the time before humans would arrive was considerable, and that regul, who disposed of their own younglings so readily, would think nothing of killing a human youngling that had survived his elder, if that human youngling seemed useless to them.

Stavros' age, that had been the reason for his being assigned this mission, was also against its success. If something should befall the Hon. Mr. Stavros, it would leave Duncan himself helpless, unable to communicate with the general run of younglings, and, as Stavros had once pointed out, regul younglings would not admit him to contact with the likes of bai Hulagh, who were the only regul capable of fluent human speech.

It was not a possibility he cared to contemplate, the day that he should be left alone to deal with regul.

With hours left before debarkation on Kesrith, and with his nerves too taut to allow sleep, he gathered up his notes and started to study with an application that had his gut in knots.

Dag—Favor, please, attention. The same syllable, pronounced instead with the timbre of a steam whistle, meant: honorable; and in shrill tone: blood. *Dag su-gl'inh-an-ant pru nnugk*—May I have indirect contact with the reverence. . . . *Dag nuc-ci:* Favor, sir.

He studied until he found the notes falling from his nerveless hands, and collapsed to sleep for a precious time, before regul orderlies opened the door without warning and began shrilling orders at him, rudely snatching up their baggage without a prior courtesy.

None of the courtesies did these youngling regul use with him, even when he protested their rough handling of their belongings; they maintained a surly silence toward him, a fevered haste, interspersed with a chittering among themselves, as they loaded baggage on the transport sled that was to carry it away; another vehicle waited, a passenger sled.

"Now, now," one said, probably the extent of the human vocabulary he had troubled to hear, urging their haste; and only when Stavros himself appeared did the younglings assume decorum.

Even an elder human had his honor from the regul: they seemed to regard Stavros with a healthy fear.

But Duncan, when he looked back as they were boarding, chanced to look directly into the face of one of the younglings that bent, assisting them into the sled, and nostrils snapped shut and lips clamped, a look of hate that transcended species.

They were on Kesrith, among regul, who would be their companions and counselors in dealing with the evacuation of other regul who had made their homes here for centuries. They had come to take this world as conquerors, conquerors who, at least for thirty days, were only two, and vulnerable. The world had belonged to regul and to mri; and it was likely that certain of the crew of *Hazan* had called Kesrith their home.

It dawned upon him with immediacy that there could be more than simple racial or political hatred among regul toward their presence on Kesrith.

And perhaps there were many residents on Kesrith who had never consented to the treaty that disposed of their world and brought humans to it.

The inconvenience is minor, Stavros had translated the bai's assurance. Perhaps in the bai's eyes it was minor: the regul were not supposed to be able to lie; but in the eyes of the regul younglings that attended them there was no lie either, and it told a different story.

While they were on Kesrith, they would be housed in a building called the Nom, in the center of the chief city of Kesrith, and they would be thus protected for the first and most critical days against the irritations of Kesrith's natural atmosphere and the other minor inconveniences of the local climate: they would be expected to adapt.

And he saw Stavros' face when they first broke out of the ship's warmth into the wide world, and had their first sight of the place: hills, mountains, white plains, strangely lit by a ruddy pink sun.

For Stavros this was home, forever. His assignment was to prepare for other humans, to direct them after they had come, to build civilization again; and already Duncan was considering that five years here might be a very long time.

Regul, and alkali flats, and geysers, dust and mines and a sun that looked sickly and too large in the sky. He had been on half a score of worlds in his travels in the service, from bare balls of rock to flowering wildernesses, but he had never been on one so immediately alien as Kesrith.

Forbidding, unfriendly to humans. The very air smelled poisonous, laden with irritants.

If Stavros felt regret, he did not show it. He let himself be handled like a regul elder, already playing the part, and the younglings handed him down to the land sled that waited below. It was well after dawn, the sun a quarter of the way up the sky. There was, instead of the welcome they had expected—like most regul courtesies, carefully controlled and managed—a still and ghostly quiet about the port, as if they and the younglings were the only living things about the premises.

And far away, on the heights, was visible something that set Duncan's heart to beating more rapidly, a clutch of fear at the stomach that had nothing to do with reason, for there was the peculiar silhouette of four slanted towers that formed a flat-topped, irregular pyramid.

A mri edun. He had known there was one onworld. He had seen pictures of the ruins of Nisren. He was unprepared for it to be here, so close. It overlooked the city in such a way that nothing that was done on the plains could be hidden from it.

It brooded, an ominous and alien presence, reminding them all that there was a third party to the transaction that promised peace.

"Now. Now!" the regul repeated, impatient of the delay or at the object of his attention, it was unsure; but Duncan did not want to contest the matter, and he lowered his head and entered the sled, where the air was filtered and cleaned of the acrid biting taste that contaminated the air of Kesrith.

The sled lumbered off toward the city on pavement made rough by inroads of sand from the flats, taking them to what he thought with increasing conviction was a confinement only wider in space than their last.

Chapter Six

The sun was climbing the east, and on another day Niun would have been out about the hills, walking, hunting, practicing at arms, all other such things as he used to fill the solitary hours and relieve the sameness of his days.

But on this day nothing could have persuaded him from the vicinity of the edun. He haunted the communications station in the top of the Sen tower, where, in an edun grown informal by reason of its small size, he was permitted to be on occasion; he hovered about the main entrance; and finally, consumed by his impatience, he went to the rock at the top of the causeway, to stare into the growing glare off the white flats and strain his eyes for any movement from the direction of the port.

He had for so very, very long had nothing good to anticipate. Now he savored the feeling, hating the waiting, and yet relishing the feeling of waiting: with mixed feelings about the meeting, and yet longing desperately for the comradeship it promised. He had not loved Medai. He remembered the rivalry with his cousin; his—he could be honest with himself after so many years—jealousy of his cousin; and he strove to forget any such feelings he had ever cherished: he wanted Medai's presence, wanted it desperately, fervently. Anything was better than this long loneliness, this knowledge that the edun was slowly, irrevocably perishing.

And there was, at the foundation of all the thoughts, the least stirring of hope, the suspicion that Medai had been summoned, that he was the first of many to come—that the she'pan had stirred to action, and that something was moving in the future of the People.

On a thousand previous days, he had sat as he sat now, seeking any tiny deviation in events to occupy him, the struggles of an insect, the slow, perilous blooming of a windflower, the rise or descent of ships at the port—ill-wishing such ships, imagining disasters, imagining important arrivals that would somehow change the pattern of his existence. He had done this so often that it was hard to realize that this time it was real, that the game was substance on this morning so like a thousand other mornings. The very air seemed alive. His heart beat so strongly, his muscles were so taut that his chest and stomach hurt, and he almost forgot to breathe whenever his eyes would deceive him into believing that he had seen movement below.

But in the full light of noon, there was a plume of dust on the flats, at the beginning of the causeway, a line of dark figures moving slowly upward. He sat upon his rock at the top of the causeway and lowered his visor to remove the haze of daylight, trying to discern the figures individually.

He had seen vehicles come up the road years before. Judging the distance and the size of the objects and the amount of dust, that was what it looked to be. A sense of wrongness grew in him, a weight in his stomach counterpoised against the beating of his heart. He clenched his limbs together, long arms wrapped about his knees, and watched, unwilling to run and tell the others. Regul. Regul were coming up.

Once he would have been delighted at such an unaccustomed visitation; but he was not so on this morning of all mornings. Not now. Not with mri business afoot that was more important than regul.

Not with mri business in the working, in which regul might seek to interfere.

Of a sudden he realized that the she'pan desperately needed to know what was coming up the hill: he made them out—six vehicles and a moving dot further back that his eyes could not resolve; but it looked to be a seventh.

No such number of regul had ever called on the edun in his memory.

He slid down from his rock and started downhill, his long strides carrying him at what swiftly became an uncontrollable run, undignified, but he was too alarmed to care for appearances. He raced toward the edun, breathless.

Others were coming out the doorway even before he arrived with his warning—black-robes of the Kel, and none of gold: he slowed his pace and came to them, out of breath and trying to conceal his pain. Sweat filmed his skin, quickly dried as the moisture-hungry air stole it. One did not run on Kesrith: a hundred times he had been taught so, the sober necessities of the world imposed over the nature of youth. His lungs burned; there was the sharp edge of blood in the air he breathed. None of the Kel rebuked him for his rashness: and he felt the mood of them, saw it in the attitude of the attendant dusei that had come out of the edun with them. One of the dusei reared up, towering, snuffing the wind. It came down heavily on all fours again, an action that stirred the white dust, and blew a snort of distress.

"Yai, yai!" kel Dahacha rebuked the lot of the dusei, that meaningless word that had a thousand meanings between dus and kel'en. They shied away, the nine of them, dismissed, hovering in a knot near the edun, ears pricked. Some sat. Now and then one would rise and walk the circuit of the group of dusei, a different one each time, and constantly that one would eye the advancing caravan of regul vehicles and utter small whuffs of warning.

The Kel was veiled, for meeting outsiders. Niun secured the *mez* a proper degree higher, and took his place in their black rank, one among others; but kel'anth Eddan took him by the elbow and drew him to the front of the group.

"Here," said Eddan, and no more. A man would not jabber questions with the Kel in such a mood. Niun held himself silent, his heart constricted with panic at Eddan's gesture. He was a novice, even at his age; he did not belong in the fore of question-and-answer with regul, here between Eddan and kel Pasev, oldest masters of the Kel.

Unless it involved him personally.

Or a kinsman.

Of a sudden he knew a message must have been passed to the edun through the Sen-tower, some intelligence of events that the edun possessed and that he had missed, sitting alone, vainly anticipating pleasure in this day.

Something was fearfully amiss, that regul had intervened between mri kinsmen.

The regul caravan ground its slow way upward, the sound of its motors audible now. The sun beat down, wanly red. Out on the flats a geyser spouted: Elu, one of the dangerous random ones, that kept no schedule. The plume continued a time, ten times the height of a man, and with its characteristic slant. Then it quickly dissipated. It was possible to recognize each of the geysers of the flats by its characteristic pattern and location. Niun reckoned that if Elu had erupted, Uchan would not be long after. It was a precious moment of distraction, in which it was not necessary to consider the sinister line of dark vehicles laboring their way upslope.

One—two—three—four—five—six.

Six landsleds. No more than two had ever come to the edun at once. He did not make this observation aloud. The Kel about him stood utterly rigid, like images against which black robes fluttered in the strong wind. Each kel'en's right hand was at the belt where the *as'ei* were sheathed, fingers slipped within the belt. This was a warning, to another kel'en. The regul, being mere tsi'mri, had likely not the sense to recognize it; but it was courtesy all the same, to advise intruders that they were not wanted, whether or not the intruder had the wit to recognize a warning.

The sleds bounced over the final ruts in the ascending road, came at last to a dusty halt even with the front entry to the edun, fronting the Kel. Motors were cut off, leaving sudden silence. Regul opened doors and began laboriously to disembark: a full ten of regul younglings, sober and joyless, without even visible arrogance. One of them was the Nomguard, Hada Surag-gi: Niun recognized that one by the badges and the robes, which was the best way to recognize any individual regul. It was also likely, he reflected bitterly, that the regul Hada Surag-gi recognized him by his distinctive lack of badges; but the youngling came forward to face Eddan, and consequently himself, and gave no sign of recognizing him. Hada's eyes did not even linger. There was no hint of insolence. Hada Surag-gi sucked air and rocked forward, a regul courtesy.

There was a proper mri response to this, a gesture of reciprocal goodwill. Eddan did not make it, and therefore no mri moved. Hands stayed by the *as'ei*.

"Favor," said Hada Surag-gi. "We bring most tragic news."

"We are prepared to hear what you say," said Eddan.

"We trust that our elder informed you—"

"Do you bring us Medai?" asked Eddan harshly.

Hada turned, an awkward motion for a regul, a shifting of feet. It closed its hands and made the gesture that wished its assistants to perform their duties. They shuffled about the second sled and opened its storage, lifted out a white, plastic-encased form on a litter. They bore it forward and carefully set it down at the feet of Hada Surag-gi, before the Kel.

"We have brought you the remains of Medai," said Hada.

Niun knew, already, had known from Hada's first words; he did not move, nor even lower his visor. This steadiness might be mistaken by some of his brothers for self-control. It was numbness. He heard their movings, their stirrings about the scene as if they and he were in different places, as if, divorced from the scene, he watched from elsewhere, leaving the flesh of Niun s'Intel, like that of Medai s'Intel, senseless and unparticipant.

"Are the humans then that close?" asked Eddan, for it was the custom to give the dead of the People who had died in the war to cold space where they had died, or, better still, to the fires of suns, recalling the birth of the People, rather than to make a long and inconvenient journey from the fighting front to inter them in earth. All the People would choose, if they had the choice, to avoid earth-burial. It was strange that regul, knowing mri even slightly as they did, could have misunderstood this and made the mistake of returning a dead mri to his edun.

The regul younglings—no arrogance at all in their manner now—let air flutter their nostrils and by other signs looked uncomfortable in their mission.

Guilty, was the bitter thought that came to Niun, watching them. He came back to his own body and fixed his eyes on the eyes of Hada Surag-gi, willing that youngling to meet his gaze directly. For an instant Hada did so, and flinched.

Guilty and uncomfortable in this whole meeting, and trying not to say the half of what they knew. Niun trembled with anger. He found his breath short. There was no move from the Kel. They stood absolutely still, one with the mind of Eddan, who led them, who with a word could lead them to a thing no mri had ever done.

Hada Surag-gi shifted weight on bowed legs and backed a little from the shrouded corpse between them. "Kel'anth Eddan," Hada said, "be gracious. This kel'en wounded himself and would not have the help of our medical facilities, although we might perhaps have saved him. We regret this, but we have never attempted to violate your beliefs. We bring you the regrets also of bai Hulagh, in whose service this kel'en gained great distinction. It is bai Hulagh's profound regret—his most profound regret, that this meeting is an inauspicious one, and that he makes the acquaintance of the People in such a sad moment. He sends his condolences and offers his extreme personal distress at this most unhappy event—"

"Bai Hulagh is then the new commander of this zone. What of bai Solgah? What of the Holn?"

"Gone." The word was almost swallowed, momentum quickly resumed. "And the bai wishes, kel'anth, to assure you—"

"I surmise," said Eddan, "that the death of kel Medai is very recent."

"Yes," said Hada, deterred from the prepared speech: Hada's mouth worked, seeming to search for words.

"Suicide." Eddan used the vulgar regul word, although regul knew the meaning of the mri word *ika'al,* where it regarded the ritual death of a kel'en.

"We protest—" In gazing directly at the kel'anth, the youngling seemed to lose its thread of thought, which was an impossibility with the eidetic regul. "We protest vehemently, kel'anth, that this kel'en was in deep melancholy that had nothing to do with the accession of bai Hulagh to command or the fall from power of the Holn. We fear that you are drawing the wrong inference. If you suppose that—"

"I did not advance any statement of inference," said Eddan. "Do you suggest that one might be made?"

The regul, interrupted more than once, confounded by argument that was no argument, confused as regul easily were when dealing with mri, blinked rapidly and tried to regroup. "Kel'anth, I protest, be gracious, we only stated that this kel'en was in deep melancholy prior to his act, that he had been confined in his quarters by his own choice, refusing all attempts to inquire into his needs, and this had nothing to do with the accession of bai Hulagh, in no wise, sir, in no wise. Bai Hulagh became employer to this kel'en and this kel'en served him with great distinction in several actions. There was nothing amiss. But after the peace was announced, kel Medai evinced an increasing melancholy."

"You are of the Nom," Niun interrupted, unable to bear it longer, and Hada Surag-gi looked in his direction, black eyes wide, showing whites in amazement. "How is it that you report accurately on the state of mind of a kel'en who was on a ship far removed from you?"

It was not his place to have spoken. From a kel'en youth before strangers, it was an outburst, not an acceptable behavior; but the Kel stood firm, and as for Hada Surag-gi, its mouth flew open and shut again in a taut line.

"Elder," it protested to Eddan.

"Can the bai's spokesman answer the question?" asked Eddan, a vindication that sent a flood of fierce gratitude through Niun.

"Most gladly," said Hada. "I know these things to be fact because they are exactly as given to me by the bai himself, face to face, by his word. We had no idea that the kel'en contemplated such an action. It was not due to any animosity toward his service."

"Yet it is abundantly evident," said Eddan, "that kel Medai considered that he had sufficient reason to quit your service, such strong reason that he chose *ika'al* to be free of you."

"This was doubtless because of the end of the war, which this kel'en did not desire."

"It is," said Eddan, "curious that he would have elected *ika'al* when he knew that he was returning to homeworld."

"He was despondent," said Hada Surag-gi, illogicality that the regul did not seem to comprehend as illogical. "He was not responsible for his actions."

"You are speaking before his kinsman," said Eddan sharply. "This was a kel'en, not a dus, to go mad. He was bound for homeworld. What you say he did is not reasonable unless the bai offended against his honor. Is it possible that this was what happened?"

The regul, under the sting of Eddan's harsh voice, began to retreat slightly, a sidling backward by the hindmost.

"We are not done with questions," Eddan said, fixing Hada Surag-gi with his stare. "Tell us where and when kel Medai died."

The regul did not want to answer at all. It sucked air and visibly changed color. "Favor, kel'anth. He died during the previous evening on the ship of the bai."

"On the ship of bai Hulagh."

"Kel'anth, the bai protests—"

"Was there any manner of discussion passed between the bai and the kel'en?"

"Be gracious. The kel'en was despondent. The end of the war—"

"The bai made this mri despondent," Eddan said, discomfiting the youngling utterly.

"The bai," said Hada, nostrils dilating and contracting in rapid breaths, "requested of this mri that he remain in the ship and remain in service; the kel'en refused, wishing to leave at once, a privilege the bai had denied to everyone, even himself. There were matters of business to attend. It is possible—" the skin of the youngling went paler and paler as it spoke: its lips faltered upon the words. "Kel'anth, I realize that there is possible blame in your eyes; yet we do not understand the actions of this kel'en. The bai commanded him to wait. Yet the kel'en found fault with the order sufficient that he committed this act. We do not know why. We assure you we are greatly distressed by this sad event. It is an hour of crisis for Kesrith, in which this kel'en would have been of great service to the bai and to yourselves, surely. The bai valued the service of kel Medai. We protest again that we do not understand the source of his bitterness with us."

"Perhaps you did not inquire or listen," said kel'anth Eddan.

"Be gracious. Kesrith has been ceded to humans. We are in the process of the evacuation of all residents of Kesrith. Arrangements are being made also for the mri of Kesrith. The bai wishes his ship manned at all hours, and he wishes the crew, naturally—" The youngling moved uneasily, looking at Eddan, who did not move. "These are affairs over which we have no control. If the kel'en had only informed the bai of his extreme desire to have an exception granted in his case—"

"Kel Medai chose to leave his service," said Eddan. "It was well done. We do not want to talk to youngling regul on this subject any longer. Go away now."

And this was plainly put, and the regul, degree by degree, retreated, more rapidly as they neared their sleds. Hada was neither the first nor the last seated. Hatches were closed, engines started; the landsleds lumbered clumsily into a turn on the narrow and rutted roadway and retreated down the long slope as slowly as they had come.

No one moved. There was a numbness in the air now that the regul had gone, leaving them alone with their dead.

And suddenly in the doorway, gold-robes and white, the sen'anth and Melein, and the she'pan herself, on their arms.

"Medai is dead," said Eddan, "and the world is going to humans soon, as we suspected." He lifted his robed arms to shield the she'pan from the sight; and Melein started forward a step, only a step: it was forbidden her. She veiled herself and turned her face away, bowing her head; and likewise the she'pan and the sen'anth veiled, which they did not do save in the presence of the unacceptable.

They went away into the edun. Death was the peculiar domain of the Kel, either in inflicting it or mourning it; and it was for them to attend to the proprieties.

For a kinsman within the Kel it was a personal obligation.

Niun knew that he was expected in this to take charge; and he saw that the others longed to help, to do something, and he opened his hands, gave them leave. He had only heard the rites, had never done them, and he did not wish to shame himself or Medai by his ignorance. They gathered up the litter, he and all who could find space to help, and passed within the doors of the edun, toward the Pana'drin, the Shrine, to present Medai at his homecoming, where he would have presented himself first if he had lived.

Niun's hands felt the warm metal of the litter frame; he looked down on the object in white that had been his cousin, and the shock that had held him numb until now began to meld into other feelings, into a deep and helpless rage.

It was not right that this had happened. There was no justice in things if this could happen. He found almost trembling with anger, a violence in which he could kill, if there were anyone or anything against which to direct that rage.

There was no one. He tried to feel nothing; that was easier, than to try to find a direction for the resentment that boiled in him. He had hoped: he schooled himself not to hope, henceforth. The world was mad, and Medai had added himself to the madness.

My last son, the she'pan had called him. Now it was true.

Chapter Seven

There was a screen in the Shrine of the Edun of the People, worked in metals and precious stones and overwritten with ancient things. It was old beyond reckoning, and in every Shrine that had ever existed, this very screen had stood, between the lamps of bronze that were of equal age with it. In life it marked the division between the Kel and the Sen, the point past which the Kel might not tread: in death it was no more crossable.

Before the screen, at its very base, they laid the white-shrouded body of Medai s'Intel Sov-Nelan, as close to the dividing line as a kel'en could ever come. Incense curled up from burners on either side of the screen, heavy and cloying, overhanging the room and obscuring the ceiling like an immaterial canopy.

For Niun, attendant to his cousin, that scent of incense held its own memories, of being in the Kath and of watching holy rites from that least, outermost room, when he had been a child with Melein and Medai beside him, and others now gone, whose deaths he knew. From that outer room the small shrine of the Kel had seemed mysterious and glorious, a territory where they might not yet venture, where warriors in their *sigai* might move, disdaining the Kath.

His mind ran to a later day, when they three had been taken among the black-robes, one with the Kel, and had been allowed for the first time to enter the middle shrine, and to realize that yet another barrier lay between them and the Pana, the Mysteries; and a day later yet, that they had prayed for the welfare of Medai, who was leaving the edun for service, greatly honored—and Niun had died inwardly that night with jealousy and bitterness, his prayers insincere and hating and mingled with thoughts that came back now like guilty ghosts.

He felt no differently now than then. Medai had taken another departure, leaving him the ugliness, the loneliness of Kesrith.

Medai had never endured the things he had endured, left here, last guard to the House, servant to the others.

Medai was counted a great kel'en for what he had done.

There was a whisper of robes in the holiness dimly visible beyond the screen, where the Sen met and tended the Holy Objects. Melein would be there, with Sathell.

Three children an age ago had stood within the outer Kath-hall, and longed for honor; and they had gotten their prayers in strange and twisted ways: Niun within Kel-shrine, where they had all longed to go; Medai possessing the honors of a warrior, newly wandering the Dark; and Melein, Melein the light-hearted, had passed through Kel-shrine to the place beyond, to the Mysteries that were never for a kel'en to see.

He bowed down, shaking with rage and frustration, and remained so for a time, trying to take his breath back again and compose himself.

A hand touched his shoulder. A dark robe brushed him with shadow as Eddan sank down beside him. "Niun," the kel'anth said in a soft voice. "The she'pan calls you. She does not want you to have to sit this watch. She says that she wants you to come and sit with her this night, and not to go to the burial."

It took him a moment to be sure of his voice. "I do not believe it," he said after a moment, "that she will not loose me even for this. What did she say? Did she give no reason?"

"She wishes you to come, now."

He was stunned by such an attitude. There had been no love between himself and Medai: the she'pan knew that well enough; but there was no decency in what she asked him to do, publicly. "No," he said. "No, I will not go to her."

The fingers dug into his shoulder. He expected rebuke when he looked up. But the old man unveiled to him, showing his naked face, and there was no anger there. "I thought you would say so," Eddan said, which was incredible, for he had not known himself: it was impulse. But the old man knew him that well. "Do as you think right," Eddan said further. "Stay. I will not forbid you."

And the old man rose and ordered the others, who moved about their separate tasks. One brought the vessels of ritual, given by the Sen, that were for burying, and set them at Medai's feet; Pasev brought water; and Dahacha, cloths for washing; and Palazi filled the lamps for the long vigil; and Debas whistled softly to the dusei and took them from the outer hall, herding them away into the tower of the Kel so that they should not disturb the solemnities. In the midst of the activity Niun sat, conscious finally that he had torn his robe in his haste for descending from the hills, and that he was dusty and his hands were foul with dirt. Feet pattered about him. Sirain came, half-blind Sirain, and gave him a damp cloth, and Niun unveiled and washed his face and veiled again, grateful for his thoughtfulness. Liran brought a robe for him, and he changed his *siga* in the very Shrine, for it was not respect to sit the watch in disorder. He sat down again, and began to be calmer at their quiet, efficient ministering.

Then at Eddan's whispered word, they began to take the ugly white shroud from Medai, and patiently, patiently the fingers of one and the other of them tore the webbing that was as close-spun as a cocoon and well-nigh impenetrable—like *cho*-silk it was, having to be unraveled with the fingers. But Pasev knew to touch the regul fiber with a burning wick, and so to part the strange web. The material burned sullenly, but it gave way, shedding its chemical smell into sickening union with the incense that lowered overhead.

It was something on which they all silently agreed, that they would not give to burial a kel'en in a regul shroud, whatever the inconvenience; and gradually they recovered Medai from the web, a face that they remembered, a countenance still and pale. The body was small and thin in death, pitifully so; it weighed very little, and Medai had been a strong man. The honors that they found laced to his belts were many, and the *seta'al* were weathered to pale blue on his face. He had been a handsome youth, had Medai s'Intel, full of the life and the hope of the edun in brighter days. Even now he was very fine to see. The only marring of him was the blood that stained the fiber under his central ribs, where he had dealt himself his death wound.

Suicide.

Niun worked, not looking at Medai's face, trying not to think what his hands did, lest they tremble and betray him. He was trying to remember better days, could not. He knew Medai too well.

His cousin was in his dying as he had been in life: selfish, arrogant to match regul arrogance, and stubborn with it all. It was wrong to hold anger with the dead, impious. But in the end Medai had been as useless to his kinfolk as he had always been. Medai had lived for himself and died for his own reasons, nothing regarding what others might need of him; and there was precious little honor for a cold corpse, whatever the high traditions of the Kel.

They had parted in anger. He remembered, each day of his life for six years he had remembered, and he knew why the she'pan had wanted him upstairs, and what was surely in the minds of his brother kel'ein who sat with him. There had been a quarrel, the *av'ein-kel*, the long blades drawn; it had been his own fault, drawing first, in the Shrine hall, outside. It was the day that Medai had laid hand on Melein.

And Melein had not objected.

The she'pan herself had put an end to that quarrel—abler in those days six years gone—had descended the tower stairs and intervened. Had called him *eshai'i*, lack-honor, and *tsi'daith'*, unson, and because then he had loved her, it had crushed him.

But not a word, never a word of rebuke to Medai.

And for Medai within a hand of days came the honor of service to the bai of the regul, an honor that might have gone to one of the Husbands; and for Melein came the chastity of the Sen.

And for Niun s'Intel came nothing, only a return to study, a long, long waiting, crushed to the Mother's side and held from any hope of leaving Kesrith.

There had never been a way to undo that one evil day. Intel would not let him go. He had hoped for peace with Medai, for a change in the affairs of the People.

But Medai had robbed him of that too. It was on him alone, the service of homeworld, and there had never been any justice in it.

When you have made up your mind what it is the People owe you, Eddan had said, *come and tell me.* He would have settled for half of what Medai had had.

But then, beginning with Eddan, the Kel spoke of Medai, each praising him: ritual, the *lij'alia,* beginning the Watch of the Dead; and the voices of the old kel'ein shook in the telling of it.

"It is hardest," said Liran, "that the old bury the young."

And last of all but himself, Pasev: "It is certain," she said, touching the medallions, the *j'tai* that glittered in the lamps' golden light, the honors that Medai had won in his services, "that though he was young, he has travelled very far and seen a great deal of war. I see here the service of Shoa, of Elag, of Soghrune, of Gezen and Segur and Hadriu; and it is certain that he has served the People. Surely, surely he has done enough, this brother of ours, this child of our house; I think that surely he was very tired. I think he must have been very weary of service to the regul, and he would have come home as best he could, with what of his strength he had left. I understand this. I am also very tired of the service of regul; and if I knew my service was at an end, I would go the road he took."

And then it should have been Niun's time to speak, praising Medai, his cousin. He had gathered angry words, but he could not, after that, speak them or contradict the feelings of Pasev, whom he loved with a deep love. He sank down and lowered his head into his crossed arms, shaking with reaction.

And the Kel allowed him this, which they seemed to take for a kinsman's grief. But theirs was a true, unselfish sorrow for a child they had loved. His was for himself.

In this he found the measure of himself, that he was capable of meanness and great selfishness, and that he was not, even now, the equal of Medai.

The others talked around him, whispering, after such a time as it became clear that he would not choose to speak in the ritual. They began finally to speak of the high hills, the burial that they must accomplish, and woven into their speech and their plans was a quiet desperation, a shame, for they were old and the hills were very far and the trail very steep. They wondered unhappily among themselves whether the regul might not, at their request, give them motorized transport; but they felt at heart that they dishonored Medai by asking such help of the regul. They would not, therefore, ask. They began to consider how they might contrive to carry him.

"Do not worry," said Niun, breaking his long silence. "I can manage it myself."

And he saw in their faces doubt, and when he thought of the steep trails and the high desert he himself doubted it.

"The she'pan will not allow it," said Eddan. "Niun, we might bury him close at hand."

"No," said Niun, and again, thinking of the she'pan, "no." And after that there were no more suggestions to him. Eddan quietly signed at the others to let be.

And they left him, when he asked of them quietly and with propriety to be left alone. They filed out with robes rustling and the measured ring of honors on their garments. The tiny high sound of it drew at Niun's heart. He considered his own selfishness, lately measured, and the courage of his elders, who had done so much in their lives, and was mortally ashamed.

But he began to think, in the long beginning of his nightlong watch, in the silences of the edun, where elsewhere others were in private mourning—and knew that he was not willing to die, whatever the traditions of his caste, that he did not want to die as Medai had died, above all else; and this ate at him, for it was contrary to all that he was supposed to be.

Medai had been able to accept such things, and the she'pan had accepted Medai. And this was what it had won him.

It was blasphemy to entertain such thoughts before the Shrine, in the presence of the gods and of the dead. For himself he was ashamed, and he longed to run away, as he had done when he was a child, going into the hills to think alone, to try himself against the elements until he could forget again the pettinesses of men, and of himself.

But he was reckoned a man now, and it had been long since he had had that freedom. Dangerous times were on the edun, hard times, and it was not an hour that Niun s'Intel could afford to play the child.

There was a matter of duty, of decencies. Medai had lived and died by that law. He could not manage the inner part of him, but he could at the least see to it that the outer man did what was dutiful to those who had to depend on him.

Even if it were totally a lie.

"Niun."

The stir, the whisper from beyond the screen he had taken for the wind that blew constantly through the shrine. He looked up now and saw a hazed golden figure through the intricate design, and knew his sister's voice. She crossed the floor as far as the

screen that divided them, religiously, though they could meet
face-to-face elsewhere in the edun and outside its limits.

"Go back," he wished Melein, for she violated the law of her
caste by being in the presence of the dead, even a dead kinsman.
Her caste had no debts of kinship; they renounced them, and all
such obligations. But she did not leave. He rose up, stiff from
kneeling on the cold floor, and came to the grillwork. He could
not see her distinctly. He saw only the shadow of her hand on the
lacery of the screen and matched it with his own larger one in
sympathy, unable to touch her. He was unclean and in the presence of the dead, and would remain unapproachable until he had
buried his kinsman.

"I am permitted to come," she said. "The she'pan gave me
leave."

"We have done everything," he assured her, struck to the heart
remembering that there had been affection between Melein and
Medai, cousinwise, and at the last, perhaps more than cousinly.
"We are going to take him to Sil'athen—everything that we can
do we will do."

"I had not thought you would watch here," she said. And then,
with an edge of utter bitterness. "Or is it only because you were
directly ordered not to?"

Her attack confused him. He took a moment to answer, not
knowing clearly against what manner of assumption he was answering. "He is kin to me," he said. "Whatever else—is no matter
now."

"You would have killed him yourself once."

It was the truth. He tried to see Melein's face through the
screen; he could only see the outline, golden shadow behind gold
metal. He did not know how to answer her. "That was long ago,"
he said. "And I would have made my peace with him if he were
alive. I had wanted that. I had wanted that very much."

"I believe you," she said finally.

She left silence then. He felt it on him, an awkward weight. "It
was jealousy," he admitted to her. The thing that he had pondered
took shape and had birth, painfully, but it was not as painful as he
had thought it would be, brought to light. Melein was his other
self. He had been as close as thought to her once, could still imagine that closeness between them. "Melein, when there are only

two young men within a Kel, it is impossible that they not compare themselves and be compared by others. He had first all the things I wanted to excel in. And I was jealous and resentful. I interfered between you. It was the most petty thing I have ever done. I have paid for it, for six years.

She did not speak for a moment. He became sure that she had loved Medai; only daughter of an edun otherwise fading into old age, it was inevitable that she and Medai should once have seemed a natural pairing, kel'en and kel'e'en, in those days when she had also been of the Kel.

Perhaps—it was a thought that had long tormented him—she would have been happier had she remained in the Kel.

"The she'pan sent me," she said finally, without answering his offering to her. "She has heard of the intention of the Kel. She does not want you to go. There is disturbance in the city. There is uncertainty. This is her firmest wish, Niun: stay. Others will see to Medai."

"No."

"I cannot give her that answer."

"Tell her that I did not listen. Tell her that she owes Medai better than a hole in the sand and that these old men cannot get him to Sil'athen without killing themselves in the effort."

"I cannot say that to her!" Melein hissed back, fear in her voice, and that fear made him certain in his intentions.

It made no more rational sense than the other desires of Intel, this she'pan that could gamble with the lives of the People, that could bend and break the lives of her children in such utter disregard of their desires and hopes. *She has given me her virtues,* he thought, with a sudden and bitter insight: *jealousy, selfishness, possessiveness, . . . ah, possessive, of myself, of Melein, the children of Zain. She sent Melein to the Sen and Medai to the regul when she saw how things were drifting with them. She has ruined us. A great she'pan, a great one, but flawed, and she is strangling us, clenching us against her until she breaks our bones and melts our flesh and breathes her breath into us.*

Until there is nothing left of us.

"Do as you have to do," he said. "As for me, I will do him a kinsman's duty, truesister. But then you are sen'e'en and you do

not have kinsmen anymore. Go back and say what you like to the
she'pan."

He had hoped, desperately, to anger her, to pierce through her
dread of Intel. He had meant it to sting, just enough. But her hand
withdrew from the screen and her shadow moved away from him,
becoming one with the light on the other side.

"Melein," he whispered. And aloud: "Melein!"

"Do not reproach *me* with lack of duty," her voice came back to
him, distant, disembodied. "While he lived, I was a kinswoman to
him and you were grudging of everything he had. Now I have
other obligations. Say over him that the she'pan is well pleased
with his death. That is her word on the matter. As for me, I have
no control over what you do. Bury him. Do as you choose."

"Melein," he said. "Melein, come back."

But he heard her footsteps retreat up hidden stairs, heard doors
close one after another. He stayed as he was, one hand against the
screen, thinking until the last that she would change her mind and
come back, denying that answer she had made him; but she left.
He could not even be angry, for it was what he had challenged her
to do.

Intel's creation. His too.

He hoped that somewhere in Sen-tower Melein would lay
down her pride and weep over Medai; but he doubted it. The
coldness, the careful coldness that had been in her voice was beyond all repentance, the schooled detachment of the Sen.

He left the screen finally, and sat down by the corpse of Medai.
He locked his hands behind his neck, head bowed on his knees,
twice desolate.

The lamps snapped and the fires leaped, the door of the edun
having been left open this night, an ancient tradition, a respect to
the dead. Shadows leaped and made the writings on the walls
seem to writhe with independent life, writings that the she'pan
said contained the history and wisdom of the People. All his life
he had been surrounded by such things: writings covered every
wall of the main hall and the Shrine and the she'pan's tower, and
the accesses of Kath and Kel—writings that the she'pan said were
duplicated in every edun of the People that had ever existed, exact
and unvaried. Through such writings the sen'ein learned. The
Kel'ein could not. He knew only what had happened within his

own life and within his sight, or those things he heard his elders recall.

But Melein could read the writings, and knew what truth was, as did the she'pan, and grew cold and strange in that knowledge. He had asked once, when Melein was taken into the Sen, if he could not be taken too: they had never in their lives been separated. But the she'pan had only taken his hands into hers, and turned the calloused palms upward. Not the hands of a scholar, she had said, and dismissed his appeal.

Something stirred out in the hall, a slow shuffling, a click of claws on stone—one of the dusei that had strayed from the Kel-tower. They generally went where they chose, none forbidding them, even when they were inconvenient or destructive. It was not even certain that one could forbid them, for they were so strong that there could be no coercion. They sensed, in the peculiar way of dusei, when they were wanted and when not, and rarely would they stay where they were not desired.

They understood the kel'ein, the belief was, whose thoughts were unfearing and uncomplex, and for this reason each dus chose a kel'en or kel'e'en and stayed lifelong. One had never set affection on Niun s'Intel, though once he had tried—shamefully desperate—to trap a young one and to coerce it. It had fled his childish scheme, smashing the trap, knocking him unconscious.

And never after that had he found any skill to draw one after him, as if that one, betrayed, had warned all its kind of nature of Niun s'Intel.

The elder kel'ein said that it was because he had never truly opened his heart to one, that he was too sealed up in himself.

He thought this false, for he had tried; but he also thought that the sensitive dusei had found him bitter and discontent and could not bear it.

He believed so, hoping that this would change; but in the depth of his heart he wondered if it were possibly because he was not a natural kel'en. For a woman of the People all castes were open; for a man, there were only Kel-caste and Sen; and he had been both deprived in one sense and overindulged in others, simply because he was the last son of the House. It had meant that he received the concentrated efforts of all his teachers, that they had worked with him until he had understood, until his skill was acceptable. But in an edun full of sons and daughters, he thought that he might have failed to survive; his stubbornness would have brought him early challenge, and the People might then have been rid of his irritance in the House. He thought that he might have been a better kel'en if not for the Mother's interference; but then many things might have been different if he were not the last; and so might she.

Medai had pleased the Mother; and Medai was dead; but he sat here living, a rebel son to the Mother. She would have somewhat to say to him after Medai's burying in the hills, when he must come back and face her. Thereafter would be bitter, bitter words, and himself without argument, and Melein on the she'pan's side in it. He shrank from what the she'pan might say to him.

But she would have to say it. He would not unsay what he had said.

Again the scrape of claws. It was a dus. The explosive sough of breath and the heavy tread made it clear that the intruder was coming closer, and Niun willed it away from the Shrine, for dusei were not welcome here. Yet it came. He heard it enter the outer room, and turned and saw it in the dark, a great slope-shouldered shadow. It made that peculiar lost sound again, and slowly edged closer.

"Yai!" he said, turning on one knee, furiously willing it out.

And then he saw that the dus was dusty and that its coat was patched with crusted sores, and his heart froze in his chest and his breath caught, for he realized then that it was not one of their own tame beasts, but a stranger.

Sometimes wild dusei would come down off the high plains to hover round the lands of the edun and create havoc among the tame ones; in his own memory kel'ein had died, trying to approach such an animal, even armed. Dusei sensed intentions, uncannily prescient: there were few animals more dangerous to stalk.

This one stood, head lowered, massive shoulders filling the doorway, and rocking back and forth, uttering that plaintive sound. It forced its way in, making the plaster crumble here and there, though the door was purposely made small and inconvenient for them, to protect the Mysteries from their mindless irreverence.

It came, irresistible, thinner than the well-fed dusei of the edun. Niun edged aside, one of the lamps crashing down as the dus shouldered it. It whined and whuffed and fortunately the spilled fire went out, though the hot oil stung its foot and made it shy aside. Then it approached the body of Medai and pawed at it with claws as long as a man's hand—poisonous, the dew claw possessing venom ducts, the casual swipe of them capable of disemboweling mri or regul. Niun crouched in the shadow by the overturned lamp, as immobile as the furniture. The beast's body filled much of the room and blocked the doorway. It had a fearsome, sickly stench that overrode even the incense; and when it turned its massive head to stare at the frail mri huddled in the corner, its eyes showed, running, dripping rheum onto the hallowed floor.

Miuk! The Madness was on him. The secretions of his body were out of balance and the *miuk,* the Madness of his kind, was to blame for his behavior, sending him into a mri dwelling. There was nothing Niun knew, neither beast nor man, more to be feared than this: if the dusei of the edun had not been locked upstairs this night, they would never have let a *miuk'ko* dus come near the edun; they would have died in defense of that outer doorway, rather than let that beast in.

And Niun s'Intel prepared himself to die, most horribly, in a space so small that the dus could not even cast his body from underfoot; his brothers would find him in shreds. It prodded at the body of Medai, as if in prelude to this, but it hesitated. Grotesque, horrid, the beast rocked to and fro, straddling the corpse, its eyes streaming fluid that blinded it. From some far place in the Kel-tower there was a deep moan, a dus fretting at its unaccustomed confinement, at the mood of the mourning Kel—or sensing invasion downstairs, trying desperately to get out. Others joined in, then fell abruptly silent, hushed perhaps by the order of the kel'ein.

Niun held his breath while the rogue lifted his rheum-blinded eyes toward that sound, mobile lips working nervously. It rocked. It gave another explosive snort and shifted its weight, easing aside. The shoulder hit the screen. It toppled with a brazen crash, and the beast whirled, bathed in the glow from the inner shrine. Niun flung his arm over his eyes in horror lest he see the Forbidden, and then, surety in his heart, he reached for his gun, futile against a dus.

He must attack whatever threatened the Forbidden, to prevent, if he could, the invasion of the Sen-shrine. He sighted for the brain, the first of the two brains, knowing full well the following convulsions would destroy him with the dus.

But the dus did not take that step beyond. It lowered its weeping head and nosed at the corpse, disarranging the veil; and when it had done so, it moaned and slowly, almost distractedly, swung its head about, putting its shoulder between its head and the gun, and began to withdraw from the Shrine.

And when it had done so, when it walked the hall outside, still giving that lost-infant sound, for the first time Niun clearly knew it.

Medai's dus.

There was no mri who could claim, other clues removed, to know any dus but his own, and not even that one, given much passage of time. Dusei were too similar and too mutable, and one could only say that this one was *like* the dus he knew.

But that this particular one had not killed him, that it had been primarily interested in the body, and departed unsatisfied—that action he understood. Dusei were troubled at death. Other animals ignored the dead, but dusei did not understand, did not accept it. They grieved and searched and fretted, and eventually died themselves, more often than not. They rarely outlived their masters, pining away in their search.

And this one was hunting something it had not found.

Medai's dus, come looking for him.

A dus that was sickly and covered with sores and deep in the throes of a madness that did not come on swiftly, although regul said that Medai had died but a night ago.

A dus that was thin and starved as its dead master.

A chill feeling grew in Niun, until he was physically shivering, not alone from dread of the dus. He holstered his gun and glanced fearfully at the nakedness of the inner shrine, on which he ought never to have looked.

It should not have happened. He washed his hands with the water of the offerings, and without setting foot across the forbidden line, he set the screen in place again, his fingers reverent on the inanimate metal. He had lived. The gods, like men, could forgive the irreverence of dusei; and he had looked within the Sen shrine, and felt shaken, but not to the death. He had seen brightness, but nothing of the Objects, or nothing that he could identify as the Holy. He tried to put this from his mind. It was not for a kel'en to have seen. He did not want to remember it.

And Medai—

He set up the lamp again, and refilled it, and lighted it, restoring its comforting glow. Then on his knees he mopped up the spilled oil that by the mercy of the gods had not kept burning; and all the while he worked, exhausted and trembling from his vigil, he thought, and nursed that cold feeling that lodged under his heart.

At last he washed his hands for respect and laid hands on Medai for the irreverence he had to commit: the thought borning in his mind gave him no peace otherwise. He did it quickly, once he had gathered his courage, carefully unfastened the clothing and examined the wound, and found it—shaming his suspicion and his act—as the regul had said.

Ika'al.

"Forgive me," he said to the spirit of Medai; and reverently reclosed the robes and washed the face and replaced the veils. Then he cast himself on his face before the shrine and made the proper prayers to the several ancestor-gods of his caste for rest for the soul of Medai, with more sincerity than he had ever used on his cousin when he was living.

This should have absolved him and given him peace, having surrendered to that which was proper and honest, but it did not.

He had in him a gathering certainty that, whatever the evidence of his eyes and the testimony of the regul, Medai had not laid down his life willingly.

The dus, so close to a kel'en's mind, was *miuk'ko* and grown so thin that it could pass shrine doors; and the body of Medai, once solid with muscle, was thin as the mummified dead.

Kel-quarters were independent units within the regul ship plan, because of the dusei, which the regul feared beyond all logic; and because of the stringent caste laws that a kel'en must observe with respect to contact with outsiders.

But essentially that kel'en was always at the mercy of the regul, who supplied that unit with food, water, even the air he breathed. All that a kel'en could do to assert his independence was lock the door.

Had they wanted him dead, they could have stopped the air and cast him into cold space afterward. But these were tsi'mri, and more than that, they were strangers to the People, a strange new branch of regul; and they might not have known enough to deal with a kel'en. Regul were not fighters.

Not directly.

Consumed by the thought that took shape in him, he rose up and left the shrine, took an offering vessel of water and a pannikin, and went out to the outer hall, to the door, where the mad dus still crouched before the edun.

He had known it must be there, waiting. It was near what it desired, but could not find it. He had been as sure of its lingering there as he was sure how it had been driven mad. It was no less dangerous for its once having been tame; it could still rise up and kill on impulse. But when he set the water before it, it sniffed at the offering curiously and at last bestirred itself, nosing down into the water. The contents of the pannikin disappeared. Niun filled it a second and a third and a fourth time, and only at the fourth did the beast suddenly avert its head in refusal.

He sank down on his heels and studied the creature, thin as it was and its fur gone in patches. A great open wound was fresh on its side.

Medai's dus, come from regul care, from violence, from starvation. It would not have left Medai of choice even after he was dead.

Regul would not act as mri would act. They were capable of collusion, of bribery, of deceit, of slaughter of their own young, but never of murder of an adult, never of that. They could neither kill nor lie in cold blood; they hired mri to attend to their enemies.

So he had always been taught, by those who knew the regul better than he, by those who had dealt with regul lifelong.

So he had implicitly believed.

As had Medai.

He rose and walked inside, back to the Shrine, and sat down beside the body of his cousin, arms locked about him, staring without comprehension at the serpentine writings that recorded and concealed the history of the People.

Murder had been done, in one manner or another, whatever name the regul gave it. A kel'en had been killed by his own employers, and his dus weakened to the point that they could drive it out to die naturally—one body to return to the Kel, the act of ignorant regul; another disposed of by predators and scavengers, or at best those incapable of betraying what had happened. Regul hands and regul conscience were doubtless clean. Medai had finally done as they had wished.

He wished desperately to go upstairs and tell someone. He wished to run to Eddan for counsel, to alert the she'pan. But he had nothing for proof but a beast that lay outside the door. He had nothing on which to hang such an accusation, no shape to his suspicion, no motive he could reckon which would have driven the regul to compel a kel'en to such an action.

It was irony of a kind, he thought, that of all whom Medai might have trusted to see to his avenging, he had come to the hands of his oldest rival; and the only likely witness of the truth was a *miuk'ko*.

Dusei, it was said, lived in the present; they had no memories for what had happened, only for persons and places. It had sought home, the House where it had first lived; it had sought Medai; it had found the one, and not the other.

Chapter Eight

Niun had begun, before the others had even stirred, to prepare for the journey to Sil'athen. There was the water drawn, and the ritual store of food, a token only, and the real provisions that were for the living.

With much effort he took the body of Medai from the small Shrine and bound it with cords to the regul litter on which it had come. The dus that waited by the doorway saw, but paid no heed to what he did.

Then the others began to come: Eddan and Pasev and Dahacha and the rest of the Kel. The dusei came down too, and the *miuk'ko* by the door withdrew a space. There in the sunlight it subsided, massive head between its paws, sides heaving. It was deep in shock.

"*Miuk,*" murmured Debas, horrified to see what sat at their gates.

But Pasev, who was, despite having killed many humans, a gentle soul, went and tried to call to it, staying out of its reach. It reared aside with a plaint of rage and sank down again a little distance away, exhausted by its effort. The dusei of the edun drew aside from it, agitated, sensing the distress of their fellow and the danger he posed. They formed a tight knot about the Kel and commenced that circling action by the guard dus, protecting the Kel from the threat of the rogue.

And eyes were on Niun, questioning. He shrugged and picked up the ropes of Medai's improvised sled. "It came," he said, "into the shrine last night." He looked at Eddan. "It was hunting someone."

And he saw the ugly surmise leap into the kel'anth's eyes: a wise man, Eddan, if he were not kel'en. And quietly Eddan turned and gestured to Pasev, to Liran and Debas and Lieth. "Stay here," he said. "Guard the she'pan."

"Eddan," said Pasev, "the she'pan forbade—"

"Any who wish to stay besides these may stay. Guard the she'-pan, Pasev."

And Niun, not waiting for them, started out, knowing already by the resistance of the sled that he was going to pay dearly for his obstinacy, when the she'pan and all the rest had given him a way to escape this kinsman's duty.

Slowly, painfully, the *miuk'ko* heaved itself up and tried to follow the sled. It went only as far as the roadway, and there sank down, exhausted, at the end of its strength.

The other dusei flanked it, one still pacing between the dus and the remaining Kel, watching the rogue. They did not follow the burial party. They were not wanted. They guarded the edun.

And Eddan and the other kel'ein overtook Niun on the slope that led to the hills, and offered their hands to the rope. He did not object to this. He felt pained that they must make this gesture, showing him their fellowship, as if that needed to be shown.

He veiled himself, one-handed, lowered the visor, already conserving the moisture his panting breaths tended to waste. He had taken along more than the usual quota of water, knowing the toll it would exact of them. One did not work on Kesrith: this was for youngling regul and for regul machines. Exertion would wring the moisture from the body and bring hemorrhage without proper caution.

But none of them said the obvious, that the journey was ill-advised.

Never had the Kel defied the Mother, not directly.

And it came to Niun then that the Mother had recourse available: she might have directly ordered Eddan. She had not done this.

Uncharitably, he attributed it not to love, but that she drank again of *komal,* and therefore could not be awakened when Melein brought his refusal back to her: such was Intel, she'pan of Kesrith. It had happened before.

He held to this irreverent anger, refusing to believe that she had relented, for this, at least, had never happened before, not in all the years that he had made requests of her. He did not think that she would begin now that he defied her.

He refused to repent his stubbornness even when the trail grew steeper, and the rocks tormented his feet and the air came like cold fire into his lungs.

In the sky, the regul ships continued to come and go, their speed making mock of the agony of the small figures of mri— ships carrying more and more of their kind into refuge before humans should come and claim the world.

The trail to Sil'athen was no trail, but a way remembered by all mri that had ever walked it. There was no real trace of it among the rocks, save that it was devoid of the largest obstacles and tended from landmark to landmark. Niun knew it, for burials had been common enough in his life, though he had never seen the ceremonies surrounding a birth; he had been too young for Melein's. He drew on the sled's ropes alone now, following after Eddan's tall slim figure, wrestling the sled among among the small rocks until he had to wrap a fold of his robes about his torn hands to save them. His breath came hard and his lungs ached; he was accustomed to weapons-work, not to labor like tsi'mri; and every few paces of altitude gained made breathing that much more difficult.

"Niun," one and another of the brothers would say, "let me take it a time." But he shook off their offering hands here. Only the oldest, save Pasev, whom Eddan had placed in command back at the edun, had come on this trek. His conscience tormented him now, that his stubbornness might prove the death of one of these brave old men; and surely, he thought, the she'pan had foreseen this, and he had been too blind with his own self-importance to consider that her reasons might not have involved him. He had thought the worst of Medai, and repented it now; and it began to dawn on him that he might have been mistaken in other things.

But it would shame these men now, having begun, to turn back. He had brought them out here, he with his stubborn pride; he welcomed the pain, that drove clear thought from his mind, atonement for his pettiness, against them, against the dead. Medai had been no coward, no man light-of-thought; he was certain of that

ow, that his cousin had held a long time, against perfidy of his
masters, against the gods knew what else.

And why these things had been: this was still beyond him.

"Eddan," he said quietly, when they rested in the shadow of a
high crag, and the sand beyond them rippled in the ruddy light of
Arain's zenith. A burrower had his lair out on the flat beyond. He
had seen it pock the surface, sand funnelling down as it reacted to
the breeze, thinking it had prey.

"Ai?"

"I think you believe Medai's death was not what the regul
said."

Eddan, veiled, moved his hand, a gesture that agreed.

"I think," Niun continued, "that the Kel has already discussed
this, and that I was probably the only one in the Kel who was surprised to find that so."

Eddan looked at him long. The membrane nictitated across his
eyes, flashed clear again. "Niun," he said, "that is an uncharitable
thing, to assume that we would willfully keep you from our
thoughts in such a matter."

"But perhaps it is still so, sir, that you had reasons."

Eddan's hand closed on Niun's wrist, a hard grip. Eddan had
taught him the yin'ein; there was none more skillful than Eddan
and Pasev, to divide a man body from soul with delicacy; one
could not see the blade move. And the strength was still in his
hand. "Do not look to serve regul, Niun s'Intel Zain-Abrin. You
serve the she'pan; and one day you will be in my place. I think
that day is coming soon."

"If I should be kel'anth," said Niun, cold at the words of omen,
and unsure what he meant by that, "then it will be a very small
Kel. Everyone else is senior to me."

"You will have your honor, Niun. There was never doubt of
this in our minds, only in yours. It will come."

He was disturbed to the heart by the deadly urgency of this, at
Eddan's pressing this upon him. "I have never fought," he objected. "How am I fit for anything?"

Eddan shrugged again. "We are the Hand; others do the planning. But be sure that you have a use and that the she'pan has
planned for it. Remember it. Medai was considered and rejected.
Remember that too."

He sat stunned, all his surmises torn down and laid waste at once. "Sir," he said, but Eddan thrust away from him and rose, turning his face from him, making it plain that he wanted no further question on the matter. Niun rose to his feet, seeking some way to ask, let his hand fall helplessly: when Eddan would not answer, he would not answer, and quite probably it was all Eddan could say, all that he knew how to say.

The she'pan is well-pleased with his death, Melein had said; the coldness of that still chilled him. And: *Medai was considered and rejected,* Eddan had told him.

For the first time he pitied his cousin, saw everything turned inside out.

Himself, in his youthful jealousy—Medai, whose crime had been only that he had looked on Melein, and that the she'pan had planned otherwise. Kesrith was a hard and unforgiving world. The Mother of Kesrith was like her world, without mercies.

His own stubbornness had run counter to her will. He had defied her, knowing nothing of her reasons. He had done a thing which kel'ein did not do and tested her resolve to stop him, at a time when the People could least afford division.

It was possible, he thought, that not alone the regul had killed Medai—that the she'pan and even Melein had had their part in it.

He pitied Medai, fearing for himself. He would have wished to have spoken with his cousin, both of them men now, and not one only—to have learned of Medai the things Eddan could not tell him. He looked at the black-shrouded form on the litter as he took up the ropes again, and found that all his confidence had left him.

He need not have been alone these years, he thought suddenly, and Medai need not have died, and so many things need not have happened, if he had not made the she'pan choose between them.

It was not alone the regul that had killed Medai.

It was evening when they reached the holy place, the cliffs, the windy recesses where the caves of Sil'athen hid the dead of the People that had died away from sun-burial. There were many, many graves, the oldest dating from before Kesrith had known regul, the last those that had been born on Nisren, and had fled here for refuge.

The valley was a long retreat where the cliffs marked a new level of the uplands. Here the sands were red, beginning with the cliffs, in contrast to the pale lowlands, and the red rock was banded at times with white. Where rock formed a hard cap, erosion by wind and the burning rains had made strange pillars and hulking shapes that guarded the way through Sil'athen, and cast strange shadows in the setting light of ruddy Arain. A windflower had occupied one of the crags; its tendrils glistened like threads of glass, red-stained, in the sunset. On the left of the entry a burrower had laired for many years: they swung wide, avoiding this guardian.

It was shaming to stumble here, at the end: Niun felt the sand shift underfoot and caught himself, fearing at first a smaller burrower, undetected; but it was an old hole, only soft sand. He gathered himself up, dusting the knee on which he had fallen, and leaned against the ropes, shaking off the several offered hands. There was a black shadow over his vision, tinged with red; the membrane half closed, no longer responsive to conscious will. The air he breathed was salt with his own evaporating moisture.

They passed the old graves, the thousands of the old Kath, from days before the regul. Then there were the lonely twelve of their own Kath, buried westward according to tradition, facing the rising sun, dawning hope: they were the childbearers, and with them were buried the few sad children, those too gentle for Kesrith's harsh winds, lives that should have preserved the People, had Intel not chosen Kesrith for homeworld. Many worlds the regul had offered, fair, green worlds; but Intel had desired Kesrith. She had told them this. *The forge of a new people,* she had said of Kesrith. But the gentle Kath had died in that forging, leaving them desolate.

Facing the sun's setting were the Sen in their thousands, and the nineteen recent graves of their own Sen. These also, in their way, gentle and vulnerable, had failed in Intel's refining, leaving Melein and Sathell alone to serve.

In the highest cliffs were the graves of she'panei and the kel'ein who guarded them in death. It was not certain how many she'panei had been on Kesrith. Niun knew of fifty-nine. He also knew that no kel'en knew a whole truth. He thought on this through the red and black haze of other thoughts, as they turned toward the graves of the Kel.

There were only a few hundred, to the others' thousands, almost as few as the graves of the she'panei—on Kesrith. Their dead would many times outnumber the Sen; but very, very few found their graves in earth.

They stopped at the newest cave, where the veterans of Nisren were entombed; and Niun forced himself to stay on his feet, to help them in unsealing it, moving rock until his hands were numb, for these stubborn old men would do everything if he did not forestall them. He ached and his own blood was on the rocks with which he made place for Medai.

Kel'ein were not buried like others: other castes faced into the valley of Sil'athen; but the Kel faced outward, toward the north, the traditional direction of evil. Row on row the other dead lay in the dark. When they lit their single lamp they could see them, musty black shadows in veils and robes moldering into ruin, veiled faces turned toward the north wall of the cave.

The air inside was cold and strange with decay. The dark oppressed. Niun stood, content for a moment only to stand, and let the old men set Medai in place among the others. They stopped then and faced north, and spoke over him the *Shon'jir,* the Passing ritual. Niun repeated the words—spoken at birthings and burials, heralding a life of the People into the world and out of it.

> *From Dark beginning*
> *To Dark at ending,*
> *Between them a Sun,*
> *But after comes Dark,*
> *And in that Dark,*
> *One ending.*

The words echoed in the cavern, in darkness wrapped about them; and Niun looked at the dead, and at his companions, and considered the frailty of them that chanted of the Dark; and the fragile breath's difference between lips that moved and those that could not. Terror possessed him, rebellion, to rush out into the open; but he did not give way. His lips continued to form the words.

From Dark to Dark
Is one voyage.
From Dark to Dark
Is our voyage.
And after the Dark,
O brothers, o sisters,
Come we home.

He had never thought the words. He had mouthed them; he had
never felt them. He felt them now, looking about him.
Home.
This.
He held himself still while the others filed out, forced himself
to be the last, mastering his fear; but even when he had the light
of stars and Kesrith's first moon overhead, he felt that cold inside
him, that many suns would never warm away.
"Seal it," said Eddan.
He gathered up the rocks one by one, and fitted them into
place, making tight their joinings, sealing them between himself
and Medai. His breath came hard. He found himself with tears
flooding his cheeks, for his shame before Medai.
Not like you, cousin, not like you, he kept thinking, as he set
each stone in place, a determination, a wall that he built, a protection for the hallowed dead against the winds and the sands and the
prying fingers of the suruin that ranged the high hills: a protection
for himself, against the truth inside.
And they were done, all debts paid. The brothers blew dust
upon the wind; he gathered up his handful and did likewise, bidding farewell. Then they rested a time, before beginning the long,
hard trek back to the edun.
Soah joined the first moon overhead, making their passage
safer, and they set forth. Eddan went first, using his staff to probe
for windflowers in the dark air, wary as those who walked the
wilds of Kesrith dus-less had to be; but Niun lent his company to
Sirain, who was half blind and very frail, and too proud to accept
help. Often he gave way to exhaustion himself to slow their
progress, as if the sores on his hands and the long walk and the
sleeplessness had utterly undone him; but of a sudden pride was
not important to him: it was only important that Sirain's pride be

saved, that he not die. He did not flaunt his youth at them any longer. He found comradeship with them, as if they and he had finally understood a thing that he should have understood long ago.

They shared water and food together—sat, the six of them, in the dark after the moons had set, and broke fast; and the brothers were sorry for his hands, and offered of their own experience various advice to heal them. But Eddan cut the stalk of a young luin and rubbed the juice of it on the sores, which was a remedy counted sovereign for every wound: it eased the pain.

In the journey after that the pace was slower still, and perhaps Sirain had seen through his careful pretense from the beginning, for at last he clasped Niun's arm in a feeble grip and admitted that this time it was himself who must rest a time.

By such degrees they came homeward.

And it was evening again when they returned, and the edun's entry was lit for them, and the great bulk of the ailing dus still was to be seen at the door.

In the end there was no hurrying. Niun had been anxious lest he have to take up Sirain and carry him, which would have been a crushing shame to the old warrior. And for Sirain's sake, and for Eddan's, who labored now, they walked slowly despite their anxiety to reach the edun, their dread of things that might have gone amiss in their absence.

But there in the doorway Melein waited, and gave them gentle welcome, unveiled, as they unveiled themselves, coming home.

"Is all well?" Eddan asked of her.

"All is well," she said. "Come in. Be at ease."

They entered, footsore and cold, and passed the long hall to the Shrine, that first of all, making their individual prayers and washing of the hands and face. And when they were done they turned toward the steps of the Kel-tower, for they were exhausted.

But Melein waited, outside the Shrine.

"Niun," she said. "The Mother still sends for you."

He was tired. He dreaded the meeting. He turned his shoulder to her rudely and walked out of the hall, to the step, to see how the dus fared. He gave it a scrap of meat that he had saved from his own rations on the journey; but someone else had filled the pannikin with water.

It turned from his gift, and would have none of him. He had thought that this would be the case, but he had tried. He sank down in exhaustion on the step and stared at the dus helplessly.

Never would the beasts tolerate him, and this one, bereaved and suffering, he could not help.

He gave a great sigh that was almost a sob, and stared at his bloody hands in the light, so sensitive, so delicate to wield the yin'ein, and reduced to this. There was no warrior here, none that the dus could detect. It chose to die, like Medai. It found nothing in him to interest it in living.

He had the *seta'al* and the weapons and the black robes; he had the skill, but the heart in him was terrified, and angry, and the dus, being sensitive to such things, would not have him.

He swept off *mez* and *zaidhe,* bundled them into the crook of his arm, and with his right hand he gathered a handful of dust from the side of the step and smeared his brow with it, a penance for his jealousy.

Then he went inside, ascended the stairs of the inmost tower, that of the she'pan. He opened the door to the she'pan's hall cautiously, and saw that Melein knelt at the she'pan's left hand, arranging the cushions.

"Hush," said Melein, accusing him with her eyes. "She has just now fallen asleep. You are too late tonight. Be still."

But the she'pan stirred as he came near her, and her golden eyes opened and the membrane receded, leaving them clear.

"Niun," she said very softly.

"Little Mother." He sank down on her right, and offered his bowed head to her gentle touch, an intimacy the Kel offered no others but the she'pan or a mate. Her hands were warm against the chill of his skin.

"You are safe," she said. "You are back safely." And as if that were all the burden of what she desired, like a child sleeping with a favorite toy at hand, she settled back into her dreams.

Niun stayed still, leaned his head against the arm of her chair, and gradually gave himself to sleep, her hand still resting on his shoulder. His dreams were troubled. At times he woke, seeing the cave and the dark; and then he saw the golden light that surrounded them, and felt the weight of the she'pan's hand, and knew where he was.

She dreamed, did the Mother, and reclaimed him; possibly she confused him with another. He did not know. He was kel'en, like the other. He sat at her side and slept at times, and knew that the sum of his duty to her was to live, to stay by her. She had rejected Medai, and never from her had come a word of regret, of sorrow for him.

You are safe, she had said.

The bonds, so lately slipped, ensnared him again; and at last he gave up his struggle and knew that he must serve to the service that had claimed him.

The *su-she'pani kel'en a'anu.*

The she'pan's kel'en, like those in the cliffs.

In the whispered long-ago days, when there was no war, there had been such, when mri fought against mri and house against house, when she'pan contended against she'pan.

Her last kel'en, the one—he foresaw with what he thought was a true vision—would never indeed know the Dark of the caves of Sil'athen: the one to seal the barrier for the others, and to remain outside, a guardian.

He slid a glance toward Melein, saw her awake also, her eyes staring into the shadows; he realized what it had surely been for her, alone here, with Intel.

For her also, he was afraid.

Chapter Nine

It was, in the Nom, the twentieth day.

It was possible finally for human nerves to adjust to Kesrith's longer day. Duncan rose and wandered to the private bath—that luxury at least their onworld accommodations had afforded him, though he must content himself with the recycled ration of water available within the Nom's apparatus.

The Nom depended entirely on life-support systems like those of a ship: regul did not find surface existence comfortable, although it was tolerable.

Neither was it, he suspected, comfortable for humans.

Filtered air, recycled water, and that originally reclaimed from a sea so laden with alkali that nothing would live in it. The world's little animal life was confined to the uplands, and from what information he had obtained from the translated regul advisories on that score, there was little born of Kesrith that was harmless.

The interior of the Nom held gardens that somewhat humidified their air and provided pleasantness, but the alien harshness of the foliage and the accompanying scent of regul made the gardens less pleasant than they might have been.

He was, he reckoned, growing used to regul. He was learning to tolerate a number of things he had once thought impossible to accept, and that in twenty days of close contact.

It was close contact. There were no restricted hours, no confinement to quarters, but the regulations forbade them to leave the Nom at any time. Stavros, of course, would not do so as long as regul remained on Kesrith—a reasonably brief time to wait: ten days until the first human ships should come in and replace the regul.

Duncan reckoned, at least, that their sanity might hold that long. He had a mental image of their first encounter with those humans incoming: that the landing party would find them both changed, bizarre and altered by their stay on Kesrith. He was not the man that had begun the voyage; SurTac Sten Duncan on Haven had been capable of far more impulsive behavior than Sten Duncan, aide to the new governor of Kesrith. He had acquired patience, the ability to reckon slowly; and he had acquired something of regul manners, ponderous and unwieldy as their conventions were. They began to come as naturally as yes, sir and no, sir: Favor, my lord; and, Be gracious, elder.

They had promised him retirement after five years; but five years in this sullen environment would make him unfit for human company: five years from now he might find clean air a novelty and Haven daylight strange to the eyes—might find human manners banal and odd after the stark, survival-oriented settlement that men would have to make of Kesrith. He was in the process of adapting: any world, any climate, any operation in hostile terrain that wanted human hands directly at work onworld was a SurTac's natural job, and he was learning the feel of Kesrith.

Stavros was doing the same thing in his intellectual way, absorbing every oddity within his reach—like the regul, never seeming to need notes, simply looking and listening, on his rare excursions from his room to the gardens.

This morning he had an appointment in Hulagh's offices. It was an important occasion.

Something rumbled outside, different from the accustomed thunder of departing ships. Duncan switched the view to let light through the Nom's black windows. They had a view of the whole horizon from the sea at the right to the hills at the left, save that they could not see the mri edun and could not see the port, the two things in which they had the greatest interest: it was of course no accident that they were arranged as they were. Nothing in that desolation had changed in twenty days; but now above the hills there was a change. A storm was moving in, the clouds grey, red-tinged, shadowing the sea in one quarter. Lightning flashed with impossible rapidity.

The weather, said the prepared statements of the bai's staff, *is unpredictable by season, and occasionally violent. The rain is mildly caustic, especially in showers following duststorms. It will be desirable to bathe if one is caught in the rain. Above all it is necessary to seek suitable cover at the earliest indication of a storm. The winds can achieve considerable violence. If fronts converge on the seaward and hillward sides, cyclonic action is frequent.*

The red light in the ceiling mount flared, summoning him. Stavros was awake. Duncan quickly obtained a cup of soi from the wall dispenser—soi being the regul liquid stimulant, and only mildly flavored, unlike most regul foods. It was one of the few regul graces they had come to enjoy. A touch of sweetener made it completely palatable. He added the two drops, set the cup on a small tray, gathered up the morning dispatches from the slot, and carried the offering in to Stavros' quarters—again accessible only from his own apartment.

"Good morning, sir," he murmured, courtesy which was regularly answered with only a civil nod, and that sometimes belated. Stavros was in exceptional spirits this morning. He actually smiled, a gesture which made his thin mouth the tighter.

"Do the windows," Stavros said. It was thundering again.

Duncan switched them over and let in the day's sullen light.

The first drops began to spatter the dust on the panes. A crack of thunder made the glass bow and rattle, and Stavros walked over to enjoy the view. Duncan himself felt a heightening of senses, a stimulation unaccustomed in their carefully controlled environment. This was something the regul could not schedule or censor, the violence of nature. He could see it sweep down on the sea, where the waves white-capped, dyed pink. The whole day was enveloped in reddish murk, and fitful with lightning.

"This," said Stavros, "is going to be one of the major obstacles to settlement here."

Duncan felt he was called on to discuss the matter. He did not know precisely how; his training was not in civilizing worlds, but in taking them. "The regul gave us an edge there," he said, "with this city for a base."

"There's considerable attrition in machinery on Kesrith, so I'm told; and for some idiotic reason they've followed the mri example and built a number of outposts out of rammed earth and binder, cheap but remarkably unsuited for the climate."

"If you have a lot of labor you can keep rebuilding, I suppose."

"Humans can't run a colony that way." Stavros went off on another tangent of thought, sipping at the warm drink. Thunder rattled at the glass again. Wind hit with a force that sent a sheet of water between them and the world, obscuring everything. Duncan swore in surprise and awe.

"The storm shields," Stavros advised him. It was hailing now, a rapid patter that threatened the window. It was coming from their direction.

Duncan quickly activated the shutters. They whisked across and cut off the daylight; the room lights compensated. Then he went back at once to see to the windows in his own quarters, appalled, even afraid to approach the glass under the violence that battered against it.

The thunder broke overhead as he reached for the switch. His heart was pounding as the storm shield slid over the window. Distantly he could hear an alarm in the building, and for a moment the hiss of air in the ducts ceased and he could feel a pressure in his ears like ascent in an aircraft.

He went to the door, opened it. Regul were whisking about in sleds along the corridors in mad confusion. The pressure eased then. He heard a sound that was too deep for sound, shuddering through the building.

"Nai chiug-ar?" —What is it?—he asked the first regul he saw afoot. *"Nai chiug-ar?"*

"Sak noi kanuchdi hoc-nar," the youngling spat back, which had something to do with the port, but nothing else he could understand. *"Sak-ak toc dac,"* it hissed at him then. Keep to quarters, favor.

He retreated, closed the door and called the main desk for information. No one would respond to his calls. Eventually everything seemed to grow calm outside, only a rush of rain against the storm shields. He ventured finally to open the shields and saw nothing but a wash of water, distorting everything outside. He closed them again.

And from Stavros' room, long silence.

He gathered together his shaken faculties, berating himself for his panic, and went in to see about the old man, expecting cynical amusement at a SurTac who feared storms.

The cup was on the floor, a brown stain on the carpet. He saw the old man half across the bed, still in his nightclothes.

"Sir?" he exclaimed. He went and touched his shoulder fearfully, then turned him over and obtained faint movement, a gasp for breath, a flutter of the right eye. The left remained drawn, that side of the mouth peculiarly distorted. Stavros tried to talk to him, unintelligible.

In the next instant Duncan ran from the room, from his quarters to the hall and the duty desk, trying every word that would come to mind to express his need.

"Stavros," he said at last, "Stavros!" and this finally seemed to impress itself on the youngling. It rose, lumbering in its gait, and came with him.

It stood, for a considerable time, at the foot of the bed. "Elder," it said finally, with the regul equivalent of a shrug. Here was an elder. It did not seem capable of rising; this was natural for an elder. Duncan seized its massive arm and raised his voice.

"Sick," he insisted.

Slowly, with ostentatious slowness, the youngling turned and went to the console, coded in a call and spoke to higher authority.

Authority responded, in a bewildering patter of words. Duncan sank down and bowed his head into his hands, despair knotted in his stomach.

And when an array of important regul arrived, and began with dispatch to load Stavros into one of the sled transports, Duncan stayed nearby constantly, and insisted with forceful gestures that he intended to come with Stavros.

A regul seized him, firmly but without violence, and held him, while the sled moved and departed. Then the regul let him go. It was all the restraint that need have been applied; there was no way for him to follow down that web of tracks.

He sank into a chair in his quarters, shivering with anger and terror, and utterly, utterly helpless to do anything for Stavros.

Outside the storm pattered against the shields. It continued for an hour or more. He left the room four times during that period to go down to the duty desk and demand information on Stavros' condition, each time arming himself with applicable phrases from his dictionary and lesson sheets.

The regul on duty had learned quickly enough that it need not be silent to express disdain; it needed only to shower words at him as rapidly as it could speak, impressing on him his incapacity to understand.

"Dal," it said finally, *"seo-gin."*

Go away. It repeated it several times more.

He turned away, not for the apartment, but for the forbidden first-level ramp, down which bai Hulagh had his offices. Words shrilled after him. A trio of regul closed in on him and marched him firmly enough to his door, pushing at him to make him enter.

"Stavros sick," one said finally.

It was the sum of information available until the morning, an entire night in sleepless anxiety.

But with dawn they came in numbers, and transferred a brown wrapped bundle from a sled to the bed; and Duncan, roughly thrusting himself into their midst, saw Stavros conscious, but still with that deadness about his left side.

And then there was deference in plenty among the younglings, for a hum sounded at the door and a sled console eased through the ample doorways to rest in their midst.

Bai Hulagh.

Words came from Stavros, distorted, unrecognizable in either language.

"Honorable Stavros. Rest now." The bai rose within his sled with great effort and looked directly upon Duncan. "Youngling, the affliction is to the nervous system."

"Bai," Duncan said, "help him."

The regul shrugged. "Human structure is strange to us. We regret. We are in the midst of considerable disaster. The storm toppled a tower at the port. There was a great loss of life. Our facilities are strained by this emergency. Our information on the human system is very scant."

"I can provide you—I can provide you myself, bai, if your medics would—"

"Youngling," said the regul, a basso profundo that vibrated with disdain, "we do not have information. We do not experiment on living beings. This moderate restoration of function we could accomplish, no more. This is an elder of your people. He will be made comfortable to the utmost of our abilities. Do you, youngling, question this statement?"

"Be gracious," he murmured, reserving decisions to others; he moved to Stavros' side, took the good hand in his. A mild pressure answered. Stavros' pale eyes glittered wetly, alive, fully cognizant and trying to command him something, a stern and reprimanding look. He tightened his hand in reassurance and looked up at the bai.

"Favor, reverence," he said. "I am distressed for him."

The bai gestured him to come. He let slip Stavros' fingers and did so, submitted to the touch of the regul bai, whose rough fingers rested on his shoulder, a considerable weight.

The bai spoke curtly to his servitors, who hastened about their business. Then the wrinkle-enfolded eyes looked into Duncan's, and the bai's fingers tightened until it was hard not to wince.

"Youngling, I am informed you have neglected food and drink. This is an expression of grief? This is religion?"

"No, reverence, I will eat."

"Good." The word rumbled forth, almost incomprehensible in its depth. The pressure increased until Duncan felt the joint give. He flinched. The bai dropped the hand at once.

And the bai turned ponderously and levered himself back into his sled, settled. It whined, backing, and turned and retreated.

Duncan stood and stared after it, after the others, who withdrew almost as quickly. A sound came from Stavros.

"Sir?" he asked at once, trying to keep his voice natural. He turned and saw Stavros beckon toward the table. Stavros' notes were there. He gathered them up and offered them, but Stavros with his right hand fumbled after the tablet only. Duncan understood and found the pen to give him. He knelt down and braced the tablet as Stavros wrote, heavily, with childlike awkwardness.

Regul not upset, he read. *Process with them natural to age. Mobility may return. No reason for panic.* The awkward, slanted writing reached the accessible limits of the page. Duncan reversed the tablet, braced it higher.

Humans due soon, Stavros resumed. *Disaster at port—truth. Regul evacuation schedule hampered; Hazan damaged. Regul much concerned. Mri—need to find out what mri doing. This most urgent. Listen to regul talk, learn of mri, don't provoke.*

"Even leaving the Nom if I have to?"

SurTac—now become diplomat. Careful. Take my instructions. Regul kill younglings here—many. Consult first on everything. Move me. Now. Console.

He did not want to move him; but Stavros cursed at him thickly and ordered him aloud, and evidently was determined. Duncan carefully, tenderly gathered up the old man and placed him within the sled console in the corner, supported him, adjusted the form-fitting cushions to hold him securely. Stavros' right hand sought after controls, made further adjustments. The sled console turned. The screen turned independently. A message, hand-keyed, crawled across the small screen.

Can learn even this.

"Yes, sir," Duncan said with a tightness in his throat. He was suddenly concerned for this man, for Stavros personally.

The message-crawl resumed. *Order food for you. Rest.*

"And for yourself, sir?"

Stavros turned the sled, jerkily maneuvered it next to the bed. He operated the console arm to dim the lights. *I wait,* the screen said. *No needs.*

Chapter Ten

"Truebrother."

On the step beside the dus, Niun looked over his shoulder. It was seldom now that he met his sister informally, brother and sister, daithen and daithe, as they had been before. She surprised him with the dus. He was embarrassed to be found at this charity: there had been a distance between them, though they had been much together in the she'pan's hall. He did not like to be with her, alone, not any longer. It was painful, that the closeness between them was gone.

He continued a moment, trying to tempt the dus with a scrap of food, for until she had come, he had deceived himself that there was the slightest flicker of interest in the dark eyes of the dus. Now it would not come. But he had so deceived himself many a time since its coming to the edun. He shrugged and casually tossed the prize to the dus, letting it land between its massively clawed forepaws. Sometimes, eventually, it would eat. It accepted just enough to stay alive; and sometimes he would see the scrap shrivelled and neglected that evening, and the dus moved slightly elsewhere until it was taken away; for the dus was very proud, and did not really want to eat.

Someone else saw that the waterbowl by the step was constantly full. This was great extravagance on Kesrith. Ordinarily a sick dus simply complained when thirsty and received what it needed; and a healthy one derived all its moisture requirement from food it ate. Niun suspected kel Pasev of this wasteful charity. She had her own dus, but she was capable of such feelings toward a good animal. He was not himself so deft in his offerings as was Pasev. Doubtless everyone in the edun knew how desperately he tried to feed the creature, and claim it, and how it stubbornly refused him.

Doubtless another kel'en would be feeding it if he did not. The dus shamed them all in its loyal grief. It found not one of them worthy to take it; and rarely would they transfer affection, but he still hoped, desperately, for the life of this one.

"Sometimes," said Melein, "they simply cannot be saved."

She sat down on the dusty step with him, heedless of her robes of caste: but the granular sand of the edun grounds did not cling so much as white lowlands powder. She wore the light veil over her silken mane in the out-of-doors, for the Sen disdained to cover.

The body of a kel'en is itself a Mystery of the People, the teachings held, *and therefore the Kel veils; the body of a sen'en is a veil to that within, which is a Mystery of the People, and therefore the Sen veils not.*

Save to the unacceptable.

The weather was fair after the storm of days past, in which wrack and disaster had blown down the passes and dealt havoc in the regul town. The smoke of the destruction in the lowlands had been visible even through the rain, and when the worst of the storm was done, the kel'ein had looked out from the summit of the Sen-tower with a new and bitter satisfaction.

"Ah," Eddan had said, when they noted the smoke and the fire, "Kesrith has her way with the masters even yet."

It was likely that many regul had perished in the conflagration. Such satisfaction was a thing that once no mri would have thought or felt. But that was before the death of a kel'en unaccounted for on a regul ship, and before it was clear that humans would possess the world.

Now the stars of evening began to show in a clear sky, and there was no wind to stir the sand and make the *mez* advisable. Such crystal evenings were frequent after the greatest storms, as if the very world lay exhausted after the recent violence.

He dropped his own veil and looped it under his chin, refastening it. There was no likelihood of tsi-mri here, and he did not need it.

"Shall we walk?" Melein suggested.

He had no such thing in mind; but rarely did Melein ask anything of him any longer. He arose and offered her his hand to help her up. Thereafter they walked, side by side in the direction Melein chose, on the small trail that led from the corner of the edun to the rocks at the top of the causeway. He found himself remembering the times that they had run that distance, they three, agile as the dusty lizards, children without the veil, small slim-limbed boys and smaller girl, racing illicitly for the vantage point from which they could see the ships at the port come and go.

They had been ships with magical names then, mri ships, regul ships: *Mlereinei, Kamrive, Horagh-no,* that came from distant stars and the glory of battles. As children they had played at war and duel, and imagined themselves great kel'ein, glittering with honors like the far-travelled kel'ein that visited from the ships and departed their own ways again—like their truemother and their father that left separately with the ships and never visited home-world again.

Tonight they walked, he of the Kel, she of the Sen, weighted with their robes of caste and their separate laws. When they reached the rock that overlooked the valley, he leaped up first and pulled her up after with a single tug—there was still the girl Melein within the golden robes, agile and quick as a kel'e'en, un-becoming the gravity of her caste.

They sat together while the red sun vanished, and watched the whole of the valley, and the glow of lights where the port was, and the wound the storm had made there, a darkness amid the lights near *Hazan.*

"Why did you ask me here?" he asked of her at last.

"To talk with you."

He did not like this manner in her. The last light touched her face. It was that of a stranger for a moment, someone he should remember, and did not, quite. It was not Melein as he knew her, but a sen'e'en that contained quiet, secret thoughts. He suddenly wished she would not pursue the opening he had given her. He foreknew that she might rob him of his peace; and he could not stop her from doing it.

"You do not smile anymore," she said. "You do not even look up when you are named."

"I am not a child."

"You do not love the she'pan."

"I come. I sit. I wait. This seems to be all she wants of me. It is her right."

"You do not much go out of the edun."

"I have given up, Melein. That is all."

She looked up, where the stars glittered. Her arm resting on her raised knee pointed toward Elag's star, that shone and danced above the hills. "There are humans now," she said. "But this is different, here—Kesrith. This is homeworld. Sanctuary for the People. The Holy."

He looked at her, sullen, frightened. "Remember that I am kel'en."

"The Kel must remain unlearned because the Kel ventures where our enemies are, and where knowledge that cannot serve the Kel cannot be permitted. For all traditions, however minor, there are reasons. You are a kel'en of homeworld, and you will hear what it would not be good for a kel'en elsewhere to hear."

He rose and set his back against the rock, leaning there with his arms folded and the rising breeze touching him with more chill than was comfortable. It was night now, the last of the sun slipped from view. He did not know why she had wished to come out here. The hills were full of menace. The ha-dusei, wild relatives of the tame companions of the kel'ein, were not to be trusted. There were windflowers and burrowers, and serpents that hid in the rocks. He owed a sen'e'en his protection; and it was arrant stupidity to be out here with Melein in his charge after dark. Her value to the edun was incalculably above his.

"We can talk elsewhere, later," he said. "I do not think we should have come here at this hour."

"Listen to me!"

Her voice was edged, cruel, a blow that stunned. Melein was his little sister. She had never used that tone with him.

"Today," she said, "the she'pan called me in private. Today she gave me rank with Sathell. And you understand this."

She'pan's successor, her Chosen.

In the nethermost parts of his mind he had known it would come, this the only reasonable purpose behind Intel's snatching Melein out of Kel and into Sen.

Not to bear children, but to learn the Pana, the Mysteries; not to continue the People, but to rule them.

And Intel had taken him likewise, to defend challenge herself, to guard her—to kill, if need be, any overanxious successor, and the kel'en that supported her challenger's cause.

He gave a single bitter curse, understanding; and saw the hurt leap into Melein's eyes.

"I am sorry that you take it so," she said.

"Why must she have kept me by her and not Medai?"

"She trusted you, and never Medai."

He considered that, and its reasons. "She trusted you," he said softly, "while I guard her sleep. While she could set me against you."

The hurt became shock. The thought seemed to startle her. "No," she said. "I am not apt to challenge her."

"Not so long as you have regard for me," he answered. "She feels her mortality on her or she would not have named you yet. And some kel'en will guard her tomb."

"She would not take you. Eddan—Sirain—they would seek the honor. But not you.

"Maybe with the humans at hand the question is pointless. I am thinking ahead of the hour, and that is beyond my caste. You will have to think that through, truesister. I am far from knowing the future. I can only speak for what is true now."

"She is not preparing to cede homeworld quietly. Niun, I am young, I am nothing compared to Intel's experience. Other she'-panei would hesitate to challenge her: she knows too much. Killing her would rob the People of so much, you do not know how much. It would be an act of—I do not know, Niun, I do not know. If I should succeed her as she'pan of homeworld, here am I—young, inexperienced,. I know that some older she'pan will come then and challenge, and it will be my place to die. I want her to live, I desperately want her to live, and she is dying, Niun."

He found himself trembling, hurting to reassure her; and there was no comfort. She spoke of things beyond his caste; and yet he thought that she had laid out all the truth for him, and stole what remained of his peace and hope. He had always thought that she would survive him.

"We were unlucky," she said, "in being last-born of the People: not alone of Kesrith, Niun, but of all the People. We were without choice because we were simply the last. I wish it were different."

What she said struck at other confidences. He looked at her with the wind whipping at them and chilling to the skin and ceased even to shiver. "Of all the People?"

"Edunei have fallen," she said, "and children have died; and kel'e'ein are occupied with war, and nothing else. I should not have answered," she added. "But of our generation, there is little left. Those older—they will get other children. It is not too late."

She tried to comfort him. He reassured himself that she had faith in their future, and this was enough. "But then," he said, catching up a thought, "then Intel will not plan to lose you. You might be after all the ablest after her; and if she bequeaths my service to you—if you should challenge or return challenge, Melein, I can defend you. I am not unable to defend you: I am skilled in the yin'ein. Nine years they have kept me in training. I must be capable of something."

She was silent a long time. Finally she arose. "Come," she said. "Let us return to the edun. I am cold."

And she was silent as they climbed down to the trail and walked back; she wept. He saw it in the starlight, and took off his own veil and offered it to her, a gesture of profound tenderness.

"No," she said fiercely. He nodded, and flung the *mez* over his shoulder, walking beside her. "You are right," she said finally. "I will not surrender the office and die without challenge if it comes to me. I will kill to hold it."

"It is a great honor for you," he said, because he thought that he should have said something of the kind when she first told him.

She let go her breath, a slow hiss. "What honor—to go into some strange edun, and into a strange Kel, and kill some woman who never did me hurt? I do not want that honor."

"But Intel will arm you for this," he said. "She will make you able. She has surely planned for this for many years."

She looked up at him, her shadowed face set and calm. "I think you are not far wrong," she said, "that she wanted you by her because she knows I could make trouble in the House. She trusts you. She does not trust me."

He shivered, hearing in her voice the bitterness he had always suspected was there, and shadows tore away between himself and the Sen-tower and the she'pan. He remembered Melein preparing the cup each evening, the cup that helped she'pan sleep; and each evening, the she'pan drinking, nothing questioning. He suspected what ungentle things might run in Intel's drug-hazed mind—a she'pan foreseeing her own death and mistrusting her successor with good reason.

Intel had wanted Melein disarmed: had sent Medai into service, had kept her brother close by. Some kel'en would guard Intel's tomb: normally it would be one of her Husbands, not a son. But there might be one instruction if she passed of age, and another if by Melein's hand.

And Melein would have to challenge against him to challenge Intel: he would die before Intel would; but Melein would have to find a kel'en to champion her—and there was none who would agree to that.

Intel had done well to banish Medai.

But Melein was not capable of the things of which Intel suspected her; he insisted on believing that she was not. Caste and teaching and the bitterness of her imprisonment could not have changed his truesister to that extent. He would not believe that Intel's fears were justified.

I want her to live, I desperately want her to live, Melein had said.

"How much," he asked finally, "did she bid you tell me?"

"Less," she said, "than I told you."

"Yes," he said, "I had thought so."

They came back to the edun, she drawing ahead of him as they entered. He looked aside at the dus that turned its head from him. When he looked up, she had gone on into the shadows, toward the stairs of her own tower.

She did not look back.

He went toward the she'pan's tower, to take up his duty, where he belonged.

Chapter Eleven

There was quiet over Kesrith. After so many hazards, after two days stalled with the port in chaos from the storm, that last shuttle had lifted with its cargo of refugees, to the station where the freighter *Restrivi* was forming the last regular civilian list that would leave the world. Hereafter there was time, necessary time, for setting final matters in order. Against the ruddy sun of Kesrith there was only *Hazan* remaining—armed and, when her minor repairs were completed, star-capable; she waited with her crew constantly within her. She carried in her tapes the way to Nurag, to regul homeworld, to safety and civilization for the few hundred left on Kesrith.

A ten of times each passing day bai Hulagh Alagn-ni, working in his heated offices in the Nom complex, looked up at the windows and concerned himself with the condition of *Hazan*. The dual-capable ship, strong enough behind her screens for combat, was yet a perilously fragile structure when grounded. He had hesitated to take her down in the first place; he had suffered agonies of mind in the hours of the storm's approach, had decided against lofting her to stationside.

And then—then, to have a witless aircraft pilot attempt to outrun the storm and risk the crosswinds, a known peril at Kesrith's field—on such an occurrence the whole mission was almost lost. Hulagh cursed each time he thought of it, the youngling pilot and passengers, of course, beyond retribution. He was relieved that, at the least, damage had been confined to the tower and loading facilities, and that to *Hazan's* structure was minimal. Luck had been with him. *Hazan* was in his trust over the objections of powerful influences back on homeworld. He had risked everything in securing for himself and his interests this post, replacing old Gruran and Solgah Holn-ni—an assignment for which his personal age and erudition had qualified him, and thereby won doch Alagn the status it was long overdue.

But as with !anding the ship, as in other decisions he had made along the way, it was necessary to risk in order to gain. It was necessary to demonstrate to homeworld his claimed ability and that of doch Alagn in order to obtain the influence permanently.

He could do so by salvaging the most possible benefit of Kesrith, after its loss by Gruran Holn-ni and his get; and Solgah Holn-ni—he thought with disgust and contempt of the prolific female who had ruled Holn's establishment of Kesrith, and lorded it so thoroughly over the zone and over the war that was her creation—Solgah was on her way to homeworld in utter confusion, stripped of her command, most of her younglings left behind, their ranks decimated by Holagh's own orders, survivors parcelled out to many different colonies, the doch in complete disorganization. She would be lucky if her influence on homeworld enabled her to escape sifting and the execution of her younglings. At the least, Holn was due for some years of obscurity.

The memory still pleased him, how Solgah had received the shock of *Hazan's* unscheduled and unauthorized landing: how she had fluttered and blustered with prohibitions and objections, until he had made known to her his homeworld-granted authority to assume control.

Now it was his office to complete the evacuation Solgah had begun, to save as much as possible from the concessions her weak kinsman Gruran Holn-ni had granted in negotiations at Elag, trying to save the inner portions of the vast Holn empire. It was his task to prepare Kesrith to receive human occupation, and to remove regul properties as much as could be saved, and regul personnel, as many as could be saved; and to ensure that humans drew the least possible benefit from what they had won in war and in negotiations.

Hulagh had dealt with humans indirectly for three homeworld years, and met with a few after replacing Gruran, and knew them—including the two that had come in on *Hazan*—with a quiet but mild distaste, less distaste, in fact, than he had ever felt for mri, who served regul. The human war, of course, had been a complete mistake, an error in calculations, and not one attributable to doch Alagn. It had been abundantly clear to wiser regul minds for the better part of five years that the companies of Holn doch had involved themselves in an utter fiasco, from which the mri were unable to rescue them, and that error would have been corrected then, if it had been possible to restrain the obstinacies and military power of such as Holn, whose employ of mercenary kel'ein and whose obvious self-interest in retaining the disputed territories had stalled off any change in policy.

Now, at last, after the consequences of the original error were multiplied to great cost, after regul lives and properties and home territory itself had been lost, the Holn empire tottering on the brink, now the military Holn handed the tangled and dangerous situation—reluctantly even so—over to older, wiser minds on Nurag.

And politics, in a turn of events unforeseen by the Holn, had served to turn the Holn authority finally into the hands of Alagn, and to elevate Alagn to a status in which Alagn, with the right Alagn in command, could utterly ruin doch Holn.

Holn had left a tangle behind them. Bai Hulagh was far from satisfied with the treaty terms within which he must operate, but they were Holn's legacy, sealed, legal, recorded and beyond his power to adjust. Yet if the cession of three colonial systems, costly as that was, had created a permanent and reliable boundary between human and regul claims, it could turn out to be one of the wiser things doch Holn had done in its administration. Doubtless, Hulagh felt, the humans now clearly knew that they had made all the cheap gain they could reasonably expect in this adventure, and that hereafter regul would resist with more vigor. The humans were apparently perplexed and disturbed by this sudden change of authority on the frontier, and yet they seemed anxious to honor the treaty. Kesrith was a likely and sensible boundary: the dead space of the Deep discouraged exploration regulward without considerable routing round by Hesoghan, an old and firmly regul holding; and the lure of the Haze-stars would lead humans from Kesrith rimward in due time. So Hulagh planned in his strategies, mapping what he considered might be new directions in regul policy. The humans would be attracted by the wealth toward which Kesrith had been reaching; but likewise the regul stars had mineral wealth sufficient to sustain industries without the convenient luxury of doch Holn's outermost colonies. Economic effects would be felt, but only in small degree on homeworld; and so long as the elders of homeworld were well-supplied in their needs, the Alagn operation would be favorably judged.

And afterward, it was only one arm of regul expansion that had been cut off. Two others remained. One of them was the presently meager holding of doch Alagn.

To direct, to shape, to rule, to settle himself eternally into the memory not alone of doch Alagn, but of the center of Nurag—this was the dream Hulagh savored. In his vast age he had outlived his rivals, had seen them dust; and he remembered, and planned long. He had obliterated the younglings of his chiefest enemies. He risked everything now in assuming personal command of Kesrith: if matters went amiss, it would be remembered that Hulagh of Alagn was in charge when they did so; but here on Kesrith also lay wealth he desperately needed.

The terms of the human/regul treaty surrendered only the bare earth of the ceded worlds. There was no specified claim of valuable hardware, cities, resources. Bare earth was all the encroaching humans need find when they arrived; and redeveloping the stubborn wilderness of Kesrith would occupy them long enough to give regul-kind a breathing space—while the plunder of Kesrith would go into the stores of Alagn doch, legitimate salvage on which Holn had no claim.

And all this under the very eyes of the human envoys.

This satisfied Hulagh no less, to discredit the human who had been sent to oversee the transition of power. The sudden illness of the human elder and the natural timidity of its single youngling were a convenience beyond measure. A regul elder would have demanded constant and detailed reports of actions by his hosts; a competent one would have demanded them in such volume and at such a pace that nothing escaped his notice; a resourceful one would have used his youngling's eyes to see what he was not meant to see. But none of this had the human envoy managed on any great scale. The human concentrated on the wrong materials, learned the language assiduously and reheard reports which he had already been given in his own language, going over old information as if he suspected he could learn something new from it, as if there were discrepancies or untruths in plain statements. Such deceptions might be the human practice; they were not regul. What was happening was as wide as the port and as plain as the ships that daily lifted, and when humans arrived some few days hence they would find a stripped and ruined possession and their delegate in command of a barren wilderness incapable of sustaining life on any large scale.

This was itself a coup that the council on Nurag would savor when it heard.

Hulagh had been perplexed originally that the two humans had contrived no means of circumventing the onerous restrictions placed on them. Only once had they broken quarantine, a quarantine no regul would have accepted in principle in the first place; and that one success seemed without forethought and was embarrassedly, tacitly ignored by the envoy. It had succeeded only because it had been uncharacteristic of the humans, a minor victory in the sense of its unhappy result, but actually of no possible benefit to them. In the end only the kel'en had suffered for it, and that needlessly, as impractical as all his kind. The mri had been a man of importance among their bloody, stubborn species. He had promised perhaps to be valuable; but he had been ruined. The humans remained ignorant even of this small revenge they had inflicted on their old enemies. They sat, helpless, obedient.

And hereafter there remained nothing much on Kesrith but what waited loading, now that work crews were free to clear the debris at the docks. There were charges to be set, a few small installations to be stripped, mines to be closed, but the most valuable cargo waited at the dock already.

Of personnel there remained only the lowest priority evacuees, who would leave with him on *Hazan*.

Records bequeathed him from doch Holn indicated that there had been some eighteen million regul adults on Kesrith at the beginning of the evacuation procedure, a colony once exceedingly prosperous and supporting a university and a few first-rate elder minds (excluding the Holn, whom he despised as overvalued). He knew the exact number, and the disposition Holn had made, and the disposition he himself had made of the remaining citizens and properties from the instant he had taken charge, and what goods he had placed on the evacuation ships to be consumed enroute, and what to be allotted as personal baggage, and what he was salvaging to take himself, down to fractional weight and space requirements for shipping. He had absorbed all this data in minute detail. He made occasional written records, against the event of his sudden death and the passing of Alagn doch to his immediate heirs—he did not entirely trust humans—or his sudden incapacity; but these were only for such an event. In the ordinary course of transactions he did not consult written records at all. It was physically impossible for a sane and healthy regul to forget anything he had ever determined to remember, and it was also quite likely that he would remember what he heard only casually. Hulagh believed implicitly in the accuracy of the record he had obtained from Solgah Holn-ni, his enemy, as he believed implicitly in her sanity. It was inconceivable that Solgah, however lacking in astuteness and over-impressed with her own ability as an administrator, would not have at least recalled accurately what was the number of regul on her world, and what their resources, and how disposed.

He knew therefore that 327 regul young remained with him outside the ship, the barest minimum necessary to carry out the dismantling operation, and three of those were almost adult. The majority were younglings below the age of twenty-five, as yet undetermined in sex—this would manifest itself at about thirty—and far more mobile than would be possible for them as they began to attain their adult weight. They were of use to him when it came to errands or heavy labor, for the observations of the evacuation that later would be gleaned from their memories by expert scholars on Nurag. Their memories, presently, save in their most recent unique experiences and knowledge of the events passing around them, had not yet acquired any data that would make them intrinsically valuable to any elder, simply because they had not lived long enough or traveled far enough to have rivaled the experience or comparative observatory powers of an elder. They belonged only to the doch of their birth, and had not seen what they might yet accomplish, and since they would not sex and reproduce for another several years, they were not distracted by these considerations.

Only those fully mature and those protected by adult choice of a doch (even Holn) had been lifted off to safety in the main evacuation—they and such infants as could be contained in their mothers' pouches for the duration of the voyages, life-supported without undue expenditure of resources by the crowded rescue ships.

These last younglings, more fortunate than the masses of Holn that had not fitted into either category, knew that they were still expendable, and why, and they were accordingly nervous about the coming of humans and petulant about their personal losses—and, which was the common quality of the young—abysmally stupid in their anxieties, believing, for so their limited experience misled them, that they were the first and most important younglings in the history of the race to suffer such things.

One fretted outside now and craved admittance for the fifth time, urgent with some message doubtless protesting the conditions under which they were confined in the Nom and forbidden to wander the square during off-hours, or protesting the long hours that they had been required to work since the crisis at the port, or their increasing fear of the coming humans and the fact that they were not yet on board the safety of *Hazan,* which was at the root of everything. Hulagh had answered enough such requests for attention, both from regul younglings and from dull-witted humans. He was busy. The youngling in question was not assigned anywhere near the human delegate, so it could not be an emergency in that quarter, which was all that would have truly interested him within the Nom. He dealt with the destructions of the storm as best he could, covering the one error he had committed, in failing to ask of Solgah concerning the behaviors of the seasons and the climate of Kesrith. He had little time for petulant and frightened assistants.

The youngling persisted. Hulagh sighed at last and pressed a button and admitted the youngling, whose agitation was extreme.

"Be gracious, bai." It was the one named Suth Hara-ri, bred of the university bai-dach. It gave a polite suck of breath.

Hulagh reciprocated. There was at least some grace in Suth, who had been unmannered and fearful to a degree unbecoming any age when it began service. This former gracelessness on the part of Kesrith's younglings in general was surely due to the years of war which had encompassed the younglings' entire experience. The Kesrithi younglings left in Hulagh's charge were acquiring some graces. Hulagh continually took care to reprimand them, so that they would not arrive ashamed and misfit in the inner worlds: this also he took for part of his duty in salvaging what he could of Kesrith—and also anticipated winning the best of them to Alagn's enlistment as adults, hand-trained, augmenting his private staff to that of a colonial governor.

He reached a place where stopping would not overmuch inconvenience him, but he let the youngling wait with the petition awhile more, while he enjoyed a cup of soi, and midway through it saw fit to gesture his willingness to listen.

"Be gracious," Suth breathed, then blurted in desperate haste: "Bai, the station reports a mri vessel incoming."

This struck through all courtesies and lack of them, commanding Hulagh's attention. Hulagh leaned back, the cup forgotten on the console, and looked at the youngling in unconcealed dismay.

The mercenary Kel—in this situation with humans but a few days removed from Kesrith. Hulagh's hearts became at once agitated and anger heated his face. It was like the mri to be inconvenient.

To arrive always in the moment other elements had reached their maximum vulnerability.

"They have given notice of their intentions?" Hulagh asked of Suth.

"They say that they will land. We urged them to make use of the station facilities. They did not respond to this. They said that they have come for their people onworld and that they intend to land."

"Mri never lie," said Hulagh, for the youngling's reference, if it had never dealt face-to-face with the mercenaries. "Neither do they always tell the truth. In that, they resemble regul."

Suth blinked and sucked air. Subtleties were wasted on this one. Hulagh frowned and blew heated air through his nostrils.

"Are they to have their permission to land?" asked Suth. "Bai, what shall we say?"

"Tell me this, youngling: Where are our station ships?"

"Why, gone, gracious lord, all but the freighter and the shuttles, with the evacuation."

"Then we cannot very well enforce our instruction not to land, can we? You are dismissed, youngling."

"Favor," Suth murmured and withdrew, hasty and graceless in departure. Hulagh, already deep in thought, failed to rise to the provocation.

Mri.

Inconvenient as the stubborn kel'en he had inherited from Gruran. Bloody-handed and impulsive and incapable of coherent argument.

His memory informed him that there were constantly some few mri on Kesrith, and that this was true of no other world since Nisren had fallen to humans forty-three years ago. There were thirteen mri in residence. There was nothing to indicate why Kesrith had been so favored, save that mri had a tendency to choose one or another world as a permanent base, designating it as homeworld, and thereafter behaving as irrationally and emotionally as if this were indeed the true land of their birth. There had been three such homeworlds thus far in the regul-mri association, all within the Holn domain, since the mri had constantly come within Holn jurisdiction and remained unknown in home territories of the regul. This employment of the mercenaries was, curiously, not an arrangement of regul seeking, but an arrangement which the mri had offered the regul 2,202 years ago—for no apparent reason, for no apparent compulsion, save that this arrangement seemed to satisfy some profound emotional need of the mri. Regul had inquired into this mri peculiarity, but remained unsatisfied. There was a regul joke about mri, that mri had made records about their home and origin, but had forgotten where they had left them: hence their nomadic condition. The fact that mri had no memories was a laughable matter to one who had not dealt personally with the intractable mri.

One could not argue with them, could not reason, could not persuade them from old loyalties, and could not—above all could not tamper with their sense of proprieties. He remembered Medai's suicide with a shudder; stubborn and without memory and prone to violence. It was like the mri to prefer bloodshed to reason, even when it was one's own blood that was shed. Medai, Kesrith-born, would not compromise: the mri treaty held only so long as regul maintained a homeworld for mri, so long as that homeworld was inviolate from invasion. Medai had seen what he had seen, and could not reason otherwise; and therefore he had chosen to set himself against his lawful employers.

His suicide was supposed, Hulagh recalled, to put some burden of shame or social stigma on the man who had offended against the mri in question. This self-destruction was an act of reproach or of complete repudiation supposed to have devastating effect on the emotions of his superior.

A mri kel'en would do such a thing, even knowing that regul were not impressed, casting away his precious life rather than compromise on a small point of duty that could make no ultimate difference to him personally. Mri doubtless imagined that it made a difference.

It was that mri ferocity that had originally appealed to the regul, an amazement that this savage, fearsome species had come peacefully to the regul docha and tendered their services—services without which the colonizing of the humanward worlds and the rise of the Holn might never had occurred, not in the manner in which Holn had created monopoly. And this very ferocity ought by rights to have warned sensible regul of the nature of mri. Mercenaries by breeding and choice, their strict, dull-witted codes made them in the beginning utterly dependable as guards in commerce of the outworld docha. They did not change allegiance in mid-service; it was impossible to bribe them; it was impossible even to discharge them save by the completion of a service or by suicide. They had not sense enough to retreat; they had no strong instincts of self-preservation, a fact which balanced their prolific breeding, in which all males of the Kel were free to mate with the low-caste females, besides the mates of their own caste: they therefore tended in the years of peace to multiply at an alarming rate, if it were not for the attrition worked on them by their way of life, their rejection of medical science, and their constant passion for duelling. How these fierce warriors had supported themselves before they found the regul to hire them was another mystery to regul, which the mri had never chosen to reveal. Mri would not do manual labor, not even sufficient to provide themselves food. A mri would starve rather than bear burdens or work the earth for another. They broke this rule only for the building and maintenance of their towers and the managing of the few ships they were allotted personally; but beyond those two exceptions, they would not turn a hand if there were regul available to take over the menial tasks. Once in Hulagh's recall a certain ship with a kel'en aboard had met a difficulty other than human, a navigational malfunction that had the crew in a panic; they had summoned the ship's kel'en—an old kel'e'en it was—who had leisurely come to see the difficulty, sat down at the console, and made the appropriate adjustments; then, with consummate arrogance, the kel'e'en had retired to the solitude of her own quarters, neither speaking nor offering courtesies nor accepting thanks.

Yet this kel'e'en could not read a simple sign to direct herself to the mess hall on station liberty, but had to be directed by her regul employers.

There was nothing to match either the arrogance or the ignorance of the mri Kel: touchy, suiciding when offended by regul, fighting when offended by other mri—there was no knowing what truly motivated the species. Hulagh himself reckoned that he knew humans better than he knew mri, although he had dealt with humans for three years and his ancestors had dealt with mri for 2,202 years. Humans were simply territorial like regul, and while they were creatures of brief memory and small brain like the mri, they did have the industry to work, and to mend the deficiencies of their talents with an admirable technology.

It was a curious thing that in the forty-three-year-war, the regul had come to trust humans far more than they did the mri; they had come to fear humans far less than they feared mri. Constantly regul had to command the mri to observe the decencies of restraint, actually had to intervene to prevent the mri escalating the war out of the territorial zone of conflict and into reaches far beyond regul limits, into a scale in which regul technology was inadequate to maintain defenses around vital homeworlds. The mri, who were specialists in war, yet had not been able to perceive this; even the Holn had done so, and had put restraints to the war, or there would have been incredible devastation and economic collapse. Mri might lose one homeworld after another and move on, but they were nomadic—perhaps, Hulagh estimated, the source of their contempt for national boundaries. Regul could not contemplate the loss of even one world of home space, with artwork, technology, trade routes: they did not intend at any time to enter war with the all-out dedication of mri.

The most serious losses were, at the end of matters, to the mri themselves. Mri had begun the war with one million, nine hundred fifty and seven kel'ein according to regul census; and this small figure was still a great increase over their former numbers, reflecting the prosperity that had been theirs in regul service over the span of 2,202 years. Only a hundred thousand had they numbered when their leaders had first approached the regul and begged to be allowed to take service with the regul species. But now most recent records indicated that there were but 533 mri of all castes surviving in known space.

It was impossible, considering that small number and the mri's unrestrainably fierce inclinations, that the species could survive at this low ebb—ironically—without regul protection during their recovery. An era had ended, with the passing of the basis of Holn power, with the passing of the kel'ein. A few could be preserved by Alagn, if the mri would in extremity permit themselves to see reason: and Hulagh could see use for them, if only in the regul awe of the ferocity of the Kel. But they must be removed from the path of the human advance or the mri would continue like automatons to dash themselves to death against the inevitable.

And in the midst of other confusions, one mri must suicide and now a mri ship must come interfering in the evacuation of the mri homeworld. It would be an armed ship. Mri vessels, at least vessels totally mri, were small, but mri did not go anywhere unarmed.

The humans who were coming to take possession of Kesrith would likewise be armed.

Hulagh considered for one wild moment making a graceless withdrawal from his duty on Kesrith, bundling surviving younglings and himself aboard *Hazan* tonight and leaving the mri and the humans to each others' mercies.

But *Hazan* was not ready, not fully repaired, her important cargo impossible to load until the dock machinery had been repaired.

And he would not retreat in such fashion, which would be told on homeworld to his discredit; in that much he understood the mri compulsion to stand fast when pushed.

He reached to his left and pressed a button, contacting the youngling Hada Surag-gi, kosaj of the Nom, who served him personally for sufficiently important errands: a twenty year old, Hada, extraordinarily competent in its advanced post. "Hada," he said, "send the records of mri settlement on Kesrith."

"Be gracious," replied Hada's voice. "Such records go back 2,202 years. Kesrith was among the first worlds possessed by the mri and it is locally believed that they were here before first contact. What information does the bai wish in particular? I may perhaps recall what is of help."

This was utter impudence, that such a youngling supposed its own personal knowledge sufficient to remedy the desire of an elder.

"O young ignorance," said Hulagh peevishly, remembering that he was the only elder presently on Kesrith and that the youngling, though impudent and self-important, was probably offering with the best of intentions, to save him valuable time and effort. This was not, after all, Nurag; there was a limit on everyone's time and patience, most particularly his own. "Hada, what do you suppose would bring a mri ship now to Kesrith?"

"This is," said Hada, "the present mri homeworld. Perhaps they mean to defend it. They are not accustomed to retreat."

It was not a comforting conjecture, and precisely the one that Hulagh had made for himself. Yet the mri had accepted the treaty that regul had made with humans; mri had been advised at every step of the negotiations that they might not carry on further war with humans.

"Hada what is the present number of mri on Kesrith?"

"Bai, there are thirteen, mostly elders of the edun and entirely unfit for war."

He was surprised by this. He had not been interested in the small edun, since it had not intruded into his notice; he had known the number accurately but not the incapacity of its members.

"Send the records anyway, whatever you possess on the leaders personally and on the history of the species here." *Perdition,* thought Hulagh miserably, *mri have been on Kesrith for far too many years that I can sift through such as this. There is no time. The records will be mountainous.* "Hada."

"Favor?"

"Contact their kel'anth. Tell him I want him to report to this office immediately."

There was a very long pause. "Be gracious, bai," ventured Hada at last. "The Kesrithi edun is headed by a she'pan, one Intel. Onworld, a kel'anth must defer to a she'pan. He is not the leader of the mri on Kesrith."

Hulagh's oath cut short the youngling. There was silence in the chatter for a moment, welcome silence. He absorbed the new information, embarrassed by his reliance on a youngling's knowledge, aware that, where mri were concerned, no one actually knew what the chain of command was within their community. Hada claimed to possess this knowledge. Perhaps Hada had acquired it from elders of Holn doch, who had commanded mri for generations. *Plague and perdition,* thought Hulagh, *there is no time, there is no time. Confound all mri to perdition.* But neither did one summon a she'pan: he knew that much. None but Kel caste would respond to a summons to leave their community and meet with outsiders. There was the necessity to brave the process of records search, or the necessity to ignore the incoming ship, with all its ugly possibilities.

Or there was the necessity to leave his desk and his work and his important duties to the incompetent mercies of youngling assistants at such a crisis, while he paid slow courtesies to a mri religious leader, whose memory was fallible and whose graces were probably lacking, who trammeled up the cleanly relations between regul doch and mri kel'anth. He and the war leader of the Kel might have settled things with a simple exchange; with one of the ceremonial leaders of the mri involved, whose power was nebulous and whose authorities and compulsions were somehow linked to the mri religion, whatever it was—a regul petitioner must suffer tedious and pointless discussion that might only perhaps produce what he wanted.

"Hada," said Hulagh, surrendering, "fetch me my car and the most reliable driver, a youngling who does not flinch from mri."

Many humiliations had he accepted in dealing with the invading humans, in negotiations concerning arrangements, in accepting two inconvenient observers whose presence, if known, could cause impossible complications with the mri treaty. He had succeeded in handling the humans, which was thought to have been the most difficult matter; he had outmaneuvered them in a way that would bring him prestige. And now it came to this, that he must interrupt the saving of regul lives and regul properties to counsel with mri hirelings, to rescue an ungrateful people who most likely would not treat with him courteously for his efforts.

A thought struck him. "Hada," he said.

"Favor?"

"Is it or is it not possible that the mri would know that one of their ships is coming?"

"That information has not been released by this office," said Hada. Then: "Be gracious, bai; mri have learned things before this that have not been released by this office. They have their own communications."

"Doubtless," said Hulagh, and broke the connection and went about the laborious and painful business of rising. He was 290 years removed from the class of younglings. His legs were proportionately shorter, his senses duller, his body many times heavier. His rugose skin was prone to cracking and developing sores when directly exposed to the dry cold of Kesrith's air. His double hearts labored under the exertion of lifting his adult bulk, and his muscles trembled with the unaccustomed strain. As an elder of the regul, his principal business was of the mind and the intellect.

And he was reduced to this, to visit mri.

Chapter Twelve

The Mri Edun hove into view, a set of truncated, common-based cones ominously alien—and located, inevitably, in the most inconvenient and inaccessible place available. Hulagh settled uneasily into his cushions in the rear of the landsled and saw it grow nearer: built of the soil of the mineral flats, cemented and dull-surfaced, it was of a color with the earth, but startling to the eye and forbiddingly sterile in its outlines. It wasted space with its slanting walls—but then, mri never did anything the simple way. It was, he reflected, indicative of the mri mind, nonutilitarian, alien in its patterns, deliberately isolate. The sled labored in the climb up the causeway, which the rains, that other of Kesrith's terrestrial nuisances, had left in ill-repair, dissolving the salts that lay in thick deposits thereabouts and creating alarming channels in the earth and rock of the causeway. On either side lay a fatal plunge to the thin crusts of the flats, volcanic and constantly steaming at one or another vent. Hulagh tried not to think of what depths lay beside the treads of the sled as it ground its way over a series of ruts that had almost eaten the road away.

Mri did not choose to repair it. Old they might be, but even if they had been physically capable, they would have disdained to do it, not as long as there remained onworld a single regul on whom to cast the responsibility. The road would wash away before mri would stir to mend it, and there was no intention in Hulagh's mind to do so for human benefit.

He only hoped it would suffice to carry him to and from, and that once only.

The car jolted up the last few feet of incline and came to the main entry of the edun. The structure itself was in similar disrepair, already yielding to the rains that would claim it in the end, that would reduce it to the white earth again. The slanted walls bore dim traces of colors that must once have made it bright.

He had seen pictures of edunei, but he had never seen one in reality, and never seen one in such a state. This was surely an ancient structure, and declined sadly. Mri were usually more proud. Even the front walk was guttered with erosion channels, and with the sled grinding to a halt, bai Hulagh looked on that irregular surface with dread. It was a long walk, a difficult walk on soft ground. And there was a dus guarding the entry, a massive brown lump, all wrinkles and folds of flesh, rising to a hump at the shoulders and descending at either end. It seemed to be asleep, resting with its back a quarter as high as the door—higher by more should it stir, which Hulagh fervently hoped it would not do. Dusei were wherever mri traveled, but on ship they kept entirely to the kel'en's cabin and were not allowed to range the premises. He had never encountered one at close range, had let his younglings tend to that unpleasantness. He knew only what he had heard: that while mri were legally class-two sapients on a scale which rated regul as one, dusei were tentatively classed at ten, although many who had dealt with the frustrating creatures reckoned that dusei should be considerably higher or lower. They were Kesrith's native dominant species; he knew this too, although they ran wild wherever mri had been for long, which was every world where mri had ever been permitted—none, happily, in the inner territories of regul space—this was their origin. They were a plague in the wilds of whatever world they adopted, and they were dangerous. There were surely wild ones prolific in the hills and plains—slow, patient omnivores, a gift such as regul gladly bestowed on the humans. Mri purchased with their service food to feed their dusei, which accordingly haunted their dwellings and accompanied them into space; but dusei did nothing, contributed nothing, did not fight unless cornered, and were never eaten. Their only visible benefit was that to keep them nearby pleasured the mri, who apparently derived some social status among their own kind for the keeping and support of such useless and expensive creatures. Hulagh himself collected gems, stones, geological curiosities. He attempted to comprehend the mentality of the mri, who treasured such live and dangerous specimens.

This one in particular looked diseased. Its hide was patched and his attitude was more sluggish than was natural even for a dus. It had not even lifted its head as the car drew up at the walk.

The sight of the ugly creature did more than the decay of the edun itself to distress Hulagh's aesthetic sense. He looked at it and did not wish to look, as he forced his own considerable bulk from the confines of the sled and waited for his driver, one Chul Nag-gi, to assist him up the walk. Chul also seemed to regard the dus with distaste, and as they walked together toward the step, Chul dutifully walked on the side nearest the creature and kept a constant eye on it. The dus lifted its head to investigate them as they came to the doorway. Its eyes were running and unhealthy.

Perdition, thought Hulagh uneasily, *the thing is dying of disease on their doorsill, and will they not destroy it?—for the sake of hygiene, if not mercy.*

The dus investigated them, snuffling wetly, emitted a strange sound, a low rumbling and whuffing that was not pleasure and not quite menace. "Away!" Chul exclaimed, in a voice edged with panic. Hulagh edged past with all possible speed, while Chul fended the creature away with a violent kick. Chul overtook him just inside the dark door, and offered an arm once more, whereupon they began the long walk together.

A mri saw them and vanished, a black shadow among shadows, and none offered to guide them. Hulagh needed no guidance. He had been acquainted before they left the Nom with the plan of edunei, which was universal. He knew the general design of the ground level, and where the fourth cone of the she'pan ought to sit, and to this cone he walked slowly, panting, struggling as the approach offered, to his horror, stairs, winding up and up toward the crest.

A shout echoed above. Yet he saw no one and came at his own agonized pace, step by step, past mud-plastered walls cheaply decorated with rough designs or symbols, so irregularly and stylistically painted that they seemed impossible of decipherment even if one knew the mri system. Designs in black and gold and blue serpentined round the windings of the corridor upon walls and ceilings. They might be religious in nature: it was another thing the mri had never revealed—to avert evils or call them down on intruders; or perhaps they simply thought it beautiful. It was difficult to reconcile this with the modern lighting and the other evidences of mri sophistication with regul machinery—a people that could handle starflight and yet lived in this primitive manner. The doors that shielded the hall where the she'pan would hold state, most of the doors in the edun, in fact, were steel, of regul manufactury, and steel likely reinforced the mud-and-binder architecture.

"They do not mind furnishing their mud hovels with good regul metal," Chul said, an undertone, but the youngling saved its comments for itself when Hulagh gave it a hard look, for the acuteness of mri hearing was legendary.

"Open the door," said Hulagh.

And when Chul had done so, the youngling gave a sharp intake of breath, for there was a mri directly confronting them, a black-veiled kel'en, a mere youngling himself; Hulagh reckoned so, at least, by the unmarred brow and clear golden skin. He was grim, impudent, barbarous, a golden man bedecked in black and weaponry, warlike gear that even included the archaism of a long knife at his belt. Hulagh was minded instantly and painfully of Medai, who had been such as this. It was like meeting a ghost.

Youngling fronted youngling, and it was the regul that backed a pace, a weakness that sent a wave of angry heat to Hulagh's head.

"Where is the she'pan?" Hulagh asked sharply, embarrassed by his driver's discomfiture and seeking to recover regul dignity. "Young mri, get out of the door and call someone of authority. You were advised that I would call on the she'pan."

The mri turned neatly on his heel and walked away, silent, graceful, disrespectful. Mri warrior. Hulagh hated the whole breed. They were utterly unmannered as a nation, and encouraged it in their younglings. The youth, like the whole edun, stank of incense. It lingered in the air, and Hulagh fought a tendency to sneeze, to clear his violated air passages. His legs were shuddering from the long walk upstairs. He walked in and bent his knees and lowered his heavy body the necessary small degree to sit on the carpets. Mri furniture, of which there was only the she'pan's chair of honor and two benches near the entry, was too high and too fragile for an adult regul, nor could a regul stand and bear his own weight for any length of time.

In proper courtesy the youngling should have summoned some of his kind to bring furniture apt to him; but this was a very poor edun by all evidences, and perhaps unused to regul callers at all. The carpets were at least clean.

Shouting echoed in the depths of the hall beyond the partition that screened the privacies of the central chamber. Hulagh mentally winced at the unseemliness of this behavior, and Chul stirred uneasily. In a moment more the room began to admit other warriors, likewise veiled and armed.

"Bai," said Chul. There was fear in that tone. Hulagh dealt with it with a foul look: ignorant, this youngling. The mri, while graceless and arrogant, were still subjects of the regul, and they were subjects by choice, not compulsion. Mri were many things, and they were unpleasant, but they were not dangerous, at least in the personal sense—not to regul.

Several dusei wandered in, heavy-boned heads held low to the carpet, looking as if they had lost something and forgotten just what it was. They settled their great bulks into the corner and lowered their heads between their paws and watched, their tiny, almost invisible eyes glittering. One rumbled an ominous sound, quieted as a kel'en settled against him, using his broad shoulder for a backrest.

The sneeze came, unexpected and violent. Hulagh contained it as best he could. None of the mri affected to notice this terrible breach of etiquette. He counted those present. There were eleven, and nine of these were veiled, males and perhaps a female of the Kel; one young female was unveiled, robed in gold; and with her was one of the oldest, a presumed male of the gold-robed caste. They were the only mri whose faces he had ever seen. He could not help staring, amazed at the graceful delicacy of the young female.

Odd, Hulagh reflected, that this backward species sexed when young and aged into sameness. He stored that thought away for further pondering, did mri chance to survive this era and remain relevant to the living.

And with a soft rustling, the she'pan herself arrived, leaning on the arm of the young kel'en; she settled among them, in her chair, veilless. She was also very, very old, and, Hulagh thought, although he was not sure, that she had been disfigured on one side of her face. Young mri were smooth-skinned and slim; and the young woman's hair shone in the light like textured bronze, but the she'pan's was faded and brittle, and on the side with the apparent injury it was dark at the temple. The young warrior knelt at her side, golden eyes darting mistrust and hostility at the visitors. The she'pan's look contained the placidity of age and long, long experience, qualities which Hulagh valued, and he suddenly revised his opinion and reckoned that it might be better after all to deal with this aged female than with an intractable war-leader, if she could indeed guide her people in areas other than in the obscure mri religion.

She had no great awe of regul, this was plain enough; but neither was she hostile or slow-witted. Her eyes were quick and appraising. There was the look of higher sentience there.

"She'pan," said Hulagh, recognizing age's right to dignity, even if she were mri.

"Hulagh," she said, stripping him of titles.

His nostrils snapped shut, blew air in irritation. He remembered the presence of the youngling Chul at his elbow, Chul, whose witness he did not particularly want at this moment, and the heat of anger seethed in him as it had not in many sheltered years.

"She'pan," said Hulagh, persistent in proprieties, "we have made room for your people on our ship." This was, basically, the truth: he had allotted space, which he had hoped would not have to be too extensive, and he had hoped for younglings, who could be civilized and molded anew under Alagn guidance; but he saw only two. He revised opinions quickly. These elders, it might be, could control young mri loose elsewhere, render them tractable, perhaps—gather a colony of mri in Alagn territory. He thought again of the young kel'en who had suicided, and thought perhaps that that would not have happened if there had been an elder mri to provide that youngling with a proper perspective on his act.

If there were not that restraint and sense even in elders like this, and they would not have dissuaded him, then the whole of mri civilization had failed, and there was no rescuing it from itself.

"We would desire," he told the she'pan, "for you to board within the coming night."

The she'pan stared at him, neither joyed nor dismayed by that short time. "Indeed, bai?"

"As soon as possible. We are at that stage of our loading."

The she'pan stared at him and considered that in silence. "And our dusei?" she asked.

"And the dusei, one for each," Hulagh painfully conceded, mentally deducting two times the resources that would have been necessary to accommodate the mri; he had hoped to take no dusei at all; but when he considered the matter, he reflected that the unpleasant beasts might keep the mri content, representing their wealth, and it was very desirable that the mri remain content.

"We will consult upon the matter," said the she'pan, her hand on the shoulder of the young warrior who sat beside her, and at her other side, silent, settled the gold-robed young female.

"There is no time for lengthy consultations," Hulagh objected.

"Ah," said the she'pan, "then you have heard about the ship."

Blood drained from Hulagh's face, slowly resumed its proper circulation. He did not look at the youngling, hoping for once its wits would prevent its repeating this insult and humiliation elsewhere, among its youngling fellows. He had scant hope that this would be the case.

"Yes," said Hulagh, "we have naturally heard. Nevertheless we are anxious to speed our departure. We are not familiar with this incoming ship, but doubtless—" he stammered over the not-truth, compelled to lie, for the first time in his life, for the sake of regul, for the welfare of the younglings in his protection, and most of all for his own ambitions and for the survival of his knowledge; but he felt foul and soiled in the doing. "Doubtless after you are aboard, we may intercept this ship of yours and divert it also toward the safety of our inner zones."

"Would you permit that?" The dry old voice, heavy with accent, was careful, devoid of inflections that could have betrayed emotion and concealed meanings. "Shall mri go to the regul homeworld at long last? You have never permitted us knowledge of its location, bai."

"Nevertheless—" He could not build upon the lie. He was not able to consummate this, the supreme immorality—to falsify, to lend untruth to memory, which could not be unlearned. He had learned this practice of aliens. He had watched them do it, amazed and horrified; he had learned that humans lied as a regular practice. He felt his own skin crawl at the enormity of it, his throat contract when he tried to shape more to his fiction, and knew that if he refused to build upon it, it would not be believed at all; and then he would be caught, lose credibility, with fatal consequences for the mri, with unfortunate result for the regul under his command, and for his own future.

If it were known on Nurag—

But they were only mri, lesser folk; they had no memories such as regul had; and with them the lie could not live as it would among regul. Perhaps therein lay at least a lesser immorality.

"Nevertheless, she'pan," he said, controlling his voice carefully, "this is so. Matters are different now. We will not delay here as long as we had planned. We will board with all possible speed."

"Do you fear lest the humans should gain us?"

This came too near the mark. Hulagh sat still, looking at the she'pan and suspecting deeper things within her words. Mri were, like regul, truthful. He had this on the tradition of all his predecessors who had made the records which he had learned, and an ancestry that made the records on the truth of which all the past and therefore all the future depended.

Had the ancestors also been tempted to lie, to play small games with truth and reality?

Had they in fact done so? The very doubting increased the pace of Hulagh's overtaxed hearts, pulled the foundations from beneath his firmest beliefs and left everything in uncertainty. Yet in spite of this tradition of the ancestors, a bai now lied, to save lives, for a good cause and the welfare of two species: but the truth had been altered, all the same, and now the lie shaped truth to cover it.

"We are anxious," said Hulagh, wading deeper into this alien element, "that you be safe from humans. We are anxious to speed our own departure, for our safety's sake, and for yours. Our own younglings are at stake, and myself, and my reputation, and I am extremely valuable in the eyes of my people, so you may know that we will take unusual care to ensure the safety of this particular ship. If you wish to go with us, and I advise it, she'pan, I strongly advise it, then prepare your people to embark at once."

"We have served regul," said the she'pan, "for 2,000 years. This is very long service. And scant have been the rewards of it."

"We have offered you what you ask and more: we have offered you technicians who would give you all the benefits of our experience; we have offered you our records, our histories, our technology."

"We do not," said the she'pan, "desire this knowledge of yours."

"It is your own misfortune then," said the bai. He had met this stupidity in mri before, in Medai. "She'pan, you keep to your own dwellings and to ships, but they are regul-built ships; even your weapons are regul-made. Your food is produced by regul. Without us you would starve to death. And yet you still affect to despise our knowledge."

"We do not despise your knowledge," said the she'pan. "We simply do not desire it."

Hulagh's eyes strayed past her shoulder to the chamber itself, a gesture of contempt for the conditions in which the she'pan held state, in rooms barely sanitary, in halls innocent of amenities, decorated with that frighteningly crude and powerful art of symbols, the meaning of which he doubted even the mri remembered. They were superstitious folk. If ill or injured, mri would turn from regul help and die rather than admit weakness, desiring only the presence of other mri or the presence of a dus. This was their religion at work.

Usually they died, all the same. *We are warriors,* regul had heard often enough, *not carriers of burdens, sellers of goods, practitioners of arts, whatever the offered opportunity or benefit.* Medicine, engineering, literature, agriculture, physical labor of any sort as long as there was a single regul to do it for them—all these things the mri despised.

Animals, Hulagh thought, *plague and pestilence—they are nothing but animals. They enjoy war. They have deliberately prolonged this one in their stupidity. We ought never to have unleashed them in war. They like it too well.*

And to the youth, the arrogant young kel'en who sat by the she'pan's knee, he asked, "Youngling, would you not wish to learn? Would you not wish to have the things that regul enjoy, to know the past and the future and how to build in metals?"

The golden eyes nictitated, a sign of startlement in a mri. "I am of the Kel," said the young warrior. "And education is not appropriate for my caste. Ask the Sen."

The young woman in gold looked on him in her turn, her unveiled face a perfect mask, infuriating, expressionless. "The Sen is headed by the she'pan. Ask the she'pan, bai, whether she desires your knowledge. If she bids me learn, then I will learn what you have to teach."

They played with him, games of ignorance, mri humor. Hulagh saw it in the eyes of the she'pan, who remained motionless through this circular exchange.

"We know," said the she'pan finally, "that these things have always been available to us. But the rewards of service that we desired were other than what you offer; and of late they have been scant."

Enigmas. The mri cherished their obscurities, their abstruseness. There was no helping such people. "If one of you," Hulagh said with deliberate patience, "had ever deigned to specify what reward you sought, then we might have found the means to give it to you."

But the she'pan said nothing to this, as the mri had always said nothing on this score: *We serve for pay,* some had said scornfully, similarly questioned, but they offered nothing of the truth of the whole; and this she'pan like her ancestors said nothing at all.

"It would be a comfort to my people," said Hulagh, trying that ancient ploy, the appeal to legalities of oath and to mri conscience, and it was partly truth at least. "We are accustomed to the protection of mri with us. We are not fighters. Even if one or two mri should be on the ship as we leave, we would feel safer in our journey."

"If you demand a mri for your protection," said the she'pan, "I must send one."

"She'pan," said Hulagh, trying again to reach some point of reason, forgetful of his dignity and the watching eyes of Chul. "Would you then send one, alone, without his people, to travel so far as we are going, and without the likelihood of return? This would be hard. And what is there possibly in these regions to detain you once we have gone?"

"Why should we not," asked the she'pan, "bring our own ship in your wake—to Nurag? Why are you so anxious to have us aboard your own, bai Hulagh?"

"We have laws," Hulagh said, his hearts pounding. "Surely you realize we must observe cautions. But it will be safer for you than here."

"There will be humans here," said the she'pan. "Have you not arranged it so?"

Hulagh found nothing in his vast memory with which to understand that answer. It crawled uneasily through his thoughts, rousing ugly suspicions.

"Would you," Hulagh asked, compelled to directness, "change your allegiance and serve humans?"

The she'pan made a faint gesture, meaningless to a regul. "I will consult with my Husbands," she said. "If it pleases you, I will send one of my people with you if you demand it. We are in service to the regul. It would not be seemly or lawful for me to refuse to send one of us with you in your need, o Hulagh, bai of Kesrith."

Now, now came courtesy; he did not trust this late turn of manners, though mri could not lie; neither had he thought that he could lie, before this conference and his moment of necessity, which had been spent all in vain. Mri might indeed not lie; but neither was it likely that the she'pan was without certain subtleties, and possibly she was laughing within this appearance of courtesy. And the Kel was veiled and inscrutable.

"She'pan," he said, "what of this ship that is coming?"

"What of it?" echoed the she'pan.

"Who are these mri that are coming? Of what kindred? Are they of this edun?"

Again the curious gesture of the hand that returned to stroke the head of the young female who leaned against her knee.

"The name of the ship, bai, is *Ahanal*. And do you make formal request that one of us accompany you?"

"I will tell you this when you have consulted with your Husbands and given me the answer to other questions," said Hulagh, marking how she had turned aside his own question. He smoldered with growing anger.

These were mri. They were a little above the animals. They knew nothing and remembered less, and dared play games with regul.

He was also within their territory, and of law on this forsaken world, he was the sole representative.

For the first time he looked upon the mri not as a comfort, not as interestingly quaint, nor even as a nuisance, but as a force like the dusei, dull-wittedly ominous. He looked at the dark-robed warriors, this stolid indifference to the regul authority that had always commanded them.

For mri to challenge the will of the regul—this had never happened, not directly, not so long as mri served the varied regul docha and authorities; Hulagh sorted through his memory and found no record of what the mri had done when it was not a question of traditional obedience. This was that most distasteful of all possible situations, one never before experienced by any regul on record, one in which his own vast memory was as helpless as that of a youngling, blank of helpful data.

Regul in the throes of complete senility sometimes claimed sights of memories that were yet in the future, saw things that had not yet been and on which there could not possibly be data. Sometimes these elders were remarkably accurate in their earliest estimations, an accuracy which disturbed and defied analysis. But the process then accelerated and muddled all their memories, true and not-yet-true and never-true, and they went mad beyond recall. Of a sudden Hulagh suffered something of the sort, projected the potentials of this situation and derived an insane foreboding of these warlike creatures turning on him and destroying him and Chul at once, rising against the regul docha in bloody frenzy. His two hearts labored with the horror not only of this image, but of the fact that he had perceived it at all. He was 310 years of age. He was bordering on decline of faculties, although he was now at the peak of his abilities and looked to be for decades more. He was terrified lest decline have begun, here, under the strain of so much strangeness. It was not good for an old regul to absorb so much strangeness at once.

"She'pan," he said, trying the last, the very last assault upon her adamancy. "You are aware that your ill-advised delay may make it impossible in the end to take any of your people aboard to safety."

"We will consult," she said, which was neither aye nor nay, but he took it for absolute refusal, judging that he would never in this world hear from the she'pan, not until that ship had come.

There was something astir among mri, something that involved Kesrith and did not admit regul to the secret; and he remembered the young kel'en who had suicided when he was denied permission to leave—who would have borne the news of human presence to the she'pan already if he had been allowed off that ship; and there was that perversity in mri, that, deprived of their war, they might be capable of committing racial suicide, a last defense against humans, who came to claim this world—and when humans met this, they would never believe that the mri were acting alone. They would finish the mri and move against regul: another foresight, of horrid aspect.

Mri would retreat only under direct order, and if they slipped control, they would not retreat at all. Of a sudden he cursed the regul inclined to believe the mri acquiescent in this matter—Gruran, who had passed him this information and caused him to believe in it.

He cursed himself, who had confirmed the data, who had not considered mri as a priority, who had been overwhelmingly concerned with loading the world's valuables aboard *Hazan,* and with managing the humans.

Hulagh heaved himself up, found his muscles still too fatigued from his first climb to manage his weight easily, and was not spared the humiliation of having to be rescued from relapse by the youngling Chul, who flung an arm about him and braced him with all its might.

The she'pan snapped her fingers and the arrogant young kel'en at her knee rose up easily and added his support to Hulagh's right side.

"This is very strenuous for the bai," Chul said, and Hulagh mentally cursed the youngling. "He is very old, she'pan, and this long trip has tired him, and the air is not good for him."

"Niun," said the she'pan to her kel'en, "escort the bai down to his vehicle." And the she'pan rose unaided, and observed with bland face and innocent eyes while Hulagh wheezed with effort in putting one foot in front of the other. Hulagh had never missed his lost youth and its easy mobility; age was its own reward, with its vast memory and the honors of it, with its freedom from fear and with the services and respect accorded by younglings; but this was not so among mri. He realized with burning indignation that the she'pan sought this comparison between them in their age, furnishing her people with the spectacle of the helplessness of a regul elder without his sleds and his chairs.

Among mri, light and quick, and mobile even in extreme age, this weakness must be a curiosity. Hulagh wondered if mri made jest of regul weakness in this regard as regul did of mri intelligence. No one had ever seen a mri laugh outright, not in 2,202 years. He feared there was laughter now on their veiled faces.

He looked on the face of Chul, seeking whether Chul understood. The youngling looked only bewildered, frightened; it panted and wheezed with the burden of its own and another's weight. The young mri at the other side did not look directly at either of them, but kept his eyes respectfully averted, a model of decorum, and his veiled face could not be read.

They left the steel doors and entered the dizzying windings of the painted halls, down and down agonizingly painful steps. For Hulagh it was a blur of misery, of colors and cloying air and the possibility of a fatal fall, and when they finally reached level ground it was blessed relief. He lingered there a moment, panting, then began to walk again, leaning on them, step by step. They passed the doors, and the stinging, pungent air outside came welcome, like the hostile sun. His senses cleared. He stopped again, and blinked in the ruddy light, and caught his breath, leaning on them both.

"Niun," he said, remembering the kel'en's name.

"Lord?" responded the young mri.

"How if I should choose you to go on the ship with me?"

The golden eyes lifted to his, wide and, it seemed, frightened. He had never seen this much evidence of emotion in a mri. It startled him. "Lord," said the young mri, "I am duty-bound to the she'pan. I am her son. I cannot leave."

"Are you not all her sons?"

"No, lord. They are mostly her Husbands. I am her son."

"But not of her body, all the same."

The mri looked as if he had been struck, shocked and offended at once. "No, lord. My truemother is not here anymore."

"Would you go on the ship *Hazan*?"

"If the she'pan sent me, lord."

This one was young, without the duplicities, the complexities of the she'pan; young, arrogant, yes, but such as Niun could be shaped and taught. Hulagh gazed at the young face, veiled to the eyes, finding it more vulnerable than was the wont of mri—rudeness to stare, but Hulagh took the liberty of the very old among regul, who were accustomed to be harsh and abrupt with younglings. "And if I should tell you now, this moment, get into the sled and come with me?"

For a moment the young mri did not seem to know how to answer; or perhaps he was gathering that reserve so important to a mri warrior. The eyes above the veil were frankly terrified, agonized.

"You might be assured," Hulagh said, "of safety."

"Only the she'pan could send me," said the young kel'en. "And I know that she will not."

"She had promised me one mri."

"It has always been the privilege of the edun to choose which is to go and which to stay. I tell you that she will not let me go with you, lord."

That was plainly spoken, and the obtaining of permission through argument would doubtless mean another walk to the crest of the structure, and agony; and another debate with the she'pan, protracted and infuriating and doubtful of issue. Hulagh actually considered it and rejected it, and looked on the young face, trying to fix in mind what details made this mri different from other mri.

"What is your name, your full name, kel'en?"

"Niun s'Intel Zain-Abrin, lord."

"Set me in my car, Niun."

The mri looked uncertainly relieved, as if he understood that this was all Hulagh was going to ask. He applied his strength to the task with Chul's considerable help, and slowly, carefully, with great gentleness, lowered Hulagh's weight into the cushion. Hulagh breathed a long sigh of exhaustion and his sight went dim for a moment, the blood rushing in his head. Then he dismissed the mri with an impatient gesture and watched him walk back to the doorway, over the eroded walk. The dus by the door lifted his head to investigate, then suddenly curled in the other direction and settled, head between its forelegs. Its breath puffed at the dust. The young mri, who had paused, vanished into the interior of the edun.

"Go," said Hulagh to Chul, who turned on the vehicle and set it moving in a lumbering turn. And again: "Youngling, contact my office and see if there are any new developments."

He thought uneasily of the incoming ship, distant as it surely was, and of everything which had seemed so simple and settled this morning. He drew a breath of the comfortably filtered and heated air within the vehicle and tried to compose his thoughts. The situation was impossible. Humans were about to arrive; and if humans perceived mri near Kesrith and suspected treachery or ambush, humans could arrive sooner. They could arrive very much sooner.

Without a doubt there would be confrontation, mri and human, unless he could rid Kesrith and Kesrith's environs of mri, by one method or another; and of a sudden reckoning she'pan Intel into matters, Hulagh found himself unable to decide how things were aligned with mri and regul.

Or with mri and humans.

"Bai," came Hada Surag-gi's voice over the radio. "Be gracious. We have contacted the incoming mri ship directly. They are *Ahanal*."

"Tell me something I do not already know, youngling."

There was a moment's silence. Hulagh regretted his temper in the interval, for Hada had tried to do well, and Hada's position was not enviable, a youngling trying to treat with mri arrogance and a bai's impatience.

"Bai," said Hada timidly, "this ship is not based on this world, but they are intending to land. They say—bai—"

"Out with it, youngling."

"—that they will be here by sunfall over Kesrith's city tomorrow. They have arrived close—dangerously close, bai. Our station was monitoring the regular approaches, the lanes—but they ignored them."

Hulagh blew his breath out softly, and refrained from swearing.

"Be gracious," said Hada.

"Youngling, what else?"

"They rejected outright our suggestion to dock at the station. They want to land at the port. We disputed their right to do so under the treaty, and explained that our facilities were damaged by the weather. They would not hear. They say that they have need of provisioning. We protested they could obtain this at the station. They would not hear. They demand complete re-provisioning and re-equipage of a class-one vessel with armaments as on war status. We protested that we could not do these things. But they demand these things, bai, and they claim—they claim that they number in excess of 400 mri on that ship."

A chill flowed over Hulagh's thick skin.

"Youngling," said Hulagh, "in all known space there are only 533 of the species known to survive, and thirteen of these are presently on Kesrith and another is recently deceased."

"Be gracious," pleaded Hada. "Bai, I am very sure I heard accurately. I asked them to repeat the figure.—It is possible," Hada added in a voice trembling and wheezing with distress, "that these are all the mri surviving anywhere in the universe."

"Plague and perdition," said Hulagh softly and reached forward to prod Chul in the shoulder. "The port."

"Bai?" asked Chul, blinking.

"The port," Hulagh repeated. "O young ignorance, the port. Make for it."

The car veered off left, corrected, followed the causeway the necessary distance, then left along the passable margin of the city, bouncing over scrub, presenting occasionally a view of the pinkish sky and the distant mountains, Kesrith's highlands, then of white barren sands and the slim twisting trunks of scrub luin.

To this the humans fell heir.

Good riddance to them.

He began to think again of the mri that had suicided, and with repeated chill, of the remaining mri that had by that time already tended toward Kesrith—all the mri that survived anywhere, coming to their homeworld, which was to go to the control of humans.

To die?

He wished he could trust it were so simply final. To stop the humans; to breathe life into the war again; to ruin the peace and the regul at once, and then, being few, to die themselves, and leave the regul species at the mercy of outraged humans: this was like the mri.

He began to think, his double hearts laboring with fear, what choice he had in dealing with the mercenaries; and as he had never lied before he dealt with mri, so he had never contemplated violence with his own hands, without mri hired as intermediaries.

The sled made a rough turn toward the port gate, bouncing painfully over ruts. The disrepair was even here.

He saw with utter apprehension that clouds had gathered again over the hills beyond the city.

Chapter Thirteen

The rain came, a gentle enemy, against the walls of the edun. The winds rushed down, but the mountain barrier and the high rocks broke their force and sent them skirling down slopes toward the regul town and port instead. No strong wind had ever touched the edun, not in 2,000 years.

It was comfortable on such a night to take the common-meal, all castes together in the she'pan's tower. All evening long there had been a curious sensitivity in the air, a sense of violent pleasure, of satisfaction as strong as the storm winds. The dusei, mood-sensitive, had grown so restive that they had been turned out of the edun altogether, to roam where they pleased this night. They disappeared into the dark, all but the *miuk'ko* at the gate, finding no discomfort at all in the world's distempers.

And the spirits of the kel'ein were high. Old eyes glittered. There was no mention of the ship that was coming, but it was at the center of everything.

Niun likewise, among the kel'ein, felt the surge of hope at the arrival of *Ahanal*. Of a sudden, dizzying views opened before his feet. Others. Brothers. Rivals. Challenge and hope of living.

And himself, even unfledged, even without experience in war, hitherto no person of consequence: but this was homeworld, and he of homeworld's Kel; and he was, above all, the she'pan's kel'en. It was a heady, unaccustomed feeling, that of being no longer the least, but one among the first.

"We have been in contact with a mri ship," was all the word the she'pan had given them that morning, before the arrival of the regul bai; and that, outside its name, was all that they knew. The Lady Mother had gathered them together in the dawning, and spoken to them quietly and soberly, and it was an effort for her, for she lay insensible so much of the time. But for a moment, a brief moment, there had been an Intel Niun had never seen: it awed him, that soft-voiced, clear-headed stranger who spoke knowledgeably about lanes and routings around Kesrith that were little-monitored by regul—in riddles she spoke at times, but not now: "Soon," she had said, "Very soon. Keep your eyes on the regul, kel'ein."

And quickly then, more quickly than they had anticipated, the regul bai had come making them offers.

The regul were concerned. They were presented something that had never happened before, and they were concerned and confused.

"Intel," said Eddan, her eldest Husband, when dinner was done and Niun had returned from carrying the utensils to the scullery—that and the storerooms the only part of the Kath-tower that remained open. "Intel, may the Kel ask permission to ask a question?"

Niun settled among the kel'ein quickly, anxious and at once grateful that Eddan had waited until his return; and he looked at Intel's face, seeking some hope that she would not deny them.

She frowned. "Is the Kel going to ask about the ship?"

"Yes," said Eddan, "or anything else worth the knowing."

The she'pan unfolded her hands, permission given.

"When it comes," asked Eddan, "do we go or do we stay?"

"Kel'ein, I will tell you this: that I have seen that Kesrith's use is near its end. Go, yes; and I will tell you something more: that I owe the regul bai one kel'en, but no more. And I do much doubt that he will come back to collect that promise of me."

Old Liran, veilless as they all were veilless in the intimacy of the common-meal, grinned and made a move with his scarred hand. "Well, she'pan, Little Mother, if he does come back, send me. I would like to see whether Nurag is all it is claimed to be, and I would be of scant use in the building of another edun. This one, all cracks as it is, is home; and if I am not to stay with this one, why, I might as well take service again."

"Would a service among the People not do as well, Liran?"

"Yes, Little Mother, well enough," Liran answered, and his old eyes flickered with interest, a darted glance at Eddan—an appeal:

ask questions, eldest. The whole Kel sat utterly still. But the she'-pan had turned their question aside. Eddan did not ask again.

"Sathell," said Intel.

"She'pan?"

"Cite for the Kel the terms of the treaty that bind us to the service of regul."

Sathell bowed his head and lifted it again. "The words of the treaty between doch Holn and mri are the treaty that keeps us in service to the regul. The pertinent area: *So long as regul and mri alone occupy the homeworld, whereon the edun of the People rests . . . or until regul depart the homeworld, whereon the edun of the People rests . . .* This long we are bound to accept service with regul when called upon. And I hold, she'pan, that in spirit if not in letter, regul have already failed in the terms of that treaty."

"Surely," said the she'pan, "we are not far from that point. We contracted with doch Holn. Doch Holn might have known how to deal with us; but this bai Hulagh is apparently of Nurag itself, and I do not think he knows the People. He erred seriously when he did not take urgent care to see to our evacuation long before now."

"Holn knew better," said Sathell.

"But Holn neglected to pass on to her successor all that she might have told him. The old bai Solgah kept her silence. Neither do regul tend to consult written records. The regul-kind do not make good fighters, but they are, in their own way, very clever at revenge."

And Intel smiled, a tired smile that held a certain satisfaction.

"May the Kel," asked Eddan, "ask permission to ask a question?"

"Ask."

"Do you think the Holn deliberately excluded us from the assets she turned over to this bai Hulagh?"

"I believe the Holn will consider this a stroke of revenge, a salve to their pride, yes. Bai Hulagh has lost the mri. In such manner regul fight against regul. What is that to us? But I am sure of this," she said in a hard tone, "that Medai was the last of my children to leave on a regul ship, the last of my children to die for regul causes. And hereafter, hereafter, kel'ein, do not plan that mri should fight mri again: no. We do not fight."

There was palpable dismay in the whole Kel.

"May the Kel ask?—" Eddan began, unshakably formal.

"No," she said. "The Kel may not ask. But I will tell you what is good for you to know. The People are dangerously declined in numbers. Time was when such fighting served the People: but no longer, no longer, kel'ein. I will tell you a thing you did not ask: the ship *Ahanal* bears what remains of all the People; and we are the rest. There are no more."

There was cold in the room, and no one moved. Niun locked his arms tightly about his knees, trying to absorb personally what the Mother said, hoping that it was allegory, as she often spoke in riddles: but there was no way to believe it a figure of speech.

"At Elag," said Intel in a thin hard voice, "while regul evacuated their own kind, they threw the kel'ein that served them against humans again and again and again, and summoned the kel'ein of Mlassul and Seleth edunei, and lost them as well. But this mattered little to regul, to this new bai, Hulagh—to this new master sent out from Nurag."

There was a sudden sound, an impact of fist on flesh: and Eddan, who did not swear, swore. "She'pan," he said then. "May the Kel ask—"

"There is nothing more to ask, Eddan," said Intel. "That is the thing that happened: that cost 10,000 mri lives, and ships—ships of which I do not know the tally; many, many of the ships were regul, without regul personnel aboard, because the regul feared to stay. They killed 10,000 mri. And I curse the she'panei who lent their children to such as that."

A fine sweat beaded Intel's face, and pallor underlay her skin. The sound of her breathing was audible, a hoarseness, above the sound of the rain outside. Never had the gentle Mother cursed anyone; and the enormity of cursing she'panei chilled the heart; but neither was there repentance on her face. Niun drew his breaths carefully, sucking in air as if he drew it off the noon-heated sands. His muscles began to tremble, and he clenched his hands the harder lest someone notice it, if anyone could notice anything but his own heartbeat in that terrible silence.

"Little Mother," Sathell pleaded. "Enough, Enough."

"The Kel," she said, "finds it necessary to ask questions. They are due their answer." And she paused a moment, drawing great breaths, as if she intended next something necessary, something urgent. "Kel'ein," she said, "chant me the *Shon'jir*."

There was a stirring among the kel'ein, outright panic and dismay. *She is dying,* was Niun's first thought, and: *O gods, what an ill omen of things!* And he could not say the words she asked of them.

"Are you children," she asked of her Husbands, "to believe any longer in luck either good or bad? Chant me the Passing ritual."

They looked at Eddan, who inclined his head in a gesture of surrender, and began, softly. Niun joined them, uncertain in this insanity in which they were bidden join.

> *From Dark beginning*
> *To Dark at ending,*
> *Between them a Sun,*
> *But after comes Dark,*
> *And in that Dark*
> *One ending.*
>
> *From Dark to Dark*
> *Is one voyage,*
> *From Dark to Dark*
> *Is our voyage.*
> *And after the Dark,*
> *O brothers, o sisters,*
> *Come we home.*

Intel listened with her eyes closed, and afterward there was a long silence; and her eyes opened, and she looked on all of them as from a far place.

"I give you," she said, "a knowledge which kel'ein knew long ago, but which passed from the Kel-lore. Remember it again. I make it lawful. Kesrith is only a between, and Arain only one of many suns, and we are near an ending. In the People's history, kel'ein, are many such Darks; and the regul have afforded us only the latest of our many homes. For this reason we call it *Shon'jir,* and in the low language, the Passing ritual. For this reason we say it at the beginning of each life of the People and at each life's ending; and at the beginning of each era and at its ending. Until another she'pan shall bid your children's children, Niun, forget what I have told you, the Kel may remember."

"Mother," he said, raising hand to her in entreaty, "Mother, is it the moving of homeworld you mean?"

Too long she had been mother to him, and he realized after he had spoken his question that she was due more courtesy; he sat with his heart pounding and waited to hear her coldly rebuff him by asking Eddan if the Kel had a question to pose.

But she neither frowned nor refused his question. "Niun, I give you more truth to ponder. The regul call themselves old; but the People are older. The 2,000 years of which you know are only an interlude. We are nomads. I say that the Kel shall not fight; but the Kel has other purposes. Last of my sons, the Kel of the Darks is a different Kel from the Kel of the Between. Last of my daughters, the she'panate of the Darks is a duty I do not envy you."

Upon an instant the whole Kel was torn from one to the other of them, a fearful, astonished attention.

The succession was passed, not in fact, but in intent; and Niun looked at his onetime brothers, and saw their dismay; and looked at Melein and saw her pale and shaken. She veiled herself and turned away from them; and of a sudden he felt himself utterly alone, even amid the Kel. He bowed his head and stayed so while the voice of Eddan, subdued, begged leave to question, which the she'pan refused.

"The Sen asks," said Sathell's voice then, and by that, posed a question that could not be refused. "She'pan, we cannot make these plans without consulting together."

"Is that a question, Sen?" the she'pan asked dryly, and in the shock of that collision of wills, there was silence. Niun looked at them, from one to the other, appalled that those who ruled his life did not agree.

"It is a question," said Sathell.

The she'pan bit at her lip and nodded. "Yet," she said, "we have made these plans without consulting. I did not consult when I made sure that *Ahanal* was reserved from the madness of Elag. I did not consult when I maintained our base on Kesrith against the urging of some to leave. I have made these plans without consulting—and I have left the People no other choice."

"To the death of our Kath and most of our Kel, when we might have had Lushain for homeworld instead, where there is water and gentle climate, where we might have had a rich world, she'-pan."

"That old quarrel," she said in a still voice. "But I had my way, Sathell, because the she'pan, not the sen'anth, leads the People. Remember it."

"The Sen asks," said Sathell in a trembling voice, "*why. Why* must it have been Kesrith?"

"Is your knowledge adequate? Do you know the last Mysteries, sen'anth?"

"No," Sathell acknowledged, an answer wrung from him.

"Kesrith was the best choice."

"I do not believe it."

"I said at the time," said Intel softly, "that I decided as I saw fit. That is still true. I do not require your belief."

"This I know," said Sathell.

"Kesrith is hard. It kills the weak. It performed its function."

"This forge of the People, as you called it, performed its function too well. We are too few. And Elag has left us with nothing."

"Elag has left us with a remnant like the remnant of Kesrith," said Intel. "With what has been through fire."

"A handful."

"We have given the People," she said, "a place to stand, and stand we shall until humans stand on Kesrith. And then the Dark. And then a decision that will belong to others than you and me, Sathell."

There was silence. Sathell rose suddenly and caught at the wall for support, his weakness betraying him. "To others then," he said, "let it pass now."

And he walked out. His footsteps descended the tower.

Eddan bowed himself, came to Intel and took her hand. "Little Mother," he said gently, "the Kel approves you."

"The Kel knows little," she said, "even now."

"The Kel knows the she'pan," he said in a faint voice. And then he looked about him at the others, at Melein last of all. "Sen Melein—make the cup for her."

"I will not drink it tonight, Eddan," Intel said.

But Eddan's look said otherwise, and Melein nodded, silent conspiracy against Intel's will, and rose and poured water and *komal* into a cup, preparing the draught that would give Intel ease.

"Go," said Eddan to the Kel.

"Niun will stay," said Intel, and Niun, who had risen with the others, stopped.

And downstairs the main door opened and closed, a hollow crash.

"Gods," Pasev breathed, and cast a look at Intel. "He is leaving the edun."

"Let him go," said Intel.

"She'pan," said Melein's voice, a clear note of anguish. "He cannot stay the night out there in the weather."

"I will go after him," said Debas.

"No," said the she'pan. "Let him go."

And after a moment it was clear that there was no changing her mind. There was nothing to be done. Melein settled at Intel's side, still veiled, her eyes averted.

"The Kel is dismissed," said Intel, "except Niun. Sleep well, kel'ein."

Eddan did not wish to be dismissed. He stayed last of all; but Intel gestured him away. "Go," she said. "There is nothing more I can tell you tonight, Eddan. But in the morning, set one of the kel'ein to watch the port from the high rocks. Sleep now. This storm will keep the regul inactive, but tomorrow is another matter."

"No," said Eddan. "I am going after my brother."

"Without my blessing."

"All the same," said Eddan, and turned to go.

"Eddan," she said.

He looked back at her, "We are getting too few," he said, "to make too many journeys to Sil'athen. Sathell would not willingly have left Nisren. Neither would I. Now we will not leave Kesrith. We will walk toward Sil'athen, he and I. We will be content."

"I give my blessing," she said after a moment.

"Thank you," he said, "she'pan."

And that was all. He left; and Niun stared after him into the dark of the hall and trembled in every muscle.

They were as dead, Eddan and Sathell. They had chosen, Sathell after the fashion of his kind, and Eddan, untypical for his caste, to go the long walk with him. And he had seen Eddan's face, and there was no heaviness in it. He heard the kel'anth's steps going down the spiral, a quick and easy stride, and the door closed behind him too; and it was certain that the edun was less by two lives, and they had been great ones.

"Sit by me," Intel bade them.

"She'pan," said Melein in a thin, strained voice, "I have made your cup. Please drink it."

She offered it, and the tray shook in her two hands. Intel took the cup from her and drank, then gave it back, leaning back as Niun settled, kneeling, on her left hand, and Melein on her right.

So they had spent many of the nights since Medai's death, for Intel's sleep was not easy and she would not sleep without someone in the room.

This night, Niun envied her the draught of *komal;* and he would not look at her while she waited for the draft to have effect, but bowed his head and stared at his hands in his lap, shaken and shattered to his inmost heart.

Eddan, Eddan and Sathell, that had been a part of all his life. He wept, naked-faced, and the tears splashed onto his hands, and he was ashamed to lift a hand to wipe them away, for the Kel did not weep.

"Sathell is very ill," said Intel softly, "and he knew well what he did. Do not think that we parted hatefully. Melein knows. Eddan knows. Sathell was a good man: our old, old quarrel—he never agreed with me, and yet for forty-three years he has given me his good offices. I do not grudge that he simply stated his opinion at the last. We were friends. And do not feel badly for Eddan. If he did otherwise, I would have been surprised."

"You are hard," said Niun.

"Yes," she said. And her slight touch descended on his shoulder, brushed aside the *zaidhe*. He slipped it off, wadded his cloth in his clenched fists, head still bowed, for his eyes were wet. "Last son of mine," she said then, "do you love me?"

The question, so nakedly posed, struck him like a hammer blow; and in this moment he could not say smoothly, yes, Mother. He could not summon it.

"Mother," he said painfully, of her many titles, the best and dearest to the Kel.

"Do you love me, Niun?" Her soft fingers brushed past his mane, touched the sensitivity of his ear, teasing the downy tufts at its crest, an intimacy for kinswomen and lovers: *Here is a secret,* the touch said, *a hidden thing; be attentive.*

He was not strong enough for secrets now, for any added burden; he looked up at her, trying to answer. The calm face looked down on him with curious longing. "I know," she said. "You are here. You pay me duty. That is still a good and pious act, child of mine. And I know that I have robbed you and denied you and compelled everything that you have done and will ever do."

"I know that your reasons are good ones."

"No," she said. "You are kel'en. You do not know; you believe. But you are proper to say so. And you are right. Tomorrow—tomorrow you will see it, when you see *Ahanal*. Melein—"

"She'pan."

"Do you mourn Sathell?"

"Yes, she'pan."

"Do you dispute me?"

"No, she'pan."

"There will be a she'pan on *Ahanal*," said Intel, "That she'pan is not fit as I have made you fit."

"I am twenty-two years old," protested Melein. "She'pan, you could take command of *Ahanal*, but if they challenge, if they should challenge—"

"Niun would defend me, defend me well. And he will defend you in your hour."

"Do you pass his duty to me?" Melein asked.

"In time," she said, "I will do this. In your time."

"I do not know all that I need to know, she'pan."

"You will kill," said Intel, "any who tries to take the Pana from you. I am the oldest of all she'panei, and I have prepared my successor in my own way."

"In conscience—" Melein protested.

"In conscience," said the she'pan, "obey me and do not question."

And the drug began to come over her and her eyes dimmed and she sank into her cushions and was still.

In time she slept soundly.

It was said, in a tale told in the Kel, that at the fall of Nisren, humans had actually breached the edun, ignoring mri attempts to challenge to *a'ani:* this the first and bitterest error the mri had made with humans. A human force had swept through the halls while the Kath in terror tried to escape: and Intel had put herself between humans and the Kath, and fired the hall with her own hand. Whether it was Intel or the fire, those humans had not come against her. She had held long enough for some of the Kath to escape, until the embattled Kel could reach that hall and get her to safety, to the regul ship.

That aspect of gentle Intel had always been incredible to Niun, until this night.

Chapter Fourteen

Duncan heard the hum of machinery. It wakened him, advising him at once that Stavros had need of something. He pulled himself off the couch and gathered his fatigue-dulled senses. He had not undressed. He had not put Stavros to bed. Storm alarms had made most of the night chaotic. There was a time that constant storm advisories were coming over communications.

He heard the storm shields in Stavros' quarters go back. He wandered in to see that the alarms were past, that the screens showed clear. The dawn came up ruddy and murky, flooding a peculiar light through the glass.

Stavros was in the center of that glow, a curious figure in his mobile sled. He whipped it about to face Duncan with a jaunty expertise. The communication screen lighted.

Look outside.

Duncan stepped up to the rain-spattered window and looked, scanning the desolate expanse of sand and rock, toward the sea and the towers of the water-recovery system. There was something wrong, a gap in the silhouette, a vacancy where yesterday towers had stood.

There was a particularly dark area of cloud over the seacoast, flattened by the winds, torn and streamered out to sea.

Stavros' screen activated.

Advisory just given: water use confined to drinking and food preparation only. 'Minor repairs at plant.' They ask we remain patient.

"We've got people coming down here," Duncan protested.

Suspect further damage at port, Regul much disturbed. Bai 'not available.'

The rain slacked off considerably, leaving only a few spatters on the windows. The murky light grew for a moment red like that from fire, only Arain through thick cloud.

And on the long ridge that lay beyond the town there was a shadow that moved. Duncan's eyes jerked back to it, strained upon that one spot. There was nothing.

"I saw something out there," he said.

Yes, the screen advised him when he looked. *Many. Many. Maybe flood drove beasts from holes.*

In a moment another shadow appeared atop the ridge. He watched, as yet another and another and another appeared. His eyes swept the whole circuit of the hills. Against the sullen light there was a gathering row of black shapes, that moved and milled aimlessly.

Mri, he had feared.

But not mri. Beasts. He thought of the great unpleasant beasts that had been found with dead mri, ursine creatures that could be as dangerous as their size warned.

"They're mri-beasts," he said to Stavros. "They've got the whole area ringed."

Regul call them dusei. They are native to Kesrith. Read your briefings.

"They go with mri. How many mri are supposed to be here? I thought it was only a handful."

So the bai assures us—a token presence—to be removed.

He looked at the horizon. The clouds stretched unbroken.

And the dusei were a solid line across the whole ridge, encompassing the visible circuit of the sea to the town.

Duncan turned from the sight of it, shivered, looked back again. He considered the rain, and the land—worked his sweating hands and looked at Stavros. "Sir, I'd like to go out there."

"No," Stavros murmured.

"Listen to me." Duncan found it awkward to talk at such an angle, dropped to one knee so that he could meet the old man eye to eye, set a hand on the cold metal of the sled. "We've got only regul word for it that the regul don't lie; we've got mri out there; we've got a colony mission coming in here in a matter of days. You took me along. I assume you had some feeling then you might need me. I can get out there and take a look and get back without anyone the wiser. You can cover for me that long. Who cares about a youngling more or less? They won't see me. Let me go out there and see what kind of situation we're facing with those ships coming in. We don't know how bad it is with the water; we don't know what shape the port is in. Are you that confident we're always told all the truth?"

Weather hazardous. And incident with regul likely.

"That's something I can avoid. It's my job. It's what I know how to do."

Argument persuasive. Can you guarantee no incident?

"On my life."

Estimate correct. If incident occurs, then regul law prevails out there. You understand. Survey facilities, plant, port, return. Can cover you till dark.

"Yes, sir." He was relieved in some part; he did not look forward to it: he knew the hazard better perhaps than Stavros did. But for once he and the honorable Stavros were of one mind. Hunting out the hazards was more comfortable than ignoring them.

He rose, looked outside, found the dusei's dark line vanished in that brief interval. He blinked, tried to see through the haze of rain, made out little in the distance.

"Sir," he murmured to Stavros by way of farewell; Stavros inclined his head, dismissing him. The screen stayed dark.

He went quickly to his own quarters and changed uniforms, to khaki weatherproofs and sealed boots, still common enough in appearance that he did not think regul would notice the difference. He put into the several pockets a tight roll of cord, a knife, a packet of concentrates, a penlight, whatever would fit without obvious outlines. He flipped the hood into the collar and zipped the closures.

Then he strolled out into the hall on a pattern he had followed several times a day since he had studied the layout of the building, down the hall to the left and out toward the observation deck window. No one was in the hall there. He opened the door and went out into the rain-chilled air, walked the circuit of the low-walled observation deck, looked over his shoulder to see that the hall beyond the doors was still clear.

It was.

He quite simply sat down on the edge of the wall, held with his hands as he dropped, and let go. The regul stories were short by human standards. He landed on cement at the bottom, but it was not a hard drop at all, only a flex of the knees; and the cement showed no tracks. By the time that he reached the edge of the concrete and disappeared into the gentle rolls of the landscape, he was confident that he was unobserved.

He walked toward the water plant, turning up the hood of his uniform as he went, for he knew the warnings about the mineral-laden rains and cared to expose as little of his skin as possible. Now off the pavements of the city he left tracks as plain as wet sand could show them, but he did not reckon to be tracked at all. He felt rather self-pleased in this, which he had thought about for days, idle exercise of his professional mind during the long inactivity in the Nom: the fact was that no regul could have possibly done what he had just done, and therefore the regul had not taken precautions against it. Such a drop would have been impossible to their heavy, short-legged bodies, and likewise there was no regul that could come tracking him crosslands.

That would take a mri.

And that was the only possibility that made him a little less self-pleased than he might have been under the circumstances. He had wanted arms at the outset of the voyage, but the diplomats had denied them to him: unnecessary and provocative, they had reasoned. Now he was unarmed but for the kit-knife in his pocket, and a mri warrior could carve him in small portions before he could come close enough to make use of that for defense.

The fact was plainly that if regul would set a mri on his trail, he was dead; but then, he reasoned, if regul would dare do that, then the treaty was worth nothing, and that fact had as well be known early.

There was also the possibility that the mri were out in force, and that they were not under regul control; and that most of all needed to be known.

For that reason he exercised more caution in his walking than he would have shown if he feared only regul: he watched the ridges and the shadows of gullies, and took care to look behind him, remembering the dark shapes that had moved upon the hills, the dusei that were out somewhere: he crossed dustracks, long-clawed, ominous reminders that there were hunters aprowl other than regul or mri.

Briefings said that the beasts did not approach regul dwellings.

Briefings also said that crossing the flats off the roads was not recommended.

The jetting stream of geysers, the crunch of thin crusts underfoot, warned him that there was reason for this. He had to draw a weaving course around hot zones, approaching the lowest part of the flats, that near the seashore and the water plant.

There was a road of sorts, badly washed, along the seacoast. Parts of it were underwater. A regul landsled was down in a trench where it had run off the edge.

Duncan sat down, winded in the thin, cold air, his head and gut aching, and watched from a distance as a regul crew tried to extricate it. He could see the water plant clearly from this vantage point. There was chaos there too, beyond its protective fences. The towers extended far out into the whitecapped water, and several of those towers were in ruins.

From what he could see there was no possibility those towers could even be cleared for repair in the few days before human ships would arrive, certainly not with prevailing weather. What was more, he could not see any evidence of heavy machinery available to do repairs.

Realistically estimating, it was not going to be done at all. A large human occupation force was going to land, having to depend totally on ships' recycling: irritating, but possible—if there was a place to land.

He looked to the right along the shoreline, toward the city and beyond, where he could see the low shape of the Nom—no building high enough to obstruct his view of the port. He recognized *Hazan,* saw its alien shape surrounded by gantries, a web of metal.

There was no way to set a ship down on the volcanic crusts that overlay most of the lowlands. If the port was in the same condition as the water plant, then there was going to be merry chaos when the human forces tried to land.

And the regul had not been forward to inform them of the extent of damages to the facilities at the plant: they had not lied, but neither had they volunteered all the truth.

Hew drew a breath of tainted air and looked behind him suddenly, chilled to realize that he had been thinking about something other than his personal safety for a few seconds.

The horizon was clear. There were only the clouds. A man did not always find himself that fortunate in his lapses.

He let go that breath slowly and gathered himself up, conscious of the pounding of his head and the pounding of his heart in the thin air. He saw a way to work around some low rocks and a sandy shelf and so cross between the city and the sea, working toward the port. Regul were reputed to have dim eyesight—to be dull, as it happened, in all sensory capacities. He hoped that this was so.

Stavros, sitting back in the embrace of his regul machine, had said that he could cover his absence. He reckoned that Stavros might be good at that, being skilled at argument and misleadings.

Out here, he knew his own job—knew with a surety that the instinct that had drawn Stavros to choose a SurTac for Kesrith had been a true one. Stavros had not ordered him, had only relied on him, quietly—had waited for him to move of his own accord, sensing, perhaps, that a man trained in the taking of alien terrain would know his own moment.

He could not afford a mistake. He was afraid, with a different sort of fear than he had ever known in a mission. He had operated alone before, had destroyed, had escaped—his own life or death on his head. He was not accustomed to work with the life or death of others weighing on his shoulders, with the weight of decision, to say that an area was safe or not safe for the landing of a mission involving hundreds of lives and policies reaching far beyond Kesrith.

He did not like it; he far from liked it. He would have cast it on any higher authority available; but Stavros, bound to his machine, had to believe either the regul or his own aide, and he desperately wanted to be right.

Chapter Fifteen

The Edun woke quietly; the People moved quietly about the daily routine. Niun went back to the Kel, which was now empty-seeming; and the Kel sat in mourning. Eddan did not return.

And Pasev's eyes bore that bruised look that told of little sleep; but she sat unveiled, in command of her emotions. Niun brought her a special portion at breakfast, and it tore his heart that she would not eat.

After breakfast the brothers Liran and Debas spoke together and rose up and put on the belts with all their honors, and *mez'ein* and *zaidh'ein,* and gave their farewells.

"Will you all leave?" asked Niun, out of turn and out of place and terrified. And he looked then at Pasev, who had most reason to go, and did not.

"You might be needed," said Pasev to the brothers.

"We will walk and enjoy the morning," said Liran. "Perhaps we will find Eddan and Sathell."

"Then tell Eddan," she said softly, "that I will be coming after him when I have finished my own duties, which he left to me. Goodbye, brothers."

"Goodbye," they said together, and all the remaining Kel echoed, "Goodbye," and they walked down from the tower and out across the road.

Niun stood in the doorway to watch them go, a deep melancholy upon him; and a knot settling in his throat to consider their absence hereafter. They continued to the horizon, two shapes of black; and the sky was shadowed and threatening, and they had not so much as the comfort of their dusei in their journey, for none of the beasts had come home. The *miuk'ko* from the door had disappeared also, dead, perhaps, in the storm: dusei went away to die, alone, like kel'ein that found no further hope in their lives.

Loyal to Intel, he thought, and loyal to Kesrith, and foreseeing the end of both; they could not help now, and so they departed, with their honors on them, not seeking burial of a young kel'en too overburdened with duties to see to them.

They had chanted the rites last night. It was ill-omened; they all knew it. It was as if they had chanted them over Kesrith itself, and he suddenly foresaw that few of the old ones at all would board the ship.

They did not want Intel's dream. She had shown them the truth of the rites and they had not wanted it; they had seen only the old, familiar ways.

She had promised them change, and they would have none of it.

He was otherwise shaped, formed by Intel's hands and Intel's wishes, and loyalty to Melein would hold him bound to Intel's dream. He looked on the place in the rocks where the brothers had disappeared and could have wept aloud at what he then realized of them and him, for Pasev would follow, rather than take ship into uncertainties for which she had no longing; and after her would go the others. He would never be one with the like of them: black-robe, plain-robe, honorless and untested, shaped for different ways. *The Kel of the Darks,* she had said, *is a different Kel.*

It was he who already stood in the Dark; and they had walked away from the shadow, into what they knew.

He turned, to seek the edun, the Shrine's comfort for his mood; and his heart chilled at what he saw along the lower ridges, with row upon row of shadows moving there.

Dusei.

They ringed the regul town in every place that offered solid ground. Ha-dusei, wild ones, and dangerous.

The dusei of the edun had not returned.

And there were far too many of the ha-dusei, far too many.

The sky roiled overhead, stained with red and sullen gray: stormfriends, the dusei, weather-knowing. In the days before the edun stood, they had watered here below: the Dus plain, the low-land flats were called. They came as if they sensed change in the winds, they came as if waiting the regul departure, which would give the Dus plain back to the dusei.

Waiting.

It was told of regul stubbornness that the first mri had warned the regul earnestly that they should build their city elsewhere, as the edun itself had been carefully positioned off the plain, in respect to the bond between mri and dusei; but regul had wanted rock for their ships to land on, and they had sounded the area thereabouts and found only on the Dus plain rock suitable for a port near the sea. Therefore regul had built there, and there had grown a city, and the ha-dusei had gone.

But dusei returned now, with the unseasonal rains and the destroying winds. They sat and waited.

And the dusei had left even the mri.

He shrugged, half a shiver, and walked inside and stopped, not wishing to bear that news to the Kel or to the she'pan. The Kel was in mourning, the she'pan still lost in dreams; and Melein, her Chosen, had veiled herself and sealed herself alone in the Sen-tower.

He cast a yearning thought skyward, through the spiral corridors that massed over him, that *Ahanal* hasten its coming, for he did not think that he could bear the endless hours until the evening.

And each thing that he thought of doing this day was pointless, for it was a house to which they would never return; and outside, the weather threatened and the lightning flashed in the clouds and the thunder rumbled.

So he sat down in the doorway, watching all the flats below, the geysers' plumes, predictable as the hours, their clouds torn and thrown by gale-force winds. It was a cold day, as few days on Kesrith were chill. He shivered, and watched the heavy drops pock the puddles that reflected a sky like fire-on-pewter.

A heavy body trod the wet sand: a whuff of breath, and a great dus lumbered round the corner, head hanging. Others followed. He scrambled up in terror, not sure of their mood; but wet and muddy-pawed, they came, and nosed their way past him into the edun, rumbling that hunger sound that betokened a dus with a considerable impatience. He counted them in: one, two, three, four, five, six. And last came the *miuk'ko,* the seventh, bedraggled and angular, to cast itself down in the puddle at the base of the slanted walls, drinking with great laps of its gray tongue at the water between its massive paws.

Three did not come. Niun waited, a relief and a disquiet growing in him at the same time—relief because a bereaved dus was dangerous and pitiable; and disquiet because he did not know how they had known. Perhaps the three that were missing had encountered their kel'ein.

Or perhaps, with that curious sense of dusei, they had known and sought them.

Perhaps they were far along the trail to Sil'athen. He earnestly hoped so. It would be best for both men and dusei.

He went to the storerooms in the cellar of Kath. The dusei must have care.

And first of all of them, he waited on the *miuk'ko*, that had left its post of mourning for the first time and then returned. He hoped it would be in a different mind.

But it would not eat. Perhaps, he thought, it had fed during its hours of wandering. But he did not believe it. He left the food on the dry edge of the step and went to carry portions to the others.

Save for the insistence and irreverence of the dusei, save for Melein, who grieved in her tower, the edun had become a place of dreams, and a sense of finality hung over everything: the dus by the gate, the old men and the old women. He crept about his tasks with the utmost quiet, as if he, living, walked in the caves at Sil'athen.

And in the evening the ship came.

The she'pan was asleep when they heard it descending; and they that were left of the Kel hurried out to the road to see it, and on tired faces there were smiles, and in Niun's heart there was misgiving. Dahacha took his arm on impulse and pressed it, and he looked at the sun-wrinkled eyes and felt an unspoken blessing pass between them.

"Dahacha," he whispered. "Will you come, at least?"

"We that have not walked will come," said the old man. "We will not send you alone, Niun Zain-Abrin. We have made our reckoning. If we would not, we would have gone with Eddan, like Liran and Debas."

"Yes," said Palazi at his other side. "We will reason with the kel'anth."

And it struck him like a blow upon a wound, that this now referred to Pasev.

The commotion of the ship's landing was visible in lights, in flares of regul headlights that crawled serpent-wise toward that far side of the field, half-glow in the red twilight: regul eyes were not adapted to the night.

"Come," said Pasev, and they followed her into the halls and to the she'pan's tower.

Melein was there, beside Intel, and she touched the she'pan's hand and tried to wake her, but it was Pasev who laid a firm grip on the she'pan's arm and shook her from her dreams.

"She'pan," said Pasev, "she'pan, the ship has come."

"And the regul?" In the she'pan's golden eyes the dream finished and that keenness returned, focused and struggling for control. "How do the regul bear it?"

"We do not know that yet," said Pasev. "They are all astir, that is all we saw."

Intel nodded. "No contact by radio. Regul will be monitoring; *Ahanal* will observe that caution also." She struggled with the cushions, a small moue of pain upon her face, and Melein adjusted them for her. She sighed and breathed easily a moment.

"Shall we," asked Dahacha, "Little Mother, carry you to the ship? We can bear you."

"No," she said with a sad smile. "A she'pan is guardian of the Pana: there is no ship-going for me until that care of mine is finally discharged."

"At least," said Dahacha then, "let us take you down to the road, so that you can see toward the port."

"No," said Intel, firmly. And then she touched Dahacha's hand upon the arm of her chair and smiled. "Do not fear: I am in possession of my faculties and in possession of this edun and this world, and so I will remain until I am sure that it is my time; and yours will not be until mine is. Do you hear me?"

"Aye," said Pasev.

Intel met the eyes of the kel'anth and nodded, satisfied; but then her glance strayed about the room, perhaps counted faces, and her eyes clouded.

"Liran and Debas left some time ago," said Pasev. "We gave them farewell."

"My blessing," she murmured dutifully.

Pasev bowed her head in acknowledgment. "Until the she'pan dismisses me," she said, "I serve you, and there are still enough of us to do what needs doing."

"We will not be long about it," said Intel. "Niun, child," she said, and held out her hand.

He knelt at her knee and took her hand in his, bowed his bared head to her touch, felt her fingers slip from his and give that gesture of blessing.

"Go crosslands," she said. "Go to the ship and talk with the visitors face to face, and hear what they have to say. Answer wisely. You may have to take decisions on yourself, young kel'en. And do not go carelessly. We have almost ceased to serve regul."

Something passed his bowed head: he felt weight settle on his neck, and caught at it, and his fingers closed on cold metal. When he turned it and looked at the amulet on the chain he saw the open hand emblem of Kesrithun edun, and Intel's silken fingers touched his chin and lifted his face to meet her eyes.

"Only one j'tal," she said softly. "But a master-one. Do you recognize it, my last son?"

"It is an honor," he said, "of a she'pan's kel'en."

"Bear yourself well," she said. "And make speed. Time is important now."

And she pushed at him with her fingers and he rose, almost fearing the eyes of the others, the kel'ein who might have been honored with such a j'tal; and he the youngest and least. But there was no envy there, only gladness, as if this were something in which they were all agreed.

He took off his houserobe, and there in the she'pan's chamber, they all took hand in preparing him for the journey, hastening to bring him the *siga* that he should wear in walking the dusty lands, and *zaidhe* and *mez;* and they gave him their own weapons, both yin'ein and zahen'ein, finer than his own; and with a smile, a laugh that deprecated superstition older than memory among the People, Palazi unclipped a luck amulet from his own belts and gave it him, a maiden warrior, giving him of his luck.

"Years and honors," said Palazi.

He hugged the old man, and others, and returned to the she'pan for a last hasty bow at her feet, his heart pounding with excitement. But as he received her kiss upon his brow she did not let him go at once, but stared into his face in such a way that it chilled all the blood in him.

"You are beautiful," the she'pan said to him, her golden eyes brimming with tears. "I have a great fear. Be careful, youngest son."

The People no longer believed in presciences with any great fervor, no more than he really trusted Palazi's luckwish; but he shivered. There was mri-reason and regul-reason, and always to believe only what could be demonstrated by experience was the regul way, not the mri.

One who had lived so many years as Intel might have reasons he did not understand. His whole life had been spent in the presence of the forbidden and the incomprehensible; and she'pan Intel had been involved in most: *she'pan*—keeper of mysteries.

"I shall be careful," he said, and she let him go then; he avoided the eyes of Melein when he rose, for if she'pan and Chosen shared anything concerning him, he did not want to carry it with him on this mission.

"Do not trust any regul," said the kel'anth. "See all that you look upon."

"Yes," he agreed earnestly, and took Pasev's hands and pressed them gently by way of farewell to the brothers and sister of his caste.

He turned away quickly and left, long strides carrying him hurriedly down the spiraling stairs, past the written names of the history and heroes of the People and the truth of all the things that Intel had hinted at, that he could not read. He felt their meaning this day, the remembrance of his ancestors.

All, all that Intel had desired had come down to him; and she had been able, at the last, to let him go, to cast him like the *as'ei* in *shon'ai*. And she had not lost him. There was too much of love poured into him by these old ones that he could fail the wishes of Eddan, of Intel, of Pasev and Debas and Liran. They had made sure that he would succeed before they had launched him upon the she'pan's mission.

He passed the main doors and closed them against the night, and saw there the monstrous bulk of the *miuk'ko,* a shadow beside the door. The great head lifted and the eyes stared at him invisibly in the dark.

Perhaps, he thought, optimism uncrushed in a hundred repetitions of this coming and going, *perhaps this time. It would be good if it were this time at last, who needs me, who need him.*

But it murmured and turned its face and laid its massive head in the mud. Male, female, or neither; no one had ever ascertained the sex of a dus, nor reckoned why they came to one mri or why they refused to come to another; whether this one had yet comprehended that Medai would never return, whether it grieved, or whether it starved out of simple stupidity, waiting for Medai to feed it, Niun could not fathom.

With a sad shrug he went his way, hardly having paused that half-step; but in this passing there was a difference, for things the dus did not understand had changed, were changing, were about to change. And it was doomed, having rejected him.

Likely the humans would destroy the dusei. Regul would have done so gladly, if not for mri protection. The size and the slow-moving power of dusei was very like that of regul, but regul instinctively hated the dusei. Regul could not, as mri could, become immune to the poison of the claws; they could not, as mri could, abandon themselves to the simplicity of the beasts. Therefore regul fled them.

And the unease the contact of the dus had left in him stayed the while he walked down toward the flats, toward the ghostly plumes of geysers under the windtorn clouds. He smelled the wind, felt the familiar force of it, like some living thing.

He found himself looking at the familiar places that he had seen and known all his life, and thinking of each: *this is almost the last time.* There was excitement in his heart and an uncertainty in his stomach that was far from heroic and cheerful. His senses were alive to the whole world, the scents of the earth, acrid and wet, the feel of the damp hot breath of the geysers, that each had their name and manner.

His world.

Homeworld.

Impermanent as the wind, the Kel, but capable of loving the earth. It struck him that they did not know where they were going, that Intel spoke of the Dark as if it were a place, as if it had dimension and depth and duration like the world itself. It came to him that after leaving Kesrith he might never feel earth under his feet again: a Dark with promise, the she'pan had insisted; but he could not imagine what it promised.

And hereafter to deal with kel'ein who were not old, long-thinking men—kel'ein who knew only war and were touchy of their pride and their prerogatives of caste, in a way that the gentle Kel of Kesrith had never been.

To live among the Kel of strangers, where there were kath'ein, who would be his for the asking, and the chance to get children, and to see his private immortality. He would be son to one she'-pan, truebrother to another, honored next whatever fen'ein, Husbands, she would choose to sire her children on the kel'e'ein and the kath'ein of the edun, if first he survived the combat of succession.

Choices spread before him in dazzling array, in dizzying profusion, a future full of things neither stale nor predictable nor sure.

He walked swiftly, where reeking sulphur and steam obscured his way, where water dripped from recently sprayed rocks and the heat underground prepared further eruptions. He knew his timing to a nicety. The thin crusts on the right—boiling water and mud underlay much of that ground. The edge that he trod would bear a mri's weight, but not that of a dus or a regul. Regul had learned bitter lessons about Kesrith's flatlands; they did not stray now from the safety of their vehicles and aircraft and carefully chosen roads and landing sites. It would take a long time for humans to learn the land, if they would ever dare leave the security of the regul city.

Some would surely die learning it. A few mri had done so.

He could cease to care what humans did. They would gather up the People and go, all of them, Dahacha and Palazi and the others; and Intel too—they would persuade her too, though she was old and very tired of struggles; she could at least begin their journey.

And then they could leave without even wanting to look back.

He gazed at last from the long white ridge that was above the port and saw the shape of the regul ship *Hazan* and opposite it, the new one of *Ahanal.*

Ahanal—the Swift.

He slid down the moonlit ridge in a white powdering of dust, and crossed the long slope to the lower ground.

And a shadow flowed among the rocks, large and menacing. He turned, hand on his pistol, and looked up at the hulking form that had mounted a ridge.

Ha-dus. For a moment he did not breathe, did not move. Three others showed. Silent, the great beasts could be, when they stalked; but they did not stalk him. He had only disturbed their vigil.

He remained still, respectful of their right to be here, and they snuffed the air and regarded him with their small eyes, and finally gave that explosive question sound that indicated the fighting mood was not on them.

Pardon, brothers, he wished them in his mind, which was the best way to deal with a strange and skittish dus, and backed a few paces before he edged on toward his former course: language the dus understood, a matter of movements that one made and did not make.

His hand shifted from the pistol to the amulet at his breast. Not the moment to risk his life with the ha-dusei, far from it; he walked more slowly, more cautiously, remembering Pasev's admonishment to use his eyes and his wits.

They let him go, and when he looked back they were no longer there.

He walked from the white dust to the artificial surface that covered the firm rock of the north rim area; and there was a fence, a laughable affair of wire screen that could stop nothing that was truly determined, not on Kesrith. He burned it, made himself a door in it, with fine disregard for regul obstructions on the free land. Any mri would do the like rather than walk round a fence, and regul met the like with outrage; but it was the mri way, and in this mri would not oblige the masters.

Bloody-handed savages, he had heard one of the regul younglings call him in the town.

But regul built fences and made machines that scarred the earth, and tried to divide up space itself into territories and limits and parcels to be traded like foodstuffs and metals and bolts of cloth. It was ludicrous in his eyes.

He walked amid the great tangle of abandoned equipage and skeletal braces and vehicles—as he had foreseen, a vast graveyard of vehicles and machines, a clot of metal so tightly jammed together that he had to detour round the whole of it, a heap of vehicles and sleds and aircraft indiscriminately mixed as if some giant hand had piled them there, the vehicles that had brought out the inhabitants of all the settlements the regul had ruled. And there, there a great burned area, a tower in charred and jagged outline against the port lights, an angular tangle of braces and more goods that the regul had cast aside as waste. Storm-shattered, burned: the damage at the port had then been very extensive. He looked about him as he walked, taking inventory of things he had once seen whole and what he saw now damaged, and he began to see reason for the regul's distressed behavior.

Hazan stood in a vast assemblage of gantries and hoses and fragile extensions, and about that ship too he saw evident damage. She was aglow with lights, acrawl with black figures that labored on her like carrion insects; and a steady line of vehicles crawled toward her, bearing goods, no doubt, for loading and for repairs.

He passed this area, careful of being seen, and rounded the shape of *Hazan*. There, a tower before him, stood *Ahanal* once more, looming against the sky with only one light brought to bear upon her hull.

He drew near and saw that she was old, her metal pitted as with acids, her markings seared almost beyond recognition. Long scars marked where shields must have failed.

He voice-hailed them, conscious of the nearness of regul sentries; of a sled that had already started his way.

"Ahanal!" he cried. "Open your hatch!"

But either they were not prepared to hear or they had reason to be uneasy of the regul; and there was no response from *Ahanal*. He saw the sled veer sharply, coming to a halt near him, and a youngling regul opened the sidescreen to speak to him.

"Mri," said the regul, "you are not permitted."

"Is this the order of the bai?" he asked.

"Go away," the regul insisted. "Kesrithi mri, go away."

There was a crash of metal: the hatch had opened. He ignored the regul to glance upward at the ship, from which a ramp began to extend. He walked toward it, simply ignoring the regul.

The sled hummed behind him. He moved, narrowly missed: its fender clipped the side of his leg, and the sled circled in front of him, blocking his path.

The window was still open. The youngling regul was breathing hard, his great nostrils opening and shutting in extreme agitation.

"Go back," it hissed.

He began to step round the sled; it lurched forward and he rolled on his shoulder across its low nose, landed on the other side and ran, shamed and frightened: mri were watching from the ramp, doubtless outraged at his discomfiture. His legs were weak under him with terror for what he had done, a thing which no mri had ever done: he had defied the masters directly; but he was the she'pan's messenger, and if he delayed to argue with the youngling there would be regul authority involved, with orders to obey or disobey, with a crisis for the she'pan that a mere kel'en could not resolve without direct violence.

He ran, hit the echoing solidity of the ramp and raced up it as quickly as he could to meet the mri of the ship, but they were already fading back into the ship and did not stay for him. He heard and felt the ramp taking up behind him, shortening its length as he overtook the last of them. Lights came on, blinding; doors shut, sealing them safely inside.

Ten kel'ein: Husbands, by their age and dignity. There was cold light and air piercing in its sterility after the air of Kesrith. The final seal of the lock closed between them and the outside, the ramp in place. There was silence.

"Sirs," he remembered to say, and stopped looking at them, with the many j'tai and their grim, stranger's manner, long enough to touch his brow and pay proper respect. He looked up again and unveiled, a courtesy which they grudgingly returned.

"I am Niun s'Intel Zain-Abrin," he said in the high language, as all mri used in formalities. "I bear service to Intel, she'pan of Edun Kesrithun."

"I am Sune s'Hara Sune-Lir," said the eldest of them, an old man whose mane grayed at the temples and who looked to be of the age of Pasev or Eddan; but his fellows were younger, more powerful-looking men. "Does the she'pan Intel fare well?"

"The edun is safe."

"Does the she'pan intend to come in person?"

"As to that, sir, not until I return with the word of your she'-pan."

He understood somewhat their attitude, that of men who loved and defended their own, who must yield to she'pan Intel, who must yield them too. It was natural that they look on Intel's messenger with resentment.

"We will take you to her," said Sune s'Hara, with formal grace. "Come." And with better courtesy: "You are not injured?"

"No, sir," he said, and remembered with a sudden flush that it was not proper for him to defer to this man, that he was a messenger, and more than that; he betrayed himself for a very young kel'en and inexperienced in his authority. "Regul and mri are not at ease in Kesrith," he added, covering his confusion. "There have been words passed."

"We were met with weapons," Sune said. "But there were no casualties."

He walked with them, through corridors of metal, in halls designed for regul. He saw kel'ein and he saw kel'e'ein, veiled and youthful as he; and his pulse quickened—he thought them glorious and beautiful, and tried not to stare, though he knew that their eyes were taking close account of him, a stranger among them. Some unveiled in brotherly welcome when he met them, and a great company of them went through the corridors to the main-room, to that center of the ship that was now the hall of a she'-pan.

She was middle-aged. He came and bowed his head under her hands, and looked up at her, vaguely disturbed to be greeted by a she'pan not in the familiar earthen closeness of a tower but in this metal place, and by greeting a she'pan who was not kin, whose emblem on her white, blue-edged robes was that of a star, not the hand emblem of Edun Kesrithun.

She was a stranger who must die, who must choose to die or whose champion he must defeat, if she challenged; and he prayed silently to all the gods that this one would be brave and gracious and forego challenge.

Her eyes were hard and she existed in light harsh enough to hurt; and the world that surrounded her was cold and metal. Many, many of the ship-folk surrounded them now, their she'pan, their beloved Mother, and not his: he an intruder, a threat to her life.

They saw a she'pan's messenger, but one innocent of *j'tai* won in battles—a youth unscarred, untried, and vulnerable to challenge.

He felt her eyes go up and down him, reckoning this, reckoning his world and those who sent him. And beyond her, about her, he saw gold-robed sen'ein; and black-robed kel'ein; and shyly observing from the recesses of the further hall, he saw kath'ein, blue-robes, veilless and gentle and frightened.

And about them, within the other corridors, row on row of hammocks slung like the nestings of Kesrith's spiders, threads of white and webbings that laced the room and the sides of the corridors. He was overwhelmed by the number of those that crowded close: and yet it struck him suddenly that here was his whole species, all reduced to this little ship, and under the present command of this woman.

"Messenger," she said, "I am Esain of Edun Elagun. How fares Intel?"

Her voice was kinder than her face, and shot through him like sun after night. His heart melted toward her, that she could speak kindly toward him and toward Intel.

"She'pan," he said, "Intel is well enough."

He put kindness in his voice, and yet she understood, for a shadow passed through her eyes, and fear; but she was a great lady, and did not flinch.

"What does Intel wish to tell me?" asked Esain.

"She'pan," he said, "she gave me welcome for you; and sent me to listen to you first of all."

She nodded slightly, and with a move of her hand bade council attend her: kel'anth and sen'anth and kath'anth came and sat by her; and the fen'ein, her Husbands of the Kel; and the body of the Sen; and while these took their places the others withdrew, and doors were closed.

He remained kneeling before her, and carefully removed his *zaidhe* and laid that before him; and on it he laid the *avkel*, the

Kel-sword that was Sirain's lending, sheathed before him, hilt toward her, a token of peace. His hands he folded in his lap. Her kel'ein did the same, hilts toward him, the stranger in their midst, the visitor admitted to council.

"We send greetings to Intel," said Esain quietly. "Of her wisdom long ago was *Ahanal* reserved for the People, and of her wisdom was *Ahanal* freed to come. She placed such a burden on the Kel, refusing regul assistance, that there was no honorable choice. Honor outweighed honor. This was wisely done. All aboard understand and are grateful that it was done in time, for nothing else could have compelled us from the front. Is it true as we guess, that she intends to leave regul service?"

"Her words: We have almost left regul service. Your fen'ein and the kel'anth saw the result of it when I came toward the ship."

She looked at the kel'anth. He gave agreement with a gesture.

"I have seen a thing I have never seen," the old man said. "A regul attacked this messenger—not with hands, to be sure; but with his machine. These regul are desperate."

"And the edun?" the she'pan asked, her brow crossed with a frown. "How fares the Edun of the People, with the regul in such a mood?"

"Presently secure," he said, and, for he saw the real question burning in her, that she would hesitate to ask a mere kel'en: "She'pan, the Forbidden is in her keeping; and the regul are busy with the damage the weather has done them. Humans are close, and the regul fear delays that could hold them grounded. I think what happened out there was the act of a youngling without clear orders."

"Yet," said the she'pan, "what if we were to leave the ship in a body?"

"We are mri," said Niun with supreme confidence, "and regul would give way before us, and they would dare do nothing."

"Did you so judge," asked the she'pan, "of that youngling that attempted your life?"

Heat mounted in his face. "She'pan," he said, made aware of his youth and his inexperience. "I do not think that was a serious threat."

She thought, and looked at the Sen and the others, and finally sighed and frowned. "I bear too great a charge here to risk it. We will wait until Intel has made her decision. We have force here at her call; I will send it or reserve it as she says. And, messenger, assure her that I will respect her claim on the People."

He was shocked and relieved at once, and he bowed very low to her, hearing the murmur of grief run the length and breadth of the room. He could hardly bear to meet her eyes again, but found them gentle and unaccusing.

"I will tell her," he said, recovering the courtesies trained into him, part of blood and flesh and bone, "that the she'pan of Edun Elagun is a grand and brave lady, and that she has earned great honor of all the People."

"Tell her," she said softly, "that I wish her well with my children."

Many veiled themselves, hearing her, and he found his own eyes stinging.

"I will tell her," he said.

"Will you, messenger, stay the night with us?"

He thought of it, for it was a walk of the rest of the night to come again to the edun, and likely a great deal of sleep lost thereafter, once Intel had begun to give orders; but he thought of the regul that had crossed his path, and the weather, and the uncertainties that hemmed him about.

"She'pan," he said, "my duty is to go back now—best now, before the regul have time to take long consultations."

"Yes," she said, "that would be the wisest thing. Go, then."

And she, when he had gathered up the *av-kel* and replaced the *zaidhe*, and come to touch her hand and do her heartfelt courtesy, gave into his hand a ring of true gold, at which his heart clenched in pain; for it was a gracious, brave thing to do, to give a service-gift as if he had well-pleased her. Off her own finger she drew it, and pressed it into his hand, and he bowed and kissed her fingers, before he stood and took his leave. He laced the ring into one of the thongs of his honors, to braid it in property later, and bowed her farewell.

"Safe passage, kel'en," she said.

He should wish her long life, and he could not; he thought instead of that parting of kel'ein: "Honors and good attend," he
said, and she accepted that courtesy with grace.

The Kel veiled, and he did so likewise, grateful for that privacy
as they led him back to the doors, to let him out into the dark.

He heard the mournful protest of a confined dus, attuned to the
mood of the Kel it served; and with that he entered the lock, and
the lights were extinguished, to make them less a target.

For a moment the darkness was complete. Then the opening
ramp and the double doors let the light in, the floodlights on the
field, and the acrid wet wind touched them.

They did not speak as he left. There had not been a word
passed. It was due to their Lady Mother's courage that he and one
of hers would not shed blood in the passing of power; but it was
settled.

When there was only one she'pan on Kesrith, then there would
be time for courtesies, for welcome among them.

He did not look back as he started down the ramp.

Chapter Sixteen

Niun had expected trouble at the bottom of the ramp: there was nothing, neither regul guard nor the assistance that guard might have summoned. He questioned nothing of his good fortune, but ducked his head and ran, soft-soled boots keeping his steps as quiet as possible across the pad.

He threaded again the maze of machinery, and there, there were the regul he had feared, a flare of headlights beyond the fence. He caught his breath and paused half a step to survey the situation, slipped to the shadows and changed course, reckoning that there was no need to use the same access twice. He burned through the wire fence and kicked the wire aside, and ran for it, his lungs hurting in the thin air. Somewhere a dus keened, over the rumble of machinery that prowled the dark.

He reached the edge of the apron and bolted for the sand, startled and shocked as a beam hit the sand across his path. He gasped for air and changed directions, darted round the bending of a dune and ran with all the strength he had remaining.

After a moment he reckoned himself relatively safe, enough to catch his breath again. Regul could not outrace him and the noisy machines could not surprise him. He smothered a cough, natural result of his rash burst of speed, and began uneasily to take account of this new state of affairs, that regul had premeditatedly sought not to catch him, but to kill him.

He lay against the side of the dune, his hand pressed to his aching side, trying to keep his breathing normal, and heard something stir—dus, he thought, for he knew that the hills were full of them this night, and did regul come out very far into the wild after him, they would meet a welcome they would not like. The dusei

of the edun would do no harm to regul; but these were not tame
ones, and the regul might not reckon that difference until it was
too late to matter.

He gathered himself up and started to move, hearing at the
same time a rapid sound of footsteps, mri-light and mri-quick,
and following his track through the dunes. He reckoned it for one
of Esain's kel'ein, on some desperate second thought; and for that
reason he froze, hissed at the shadow a warning as it fronted him,
respectful of it, another kel'en.

But no kel'en.

Half a breath they faced each other, human and mri; and in that
half-breath Niun whipped up his pistol and the human dived desperately to retreat, vain hope in that narrow, dune-constricted
area.

And in the next instant another thought flashed into Niun's
mind—that a dead human could provide little answer to questions. He did not fire. He followed; and when he overtook the
human he motioned with his hand, come, come. The human, casting desperate looks behind and at him, was a fair target if he fired.

And the human chose regul and whirled and ran.

A creature that had no business on Kesrith.

Niun thumbed the safety on, holstered the pistol and chose a
new direction, a direction the regul could not, up over the arm of
a dune; and cast himself flat, scanning the scene to know what
manner of ambush he had sprung. Indeed the human had run directly into regul hands, in the person of one daring youngling who
had him cornered against a ridge the human could easily climb if
he had the wit to think of it; and the human did think of it and
scrambled for his life, fighting to gain the top. But the regul laid
hold on his ankle, and dragged him back again, inexorably.

They noticed nothing else. Niun retreated behind the ridge,
raced a distance, came over and down in a plummeting slide, hit
the solid mass of the regul and staggered it; and when it rounded
on him clumsily, making the mistake of aiming a weapon at a
kel'en, it was the youngling's final mistake. Niun did not think
about the flash of the *as'ei* that left his hand and buried themselves in the youngling's throat and chest: they were sped before
the thought had time to become purpose.

And the human, scrambling to reach the regul's gun—Niun hit him body to body, and if there had been a knife in Niun's intentions, the human would have been dead in the same instant.

No mean adversary, the human: Niun found himself countered, barehanded, in his attempt to seize hold of him; but the human was already done, bleeding from the nostrils, his bubbling breath hoarse in Niun's ear. He broke the human's hold: his arm found the human's throat and snapped his head back with a crack of meeting teeth.

Not yet did the human fall, but a quick blow to the belly and a second snap to the head toppled him writhing to the sands; and Niun hit him yet another time, ending his struggles.

A strip from his belt secured the human; and he recovered his *as'ei* and sheathed them quickly, hearing the slow grinding of machinery advancing on this place, and both of them having made tracks even the night-blind regul could read.

The human was showing signs of consciousness; he gave him a jerk by the elbow and dragged him until the man tried to respond to the discomfort. Then he gave him slack to drag his legs under him and try to stand.

"Quiet," Niun hissed at him.

And if the human thought to cry out, he thought better of it with the edge of the *av-tlen* near his face; he struggled up to his knees and, with Niun's help, to his feet, and went silently where he was compelled to go. He coughed and tried to smother even that sound. His face was a mask of blood and sand in the dim light that shone from the field, and he walked as if his knees were about to fail him.

Onto the edge of the flats they went, and slow, ominous shadows of dusei stood watching them from the dunes, but gave them no threat. There was no sound of pursuit behind them. Perhaps the regul were still in shock, that a kel'en had raised hand against the masters.

Niun knew the enormity of what he had done, had time to realize it clearly; he knew the regul, that they would take time to consult with authority, and beyond that he could not calculate. No mri had ever raised hand to his sworn authority. No regul had ever had to deal with a mri who had done so.

He seized the human's elbow and hurried him, though he stumbled at times, though he misstepped and cried out in shock when a crust broke under him and he hit boiling water. They went well onto the flats, where neither regul nor regul vehicles could go, into the sulphuric steam of geysers that veiled them from sight. By now the human coughed and spat, bleeding in his upper air passages if not in his lungs, Niun reckoned.

In consideration of that he found a place and thrust the human down against the shoulder of a clay bank, and let him catch his breath, himself glad enough of a chance to do the same.

For a moment the human lay face down, body heaving with the effort not to cough, correctly reckoning that this would not be tolerated. Then the spasms eased and he lay still on his side, exhausted, staring at him.

Unarmed. Niun took that curious fact into account, wondering what possessed the humans; or what had befallen this one, that he had lost his weapons. The human simply stared at him, eyes running tears through sand: no emotion, no other expression than one of exhaustion and misery. Unprotected he had come into Kesrith's unfriendly environment; unwisely he had run, risking damage to his tissues.

And he had run from regul, with whom his people had made a treaty.

"I am Sten Duncan," the human whispered at last in his own tongue. "I am with the human envoy. Kel'en, we are here under agreement."

Niun considered the volunteered information: human envoy, human envoy—the words rolled around in his mind with the ominous tone of betrayal.

"I am kel Niun," he said, because this being had offered him a name.

"Are you from the edun?"

Niun did not answer, there seeming no need.

"That is where you're taking me, isn't it?" And when again the human had no answer of him, he seemed disquieted. "I'll go there of my own accord. You don't need to use force."

Niun considered this offer. Humans lied. He knew this. He had not had experience to be able to judge this one.

"I will not set you free," he said.

It was not the custom of humans to veil themselves; but Niun was sorry, all the same, that he had so dealt with a human kel'en, taking dignity from him—if he was kel'en. Niun judged that he was: he had handled himself well.

"We will go to the edun," he said to Duncan. He stood up and drew Duncan to his feet—did not help him overmuch, for this was not a brother; but he waited until he was sure he had his balance. The man was hurt. He marked that the human's steps were uneven and uncertain; and that he walked without knowledge of the land, blind to its dangers.

And deaf.

Niun heard the aircraft lift from the port, heard it turn in their direction; and the human had not even looked until he jerked him about to see it—stood stupidly gazing toward the port, malicious or dull-witted, Niun did not pause to know. He seized the human and pulled him toward the boiling waters of Jieca, that curled steam into the night; and by a clay ridge, their lungs choked with sulphur, they took hiding.

Regul engines passed. Lights swept the flats and lit plumes of steam, fruitlessly seeking movement. Heat sensors were of limited usefulness here on the volcanic flats. The boiling springs and seething mud made regul science of little value in tracking them.

"Kel'en," Duncan said. "Which one are they looking for? Me or you?"

"How have you offended the regul?" Niun asked, reckoning it of no profit to give information, but of some to gain it; and all the while the beams of light swept the flats, lighting one plume and another. "Were you a prisoner?"

"Assistant to the human envoy, to come—" A burst of fire lit their faces and spattered them with boiling water. They made a single mass against it, and as the firing continued and the water kept splashing, a rumble began in the earth and a jet of steam broke near them, enveloping them, uncomfortably hot but not beyond bearing.

"Tsi'mri," Niun cursed under his breath, forgetting with what he shared shelter; and as the barrage kept up he felt the human begin trembling, long, sickly shudders of a being whose strength was nearly spent.

"—to come ahead of the mission," the human resumed doggedly, still shaking. "To see that everything is as we were promised. And I don't think it—"

A near burst threw water and mud on them. The human cried out, smothered it.

"How many of you are there?" Niun asked.

"Myself—and the envoy. Two. We came on *Hazan*—back there."

Niun grasped Duncan's collar and turned his face to the light that glared from the searching beams. He saw nothing to tell him whether this was truth or lie. This was a young man, he saw, now that the face was washed clear by the moisture that enveloped both of them—a kel'en of the humans: he shrank from applying that honorable title to aliens, but he knew no other that applied to this one.

"There was a kel'en on *Hazan*," said Niun, "who died there."

For the first time something seemed to strike through to the human: there was a hesitancy to answer. "I saw him. Once. I didn't know he was dead."

Niun thrust him back, for the moment blind with anger. Tsi'mri, he reminded himself, and enemy, but less so now than the regul. *I saw him. I didn't know he was dead.*

He turned his face aside and stared bleakly at the rolling steam and the lights that crisscrossed the flats, searching.

Forgive us, Medai, he thought. *Our perceptions were too dull, our minds too accustomed to serving regul or we could have understood the message you tried to send us.*

He made himself look at the hateful human face that had not the decency of concealment—at the nakedness of this being that had, unknowingly perhaps, destroyed a kel'en of the People. *Animal,* he thought; *tsi'mri animal.* The regul-mri treaty was broken, from the moment this creature set foot on Kesrith; and that had been many, many days ago. For this long the People had been free and had not known it.

"There is no more war," Duncan protested, and Niun's arm tensed, and he would have hit him; but it was not honorable.

"Why do you suppose that the regul are hunting us?" he asked of Duncan, casting back his own question. "Do you not under-

stand, human, that you have made a great mistake in leaving
Hazan?"

"I am going with you," the human said, with the first semblance of dignity he had shown, "to talk to your elders, to make
them understand that I had better be returned to my people."

"Ah," said Niun, almost moved to scornful mirth. "But we are
mri, not regul. We care nothing for your bargains with the regul,
much good they have done you."

The human stayed still and reckoned that, and there was no
yielding at the implied threat. "I see," he said. And a moment
later, in a quiet, restrained tone: "I left the envoy down there in
town—an old man, alone with regul, with this going on. I have to
get back to him."

Niun considered this, understanding. It was loyalty to this
sen'anth for which he endured this patiently. He gave respect to
the human for that, touched his heart in token of it.

"I will deliver you alive to the edun," he said, and felt compelled to add: "It is not our habit to take prisoners."

"We have learned that," Duncan said.

Therefore they understood each other as much as might be.
Niun considered the flats before them, reckoning already what
might have been done to familiar ground by the bombardment:
what obstacles might have been created on the unstable land,
where they might next find securest shelter if the regul swept
back sooner than anticipated.

It was well that he and the human had come to an understanding, that Duncan considered his best chance and most honorable
course was to cooperate for the moment. A man unburdened could
make the journey by morning, all things in his favor; but not with
regul blasting away the route about them; and day would show
them up clearly, making it next evening before they could reach
the edun if things kept on as they were.

A sick dread gathered in Niun's stomach: for very little even
so, he would have killed the human and run for the edun at all
speed.

He cursed himself for his softness, which had put him to such a
choice between butchery and stupidity, and gripped the human's
arm.

"Listen to me. If you do not keep my pace, I cannot keep you; and if I cannot keep you, I will kill you. It is also," he added, "very likely that the regul will kill you to keep you from your superior."

He slipped from cover then, and drew the human with him by the arm, and Duncan came without resisting.

But the regul craft, lacing the area, swept back, and they made only a few strides before it was necessary to hurl themselves into other cover.

The barrage began again, deafening, spattering them with boiling water and gouts of mud.

The edun would be aware of this. They were doubtless doing something; perhaps—Niun thought—Duncan's sen'anth likewise knew and was doing something; and there was also *Ahanal,* independent of Intel.

He understood the human's helpless terror. Of all who had power on Kesrith, they two had least; and the regul, who did not fight, had taken up arms, impelled by malice or fear or whatever driving motive could span the gap between cowardice and self-interest.

Chapter Seventeen

There was firing, a sound unmistakable to a man who had lived a great part of his life in war.

Stavros turned his sled to view the window and saw the lights of aircraft circling under the clouds. His fingers sought the console keyboard, adjusted screens with what had grown to be some expertise: simple controls, a phenomenal series of coded signals, each memorized. The regul had provided him the codings with an attitude of smug contempt: learn it, they challenged him with that look of theirs that rated beings of short memory with subsapients.

Stavros was not typical in this regard, had never been typical, not from his boyhood on remote Kiluwa, to his attachment to the Xen-Bureau to his directorate on Halley during first contact. He found nothing difficult in languages, nor in alien customs, nor in recognizing provincial shortsightedness, whether offered by humans or by others.

He was Kiluwan by allegiance, a distinction the regul and most humans did not appreciate: remote, first-stage colony, populated by religious traditionalists, among whom writing was a sin and education an obsession. He had been born there a century ago, before peaceful, eccentric Kiluwa became a casualty of the mri wars.

A number of Kiluwans had distinguished themselves in Service; they were gone now, among casualties forty years ago, retaliation for Nisren. Stavros survived. It was characteristic of his Kiluwan upbringing that he should be driven to understand the species that had ordered Kiluwa obliterated. Regul had done this, not mri. Therefore he studied the phenomenon of regul—minds much like the perfection Kiluwa had sought; and they had destroyed all that Kiluwa had built. There was, as the university masters had once said, a 'rhythm of justice' in this, a joining of cancelling forces. Now a Kiluwan came to displace regul, and the rhythm continued, binding them both.

He learned regul ways, looking for resolution to this; he observed meanness and coldness and self-seeking ambition, as well as reverence for mind. He had come from fear of regul to a yearning over them—not a little of sorrow for Kiluwa, whose dream in the flesh had come to this flawed reality; and there were truths beyond what he had been able to grasp, vices and virtues inherent in the biology of regul. He saw these, began to understand, at least, constraints of species perpetuation and population control—division into hive structures, breeding-elders and younglings, the docha that answered roughly to nations: he acquired suspicions about the value of treaties, which bound and yet did not bind docha which had not been party to the agreement.

They had contracted with Holn and suddenly found themselves dealing instead with Alagn; and Alagn honored the agreement.

Outwardly.

It had come to the point of truth. He had sat the long hours through the day and into dark and covered for Duncan's absence and committed every deception but the outright lie which the regul would not forgive. In the hours' passage he had grown more and more certain, first that Duncan had found something amiss or he would have returned quickly, certainly by the time dark gave him concealment—and when the fall of night did not bring him back, he became well sure that something amiss had found Duncan.

The pretenses with the regul became charade bitterly difficult to maintain. They could murder the SurTac and blandly fail to mention it with the morning's reports. And there was not a human going to land on Kesrith without Stavros' clearance: not in peace, at least, not without removing all possible resistance.

The regul surely understood this.

He sat and listened to the firing, knowing while it continued that Duncan was likely still alive.

He had been a shaper of policy in his day, had settled a new world and founded a university; had plotted strategies of diplomacy and war, had disposed of lives in numbers in which ships and crews were reckoned expendable, in which the likes of Sten Duncan perished in their hundreds.

But he heard the firing, and clenched his right hand and agonized in a desperate attempt to move his unwilling left with any strength at all. He was held to the sled. He was constrained to be patient.

There was new catastrophe at the port. There were hints in regul communications, into which he had intruded, that a ship had come down, that it was not friendly to regul.

Human, rival regul, or mri. He could guess well enough what had drawn Duncan to overstay his leave. Create no incident, he had told the lad, knowing then that there was little Duncan could do to create anything: it waited to happen, all about them. He had felt it increasingly, in the silences of the regul, the tension in the atmosphere of the Nom.

The regul were trying something illicit. Human interests were endangered. And there was no word of approval going from him to the human mission when it arrived, no matter what the coercion.

If that was not what had already happened.

Stavros was not a man of precipitate action: he thought; and when he had concluded chances were even, he was capable of rashness. He found no need to cooperate further with hosts that would either kill them or not dare to kill them: it was time to call their bluff.

He fingered the console, whipped the sled about and opened doors. He guided it through Duncan's apartment and with a smooth, well-practiced series of commands, and a turn to the right, locked it into the tracking that ran the corridors.

Youngling regul saw him and gaped, jabbering protests which he ignored. He knew his commands, calculated the appropriate moves, and locked into a turn, whisked into the side of the building that faced the port. There he stopped and keyed into the window controls, brightening windows, commanding storm shields withdrawn.

A new ship, indeed.

And lights glared over the countryside, flaring garishly in the haze of smoke and steam, aircraft lacing the ground with their beams.

Ah, Duncan, he thought with great regret.

A youngling puffed up to him. "Elder human," it said. "We regret, but—"

Bai Hulagh. Where? he demanded via the screen, which took the youngling considerably aback. *Youngling, find me the bai.*

It fled, at least with what dispatch a regul could manage, and Stavros whipped the sled about and took it to the left, engaged a track and shot down the ramp, whipped round the corner and entered the first level of the Nom, from which they had been carefully excluded.

Here he disengaged and went on manual, edging through the gabbling crowd of younglings. *Mri,* he heard, and: *mri ship;* and: *alert.*

And they made way for him until one noticed that the sled, the symbol to them of adult authority, contained a human.

"Go back," they wished him. "Go back, elder."

Bai Hulagh. Now, he insisted, and would not move, and there was nothing they dared do about it. When they began to murmur together in great confusion, he directed the sled through them and toured the ground floor in leisurely fashion, with the air vibrating with the attack out on the flats and the building vibrating to the shocks. Mentally he noted where doors were located, and where accesses were, and where it was possible to come and go with the sled.

A message flashed on his receiver.

It was Hulagh's sigil. Hulagh's face followed. "Esteemed elder human," Hulagh said. "Please return at once to your quarters."

I am unable to believe that they are secure, Stavros spelled out patiently. *Where is my assistant?*

"He has disregarded our advice and is now involved in a situation," said Hulagh with remarkable candor, such that Stavros' hopes abruptly lifted. "Mri have landed, I regret to admit, honorable representative. These mri are outlaws, bent on making trouble. Your youngling is somewhere in the midst of things, quite contrary to our warnings. Please make our task easier by returning to the safety of your quarters."

I refuse. Stavros keyed a window clear. *I will observe from the windows here.*

Hulagh's nostrils snapped shut and flared again. "This lack of cooperation is reprehensible. We are still in authority here. We do not lose this authority until the arrival of your mission. You are here only as an observer, on our agreement."

Therefore I shall observe.

Again the flare of anger. "Do so, then, at your own hazard. I shall inform your youngling if he is found that you miss his services and he would be well advised to return to you."

I should be grateful, Stavros spelled out with deliberation. *I shall inform my people when they come that you are not responsible for any delay in withdrawal—if it should happen that my aide is recovered safely and there is no damage to our chosen landing site, or to necessary facilities, such as this building or the water or power plant. However, if these things do occur, other conclusions may be drawn.*

There was silence, bai Hulagh still on the screen, while the bai reflected on this statement of intent. Stavros had expected anger, threat, bluster. Instead some quieter emotion passed within the bony mask of a face, betrayed only by the rapid flare of nostrils.

"If the human envoy will assure us that this is indeed the case and accommodation may be made, then we will make every effort to preserve these facilities and to accomplish the recovery of your youngling alive. It will, however, be necessary to warn the human envoy that there will be necessary operations at the port and, for the security of the Nom and all within, it will be preferable for the honorable human elder to observe through remote channels and not through the windows. Your consideration, favor, sir."

I understand. Favor, sir. I am presently satisfied that you are doing your utmost. He would not, voluntarily, have surrendered his view through the windows, not trusting the limited view provided by regul services; but the barrage was intense and the windows rattled ominously, and he began to believe the bai's warning. The regul building was undergoing repeated shocks. He knew the bai's warning for an honest one.

It only remained to question what was happening to occasion the firing. The regul, he reminded himself, closing the storm shield, did not lie.

Therefore it was true that mri had landed and that Sten Duncan was somewhere out on the flats, but one never assumed anything with the regul.

Then the floor shook, and sirens wailed throughout the building.

Stavros locked the sled onto a track and whisked himself back to the main lobby, where a group of younglings frantically waved at him, trying to offer him instructions all at once.

"Shelter, reverence, shelter!" they said, pointing at another hall, a ramp leading down. He considered and thought that it might at the moment be wise to listen.

Chapter Eighteen

Duncan was spent, a burden, a hazard. Niun set hands on him and pushed him downslope, to shelter under an overhang by a boiling pool, forcing him farther under as he wedged his own body after.

It was scantly in time. A near burst of fire hissed across the water and crumbled rock near them: blind fire, not aimed. The searching beams continued, lacing the area. Niun saw the face of Duncan in the reflected light, haggard and swollen-eyed—unprotected by the membrane that hazed Niun's own vision when the smoke grew thick. Duncan's upper lip showed a black trail that was blood in the dim light. It poured steadily, a nuisance that had become more than nuisance. The human heaved with a bubbling cough and tried to stifle it. The reek in the air from the firing and from the natural steam and sulphur was thick and choking. Niun twisted in the narrow confines, fastidious about touching the bleeding and sweating human, and at last, exhausted, abandoned niceties in such close quarters. They lay in a space likely to become their tomb should another shot crumble the ledge over them; mri and human bones commingled for future possessors of Kesrith to wonder at.

This was delirium. The mind could not function under such pounding shocks as bracketed them constantly. Niun found the regul amazing in their ineptness. They two should have been dead over and over, had the regul had any knowledge of the land; but the regul had not, were firing blind at a landscape as unknown and alien to them as the bottom of the sea. The world was lit in constant flares of white and red, swirled in mists and steam and smoke and clouds of dust, like the Hell that humans swore by— that of mri was an unending Dark.

The water splashed, singing and bubbling; Niun lowered the visor of the *zaidhe,* he the outermost, shielding the human with his own body: ironic arrangement, chance-chosen, one he would have reversed at the moment if it were possible.

An explosion heaved the earth, numbed the senses, drove their numbed bodies into a fresh convulsion of terror.

And hard upon that a white light lit the rocks, grew, ate them, devoured all the world; and a pressure unbearable; and Niun knew that they were hit, and tried to move to roll out into the open before the ledge came down. The pressure burst over him, and it was red . . .

. . . wind, wind in great force, skirling away the smoke and mist, making the red swirl before his membraned, visored eyes. Niun moved, became aware that he moved, and that he lived.

And all about them was light, sullen and ugly red.

He gathered himself up, the light at his back, and turned to the light, and saw the port.

There was nothing.

He stood—legs shuddering under him. He thought that he cried out, so great was his pain, and shut his eyes, and opened them, trying to see through the flame, until the tears poured down his face. But of *Ahanal,* of *Hazan,* there was nothing to be seen. Within the city itself, fires blazed, sending smoke boiling aloft.

And even while he watched, an aircraft lifted from near the horizon, circled for a distance out to sea, and came back again, lights blinking lazily.

He followed it with his eyes, the aircraft circling, rounding over the city, through the smoke—beginning to come about toward the hills.

Toward the edun.

He wished to turn his face from it, knowing, knowing already the end. He turned with it, watched, a great knot swelling in his throat, and his body cold and numb, and the center of him utterly alive to what began to happen.

The first tower of the edun, that of the Kel, flared in light and went, slowly tumbling. The sound reached him, a numbing shock, and after that the wind, as the towers fell, as the whole structure of the edun hung suspended and crumbled down into ruin.

And the ship circled, light and free, lazily winking in the dark as it rose above the smoke and came, insolently, over their heads.

His pistol was in his hands: he turned and lifted it, and fired one futile burst at those retreating lights, none others in the sky. The lights blurred in his eyes, the betraying membrane, or tears: it flashed and cleared, and he fired again.

And the lights continued on a moment, and a red light blossomed and fragments went spinning in various trajectories, ruin upon ruin, pistol shot or the turbulence that must surround the port.

It healed nothing. He turned, looked again at the edun where not even flames remained, and his stomach spasmed, a wrench that weakened his joints and made him dizzy. In that moment he would have wished to be without senses, to be weak, to fall, to sink down, to do anything but continue to stand, helplessly.

Dead. Dead, all of them.

He stood, not knowing whether to return to the ruin at the port, to go on as he was going, or whether there was reason to go, or to do anything but sit where he was until morning, when the regul would come to finish matters. He found no limit to what senses could absorb. He felt. He was not numb. He only wished to be, battered by the wind that stole the sound from the night, whipping at his robes, a steady snap of cloth that was, here, louder than the silence that had fallen over everything.

The People were dead.

He remained. For survivors there were duties, respects, rites that wanted doing. He was not of Medai's temperament.

He slipped pistol into its holster, and clenched his icy hands under his arms, and began to reckon with the living.

The Hand of the People, a kel'en; and there were his kin to bury, if the regul had not done it in killing them, and after that there was a war the regul perhaps did not look to fight.

And then he looked toward the ledge, and looked on his human prisoner, and met his eyes. Here also was a man that waited to die, that also knew, in small measure, what desolation was.

He could kill, and be alone thereafter, a vast, vast silence; a tiny act of violence after the forces that had stormed across the skies of Kesrith and ruined the world.

A tiny and miserable act. Vengeance for a world deserved something of equal stature.

"Get up," he said quietly, and Duncan gathered himself up, shoulder to the rock, staring back at him.

"We will go up to the hill," he told Duncan. "The house of my people—I do not think there will be more aircraft."

Duncan turned and looked, and without demur, without question, started walking ahead of him.

The world was changed about them. Landmarks that had been on the Dus plain for eons were gone. The ground was pocked with scars that filled with boiling water. Duncan, leading the way, blind, bound, misstepped and went in up to the knee, with nothing more than a hoarse sob of shock; and Niun seized him and pulled him back, steadying him, while the human stood and gasped for air.

He kept a hand on Duncan's arm thereafter, and guided him, knowing the way; and preserved the human against another time.

The light came, the red light of Arain, foul and murky. Niun looked back toward the port, and saw in the first light the full truth of what he had already known: that nothing survived.

Neither *Ahanal* nor *Hazan*.

And when he looked on the hill where the Edun of the People had stood, it was one with the sand and the rocks—as if nothing built by hands had ever stood there.

He saw also in the light what prize he had taken, an exhausted creature that struggled for every upward step, whose face and mouth and chest were spattered with blood that poured afresh from the nose, injury or atmosphere, it was uncertain. The eyes were almost shut, streaming tears not of seeming emotion but of outraged tissues—a face naked in the sun, and indecent, and more bewildered than evil: he did not know why the human kept walking at such cost, toward such little reward—easier by far the death of the land's violence than what mri and human had exchanged for forty years.

But there was a point past which there was no thinking, only the fact that one lived; and that continued whether one wanted or wished otherwise.

He understood such a mind, that deep shock which admitted no decisions. He had never thought that he would freeze in crisis; yet he had frozen, and the cold of that moment when the People died was still locked round his mind and his heart and seemed never apt to go away, not though he had revenge, not though he killed every regul that breathed and heaped humanity on the desolation as well.

It was a shock in which their two lives were of like value, which was nothing at all.

He pushed the human ahead, neither hating now nor pitying, finding no reason for sparing a human when he had the ruin of the edun to face for himself. He thought perhaps that Duncan sorrowed for his own failed duty, which lay lost in burning Kesrith; that Duncan also mourned failure, as miserable as he.

But Duncan had all the human worlds for kinsmen, knowing that they survived; and it was possible to hate the human when he let himself think on this. He would not return this one to his kind: while he lived, Duncan would live. While he had to face what had become of Kesrith, the man Duncan would do the like.

They came to the edun by full daylight, untroubled by ships or any sign of life from the skies. Down in the city there might be. It did not extend to them. When Niun thought of it, he thought of going down and destroying them—methodically, joylessly: regul, who had no capacity for war.

Who had finally, in one cowardly act, destroyed the People.

There was irony there that was worth bitter laughter. He looked on the mound of rubble that had been the edun and felt moved to that or to tears; and Duncan, no longer forced to walk, simply slumped to his knees and leaned against the shoulder of the causeway. Niun heard his hollow cough and kicked him gently, reached down when that was not enough to rouse him, and caught his arm, pulling him up again.

There was work to be done, at least so far as they could try; and he was loath to have the ruin touched at all by tsi'mri hands, but he had not the strength alone. He drew the *av-tlen* and pried loose the knots at Duncan's wrists with its point, carefully unwound the thongs that were embedded in Duncan's swollen flesh and looped the recovered leather through its ring on his own belts.

Duncan, trying to work his hands to life, looked at the edun, and looked at him, a question. Niun jerked his head in response and Duncan comprehended and began to walk. They waded through rubble, stepped carefully among chunks of the walls that were cast down and shattered. Here had been simple fire, not the radiation that doubtless bathed the city and made the place uninhabitable. Niun pushed at the heap of rubble that blocked their way, and saw that beneath that pile of heavy stone and fine dust lay at least one of the Kel.

There was no use to move that mass, no hope of moving it entirely. Instead Niun took stones and began to heap them round the visible body like a cairn, and Duncan, seeing what he was about, began to gather up rocks of the proper size and pass them to him.

This offended him bitterly, that the human offered rather than suffered compulsion; but it was needed, and he would not suffer the human to touch the grave itself. And it occurred to him at the same moment that Duncan might well smash his skull with one of those self-same stones the moment he turned his back entirely, and that this might be what the human was preparing, so he kept from turning his head while he worked.

They finished, and from this place they went deeper into the ruin and into places dark and difficult, where heaps of rubble towered overhead and sifted dust and pebbles downslope at them. And the core of all the deepest ruin was the Shrine that he had sought.

It was all too deeply buried.

If it had been possible, he would have sought out whatever relics he could carry and taken them away into the sanctity of Sil'athen, where his kinsmen also would have been buried; but perhaps humans would never be curious enough to desecrate this place with their machines, to sift out the debris and leavings of a species which no longer mattered in the universe.

And here the destruction reached that central citadel of himself that had yet to feel it; and he trembled and his senses almost left him. He reached out and sought support, and touched the wrong stone, bringing a slide that buried the place at their feet and brought a sift of powder down on them. The only thing he saw clearly was Duncan's face, terror in his eyes as for an instant they seemed likely to go under the weight of rubble and earth; and then the sifting stopped and the place grew still.

A stone shifted somewhere, and another; there was another slide, and silence, the fall of a few pebbles.

And in that silence came a thin and distant cry.

Duncan heard it: if not for that confirming glance sideward, Niun would have thought it illusion. But it came from the direction that had been Kath, where the deepest storerooms were.

He turned and began to pick his way through the ruin, careful, careful with his life now, and that of her who had cried aloud, down in the dark.

"Melein!" he cried, and paused and listened, and that same thin sound returned to him.

He reached the place, estimating where it lay, and a wall had fallen there, and finer rubble atop it; but the steel regul-made doors had held.

Too well. They were barred by a weight that could not be moved, that they lacked tools to chip away and machines to lift. Niun tore his hands on it, and his muscles cracked, and Duncan added his force, but it would not slide; and at last they both sat down, gasping for air, coughing. Duncan's nose started pouring blood again. He wiped it in a bloody smear and his hands were shaking uncontrollably.

"Is it," Duncan asked, "ventilated down there?"

It was not. It added a fear atop the others. "Melein," Niun called out. "Melein, do you hear?"

He heard some manner of answer, and it was a woman's voice and a young voice, high and thin and clear: it was Melein. He reckoned it below them, and tried to figure the exact location of it, and marked with a heel a spot on the floor.

Then he wrenched a reinforcing rod from the ruin and began with careful chips to dig—no firing down into that sanctuary, no such recklessness. He dug with that and with his fingers, and Duncan saw what he was doing and helped him, alternating strokes that pounded deeper into the cubit-thick flooring, and now and again they paused to paw away the dust they had made. The sun grew hot, and the only sound now was the steady chink of steel on the cemented earth, and he had heard no word from Melein in a very long time. He was tormented with fear, knowing how small the space below was, how scant the air must be; and fear lest the gap they were making miss the small space where she was sheltered; and fear lest the whole floor give way.

They broke through. Air flooded out of that blackness, stale and depleted and cold.

"Melein," he shouted down, and had no answer.

He began to work yet harder, ramming chips from the edges of the hole, widening it, admitting more and more air, sending a shaft of sunlight down into that place. They exposed steel rods, and worked in the other direction, where they could make a wider hole, and from time to time he would call down to her, and hear nothing.

It was at last a size to admit a body; and he considered it, and the human who would remain above, and how they were to get up again, and thought desperately of killing Duncan; but he could not come up with Melein in his arms, not so easily; and he was not sure whether the cloth of his robes could bear his weight, or what else might avail.

"I will go down," said Duncan, and opened a pocket and took out a length of cord, and from another a small light. He offered these precious things with a naive forthrightness that for a moment disarmed Niun.

"The drop," Niun said, inwardly shuddering at the thought of him near Melein, "is my height and half again." He did not add what revenge he would take if Duncan were careless, if he harmed Melein, if he could not recover her alive: these things were useless. He sat helpless and watched as Duncan worked his body—a little heavier than his—into that gap and dropped, with a heavy sound, into the dark.

Niun listened as he searched below, through things that rattled and moved, through the shifting of rock. He leaned close and tried to see the tiny glow of the light he held.

"I have found her," Duncan's voice floated up out of that cold. And then: "She's alive."

Niun wept, safe, where the human could not see him; and wiped his eyes and sat still, fists clenched on his knees. He knew that the human could claim her for hostage, could harm her, could exact revenge or some terrible oath of him; he had not thought through these things clearly, a measure of his exhaustion and his desperation to reach her in time; but now he thought, and poised himself on the edge of the pit, to go down.

"Mri! Niun!" Duncan stood in the light with a pale burden in his arms, a gold bundle of robes that lay still against him. "Let down the cord. I will try to guide her up."

Even while he watched, Melein stirred, and moved, and her eyes opened on the light in which he above could be only a shadow."

"Melein," he called down. "Melein, we will pull you up. This is a human, Melein, but do not fear him."

She struggled when she heard that, and Duncan set her feet on the floor. Niun saw her look at his face in the dim light and draw back in horror.

But she suffered him then to put his hands on her waist, and to lift her up, by far the easiest and least hurtful way for her: but she could not lift her hands to reach Niun's, and protested pain—she once kel'e'en. "Wait," Niun objected, and with a turn of cord and a knot fashioned a sling and cast it down. He wrapped it about hand and arm and took the weight carefully as she settled in the sling he had made: Duncan helped lift, but for a time the thin, cutting cord and an upward pull bit into Niun's hands. He tried not to rake her against the jagged opening, pulled ever so carefully, and braced his feet and ignored the pain of his hands. She came through and levered herself out onto the sunlit dust, tried to rise: he had her, he had her safe; and he hugged her to her feet and held to her as he had held to no living being since childhood, they both entangled in the cord. He brushed dust and tears from her face, she still gasping in the outside air.

"The ship is destroyed," he said, to have all the cruelty done with while wounds were still numb. "Everyone else is dead, unless there is someone else alive down there."

"No. None. They had no time. They were too old to run—they would not—they sat still, with the she'pan. Then the House—"

She began to shake as if in the grip of a great cold; but she was once of the Kel, and she did not break. She controlled herself, and after a moment began to disentangle them both from the cord.

"None," he said, to be sure she understood it all, "could have possibly survived on the ship."

She sat down on the edge of the section of wall that blocked the doors, and smoothed back her mane with one hand, her head bowed. She found her torn scarf at her shoulder and smoothed it and carefully covered her head with that light, gauze veil. She was quiet for a time, her head still turned from him.

At last she straightened her shoulders, and pointed over to the hole in the rubble, where Duncan waited. "And what is he?" she asked.

He shrugged. "No matter to us. A human. A regul guest. They tried to kill him when we met; then—" The surmise that it was this, partly his own action, which had killed the People and left them orphan, was too terrible to speak. His voice trailed off, and Melein arose and walked from him, to look at the ruin, her back to him, her hands limp at her sides. The sight of her despair was like a wound to him.

"Melein," he said to her. "Melein, what am I to do?"

She turned to him, gave a tiny, helpless gesture. "I am nothing."

"What am I to do?" he insisted.

Sen and Kel: Sen must lead; but she had become more than Sen, and that was the heaviness on her, which he saw she did not want, which she had to bear. He stood waiting. At last she shut her eyes and opened them again.

"Enemies will come here," she said, beginning clearly to function as she had been prepared for years to function, to command and to plan: she assumed what she must assume, she'pan of the People, who had no people. "Find us what we need for the hills; and we will camp there tonight. Give me tonight, truebrother—I must not call you that; but tonight, that only, and I will think what is best for us to do."

"Rest," he urged her. "I will do that." And when he had seen her seated and out of the direct sun, he bent down over the hole and cast the cord down. "Duncan."

The human's white face appeared in the center of the light, anxious and frightened. "Lift me up," he said, laying hand on the cord, which Niun refused to give solidity. "Mri, I have helped you. Now lift me out of here."

"Search for the things I name and I will draw them up by the cord. And after that I will draw you up."

Duncan hesitated there, as if he thought that, like humans, a mri would lie. But he agreed then, and sought with his tiny light until he had found all the things that Niun then requested of him. He tied each small bundle on the cord for Niun to draw up: food, and water flasks, and cording and four bolts of unsewn black cloth, for they could not reach better without delaying to pierce a new opening, and Duncan avowed he did not think it safe. A last time the cord came up, with a bolt of cloth; and a last time he cast it down, this time for Duncan, and braced it about his body and his arm.

It was not so hard as with Melein's uncooperating weight: he leaned and braced his feet, and Duncan hauled himself up—gained the lip of the hole and heaved himself to safety, panting, bent double, coughing and trying to stop the bleeding. The coughing went on and on, and Melein came from her place of rest to look down on the human in mingled disgust and pity.

"It is the air," Niun said. "He has been running, and he is not acclimated to Kesrith."

"Is he a manner of kel'en?" asked Melein.

"Yes," Niun said. "But he does not offer any threat. The regul hunted him; likely now they would cease to care—unless this man's superior is alive. What shall we do with him?"

Duncan seemed to know they spoke of him; perhaps he knew a few words of the language of the People, but they spoke the High Language, and surely he could not follow that.

Melein shrugged, turned her head from him. "As you please. We will go now."

And she began, slowly, to walk through the ruin, picking her way with care.

"Duncan," said Niun, "pick up the supplies and come."

The human looked outrage at him, as if minded to dispute this as a matter of dignity; and Niun expected it, waited for it. But then Duncan knelt down and made a bundle of the goods with the cord, heaving it to his shoulder as he arose.

Niun indicated that he should go, and the human carried the burden where Niun aimed him, his footsteps weaving and uncertain in the wake of Melein.

*   *   *

No firing had touched the hills. They came into a sheltered place that was as it had been before the attack, before the discords of regul or mri or humans—a shelter safe from airships, withdrawn as it was beneath a sandstone ledge.

With a great sigh Melein sank down on the sand in that cold shadow, and bent, her head against her knees, as if this had been all that she could do, the last step that she could take. She was hurt. Niun had watched her walk and knew that she was in great pain, that he thought was in her side and not her limbs. When she was content to stop, he took the supplies from Duncan, and made haste to spread a cloth for a groundsheet and a cover for Melein. He gave her drink and a bit of dried meat; and watched, sitting on his heels, as she drank and ate, and leaned against the bare rock to rest.

"May I drink?"

The human's quiet request reminded him he had another charge on him; and he measured out a capful of water and passed it to Duncan's shaking hands.

"Tomorrow maybe," said Niun, "we will tap a luin and have water enough to drink." He considered the human, who drank at the water drop by drop, a haggard and filthy creature who by appearances ought not to have survived so far. It was not likely that he could survive much farther as he was. He stank, sweat and sulphur compounded with human. Niun found himself hardly cleaner.

"Can you—" he said to Melein, almost having forgotten that her personal name was not for him to speak freely now. He offered her his pistol. "Can you stay awake long enough to watch this human a time?"

"I am well enough," she said, and drew up one knee and rested wrist and pistol on it in an attitude more kel'e'en than she'pan. By caste, she should not touch weapons; but many things ought to be different, and could not be.

He left them so, and went out of sight of the ledge, and stripped and bathed, as mri on dry worlds did, in the dry sand, even to his mane, which when he shook the sand out recovered its glossy feel quickly enough. He felt better when he had done this, and he dressed again, and began to retrace his steps toward the cave.

A heavy body moved behind him, an explosive breath and plaintive sound: dus. He turned carefully, for he had left his gun with Melein, and nothing else could give a ha-dus pause.

It was the *miuk'ko,* gaunt, forlorn, scab-hided. But the face was dry and it shambled forward with careless abandon.

His heart beat rapidly, for the situation was a bad one in potential, for all the dusei were unpredictable. But the dus came to him, and lifted its head, thrusting it against his chest, uttering that dus-master sound that begged food, shelter, whatever things mri and dus shared.

He knelt down there, for the moment demanded it, and embraced the scrofulous neck and relaxed against the beast, letting it touch and be touched. A sense of warmth came over him, a feeling deep and almost sensual, the lower beast functions of the dus mind, that could be content with very little.

This it lent him. He looked up, aware of presence, saw two stranger-dusei on the sandstone ridge above; he was not afraid. This dus knew them, and they knew him, and this, like the warmth, came at a level too low for reason. It was fact. It was dependable as the rock on which they stood, mri and dus. It absorbed his pain, and melted it, and fed him back strength as slow and powerful as its own.

And when he came back to the cave, the great beast lumbered after him, a docile companion, a comical and friendly fellow that—beholding the human—was suddenly neither comic nor friendly.

Distrust: that reached Niun's mind through the impulses of the dus; but that subsided as the dus felt the human's outright terror. This one feared. Therefore he was safe. The dus put thought of the human aside and settled down athwart the entrance, radiating impulses of ward and protection.

"He came," said Niun, gathering his pistol from Melein's hand. "There are more out there, but none even vaguely familiar."

"The old pact," she said, "is still valid with us and them."

And he knew that they might have no better guardian; and that he could sleep this night, sure that nothing would pass the dus to harm Melein. He was overwhelmingly grateful for this. The exhaustion he had held back came down like a flood. The dus lifted his head and gave that pleasure moan, a gap-mouthed smile, tongue lolling. It flicked and disappeared into a dusine smugness.

Niun spoke to it, the small nonsense words the dusei loved, and touched its massive head, pleasing it; and then he took its paw and turned it, the size of it more than a man could easily hold in his hands. The claws curled inward, drawing his wrist against the dew-claw: reflex. It broke the skin, admitting the venom. He had sought this. It would not harm him in such small doses; by such degrees he would become immune to this particular dus, and need never fear it. He took his hand back and caressed the flat skull, bringing a rumbling sound of contentment from the beast.

Then, because he could not bear the thought of bedding down with the human's filth, he took up an armload of cloth and bade the human come with him, and took him out beyond the ledge.

"Bathe," he told Duncan, and, casting down the cloth when Duncan seemed dismayed, he bent and with a handful of sand on his own arm, demonstrated how; he sat with arms folded, eyes generally averted somewhat, while the human cleansed himself, and the curious ha-dusei watched from the heights, grouping and circling in alarm at the strange pale-skinned creature.

Duncan looked somewhat more pleasant when he had scrubbed the blood from his face and the tear streaks had been evened out to a dusty sameness. He shook the dust from his hair and picked up his discarded clothing and started to dress; but Niun tore a length from the cloth and tore it in such a way that it could be worn. He thrust it at the human, who doubtfully put it on, as if this were some intended shame to him. Then he thought to search the clothing that the human had taken off, and found pockets full of things of which the human had not spoken.

He opened his hand, demonstrating the knife that he had found. Duncan shrugged.

Niun gave him credit at least that he had not attempted any rashness, but bided his time. The human had played the round well, though he had lost it.

Niun thrust a second wad of black cloth of him. "Veil yourself," he said. "Your nakedness offends the she'pan and me."

Duncan settled the veil over his head, ineptly attempting to make it stay, for he had not the art. Niun showed him how to twist it to make a band of it, and how to arrange the veil; and Duncan looked the better for it, decently covered. He was not robed as kel'en, which would have been improper; but he was in kel-black and modestly clothed as a man and not as an animal. Niun looked on him with a nod of approval.

"This is better for you," he said. "It will protect your skin. Bury your clothing. You will find when we travel in the day that our way is best."

"Are we moving?"

Niun shrugged. "The she'pan makes that decision. I am kel'en. I take her orders."

Duncan dropped to his knees and dug a hole, animal fashion, and put his discarded clothing in it. He paused when he had smoothed it over, and looked up. "And if I could offer you a safe way off this world—"

"Can you?"

Duncan rose to his feet. He had a new dignity, veiled. Niun had never noticed the color of his eyes. They were light brown. Niun had never seen the like. "I could find a way," Duncan said, "to contact my people and get a ship down here for you. I think you have something to lose by not taking that offer. I think you would like very much to get her out of this."

Niun moved his hand to his weapons, warning. "Tsi'mri, you do assume too much. And if you make plans, present them to her, not to me. I told you: I am only kel'en. If something pleases her, I do it. If something annoys her, I remove it."

Duncan did not move. Presumably he reconsidered his disrespect. "I do not understand," he said finally. "Evidently I don't understand how things are with you. Is this your wife?"

The obscenity was so naively put, in so puzzled a tone, that Niun almost laughed in surprise. "No," he said, and to further confound him: "She is my Mother."

And he motioned the human to cease delaying him, for he grew anxious for Melein, and there were the ha-dusei about them, that snuffed the air and called soft cries from their higher perch. One came down as they left the area. Doubtless the clothes would not stay buried, but neither would there be much left of them to catch the eye of searchers.

The dus at the entry of their refuge lifted his head and pricked his tiny ears forward at their approach, radiating feelings of welcome; and Niun, already feeling the flush of the poison in him, and knowing he would feel it more in the hours of the night, offered his fingers to its nose and brushed past, putting his body between it and Duncan.

Melein took note of the human and nodded in approval of the change; but no further interest in him did she show this night. She settled down to rest in peace now that they had returned. And Niun drank a very small ration of water and lay down and watched as the human likewise stretched himself out as far from them and the beast as he might in the little space.

In time Niun let his eyes close, his mind full, so overburdened that at last there was nothing to do but abandon all thought and let go. The dus-fever was in him. He drifted toward low-mind dreams, that were the murky, sometimes frightening impulses of the dus; but he feared no harm from the impulses because it was in the lore of the Kel that no kel'en had ever been harmed by his own dus, it being sane.

And he was owned by this beast, and the beast by him; and he compassed his present world by this and by Melein. He had been utterly desolate in the morning, and at this evening he rested, kel-ignorant, with a dus to guard his sleep and touch his mind, and with once more a she'pan to take up the burden of planning. His heart was pained for Melein's burden, but he did not try to bear it. She would have her honor. He had his, and it was vastly simpler.

To obey the she'pan. To avenge the People.

He stared at the human during his waking intervals and once, in the dark, he knew that the human was awake and looking at him. They did not speak.

Chapter Nineteen

The day came quietly, with only the sounds of the wind and the dus's breathing. Niun looked and found Melein already awake, sitting cross-legged in the doorway, outlined by the dawn. She was composed as if she had sat so for a long time, arranging her thoughts in private in the last hours of the night.

He rose, while Duncan still lay insensible; and came to her and settled on the cold sand, near the fever-warmth of the drowsing dus. His legs were weak with the poison and his arm was stiff and hot to the shoulder, but it would pass. His mind was still calm, with the muddled thoughts of the dus still brushing it; and he was not afraid, even considering their situation. He knew this for dus courage, that would melt when crisis came and a man needed to think; but it was rest, and he was glad of it. He thought perhaps Melein had enjoyed something of the same, for her face was calm, as if she had been meditating on some private dream.

"Did you rest long?" he asked of her.

"So long as I needed. I was shaken yesterday. I think I shall still find a long walk difficult. But we will walk today."

He heard this, and knew that she had come to some ultimate decision, but it would not be respectful to ask, to go on assuming that he was her kinsman, which he could not be any longer.

"We are ready," he said.

"We are going by the way of Sil'athen," she said, "and further into the hills; and we will find a shrine of which the Kel has known nothing in our generation. Before we two were born it was ordered forgotten by the Kel. The Pana, Niun, never rested in the Edun. It was a time of war. The she'pan did not think it good that the Pana be in the edun, and she was right."

He touched his brow in reverence, his skin chilled even to hear the things that she said; but his spirit rose at what she said. It changed nothing, had no bearing on their own bleak chances; but the Holy existed, and even if they went to destroy it with their own hands, it would not have perished by enemies.

The gods' mission, then. That was something worth doing, something he could well comprehend.

"Know this," she said further. "We will recover the Pana for ourselves, and we two will bear it to a place where we can be safe. And we will wait. We will wait, until we can find a way off Kesrith or until we know that there can be none. Does the Kel have an opinion?"

He considered, thought of Duncan's offer, of bringing it to her, and put it away in his thoughts. There would be a moment for that, if they lived to do the one thing. "I think," he judged carefully, "that we will end by killing humans and then by being hunted to our end. But for my part I had as lief go to the human authorities and contract with them against regul. I am this bitter."

She listened to him attentively, her head tilted to one side, and she frowned. "But," she said, "there is peace between regul and humans."

"I do not think it will last. Not forever."

"But would humans not laugh—to consider one kel'en alone, trying to take service against all regul?"

"The regul would not laugh," said Niun grimly, and she nodded, appreciative of that truth.

"But I will not have this," she said. "No. I know what Intel planned: to take us into the Dark again, to take the long voyage and renew the People during that Dark. And I will not sell you into hire for any promises of safety. No. We two go our own way."

"We have neither Kath nor kel'e'ein," he cried, and dropped his voice at once to half-whisper, for he did not want Duncan waking. "For us there are no more generations, no renewing. We will never come out of that Dark."

She looked up tranquilly at the dawning. "If we are the last, then a quiet end; and if we are not the last, then the way to surest extinction for the People is to waste our lives in pursuit of tsi'mri wars and tsi'mri honors and all the things that have occupied the People in this unhappy age."

"What is there else?" he asked; which was a forbidden question, and he knew it when he had spoken it, and canceled it with a gestured refusal. "No, do as you will."

"We are free," she said. "We are *free,* Niun. And I will commit us to nothing but to find the Pana and to find whether others of our kind survive."

He looked up and met her eyes, and acknowledged her bravery with a nod of his head. "It is not possible that we do this," he said. "The Kel tells you this, she'pan."

"The Kel of the Darks," she said softly, "is not wholly ignorant; and therefore it is a harder service. No, perhaps it is not possible. But I cannot accept any other thing. Do you not believe that the gods still favor the People?"

He shrugged, self-conscious in his ignorance, helpless as a kel'en always was in games of words. He did not know whether she played ironies or not.

"I cast us both," she said then. *"Shon'ai."*

This he understood, a mystery that Kel easily fathomed: he made a fist, a pantomime of the catch of *shon'ai,* and his heart lightened.

"Shon'ai," he echoed. "It is good enough."

"Then we should be moving," she said.

"We are ready," he said. He gathered himself up and went to Duncan and shook at him. "Come," he told Duncan, and while Duncan began to stir about he made a pack of their remaining belongings. The water he meant to carry himself, and a small light flask also he meant for Melein, for it was not wise to make Duncan independent in that regard or to make her dependent, should it come to trouble—though neither he nor she, whole of limb and untroubled by enemies, needed a flask in a land where they knew every plant and stone.

He threw the bundle of supplies at Duncan's feet.

"Where are we going?" Duncan asked, without moving to pick it up. It was a civil question. Niun shrugged, giving him all the answers he meant to give, with the same civility.

"I am not your beast of burden," Duncan said, a thin, under-the-breath piece of rebellion. He kicked at the bundle, spurning it.

Niun looked at it, and looked at him, without haste. "The she'-pan does not work with the hands. Being kel'en. I do not bear burdens, while there are others to bear them. If you were dead, I would carry it. Since you are not, you will carry it."

Duncan seemed to consider how seriously that was meant, and reached the correct conclusion. He picked it up, and slid his arms into the ropes of the pack.

Then Niun did find some pity for him, for the man was a manner of kel'en, and avowed he was not of a lower caste, but he would not fight for it. It was a matter of the yin'ein, *a'ani*, honorable combat; and he reckoned that with mri weapons the human was as helpless as a kath'en.

Perhaps, he thought, he had been wrong to insist upon this point, and to have taken some small part of the weight for himself would not have overburdened his pride. It was one thing to war against the tsi'mri kel'en's species; it was another to break him under the weight of labor in Kesrith's harsh environment.

He said nothing, all the same. It troubled him, the while they started out together, the three of them, and the dus lumbering along by his side. It was a difficult question, how it was honorable to deal at close quarters with a human.

It had been the death of the People, that humans refused *a'ani* and preferred mass warfare; and he began to realize now that humans simply could not fight.

Tsi'mri.

He felt fouled, deeply distressed by what he had discovered. He wished to change what he had said, and could not, for his pride's sake. And he began to think over and over again how bitter the war had been, that so many had perished without knowing the nature of the enemy.

But it was not his to change this, even now. He was not a caste that made ultimate decisions. He reminded himself of this, wondering how much Intel had known.

By the Deog'hal slash they ascended into the high hills, not following the usual track to Sil'athen, lest some survivor down in the city find them the more easily and finish what they had begun at the edun. It was a hard climb, and one which took a great deal from Melein, and from Duncan, laboring as he was under his burden.

"I was too long sitting in the she'pan's tower," Melein breathed when they had come to the crest. She coughed and tried to smother it, while Duncan sank down in a heap, disengaged himself from the ropes and lay upon his pack. Niun poured a little water to ease Melein's throat, and deep in his heart he was afraid for her, for Melein was not wont to be so easily tired; and he marked how she limped, and sometimes held her arm to her side.

"I think that you are hurt," he said softly.

She made a deprecating gesture. "I fell, closing the door to the storeroom. It is nothing."

He hoped that she was right in that. He gave her to drink again, spendthrift with the water, but it was likely that they would come on more soon enough. He drank enough himself to moisten his mouth, and saw the human looking at him with an intent gaze, unwilling to plead.

"For moisture only," he said, giving him half a measure. "Be slow with it."

The human drank as he had drunk, beneath the veil, keeping his face covered, and handed back the cap with a nod that achieved some grace.

"Where are we going?" Duncan asked again, his voice gone hoarse.

"Human," said Melein, startling them both. "Why does it matter to you to know?"

Duncan drew a breath to answer at once; Niun reached out and caught his arm in a hard grip.

"Before you speak," Niun said to him, "Understand that she is a she'pan. The Kel deals with outsiders; the she'pan does not. You are honored that she even looks at you. If you speak a word that offends her, I will surely kill you out of hand. So perhaps you will be more comfortable to direct your words to me, so that you will not offend against her."

Duncan looked from one to the other of them, as if he thought they were making mock of him, or threatening him in some way he could not comprehend.

"I am very serious," said Niun. "Direct your answer to me."

"Tell her," said Duncan then, "that I'm more interested in returning to my own people alive. Tell her what I told you last night. That offer still stands. I may be about to get you offworld."

"Duncan," said Melein, "I already know what you would like to ask, and I will not answer yet. But you may tell us when your people will come. You know that, surely."

Duncan hesitated in evident distress, surely weighing their purposes. "A matter of days," he said in a low voice. "A very few days—maybe sooner than I would figure. And they're going to find ruins at the city; and the regul will be left to tell them whatever story they like about what happened night before last."

"Tsi'mri," said Melein deprecatingly, which Duncan did not understand.

"The she'pan means," Niun answered that look, "that what outsiders do is not our concern. We have no brothers and no masters. We do not serve regul any longer. Perhaps you do not understand, Duncan, that we are the last mri. The ship *Ahanal* contained all the survivors of the war and the edun contained the rest; and the regul know us, that if they do not finish what they began at the port, then we are likely to deal them hurt. Being regul, they will not wish to meet us face to face to do this, and they will probably try to convince your species to do the work for them. You see how it is. You do better not to press us with questions. There are things to be thought of in their time, if this happens or if that happens—but you do well not to ask so that we will not have to think of it."

Duncan absorbed all that answer in silence, and sat with his arms wrapped about his knees, hands clenched until the knuckles went white.

"Duncan," Melein said then, "it is a saying among us that *Said is done.* So we do not say, so that we are not obligated to do. We do not trap with words, like the regul do. Ask no more questions."

And she held out her left hand to Niun, gesturing that she wanted help to rise. It hurt her, thought he was very careful.

"There are clouds," she observed, looking toward the east. "May it descend to the regul."

By afternoon the sky was entirely overcast, sparing them the heat of the direct sun, bringing a chill to the air; and it became clear that the clouds were doing as Melein had wished they would do: that upon the ruin of the city and the port would come storm.

Once, when she gazed over her shoulder toward the plain and looked upon the lightning that flashed in that shadowed quarter, she held some impulse that made the dus moan in startlement and shy off from her: it was Melein that had done it, for Niun knew himself innocent, and the dus sought his side afterward.

But the clouds shed no water on them, and their flasks were only a quarter full when they came to the end of the long upland rise and entered the flat highland. By late afternoon Duncan was staggering with weariness and would gladly have stopped at any time, but Niun considered the possibility of aircraft seeking them and was not willing to stop in the open, not for Duncan's sake.

He looked often at Melein, anxious for her, but she walked without appearing to suffer overmuch.

And toward sunset there was a luin-cluster on the horizon, twisted trunks like a mirage against the red sun, bare limbs tufted with small leaves only at the ends.

"There is water," Niun told Duncan. "Tonight will be an easy camp and you will have enough to drink."

And Duncan, who had begun to lag, expended a last effort, and kept the pace they, unburdened, set toward the trees.

And walked among them, careless.

"'Ware!" Melein cried, seeing it, even as Niun did, the glassy strands spread in the evening light.

Niun whipped up his pistol and fired before Duncan had time to know what had befallen him: and the windflower died, a stench, glassy tendrils blackened. But where it touched Duncan's flesh, on hands and forehead, the red sprang up at once, and Duncan, his clothing covered with the tendrils, fell and writhed on the sand in agony.

"Ch'au!" Niun cursed his stupidity. "Still! Lie still!" And Duncan lay quietly then, shuddering as with the av-tlen's point he lifted the tendrils from Duncan's flesh. He pulled them from the cloth too, and urged Duncan to his feet, there to stand while he inspected the black cloth for any transparent remnant.

Then Duncan went a few feet away and was dryly sick for some few moments.

Niun cleansed the *av-tlen* in the sand and with it cut the trunk of a luin that had not been poisoned by the windflower. He took from his belt a small steel tube and drove it easily into the soft wood, and the sweet liquid began to flow, pure and clean of Kesrith's dust.

He filled the first flask and gave it to Melein, so that she might indulge her thirst to the full, for there were many luin. He drank the second, rapidly filled from a second tree; and the third he filled he took to Duncan, who had not succeeded in being as sick as he doubtless wished to be after his shock. The human simply lay on the ground and shuddered.

"It is a point worth remembering," Niun echoed Eddan's words to him on a less painful encounter, "that where there is water on Kesrith, there are enemies and predators. The pain is all, and you are lucky. It will pass. If you had been alone, you would have been wholly ensnared and the windflower would have been the end of you."

"I saw nothing," Duncan said, and swallowed a sip of the water, fighting the pain.

"When you walk among luin, walk with the light in your face, so that the strands of windflowers cast across the sun and shine; and mind where you step." He indicated where a little burrower had his lair, a place marked by a flat and a tiny depression. He flung a pebble. The sand erupted, and there was a flash of a pale back, gone again as the little burrower dived and fluttered his mantle, settling sand over himself again.

"They are venomed," said Niun, "and even a little one can make a man very sick. But since they grow large enough to engulf a dus whole, the venom does not matter much to us. Burrowers lair among the luin, and in shadowed places and among rocks where there is sand to cover them. There are not many large ones. The ha'dusei eat them, if they do not eat the dusei, before they grow to great size. There is a very large old one by the way we will pass tomorrow. I think he has been there all my lifetime. Burrowers are like regul: when they grow so big, they do not move much."

The little one, disturbed and angry, fluttered off under the sand, a moving ripple, to settle again deeper among the luin.

There was a general shifting about of others of his kind, and a jo, harmless, detached itself from its successful bark-imitation on a luin and fluttered away through the twilight.

"Drink your fill," Niun said to the distressed human, feeling pity for him, and Duncan slowly did so, while Niun made them a supper of the supplies they had brought. They would make many a meal off the burrowers themselves, meat unpalatable and tough as rubber; but this night Melein was suffering, and they had starved the night before and most of the day. He was extravagant, and gave to Duncan an equal share with them, considering that he had confiscated what of Duncan's gear was useful, including his rations.

Across the sky toward the lowlands there was continued lightning, ill luck for the regul.

And they rested with the dus for warmth, and with its ward impulse to keep the ha-dusei at bay, so that they slept secure in the luin grove.

In the morning they gathered up their gear once more; and Niun considered the matter with a gnawing of his lip and a frown, and finally, brusquely, snatched several rolls of cloth and the food from the human's burden and did them up himself.

"In the case that you do not watch where you walk," Niun said in a harsh tone, "the burrower that gets you will not have our shelter and our food."

The human looked at him, marked across the brow by a bloody stripe of his encounter with the windflower; and Niun did not think that the human would have forgotten his words of the day previous, that he would carry no burden. He glowered at Duncan, discouraging any reminder of this.

"I learn quickly," Duncan said, and Niun reckoned that among the things Duncan had learned was the art of answering a kel'en civilly.

Chapter Twenty

The air was unimaginably foul, tainted by so many frightened regul. It was dark, save for the lights on the two sled consoles and the four life-battery lamps the shelter provided. Power elsewhere was out. The water plants were down. There was talk of seeking water Kesrithi style, from the land, but none of the younglings were sure that they could accomplish this; and they were not anxious to go out into the contaminated exterior, or across the seething flats.

Hulagh had not yet ordered them. He would do so, Stavros did not doubt, when he himself began to thirst.

The sleds were on battery. To this also there was a limit; but Stavros and Hulagh, elders, consumed vital power as they consumed food and water unrationed, because it was unquestioned that elders must be supported by the young. Stavros found it in him to pity the harried secretary, Hada, who dispensed food and water that remained to 300 other younglings, and likewise ministered to Hulagh and himself. They were jammed into the shelter so tightly that the youngest and least could not lie down to sleep; but the sleds were accorded their maneuvering room. The younglings gave back from them with deference that was next to worship; indeed their whole hope for survival centered on the presence of elders among them. They talked little. They all faced Hulagh, row on row of bone-shielded faces and blunt heads, and eyes glittered in the almost-dark and nostril-slits worked in a slow rhythm that seemed to Stavros, in a moment of bizarre humor, to be tending toward unison.

And in the long hours he noted something else, that there were not a few who fell asleep and did not waken.

Bai, favor, he signaled, spelling slowly in regul symbols on the screen. *I think some of the younglings are ill.*

Hulagh's great body heaved as he looked, and heaved again with a hiss of mirth. "No, reverence-human, they are asleep. They are to sleep until your assistance comes. They consume less in that state."

And in increasing numbers the young, beginning with the youngest, slipped into that state, until almost all were dormant.

And bai Hulagh himself began to drowse. He recovered from this with a jerk and a rumbled curse, and called to Hada. "Food," he ordered. "Be quick, witless."

The thick, sour-smelling soup was offered likewise to Stavros, but he declined it, almost retching. This troubled Hada, but it gave the portion to Hulagh, between whose thin lips the paste disappeared rapidly.

"You do not eat," Hulagh observed.

I do not need to eat, Stavros replied, and in honesty: *Your food does not agree with me. But I would have soi.*

Hada scrambled to accommodate this wish, feverish, almost maniac in its desire to please. It offered the hot liquid to Stavros' good hand, with a straw for his ease, and hovered near him.

Hulagh laughed, a rumbling, a series of hisses. "Go, egg-stealer, and sit with the other younglings." And Hada visibly cringed, and slunk aside, on small tottering steps.

"Hada knows," Hulagh explained, waxed almost affable under the pressure of their long wait, under the need to be pleasant with humans and human ways, "that if we are here much longer, there will be shorter rations; and Hada is greedy. I indulge this youngling. I shall keep it if it continues to please. I may keep all. I have lost," he added sadly, "my own."

With the ship, Stavros understood. *My sorrow, reverence.*

"And mine for the loss of your own youngling." The great gossamer-clad monster sighed and lapsed into a long reverie.

And Stavros, his sled nose-to-nose with that of Hulagh, hurled his temper at the weak fingers of his left hand. They gave only slightly. The right hand clenched. He had ceased to fear that the paralysis would spread or that it would affect his mind, but he was ceasing to hope that it would ever ease completely. He remained grateful for regul technology, if not for regul.

Hulagh's condolences were honest, doubtless, but it did not
mean that the regul's hands were clean in the matter. Stavros regarded the drowsing regul with narrowed eyes. Now, shut in a
shelter with the regul, was an inopportune moment to state the obvious, that Hulagh had had somewhat to do with the disappearance of Duncan, and that Stavros, conversely, was innocent in the
loss of the bai's ship and the younglings aboard it.

In regul morality, disposing of a youngling was a serious matter, but only in terms of the affront offered its elder and its doch.
A regul would as soon face an elder's wrath over the loss of a
youngling as that same elder's wrath over some matter of shady
dealing discovered in trade; and Stavros reckoned that the same
ruthless logic just might apply to eliminating a lone elder whose
doch could prove hostile, given the information which that elder
possessed.

Regul did not lie, he still believed, but they were fully capable
of murder, whereby lies could be rendered unnecessary. And they
feared him on the one hand and hoped for his help on the other,
and he fostered that hope in them as he cherished his own life.

He began to reckon the mind of bai Hulagh of doch Alagn, that
here was a desperate fellow, who had suffered a very dangerous
loss in the eyes of his kind. And therefore, while it seemed profitable, Hulagh, like a good merchant prince, was dealing for compromise.

It was a compromise out of which humankind could win a great
deal.

But part of that settlement, Stavros was determined, would be
an accounting for a certain lost SurTac, on whom Stavros had settled rather more affection than he had admitted to himself. He had
not loved his own children, of whom he had seen little, locked as
he was in the reclusive life of a scholar of Kiluwa, or later, while
he was busy in government and at the university. He had found
many other things more important than to trouble himself with
the issue of several of his young passions, that had given him
first an assortment of sons and thereafter grandchildren and
great-grandchildren—who sought him out mostly because a
Kiluwan connection was prestigious. Some of them, he knew,
hated him with the same dedicated zeal with which they sought
promotions based on his influence.

But he missed Duncan. Duncan had come, like others who had ridden Stavros' reputation to reach for wealth, with the motives of the others; and yet Duncan had given him a constant and earnest duty, earnest in his attempts to penetrate Kiluwan formality, simply because it was Duncan's nature to do so.

Stavros had never learned how to answer that. Nor, for the regul, did he admit to grief which they would not have understood. But in addition to an accounting which the regul owed for Kiluwa, there was that for an inconsequential SurTac.

He did not, all the same, regret having sent Duncan, even at such cost. Events had damaged the regul and exacted satisfaction of them, and placed them at human mercy; and this was very much to Stavros' satisfaction. This was partial payment for Kiluwa.

It would be full payment, when he seized the reins of control from bai Hulagh, and began to bend doch Alagn into agreement with humans. This was revenge of a sort that both Hulagh and Kiluwa could appreciate—the more so when he ascertained who among regul was directly responsible for Kiluwa and found the means to deal with them. Being Kiluwan, Stavros entertained a hatred specific and logical: there was a species called regul; but the species called regul had not destroyed Kiluwa. It was one doch; and its name was Holn, and it was not represented here.

There had been a decimation of Holn at their landing. This did not satisfy Stavros, who was not interested in bloodshed. It was the decline of Holn he wanted, its elimination from power among regul.

And Hulagh, controlled, an ally of humans, could become the instrument of this policy.

"Elder," Hulagh rumbled at last, "it is certain that you have authority over your people?"

Unless mri intervened and started something wider, Stavros replied. *I have authority over the force that is coming to Kesrith.*

"Favor," said Hulagh. "The mri will no longer be a factor in relations between us. They are gone. There are no more mri."

This was news. Stavros flashed a question sign, unadorned by words.

"The ship," said Hulagh, "contained all the survivors of mri-kind. We have disposed of this plague that kept our two species at war."

Hulagh had waited to divulge that piece of news. Stavros heard it, at first appalled at such a concept, the destruction of a sapient species; and then suspicious—but the regul did not lie. He began to contemplate the possibilities of a universe without the mri, and found the possibilities for human profit enormous.

"It is clear," said Hulagh, "that total rearrangement of human-regul relations is in order. Doch Alagn might find interest in helping this come about."

Stavros was shocked a second time, and recognized that dismay for a human reaction, based on a morality to which Hulagh could not possibly subscribe. There was no particular reason that doch Alagn should refrain from an offer that, in a human state, would amount to treason. Doch Alagn was in financial and political difficulty. Hulagh was seeking alignment with the powers that had control of the resources he desired.

Humanity's grudge, Stavros answered after due thought, *is with doch Holn. It would be possible to arrive at new accommodations with advantage to both our interests.*

Hulagh's lips parted in a regul smile. A slow hiss betokened his pleasure. "We shall explore this," he said. "We shall, most excellent Stavros."

And he wakened Hada and ordered soi, and remembered this time to order it sweetened, to Stavros' personal preference.

But before it was prepared, Hada came puffing back, waving his hands in agitation. "The ship," he breathed. "Be gracious, elders, the human ship, early—communications report—"

Hulagh's gesture cut the youngling off abruptly. The bai's lips continued parted, his nostrils dilated in what Stavros had learned was an expression of anxiety. The bai's total attitude was that of a man with a nervous smile, displaying good manners amid subdued terror.

"You will surely wish then," said bai Hulagh, "to greet these representatives of your people and explain the situation. Assure them of our regret for the condition of the port, reverence."

We will manage, Stavros answered, beside himself with anxiety and restraining it, remembering how important it was that Hulagh be reassured. *Have confidence, reverence, that you have nothing to dread if your younglings will remain calm and not hamper operations.*

And he turned his sled toward the control section of the shelter, following the rolling gait of Hada Surag-gi, who by regul standards, was almost running.

The big doors of the shelter opened, and beams glared through the dim interior, handled by the fantastic shapes of suited men, who walked heavy-footed through the ranks of dormant younglings. The door was closed again, a precaution. The second man used a counter, reckoning what radiation might have gotten into the shelter. Conscious younglings scurried to clear them a path, chittering in terror.

Stavros slid his vehicle forward, faced a suited form and saw the blind-glassed head pause in an attitude of astonishment.

"Consul Stavros?"

The tab on the suit said GALEY and the rank was lieutenant.

"Yes," Stavros said, turned the communications screen by remote and spelled out a message on the basic-alphabet module, not trusting his slurred speech for complicated messages. *I am inconvenienced by an accident. Speech is awkward, but prosthetics are very adequate. Speak normally to me and watch the screen. Be respectful of these regul. It will be necessary to transfer them to safety if you cannot guarantee normal operations here in the building.*

"Sir," Galey said, seeming confused by the situation, then drew a breath and let it go again. "You're in command down here. What instructions? I'm afraid the power is going to be a major problem. We can possibly get a crew working on it, and you seem clean of contamination, but there are some considerable hot spots toward the port. The station is intact. We would rather evacuate."

Buidling can be occupied? Livable?

"This building? Yes, sir. It seems so."

Then we stay. Untoward weather a problem here. I have rest under control.

"The mri, sir—" Galey said. "We're not clear what happened here."

We have a problem, Lt. Galey, but we're resolving it. Kindly dispose your men so that we can resume normal operations here in the building. The communications station is accessible through that door. You will excuse me if I do not go with you.

"Yes, sir," said Galey, and gave his courtesies to the regul also, wooden and perfunctory. The marines with him began to move about various duties, on suit phones, doubtless, where regul would not be privy to exchanges of comment and instruction.

"You deal with younglings," Hulagh observed. "Favor. Are there other elders involved here?"

Other authorities, Stavros reckoned the bai's meaning, authorities who could complicate agreements made between them. *My apologies, bai Hulagh. This was an older youngling. And the elder who commands them must, as you surely remember from the treaty, defer to me where it regards the administration of Kesrith and its area. There is, however, one matter wherein his authority and mine might tend to cross.*

"And this one matter, human bai?"

My missing assistant is military personnel. The bai of the arriving ship may feel that he can settle this matter best. This would be an occasion for him to intrude his authority into my domain here. Naturally I do not wish this. I feel that it would smooth matters over if it were possible for answers to be given in this matter.

Hulagh's nostrils fluttered in rapid agitation. "Favor, reverence. We might suggest a search of the Dus plain, where there was conflict between my younglings and the mri outlaws. This is an unpleasant surmise, but if there are remains to be found—"

Stavros looked on the anxious bai without mercy. *It is then the conclusion of the bai that this youngling is dead?*

"It is most probable, reverence."

But if he were not, it is more likely that one of your staff could direct a search with more success than one of the ship's officers might. This is possible, is it not, bai? It would greatly augment my authority here and ease negotiations between us if it were possible that this lost youngling could be recovered. He is, of course, merely a youngling, and his experiences during the mri action would doubtless influence his mind to hysteria and cloud his judgments, so that no testimony he could give could be taken seriously. But it would please me if he were recovered alive.

The bai considered these things, and the understandings implicit in the words. "Indeed," said bai Hulagh, "there is such an expert on my staff, a person familiar with the terrain. With your staff's cooperation, this could be arranged at once."

My gratitude, reverence. I will see to the disposition of necessities with the ship. And Stavros turned his sled away, seeking out Galey, while his hearing caught bai Hulagh urgently summoning Hada Surag-gi.

The reaction began to strike him. He found it difficult for the moment to concentrate on the numerical signals that activated the various programs of the sled. He found his eyes misting. This was unaccustomed. He had the emotional reaction under control again by the time he swung the sled in with casual nonchalance beside Galey, who did not seem to know whether to offer condolences or congratulations on survival.

"You're alone here, sir?" Galey asked.

As you have noticed, difficulties abound. No delays. Is Koch in command up there?

"Yes, sir."

Then get me contact with him directly. I can patch this console in with the main board. Are you able to get a ship down here with sufficient personnel to staff work crews and give me office staff?

"Not quickly. The port's completely gone. But the station is in good shape. Servos everywhere." Galey bent over the console of the com unit, fingering regul controls helplessly.

"Here," Stavros said, with some satisfaction, keyed in and started the sequence of changes that put them through to the warship *Saber,* which had brought them all that clutter of personnel that would begin to make Kesrith human: soil experts, scientists.

And weapons.

His command, Kesrith, his. There was no med staffer going to rule him unfit to govern; and deep in his heart he knew that he needed that hulking merchant prince of the Alagn as much as doch Alagn presently needed him.

He saw the shock on the face of the com officer of *Saber;* and at once that face vanished, replaced by that of Stavros' military counterpart, Koch.

"Stavros?" Koch asked.

A little difficulty speaking, he keyed the answer, replacing the visual. *We have regul stranded down here. Stand by to assist us with on-world operations. We need food, drinkable water.*

"We were not prepared for regul nationals."

Unforeseen circumstances. All decisions regarding Kesrith and regul are mine. Situation here is under control. Presently seeking my aide, possible casualty of attack by mri. Hot areas reportedly confined to port. I request military personnel detached from Saber *to my command until we can clean up.*

"Excellency," said Koch, "the medical facilities of *Saber* are at your disposal if you will care to come up to the station."

Negative. Regul services are adequate. The situation is too urgent. My condition is good, considering. I am pursuing matters under my authority granted as governor of Kesrith. Send down scientists, military aides, all attached personnel and equipment as soon as area is cleared.

"It may be advisable to wait."

Send down personnel as requested.

There was a long delay. "All right," said Koch. "A medic will accompany the party."

On Kesrith, said Stavros, *medic will await my convenience.*

Koch digested this also. At last he nodded, accepting. "You have the authority, right enough. But ship's personnel stay under my command. You'll have the civs as soon as we can find solid ground for them. Starship *Flower* is attached to your personal service, with my compliments, sir. She's probe, though, not combat. Does the situation warrant immediate armed support?"

Negative.

"There is weather down there."

This is evidently frequent. Wait, then. We are pursuing operations here with available personnel. You are invited to come planetside and exchange courtesies when we get the wreckage cleared.

A sled hummed into the vicinity. Stavros heard it, and put them momentarily on visual from his side again, watching with satisfaction as Koch beheld a regul elder for the first time.

This is bai Hulagh, Stavros told him, cutting out the visual again. *A most influential regul, sir, if you please. We have achieved a certain necessary cooperation here, which is to the advantage of both species.*

"Understood," Koch said slowly, and seemed utterly taken aback: a military man, Koch, born and bred. He had been presented a situation with which he could not deal, and fortunately recognized it.

"You'll get your help," Koch said, and Stavros closed out the communication with an inward satisfaction, cast a look at Galey. *Scan the area here,* he said to the lieutenant. *And when you've made sure where it's safe, we'll start clearing these younglings back to normal duties. This is the bai's staff. All due considerations to them, Lt. Galey.*

"Reports are coming in," he said. "The whole area seems cool and secure. The building seals held very well."

Stavros breathed a sigh of relief.

"My younglings," said Hulagh, "will find means of restoring the water and repairing the collectors for the power." He waved a massive hand. "Hada will attend other matters, given use of transport. I believe some of the vehicles at the water plant may have survived intact."

Chapter Twenty-one

At the entrance to Sil'athen a dus met them, warding with such strength that Niun's dus shied off. And there in the rocks, half buried in the sands, lay Eddan's remains; and not far away lay a tangle of black that had been Liran and Debas, and gold that had been Sathell.

Melein veiled herself and drew aside, being she'pan and unable to look upon death; but Niun came and reverently arranged the visor over Eddan's face, and it was long before he could look up and face the human that hovered uncertainly by.

He cleansed his hands in the sand, and made the reverence sign and rose. The human also made such a sign, in his own fashion, a respect which Niun accepted as it was given. "They chose this end," he said to Duncan, "and it was better for them here than for those that stayed."

And he poured a little of their precious water, and turned his back to wash, hands and face, and veiled again. When he looked up at the rocks he saw two other dusei, that began to come down from their heights; and he gave back at once.

His own dus came between, and tried to approach the three warding beasts that had formed a common front against them. Noses extended, they circled back and forth, and then the great gentle creature that had been Eddan's, or so Niun thought it, reared up and cried out, driving the dus away. But the smallest of the three hesitated between, and followed the stranger-dus of Niun, and its fellow came after.

The largest, Eddan's, gave a plaintive moan and retreated from these traitor-dusei, that he no longer knew. Niun felt its anger, and trembled; but when he moved away from this place, not alone his own dus came, but the two that had been of Liran and Debas, a tight triangle with his own. They called and moaned, and would not yet suffer Niun to come near them, but they came away from their duty all the same, choosing life, leaving matters to the dus of Eddan, who settled by his dead and remained faithful.

"Lo'a'ni dus," Niun saluted that one softly, with great respect; but he shut his heart to it, because the warding impulse was too strong to bear.

And he shouldered his burden again and began walking, his course and Duncan's converging with that of Melein.

There was no need to speak of what they had found. The dusei walked ahead of them, and now and then one would make to go back and go toward Duncan, but Niun's dus would not allow this, and constantly circled toward the rear to prevent them when they did so. Soon they seemed to understand that this particular tsi'mri was under safe-conduct and gave up their attempts on him.

They were at the entrance to the inner valley of Sil'athen, and here was another sort of warder. Niun saw it across the flat sweep of sand, and, touching the human on the arm, he bent and picked up a tiny stone. He hurled it far, far out across the flat sand, toward the central depression.

It erupted, a circumference twenty times the length of a dus, a cloud of sand from the edge of the burrower's mantle and it rose and dived again a few lengths farther.

The human swore in a tone of awe.

"I have shown you," said Niun, "so that you will understand that a man without knowledge of this land—and without a dus to walk with him—will not find his way across it. Across the great sands, there are said to be larger ones than what you saw. The dusei smell them out. They smell out other dangers too. Even mri do not like to walk this country alone, although we can do it. I do not think you can."

"I understand you," said Duncan.

They walked quietly thereafter, near the wall of the cliffs, where the safe course was, past caves sealed and marked with stones, and the strange shapes of Sil'athen's rocks one by one passed behind them, ringing them about and shutting off view of the way they had come.

"What is this place?" Duncan asked in a lowered voice, as they passed the high graves of the she'panei.

"Nla'ai'mri," said Niun. "Sil'athen, the burying place of our kind."

And thereafter Duncan said nothing, but looked uneasily from one side of the valley to the other as they passed, and once backward, over his shoulder, where the wind erased their tracks, wiping clean all the trace that men had ever walked this way.

Melein led them now, walking at their head, her hand on the back of Niun's dus, which ambled slowly beside her, and the beast even seemed to enjoy that contact. Deep into the canyons they went, by a path that Niun had never walked, down the aisle of rock that belonged to the tombs of the she'panei. Here there were signs graven on the rocks—names, perhaps, of ancient she'panei, or directions: Melein read them, and Niun trusted her leading, that she knew their way though she herself had never walked it.

She tired, and it seemed at times that she must surely stop, but she would not, only paused for breath now and again, and went on. The sun that was at noon became the fervent blaze of afternoon, and sank so that they walked in the cold shadow of the cliffs, dangerous if not for the protecting dusei that probed the way for them.

Deep in that shadow they came to the blind end of the cliffs, and Niun looked to Melein, suddenly wondering if she had not after all lost their way, or whether this was where she meant that they should stop. But she gazed upward at a trail that he had not seen until he followed the direction of her gaze, that could not be seen at all save from this vantage point. It led up and up into the red rocks, toward a maze of sandstone pillars that thrust fingers at the sky.

"Niun," Melein said then, and cast a glance backward.

He looked where she did, toward Duncan, who, exhausted in the thin air, had slumped to rest over his pack. The dusei were moving toward him. One extended a paw. Duncan froze, lying still, his head still pillowed on the pack.

"Yai!" Niun reproved the dus, who guiltily retracted the curious paw. The dusei in general retreated, radiating mingled confusion.

And in his own mind was unease at the thought of entering that steep, tangled maze with the human in their company, where a misstep could be the end of them.

"What shall I do with him?" he asked of Melein, in the high language, so that Duncan could not understand. "He should not be here. Shall I find a way to be rid of him?"

"The dusei will manage him," she said. "Let him alone."

He started to protest, not for his own sake, but for fear for her; but she did not look as if she were prepared to listen.

"He will go last when we are climbing," he said, and gathering in his belly all the same was a knot of fear. Intel had seen the future clearly; *I have an ill feeling,* she had said the night they all died; and he had such a dread now, a cold, clear premonition that here was a point of no return, that he was losing some chance or passing something; and the human wound himself deeper and deeper into his mind.

He did not want him. He carried Duncan in his mind the way he carried the memories of the attack, indelible. He looked at the human and shuddered with sudden and vehement loathing, and found himself carrying the human's due burden, and not knowing what else to do with it. He fingered the pistol.

But he had been made kel'en for the honor of the People, not for outright butchery; and Melein had ordered otherwise, easing his conscience. He was not able to make such a decision. It was hers to say, and she had said, agreeing with his better conscience.

And suddenly Duncan was looking at him, and he slipped his fingers into his belt, trying to cover his thoughts and the motion at once. "Come," he said to Duncan. "Come, we are going up now."

He set himself first on the narrow climb, and saw at once that Melein was scarcely able to make the climb on that eroded, unused track. He braced his feet where he could and reached for her hand, and she took his fingers crosshanded, to favor her injured side. He moved very carefully, each time that he must give a gentle pull to help her, for he saw her face and knew that she was in great pain.

Duncan came after, and the dusei last of all, clumsy and scattering rocks that rattled into the deep canyon, but their claws and great strength made them surer-footed than they looked.

And halfway, the sound of an aircraft reached them.

It was Melein's keen hearing that caught it first, between steps, as she was resting: and she turned and pointed where it circled above the main valley. It could not see or detect them where they were, and they were free to watch it, that tiny speck in the rosy halflight that remained.

Niun had view not only of that, but of Duncan's back, as the human stood holding his place against a great boulder and looking outward at that ship; and he could not think how gladly Duncan would have run to signal it, and how he might well do so if he had some future chance.

They were no longer alone in the world.

"Let us climb," said Melein, "and get off this cliffside before it circles this way."

"Come," said Niun sharply to Duncan, with hatefulness in his tone; and Duncan turned and climbed after them, away from what in all likelihood was hope of rescue.

Looking down another time to help Melein, Niun looked out and did not see the aircraft; and that gave him no comfort at all. It could as easily appear directly overhead, passing the cliffs and sandstone fingers that gave them only partial cover.

And to his relief, once they gained the top of the cliffs, they were not faced with another flat, but went down a slight decline, and followed a winding track among sandstone pillars that were now burning red against the purpling sky. There was strong wind, that skirled small clouds among the pillars and erased their tracks as they made them.

Duncan's dry cough began again and continued a time until the human had caught his breath from the climb. They were at high altitude, and it was far drier air than the lowlands. Here on the highlands, over much of the rest of the land, there was no rain, only blowing sand. A sea lay beyond, the The'asacha, but it was small and dead as the Alkaline Sea that bordered the regul city; and beyond that sea was a mountain chain, the Dogin, the mere skeletons of eroded mountains that still were tall enough to cast the winds this way and that across the backbone of the continent, and generated storms that never fell on the uplands plain, but down-country, in the flats.

The clouds that rimmed the sky now were headed to shed their load of moisture on the lowlands, affording them neither concern for the storm nor hope of water from it. All that it would bring them was a dark sky and a hard and dangerous walk without the stars.

The sound of the aircraft intruded suddenly upon Niun's hearing: he shepherded human and dusei toward the deepest shadows, in the gathering dark—Melein had sought shelter at once. If the aircraft saw anything it would be the image of a dus, a hot, massive silhouette for their instruments, something that was common enough to see in the wilds. If they fired at every dus on Kesrith, they would be a long time in their searching.

It passed. Niun, his fist entangled in the human's robes, a grip he had not relaxed since he herded them in together, let go and drew his first even breath.

"We may rest here a moment," said Melein in a thin, tired voice. "It is a long walk from here—I must rest."

Niun looked at her, seeing her pain, that she had tried so long to hide. On the climb he had felt her every wince in his own vitals. And they were not to rest long. He was distressed with this, feeling that she was spending her last strength against this urgency to go farther.

And without her, there was nothing.

He took the cloth for a blanket, and settled her against the side of the dus, into that friendly warmth, and was glad when she relaxed against that comfort he offered, and the line of pain knit into her brow, eased and began to vanish.

"I will be all right," she said, touching his hand.

And then her eyes widened and he whirled about upon a shadow—a darting reach for a water flask and Duncan was gone, into the maze of rocks in the dark.

Niun swore and sprang after him, hearing the moaning roar of the dusei at once behind him. He came round the side of a pillar, half expecting ambush, which would have been idiocy on the human's part, and did not meet it.

Nor was there sight or sign of Duncan.

And he had left Melein, and sweat broke out on him, only to think what could happen if Duncan circled on them and attacked her, hurt as she was.

Then the sound of a dus hunting arose, moaning carried on the wind, and that cry meant quarry sighted. He blessed the several gods of his caste and ran toward that sound, pistol in hand.

So he met Melein, a pale wraith in the dark, and a dus beside her: and together they found the blind way where the other dusei had Duncan pent.

"Yai!" Niun called the beasts, before they should close in and kill; and they wheeled in a slope-shouldered and truculent withdrawal, only enough to let Duncan rise from the ledge where he had been cornered. He would not. He huddled there, unveiled in the scramble he had made, his naked face contorted with exhaustion and anger. He coughed rackingly, and his nose poured blood.

"Come down," said Melein.

But he would not, and Niun went in after him, pushing the dusei aside. Then Duncan made to move, but he fell again, and sat still and dropped his head on his folded arms.

Niun took the strap of the water flask and ripped it from Duncan's hand, and let him rest the moment, for they were all hard-breathing.

"It was a good attempt," said Niun. "But the next time I will kill you; it is a wonder that the dusei did not kill you this time."

Duncan lifted his face, jaw set in anger. He shrugged, a gesture of defiance, a gesture spoiled by an attack of helpless coughing.

"You would have signaled the airship," said Melein, "and brought them down on us."

Duncan shrugged again, and came to his feet, went with them of his own accord in leaving the blind pocket. The dusei were still blood-roused, and confused by being set on and drawn off their quarry; and Niun walked between them and the human. Melein followed after them as they went back to the place where they had abandoned their gear in the chase.

There they sank down where they had begun to rest, doubly exhausted now; and Niun stared at Duncan thoughtfully, thinking what might have happened, and what damage might have been done them.

There was Melein, fragile with her injury.

And there was an aircraft in the vicinity that wanted only the least error from them, the least slip into the open at the wrong moment, in order to locate and put an end to them.

"Cover your face," Niun said at last.

Duncan stared at him sullenly, as if he would defy that order, but in the end he lowered his eyes and arranged the veil, and stared at him still.

The dus moaned and reared up.

"Yai!" Niun ordered him, and he subsided, swaying nervously. The dus-anger stirred his own blood. He fought it down and mastered it, as a man must, who went among dusei, be more rational than they.

Duncan shifted aside, tearing his glance from them and the beasts, fixing it instead on the rock before them.

"We will move on," said Melein after a time, and pulled herself to her feet, carefully, painfully. She faltered, needed Niun's immediate hand to steady her.

But she set her hand then upon the dus, and the beast ambled out to the fore, and she was able to walk at its side, a slow pace and deliberate—the beast the only safety they had in this dark and close passage through the rocks.

Niun gathered up the water flasks, and left the human all the rest of the burden to carry, and hurried him on with a heavy hand, in among the two other dusei, before they should lose sight of Melein's pale figure.

The dusei, their oily hides immune to the poison of windflowers, their keen senses aware of other dangers, were the only means by which they could dare to move after dark in this place; and the dark, as Melein was surely reckoning, was friendly to them as it would not be to those that pursued them.

The long walk led them into more open areas, where they crossed fearfully exposed stretches of sand under the ragged clouds; and they made it in among the sandstone formations again as they heard the distant sound of the aircraft still in the area.

It came close. Duncan looked to the skies as if in hope, looked back sharply as Niun whipped the *av-tlen* from its sheath, a whisper of edged metal.

They faced each other, he and Duncan, standing still as the aircraft circled off again, out of hearing. Niun put the weapon back into its sheath with a practiced reverse.

"Someone," Duncan said, his voice almost unrecognizable from his raw throat, "someone knows where to look for you. I somehow don't think my people would know that."

It was sense that struck cold to Niun's heart. He glanced at Melein.

"We cannot stop again for rest," she said. "They must not find us, not here. We must be at the place before light and come away again. Niun, let us hurry."

He pushed the human gently. "Come," he said.

"Is it her?" Duncan asked, nodded back toward Melein without moving from where he stood. "Is it somehow to do with her that the regul keep after you?"

"It could not be," he said with assurance; and then another thought began to grow in him with horrid clarity, mental process working again where for a long time there had been only shock. He looked again to Melein, spoke in the hal'ari, the high language. "It could not be that they are hunting us. They could not know that we exist. What are two mri to them, with others dead? Or how could regul have reached the edun to know survivors left it? They could not have climbed among those ruins. It is this human, this cursed human. He has ties back in the city, a master, and for his sake the regul tracked me across the flats. If it is the regul, they are still on that trail. There are regul and humans at work in this thing."

Her eyes grew troubled. "Let us go," she said suddenly. "Let us go now, quickly. I do not know what we will do with him, but we cannot settle it now."

"What are you saying?" Duncan demanded of them suddenly in his hoarse voice. Perhaps there were certain words, a sideward look, that he had caught amid what they had said. Niun looked on him and thought uneasily that Duncan did suspect how little his life might weigh with them.

"Move," Niun said again, and pushed him, not gently. Duncan abandoned his questions and moved where he was told without arguing.

And if it were Duncan that was hunted, and regul were tracking them for his sake, then, Niun thought, Duncan would ultimately have to go to the enemy in such a manner to stop that search, in such a manner that he could not betray to them the fact that a she'pan of the People was still alive.

O gods, Niun mourned within himself, urged toward murder and dishonor, and not seeing any other course.

But the aircraft did not come again, and he was able to forget that threat in the urgency of their present journey—to put off thinking what he might have to do if the search resumed.

Twice, despite Melein's wishes, they had to rest, for Melein's sake; and each time, when Niun would have stayed longer, she insisted and they walked again, at last with Niun holding her arm, her slim fingers clenching upon his against the unsteadiness of her legs.

And after the mid of the night, they entered a narrow canyon that wound strangely, dizzily, and began to be a descent, where the walls leaned together threateningly over their heads and cast them into dark deeper than the night outside.

"Use your light," Melein said then. "I think there is stone overhead now entirely." And Niun used Duncan's penlight, ever so small a beam to find their footing. Down and down they went, a spiralling course and narrow, until they suddenly came upon a well of sky above them, where the night seemed brighter than the utter black they had travelled. Here was a widening, where walls were splashed with symbols the like of which had once adorned the edun itself.

The foremost dus reared aside, gave a roar that echoed horridly all up and down the passage, and Niun swung the beam leftward, toward the dus. There in a niche was a huddled knot of black rags and bones.

A guardian's grave.

Niun touched his brow in reverence to the unknown kel'en, and because he saw Duncan standing too near that holy place, he drew him back by the arm. Then he turned his light on the doorway where Melein stood, a way blocked by stones and sealed with the handprint of the guardian who had built that seal and set his life upon it.

Melein signed a reverence to the place with her hand, and suddenly turned to Duncan and looked at him sternly. "Duncan, past the grave of the guardian you must not go or you will die. Stand here and wait. Touch nothing, do nothing, see nothing." And to Niun: "Unseal it. It is lawful."

He gave the light to her and began, with the uppermost stones, to unseal what the guardian had warded so many years, a shrine so sacred that a kel'en would wait to the death in warding it. He knew what choice the man had made. Food and water the kel'en had had, the liberty thereafter to range within sight of his warding-place, to hunt in order to survive; but when the area failed him, when illness or harsh weather or advancing age bore upon the solitary kel'en, he had retreated to this chosen niche to die, faithful to his charge, his spirit hovering over the place in constant guardianship.

And perhaps Intel herself had stood here and blessed the closing of this door, and set her kiss upon the brow of the brave guardian, and charged him with this keeping.

One of the kel'ein who had come with her from Nisren, forty years ago, when the Pana had come to Kesrith.

The rocks rattled away from the opening with increasing ease, until Melein could step over what was left, setting foot into the cold interior. The light held in her hand ran over the walls, touched writings that were the mysteries of the Shrine of shrines, convoluted symbols that covered all the walls. For an instant Niun saw it, then sank down to his knees, face averted lest he see what he ought not. For a time he could hear her tiniest step in that sacred place; and then there was no sound at all, and he dared not move. He saw Duncan against the far wall of the well, the dusei by him, and not even they moved. He grew cold in his waiting and began to shiver from fear.

If she should not come back, he must still wait. And there was no stir of life within, not even the sound of a footstep.

One of the dusei moaned, its nerves afflicted with the waiting. It fell silent then, and for a long time there was nothing.

Then came a stirring, a quiet rhythmic sound at first from within the shrine; and at last he recognized it for the sound of soft weeping that became yet more bitter and violent.

"Melein!" he cried aloud, turning his eyes to that forbidden place; and shadows were moving within the doorway, a soft flow of lights. His voice echoed impiously round the walls and startled

the dusei, and he scrambled to his feet, terrified to go in and terrified not to.

The sound stopped. There was silence. He came as far as the
door, set his hand on it, nerved himself to go inside. Then he
heard her light steps somewhere far inside, heard the sounds of
life, and she did not summon him. He waited, shivering.

Things moved inside. There was the sound of machinery. It
continued, and yet at times he heard her steps clearly. And he remembered with a panic that he had turned his back on Duncan,
and whirled to see.

But the human only stood, no closer than Melein had permitted, and made no attempt to flee.

"Sit down," he bade Duncan sharply; and Duncan did so where
he stood, waiting. Niun cursed himself for seeking after Melein
and forgetting the charge she had set on him, to mind matters outside. He had put them both at Duncan's mercy had the human
braved the dusei to take advantage of it. He settled on the sand
himself, at such an angle that he could watch the human and yet
steal glances toward the shrine. He wrapped his arms about his
knees, locked his hands with numbing force, and waited, listening.

It was a long, long wait, in which he grew miserable and
changed position many a time. It seemed in his sense of time that
it must be drawing toward dawn, although the overcast sky visible
above them still was dark. And for a long, long time there was no
sound at all from within the shrine.

He hurled himself to his feet finally, impatient to go again to
the door, and then persuaded himself that he had no business to
invade that place. In his misery he paced the small area he had
to pace and looked down betimes at the human, who waited as he
had been warned to wait. Duncan's eyes were unreadable in the
almost-dark.

There was the sound of footsteps again. He turned upon the instant, saw the white flash of the penlight in the doorway. He saw
Melein, a shadow, carrying the tiny light in her fingers, her arms
clasped about something.

He went as close as he dared, saw that what she carried was
some sort of casing, ovoid, made of shining metal. It had a carrying bar recessed into it at one end, but she bore it as she might

have carried an infant, as something precious, though she staggered with the weight of it and could not step over the stones bearing it.

"Take it," she said in a faint, strained voice, and he galvanized himself out of his paralysis of will and reached forth his arms to receive it, dismayed by the weight of what she had managed to carry. It was cold and strange in balance and he shivered as he took it against him.

And he was cold again when he saw her face, moisture glistening there in the reddish light that began to spread behind her, and shadows leaping within the shrine from this side and that: she had turned once to look back, and then gazed back at him as from some vast distance.

Melein, he tried to say to her, and found it impossible. She was Melein still, and sister: but something else was contained in her, and he did not know how to speak to that, to call her back. He held out his hand, anxious at the fire behind her; and she took it and stepped over the rocks at the entry, and came with him. Her skin was cold. Her hand slipped lifelessly from his when she no longer needed him.

Duncan waited, backed a little from the both of them, continuing to stare into the light that was growing behind them. Perhaps he understood that something of great value was being destroyed. He looked dazed, confused.

There was left only the strange, cold ovoid. Niun bore it in both his arms as Melein started for the passage outward. He knew that he surely bore an essential part of the Pana, which name his caste could not even speak without fear, which a kel'en ought never to see, let alone handle.

The kel'en who had borne it here had devoted himself to die afterward, to hold it secret and undisturbed. This had been an honorable man, of the old way, the Kel of the Between; such a man would have been shocked at Niun s'Intel.

But he drew courage from holding it, for by it Melein had come into her power: he felt this of a surety. She had been only half a she'pan in his eyes, appointed by violence and necessity. But now he believed that the essential things had passed, that Intel had given her all she needed. She'pan, he could call her hereafter, believing implicitly that she knew the Mysteries. She had been face to face with the Pana, understanding what a kel'en could not. He did not envy her this understanding: the sound of her weeping still haunted him.

But she knew, and she led, and hereafter he trusted her leading implicitly.

They fled, they and the human and the dusei, out of the well, where smoke began to billow up, betraying them to the sky, where flames lit the walls with red and pursued them with heat. They entered the ascending turns of the way that they had come, into the cold dark.

Chapter Twenty-two

The Nom, in its first day of new operations, was aswarm with human technicians. Stavros reveled in the sound and scurry of humanity, after so long among the slow-moving regul. Reports came in, a bustle of human experts adding their agility to the technology of regul in repairs of the damaged plants, in clearing the wreckage left by the storm and the fighting.

And at a point judged stable enough to support a ship, probe *Flower* rested her squat body out on the height to the side of the city opposite the ruined port: a small vessel for a star-capable craft, a ship without the need for vast secure landing area, her design enabling her to operate in complete independence.

It had been a fortunate decision that brought several such probes on the mission, against the need for such difficult landings, despite their lack of defense against attack. *Saber* still rested up at the station, spacemade and spacebound, a kilometer long and incapable of landing anywhere.

Flower, despite the name, was an ungainly shell, without fragility, without exposed vanes, without need of landing gantries and docks, an ugly ship, meant for plain, workman duties.

She brought technicians, scientists, who were already beginning to sift through the remnant of Kesrith's records, to sample the air, the soil, to perform the myriad tasks that would begin to appropriate the world to human colonists.

"Favor," bai Hulagh had said, seeing operations begin. "We regret in the light of this new good feeling, the unfortunate destruction of our equipment in the calamity at the port. We might have been of much assistance."

Regul younglings in general were not so easily adaptive: they fretted at the nearness of humans, and preferred to work in their own groups. They made it no secret that they would gladly be off Kesrith now, to seek the security of their own kind in regul space.

But Hulagh had taken some few of them into his own office within the Nom and when the younglings came out, they had smiles for humans and great courtesy, and a powerful fear of the bai.

Until the storms descended, and the dusei returned.

The report came in first from the water plant, Galey's group, that reported to *Flower* that there were animals moving in large numbers there upon the heights; and *Flower* confirmed it, and flashed the same to the biologists, and in the doing of it, to Stavros.

Stavros locked his sled into the track that would take him to the far side of the Nom, and whisked through several changes to the observation deck, disengaged, and went on manual through the doors and out into the acrid wind.

A ruddy bank of cloud was sweeping in, and there, there, all round the visible horizon, sat the dusei.

A chill went over him, that had nothing to do with the wind, or the biting smell of Kesrith's rains. He sat in the sled, the wind whipping at his sparse hair. He saw *Flower* squatting on her hilltop; and the distant water plant, and vehicles speeding for cover as the storm came down; and airships, running for the makeshift field before the storm should hit: miracle if the crews could get them secured in time. He clenched his fist in rage, foreseeing damage, ships picked up by Kesrith's winds and hurled like toys about the field—human equipage, that, expensive and irreplaceable.

He shifted onto *Flower's* wavelength and heard *Flower* giving frantic instructions. They were warning the aircraft off, seeking means to route them round the storm to temporary landing elsewhere. He watched as lightning lit the clouds, and the clouds bred and built, and rolled in with frightening rapidity, red-lit with Arain's glow.

And the dusei in unending rows sat, and watched, and maintained their vigil. The rains began to fall.

Stavros shivered as the first drops spattered the nose of the sled. It was not a place to sit encased in metal, with the lightning

flashing overhead. He backed, opened the doorway, entered the
Nom and sealed the door after, still hearing *Flower's* chatter, with
weather-radar on his receptor, a bow of storm that clutched at the
sea's edge, at the city itself.

Flower, he sent, breaking in on their communications. *Flower:
Stavros.*

They acknowledged, a thin metallic sound, interrupted by static.

Flower: the dusei, the dusei—

"We have observed, sir. We are regretfully busy—"

He broke in again. *Flower: drive off the dusei. Break them up,
drive them away.*

They acknowledged the order. He sat his sled feeling as if he
had lost his mind, as if all reason departed him. Doubtless *Flower*
believed that he had lost his senses. But the ominous heaviness in
the air persisted. His skin prickled. He could not bear the dus-
presence, watching, watching at the storm's edge.

Responsible?

He refused to believe it. Yet in panic he had diverted *Flower* to
deal with them. He heard them discussing the task—too wise to
discuss the wisdom of it in his hearing. He sat with his skin drawn
into gooseflesh, his teeth near to chattering, a quavering and
sickly old man, he thought, a man who had been among strangers
too long.

He could countermand his own order, break in again and bid
them tend more important matters.

But neither could he rid himself of the fear of the dusei.

His screens went all to static, robbing him of the power to communicate with anyone. The static lasted, and there came a note
over his receptors that shrilled, ear-tormenting, and passed beyond
audibility. He powered down, quickly, desperate, of a sudden consumed with the fear that the sled itself might be malfunctioning,
himself trapped, helpless to move or call for help.

He watched, through a curtain of rain against the glass, the line
of the dusei begin to break, the beasts scattering; and still he shivered, terrified as he saw many of them break not toward the hills,
but toward the city, entering its streets, ranging where dusei were
not wont to come.

Attacking.

The static continued.

A regul voice came over the loudspeaker, distorted by static, unintelligible. The address system cut in and out sporadically. Hail rattled against the windows, shaking them dangerously. Stavros hastily tried to cut in the stormshields on the observation deck, and they did not operate. He thought to put the sled on battery, and obtained responses from it, but his screens were still dead. Somewhere there was a crash, a heavy impact of falling plastiglass: and wind and the smell of rain went through the Nom halls.

Stavros backed the sled, tried to engage the track and fouled the order sequence, began again.

It took. He whisked himself out of the area and around the corner, finding the hall a wreckage, unshielded windows lying on the carpet at the end of the hall, curtains whipping loose from their bases. Regul younglings cowered in the hall.

Deprived of the screen, he could not communicate with them. They closed about him, babbling questions, seeking any elder, even human, who could advise them. He pushed the sled through them and sought the downramp, the safer side of the building, where the offices were. The hall here was clear. The public address continued to sputter.

He found Hulagh's offices open, navigated his way with difficulty, and found the bai himself frantically attempting the closure of the stormshields.

A dus was outside. I reared itself against the thin plastiglass. The glass bowed, shook under the raking impact of the claws.

Hulagh backed his sled, fingering controls desperately; and Stavros sat still, watching the attack in horror. There was not a door in the Nom that would operate, nothing they could do if the beasts broke in. The windows quivered.

"Gun!" he cried at Hulagh, trying to make himself understood aloud. "Gun!"

And he backed, and Hulagh either understood or reached the same conclusion. They moved, as rapidly as the sleds would allow; and Hulagh rounded the desk and sought a pistol, holding it in shaking hands.

But the dus retreated, a shambling brown shape quickly lost in the sheeting rain across the square.

There were others, vague brown shapes that gathered and moved, milling nervously, and slowly, as if they had forgotten what they were about, they disappeared into the streets of the city and were gone.

In time the rain slacked, leaving only pocked puddles, and the stormshields suddenly operated all at once, too late for the storm.

The public address became clear, a constant chatter of instructions. Stavros' screens sorted themselves into clarity.

"Stavros, Stavros, do you read?"

Clear, he said. *All clear;* and cut them off, for of a sudden there was a grayness before his eyes and he was content only to stay still, to breathe, to wait until the labored beating of his heart and the roaring in his ears subsided.

There is a window out on the second floor, Stavros advised Hulagh. *Injuries there, I think.*

"Younglings will attend to it."

They neither one mentioned the dus. *Flower* was still trying to advise him what its operations were doing. He heard them talking to the aircraft, that had drawn off in advance of the storm, shepherding their lost searchers home again to the city.

And one of the aircraft answering, the rough accented voice of Hada Surag-gi. "Favor, favor, seeking return to mission, *Flower*-bai, seeking return to search."

And a human voice, also from an aircraft, cursing and demanding an explanation of the jamming.

Stavros wiped his face, cut off the chatter, and looked at the bai.

"Never in my experience," said the bai. "Never, reverence." And Hulagh jabbed at buttons and summoned a youngling servitor, ordering soi, and records; and cursed the slowness of youngling wits. His breathing was at an alarming rate. It was several moments before he seemed in control of himself. "They have all gone mad," he said.

Their world, said Stavros. *Theirs, before the mri.*

The soi came, borne by a youngling so agitated that the cups danced on the tray; and Stavros drank his unsweetened and drew the welcome warmth into his chilled belly.

At length he had the courage to touch the controls to open the stormshields again, remembering the beast even as he did so; and the square was deserted. Of a surety no regul and no humans would venture out until it was known where the dusei had gone.

He felt that he would see the apparition that had attacked the window in his nightmares thereafter; if the regul were prone to bad dreams the bai would share it.

"I am very old," said Hulagh in a querulous tone. "I am too old for such things, bai Stavros. The regul who took this world were mad." He sipped at his soi. "The mri controlled them. Now nothing does."

There can be barriers, Stavros said. *We can build them.*

Hulagh was silent a long time, throughout most of the cup of soi. His nostrils worked rapidly. At last he blew a sigh and turned his sled from the window. "Holn," he said.

Reverence?

"Holn concealed records. I did not ask, and they did not say: and I know now." Nostrils worked in great flaring breaths of air. "Stavros-bai, you and I have failed to ask questions. Now, now, you and I, Stavros-bai, we have been handed only fragments of what we should have known about Kesrith. We are together in difficulty; and we share an enemy, Stavros-bai."

Holn.

"Holn," said Hulagh. "They were clever, human reverence; and I shall not be able to face the anger of my doch if I come back destitute. Ship, equipment, everything, reverence Stavros. I am ruined. But likewise Holn has cheated you."

Bai Hulagh, you have a purpose in volunteering this information.

"The fortunes of doch Alagn," said Hulagh, "are here, with myself, with these surviving younglings. I will not be sent back in disgrace on a human ship. We shall deal, Stavros."

An alliance, reverence?

"An alliance, bai Stavros. Trade. Exchange. Ideas.—Revenge."

Stavros met the dark, glittering eyes. *From Kesrith,* he said, *there are territories to be explored.*

"It is first necessary," said Hulagh, "to hold Kesrith."

As the Holn and the mri held it, said Stavros, *with its resources used. Even the dusei. Even them.*

And he fell to staring out the window, at the roiling sky, and saw the ruin of the port, and the rain, and considered the re-

sources with which they had to work; and for the first time his
hopes began to hold a taint of doubt.

When he shut his eyes he still saw the beast at the window, irrational, uncontrollable as the elements: he hated them, the more
so perhaps because they were without rationality, because they
were, like the storm, of the elemental forces.

Antipathy to all that was regul and Kiluwan, the dusei.

But they were a part of Kesrith that could neither be ignored
nor destroyed.

A combination of random elements, the world of Kesrith; and
hereafter, he foresaw, was not under the control of George
Stavros. He could no longer control. He shared Kesrith with
beasts and with regul.

He clenched his hand on controls and listened to *Flower* again,
hearing the babble of search craft that were bound out yet another
time on their continuing patterns, trying to find one lost soul in all
that wilderness, where dusei ran wild and the storms raked the
land with violence.

Almost he bade them give it up.

But he had already given *Flower* irrational orders enough. He
did not make the move. He saw one of the aircraft circle far out
over the ruins of the edun and continue west, a speck quickly lost
in the haze.

Chapter Twenty-three

Melein was asleep finally. Niun, wiping the weariness from his eyes, settled the heavy metal ovoid into his lap and leaned his head back against the warm, breathing side of the dus. Duncan lay sprawled in the sand, on his stomach, his tattered and makeshift robes inadequate to afford him much protection from scrapes and sand-sores. His skin, bare above the boots, was scored with abrasions and sunburn. His eyes, unprotected by the veil, without the membrane to ease them, ran tears that streaked a perpetual coating of dust, like a dus gone *miuk*.

Duncan was exhausted for the moment, beyond causing them any trouble. Niun noted that a jo had settled against the rock, its luin-camouflage a little too dark for the red sandstone, where it clung for shade in this hottest part of the day. The name meant mimic. The creature harmed nothing. It waited for snakes, which were its natural food. It was not a bad campmate, the jo.

Niun nodded over his charge, his arms clasped about it, and rested his head, and finally relaxed enough to sleep awhile, now that Melein had settled. She had almost fainted before they stopped in this shelter, overburdened and hurting more than she wanted to admit. She had gone aside from them, into the privacy of the rocks, and taken cloth with her, in long strips: "I think it will help my side," she said; and because there was no kath'en or kel'e'en to attend her, she attended to herself. The ribs were broken, he much feared, or at the least cracked. He was worried, with a deep cold fear, that would not leave him.

But she had come back, hand pressed to her side, and smiled a thin smile and announced that she felt some better, and that she thought she could sleep; and the tension unwound from Niun's vitals when he saw that she could do so, that her pain was less.

The fear did not go away.

He bore Duncan's presence, his dread of anything Duncan might do to him far less than fear for Melein, for losing her, for ending alone.

The last mri.

He dreamed of the edun, and its towers crumbling in fire, and woke clutching the smooth shape of the pan'en to him in the fear that he also was falling into the Dark.

But he sat on the sand, the dus unmoving behind him. The jo, with a deft swoop, descended on a lizard, and bore it back to his upside-down perch on the rock, shrouding his meal with his mottled wings, a busy and tiny movement as it fed, swallowing the lizard bit by bit.

Niun set the pan'en beside him so that he could feel it, constantly, against him, and leaned his head against the dus. He drowsed again, and awoke finding the heat unpleasant. He looked toward the advancing line of the sunlight, that had crept up on Duncan, and saw that it had enveloped him to the waist, falling on the bare skin of his knee and hand. The human did not stir.

"Duncan," said Niun. He obtained no reaction, and reluctantly bestirred himself, leaned forward and shook at the human. "Duncan."

Brown eyes stared up at him, bewildered, heat-dazed.

"The sun, stupid tsi'mri, the sun. Move into the shade."

Duncan dragged himself into a new place and collapsed again, ripped aside the veil and lay with the cooler sand against his bare face. His eyes blinked, returning sensibility within them, as Niun resumed his place.

"Are we ready to move on?" he asked in a faint voice.

"No. Sleep."

Duncan lifted his head and looked around at Melein, lay down again facing him. "Somewhere," he said in a faint whisper, "my people will have come to Kesrith by now. She needs medical help. You know that. If it were sure that those up there are humans—we could contact an aircraft. Listen: the war is over. I don't think you know us well enough to believe it, but we wouldn't pursue matters any further. No revenge. No war. Come with me.

Contact my people. There would be help for her. And no retaliation. None."

Niun listened to the words, patient, believing at least that Duncan believed what he was saying. "Perhaps it is even true," he said. "But she would never accept this."

"She will die. But with help—"

"We are mri. We do not accept medicines, only our own. She has done what can be done under our own ways. Should strangers touch her? No. We live or we die, we heal or we do not heal." He shrugged. "Maybe our way of doing things is not even a wise one. Sometimes I have thought it was not. But we are the very last, and we will keep to the things that all our ancestors before us have observed. There is no use now for anything but that."

And he fell to thinking how Melein had planned, and that they had won this last small victory over tsi'mri, that they had gathered to themselves the holiness and the history of their kind; and his fingers ran over the smooth skin of the pan'en that he kept by him.

"I have broken two traditions," he admitted at last. "I have taken you and I have carried burdens. But the honor of the she'-pan I will not compromise. No. I do not believe in your doctors. And I do not believe in your people and your ways. They are not for us."

Duncan looked at him, long and soberly. "Even to survive?"

"Even to survive."

"If I get back to my own people," said Duncan finally, "I'm going to make sure it's known what the regul did, what really happened that night at the port. I don't know whether it will do any good; I know it can't change anything for the better. But it ought to be told."

Niun inclined his head, a respect for that gesture. "The regul," he said, "would see you dead before they would let you tell those things. And if you hope on that account that I will let you leave our company and go to them, I must tell you I will not."

"You don't believe me."

"I don't believe you know what they will do, either your kind or the regul."

Duncan was silent thereafter, staring into nothing. He looked very worn and very tired. He rubbed at a line of dried blood that had settled into an unshaven trail; and he was quiet again, but seemed not apt to sleep.

"Don't run again," Niun advised him, for he disliked the human's mood. "Don't try. I have made you too easy with us. Do not trust it."

Brown eyes flicked up at him, tsi'mri and disturbing. Duncan gathered himself up to a sitting position, moving as if every muscle ached, and rubbed his head with a grimace of discomfort. "I had rather stay alive," Duncan said, "like you would."

The words stung. They were too nearly true. "That is not all that matters," Niun said.

"I know that," Duncan said. "A truce. A truce: a peace between us at least until you've got her to somewhere safe, until she's well. I know you'd kill for her; I know that under other circumstances you might not. I understand that whatever she is, she's someone very special—to you."

"A she'pan," said Niun, "is Mother to a house. She is the last. A kel'en is only the instrument of her decisions. I can make no promises except for my own choice."

"Can there not be another generation?" Duncan asked suddenly, in his innocence, and Niun felt the embarrassment, but he did not take offense. "Can you not—if things were otherwise—?"

"We are bloodkin, and her caste does not mate," he answered softly, moved to explain what mri had never explained to outsiders: but it was simply kel lore, and it was not forbidden to say. It lent him courage, to affirm again the things that had always been fixed and true. "Kath'en or kel'e'en could bear me children for her, but there are none. There is no other way for us. We either survive as we were, or we have failed to survive. We are mri; and that is more than the name of a species, Duncan. It is an old, old way. It is our way. And we will not change."

"I will not be the cause," said Duncan, "of finishing the regul's handiwork. I'll stay with you. I made my try. Maybe again, sometime, maybe, but not to anyone's hurt, hers or yours. I have time. I have all the time in the world."

"And we do not," said Niun. He thought with a wrench of fear that Duncan, wiser than he in some things, for human kel'ein were able to cross castes—suspected that Melein would not live; and it answered a fear in his own heart. He looked to see how she was resting; and she was still asleep. The sight of her regular breathing quietly reassured him.

"With time and quiet," said Duncan, "perhaps she will mend."

"I accept your truce," said Niun, and in great weariness, he unfastened his veil and looped the end of the *mez* over his shoulder, baring his face to the human. It was hard, shaming to do; he had never shown his face to any tsi'mri; but he had taken this for an ally, even for the moment, and in the rightness of things, Duncan deserved to see him as he was.

Duncan looked long at him, until the embarrassment became acute and Niun flinched from that stare.

"The *mez* is a necessity in the heat and the dryness," Niun said. "But I am not ashamed to see your face. The *mez* is not necessary between us."

And he curled himself against the pan'en, and against the solid softness of the dus, and attempted to rest, taking what ease he could, for they would move with the coolness and concealment of evening, at a time when surely regul trusted even a mri would not dare the cliffs.

There was the sound of an aircraft, distant, a reminder of alien presence in the environs of Sil'athen. Niun heard it, and gathered himself up to listen, to be sure how close or how far it was. Melein was awake, and Duncan stirred, seeking at once the direction of the sound.

It was evening. The pillars had turned red, burning in the twilight. Arain was visible through them, a baleful red disk, rippling in the heat of the sands.

Melein sought to rise. Niun quickly offered her his hands and helped her, and she was no longer too proud to accept that help. He looked at her drawn face and thought of his own necessary burden. His helplessness to do anything for her overwhelmed him.

"We must be moving," she said. "We must go down again, to Sil'athen. There is no other exit I know from this place. But with the aircraft—" Her face contracted in an expression of anger, of frustration. "They are watching Sil'athen. They believe that the place hides us—and if they have men afoot—"

"I hope they are afoot," said Niun. "That would give me satisfaction." And then he remembered Duncan, and was glad that he
had been speaking in the hal'ari, as she had used with him. But it
was likely enough that they were regul that they had to deal with,
who would not go afoot.

"The climb down," she said, "—I think it would be best to
move just at the last light, so that we can see to climb. There will
not be a moon up until sometime later. That will give us some
dark to cross the open place at the beginning."

"That is the best we can do," he agreed. "We will eat and drink
before we go. We may not have another chance to stop."

And what that journey would cost Melein weighed heavily on
his mind.

"Duncan," he said quietly, while they shared food, both of them
unveiled, "I will not be able to do more than carry what I must
carry. On the climb—"

"I will help her," Duncan said.

"Down is easier," Melein said, and looked askance at Duncan,
as if she found their arrangement far from her liking.

It was the last of the food that they had brought with them.
Thereafter they must hunt, and quickly they must find water
again, in this place where luin were not frequent. Niun's mind
raced ahead to these things, difficulties upon difficulties, but ones
more pleasant than those most immediate.

They set out again toward the trail they had used, and when
they stood finally looking down that great chasm, dim and unreal
in the faded light, shading into black at the bottom, he held the
pan'en close to him and dreaded the climb even for himself.
When he considered Melein, he turned cold.

If she falls, he thought to warn Duncan; but it would do no
good, to dishonor what small trust there was between them, and
he thought that the human must know his mind. Duncan returned
that stare, plain and accepting the charge that was set on him.

"Go first," Niun bade him, and the human looped the trailing
mez across his face and secured it firmly as Niun had already
done with his own. Then he set his feet on the downslope, bracing
them carefully, offering his hand up for Melein's.

"Niun," Melein said, a glance, a patent distress. It was the only thing at which she had shown fear, committing herself to the hands of a human, when she was already in much pain.

Then, her hand pressed to her side, she reached her fingers toward Duncan's, and carefully, carefully, she set her feet on the downslope, beginning the descent with Duncan's hand to steady her, he bracing his body against whatever security there was, his arm extended to give her a firm support should she slip. In small stages they descended; and Niun stood with the pan'en a cold and comfortless weight in his arms, watching while they disappeared together into that shadow.

The dusei waited behind him, shifting weight nervously.

And then something intruded on his hearing, from behind him.

Aircraft, skimming above the pillars.

He grasped the carrying-bar of the pan'en, the only way to carry it in the descent, and hissed to the dusei and started the descent, terrified lest he cause them to have been seen, lest in his haste now he slip and come down on Melein and Duncan.

The aircraft passed directly overhead, a roar of power that echoed off the narrow walls, and he crouched low against a rock, shuddering against the strain of holding position on that slope. Pebbles skidded under his outmost foot. He took the chance as the aircraft passed beyond view and slid a few lengths lower, into the shadow, and the great bodies of the dusei came behind him, sharing his fear, communicating back to him an anxiety that made his stomach heave. He began to think he could not hold the pan'en: his fingers felt cut to the bone; and after he had gone a distance more he could not feel much pain, only an increasing numbness and lack of control over his fingers. He braced himself against a rock and shifted hands, reversing his entire position on the cliffside, showered from above by pebbles and dust from the claws of the dusei. They were at such a place now that they could not stop, and he plunged down a desperate slide, until he entered the deepest dark.

And at a stopping place he overtook Melein and Duncan, and Duncan's face looked toward him in that faintest of light. Melein still held to his hand, bent for a moment against a boulder.

She moved on then, weakly, leaning much on Duncan; and Niun took the stable place they had had, braced his body against the weight he held, and waited, to stop the dusei, to hold them there, awkward as it was, until she was safely down. They came, shouldered against him, and he held them with a quiet will, an intense willing that they be still, hush, stop. They were patient, even in this awkward state, joined with his senses.

The aircraft passed again, lights winking against the dim sky overhead. Niun looked up at it, trembling with the strain, and held his place, helpless, with the growing conviction that they were lost.

They had surely been spotted, at the worst of all times, in the worst of all places.

It circled yet again.

He settled the pan'en in the right hand again and set out downward, hoping, desperately hoping that Melein and Duncan had had time, for there were no more resting places that he remembered. He went, boots sliding on the trail, bringing up against one and another rock with a force that his muscles were too tired to absorb. He came down and down until he could hardly control his descent, and dropped from the last turn to the sand, driven to one knee by the impact.

The dusei came after, clambering down with much scratching of claws and scattering of sand, safe at the bottom.

And Melein sat, a pale huddle of robes in the shadow, and Duncan knelt by her. Her hand was pressed to her lips, and the other hand to her side, and her robes were stained with blood.

He fell to his knees beside her, the pan'en in his arms, and she could not prevent the cough that she stanched with her veil. Blood came. He saw it, and the membrane flashed across his vision, blinding him. He shivered, unable to see for a moment, and then it cleared.

"It began on the climb," Duncan said. "I think the ribs gave way."

And the aircraft circled at the top of the cleft.

Niun looked up at it in a blindness of rage.

"Be free of us," he bade Duncan, and rose up, letting the pan'en fall to the sand. He looked last at Melein, her eyes closed, her face relaxed, her body supported in Duncan's arms—not even a sen'en to attend her.

He gave a sharp call to his dusei, and began to walk, quickly, toward the end of the small valley, toward the main valley of Sil'athen.

"Niun!" Duncan shouted after him, which he did not regard.

He saw the aircraft hovering, at the valley's end. He reached for the cords at the end of the *siga's* long sleeves, and fastened them to their places on the honor belts at his shoulders, freeing his arms from the encumbering cloth; and he worked life into his hands, scored and numbed as they were from carrying the pan'en.

Duncan was running now, trying to overtake him. He heard the human—a racking cough, immediate payment for that rashness in Kesrith's thin air. He saw the aircraft on the sand, and regul descending, standing on the ramp. The dus at his side moaned a roar of menace, and the other two scattered out, flanking them—dus-tactics in hunting, the outrunners.

He saw the regul about to fire, the weapon lifted. He was not in its line when it discharged; but his eyes were clear and his hand steady when he fired; and the regul crumpled, a mass of flesh still stirring. They did not die easily, body-shot. A moment later the ramp drew up, toppling the wounded regul: coward, Niun cursed the regul flier.

And darted into the rocks and scrambled for cover as it lifted, swinging over near him, drawing off again. He was in the open now, in the main valley, and other aircraft hovered.

They would have him, eventually. He ran low among the rocks that bordered the open sands, pursued by the aircraft with their sensors, and finally, a desperate tactic, braced and fired against the nearest—all without effect for the first several shots. Then the aircraft began having difficulty, and skidded off into a great cloud of sand amid the valley.

Others swooped in. The sky was alive with the sound of them: they passed low and drew off, warned by the fate of the other.

He ran and he rested, and by now the air was tinged with the coppery taste of too much exertion in the thin air, and he could not see clearly to fire back at them. Shots tore up the rocks where he hid, and he staggered as rock became shrapnel and tore his arm, bringing a warm flow of blood.

Lights played across the cliffs, making it impossible to stay hidden. There was scant cover, and shots tore at all of it. He ran,

and fell, and scrambled up and raced for the next rock, and what
had become of the dusei he did not know: it was not their kind of
fight, this fury of fire and light.

The valley became ruin, steles and natural formations blasted
to rubble. It was the final vengeance of the regul on his kind, to
destroy the last sanctity of the People; and to ruin the land, as
they had destroyed all that they had touched.

A near miss threw him rolling, dazed, blinded by the membrane
that shielded his eyes, and he rose up and ran, too harried to fire
any longer, only to run and run until they had him a clear target.

An aircraft pressed at him, diving low, throwing sand from the
wind of its passing. And then he thought with a sudden and clear
satisfaction, and shifted left, toward the end of the valley, toward
an old, old place, under the sightless eyes of Eddan and Liran and
Debas, his teachers.

Fight with the land; make it your ally, they had been wont to
tell him; and he heard them clear and calmly through the roar of
the aircraft.

He fell, sprawling, and the aircraft continued on over him, hovered, kicking up sand; and he lay still, still as it settled, playing
lights over the sand where he lay.

It touched; and the earth exploded, a great pale shape rearing
up, heaving the aircraft, catching the craft in the convulsions of
the mantle: burrower and machine, entangled in a cloud of sand,
and the concussions of its struggles shaking the earth. Niun rolled
and tried to run, but an edge of the mantle or a shock of air hurled
him sprawling, and then another impact, and he saw the world go
up in fire as the aircraft exploded.

And dark, thereafter.

"Niun!"

Someone was calling him out of that dark, that had not the familiarity of the brothers; but it was a familiar voice all the same.

Light broke over him. He moved limbs that were buried in
sand, and heard the sound of engines.

"Niun!"

He lifted his head and drew himself up, standing on legs that
swayed under him, shielding his eyes from the light with his arm.

Waiting.

"Niun!" It was Duncan's voice, from a ragged silhouette before the lights. "Don't fire. Niun, we have Melein aboard. She is not dead, Niun."

He went blank at that horrid shock, mind not functioning, and came near to falling. And then the kel-law echoed in his mind, reminding him that there was a she'pan to be served; and that above all else, he could not leave her alone in the hands of strangers.

"What do you want of me?" he cried, his voice breaking with fury, with rage at Duncan, and treachery, and dishonor. "Duncan, I remind you what you swore—"

"Come in," Duncan said. "Niun, come in with us. Safe conduct. I still swear it."

He hesitated, and the strength went out of him, and he made a gesture of surrender, and began, slowly, to walk into the lights, toward the silhouettes that waited for him, tall and human.

Better than the regul, at least.

And out of the tail of his eye, a squat dark form. He saw it, saw the move, knew treachery.

He palmed the *as'ei,* whirled and threw; and the fire took him, and he never felt the sand.

"Hada Surag-gi is dead," said Galey. "The mri are hanging on."

Duncan wiped his face, and in the same gesture, swept the head-cloth off and ran his fingers through his sweat-soaked hair. He stumbled back through the narrow confines of the aircraft and shouldered past the medic who had already twice ordered him to keep his seat.

He sat down on the deck, unsteady in the motion of the aircraft, and regarded the two mri, wrapped in white, a tangle of tubing and monitoring connections from the automed units keeping their lives by means that the mri would find distasteful if they knew.

But they would have the chance to know.

"They're going to make it, both of them," the medic said. And then, frowning, with a glance at the sheet-wrapped hulk to the rear: "That particular regul was an officer of the Nom, with connections. There are going to be some questions asked."

"There will be some questions asked," Duncan said in a still voice, and looked at the mri, dismissing the medic from his mind. He sat with his legs tucked under him, still in the tattered and makeshift robes, and with his mind elsewhere; and at last the medic drew off to talk to the crew.

They had spoken little to him after the first excitement of recovering him alive; they were put off, perhaps, by the look of him, the strangeness of a man who had come alive from the desert of Kesrith, keeping company with mri and insisting with such vehemence on the possession of a mri treasure.

He touched Melein's brow, smoothed the metallic-bronze of her hair, noting the steady pulse on the monitors that assured him of their lives. Melein's golden eyes opened, the membrane cleared slowly back, and she seemed to be exploring the curious place that she had seen in her intervals of waking, rediscovering the strangeness that had taken them in. She was curiously calm, as if she had accepted to be here. He took her long slim fingers in his hand, and she pressed his hand with a faint effort.

"Niun is all right," he told her. He was not sure she understood this, for there was not a flicker. "There is the object you wanted," he added, but she did not look; likely all these concerns were distant from her, for they were heavily drugged.

"Kel'en," she whispered.

"She'pan?" he answered: perhaps she confused him with Niun.

"There will be a ship," she said. "A way off Kesrith."

"There will be," he said to her, and reckoned that he had told her the truth.

The war was done. They were free of regul. A human ship—there would be that—a chance for them. It was the most the mri would ever ask of tsi'mri.

"There will be that," he said. She closed her eyes then.

"Shon'ai," she said, with a taut, faint smile. He did not know the word. But he thought that she meant acceptance.

The deck slanted. They were coming in. He told her so.

BOOK TWO

SHON'JIR

Chapter One

The mri was still sedated. They kept him that way constantly, dazed and bewildered at this place that echoed of human voices and strange machinery.

Sten Duncan came to stand at the mri's bedside as he did twice each day, under the eye of the security officer who stood just outside the windowed partition. He came to see Niun, permitted to do so because he was the only one of all at Kesrith base that knew him. Today there was a hazy awareness in the golden, large-irised eyes. Duncan fancied the look there to be one of reproach.

Niun had lost weight. His golden skin was marked in many places with healing wounds, stark and angry. He had fought and won a battle for life which, fully conscious, he would surely have refused to win; but Niun remained ignorant of the humans who came and went about him, the scientists who, in concert with his physicians, robbed him of dignity.

They were enemies of mankind, the mri. Forty years of war, of ruined worlds and dead numbered by the millions—and yet most humans had never seen the enemy. Fewer still had looked upon a mri's living and unveiled face.

They were a beautiful people, tall and slim and golden beneath their black robes: golden manes streaked with bronze, delicate, humanoid features, long, slender hands; their ears had a little tuft of pale down at the tips, and their eyes were brilliant amber, with a nictitating membrane that protected them from dust and glare. The mri were at once humanlike and disturbingly alien. Such also were their minds, that could grasp outsiders' ways and yet steadfastly refused to compromise with them.

In the next room, similarly treated, lay Melein, called she'pan, leader of the mri: a young woman—and while Niun was angular and gaunt, a warrior of his kind, Melein was delicate and fine. On their faces both mri were scarred, three fine lines of blue stain slanting across each cheek, from the inner corner of the eye to the outer edge of the cheekbone, marks of meaning no human knew. On Melein's sleeping face, the fine blue lines lent exotic beauty to her bronze-lashed eyes; she seemed too fragile to partake of mri ferocity, or to bear the weight of mri crimes. Those that handled the mri treated her gently, even hushed their voices when they were in the room with her, touched her as little as possible, and that carefully. She seemed less a captive enemy than a lovely, sad child.

It was Niun they chose for their investigations—Niun, unquestionably the enemy, who had exacted a heavy price for his taking. He had been stronger from the beginning, his wounds more easily treated; and for all that, it was not officially expected that Niun survive. They called their examination medical treatments, and entered them so in the records, but in the name of those treatments, Niun had been holographed, scanned inside and out, had yielded tissue samples and sera—whatever the investigators desired—and more than once Duncan had seen him handled with unfeeling roughness, or left on the table too near waking while humans delayed about their business with him.

Duncan closed his eyes to it, fearing that any protest he made would see him barred from the mri's vicinity entirely. The mri had been kept alive, despite their extensive injuries; they survived; they healed; and Duncan found that of the greatest concern. The mri's personal ethic rejected outsiders, abhorred medicine, refused the pity of their enemy; but in nothing had these two mri been given a choice. They belonged to the scientists that had found the means to prolong their lives. They were not allowed to wake—and that too was for the purpose of keeping them alive.

"Niun," Duncan said softly, for the guard outside was momentarily staring elsewhere. He touched the back of Niun's long-fingered hand, below the webbing of the restraint; they kept the mri carefully restrained at all times, for Niun would tear at the wound if he once found the chance: so it was feared. Other captive mri had done so, killing themselves. None had ever been kept alive.

"Niun," he said again, persistent in what had become a twice-daily ritual—to let the mri know, if nothing more, that someone remained who could speak his name; to make the mri think, in whatever far place his consciousness wandered; to make some contact with the mri's numbed mind.

Niun's eyes briefly seemed to track and gave it up again, hazing as the membrane went over them.

"It's Duncan," he persisted, and closed his hand forcefully on the mri's. "Niun, it's Duncan."

The membrane retreated; the eyes cleared; the slim fingers jerked, almost closed. Niun stared at him, and Duncan's heart leaped in hope, for it was the first indication the mri had made that he was aware, proof that the mind, the man he knew, was un-damaged. Duncan saw the mri's eyes wander through the room, linger at the door, where the guard was visible.

"You are still on Kesrith," Duncan said softly, lest the guard hear and notice them. "You're aboard probe ship *Flower*, just outside the city. Pay no attention to the man. That is nothing, Niun. It's all right."

Possibly Niun understood; but the amber eyes hazed and closed, and he slipped back into the grip of the drugs, free of pain, free of understanding, free of remembering.

They were the last of their kind, Niun and Melein—the last mri, not alone on Kesrith, but anywhere. It was the reason that the scientists would not let them go: it was a chance at the mri enigma that might never, after them, be repeated. The mri had died here on Kesrith, in one night of fire and treachery—all, all save these two, who survived as a sad curiosity in the hands of their enemies.

And they had been put there by Duncan, whom they had trusted.

Duncan pressed Niun's unfeeling shoulder and turned away, paused to look through the dark glass partition into the room where Melein lay sleeping. He no longer visited her, not since she had grown stronger. Among mri she would have been holy, un-touchable: an outsider did not speak to her directly, but through others. Whatever she endured of loneliness and terror among her enemies was not worse than humiliation. Her enemies she might hate and ignore, slipping into unconsciousness and forgetting; but before him, whose name she knew, who had known her when she was free, she might feel deep shame.

She rested peacefully. Duncan watched the gentle rise and fall of her breathing for a moment, assuring himself that she was well and comfortable, then turned away and opened the door, murmured absent-minded thanks to the guard, who let him out of the restricted section and into the outer corridor.

Duncan ascended to the main level of the crowded probe ship, dodging white-uniformed science techs and blue-uniformed staff, a man out of place in *Flower*. His own khaki brown was the uniform of the Sur'Tac, Surface Tactical Force. Like the scientific personnel of *Flower*, he was an expert; his skills, however, were no longer needed on Kesrith or elsewhere. The war was over.

He had become like the mri, obsolete.

He checked out of *Flower*, a clerical formality. Security knew him well enough, as all humans on Kesrith knew him—the humans who had lived among mri. He walked out onto the ramp and down, onto the mesh causeway humans flung across the powdery earth of Kesrith.

Nothing grew on the white plain outside, as far as the eye could see. Life was everywhere scant on Kesrith, with its alkali flats, its dead ranges, its few and shallow seas. The world was lit by a red sun named Arain, and by two moons. It was one of six planets in the system, the only one even marginally habitable. The air was thin, cold in shadow and burning hot in the direct rays of Arain; and rains that passed through it left the skin burning and dry. Powdery, caustic dust crept into everything, even the tightest seals, making men miserable and eventually destroying machinery. In most places Kesrith was uninhabitable by humans, save here in the lowland basin about Kesrith's sole city, on the shore of a poisonous sea: one small area where moisture was plentiful, amid geysers and steaming pools, and crusted earth that would not bear a man's weight.

No men were indigenous to Kesrith. The world had first belonged to the dusei, great brown quadrupeds, vaguely ursine in appearance, velvet-skinned and slow-moving, massively clawed. Then had come the mri, whose towers had once stood over toward the high hills, where now only a heap of stone remained, a tomb for those that had died within.

And then had come the regul, hungry for minerals and wealth and territory, who had hired the mri to fight against humankind.

It was the regul city that humanity had inherited, humans the latest heirs of Kesrith: a squat agglomerate of ugly buildings, the tallest only two stories, and those stories lower than human standard. The city was laid out in a rectangle: the Nom, the sole two-storied building, was outermost, with other buildings arranged in the outline of the square before it. All streets followed that bow about the Nom square—narrow streets that were designed for regul transport, not human vehicles, streets crossed by the fingers of white sand that intruded everywhere on Kesrith, constantly seeking entry. At the left of the city was the Alkaline Sea, that received the runoff of Kesrith's mineral flats. Volcanic fires smoldered and bubbled under the surface of that sea as they did below that of the whole valley, that had once been a delicate land of thin crusts and mineral spires—a land pitted and ruined now by scars of combat.

There was a water-recovery plant, its towers extending out into the sea. Repairs were underway there, trying to release the city from its severe rationing. There had been a spaceport too, on the opposite side of the city, but that was now in complete ruin, an area of scorched earth and a remnant of twisted metal that had once been a regul and a mri ship.

Of ships onworld now, there was only *Flower*, an outworlds probe designed for portless landings, squatting on a knoll of hard rock that rose on the water-plant road. Beside her, an airfield had been improvised by mesh and by fill and hardening of the unstable surface—work that would quickly yield to the caustic rains. Nothing was lasting on Kesrith. Endure it might, so long as it received constant attention and repair; but the weather and the dust would take it in the end. The whole surface of Kesrith seemed to melt and flow under the torrential rains, the whole storm pattern of the continent channeled by mountain barriers toward this basin, making it live, but making life within it difficult.

It was an environment in which only the dusei and the mri had ever thrived without the protections of artificial environments; and the mri had done so by reliance on the dusei.

To such an inheritance had humanity come, intruders lately at war with the mri and now at war with their world, almost scoured off its face by storms, harassed by the wild dusei, befriended only by the regul, who had killed off the mri for them, an act of genocide to please their human conquerors.

Duncan traversed the causeway at his own slow pace, savoring the acrid air. His bare face and hands were painfully assaulted by Arain's fierce radiation even in this comparatively short walk. It was noon. Little stirred in the wild during the hours of Arain's zenith; but humans, safe within their filtered and air-conditioned environments, ignored the sun. Human authority imposed a human schedule on Kesrith's day, segmenting it into slightly lengthened seconds, minutes, hours, for the convenience of those who dwelled in the city, where daylight was visible and meaningful, but those were few. Universal Standard was still the yardstick for the scientific community of *Flower*, and for the warship that orbited overhead.

Duncan walked with eyes open to the land, saw the camouflaged body of a leathery jo, one of the flying creatures of Kesrith, poised to last out the heat in the shadow of a large rock— saw also the trail of a sandsnake that had lately crossed the ground beside the causeway, seeking the neither side of some rock to protect itself from the sun and from predators. The jo waited, patiently, for its appointed prey. Such things Niun had taught Duncan to see.

Across the mineral flats, in the wreckage wrought by the fighting, a geyser plumed, a common sight. The world was repairing its damage, patiently setting about more aeons of building; but hereafter would come humans in greater and greater numbers, to search out a way to undo it and make Kesrith their own.

The mesh gave way to concrete at the city's edge, a border partially overcome by drifting sand. Duncan walked onto solid ground, past the observation deck of the Nom, where a surveillance system had been mounted to watch the causeway, and up to the rear door that had become main entry for human personnel, leading as it did toward *Flower* and the airfield and shuttle landing.

The door hissed open and shut. Nom air came as a shock, scented as it was with its own filtered human-regul taint, humidified and sweeter than the air outside, that sunlight-over-cold heat that burned and chilled at once. Here were gardens, kept marginally watered during rationing, botanical specimens from regul worlds, and therefore important: a liver-spotted white vine that had shed its lavender blooms under stress; a sad-looking tree with sparse silver leaves; a hardy gray-green moss. And the regul-built halls—high in the center, at least by regul standards—gave a tall human a feeling of confinement. The corridors were rounded and recessed along one side, where gleaming rails afforded regul sleds a faster, hazard-free movement along the side without doors. As Duncan turned for the ramp, one whisked past almost too fast to distinguish, whipped round the corner and was gone. At that pace it would be a supply sled, carrying cargo but no personnel.

Regul tended much to automation. They moved slowly, ponderously, their short legs incapable of bearing their own weight for any distance. The regul who did move about afoot were younglings, sexless and still mobile, not yet having acquired their adult bulk. The elders, the muscles of their legs atrophied, hardly stirred at all, save in the prosthetic comfort of their sleds.

And, alien in the corridors of the Nom, humans moved, tall, stalking shapes strangely rapid among the squat, slow forms of regul.

Duncan's own quarters were on the second level, a private room. It was luxury in one sense: solitude was a comfort he had not had in a very long time, for he had come to Kesrith as attendant to the governor; but he was keenly aware what the small, single room represented, a fall from intimacy with the important powers of Kesrith, specifically with Stavros, the Honorable George Stavros, governor of the new territories of human conquest. Duncan had found himself quietly preempted from his post by a military medical aide, one Evans, E.; he had come back from Kesrith's backlands and from sickbay to find that state of affairs, and although he had hoped, he had received no invitation to move back into his old quarters in the anteroom of Stavros' apartments—that post of regul protocol which, among their conquered hosts, humans yet observed meticulously in public. An elder of Stavros' high rank must have at least one youngling to attend his needs and fend off unwelcome visitors; and that duty now belonged to Evans. Duncan was kept at a distance; his contact with Stavros, once close, was suddenly formal: an occasional greeting as they passed in the hall, that was the limit of it. Even the debriefing after his mission had been handled by others and passed second-hand to Stavros, through the scientists, the medics and the military.

Duncan understood his disfavor now as permanent. It was Stavros' concession to the regul, who hated him and feared his influence. And what his position on Kesrith would be hereafter, he did not know.

It was, for his personal hopes, the end. He might have promoted himself to a colonial staff position by cultivating Stavros' favor. He was still due considerable pay for his five year enlistment in the hazardous stage of the Kesrithi mission—pay and transport to the world of his choice, or settlement on Kesrith itself, subject to the approval of the governor. He had been lured by such hopes once and briefly, half-believing them. He had taken the post because it was an offer, in an area and at a time when offers were scarce; and because he was nearing his statistical limit of survival on missions of greater hazard. It had seemed then a way to survive, marginally at least, as he had always survived.

He had survived again, had come back from Stavros' service scarred and sunburned and mentally shaken after a trek through the Kesrithi backlands which the lately arrived regulars would never have survived. He had learned Kesrith as no human would after him; and he had been among mri, and had come back alive, which no human had done before him.

And in his distress he had told Stavros the truth of what he had learned, directly and trustingly.

That had been his great mistake.

He passed the door that belonged to Stavros and Evans, and opened his own apartment, Spartan in its appointments and lacking the small anteroom that was essential to status in the Nom, among regul. He touched the switch to close the door, and at the same panel opened the storm shields. The windows afforded a view of the way that he had come, of *Flower* on her knoll, a squat half-ovoid on stilts; of a sky that, at least today, was cloudless, a rusty pink. There had not been a storm in days. Nature, like the various inhabitants of Kesrith, seemed to have spent its violence: there was an exhausted hush over the world.

Duncan stripped and sponged off with chemical conditioner, a practice that the caustic dust of Kesrith made advisable, that his physician still insisted upon, and changed into his lighter uniform. He was bound for the library, that building across the square from the Nom, accessible by a basement hallway: it was part of the regul university complex, which humans now held.

He spent his afternoons and evenings there; and anyone who had known Sten Duncan back in humanity's home territory would have found that incredible. He was not a scholar. He had been well-trained in his profession: he knew the mechanics of ships and of weapons, knew a bit of geology and ecology, and the working of computers—all in areas necessary for efficiency in combat, in which he had been trained from a war-time youth, parentless, single-minded in the direction of his life. All his knowledge was practical, gathered at need, rammed into his head by instructors solely interested in his survival to kill the enemy.

That was before he had seen his war ended—before he had seen his enemy murdered by regul; or shared a camp with the survivors; or seen the proud mri on human charity.

Two thousand years of records and charts and tapes lay in the regul library, truths concealed in regul language and regul obscurities. Duncan studied. He searched out what the mri had been on Kesrith, what they had been elsewhere, with an interest infinitely more personal than that of *Flower*'s scientists.

Stavros disapproved. It flaunted attitudes and interests that regul feared and distrusted; and offending the regul ran counter to humanity's new policies. It embarrassed Stavros; it angered him, who had vast authority on Kesrith and in its new territories.

But the library still remained Duncan's choice on his hours of liberty, which were extensive in his useless existence. He had begun by making himself a nuisance among *Flower*'s personnel, who themselves were mining the library for what could be gained, duplicating tapes and records wholesale for later study back in the labs of Elag/Haven and Zoroaster. Duncan searched out those particular records that had to do with mri, and made himself helpful to certain of the *Flower* personnel who could be persuaded to share his interest. With his own stumbling command of the regul tongue, he could do little himself toward solving the tapes or interpreting the charts; but he talked with the scientists who could.

He reasoned with them; he tried to make them understand, with all his insistence, that which he did not understand himself.

To learn what it was he had spent his life destroying, what he had seen—utterly—obliterated.

He gathered up his notes and his handmade dictionary and prepared to leave the room.

The light on the panel flashed.

"Kose Sten Duncan," a regul voice said, still giving him his old title as Stavros' assistant, which surprised him. "Kose Sten Duncan."

He pressed the button for reply, vaguely uneasy that anyone in the Nom chose to intervene with him, disturbing his obscurity. His earnest ambition now was simple: to be let alone, to take those assignments that might be given him through lower channels, and to be forgotten by the higher ones.

"I am here," he told the regul.

"The reverence bai Stavros sends you his order that you join him in his offices immediately."

Duncan hesitated, heart clenched at the foreknowledge that his period of grace was over. Somewhere in the labyrinth of *Flower* papers must have been signed, declaring him fit for service; somewhere in the Nom papers were being prepared that would similarly mark him down in someone's employ. Nothing on colonial Kesrith could remain without some designated use.

"Tell the reverence," he said, "that I am coming now."

The regul returned some curt syllable, ending the communication; it lacked respect. Duncan flung his notes onto the table, opened the door and strode out into the corridor.

It was no accident that Stavros had summoned him at this hour. Duncan had become precise in his habits: from his treatment before noon, to his apartment at noon, and from his apartment to the library by a quarter til.

And concerning the library, he had received his warning.

He began, feverish in his anxiety, to anticipate the worst things that might await him: a reprimand, a direct order to abandon his visits to the library—or barring him from *Flower*, and from the mri. He had already defied Stavros' hinted displeasure; and did he receive and refuse a direct order he would find himself transferred permanently stationward, to *Saber*, Kesrith's military guard.

Where you belong, he could imagine Stavros saying. *Leave the mri to the scientists.*

He stalked through the corridor that wound down the ramp, shouldering aside a slow-moving regul youngling at the turn and not apologizing. Nor would the regul apologize to him, a human it needed not fear. A hiss of anger followed him, and other younglings paused to glare at him.

Stavros' offices, again a matter of status within a regul community, were on the ground floor of the stairless Nom, beyond broad doors that afforded easy access to the regul sleds.

The office doors were open. The secretary at Stavros' reception office was human, another of *Saber*'s personnel, a ComTech whose specialized linguistic skills were wasted at this post; but at least Stavros considered security, and did not install a regul youngling at this most sensitive post, where too much might be overheard—and, by a regul, memorized verbatim at the hearing. The tech stirred from his boredom, recognized Duncan with an expression of sudden reserve. A SurTac, Duncan was outside the regular military, but he was due a ComTech's respect.

"The governor says go on in," the tech said; and with a flicker of a glance to the closed inner door and back again; "The bai is in there, sir."

Hulagh.

Elder of the regul on Kesrith.

"Thank you," Duncan said, jaw set.

"Sir," the ComTech said, "With apologies: the governor advises you to walk in softly. His words, sir."

"Yes," Duncan said, and restrained his temper with a visible effort for the ComTech's benefit. He knew how he was reputed at Kesrith base—for rashness marked with official disfavor. He also knew his way among the diplomats better than any deskbound tech.

It was not the moment for temper. His transfer to *Saber* would be complete victory for the regul bai. He could throw away every remaining influence he had on the behalf of the mri, with a few ill-chosen words between himself and Stavros or between himself and the bai, and he was resolved to keep them unspoken. The regul would not understand any difference of opinion between elder and youngling; any intimation of dissent would reflect on

Stavros, and Stavros would not ignore that, not on a personal basis, not on an official one.

The secretary opened the door by remote and Duncan entered with a meek and quiet step, with a bow and a proper deference to the two rulers of Kesrith.

"Duncan," said Stavros aloud, and not unkindly. Both human and regul bai were encased in shining metal, alike until the eye rested on the flesh contained in the center of the sled-assembly. Stavros was exceedingly advanced in years, partially paralyzed, his affliction—which he had suffered on Kesrith—still hindering his speech to such an extent that he used the sled's communication screen to converse with regul, in their difficult language; but to humans he had begun to use speech again. The stricken limbs had regained some strength, but Stavros still kept to the sled, regul-made, the prestige of a regul elder. Speed, power, instant access to any circuitry in the Nom: Duncan understood the practical considerations in which Stavros refused to give up the machine, but he hated the policy which it represented—human accommodation with the regul, human imitation of regul ways.

"Sir," Duncan said quietly, acknowledging the greeting; and he faced bai Hulagh in the next breath, serenely courteous and trembling inside with anger, smiling as he met the small dark eyes of the regul elder. Great hulking monster in silver-edged gossamer, his flesh fold over fold of fat in which muscle had almost completely atrophied, particularly in the lower limbs: Duncan loathed the sight of him. The regul's face was bony plate, dark as the rest of his hide, and smooth, unlike the rest of his hide. The composite of facial features, their symmetry, gave an illusion of humanity; but taken individually, no feature was human. The eyes were brown and round, sunk in pits of wrinkled skin. The nose was reduced to slits that could flare or close completely. The lips were inverted, a mere tight-pressed slash at the moment, edged in bony plate. Hulagh's nostrils were tightly compressed now, save for quick puffs of expelled air, a signal of displeasure in the meeting as ominous as a human scowl.

Hulagh turned his sled abruptly aside, a pointed rebuff to a presumptuous youngling, and smiled at Stavros, a relaxing of the eyes and nostrils, a slight opening of the mouth. It was uncertain whether such a gesture was native to the regul or an attempt at a human one.

"It is good," said Hulagh in his rumbling Basic, "that the youngling Duncan has recovered."

"Yes," said Stavros aloud, in the regul tongue. The com screen on the sled angled toward Duncan and flashed to Basic mode, human symbols and alphabet. *Be seated. Wait.*

Duncan found a chair against the wall and sat down and listened, wondering why he had been called to this conference, why Stavros had chosen to put him on what surely was display for Hulagh's benefit. Duncan's inferior command of the regul language made it impossible for him to pick up much of what the regul bai said, and he could gather nothing at all of what Stavros answered, for though he could see the com screen at this angle, he could read but few words of the intricate written language, which the eidetic regul almost never used themselves.

One hearing of anything, however complex, and the regul never forgot. They needed no notes. Their records were oral, taped, reduced to writing only when deemed of some lasting importance.

Duncan's ears pricked when he heard his own name and the phrase *released from duty*. He sat still, hands tightening on the edge of the thick regul chair while the two diplomats traded endless pleasantries, until at last Hulagh prepared to take his leave.

The bai's sled faced about. This time Hulagh turned that false smile on him. "Good day, youngling Duncan," he said.

Duncan had the presence of mind to rise and bow, which was the courteous and proper response for a youngling to an elder; and the sled whisked out the opened door as he stood, fists clenched, and looked down at Stavros.

"Sit down," Stavros said.

The door closed. Duncan came and took the chair nearest Stavros' sled. The windows blackened, shutting out the outside world. They were entirely on room lights.

"My congratulations," Stavros said. "Well played, if obviously insincere."

"Am I being transferred?" Duncan asked directly, an abruptness that brought a flicker of displeasure to Stavros' eyes. Duncan regretted it at once—further proof, Stavros might read it, that he was unstable. Above all else, he had wished to avoid that impression.

"Patience," Stavros counseled him. Then he spoke to the ComTech outside, gave an order for incoming calls to be further delayed, and relaxed with a sigh, still watching Duncan intently. "Hulagh," said Stavros, "has been persuaded not to have your head. I told him that your hardship in the desert had unhinged your mind. Hulagh seems to accept that possibility as an excuse that will save his pride. He has decided to accept your presence in his sight again; but he doesn't like it."

"That regul," Duncan said, doggedly reiterating the statement that had ruined him, "committed genocide. If he didn't push the button himself, he ordered the one that did. I gave you my statement on what happened out there that night. You know that I'm telling the truth. You know it."

"Officially," said Stavros, "I don't. Duncan, I will try to reason with you. Matters are not as simple as you would wish. Hulagh himself suffered in that action: he lost his ship, his younglings, his total wealth and his prestige and the prestige of his doch. A regul doch may fall, one important to mankind. Do you comprehend what I'm telling you? Hulagh's doch is the peace party. If it falls, it will be dangerous for all of us, and not only for those of us on Kesrith. We're talking about the peace, do you understand that?"

They were back on old ground. Arguments began from here, leading to known positions. Duncan opened his mouth to speak, persistently to restate what Stavros knew, what he had told his interrogators times beyond counting. Stavros cut him off with an impatient gesture, saving him the effort that he knew already was futile. Duncan found himself tired, exhausted of hope and belief in the powers that ruled Kesrith, most of all in this man that he had once served.

"Listen," said Stavros sharply. "Human men died, too—at Haven."

"I was there," Duncan returned, bitter in the memory. He did not add what was also true, that Stavros had not been. Many a SurTac had left his unburied corpse on Elag/Haven, and ten other worlds of that zone, while the diplomats were safe behind the lines.

"Human men died," Stavros continued, intent on making his point, "there and here, at the hands of mri. Humans would have died in the future—will die, if the peace should collapse, if somewhere the regul that want war find political power—and more such mercenaries as the mri. Or does that fail to matter in your reckoning?"

"It matters."

Stavros was silent a time. He moved his sled to reach for a cup of soi abandoned on the edge of a table. He drank, and stared at Duncan over the rim of the cup, set it down again. "I know it matters," he said at last. "Duncan, I regretted having to replace you."

It was the first time Stavros had said so. "Yes, sir," Duncan said. "I know it was necessary."

"There were several reasons," Stavros said. "First, because you offended bai Hulagh to his face, and you know you're lucky to have come off alive from that. Second, you were put into sickbay with an indefinite prognosis, and I need help—" He gestured at his own body, encased in metal. "You're no medic. You didn't sign on for this. Evans is useful in that regard. Your skills are valuable elsewhere."

Duncan listened, painfully aware that he was being played, prepared for something. One did not maneuver George Stavros; Stavros maneuvered others. Stavros was a professional at it; and the mind in that fettered shell had very few human dependencies, an aged man who had dealt with crises involving worlds for more years than SurTacs tended to live, who had thrown aside family and a comfortable retirement to seize a governorship on a frontier like Kesrith. For a brief time Duncan had felt there had been some attachment between himself and Stavros; he had given Stavros unstintingly of effort and loyalty—had even believed in him enough to offer him truth. But to manage others with subtlety, even with ruthlessness, that was the skill for which Stavros had won his appointment; Duncan determined neither to believe him nor to be angry that he had been used—and he knew that even so, Stavros had the skill to lie to him again.

"I have excused your actions," Stavros said, "and covered them as far as I can; but you have lost your usefulness to me in the capacity in which you signed on. Hulagh can be persuaded to tolerate your presence; but the suspicion that you have moved back into some position of direct influence would be more than he could bear, and it might endanger your life. I don't want that kind of trouble, Duncan, or the complications your murder might create. Regul are simply not prepared to believe the killing of a youngling is of equal seriousness with the killing of an elder."

"I don't want to be sent offworld."

"You don't."

"No, sir. I don't."

Stavros stared at him. "You have this personal attachment to those two mri. Attachment—obsession. You're no longer a rational man on the subject, Duncan. Think. Explain to me. What do you hope to do or to find? What's the point of this sudden—scholarship of yours, these hours in the library, in full view of the regul? What are you looking for?"

"I don't know, sir."

"You don't know. But it involves every mri record you can find."

Duncan clenched his jaw, leaned back and made himself draw an even breath. Stavros left the silence, waiting for him. "I want to know," Duncan said finally, "what they were. I saw them die. I saw a whole species die out there. I want to know what it was I saw destroyed."

"That doesn't make sense."

"I was there. You weren't." Duncan's mind filled again with the night, the dark, the blinding light of the destruction. A mri body pressed against him, two men equally trembling in the forces that had destroyed a species.

Stavros gazed at him a long time. His face grew sober, even pitying, and this was unaccustomed for Stavros. "What do you think? That it might have been you that drew the attack to them? Is that what's eating at you—that you might be responsible, as much as Hulagh?"

It hit near enough the mark. Duncan sat still, knowing that he was not going to be able to talk rationally about it. Stavros let the silence hang there a moment.

"Perhaps," said Stavros finally, "it would be better if you would go up to *Saber* for a time, into an environment more familiar to you, where you can sort out your thinking."

"No, sir. It would not be better. You took me off assignment with you. I accept that. But give me something else: I waive my transfer home, and my discharge. Give me another assignment, here on Kesrith."

"That is a request, I take it."

"Yes, sir. That is a request."

"Everything you do, since you were attached to me, is observed and taken for omen by the regul. You've persisted in aggravating the situation. You came here to assist, SurTac Duncan, not to formulate policy."

Duncan did not answer. It was not expected. Stavros' mouth worked in the effort prolonged speech cost him; he drew a difficult breath, and Duncan grew concerned, remembering that Stavros was a sick man, that he was trying, amid all other pressures, to remember something of personal debts. He put a curb on his temper.

"You took it on yourself," Stavros said at last, "to accuse bai Hulagh of murder. You created an incident that nearly shipwrecked the whole Kesrith diplomatic effort. Maybe you think you were justified. Let us suppose—" Stavros' harsh, strained voice acquired a marginally gentler tone. "Let us suppose for the sake of argument that you were absolutely justified. But you do not make decisions like that, SurTac Duncan, and you must know that, somewhere at the bottom of your righteousness."

"Yes, sir," he said very quietly.

"As it happens," said Stavros, "I don't doubt you. And I'm positive the bai tried to kill you in spite of all my efforts to reassure him. When he found you among mri, that was too much for him. I think you know that. I think you're bothered by that possibility, and I wish that I could set your mind at ease and say that it wasn't so. I can't. Hulagh probably did exactly what you charge he did. But charges like that aren't profitable for me to pursue right now. I recovered you alive. That was the best that I could do, with all else that was going on. I recovered your mri too, quite incidentally."

"What remains of them. The medics—"

"Yes. What remains of them. But you can't undo that. You can't do a thing about it."

"Yes, sir."

"The medics tell me you've healed."

"Yes, sir." Duncan drew a deep breath and decided finally that Stavros was trying to put him at ease. He watched as the governor tried awkwardly to manipulate a clean cup into the dispenser— rose and took over that task, filling the cup the governor was going to offer him. Stavros favored him with a one-sided smile.

"Still not what I was," Stavros said ruefully. "The medics don't make extravagant promises, but the exercises are helping. Makes the metal beast easier to manage, at least. Here, give my cup a warm-up, will you?"

Duncan did as requested, put it in Stavros' hand, settled again with his own cup cradled in his palms. After a moment he took his first sip, savoring the pleasant warmth. Soi was a mild stimulant. He found himself drinking more of it than was likely good for him these last few days, but his taste for food had been off since his sojourn in the desert. He sipped at the hot liquid and relaxed, knew that he was being swept into Stavros' talented manipulations, set at ease, moved, directed; but he was also being heard, for what it was worth. He believed, if nothing else, that Stavros began to listen—and cultivated the regul for reasons that did not involve naïveté.

"It was a mistake, my speaking out," Duncan admitted, which he had never admitted, not to his several interrogators or in any of the written reports he had filed. "It wasn't that I didn't know what I was saying; I did. But I shouldn't have said it in front of the regul."

"You were in a state of collapse. I understood that."

Duncan's mouth twisted. he set the cup aside. "Security got a sedative into me to shut me up and you know it. I did not collapse."

"You talked about a holy place," Stavros said. "But you never would talk about it in debriefing, not even to direct questions. Was that where you found the artifact you brought back?"

Duncan's eyes went unfocused, his heart speeding. His hands shook. He attempted to disguise the fact by reaching for the plastic cup and clenching it tightly in both hands.

"Duncan?"

Dark and fire, a gleaming metal ovoid cradled in Niun's arms, precious to the mri, more than their lives, who were the last of their kind. *Do nothing*, Melein had bidden him while he stood in that place holy to the mri, *touch nothing, see nothing*. He had violated that trust, delivering the wounded mri into human care, to save their lives, by putting that metal ovoid into human hands, itself to be probed by human science. He had spoken in delirium. He looked at Stavros, helpless to shrug it off; he did not know how much he had said, or with what detail. There was the artifact itself, in *Flower*'s labs, to make lies of any denial.

"I had better write the reports over," Duncan said. He did not know what else to say. A colonial governor had dictatorial powers in that stage before there were parliaments and laws. He himself was not a civ, and unprotected in any instance. There was very little that Stavros could not do—even including execution, certainly including shipping him to some station elsewhere, away from the mri, away from all hope of access to them and to Kesrith, forever.

"Your account was not accurate, then."

Duncan cast everything into the balance. "I was shaken. I wasn't sure, after I was silenced the first time, how much was really wanted on record."

"Don't give me that nonsense."

"I was not rational at the time. To be honest—to be honest, sir, I had the feeling that you wanted to bury everything about the mri, everything that happened. I wasn't sure I might not be put off Kesrith because I knew too much. I'm still not sure that it won't happen."

"You know the seriousness of what you're charging?"

"This is a frontier," Duncan said. "I know that you can do what you want to do. Even to having me shot. I don't know the limit of what I know—or how important it is. If an entire species can be wiped off the board and forgotten—what am I?"

Stavros frowned, sipped at his drink, made a face and set it aside again. "Duncan, the regul are living; their victims aren't. So we deal with the regul, who are a force still dangerous—and the mri—" He moved the sled, turned it, looked at him at closer range. "You have your opinions on the mri, very obviously. What would you do with them?"

"Turn them loose. They won't live in captivity."

"That simple? But it's not quite that simple afterwards. What of the regul?"

"The mri won't fight for the regul any longer—and there are only two of them. Only two—"

"Caring nothing for their lives, even two mri are considerable; and they have a considerable grudge against bai Hulagh—who heads the regul peace party, SurTac Duncan."

"I know these two mri," Duncan said. "They did nothing to anyone on this world except to defend themselves. They only tried to get to safety, and we wouldn't let them. Let them go now, and they'd leave. That's all they want."

"For now."

"There is no tomorrow for them," Duncan said, and then Stavros looked at him quizzically. "There will be no more generations. There's a taboo between those two. Besides, even if there weren't—ten, even twenty generations wouldn't make a vast threat out of them."

Stavros frowned, backed the sled, opened the door. "Walk with me," he said, "upstairs. You're going nowhere else, I trust."

"Yes, sir," Duncan agreed. Stavros undoubtedly meant to put him off his balance, and he had done so. He was asked to accompany Stavros in public, before regul. It was a demonstration of something, a restoration of confidence: he was not sure what. Perhaps he was being bribed, in subtle fashion, offered status—and the alternative was transfer to *Saber*. Stavros made it very difficult to continue the debate.

The sled eased its way through the office door, past the ComTech; it passed the outer doors, into the corridor. Duncan overtook it as Stavros waited for him. Stavros did not lock into the tracks that could have shot him along at a rate no man afoot could match, but trundled along beside him at a very leisurely pace.

"First thing," said Stavros, "no more library." And when Duncan opened his mouth at once to protest: "You have to walk among regul over there, and I'd rather not have that. *Flower* staff can find what you need, if you describe it. Do you understand me?"

"No, sir."

They walked some distance in silence, until a knot of regul had passed them, and they turned the corner into the upward corridor. "I want you," said Stavros, "to spend your time on *Flower* as

much as possible. Stay clear of the regul entirely. Work at your
private obsession through channels, and write me a decent report—a full one, this time."

Duncan stopped on the ramp. "I still don't understand you."

Stavros angled his sled to look up at him, a sidewise motion of
the eyes. "Yes, you do. I want you to apply your talents and prepare me a full report on the mri. Use any authority you want that
doesn't involve actually touching the mri themselves."

"What value is that?" Duncan asked. "I'm so scientist."

"Your practical experience," Stavros said, "makes such a report
valuable: not for the researchers, but for me."

"I'll need clearance over there."

Stavros scowled. "I'll tell you something, Duncan, and you listen to me. I don't share your enthusiasm for preserving the mri.
They were a plague in the universe, a blight, at best an anachronism among species that have learned their lessons of civilization
to better advantage. They are probably the most efficient killers in
all creation; but we didn't bring them to extinction, nor did the
regul—nor did you. They are dying because they have no interest
in comprehending any other way of life. No quarter, no prisoners,
no negotiation or compromise: everything is black and white in
their eyes, nothing gray. I don't blame them for it; but their way
of life was destruction, and they're dying now by the same standard they applied to others: nature's bias, if you like, not mine.
Convince me otherwise if you can. And be careful with them. If
you don't respect them for what they are, instead of what your
delirium remembers, then those two mri will end up killing someone: themselves certainly; you, likely; others, very possibly."

"Then I will be allowed access to them."

"Maybe."

"Give me that now, and I can talk with them as the staff can't.
Keep the medics and their drugs away from them while they have
minds left."

"Duncan—" Stavros started moving again, slowly, turning the
corner at the top of the ramp. "You were the one exception to
their no-prisoner rule, the one exception in forty years. You are
aware, of course, that there may have been a certain irrational
sense of dependency generated there, in the desert, in their environment, in your unexpected survival. They gave you food and

water, kept you alive, contrary to your own natural expectations; you received every necessity of life from their hands. When you expect ill and receive good instead, it has certain emotional effects, even when you really know nothing about the motives of the people involved. Do you know what I'm talking about?"

"Yes, sir. I'm aware of that possibility. It may be valid."

"And that's what you want to find out, is it?"

"That, among other things."

They reached the door of Stavros' apartments. Stavros opened it by remote, slipped in and whipped the sled about, facing him in the doorway. Evans stood across the room, seeming surprised at them: a young man, Evans—Duncan looked at him, who had been the focus of his bitter jealousy, and found a quiet, not particularly personable youth.

"Take the afternoon off," Stavros said to Duncan. "Stay in the Nom. I'll prepare an order transferring you to *Flower* and salving feelings among the civs over there. I'll send you a copy of it. And I expect you realize I don't want any feelings ruffled over there among the scientific staff; they don't like the military much. Use tact. You'll get more out of them."

"Yes, sir." Duncan was almost trembling with anxiety, for almost all that he wanted was in his hands, everything. "And access to their mri themselves—"

"No. Not yet. Not yet. Go on. Give me time."

Duncan tried to make a gesture of some sort, a courtesy; it was never easy at the best of times between himself and Stavros. In the end he murmured something inarticulate and left, awkward in the leaving.

"Sir?"

Stavros turned the sled about, remembered that he had ordered lunch when he returned. He accepted the offered mug of soup and scowled at Evans' attempt to help him with it, took it into his own hands. Returning function in his afflicted limbs made him arrogant in his regained independence. He analyzed his irritation as impatience with his own unresponding muscles and Evans merely as a convenient focus. He murmured a surly thanks.

"Files on the mri," he ordered Evans. "And on Sten Duncan."

Evans moved to obey. Stavros settled and drank the soup, savoring something prepared entirely by humans, seasoned with human understanding of spices. It was too new a luxury after the long stay in regul care to take entirely for granted; but after a moment the cup rested neglected in his hand.

The fact was that he missed Duncan.

He missed him sorely, and still reckoned him better spent as he had just disposed of him. The SurTac had entered service with him as a bodyguard disguised as a servant, drawn out of combat at war's end to dance attendance on a diplomat. Duncan was a young man, if any man who had seen action at Elag/Haven could ever again be called young. He was remarkable in his intelligence, according to records which Duncan had probably never seen—another of the young men that the war had snatched up and swallowed whole before they had ever known what they might have been. Duncan had learned to take orders, but SurTac-style: loners, the men of his service, unaccustomed to close direction. They were usually given only an objective, limited in scope, and told to accomplish it: the rest was up to the SurTac, a specialist in alien environment, survival, and warfare behind the enemy's lines.

Stavros himself had sent the SurTac out to learn Kesrith.

And Kesrith had nearly killed Duncan. Even the look of him was changed, reshaped by the forge of the Kesrithi desert. Something was gone, that had been there before Duncan had gone out into that wilderness—his youth, perhaps; his humanity, possibly. He bore scars of it, face half-tanned from wearing mri veils in the searing sunlight, frown lines burned into the edges of his eyes, making them hard and different. He had come back with lungs racked and his breathing impaired from the thin air and caustic dust, with his body weight down by a considerable measure, and a strange, fragile tread, as if he mistrusted the very flooring. Days in sickbay had taken care of the physical injuries, restored him with all the array of advanced equipment available on the probe ship; but there was damage that would never be reached, that had stamped the look of the fanatic on the young SurTac.

The regul bai was correct when he perceived Sten Duncan as an enemy. The regul as a species had no more deadly enemy than this, save the mri themselves. Duncan hated, and Duncan knew the regul better than any human living save Stavros himself, for they two had come alone among regul, the first humans to breach

the barriers to contact between regul and humanity, here on
Kesrith.

And most particularly Duncan hated bai Hulagh Alagn-ni: Hulagh, who had done precisely what Duncan accused him of doing,
killing the mri who had served regulkind as mercenaries, obliterating a sapient species. Hulagh had done it for desperate fear, and
for greed, which were intertwined. But bai Hulagh was moved
now by fear of disgrace among his own kind and by dawning
hope of gain from humans; he had become stranded on the world
he had hoped to plunder, among humans whom he had hoped to
cheat and disgrace. And bai Hulagh thus became vulnerable and
valuable.

The fact was that one could not, as Duncan tried to do, say
regul, and comprehend in that word the reasons and actions of a
given member of regulkind. A quasi-nation of merchants and
scholars, the regul; but their docha, their associations of birth and
trade, were each as independent as separate nations in most dealings. Hulagh was of doch Alagn, and Alagn, a new force in regul
politics, had stopped the war. The employers of the mri mercenaries who had wrought such destruction in human space were doch
Holn, the great rivals and enemies of Alagn.

Doch Holn had ceded Kesrith at war's end, compelled by the
treaty; and in the passing of Kesrith to human control, Holn had
fallen to Alagn. But Holn had had its revenge: it had cast Hulagh
Alagn-ni into command of Kesrith ignorant of mri and of the nature of Kesrith. The weather had turned: Alagn had been faced
with the collapse of their effort at evacuation and plunder of
Kesrith; and confronted with incoming humans, Hulagh had panicked. In that panic, seeking to avert human wrath, Hulagh had
done murder.

It was possible that by that act of murder, that annihilation of
the mri, bai Hulagh had saved the lives of those incoming humans, all the personnel of *Saber* and *Flower*, *Fox* and *Hannibal*.
It was possible that humanity guiltily owed bai Hulagh a debt of
gratitude, for a sweeping action that human policy could never
have taken.

Duncan, who believed in absolute justice, could not accept
such a thought; but the truth was that doch Alagn and its ruler,
Hulagh, were in every respect useful to Kesrith, most particularly

in their reliance on humans and in their burning hatred for doch Holn, who had maneuvered them into this unhappy circumstance. For Duncan, as for the mri, there was only black and white, right and wrong. It was impossible to explain to Duncan that Alagn must be cultivated, strengthened, and aimed at Holn, a process too long-range and too little honest for the SurTac.

The mri, moreover, were Holn-hired and Holn-managed throughout their history—and it was above all else necessary that what Hulagh had done on Kesrith be final: that the mri species be in fact obliterated, and that Holn not maintain in some secret place another force of the breed, those most efficient and skilled killers, for whom Duncan found such tender sympathy. The regul without the mri were incapable of war, constitutionally and physically incapable. With the mri, the regul were capable to any extent. If any mri survived, they could bear no love to doch Alagn for what Hulagh had done to their kind; and personal involvement of the mri in a war, for their own motives and not for hire, was a specter that hung over both Alagn and humanity.

The soup turned sour in Stavros' mouth while he contemplated what measures might eventually prove necessary with the remaining two mri: Duncan's mri. Duncan was a man of single sight and direct action, innocent in his way; and it was something that Stavros had no wish to do—to destroy in the SurTac that which had made him at once a valued adviser and a reliable agent.

He loved Duncan as a son.

For one of his sons, he would have felt less remorse.

Chapter Two

The order went out in the evening. Duncan read and re-read the photocopy over a solitary supper in his quarters in the Nom, at a table littered with other notes, his handmade and carefully gathered materials.

Special liaison: that was the title that Stavros had chosen to ease his transfer into *Flower*'s tight community. The order linked him to the governor's essentially civilian wing, and not to the military presence that orbited in conjunction with the station, and Duncan appreciated that distinction, that would find more grace with *Flower*'s personnel. He was given certain authorities—to investigate, but not to dispose of artifacts or records or persons: he could actually direct what lines investigations of others were to take: *fullest cooperation in pursuing his research . . .* that portion of the order began. He read that final section again and again, finding no exception in it, and he was amazed that Stavros had said it.

He began to wonder why, and found no answer.

Within the hour arrived a packet of documents—not on film, and therefore not something meant to be fed into the Nom receptors, where regul might have access to it: it came hand-delivered. Duncan signed for it and settled with the several folders in his lap—extensive files that seemed to comprise everything known and done in regard to the mri prisoners. Duncan read them, again and again, absorbing everything he could remotely comprehend.

Then followed messages, from one and another department within *Flower*—from security, from biology, from Dr. Luiz, the white-haired chief of surgery who had cared for him during his own stay aboard *Flower*. Luiz' message was warm: it was Luiz who had tacitly given him leave to conduct his daily visits aboard *Flower*, when his own treatments could as easily have been given in the Nom, far from the mri. It was Luiz who had kept the treatment of the mri as decent as it was, who had kept them alive when it was reckoned impossible; and this man Duncan trusted. From others there were more formal acknowledgements, coldness couched in courtesies.

The governor's appointee, bringing power to alter things dear to certain hearts: he began to reckon how the scientists saw him, an intruder who knew nothing about the researches and operations for which these civs had come so far to a frontier world. He did not find it surprising that he was resented. He wished that he had been given authority to alter the condition of the mri, and less authority to threaten other projects. The one he earnestly desired; the other he distrusted because it was excessive and unreasonable; and he did not know Stavros for an excessive man, and certainly not as a man who acted without reasons.

He was being aimed at someone or something: he began to fear that this was so. He had become convenient again for Stavros, a weapon to be used once more, in a new kind of warfare against some one of Stavros' enemies—be it the regul, be it some contest of authority between civs and the governor's office, or designs yet more complex, involving all of them.

He was out of Stavros' reach now, and able to think—outside that aura of confidentiality that so readily swept a man into Stavros' hands—and still he found himself willing to suspend all his suspicions and take the lure, for it was all that he wanted, all that mattered to him.

Obsession, Stavros had called it.

He acknowledged that, and went.

At *Flower*'s duty desk in the morning, more messages waited, each from a department head waiting to see him. Duncan began to find himself uneasy. He postponed dealing with them, and descended first to the medical section, intent most of all on the mri, on assuring himself as he did daily, that they were well and as comfortable as possible under the circumstances—most of all now, that no over-eager investigator had decided to be beforehand with them, to finish or initiate some research before it could be forbidden.

But before he had more than passed the door into that section, Dr. Luiz hailed him; and he found himself diverted from the mri and hastened into an assembling conference of the various departments of *Flower*.

Being involved in the meeting irked him: he hated all such procedures. He was formally introduced to them, who had known him better as a specimen like the mri, himself the object of some of their researches when he had been dragged in off the desert half-alive, from where no human ought to have survived. He forced a smile to his face, and acknowledged the introductions, then leaned back in his chair and prepared himself for the tedium to come, long exchanges of data and quibblings over objectives and items of supply. He thought it deliberate, a petty administrative revenge that he be drawn into such proceedings, in which he had no knowledge and less interest. He sat surreptitiously studying the manners and faces of the other participants, listening to the petty debates and mentally marking down to be remembered the indications of jealousies and friendships that might be useful.

But the central matter did suddenly touch his interest: the news from the military wing that there were arrivals at the station. It troubled him, this piece of news, increasingly so as he listened. Probe ship *Fox*, along with the warship *Hannibal* and the rider *Santiago*, had returned from Gurgain, a world of the star Lyltagh, neighboring Arain, a mining colony of airless moons and rich deposits, only scantly developed by regul. New information was coming in, particularly of interest to the geologists: *Flower* was sending a crew up to *Fox*. Personnel were being shifted about, reallotted on new priorities; the mri project was losing some key personnel. Duncan, beginning to perceive the reorganization, felt uneasily that his authority might be sufficient to affect the transfers: he thought that he ought to say something, that he might be expected to do something, to be well-informed in questions of staff and policies and Stavros' wishes. He was not.

He sat frowning while matters were arranged to the satisfaction of the existing powers of *Flower*, realizing miserably that he was inadequate for the position he had been given: that at the least he should have been taking notes for Stavros' benefit—and he had done nothing, not aware until late what had happened, that a major portion of the directorates had dissolved about him, ill-content, it might be, with the governor's intervention in their researches: forces wishing to assert their independence of Stavros were aiming this at him, while other departments looked in vain for his support.

Academics and politics: he was not fit for either. He was conscious of the figure he cut among them, khaki amid their blue and white, a rough-handed soldier out of his element, a hated and ridiculous presence. They concluded their business in his angry silence and adjourned. A few lingered for perfunctory courtesies with him; those bound for *Fox* pointedly ignored such amenities and walked out without acknowledging his presence. He accepted what courtesies he was offered, still not knowing friend from enemy, bitter in his ignorance. He was pleasant, having learned from Stavros to smile without meaning it.

But afterward, as he tried to leave, he found Luiz' hand on his shoulder, and Dr. Boaz of xenology smiling up at him with more than casual interest, Boaz a portly woman with the accent of Haven in her speech, her head crowned with gray-blonde braids.

"Stavros," said Boaz, "recalled you mentioned a mri shrine."

He looked at them, this pair that already held the mri's existence in their hands, the medical chief of staff and this smallish plump woman whose department held all the mri's possessions. Boaz' interest was naked in her eyes, scholarly lust. Her small department had survived the dissolution virtually intact and capable of function, while Luiz' bio-medical staff had lost key personnel to the shift, angry medical personnel choosing the more comfortable existence of the station, under the guise of setting up systems for further probe missions.

Boaz and Luiz remained with *Flower*, and had come into positions of seniority in *Flower*'s depleted staff.

And Luiz approved her. Duncan searched the surgeon's face, looked again at Boaz.

"I was at such a place," he admitted carefully. "I don't know whether it would be possible to find it again."

"Let's talk in my office," said Boaz.

* * *

"SurTac Duncan," the page said for the second time. "You are wanted at the lock."

The aircraft was waiting. It could wait. Duncan pressed a com button at a panel and leaned toward it. "Duncan here. Advise them I'm coming in a few minutes."

He walked then, as he had been granted Luiz' free permission to do, into the guarded section of the infirmary, no longer there by a bending of regulations, but bearing a red badge that passed him to all areas of the ship but those on voice-lock. It was satisfying to see the difference in security's reaction to him, the quickness with which doors were opened to him.

And when he had come into Niun's room, the guard outside turned his back, a privacy which he had not often enjoyed.

He touched the mri, bent and called his name, wishing for the latest time he had had other options. He had obtained a position of some power again; had recovered favor where it mattered; had fought with every deviousness he knew; but when he looked at the mri's thin, naked face, it felt not at all like triumph.

He wished that they would allow Niun covering for his face; the mri lived behind veils, a modest, proud people. After some days with him, Niun had finally felt easy enough in his presence to show him his face, and to speak to him directly, as a man to a man of like calling.

There is no other way for us, Niun had told him, refusing offered help, at a time when the mri had had the power to choose for himself. *We either survive as we were, or we have failed to survive. We are mri; and that is more than the name of a species, Duncan. It is an old, old way. It is our way. And we will not change.*

There were fewer and fewer options for them.

Only a friend, Duncan thought bitterly, could betray them with such thoroughness. He had determined they would survive: their freedom would cost something else again; and that, too, he prepared to buy, another betrayal . . . things that the mri regarded as holy. In such coin he bought the cooperation of the likes of Boaz and Luiz; and wondered finally for whose sake he acted, whether Niun could even comprehend his reasoning, or whether it was only selfishness that drove him.

"Niun," he urged him, wishing for some touch of recognition, some reassurance for what he was doing. But Niun was far under this noon: there was no reaction to his name or to the touch of his arm.

He could not delay longer. He drew back, still hoping.

There was nothing.

He had not expected a pilot: he had looked to fly himself. But when he climbed aboard he found the controls occupied by a sandy-haired man who bore *Saber*'s designation on his sleeve. *GALEY*, the pocket patch said, *LT*.

"Sorry about the delay," Duncan said, for the air was hot, noon-heated. "Didn't know I wasn't solo on this one."

Galey fired up, shrugged as the engines throbbed into life. "No matter. It's hot here, hot down there at the water plant on repair detail, too. I'd rather the ship, thanks."

Duncan settled into the copilot's place, adjusted his gear, the equipment that Boaz had provided, into the space between his feet, and fastened the belts.

The ship lifted at an angle, swung off into an immediate sharp turn toward the hills. Cold air flooded them now that they were airborne, delicious luxury after the oven-heat of the aircraft on the ground.

"Do you know where we're going?" he asked of Galey.

"I know the route. I flew you out of there."

Duncan gave him a second look, trying to remember him, and could not. It had been dark, a time too full of other concerns. He blinked, realizing Galey had said something else to him, that he had been drifting.

"Sorry," he said. "You asked something?"

Galey shrugged again. "No matter. No matter. How'd the kel'ein make out? Still alive, I hear."

"Alive, yes."

"This place we're going have something to do with them?"

"Yes."

"Dangerous?"

"I don't know," he said, considering that for the first time. "Maybe."

Galey absorbed that thought in several kilometers of silence, the white desert slipping beneath them, jagged with rocks. Duncan looked out, saw black dots below.

"Dusei," he said. Galey rocked over and looked.

"Filthy beasts," Galey said.

Duncan did not answer him or argue. Most of humankind would say the same, would wish the remaining mri dead, with just cause. He watched the desert slip under the airship's nose, and the land roughen into highlands over which he had traveled at great cost, in great pain—dreamlike, such speed, looking down on a world where time moved more slowly, where realities were different and immediate and he had learned for a time to live.

They circled out over Sil'athen, the long T-shaped valley remote in the highlands, a slash into the high plateau, much eroded, a canyon full of strange shapes carved by caustic rains and the constant winds that swept its length. There was wreckage there of ships not yet lifted back for salvage, aircraft that Niun had made the price of his taking; the wreckage too of nature, many an aeons-old formation of sandstone blasted into fragments.

When they landed at the crossing of the high valley and stepped out into that place, into the full heat of Arain's red light, the silence came suddenly on them both, a weight that took the breath away. Duncan felt the air at once, a violent change from the pressurized and filtered air in the ship, and began coughing so painfully that he had at once to have recourse to the canteen. Filter masks and tinted goggles were part of the gear; he put his on, and adjusted the hood of his uniform to shield his head from the sun, while Galey did the same. The mask did not overcome the need to cough; he took another small sip of water.

"You all right?" Galey's voice was altered by the mask. Duncan looked into the broad, freckled face and felt better for the company of someone in such silence; but Galey did not belong, he in no wise belonged. Duncan slung his canteen over his shoulder, gathered up the gear, and tried not to listen to the silence.

"I'm all right," Duncan said. "Listen, it's a long way down the canyon and up into those rocks. You don't have to come."

"My orders say otherwise."

"Am I not trusted with this?" Duncan at once regretted the outburst, seeing how Galey looked at him, shocked and taken aback. "Come on," he said then. "Watch your step."

Duncan walked, at the slow pace necessary in the thin air, Galey walking heavy-footed beside him. The mri were right in the dress they adopted: to have any skin exposed in this sun was not wise; but when Galey began to drift toward the inviting shade of the cliffs, Duncan did not, and Galey returned to him.

"Don't walk the shade," Duncan said. "There are things you can miss there, that may not miss you. It's dark enough where we'll have to be walking, without taking unnecessary chances."

Galey looked at him uneasily, but asked no questions. The wind sang strangely through the sandstone spires.

It was a place of ghosts: Sil'athen, burial place of the mri. Duncan listened to the wind and looked about him as they walked, at the high cliffs and caves that held their secrets.

A dead people, a dead world. Graves of great age surrounded them here, those on the east with weathered pillars to mark them, those on the west with none. There were writings, many already beyond reading, outworn by the sands, and many a pillar overthrown and destroyed in the fighting that had raged up and down Sil'athen.

And in the sand they found the picked bones of a great dus.

Sadness struck Duncan when he saw that, for the beasts were companions of the mri, and dangerous as they could be, they could also be gentle: sad-faced, slow-moving protectors of their masters.

This too, was added to the destruction of a way of life.

Galey kicked at the skull. "Fast-working scavengers," he said.

"Leave it alone," Duncan said sharply. Galey blinked, straightened, and took a more formal attitude with him.

It was a true observation nonetheless, that there were scavengers in great numbers in the seemingly lifeless wastelands: nothing dropped to the sand but that something made use of it; nothing faltered or erred but that some predator was waiting for that error. The mri themselves did not walk the desert at night without the dusei to guide them. Even by day it was necessary to watch where one stepped, and to keep an eye on rocks that might hide ambush. Duncan knew the small depression that identified a

burrower's lair, and how to keep the sun between himself and
rocks to avoid the poisonous strands of windflowers. He knew too
how to find water when he must, or how to conceal himself—the
latter an easy task in Sil'athen, where the constant winds erased
the tracks of any passage, smoothing the tablet of the sands almost as soon as the foot left the ground. Skirling eddies of dust
ran like a mist above the ground, occasionally stirring up in great
whistling gusts that drove the sand in clouds.

Such a trackless, isolated place the mri had chosen . . . such an
end Niun had chosen, as if even in passing they wished to obliter-
ate all trace that they had been.

They had been here, he had learned in his long studies, his ca-
joling of translators, for many centuries, serving regul. Here and
hereabouts they had fought—against each other . . . for regul in
the beginning had hired them against the mercenaries of other
regul, mercenaries who also chanced to be mri. The conflicts were
listed endlessly in regul records, only the names changing: *The
mri (singular) of doch Holn defeated the mri (dual) of doch
Horag; Horag (indecipherable) fled from the territory (indecipherable).*

So it had begun here—until Holn flung the mri not against mri,
but against humanity. Solitary, strange fighters: humans had
known a single mri to taunt a human outpost, to provoke a reaction that sometimes ended with more casualties in his killing than
humans were willing to suffer. Wise commanders, knowing the
suicidal fury of these mri berserkers, held their men from answering, no matter how flagrant the provocation, until the mri, in
splendid arrogance, had passed back to his own territory.

A challenge, perhaps, to a reciprocal act?

Niun was capable of such a rash thing.

Niun, whose weapons, worn on two belts at chest and hip,
ranged from a laser to a thin, curved sword, an anachronism in the
war he fought.

An old, old way, Niun had called it.

All that was left of it was here.

The place had a feeling of menace in its deeper shadows, where
the sandstone cliffs began to fold them closer, a sense of holi-
nesses and history, of dead that had never known of humankind.
And there were deeper places, utterly alien, where mri sentinels

had watched and died, faithful to a duty known only to themselves, and where the rocks hid things more threatening than the dead.

He had looked on such.

It lay there, distant above the cliffs where the canyon ended, where heaps of rock had tumbled in massive ruin.

"How far are we going?" Galey asked, with a nervous eye to the cliffs that confronted them. "We going to climb that?"

"Yes," Duncan said.

Galey looked at him, fell silent again, and trod carefully behind him as he began to seek that way he knew, up among the rocks, a dus-trail and little more.

It was there, as he remembered, the way up, concealed in dangerous shadow. He marked his way carefully with his eye, and began it, slowly.

Often in the climb he found himself obliged to pause, coughing, and to drink a little and wait, for the air was thinner still on the upper levels, and he suffered despite the mask. Galey too began to cough, and drank overmuch of their water. Duncan considered letting Galey, who had not come as he had, from a stay in sickbay, carry more of the equipment; but Galey, from *Saber*'s sterile, automated environment, was laboring painfully.

They made the crest at last, and came into sunlight, among tall spires of rock, a maze that bore no track, no enduring sign to indicate that mri had walked here: in this place, as in Sil'athen, the wind scoured the sand.

Duncan stood, considering the sinking of red Arain beyond the spires, breathed the air cautiously, felt the place with all his senses. He had land-sense, cultivated in a score of trackless environments, and it drew at him, subtle and under the threshold of reason. Galey started to say something; Duncan curtly ordered silence, stood for a time, and listened. The omnipresent wind pulled at them, frolicked, singing among the spires. He turned left.

"Follow me," he said. "Don't talk to me. I last walked this in the dark, and things look different."

Galey murmured agreement, still breathing hard. He was silent thereafter, and Duncan was able to forget his presence as they walked. He would gladly have left Galey: he was not used to company on a mission, was not used to schedules or reports or being concerned for a night spent in the open—and SurTac that he was, he had little respect for the regulars when they were stripped of their protective ships and their contact with superiors.

It occurred to him that *Flower* staff had no authority to order a regular from *Saber* to accompany him.

Stavros did.

Dark overtook them on the plateau, as Duncan had known it would, in a place where the spires were few and a vast stretch of sand lay between them and the farther cliffs.

"We might keep going," Galey volunteered, though his voice seemed strained already.

Duncan shook his head, selected a safe spot, and settled to stay until the dawn, wrapped in a thermal sheet and far more comfortable than in his previous night in this place. They removed the masks and ate, though Galey had small appetite; then they replaced them to sleep, turn and turn about..

A jo flew, briefly airborne, a shadow against the night sky. Once Duncan woke to Galey's whispered insistence that he had heard something moving in the rocks. He sat watch then, while Galey slept or pretended to sleep, and far across the sands he saw the dark shadow of a hunting dus that moved into the deeper shadow of the spires and was gone.

He listened to the wind, and looked at the stars, and knew his way now beyond doubt.

At the first touch of color to the land, they folded up the blankets and set out again, shivering in the early dawn, Galey stiff and limping from his exertion of the day before.

The spires closed about them once more, stained by the ruddy sun, and still the sense of familiarity persisted. They were on the right track; there remained no vestige of doubt in Duncan's mind, but he savored the silence, and did not break it with conversation.

And eventually there lay before him that gap in the rocks, inconspicuous, like a dozen others thereabouts, save for the identifying shelf of rock that slanted down at the left, and the depth of the shadow that lay within.

Duncan paused; it occurred to him that even yet there was time to repent what he was doing, that he could lead Galey in circles until they ran out of supplies, and convince them all that he could not remember, that the place was lost to him. It would need great and skilled effort by Boaz' small staff to locate it without him. It might go unlocated for generations of humans on Kesrith.

But relics did not serve a dead people. That everything they had been should perish, that an intelligent species should vanish from the universe, leaving nothing—there was no rightness in that.

"Here," he said, and led Galey by the way that he well remembered, that he had seen thereafter in his nightmares, that long, close passage between sandstone cliffs that leaned together and shut out the sky. The passage wound, and seemed to spiral, down into dark and cold. Duncan used his penlight, and its tiny beam showed serpentine writings on the walls, turn after turn into the depths.

Daylight broke, blinding and blurring as they arrived at the cul-de-sac that ended their descent. They stood in a deep well of living stone, open to the sky. The walls here too were written over with symbols, and blackened with the traces of fire, both the stone and the metal door that stood open at the far side of the pit.

Galey swore: the sound of the human irreverence grated on Duncan's ears, and he looked to his left, where Galey stared. A huddled mass of bones and burned tatters of black cloth rested in a niche within the stone. It was the guardian of the shrine. Niun had paid him respect; Duncan felt moved to do so and did not know how.

"Don't touch anything," he said, and immediately recalled Melein's similar words to him, a chilling echo in the deep well.

He tried to put his mind to other things—knelt on the sand in the sunlight and opened up the gear that he had carried, photographic equipment, and most of all a signal device. He activated it, and knew from that moment that human presence in this place was inevitable. Searching aircraft would eventually find it.

Then with the camera he rose and recorded all that was about them, the writings, the guardian, the doorway with its broken seal, the marks of destroying fire.

And last of all he ventured into the dark, into the shrine that not even Niun had presumed to enter—only Melein, with Niun to guard the door. Galey started to follow him, stepped within.

"Stay back," Duncan ordered; his voice echoed terribly in the metal chamber, and Galey halted, uncertain, in the doorway—retreated when Duncan stared at him. Duncan drew a careful breath then and activated the camera and its light, by that surveying the ruin about him.

Shrine: it was rather a place of fire-stained steel, ruined panels, banks of lifeless machinery, stark and unlovely. He had known what he would find here, had heard the sound of it, the working of machinery the night the place had died, destroyed by the mri.

And yet the mri, who well understood machines, revered it—revered the artifact they had borne away from it.

Mistrust recurred in him, human mistrust, the remembrance that the mri had never offered assurances to him: they had only held their hand from him.

Banks of machinery, no trace of holiness. The thing that Niun had so lovingly carried hence, that now rested in *Flower*'s belly, suddenly seemed sinister, and threatening . . . a weapon, perhaps, that could be triggered by probing. The mri penchant for taking enemies with them in their self-destruction made it entirely possible, made Niun's treasuring of it still comprehensible. Yet Boaz and security evidently had some confidence that it was no weapon.

It had its origin here—*here*, cradled in that rest, perhaps, that now was stripped and vacant. Duncan lifted the camera, completed his work among the dead, burned banks, explored recesses where the light pierced deep shadows, where yet the wind had not swept away the ash. Boaz' people would come here next; some of the computer specialists would try the wreckage of the banks, with little hope. Melein had been thorough, protecting this place from humanity, whatever it once might have been.

He had all he needed, all he could obtain. He returned to the entry, and delayed yet again, taking in the place with a last glance, as if that could fix it all in his mind and pierce through the heart of what was mri.

"Sir?" Galey said from the well.

Duncan turned abruptly, joined Galey in the daylight, moved aside the breathing mask that suddenly seemed to restrict his oxygen—glad to draw a breath of acrid, daylit air, wind-clean.

Galey's broad, anxious face seemed suddenly of another, a more welcome world.

"Let's go," he said then to Galey. "Let's get out of here."

The lower canyon was already deep in shadow when they reached the edge of the plateau, that path among the rocks that led down into Sil'athen. It was late afternoon where they stood, and twilight down in the canyon beneath them.

"Dark's going to be on us again before we reach the ship," Duncan said.

"We going to go all the way anyway?" Galey asked.

Duncan shook his head. "No. At dusk we sit down wherever we are."

Galey did not look pleased. Likely whoever had given him his orders had not well prepared him for the possibilities of nights spent in the open. Duncan's nose had started bleeding again on the return walk, irritated by the thin, dry air; Galey's cough had worsened, and if they must spend another night in the open, Galey would be suffering the like.

The regular attacked the descent first, scattering pebbles, slipping somewhat in his determination to make haste. And suddenly he stopped.

Duncan heard the aircraft at the same instant, a distant hum that grew louder, passed overhead and circled off again. He looked at Galey, and Galey likewise looked disturbed.

"Maybe it's weather moving in on us," Galey said, "or maybe it's something urgent at the port."

Duncan had the communicator; he fingered it nervously, reckoning that if either had been the case, then there should have been a call from the aircraft. There was silence.

"Move," he said to Galey.

There was no sign of the aircraft while they worked their way down the dangerous descent. They rested hardly at all; Duncan found blood choking him, stripped off the mask and wiped his face, smearing a red streak across his hand—dizziness blurred the rocks. He felt his way after Galey, stumbled to the valley floor, the soft and difficult sand.

"You're just out of sickbay," Galey said, offering with a touch on the straps to take the load that he carried. "Trust me with the gear at least. You'll be done up again."

"No," he answered, blindly stubborn. He gathered his feet under him and started walking, overwhelmed with anxiety, Galey struggling to stay with him.

Another kilometer up the canyon: this much ground Duncan made before he found his limit with the load he carried, coughing painfully; he surrendered the gear to Galey, who labored along with him, himself suffering from the cold air, rawly gasping after each breath. It was a naked, terribly isolated feeling, walking these shadowed depths among the tombs, carrying a record that did not belong to humanity, that others desired.

And there came a regul vehicle lumbering down the canyon, slow and ponderous. Galey swore. Duncan simply watched it come.

There was nothing to do, nowhere to go, no longer even any place to conceal the equipment. They were far from the rocks, in the center of the sandy expanse and under observation from the regul.

The sled rumbled up to them and stopped. The windscreen rolled back. A regul youngling smiled a regul smile at them both, a mere opening of the mouth that showed the ridge of dentition within.

"Kose Sten Duncan," said the regul. "We grew concerned. All right? All right?"

"Entirely," he said. "Go away. We do not need help."

The smile stayed. The round brown eyes flicked over his face, his hand, the equipage they carried. "Thin air. Heavy to carry, perhaps? Sit on the back, favor. I will carry you. Many bad things are here, evening coming. I am *koi* Suth Horag-gi. Bai Hulagh sent me. The reverence has profound concern—would not wish, kose Sten Duncan, accident to a human party here in the desert. We will take you back."

It was a small vehicle, a sled with a flatbed for cargo, where it was possible to sit without being confined: it was not imminently threatening, and it was pointless pride to refuse and keep walking, when the sled could easily match their best pace.

But Duncan did not believe the words he had been told—mistrusted the regul presence entirely. Galey was not moving without him, stood waiting his cue; and with great misgivings Duncan climbed aboard the flatbed of the little vehicle. He made room for Galey, who joined him, holding the gear carefully on his lap. The vehicle jolted into a slow turn on the sand.

"They must have landed down by our ship," Galey shouted into his ear. Duncan understood his meaning: regul all over their ship, that they had not secured because there was no living enemy against whom they reasonably ought to have secured it. He cursed himself for that overconfidence.

They two were armed. The regul were insane if they hoped to outmatch human reflexes in a direct confrontation; but the fact was that regul could expend younglings such as these with little regret.

And the reverence bai Hulagh had sent them—Hulagh, whose fear of the mri was obsessive and sufficient for murder.

Duncan touched Galey's arm, used the system of handsignals used in emergencies in space. *Careful. Hostiles.*

Friendlies, Galey signed back, hopeful contradiction. There was, to be sure, a treaty in effect, the utmost in courteous cooperation all over Kesrith base. Galey was confused. Humans did not like the regul, but hostiles was not a term used any longer.

Trouble, Duncan answered. *Possible. Watch.*

Shoot? Galey queried.

Possible, he replied.

The landsled lumbered on at a fair clip, enough that keeping their place on the flatbed was not an easy matter. But what would have been a long and man-killing walk in Kesrith's atmosphere— and likely an overnight camp—became a comparatively short and comfortable ride. Duncan tried inwardly to reason away his anxieties, trying to think it possible that in the intricacies of regul motives, these regul were trying to protect them, fearing Stavros' displeasure if they were lost.

He could not convince himself. They were alone with the regul, far from help.

They rounded the bend, and saw indeed that there was a regul ship on the ground near their own. They were headed directly for it. Duncan tugged at the straps in Galey's hands, took the equip-

ment to himself, all of it, then with a nod to Galey rolled off and
landed afoot on the sand, in a maneuver the heavy regul could not
have performed.

They had covered a considerable distance toward the safety of
their own ship before the regul driver reacted, bringing the sled
back about to block their path; and other younglings began to
come down the ramp out of the regul ship.

"Are you all right? You fell?" asked the regul driver.

"No," said Duncan. "No problem. We are going back to base
now. Thank you."

It did not work. The other younglings walked heavily about
them, surrounding them, smiling with gaping friendliness and at
the same time blocking their way.

"Ah," said Suth Horag-gi, dismounting from the sled. "You
take pictures. Mri treasures?"

"Property of Stavros," Duncan said in a clipped tone, and with
the dispatch he had learned was humanity's advantage over the
slow-moving regul, he shouldered a youngling, broke the circle,
and walked rapidly for the ramp of their own ship, disregarding a
youngling that tried to head them off.

"Good fortune," said that one with the proper youngling obse-
quiousness. "Good fortune you are back safe, kose Sten Duncan."

"Yes, thank you for your concern. My regards to the reverence
bai Hulagh."

He spoke in the regul tongue, as the regul had spoken in the
human. He shouldered the heavy, awkward youngling with brutal
force that to a regul was hardly painful. The push flung it slightly
off balance, and he passed it. Galey overtook him on the ramp, almost running. They boarded, found another youngling in the aircraft.

"Out," Duncan ordered. "Please return to your own ship. We
are about to go now."

It looked doubtful, and finally, easing past them, performed the
suck of air considered polite among regul, smiled that gaping
smile and waddled with stately lack of haste down the ramp.

Duncan set the gear down on the flooring and hit the switch to
lift the ramp the moment the youngling was clear, and Galey shut
the door and spun the wheel to seal it.

Duncan found himself shaking. He thought that Galey was too.

"What did they want?" Galey asked, his voice a note too high.

"Check out the ship before we lift," Duncan said. "Check out everything that could be sabotaged." And Galey stripped off the breathing mask and the visor and swore softly, staring at him, then flung them aside and set to work, began examining the panels and their inner workings with great care.

There was nothing, in the most careful examination, wrong. "Wish we could find something," Galey said, and Duncan agreed to that, fervently. The regul still waited outside.

Galey started the engines and slowly, testing out controls, turned the aircraft and hovered a few feet off the ground, running a course that vengefully dusted the regul craft, passing close enough to send the regul who were outside scrambling and stumbling ponderously toward cover.

Senior officer, Duncan should have rebuked that. He did not. He settled into the cushion while the aircraft lifted, his jaw clenched, his hand gripping the cushion with such force that when he realized it, long after they were at altitude enough that they had options if something went wrong, his fingers were numb and there were deep impression in the cushion.

"Game of nerves," he said to Galey. "Game of nerves—or whatever they were going to do, they didn't have time."

Galey looked at him. There were the patches of half a dozen worlds on Galey's sleeve, young as he was. But Galey was scared, and it was a tale that would make the rounds of the regular military of *Saber*, this encounter with regul.

"This is Stavros' business," Duncan told him, for Galey's sake, not for the regul, not even for Stavros. "The less noise made, the better. Take my example."

His reputation was, he knew, widespread among the regulars: the SurTac who had lost his head, who had gone hysterical and accused a high-ranking ally of murder. Doubtless it would stay on his record forever, barring Stavros' intervention, barring a promotion on Kesrith so high that the record could no longer harm him—and that was at present unlikely.

Galey seemed to understand him, and to be embarrassed by it. "Yes, sir," he said quietly. "Yes, sir."

The lights of Kesrith base came finally into view. They circled the area for the landing nearest *Flower*, and settled, signaling security with the emergency code. Duncan unstrapped and gathered the photographic equipment from its cushioned ride in the floor locker. Galey opened the hatch and lowered the ramp, and Duncan walked down into the escort of armed human security with a relief so great his knees were weak.

Across the field he saw another aircraft come in, close to the Nom side of the airfield, where the regul might be closest to their own authority.

A security agent tried to take the equipment from Duncan's hand. "No," he said sharply, and for once security deferred.

He lost Galey somewhere, missed him in the press and was sorry he had not given some courtesy to the regular who had done so competently; but *Flower*'s ramp was ahead, the open hatch aglow with lights in the surrounding night. He walked among the security men, into the ship, down the corridors, and to the science section.

Boaz waited, white-smocked, anxious. He did not deliver the gear to her directly, for it was heavy, but laid it on a counter.

There was nothing for him to do with it thereafter. He had completed his task for the human powers of Kesrith, and sold what the mri counted most valuable in all the world. The knowledge of it, like that of the ovoid that rested here behind voice-locked doors, was in human hands and not in those of regul, and that was, within the circumstances, the best that he could do.

Chapter Three

The majority of *Flower* personnel were in for the night after the initial excitement of receiving the records. The labs were shut down again, the skeleton night crew on duty. The ship had a different quality by night, a ghostly hush but for the whisper of machinery and ventilation, far different from the frenetic activity in its narrow corridors by day.

Duncan found the prospect of a bed, a quiet night in his own safe quarters, a bath (even the chemical scrub allowable under rationing) utterly, utterly attractive, after a three-hour debriefing. It was 0100 by the local clock, which was the time on which he lived.

The lateness of the hour did not stop him from descending to the medical section and pausing in Niun's room. There was neither day nor night for the mri, who lay, slack and deteriorating despite the therapy applied to his limbs, in the influence of sedation. Luiz had promised to consider a lessening of sedation; Duncan had argued heatedly with Luiz on this point.

There was no response now when he spoke to the mri. He touched Niun's shoulder, shook at him gently, hating to feel how thin the mri was becoming.

Tension returned to the muscles. The mri drew a deeper breath, moved against the restraints that stayed on him constantly, and his golden eyes opened, half-covered by the membrane. The membrane withdrew, but not entirely. The fixation of the eyes was wild and confused.

"Niun," Duncan whispered, then aloud: "Niun!"

The struggle continued, and yet the mri seemed only slightly aware of his presence, despite the grip of his hand. It was another thing, something inward, that occupied Niun, and the wide, golden eyes were dilated, terrified.

"Niun, stop it. It's Duncan. It's Duncan with you. Be still and look at me."

"Duncan?" The mri was suddenly without strength, chest heaving from exertion, as if he had run from some impossibly far place. "The dusei are lost."

Such raving was pitiable. Niun was a man of keen mind, of quick reflexes. He looked utterly confused now. Duncan held his arm, and knowing the mri's pride, drew a corner of the sheet across the mri's lower face, a concealment behind which the mri would feel more secure.

Slowly, slowly, the sense came back to that alien gaze. "Let me go, Duncan."

"I can't," he said miserably. "I can't, Niun."

· The eyes began to lose their focus again, to slip aside. The muscles in the arm began to loosen. "Melein," Niun said.

"She is all right." Duncan clenched his hand until surely it hurt, trying to hold him to hear that. But the mri was back in his own dream. His breathing was rapid. His head turned from side to side in delirium.

And finally he grew quiet again.

Duncan withdrew his hand from Niun's arm and left, walking slowly at first, then more rapidly. The episode distressed him in the strangeness of it; but Niun was fighting the sedation, was coming out of it more and more strongly, had known him, spoken to him. Perhaps it was alien metabolism, perhaps, the thought occurred to him, Luiz had adjusted the level of sedation, more reasonable than he had shown himself in argument on the subject.

He went to the main lock, to the guard post that watched the coming and going of all that entered and left the ship. He signed the log and handed the stylus back.

"Hard session, sir?" the night guard asked, sympathy, not inquisitiveness. Tereci knew him.

"Somewhat, somewhat," he said, blinked at Tereci from eyes he knew were red, felt of his chin, that was rough. "Message for Luiz when he wakes: I want to talk with him at the earliest."

"Recorded, sir," said Tereci, scratching it into the message sheet.

Duncan started through the lock, expecting it to open for him under Tereci's hand. It did.

"Sir," Tereci said. "You're not armed. Regulations."

Duncan swore, exhausted, remembering the standing order for personnel out at night. "Can you check me out sidearms?"

"Sign again," Tereci said, opened a locker and gave him a pistol, waiting while he put his name to another form. "I'm sorry," Tereci said. "But we've had some action around here at night. Regulations aside, it's better to carry something."

"Regul?" he asked, alarmed at that news, which he had not read in the reports. Regul was all that immediately occurred to him, and had he not been so tired, he would not have been so impolitic.

"Animals. Prowling the limits of the guard beams. They never get inside them, but I wouldn't go out there unarmed. You want an escort, sir? I could get one of the night security—"

"No need," he said wearily. "No need." He had come in from the open, and though armed, he had never thought in terms of weapons. He had walked the land in company with mri. He regarded no warnings of these men that were bound to the safety of *Flower* and the Nom, who had never seen the land they had come to occupy.

They could stand in the midst of Sil'athen and never see it, men of Galey's breed—solid men, decent.

Unwondering.

He belted on the gun, a heavy weight, an offense to a weary back, and smiled a tired thanks at Tereci, went out into the chill, acrid air. A geyser had blown out irreverently close to *Flower*. The steam made the air moist and clouded. He inhaled it deeply, not minding the flavor of it, found it grateful to walk the track by himself, in silence, without Galey. His head ached. He had not realized it before this. He took his time, and found nothing but pleasure in the night, under the larger of Kesrith's moons, with the air chill and the stars glittering, and far, far across the flats, lights illumined the geysers that spouted almost constantly. The land had become a boiling and impassable barrier, guarding the approaches to the ruins of the mri towers, that only the most intrepid of Boaz' researchers had scanned from the air.

Steel rang under his boots, the gratings that made firm the surface of the causeway. It was the only sound. He stopped, only to

have complete silence for a moment, and scanned the whole of
the horizon, the glittering waters of the Alkaline Sea, the lights of
the city, the steaming geysers, the ridges beyond *Flower*.

Rock scuffed, rattled. The sound seized his heart and held it
constricted. He heard it again, spun toward the sound, saw a
shadow shamble four-footed down a ridge.

It hit the guard beams and shied back, whuffing in alarm. Then
it reared up against the sky, twice the height of a tall man, a great,
long-clawed beast.

The dusei are lost, Niun had said.

Duncan stood still, heart pounding. He reckoned the danger
posed by these great omnivores, these natives of Kesrith. Venom-
clawed and powerful enough to rip a man to shreds. This one tried
the beam again, again, disliking the sensation, but single-minded
in its attempt.

A second beast showed on the crest of the slope, coming downhill. *Flower*'s spotlights came on, adding to confusion, her hatch
open, men pouring out.

"Stop!" Duncan shouted. "No farther! Don't shoot!"

The dus tried the beam again, heaved his bulk forward, and this
time energies of the defense system played along his great sides,
useless. He broke through, reared up and screamed, a moaning,
hollow cry that echoed off the walls of Kesrith's Nom.

A rifle beam cut the dark.

"Stop shooting!" Duncan shouted.

The second beast broke through, a sparkle of light against its
sides, a stench of singed fur. They huddled together, the two invaders, backed rump to rump, and kept shifting nervously.

Niun's beasts.

Duncan saw them head for the ramp, toward the open door,
where the men were—saw shots fired. The beasts shied off.

"No!" he cried, and the beasts backed, turned and came toward
him, snuffling the air. Back at the hatchway, men shouted at him.
They could not fire; he was too close to the beasts. Lights played
on them, blinding. The dusei, locked into their inquisitive obstinacy, paid no heed. They came, long-clawed feet turned in, claws
rattling on the mesh, heads lowered, ursine monsters—slope-
shouldered, almost comic in their distracted manner.

The larger dus nosed at him, sniffed noisily from its pug nose. Duncan stood still, heart pounding so that the blood raced in his veins. The beast nudged him, nothing gentle, and he did not fall; it nosed his hand, investigated it with the mobile center of the lip.

And they circled one before him and then the other, shifting position in a strange ballet, constantly between him and the men with the rifles, uttering low, moaning cries. He took his life in pawn and moved, found that they moved with him. He stopped and they stopped.

They were surely Niun's beasts, that had come a long, hard journey from Sil'athen—far longer a trek for them than for men's machines. And with uncanny accuracy they had found Niun, across a hundred miles of desert, and singled out the place that confined him.

He had seen dusei and mri work, had watched the beasts react, so sensitive to the voice, the gestures of the mri. He had seen the mri glance at the beast, and the beast react as if some unspoken agreement were between them.

He felt them against him, touching, giving him the heat of their vast, velvet-furred bodies. Nearly impossible to kill, the dusei, immune to the poisons of Kesrith's predators, vastly powerful, gentle and comic in their preoccupied approach to difficulties. He felt himself for a moment dizzy, the closeness of the beasts, their warmth, his exhaustion too much: he was for an instant afraid of the men with their guns, of the lights.

He thought of Niun, and there was another blurring, a desire, overwhelmingly strong, warm, determined.

The men, the lights, the guns.

Terror/desire/terror.

He blinked, caught himself with a hand against one warm back, found himself trembling uncontrollably. He began to walk, slowly, toward the open doorway, toward the security crew, who had their guns leveled, guns that could do little to a dus'massive, slow body, much to his.

He felt the savor of blood. Of heat.

"No!" he said to the dusei. They grew calm.

He stopped within easy hailing of the security personnel.

"Get out of there," one called to him. "Get out of there!"

"Go back inside," he said, "and seal all the corridors except the ones that go down to the holds. Give me a way to a safe compartment for them. Make it quick."

They did not stay to argue. Two went inside, to consult with authority, doubtless. Duncan stayed with the dusei, a hand on either broad back, calming them. They sensed Niun and Melein. They knew. They knew.

He was safe with them. It was the men with the guns that were to be feared. "Go away from the door," he wished the remaining security men. "They are no danger to me. They belong to the mri."

"Duncan?" That was Boaz' female voice, high-pitched and anxious. "Duncan, confound it, what's going on?"

"They've come for Niun. They're his. These creatures—are halfway sapient, maybe more than halfway. I want clearance to bring them inside before someone sets them off."

There was a flurry of consultations. Duncan waited, stroking the two massive backs. The dusei had settled down, sitting like dogs. They, too, waited.

"Come ahead," Boaz shouted. "Number one bow hold, equipment bay: it's empty."

Duncan made to the dusei the low sound he had heard Niun make, started forward. The dusei heaved themselves to their feet and came, casually, as if entering human ships were an ordinary thing. But no human stayed to meet them: even Boaz fled, prudence overcoming curiosity, and nothing greeting them but sealed doors and empty corridors.

They walked, the three of them, a long, long descent without lifts, down ways awkward for the big dusei—passed with a slow, measured clicking of claws on flooring. Duncan was not afraid. It was impossible to be afraid, with the like of them for companionship. They had searched him and had no fear of him: though at the back of his mind reason kept trying to urge him that he had been right to be afraid of the beasts, he began to be certain that the beasts were utterly at ease with what he was doing.

He came down into the hold, and caressed the offered noses, the thrusting massive heads that, less gentle, could stave in ribs or break his back; and again came that blurred feeling, that surety that he had given them something that pleased them.

He withdrew and sealed the doors, and trembled afterward, thinking what he had done. Food, water, other needs they had none, not at the moment. They wanted in. They had gained that, through him.

He fled, fear flooding him. He was panting as he ran the final distance to the medical wing. He saw the door that he wanted—closed, like all other doors during the emergency. He opened it manually, closed it again.

"Sir?" the sentry on duty asked.

"Are they awake?" Duncan asked, with harsh intensity. The sentry looked confused.

"No, sir. I don't think so."

Duncan shouldered past him, opened the door and looked at Niun. The mri's eyes were open, staring at the ceiling. Duncan went to the bedside and seized Niun's arm, hard.

"Niun. The dusei. The dusei. They have come."

There was a fine sweat on the mri's brow. The golden eyes stared into infinity.

"They are here," Duncan almost shouted at him. Niun blinked.

"Yes," said Niun. "I feel them."

And thereafter Niun answered nothing, reacted to nothing, and his eyes closed, and he slept, with a relaxed and tranquil expression.

"Sir?" the sentry asked, invading the room contrary to standing orders. "Do you want someone called?"

"No," Duncan said harshly. He edged past the man, walked out into the corridor, and started for the upper levels of the ship. The intercom came on, the whole ship waking to the emergency just past. He heard that Boaz was paging him, urgently.

He did not remember the walk upstairs, the whole of it a blank in his mind when he reached the area of the lock and found Boaz anxiously waiting. He dreaded such lapses, remembering the dizzy blurring of senses that had assailed him before.

"They're domestic?" Boaz asked him.

"They—seem to be. They are, for the mri. They're—I don't know. I don't know."

Boaz looked at him critically. "You're through for the day," she said. "No more questions. If they're bedded down and secure, no questions."

"No one goes down there. They're dangerous."

"No one is going to go near them."

"They're halfway sapient," he said. "They found the mri. Across all that desert and out of all these buildings, they found them."

He was shaking. She touched his arm, blonde, plump Boaz, and at that moment she was the most beautiful and kindly creature in all Kesrith. "Sten, go home," she said. "Get to your own quarters; get some rest. One of the security officers will walk you. Get out of here."

He nodded, measured his strength against the distance to the Nom, and concluded that he had enough left in him to make it to his room without staggering. He turned, blindly, without a word of thanks to Boaz, remembered nothing until he was out the door and halfway down the ramp with a security man at his side, rifle over one arm.

The mental gaps terrified him. Fatigue, perhaps. He wished to believe so.

But he had not consciously decided to enter *Flower* with the dusei.

He had not decided.

He tore his mind away, far away from the dusei, fighting a giddy return to the warmth that was their touch.

Yes, Niun had said, *I feel them.*

I feel them.

He talked to the security man, something to drown the silence, talked of banal things, of nonsensical things with slurring speech and no recall later of what he said.

It was only necessary, until he was within the brightly lighted safety of the Nom, in its echoing halls that smelled of regul and humans, that there not be silence.

The security guard left him at the door, pressed a plastic vial into his hand. "Dr. Luiz advised it," he said.

Duncan did not question what the red capsules were. They killed the dreams, numbed his senses, made it possible for him to rest without remembering anything.

He woke the next morning and found he had not turned off the lights.

Chapter Four

Stavros, seated outside his sled-console, in the privacy of his own quarters, looked like a man who had not slept. There was a thick folder of papers on the desk in front of him, rumpled and read: the labor of days to produce, of a night to read.

Duncan saw, and knew that there was some issue of his work, of the hours that he had spent writing and rewriting what he was sure only one man would ever see, reports that did not go to Boaz or Luiz, or even to security: that would never enter the records, if they ran counter to Stavros' purposes.

"Sit down," Stavros said.

Duncan did so, subject to the scrutiny of Stavros' pale eyes on a level with his own. He had no sense of accomplishment, rather that he had done all that was in him to do, and that it had probably failed, as all other things had failed to make any difference with Stavros. He had labored more over that report than over any mission prep he had ever done; and even while he worked he had feared desperately that it was all for nothing, that it was only something asked of him as a sop to his protests, and that Stavros would discard it half-read.

"This mri so-called shrine," said Stavros. "You know that the regul are disturbed about it. They're frightened. They connect all this mri business in their thinking: the shrine, the artifact, the fact that we've taken trouble to keep two mri alive—and your influence, that not least. The whole thing forms a design they don't like. Do you know the regul claim they rescued you and Galey?"

Duncan almost swore, smothered it. "Not true."

"Remember that to a regul your situation out there may have looked desperate. A regul could not have walked that distance.

Night was coming on, and they have a terror of the dark in the open wilderness. They claim they spotted the grounded aircraft and grew concerned for your safety—that they have been trying to watch over our crews in their explorations, for fear of some incident happening which might be blamed on them."

"Do you really believe that, sir?"

"No," said Stavros flatly. "I rather put it down to curiosity. To Hulagh's curiosity in particular. He is mortally afraid of what the mri might do, afraid of anything that has their hand in it. I think he's quite obsessed with the fear that some may survive and locate him. I am being frank with you. This is not for conversation outside this room. Now tell me this: was there any touching, any overt threat from the regul you encountered?"

"No hand laid on us. But our property—"

"I read that."

"Yes, sir."

"You handled it well enough," said Stavros, a slight frown on his face. "I think, though, that it does indicate that there is a certain interest in you personally, as well as in the mri relics. I think it was your presence drew them out there. And if I hadn't put Galey out there with you, you could have met with an accident. You neglected precautions."

"Yes, sir."

"They'll kill you if they can. I can deal with it after it happens, but I can't prevent it, not so long as you're within convenient reach of them. And why this shrine, Duncan? Why this artifact?"

"Sir?"

"Why do you reckon it was so important? Why did the mri risk their lives to go to that place and fetch it?"

Duncan gestured vaguely to the report that lay on the desk. "Religion. I explained—"

"You've been inside that so-called shrine. I've seen the pictures you brought out. Do you really believe that it's a place of worship?"

"It's important to them." He was helpless to say anything else. Other conclusions lay there in the photographs: computer banks, weaponry, communications—all such possibilities as regul would dread, as allies of the regul would have to fear.

"You're right: it's important to them. Boaz has cracked your egg, Duncan. Three days ago. The artifact is open."

It shook him. He had thought it unlikely—that if it were to be opened, it would need mri help, cooperation, that might be negotiated. But Boaz' plump hands, that worked with pinpoint probe and brush, with all the resources of *Flower*'s techs at her command—they had succeeded, and now the mri had nothing left that was their own.

"I hadn't thought it would be possible that soon," Duncan said. "Does the report say what it was?"

"Is. What it *is*. Boaz says it was designed for opening, no matter of difficulty to someone with the right technique, and some assurance that it was not a weapon, which I understand your pictures provided. It's some sort of recording device. The linguistic part of it is obscure—some sort of written record is there; and there's no one fluent in the mri language to be able to crack the script. For obvious reasons we don't want to consult with the regul. But there's numerical data there too, in symbols designed to be easily deciphered by anyone: there was even a key provided in graphics. Your holy object, Duncan, and this so-named shrine, are some kind of records-storage, and they wanted it badly, wanted it more than they wanted to survive. What kind of record would be that important?"

"I don't know."

"Numerical records. Series of numerical records. What sort of recording device does that suggest to you?"

Duncan sat silent a moment. In his limited experience only one thing suggested itself. "Navigational records," he said at last, because Stavros waited, determined to have such an answer.

"Yes. And is that not a curious thing for them to want, when they had no ship?"

Duncan sat and considered the several possibilities, few of them pleasant to contemplate.

"It knocks out another idea," Stavros said, "—that the mri were given all their technology by the regul: that they weren't literate or technologically sophisticated on their own." He picked up a photo that lay face-down on the desk, pushed it across, awkward in the extension of his arm. "From the artifact, ten times actual size."

Duncan studied it. It showed a gold plate, engraved with symbols, detail very complex. It would have been delicate work had the original been as large as the picture.

"Plate after plate," said Stavros. "Valuable for the metal alone. Boaz theorizes that it was not all done by one hand, and that the first of that series is very old. Techniques of great sophistication or of great patience, one or the other, and meant to last. I'm told the mathematics are intricate; they've gone to computer to try to duplicate the series of navigational tape, and to try to match it out with some reference point. Even so it seems beyond our capabilities to do a thorough analysis on it. We may have to resort to the labs at Haven, and that's going to take time. A great deal of time. But you maintain you had no idea what it was you had."

"No, sir." He met Stavros' eyes without flinching, the only defense he could make. "I didn't know then and I'm not even sure now that the mri knew; maybe they were sent by their own authorities, and had no idea why. But I'll agree it's highly likely that they knew."

"Can you get it out of them?"

"No. No. I don't think so."

"They seem to have expected a ship—if this tape is what it appears to be."

"I don't think they did. They wanted offworld, yes, but they expected nothing. That's an emotional judgment, based on the general tone of things they said and did, but I believe it."

"Possibly a very valid judgment. But they may not commit your error, Duncan, of seeing all regul as alike. The mri dealt specifically with doch Holn; Alagan is Holn's rival; and Holn . . . *does have ships*."

Cold settled from brain to stomach. The argument was plausible. "Yes, sir," Duncan said softly. "But it would be a matter of contacting them."

"The so-called shrine—is a possibility."

"No."

"Another emotional judgment?"

"The same judgment. The mri are finished. They knew it."

"So says Alagn; so, perhaps, said your mri. Perhaps neither is lying. But regul sometimes do not say all they know. Perhaps mri don't, either. Perhaps we haven't asked the right questions." Hand trembling, Stavros lifted a cup and drank, set it down again. "The mri are mercenaries. Are yours for hire?"

The question set him aback. "Maybe. I don't know."

"I think the regul as a whole fear that. I think that is one of several things Hulagh desperately fears, that having lost possession of the mri, he might find humankind possessing them. And using them. What is their usual price, do you know?"

"I don't know." He looked at Stavros, found that curious, half-mocking manner between him and the truth. He laid the picture down on the desk. "What are you proposing?"

"I'm not. I'm just wondering how well you profess to know them."

"It wasn't a thing we discussed."

"According to your records, you're a skilled pilot."

He looked at Stavros blankly.

"True?" Stavros asked.

"If the record says so."

"Elag/Haven operations required some interstellar navigation."

"I had a ship automated to the hilt. I can handle in-system navigation; but everything in transit operations was taped."

"That is rather well what we're dealing with here, isn't it?"

Duncan found nothing to say for several moments.

"Does all this come together somehow?" he asked finally. "What is it you're really asking?"

"Take the mri in charge. Take the artifact, the egg. You say that you can handle the mri. Or is that so, after all?"

Duncan leaned back in his chair, put distance between himself and the old man, drew several slow breaths. He knew Stavros, but not, he thought suddenly, well enough.

"You have doubts?" Stavros asked.

"Any sane man would have doubts. Take the mri and do what? What is this about navigation?"

"I'm asking you whether you really think you can handle the mri."

"In what regard?"

"Whether you can find out more than that report of yours tells me. Whether you can find some assurance for Kesrith that the mri are not going to be trouble, or that Holn does not have its hands on more of them."

Duncan leaned forward again and rested his arms on the front of Stavros' desk, knowing full well that there was deception involved. He looked Stavros in the eyes and was sure of it, bland and innocent as Stavros' expression was. "You're not influenced by my advice. You're going to send me off blind, and there's something else going on. Can I know what that is? Or do I guess at it?"

They had lived close, had shared, he and the old man; he leaned on that fact desperately, saw offense and a slow yielding in Stavros' expression. "Between us," Stavros said.

"Between us."

Stavros frowned, a tremor of strain in his lips. "I want the mri off Kesrith, immediately. I'm sending *Flower* up to station, where it can proceed about its work unhindered. The regul are getting nervous about the mri since your visit to Sil'athen. And a regul ship incoming is not an impossibility in the near future. Hulagh says his doch will be getting anxious because he's failed his schedule with a ship that was entrusted to him by their central organization: its loss is going to be a heavy blow to Alagn. And he's worried. He constantly frets on the topic of misunderstandings, demands a way offworld to meet his ships. If we have regul ships incoming, I don't want any of ours caught on the ground. I think moving *Flower* aloft will minimize any chance of an incident. *Saber* and *Hannibal* together have shields sufficient to protect the station and the probe ships if there should be a problem. But with the mri anywhere accessible to the regul, there could easily be a problem. The regul have a panic reaction where it concerns mri."

"I've seen it at work," Duncan said bitterly.

"Yes," said Stavros. "The bai has asked repeatedly about the artifact. I daresay the bai does not sleep easily. If you had at your disposal a ship, the mri, and the egg, Duncan, do you think you could find out the nature of that record?"

Duncan let out his breath slowly. "Alone?"

"You would have the original artifact. The mri would doubtless insist on it; and we have duplicated the object in holos—so we wouldn't be risking more than the museum value of the object, considerable though that may be. Under the circumstances it's a reasonable risk." Stavros took a long drink, rested the cup on the desk with a betraying rattle of pottery. His breath came hard. "Well?"

"Tell me plainly," Duncan said, "what the object of this is. How far. Where. What options?"

"No certainties. No clear promises. If the mri go for Holn assistance, you'll lose the ship, your life—whatever. I'm willing to gamble on your conviction they won't. You can find out what that tape is and maybe—*maybe*—deal with the mri. You tell me. If you think it's impossible, say so. But going the route of the computers at Haven will take months, a year—with the regul-mri question hanging over us here at Kesrith, and ourselves with no idea what we're facing. We need to know."

"And if I refused?"

"Your mri would die. No threat: you know the way of it. We can't let them go; they'd get the regul or the regul would get them. If we keep them as they are, they'll die. They always have."

It was, of course, the truth.

"More than that," said Stavros, "all of us are sitting on the line here at Kesrith. And there's the matter of the treaty, that involves rather more than Kesrith. You appreciate that, I'm sure. You say you can reason with them. You've said that all along. I'm giving you your chance."

"This wasn't in the contract. I didn't agree to any offworld assignments."

Stavros remained unmoved. Duncan looked into his eyes, fully aware what the contract was worth in colonial territory—that in fact his consent was only a formality.

"It is a SurTac's operation," said Stavros finally. "But back out if you don't think you can do it."

"A ship," Duncan said.

"There's probe *Fox*. Unarmed. Tight quarters too, if there should be trouble aboard. But one man could handle her."

"Yes, sir. I know her class."

"Boaz is finishing up on the holos now. *Flower* is going up to the station this afternoon, whatever you decide. If you have to have time to think about it, a shuttle can run you up to the station later, but don't plan to take too long about a decision."

"I'll go."

Stavros nodded slowly, released a long breath. "Good," he said, and that was all.

Duncan arose, walked across the room to the door, looking back once. Stavros said nothing, and Duncan exited with resentment and regret equally mixed.

There was a matter of gear to pack, that only. He had lived all his life under those conditions. It would take about five minutes.

Regul stared at him as he walked the hall to his room, were still interested when he walked back with his dunnage slung over his shoulder—carrying a burden, which neither regul nor mri would do: the regul not without a machine, and the mri—never.

They flatly gaped, which in regul could be smiles, and, he thought, they were smiles of pleasure to realize that he was leaving.

The mri's human, he had heard them call him, and mri was spoken as a curse.

"Good-bye, human," one called at him. He ignored it, knowing it was not for friendliness that they wished him farewell.

There was a moment of sadness, walking the causeway outside. He paused to look toward the hills, with the premonition that it was for the last time.

A man could not wholly love Kesrith: only the dusei might do that. But hereafter there was only the chill, sterile environment of ships, where there was no tainted wind, no earth underfoot, and Arain was a near and therefore dangerous star.

He heaved his baggage again to his shoulder, walked the ringing mesh to the lowered ramp. They expected him. He signed aboard as personnel this time, a feeling unfamiliar only because there was not the imminent prospect of combat. Old anxieties seized on him. Ordinarily his first move would be for whatever rider vessel he had drawn, to begin checking it out, preparing for a drop into whatever Command had decreed for him.

"Compartment 245," the duty officer told him, giving him his admitted-personnel tag: silly formality, he had always thought, where personnel were few enough to be known by sight to everyone on *Flower*. But they were headed for station, for a wider world, where two great warships, two probes, and an in-system rider mingled crews. He attached the tag, reckoning numbers. He was assigned near the mri. He was well satisfied with that, at least.

He went there, to ride through lift with them.

Chapter Five

The station was a different world indeed—regul-built, a maze of the spiraling tunnels favored by the sled-traveling regul. Everything was automated.

And strangest of all, there were no regul.

To walk among humans only, to hear their talk, to breathe the air breathed by humans, and never to be startled by the appearance of an alien face—in all this vast space: it was like being cast across light years; and yet Kesrith's rusty surface was only a shuttle flight away: the screens showed it, a red crescent.

The screens likewise showed the ships that clustered about the station—*Saber* foremost, a kilometer-long structure that was mostly power, instrumentation, and weaponry—and surprisingly scant of crew, only two hundred to tend that monster vessel. Shields made her strong enough to resist attack, but she would never land onworld. *Flower* and *Fox* had ridden in attached to *Saber*'s sides, as *Santiago* had ridden the warship *Hannibal*, like diminutive parasites on the flanks of the warships, although *Flower* and *Fox* were independently star-capable. Presently the probe ships were docked almost unnoticed in the black shadow of *Saber*. *Flower* had snugged into the curve to berth directly under the long ship, and from her ports and scanners there was very little visible but *Saber* and the station itself.

And the station, vast, complexly spiral, rolled its way about Kesrith, a curious dance that dizzied the mind to consider, as one walked the turning interior.

Most personnel made use of the sleds. The distances inside the station were considerable, the sleds novel and frighteningly rapid, whirling around the turns with reckless precision, avoiding collisions by careful routing at hairbreadth intervals.

Duncan walked, what of a walk was possible in the less than normal *g* of the station that was planned for regul comfort. The giddy feeling combined with the alien character of the corridors and the sight of Kesrith out of reach below, and fed his depression.

"That's the one that came in off the desert," he heard someone say behind his back. It finished any impulse he had toward mingling with these men, that even here he was a curiosity, more out of place than he was ever wont to be among regulars. He was conscious of the mask of tan that was the visible mark of the kel'en's veil, worn in the burning light of Arain; he felt his face strangely naked in their sight, and felt their stares on him, a man who had lived with humanity's enemy, and spoke for them.

On the first evening there was leisure for *Flower* personnel to have liberty, he wandered into the station mess . . . found Galey, whose face split into a broad and friendly grin at the sight of him; but Galey, of *Saber*, was with some of *Saber*'s officers, his own friends, and Duncan found no place with them, a SurTac's peculiar rank less than comfortable in dealing with officers of the regular forces. He ate alone, from the automated bar, and walked alone back to *Flower*.

He had done his tour of the station. It was enough. He had no interest even in seeking out the curiosities of the regul architecture, that the men of the warships seemed to enjoy on their hours of liberty.

He went into *Flower*'s lock, into familiarity, in among men he knew, and breathed a sigh of relief.

"Worth seeing, sir?" the duty officer asked him, envious: his own liberty had been deferred. Duncan shrugged, managed a smile; his own mood was not worth shedding on the regulars of *Flower*. "A bit like the Nom," he answered. "A curiosity. Very regul."

And he received from the man's hand a folded message of the kind that passed back and forth frequently at the desk.

He started back toward the level of his own quarters, unfolding the message as he walked.

It was Boaz' hand. *Urgent I talk with you. Lab #2.B.*

Duncan crumpled it in his hand and stuffed it into his pocket, lengthening his stride: the mri program and an urgency; if running would have put him there appreciably faster he would have run.

Number two lab contained Boaz' office. She was there, seated at her desk, surrounded by paper and a clutter of instruments. She looked up at him as he entered. She was upset, blue eyes looking fury at the world. Her mouth trembled.

"Have a seat," she said, and before he could do so: "*Saber*'s troops moved in; snatched the mri, snatched the artifact, the mri's personal effects, everything."

He sank into the offered chair. "Are they all right?"

"I don't know. Yes. yes—they *were* all right. They were set into automeds for the transfer. If they just leave them in them, they'll fare well enough for a while. Stavros' orders. Stavros' orders, they said." She picked up a sealed cylinder from the center of the littered desk and gave it to him with a misgiving stare. "For you. They left it."

He received the tube and broke the seal, eased out the paper it contained and read the message to himself. *Conditions as discussed apply. contingency as discussed has occurred. Observe patience and discretion. Stand by. Destroy message. Stavros.*

Regul troubles: ship incoming. The mri were going out, off-station, and himself with them, soon enough. He looked sadly at Boaz, wadded the message in his hand, pocketed it; he would dispose of it later.

"Well?" asked Boaz, which she surely knew she should not ask; he stayed silent. She averted her eyes, pursed her lips, and laced her fingers under her plump chin. "I belong to a ship," she said, "which is—unfortunately—under the governor's authority in some degree, where it regards putting us offworld or seizing what pertains to declared hostiles. For now, in those regards, that authority is absolute. I personally am not under his orders, and neither is Luiz. I shouldn't say this freely; but I will tell you that if you are personally not satisfied with the treatment of the mri— there can be a protest filed at Haven."

Brave Boaz. Duncan looked at her with an impulse of guilt in his heart. There was no word from her of canceled programs, interrupted researches, the seizure of work on which she had la-

bored with such care. The mri themselves occurred to her. This
was something he had not foreseen; and yet it was like her.

"Boz," he said, the name the staff called her. "I think everything is all right with them."

She made a noncommittal sound, leaned back. She said nothing, but she looked a little relieved.

"They didn't take the dusei, did they?" he asked.

Boaz smiled suddenly, gave a fierce laugh. "No. The beasts
wouldn't sedate. They tried. There was no way they would go
down into that hold with them. They asked *Flower* staff to do it,
got rather high-handed about it; and Luiz told them they could go
down for themselves and throw a net over them. There were no
volunteers."

"I don't doubt," Duncan said. "I'd better get down there and
see about them."

"You can't tell me what this business is."

"No. I'm sorry."

She nodded, shrugged. "You can't tell me whether things are
likely to reverse themselves."

"I don't think they will."

Again she nodded. "Well," she said sadly. That was all.

He took his leave of her and walked out, through the lab that
was, he saw, in a disorder that had nothing to do with research,
small items that had been on the shelves now gone, books missing.

Saber's men had been thorough.

But if they had taken the mri from the ship, then the dusei
might pine and die, like one that he had seen grieving over a dead
mri, a beast that would not leave for any urging.

He took that downward corridor that led him to the hold. His
stomach was already knotting in dread, remembering what they
could do in distress. He had been among them since that first
night, brought them food and water, and they had reacted to that
with content. But now they had been disturbed by strangers, attacked; and the fear of that feeling that had possessed him once
was as strong as any fear of venomed claws.

The sensation did not recur. He entered the hold high on the
catwalk, looked down at the brown shapes that huddled below,
and cautiously descended to them, fearing them and determined

not to yield to it. The regul avowed that the dusei thrived on synthetic protein, which was abundant enough in the station stores; that they would, in fact, eat anything they were offered, which presumably included humans and regul, as he had heard Luiz remark.

The air was remarkably fresh, a clean though occupied aroma to the hold, not so pronounced as with the fastidious regul. The beasts were very neat in their habits, and remarkably infrequent in their necessary functions, metabolizing fluids in such a fashion that Boaz and Luiz found exceedingly intriguing, with a digestion that exacted fluids and food value from anything available of vegetable or animal tissue, and gave off practically no waste compared to the bulk they had ingested—and that quite dry. Regul information on them was abundant, for regul ships had kept kel'ein and dusei for many years. Dusei seemed to go dormant during long confinement, once settled and content. In general dusei put less demand on a ship's life-support than humans, mri, or regul.

It was the awesome size of them that made them uncomfortable companions, the knowledge that there was absolutely nothing that could be done should one of them run amok.

Duncan stepped from the last tread of the stairs, saw both dusei rise with a keening moan that echoed throughout the deep hold. They stood shoulder to shoulder, nostrils working, smelling the stranger. Their small eyes, which were perhaps not overly keen, glittered in the light. The larger of them was a ragged, scarred beast: this one Duncan took for Niun's own; and he thought he also knew the smaller, sleek one for a one-time companion of theirs.

The big one shambled forward with his pigeon-toed gait, looked Duncan up and down and rumbled a deep purring that evinced pleasure in the meeting. The smaller one came, urgently thrusting with its broad nose at Duncan's leg.

He sat down on the last steps between them, and the big animals settled in an enormous mass about his feet, so that they touched. He stroked the velvet-furred hides—remarkably pleasant, that velvet-over-muscle. There was no sound at all but the rumbling of the dusei, a monotonous, peaceful sound.

They were content. They accepted him, accepted a human because of Niun, because they had known him in Niun's company, he thought, although they had disdained his touch while Niun was there. When once he had attempted escape, the dusei had hunted him, had cornered him, all the while pressing at him with such terror as he began to understand was a weapon of theirs.

I wonder that they did not kill you, Niun had said that night.

Duncan wondered now that they rested so calmly after what had been done to them, after humans had tormented them, trying to sedate them; but the dusei's metabolism absorbed poisons, and perhaps absorbed the drug. There was no evidence of harm to them, not even any of disturbance in their manner.

Neither men nor fully animal, the dusei, but four-footed halflings, shadow-creatures, that partook of the nature of both . . . that offered themselves to the mri, but were not taken: they were companions of the mri, and not property. He doubted that humanity could accept such a bargain. The regul could not.

He sat content, touching, being touched, and calm; he had not known that night whether admitting the dusei to the ship was right: now it seemed very right. He found himself suddenly full of warmth—he was receiving. He knew it all at once, knew the one that so touched him, the small one, the small one that was still more than three times the bulk of a big man. It purred with a steady, numbing rhythm, leached passion from him as water stole the salts of Kesrith from the soil and displaced them seaward.

It drowned them, overwhelmed them.

He drew back suddenly, panicked; and this the dusei did not like. They snorted and withdrew. He could not recover them. They stood and regarded him, apart, with small and glittering eyes.

Cold flooded into him, self-awareness.

They had come of their own accord, using him: they wanted— and he had given them access; and still he needed them, them and the mri, them and the mri. . . .

He gathered himself and scrambled up the narrow stairs, sweating and tense when he gained the safety of the catwalk. He looked down. One of them reared up, tall and reaching with its paws. Its voice shook the air as it cried out.

He hurled himself for the other side of the door and sealed and locked it, hands shaking. It was not rational, this fear. It was not rational. They used it. It was a weapon.

And they were where they wanted to be now: at a station orbiting Kesrith, and near the mri. He had done everything they wanted. He would do it again, because he needed them, needed the calming influence they might exert with the mri, who drew comfort from them, who relied on them. He began to suspect variables beyond his reckoning.

But he could not leave them.

The thoughts wound him in upon himself, panic-fear and the gut-deep certainty of something wrong. He realized that he had been greeted by a man in the corridor some ten paces back, and absently turned and tried to amend the discourtesy, but it was too late; the man had walked on. Duncan enfolded himself in his private turmoil and kept walking, hands in his pockets, wadding into smaller and smaller balls the messages he had thrust there, Boaz' and Stavros'.

Confound you, Niun, he thought violently, and wondered if he were sane for the mere suspicion he entertained. The dusei, whatever they were, could not touch his conscious thoughts; it was at some lower level they operated, something elemental and sensual and sensory—possible to reject if a man could master his fear of them and his need of them: that was surely the wedge they used for entry, fear and pleasure, either one or the other. It felt very good to please a dus; it was threatening to annoy one.

Yet the researchers had not picked it up. There was nothing of the kind reported in their observations of the beasts.

Perhaps the beasts had not spoke to them.

Duncan closed the door to his own small quarters, opposite the now-vacant compartments of the mri, and began packing, folding up the clothes that he had scarcely unpacked.

When he had done, he sat down in the chair by his desk and keyed in a call to *Saber* by way of *Flower*'s communications.

Transfer of dusei possible and necessary, he sent to *Saber*'s commander.

Stand by, the message came back to him. And a moment later: *Report personally* Saber *Command soonest.*

Chapter Six

There was nothing remarkable about a SurTac boarding a military ship; there should not have been, but the rumors were flying among the crew. Duncan surmised that by the looks that slid his way as he was escorted up to Command: escorted, not allowed to range at will, to exchange words with crewmen. Even the intercom was silent, an unusual hush on a ship like *Saber*.

He was shown into the central staff offices, not a command station, and directly into the presence of the ranking commander over military operations in the Kesrithi zones, R.A. Koch. Duncan was uneasy in the meeting. SurTacs had paper rank enough to assure obedience from the run of regulars, and that circumstance was bitterly resented, the more so because the specials flaunted those privileges with utter disdain for the protocols and dignity of regular officers: the gallows bravado of their short-lived service. He did not expect courtesy; but Koch's frown seemed from thought, not hostility, the ordinary expression of his seamed face.

"Pleased to make your acquaintance, SurTac Duncan." The accent was Havener, like most that had come to Kesrith, the fleet of lately threatened Elag/Haven.

"Sir," he said; he had not been invited to sit down.

"We're on short schedule," Koch said. "Regul have a ship incoming, *Siggrav*. Fortunately it seems to be a doch Alagn ship. Bai Hulagh's warning them to mind their manners; and we're probably going to have them docking here. They're skittish. Get yourself and your mri clear as quickly as possible. You're going to be given probe *Fox*. Probably your instructions are clearer than mine are at the moment." A prickle of distrust there, resentment of Stavros: Duncan caught it clearly. "*Fox* is transferring crew at the moment: some upset there. *Siggrav* is still some distance out. Your end of this operation is a matter of go when ready."

"Sir," said Duncan. "I want the dusei. I can handle them; I'll see to transferring them to *Fox.* I also want the mri trade goods that are stocked on-station, whatever you can spare me help to load."

Koch frowned, and this time it was not in thought. "All right," he said after a moment. "I'll put a detail on it now." He looked long at Duncan, while Duncan became again conscious that his face was marked with half a tan, that the admiral saw a stranger in more than one sense. Here was a power equal to that of Stavros, adjunct, not under Stavros' authority save where it regarded political decisions: and the decision that took *Fox* from Koch's command and overmanned Koch's own ship with discontent, lately transferred crew and scientists did not sit well with Koch. He did not look like a man who was accustomed to accept such interference.

"I'll be ready, sir," Duncan said softly, "when called."

"Best you go over to *Fox* now and settle in," said Koch. "Getting her underway would relieve pressure here. You'll have your supplies; we'll provide what assistance we can with the dusei. All haste appreciated."

"Thank you, sir," Duncan said. Dismissed, he took his leave, picked up his escort again at the door.

Koch had spent forty years on the mri, Duncan reckoned; he looked old enough to have seen the war from its beginning, and he doubtless had no love for the species. No Havener, who had seen his world overrun by regul and recovered by humanity at great cost, could be looked upon to entertain any charity toward the regul or toward the mri kel'ein who had carried out their orders.

The same could be said, perhaps, of Kiluwans—like Stavros; but remote Kiluwa, on humanity's fringes, had produced a different breed, not fighters, but a stubborn people devoted to reason and science and analyzing—a little, it had to be suspected, like the regul themselves. Overrun, they dispersed, and might never seek return. The Haveners were easier to understand. They simply hated. It would be long before they stopped hating.

And from the war there were also men like himself, thousands like himself, who did not know what they were, or from what world; war-born, war-oriented. War was all his life; it had made him move again and again in retreating from it, a succession of refugee creches, of tired overworked women; and then toward it, in schools that prepared him not for trade and commerce but for the front lines. His own accent was unidentifiable, a mingling of all places he had lived. He had no place. He had for allegiance now nothing but his humanity.

And himself.

And, with considerable reservations, the Hon. G. Stavros.

He exited *Saber*'s ramp onto the broad dock, his escort left behind, paused to look about at the traffic of men and women busy about their own concerns.

Haveners.

Regulars.

In the command station of *Fox*, Duncan found himself among *Fox*'s entire body of officers, unhappy-looking men and women, who exchanged courtesies with dutiful propriety.

"Sealed orders," the departing captain told him. "Crewless mission. That's as much as we know."

"I'm sorry about this," Duncan offered, an awkward condolence.

The captain shrugged, far less, doubtless, than the unfortunate man was feeling, and offered his hand. "We're promised another probe, incoming. *Fox* is a good ship, in good maintenance—a little chancy in atmosphere, but a good ship, all the same. We're attached to *Saber*, and *Saber*'s due that replacement probe as soon as it's ferried in; so we'll get it, sure enough. So congratulations on your command, SurTac Duncan; or my condolences, whichever are more in order."

Duncan accepted the handshake, in his mind already wondering what was contained in the sealed courier delivery that had come back by shuttle and resided now in the hands of the departing captain of *Fox*—in his own possession, once the passing of authorities was complete. Duncan accepted the courtesies all about, the log was activated a last time to record the transfer of command; and then, which was usual on SurTac missions, the log files were stripped and given over into the hands of the departing captain. There would be none kept on his flight.

Another, last round of ceremonies: he watched the officers and their small crew depart the ship, until there was no one left but the ever-present security detail at the hatch—four men, with live and deadly arms.

There was quiet. Duncan settled into the unfamiliar cushion and keyed in the command that played the once-only tape from Stavros: under security lock as it was, it was destroying itself as it played.

Such procedures assured that Authority would not have records coming back to haunt them: that had been the saying during the war, when SurTacs routinely expected the destruction of all records that dealt with them, records destroyed not alone for fear of the enemy, but, they bitterly suspected, destroyed to keep clear the names of men that sent them into the field, should a mission fail: losing commanders lost commands.

Stavros' face filled the screen.

"My apologies," Stavros said softly, "for what I am about to ask. I will make my proposal; and after hearing it, if you wish, you can return command of *Fox*, and accept temporary assignment at the station, pending stabilization of the situation here.

"By now you are in command of *Fox*. You are authorized to take the mri aboard, along with all their possessions, and the artifact. The probe will be equipped according to your requirements. In your navigation storage is one tape, coded zero zero one. It comes from the artifact. Proceed out on a course farthest removed from incoming regul, and maintain secrecy as much as possible. You are to follow the tape to its end. There will be no choice once the tape is activated; the system will be locked in. Gather what data you can, both military and personal, on the mri: that is the essence of your mission. Deal with them if possible. We grow more and more certain that it is in our interests to understand that tape. In those interests we are prepared to take a considerable risk. You will gather data and establish what agreement is possible with the mri.

"If you have decided by now to withdraw, wait until the end of this tape and contact *Saber*. If you have, on the other hand, decided to continue, make all possible haste.

"You will in either case say nothing of the contents of this taped message. You will exercise extreme caution in making records during your flight. We want nothing coming home with you by accident. You will have an armed self-destruct, and you will operate under no-capture priorities. If to the best of your judgment you have entered a situation which would deliver your ship into hostile hands, destruct. This is imperative. Whatever choice you make, whether accepting or rejecting this mission, is a free choice. You may refuse without prejudice."

The tape ran out. Duncan still sat staring at the gray screen, knowing that he wanted to refuse, go back to Kesrith, make his peace with the authorities—find some safe life in the Kesrithi hills.

He did not know by what insanity he could not. Perhaps it was something as selfish and senseless as pride; perhaps it was because he could not envision a use for himself thereafter—except perhaps to open the backlands to human habitation. And the world would change.

He cut the screen off, gazed around at the little command station that would be his for what might be the rest of his life, with which he could live for a little time. It was enough.

He boarded *Flower* with no change of insignia, nothing visible to indicate the change in circumstances; but the officers of *Flower* had been informed, evidently, of the authorizations granted him, for there was no demur when he asked the transfer of his gear and for preparations on the dockside.

And when he had done so, he went to Luiz, and last of all to Boaz.

It was the hardest thing, to break to her the news that all her labors were without issue so far as security would ever let her know, that he was taking her charges from her permanently—he, who had assisted her, and now returned to the military wing that she hated.

"Reasons are classified," he said. "I'm sorry, Boaz. I wish I could explain."

Her broad face was touched with a frown. "I think I have an idea what's toward. And I think it's insane."

"I can't discuss it."

"Do you know what you've let yourself in for?"

"I can't discuss it."

"Are they going to be all right? Are you yourself content with arrangements for them?"

"Yes," he said, disturbed that she seemed to guess so accurately what was in progress: but then, Boaz had done the researches on the artifact. Doubtless many on *Flower* had an idea—and surmised after one fashion and another what the military would do with the information they had found. He suffered the scrutiny of her eyes for a moment, guilty as if he were betraying something; and he did not know what power had claimed him—whether friends or enemies of Boaz' principles—or what he himself served, whether she would understand that, either.

She smiled sadly, a mask that covered other feelings. "Well," she said, "hard for us, but there's nothing to be done for it. Sten, take care." The smile died. "Take care for yourself. I'm going to worry about you."

He was touched by this, for if he had a friend anywhere about Kesrith, it was Boaz, fortyish and the only ranking woman in the civ sector. He took her by the hands and, on an impulse, by the shoulders and kissed her on the side of the mouth.

"Boz, I'm going to miss you."

"I will have to get myself some new dusei," she said. Tears were very close to the surface. "I imagine you'll be taking them, too."

"Yes," he said. "Be careful of those beasts, Boz."

"Watch yourself," she urged him hoarsely. For a moment it seemed she might say something further. At last she glanced down and aside, and together they set about the necessary business of arranging the transfer of the dusei.

The whole section was closed to foot traffic and all movement down the rails was halted while the transfer was being made—the matter of sealed canisters of supplies and Duncan's own uninteresting baggage first; and then the mri, from *Saber*, in the sealed automeds used in evacuations of wounded—not a man on the docks that could not guess who was being moved under such extraordinary security; but the precautions were as much to protect the mri as to conceal their removal. Mri were bitterly hated, and the looks that followed those sealed units were in many cases murderous.

And lastly, the docks entirely cleared, came the dusei, for whom no such protective confinement was practical. Duncan had consulted much with Boaz on the question of their transfer, considered using freight canisters, and finally, all such possibilities discarded, simply directed everyone to clear the corridors, ordered the loading crews behind sealed doors, and had the hatches opened.

Then he went down to meet the dusei, and touched them and soothed them, disturbed by their disturbance, fighting his own fear—and he felt their eagerness too, when he opened the door that let them completely free.

They walked with him, a shambling, rolling gait, broad noses snuffling the strange air as they entered the dock. About them lay a great expanse of docking area, vast room for them to stray off, get out of hand, break into freedom that could only end in harm. Duncan tried to think only of the ship *Fox*, of the mri, of the dusei going—trying to make them understand, if understand they could.

They went, the big one slightly before him and the smaller so close at his side it constantly touched. Once the big one gave a cry that echoed all over the vast station dock, a sound to send chills down the back.

In that moment Duncan feared he was going to lose control of them; but after a moment's skittishness, they walked docilely up the ramp to *Fox*, and inside. Doors were open along the way that they must go, unwanted alternatives sealed. Duncan walked them down to the hold that was prepared for them there, and let them in, himself delaying in the doorway to be sure they settled. They were excited, fretting with activity, pacing and swaying their massive bodies in the anticipation that coursed through them. One began that rumbling pleasure sound, that numbed and drew at the senses.

Duncan fled it, closed door, sealed them, retreated into the sane corridors and deathly quietude of the ship that was henceforth his.

"Clear," *Saber* control informed him. A visual on his screen showed clear space all about; a second screen showed a system mockup, with a red dot at the limit of it, which was regul, and trouble. A second dot appeared at the margin, likewise red, and flashed alarmingly.

"*Saber*," he queried the warship, "is your system mockup accurate?"

There was a long pause, someone checking for clearance to respond, no doubt. Duncan waited, pulse elevated, knowing already that the screen would have corrected itself by now if there had been any mistake.

"Affirmative," *Saber* informed him. "Further details not yet available. You have no lane restrictions, *Fox*. Officially there's no one out there but you. Clear to undock, take course of your choosing."

"Thank you, *Saber*," Duncan replied, noting the flash of data to his screen. "Stand by."

He began the checks, a few run-throughs, though the most important would check once he was clear. *Fox* was recently in from a run through nonsecure space and her sheet was impeccable.

He warned *Saber* and loosed the grapple to station, a queasy feeling as he slipped tiny *Fox* through the needle's eye of clearance between *Saber* and the station. *Hannibal* obstructed his view as he came over the crest, then fell away below.

Fox came under main systems now, aimed for the shortest run away from Kesrith and Arain's disruptive pull. He kept the world between himself and the incoming regul. He heard voices relayed from the station: the regul ship was in contact, voices harsh and dialectic. He heard the station and *Saber* respond. He made out that they were doch Alagn vessels, come for the reverence bai Hulagh Alagn-ni, for his rescue: this was a relief, to know at least that the incoming ships were not doch Holn. He was grateful that they had chosen to relay to him, a consideration that he would not have expected with his status.

He could draw a whole breath, reckoning humanity at Kesrith base safe for the moment, poised on the knife's edge of safety that Stavros had prepared, cultivating the reverence bai Hulagh.

And absenting the mri, who rested now, secretly, in the belly of a very vulnerable and very small outbound probe.

Remain invisible, he mentally read the wish that came with that relayed message, a communication they dared not send him in other terms now. He reckoned himself well-placed—reckoned with grudging admiration that Stavros might have done the right thing. If Stavros imperiled the peace by antagonizing the regul, there would be outcries at Haven, once it was known—demands for his recall, even if Kesrith remained safe. If Stavros lost the mri and *Fox,* in this present mad venture, there would be questions asked, but the whole incident would be passed off and forgotten. The mri were out of the affair at Kesrith. Accidents happened to probes: they were written off. The mri were only two prisoners; and no one had ever kept mri prisoners successfully. Mri artifacts were curiosities, obtainable wherever mri had died in numbers—meaningless curiosities now, for the species was dead: that news would have flashed back from Kesrith with all possible speed, joyous news for humankind, glory for Stavros, who had done nothing to obtain it, and who had kept his hands clean in the massacre. Reports coming from Kesrith were doubtless carefully worded, and would be in the future.

It only remained to see whether Stavros could deal with the regul. It was highly possible that he was going to succeed.

Phenomenal luck, phenomenal intelligence, a memory that missed nothing: there was nothing that escaped Stavros' notice, and his apparent gambles were less chance than calculated hazard. While extending one hand toward the regul, another directed *Fox,* covering that possibility also, trusting no one absolutely.

Duncan frowned, began to relax to the familiar sights and sounds of the ship—unaccustomed leisure, to know that he was not dropping down to combat, that Kesrith's ruddy crescent did not represent threat, but shelter. He settled into *Fox* as into his natural environment, at home in ships, in the dark worlds, in the jungle and deserts and barrenness of humanless worlds, in freefall and heavy *g* and every other place where survival was not reasonable. He had known from the time that he had been shunted into special services, in a wartime confusion of transports and destructing orders from faceless men of Stavros' kind, that he would end in some such place, light years removed from the safety of Stavros' king. Stavros at this distance became only one of a long succession.

No one special.

At this distance, from now on, there was only Sten Duncan.

On his scan he saw that something else had occurred, that there was another ship free of station. It was *Santiago,* an in-system rider, armed, but not star-capable.

He absorbed that knowledge calmly enough, a little resentful that he had not been asked whether such an escort was wanted; but with regul in the system, he did not object to it.

And he looked at the deck beside him, where in a padded support rode a silver ovoid, strangely unmarred after all the accidents that had befallen it. It did not look ever to have tumbled among the rocks at Sil'athen, ever to have been opened and examined. Its surface was unscratched.

But it was no longer unique. It had been duplicated in holos— and might be duplicated in more tangible detail one day at Zoroaster's more elaborate facilities, a museum curiosity for humans. Duncan reached down and touched it with his fingers, feeling the smoothness and the chill of it, drew his hand back and took a last check of the screens, where *Santiago* seemed locked onto his track.

He ate, the ship proceeding under automatic, silent and safe from alarms. The scan took in *Santiago* at its now accustomed distance, and the machines recognized each other. There was no other within threatening range. There was leisure finally for human needs.

And there was leisure, too, for beginning to reckon with the mri, who rode, unconscious, in the ship's labs.

He walked the corridors of *Fox*, checking to be sure that everything was in order, that nothing had come adrift in the shift from station operations to free flight. Units had reoriented themselves; the transition had gone smoothly. The dusei had ridden through it without visible difficulty: he observed them by remote, unwilling to enter that place now, disturbed as he was, and tense. The mri too rested safely, in their separate quarters. The medics had not taken them from their automeds.

Duncan did so, first the delicate, slight she'pan of the mri, Melein, arranging her into a more comfortable rest on a lab cot. Her delicate limbs felt of bone and loose flesh, appallingly slight; her eyes were sunken and stained with shadow. She did not respond when he touched her thin face and smoothed her bronze mane into order, trying to make her beautiful again. He was afraid for her, watching her breathe, seeing how each breath seemed an effort for her. He began to fear that he was going to lose her.

And in desperation he adjusted the temperature in the compartment downward, marginally reduced the pressure to something approximating Kesrith. He was not sure—no one was—what conditions were natural for the mri. It was only certain that they had less discomfort in Kesrith atmosphere than did humans or regul.

Melein's breathing became easier. After a long time of sitting in the compartment, watching, he dared leave her; and in another compartment he opened the unit to remove Niun.

Niun likewise was deeply sedated, and knew nothing of being moved, settled into yet another bed, a helplessness that would have deeply shamed the mri.

There would be no more drugs. Duncan read carefully the instructions that were clipped to the automeds, and found that medics had provided for such drugs, that they were to be found in lab storage, *sufficient*, the instructions said, *for prolonged sedation*. There were other things, meant to assist him in maintaining the mri. With two regul ships in the system and the likelihood of trouble, surely, Duncan thought it was irresponsible to ignore those precautions, at least before jump; but when he touched the mri and felt how thin and weak they had become, he could not bring himself to do it.

They were days from jump, days more of sedation, so that the mri could ride through that condition which flesh and living systems found terrifying, sealed in their automeds, limbs unexercised, muscles further deteriorating.

It was only common sense, those few days more of precaution; those who had set him in control of the mri had reckoned that these certain precautions would apply.

But those who had laid the plans did not know the mri, who, confined, would simply do what all mri captives had done, whether or not they knew their jailer—and die, killing if they could. Disabled, with their inherent loathing for medical help, they would surely make the same choice.

Duncan himself had understood from the beginning; it was on his conscience that he had never made it clear to Stavros or to others. He could not restrain the mri without killing them; and with the dusei aboard it was not likely that he could restrain them at all.

There was only one reason that would apply with the mri, amid all the powers, regul and human, that converged upon them, one thing with which the mri could not argue.

He made a final check of both mri, found them breathing easily now, and went topside, settling again into the command post.

He activated navigation storage and coded in a number: zero zero one.

Fox swung into a new orientation, her sensors locking on Arain, analyzing, comparing with data that flashed onto her screens. Lines of graphs converged, merged, flashed excited recognition.

Chapter Seven

Niun wakened, as at so many other wakings, a great lethargy on him. His eyes rested first upon Duncan, sitting as he had so often, patiently waiting by the side of his cot. Niun grew confused, disturbed at a vague memory.

"I thought," he said to Duncan, "that you had gone."

Duncan reached forth a hand, laid it on his arm. Niun tried simply to move his fingers, and that effort was beyond his strength. "Are you awake?" Duncan asked of him. "Niun, wake up."

He tried, earnestly, knowing that he was safe to do so if it were Duncan asking him; but the membrane half-closed over his eyes, hazing everything, making focus too difficult. The dark began to come back over him, and that was easier and more comfortable. He felt a touch on his mane, a mother's touch—none other would touch him so; but the fingers that touched his face then were calloused. It remained something to perplex him, and hold him close to waking.

"Drink," he was told, a voice that he trusted. He felt himself lifted—Duncan's arm: he remembered. A vessel's plastic rim touched his lips. He drank, found cool water, swallowed several times. It slid to his stomach and lay there uneasily.

Duncan took the vessel away, let him back on raised cushions that did not let him sink back into his former peace, and the elevation of his head dizzied him for a moment. Niun began to be sure that he was meant to wake in this terrible place, that there was no refuge. In his nostrils, unpleasant on the hot, heavy air, was the scent of food.

He could move his limbs. He found this a wonder. He tried to do so, began to absorb sensation again, and past and present finally merged into his mind.

He remembered fire and dark and a regul who—he thought—had killed him.

He lay now on a bed like a woman of the Kath, face-naked, his body naked and wasted beneath light coverings, his limbs without strength.

He was in an alien place. To this he had no wish to wake.

But there was dimly in his mind a belief that he had something yet to do, that there was a duty yet undone.

Someone had told him this. He could not remember.

He tried to rise, succeeded in sitting up for an instant before his arms began to shake uncontrollably and he collapsed. Duncan's arms caught him, gentle and yielding him to the mattress.

Thereafter it was easier to drift back into the Dark, where there was no remembrance at all. But Duncan would not let him. A cold cloth bathed his face, shocked awareness back into him.

"Come on," Duncan kept saying to him—lifted his head once again and poured water between his unwilling lips. Then followed salt-laden meat broth, and Niun's stomach threatened rebellion.

"Water," he asked, after he had swallowed the mouthful; and receiving it, took one sip. It was all that he could bear.

He drifted away for a time then, and came back, found himself propped half-sitting. A comfortable rumbling sound filled his ears, numbed his mind for a time; he felt warmth upon his hand, a movement. He looked and saw to his confusion that a great dus had come to sit beside him. It pushed at the cot, making it shudder, then settled, soothing his mind with its contentment.

And Duncan returned upon the instant—in the dress of humans: he noticed this for the first time. Duncan had rejoined his own kind, as was proper. It was a human place. For the first time Niun began to take account of his presence not as delirium, most real and urgent of the images that peopled his wakings, but as a presence that had logical place among humans.

Whose reasons were doubtless human, and threatening.

Disturbed, the dus looked about at Duncan, then settled again, giving only a weary sigh. It tolerated the human; and this perplexed Niun—frightened him, that even the incorruptible dusei could be seduced. He had no protection left.

Dark crossed his mind, memory he did not want, towers falling, the she'pan's pale face in the darkness, eyes closed.

The dus lifted its head again, moaned and nosed at his hand.

"Melein," he asked, focusing on Duncan, on white walls and reality, for he had to ask. He remembered that he had trusted his human: hope surged up in him, that no guilt touched Duncan's face when he asked that question.

The human came and sat by him, touched the dus in doing so, as if he were utterly easy with the beast; but fear . . . fear was in him: Niun felt it. "She is here," Duncan told him. "She is well— as well as you are."

"That is not well at all," Niun said thickly, with a twist of his mouth; but it was true, then; it was true, and he had not dreamed it among the other dreams. He could not close his eyes, lest the tears flow from them, shaming him. He stared at Duncan, and fingered the velvet skin of the dus between them, a hot and comforting sleekness.

"You are free," Duncan explained carefully, distinctly, as one would talk to a child. "Both you and she. We are on a ship, headed out from Kesrith, and I am the only one besides you aboard. I've done this because I trust you. Do me the favor of trusting me for a little while."

This, incredible, mad as it was, had the simple sound of truth in it: there was no flinching in Duncan's gaze. Niun accepted, bewildered as he was, and began at once to think of escort ships, of themselves surrounded, proceeding toward some human captivity, of a myriad other treacheries; but there was Duncan.

There was Duncan, on whom all hopes rested, who alone of human enemies and regul had understood him with honor, whose heart was honorable, a kel'en of the human folk.

He flexed his hands, trying their strength, found the numbness that had blanked his mind and weakened his limbs so long now retreating. Drugs: he recognized the probability of it; but they were losing their grip on his senses, leaving them increasingly clear. Duncan gave him water to drink again, and he drank; and more of the horrid broth, and he drank that too, and clamped his jaws and fought his stomach to keep his meal down.

The she'pan was alive: his true sister Melein, Mother of the People. She was his duty. He was kel'en, a warrior, and the sickness and the wound and the drugs had taken from him his strength and his quickness and his skill, which were all the possession he had ever owned, for the only purpose of his life, which was to serve the she'pan.

He did not let himself think of what had become of him, only of the necessity of standing on his feet, of finding again the strength to walk and go to her, wherever she was.

Until then he would bear with anything.

Duncan returned after a dark space; and in his hands he bore a black bundle of cloth, that he laid on the table by the bed.

"Your clothes," Duncan said. "If you will let me, I will help you."

And Duncan did so, carefully, gently, helping him to sit for a moment that his senses spun and went gray, then settled him back again, wrapped in the familiar comfort of a kel'en's inner robe, and propped on cushions.

Duncan sat beside him, waiting until he had his breath again. "The she'pan is doing well," he said. "She took food and demanded her belongings and told me to go away. I did."

Niun slipped a hand within his robe, where a scar crossed his ribs, and knew that he should have died: they both should have died. "Tsi'mri medicines," he objected, his voice trembling with outrage; and yet he knew that these same forbidden things had kept them both alive, and he was, guiltily, unwilling to die. He was twenty-six years old; he had expected to die before this: most kel'ein did, but most kel'ein had had honors in plenty by this time. Niun had gained nothing wherewith he was proud to go into the Dark. All that he had almost won, he had lost, being taken captive, allowing the she'pan to be taken. He should have died.

But not here, not like this.

"It was not your fault," Duncan said.

"I have lived too long," Niun answered him, which was the truth: both he and Melein had outlived their kind, outlived the People; and that was bitter fact. He did not know what she would choose to do when she found him again, or what she would bid him do. He looked on Duncan with regret. Duncan's eyes were, Niun saw, shadowed with weariness, his person unkept, as if he had slept little. At the moment he looked distraught.

"The regul would have taken you," Duncan said hoarsely. "I had the chance to put you among my people, and I took it. The she'pan did not object. She knew what I did."

The assertion shook at his confidence of things trustworthy. Niun stared at Duncan for a moment, and at last put down his pride, asked questions as he would of a brother of the Kel.

"Where are my weapons?"

"Everything you own in here," Duncan said. "I will bring you your weapons now if you insist; but you've been half asleep and you've been sick, and I thought you might not know where you are or understand what's going on. I'd hate to be shot in a misunderstanding."

This was at least sensible. Niun let go a carefully controlled breath, reminding himself that this human tended to tell the truth, contrary to the experience of the People with tsi'mri in general. "I am not sick anymore," he said.

"Do you want me to go and bring your weapons?"

Niun considered the matter, staring at Duncan's naked face; he had challenged . . . Duncan had answered with an offer, though his truth had been doubted, insulting him. "No," Niun said, making an effort to relax. "You go and come much; when you come again, you will bring them."

"I would prefer," said Duncan, "to wait until I am sure you are well. Then I will bring them."

Niun glanced aside unhappily: face-naked, he felt the helplessness of his wasted limbs and lay still, compelled to accept the situation. The dus stirred, uncomfortable in his distress. He moved his hand and comforted it.

"I have brought some food," Duncan said. "I want you to eat."

"Yes," Niun agreed. He thrust himself up against the cushion as Duncan went out into the corridor to fetch what he had brought; he took the moment to catch his breath, had steadied himself by the time Duncan returned, and determined to feed himself, though his hand shook when he picked up the bowl.

There was cold, offworld fruit, of which delicacies he had heard, but never eaten; there was a sort of bread, too soft for his liking, and thick, but it was easy to eat; and soi, for which he had a fondness. He took the bittersweet cup in both hands and drank it down to the bitter last, for it was the only familiar, Kesrithi thing, even if it were regul, and he knew that it was good for him. He had eaten a great deal for his abused stomach to absorb; he rested very still when he had eaten, reckoning that to remain very still was the only means of keeping it down.

"At that rate," said Duncan, taking the tray and setting it on the table, where immediately the dus began to investigate it, "you'll recover soon enough." He rescued the tray and took it out to the corridor, followed by the traitor dus, which trailed him with that mournful, head-lowered gait, hoping for charity.

Niun shut his eyes and rested, hearing activity down the hall and measuring the distance from him: there was the rattle of dishes; he could hear no voices, only the explosive whuff of a dus, that the beasts expressed for their own reasons.

Melein? he wondered desperately. He had asked once; he had been refused in the matter of his weapons. He would not expose his anxieties a second time. It was necessary to remember that Duncan was tsi'mri, and the enemy.

Duncan returned after a long time, in which the meal had somewhat settled and Niun felt his stomach the easier for it. Duncan showed him a panel within reach of his arm, how to dim the lights and how to call for help if he needed anything, where the sanitary facilities were, also; and with that instruction a strong admonition against attempting to walk alone.

Niun said nothing, only absorbed all the instructions he was offered, and lay staring at Duncan.

"Sleep awhile," Duncan wished him after a moment, evidently feeling the ill will. He walked to the door and looked back. "There's food whenever you want it. You only have to call me."

Niun gave no response, and Duncan left, leaving the door open, the lights dimmed, the illumination coming from the corridor outside.

And when somewhere a door closed and sealed, Niun began, methodically, to try to move, to work muscles long unaccustomed to move. He worked until he was exhausted, and when he had rested a time, and slept, he found the dus returned. He spoke to it, and it came, laying its massive head on the edge of the bed. He set his hand on its great back and used it to steady him so that he could stand. Then he walked a few steps, leaning on the beast that moved with him, and walked back again, legs trembling so that he

fell across the bed. For a while he lay still, breathing hard, close
to being ill; it was a few moments before he could even drag his
strengthless legs into bed again and rest.

But when he had rested, he began to move again, and arose
with the help of the dus and began again to essay those few possible steps.

A long sleep: a day passed, more or less, time meant nothing. It
was measured only in the arrival of food and those periods when
he was alone, that he could attempt to bring life back to his limbs.

Another sleep: on that day he wakened alone, with only the dus
for company. His limbs hurt from the exercise he forced, and
Duncan still had not found it convenient to return his weapons.
For a moment he lay still, in the darkness, staring out into the
lighted corridor.

Then he rose, without the dus this time, and walked stiffly to
the bath, washed in water and carefully dressed to the fullest in
the clothing that had lain folded on the table. Last of all he put
on the *zaidhe*, the tasseled headcloth, visored against the light of
unfriendly suns: but the visor he left raised; and with the *zaidhe*
he put on the *mez*, the veil, which he fastened under his chin—
modesty abandoned here, alone with Duncan, who knew his face.
In the black robes of the Kel he felt himself almost whole again,
and felt a pang when he touched the gold honors that were his: the
heavy symbol of Edun Kesrithun, stamped with the mark of an
open hand . . . on a chain, that *j'tal*, for it had come from the neck
of Intel, the departed Mother; and there was a small ring laced to
the honor-belt—memory flashed back at him, bitter and terrible—
from the hand of the Mother of Elag; and—more memories, full
of recent pain—a small gold luck *j'tal*, in the shape of a leaf that
had never grown on barren Kesrith: this came from an elder
brother of the Kel, and called back others to his memory, the masters who had taught him arms and the law of the Kel.

And he received them back from the hand of a human.

He rested a moment against the wall, the dus nervously pushing
at his leg; when he had caught his breath he went to the door,
looked out, and walked out into the corridor unhindered, the dus
behind him.

The very look of the place was alien: narrow, rectangular corridors, when he was accustomed to the slanting walls of his own ruined home, or the curving walls of regul interiors. It was hard to breathe, the air heavy and pungent with unfamiliar chemical scents. In his confusion he caught at the wall as his own dus shouldered him aside, and ahead of him, far down the corridor, he saw another dus thrust its broad head forth from a doorway. His shambled ahead to meet it, quite cheerfully.

He had known; somewhere in the drug-dazed depth of him, he had sensed the other presence, calming and drawing at him. Two dusei, and one with Melein, who had been of the Kel, who still might touch one of the beasts.

It was a long walk, the longest that he had tried; he thrust himself from the wall and went to that door, leaned upon the door frame and looked inside.

Melein, she'pan.

She was in truth alive; she slept—fully dressed in her modesty, in her tattered yellow robes of Sen-caste, that she had outworn. So frail she had become, Niun thought with pain, so thin; it was one thing that a kel'en should be hurt and starved and kept numbed with drugs—but that they should have dealt so with her: rage swelled up in him so that for a moment he could not see, and the dusei moaned and drew back into the corner.

He left his place at the doorway, came and knelt on the floor at her bedside, where she slept upon her side, her head pillowed upon her arm. The dusei returned, and crowded close about him; and he touched the slim fingers of her open hand.

Her golden eyes opened, nictitated in surprise. She seemed dazed at first, and then put out her hand and touched his naked face, as if to see whether he were a dream or not.

"Niun," she whispered. "Niun."

"What shall I do?" he asked of her, almost trembling in dread of that question, for he was only kel'en, and could not decide: he was the Hand of the People, and she was its Mind and Heart.

If she would not live, then he would kill her and himself; but he saw the cold, clear look of her eyes, and this was not the look of defeat.

"I have waited for you," she told him.

Niun took the dusei with him. They walked before him, single-file, for they were too big to go abreast in the corridor. Claws clicked on hard flooring, slowly, slowly. They knew whom he sought, in that curious sense of theirs—knew also that this was not a hunt in the way of game, with a kill at the end; but they were disturbed, nonetheless, perhaps because they had walked with him as they hunted.

And they met Duncan in the narrow hall just beyond the turning.

Duncan was perhaps coming as he came so faithfully to see to them. He was not armed; he never had been, Niun recalled with a sudden confusion in his anger. And perhaps Duncan had tempted them to this moment, had waited for it. He seemed to know how things lay between them; he stood still before the dusei, waiting for Niun to say or do what he would. Surely he knew that his life was in danger.

"There are no others aboard," Niun reminded him, challenging him with his own statement.

"No. I told you the truth."

Duncan was afraid. Dus-feelings were close and heavy; but he did not give way to his fear, that would have killed him.

"Yai!" Niun rebuked the dusei, attracting their attention out of that single-minded and dangerous fixation. They shifted nervously and the feeling lifted. They would not defy him. "Duncan," he said then, as directly as he would speak to a brother of the Kel, "what did you hope to do with us?"

Duncan shrugged, human-fashion, gave a faint, tired twist of the mouth. Naked-faced as he was, he looked like a man long without rest either of body or of spirit. He was naïve at times, this man Duncan, but he was capable of having guarded himself, and knew surely that he ought to have done so. Niun momentarily put aside his thoughts of violence.

"I meant," Duncan said, "to get you out of the hands of the regul."

"You simply asked your people, and they gave you this for your own pleasure. Are you so great among them that they are that eager to please you?"

Duncan did not rise to the sarcasm. His expression remained only tired, and again he shrugged. "I'm alone. And I don't plan to contest the control of the ship. You can take it. But I will point out that this is not a warship, we are not armed, and we are possibly doing already what you would wish us to do. I don't think you can take actual control; we are on taped navigation."

Niun frowned. This, in his inexperience, he had not taken into account. He stared at Duncan, knowing his own strength limited, even to go on standing. He could loose the dusei; he could take the ship; but the thing that Duncan said made Duncan's calm comprehensible, that neither of them could manage the ship.

"Where are we going?" Niun asked.

"I don't know," Duncan said. "I don't know. Come with me to controls, and I will show you what I mean."

The ovoid rested in a case lined with foam, a shining and beautiful object, unique, holy. Not a flaw was on its surface, although Niun knew that it had tumbled down rocks and withstood the gods knew what afterward to come here. He knelt down, heedless of Duncan's presence, and stretched out a reverent hand, touched that slick, cold surface as if it were the skin of a sentient being.

A piece of the mri soul, this object, this pan'en, this mystery, that he had carried until he could carry it no longer. He would have died to keep this from tsi'mri hands.

And from tsi'mri it had come to them, touched and profaned.

Duncan's doing. There was none other who could have found it.

Niun stood up, eyes blurring, the membrane betraying him for the instant; and before a stranger of the People, he would have veiled himself in anger, but Duncan had been closer to him than many another of his own kind. He did not know what manner of grace or threat was intended by this gift. He felt a counter at his back, welcome; his legs were foundering under him. The dus came, great clumsy-seeming creature, careful in this place of delicate instruments and tight spaces. It lay down at his feet, its warmth and steadiness offered to him at need.

"You know the mri well enough," Niun said, "to know that you have been very reckless to touch this."

"It is yours. I got it back for you; would you rather it had been lost out there, left?"

Niun looked down again at the pan'en, up again at Duncan still trying to reckon what lay behind that veilless face; and slowly, deliberately, he fastened the veil across his own face—a warning, did Duncan chance to have learned that mri gesture, that severed what was personal between them. "Humans are mad with curiosity. So my elders taught me, and I think that they were right. It will not have been in your hands without your scholars looking into it; and it is even possible that they will have learned what it is. Being only kel'en myself. I am not entitled to know that. Perhaps you know. I do not want to."

"You are right in your suspicions."

"Being human yourself, you knew that this would happen if you brought it to your people."

"I didn't know what it was. I didn't know that it would be more than a curiosity to them."

"But it is," Niun surmised; and when Duncan did not answer: "Is that why we are here? One thing the mri had left, one treasure we had, and here it rests, and here are you, alone, and suddenly we are given rewards, and our freedom—a ship for our leaving, at great cost. For what service to humanity is this a just reward, kel Duncan? For the forty years of war we waged with your kind, are we given gifts?"

"The war is finished," said Duncan. "Over. A dead matter."

"So are the mri," Niun said, forced himself to that bitterness, repudiating tsi'mri generosity and all its complicated demands. The weakness was on him again, a graying of senses, a shudder in muscles too long under tension. He clenched his hand on the counter, drew a deep breath and let it go, brought focus to his vision again. "I do not know why you are aboard alone," he said. "One of us does not understand the other, kel Duncan."

"Plainly put," said Duncan after taking in that fair warning. "Perhaps I am mistaken, but I thought that you would realize I tried to do well for you. You are free."

Niun cast a look about at the controls, at the alien confusion of a system unlike the regul controls that he knew only in theory. A thin trickle of sweat went down his left side, beneath the robes. "Are we escorted?" he asked.

"We are watched, so far," Duncan said. "My people aren't that trusting. And neither you nor I can do anything about that guidance system: we're on tape. Maybe you can tear us free of that, but if you do that, I don't doubt it will destruct itself, the whole ship."

This, at least, had the ring of sound reasoning. Niun thought it through, his hand absently soothing the head of the dus that sat up beside him.

"I will go present what you say to the she'pan," Niun said at last. He dismissed the dus ahead of him with a soft word and followed after it and its fellow, leaving Duncan in possession of controls. Duncan could kill them all; but Duncan could have done that long since if that had been his purpose. He could put them in confinement, but it was possible that the entire ship was a prison, guarded from the outside. The question remained why Duncan chose to be in it with them. Niun suspected that it had to do with the human's own curious feelings of honor, which apparently existed, far different from those of a mri.

Or perhaps it had nothing to do with Duncan's bond to his own kind; perhaps it was that to him, that they were both kel'ein, and lived under similar law, under the directions of others, and one chose what he could, where he could. He could comprehend that a man might find fellowship with another kel'en, that he might one day have to face and destroy. It was sung that this had happened.

It was never well to form friendships outside one's own House; it was proverbial that such attachments were ill-fated, for duty would set House loyalties first, and the commands of the she'pan first of all.

Chapter Eight

It was done.

Duncan stood and watched the mri depart, and knew that soon the she'pan Melein must come, to assume nominal control of the ship, now that Niun had assured himself that there would be no resistance or offense to her.

That was the way with the mri, that the she'pan made the decisions when she was available to be consulted. It was something that Boaz could have told the military; it was something that he himself could have told those that had laid the plans for security on *Flower*, had they asked—that the mri kel'ein, the black-robes, that had made themselves a terror wherever they had gone, were not the authority that must be considered.

Niun had not understood the artifact he revered. That also did not surprise Duncan. Niun, competent as he was, refused to know certain things that he did not consider appropriate for him; he had to consult Melein before any act of policy, given the chance to do so. Upon this, Duncan had relied desperately. It had worked. He felt vindicated, freed of a weight that had been on him for days, now that he saw Niun whole and on his feet, and bound precisely where he had calculated he would go.

He found himself with a curious lack of fear for the thing that he had done. Fear, he felt lying awake at night, remembering the ruin in the heights, the nightmare of Sil'athen, the inferno that had come down on them; or smiling at the regul who had tried to kill him and killed a sentient species instead. Of the mri he had only a knowledgeable respect.

There was still a good chance that the mri would turn on him and kill him; he had reckoned that from the beginning—but it was not the way that he had known them. If it would happen, it would proceed from the depth of some mri logic that these two mri had never shown him, even bitterly provoked.

It was long past time for regrets: there was little time left for anything he would do. He wiped the back of his hand across his blurring eyes—he had napped when he could these past four days, but he had not slept in a bed, had not dared to, not with matters aboard in a state of flux, with two regul ships loose in the system and a nervous human ship tagging him.

He settled in at the console, called forth data from the instruments that flashed their busy sequences, saw that they were prepared for transition, their guidance system locked upon its reference star and prepared to make the move as soon as *Fox*'s other systems informed the computer that they were far enough from the nearest sizable mass. It could be as much as a day: automatic tolerances were wider than they had to be. It would surely not be more.

This far out, Kesrith was lost in sunglare, and red Arain itself was assuming its proper insignificance on a stellar scale, a mere boundary beacon for men, marking as it did the edge of human territories, a star orbited by one scantly habitable world and several that were not.

And on the one screen was the mockup that still showed the regul further out than they should be after such a time: they were making a cautious approach. He did not concern himself with regul position: they were far across the system and no part of what occupied him.

On another screen appeared the tiny object that was *Saber*'s rider *Santiago*, his faithful shadow.

It was closer than it was wont to be.

He bit at his lip, his heart quickening, for he did not want to break silence or to start a dispute with his escort: the mri were at large; but the fact of the mri impelled him to rapid consultation with the computer, and he swore to himself and reached for the com switch.

"*Santiago*," he signaled it. "*Santiago*, this is *Fox*. Request you draw back a space. You're in my scan and your mass is registering on my instruments. You are preventing jump."

There was a long pause. "We copy," *Santiago* answered. And seemed to pause for consultation. "*Fox*," came a new voice, "Zahadi here. Advise you we have difficulties developing."

Santiago's captain. A chill of foreboding went through him. "Explain," he asked of Zahadi.

"*Fox*," the answer came back in due course, "advise you neither regul ship has been receptive to approach. Hulagh has shuttled up to station. Situation there is extremely tense. Hulagh has demanded boarding on regul vessel *Siggrav*, Stavros' latest message as follows: *Boarding will be granted. All conditions with probe mission are unchanged. Proceed. End message as received.*"

"*Santiago*, advise you we are prepared to jump. Situation elsewhere irrelevant. You are preventing jump. Please move out of scan."

"We copy," Zahadi replied.

There was a long silence. Duncan waited, watching the scan. There was no change. He repeated the message, irritably.

There was still no response. *Santiago* still hung within scan.

He flipped the contact again and this time swore at *Santiago* and all aboard her: a condemned man was allowed that liberty. "Get out of my scan," he repeated. "*Santiago*, get out of my way."

Again there was no answer. A chill sense of something utterly amiss was over him now; *Santiago* still remained, stubbornly using its mass to prevent him—he was sure of it now.

Stavros' orders, a leash on a ship Stavros could not fully trust, deliberate delay.

And the mri would come. He reckoned in his mind what would happen when Melein arrived down that corridor with the dusei to enforce her wishes. Niun might wait to search for his weapons; they both might wait a time, biding the return of their strength: Niun was hardly able to walk, and perhaps Melein could not. It was too much to hope that they would not intervene.

Stavros' intervention. Stavros knew him, had not trusted him let loose without restraint.

And in a sudden flash of apprehension he flicked the scan to maximum. A moving dot appeared at the limit of the field, moving in fast.

He cursed and put in a panicked call to *Santiago*, complaining of it.

"*Fox, Fox*," came the reply at last, "this is *Saber* via *Santiago*, assigned escort. Request acknowledgment."

Duncan leaned forward, adjusted the pickup, his other hand clenched. "*Saber*, this is *Fox*. Advise you no escort was in my orders. Pull off. Pull off."

There was no acknowledgment in the expected time. Nothing. *Saber* did not vary course.

"Request explanation," Duncan sent at them.

Nothing came in reply. *Saber* continued on intercept. In a very little time there would be no options at all.

Duncan swore at them. "*Saber*," he urged. "*Saber*, relay the following message to *Santiago*. Pull out of my scan: repeat, pull out of my scan. This ship is ready to jump, and your mass is registering. Request following message to be officially logged; *Santiago*, you have ignored five prior warnings. I will jump this ship on manual override in fifteen minutes. If you do not take immediate evasive action, you will be caught in my field. Advise you pull out now. Fifteen minutes, mark, and counting."

The seconds ticked off. His hand sweated on the override. The dot that was *Santiago* began to move away, but *Saber* was still coming in fast.

"*Fox*," he heard. "This is *Saber*, Koch speaking. Advise you this operation henceforth ours too. We are assigned to track. Orders of the Hon. G. Stavros, governor Kesrith territories."

It hit him at the pit of the stomach: *O God, out of this, out of this,* he wished, either them or him, he did not know. He was shaking with the strain of the long-held position.

A kilometer-long warship, with escort scout. He watched *Saber* moving in, not yet close enough for her great mass to register, but closing. They were coming in on *Santiago*'s track, and *Santiago*, not star-capable, would link and ride *Saber*'s ungainly structure into jump.

Warship, not a probe mission. He had been made a guide for warships.

No, no, no! he raged at them in his mind, and in an action both impulse and deliberate, slammed his hand forward and hit the manual override.

Jump.

He held onto the panel while the whole of his body told him lies at once, while walls flowed like water, while forms seemed to twist inside out and space was not; and was again; and the flow reversed itself, wrenching them back into normality.

The stars in the screens were different. Duncan shivered in disorientation, fighting out of it as a man must who had flown combat out of deep space.

He reached for controls to scan, finding vertigo in the tiniest imbalance of his body, the impression that interstices still existed into which he could fall, neither up nor down. If there was time in jump, the mind did not perceive it, drew nothing with it out of that abyss, only that terrible wrenching inward. He swept the scan.

There was nothing but star noise.

There was nothing.

He slumped in the cushion and fought against the emotional dissolution that often hit after transition; and this time it was more than physical. He had made a terrible, irrevocable mistake—not for the mri, not for them: he had at least bought them time, while Koch and Stavros sorted out the thing that he had done, consulted and reckoned what side he was playing, and what should be done with him.

The regul are living, Stavros had said: *their victims aren't. So we deal with the regul, who are a force still dangerous.*

Warships, not *Flower*, not the likes of Boaz and Luiz. The half of Stavros' military forces had prepared to follow in unarmed *Fox*'s wake, even with regul threatening Kesrith: warships, and himself before them, with mri aboard, to probe the defenses—an unarmed ship, and then the others.

To seek and destroy mri bases, whatever contacts the tape could locate: to finish what the regul had begun.

He bowed his head into his arms and tried to take his breath again, muscles shaking with rage and reaction. For a moment he could do nothing else; and then, fingers still shaking convulsively, he sought after the ampoule he had carried for days in his belt, never knowing at what time jump might come. He broke it, almost dropped it, then inserted the needle and let the drug enter his bloodstream.

Warmth spread through him, a sense of tranquility, ability to cope with the unnatural wrench of jump, ability to function until there should be leisure to rest. His mind cleared, but kept its distance from stresses.

He reckoned clearly what he had done: that *Saber* would track them; they had identical records, everything had been duplicated. The warships would come. There would be a court martial, if ever humanity recovered him; his direct defiance of Koch had made that a certainty. But the mri, when they learned what had been done, might themselves care for that matter, so that human justice was a very remote threat indeed.

He was calm in thinking of these things, whether the exhaustion of days without rest—he wondered distantly if that was to blame for what he had done, or whether the trigger had been pulled much earlier, much earlier, when he had sought the mri's freedom. He tried to draw information from the tape: it would tell him nothing, neither running time to go, nor number of jumps, nor any indication where they were. He looked at the star in scan. Mri base, possibly. In that case, his time could be measured in days.

He pushed himself away from controls, his senses still sending him frantic signals even through the calming effects of the drug. It was worse than he had ever felt it: fatigue made it so. He thought that if things would remain stable only for an hour, he would go to his quarters and wash and lie down, now that it was too late to worry about anything.

And a dus ambled in the door, and the second dus after him; and behind them came the mri.

He drew back. Melein came, unveiled as was her wont, her fingers laced with Niun's, who supported her. She entered the control room as Duncan stepped back, and her golden eyes swept the place, centered on the object that rested beside controls: on the artifact in its cradle. She went to it, ignoring all else, and touched the silver ovoid with her fingertips, bending with Niun to provide her balance, felt it as if to assure herself that it was real.

Then she straightened. Her amber eyes sought Duncan's, shadowed and piercingly direct.

"I will sit," she said, her voice a hoarse whisper; and Niun carefully settled her on the edge of the reclined comstation cushion as if it were a throne. She sat straight, her hand pressed to her ribs where she had been injured, and for a moment she was short of breath; but it seemed to pass, and the hand dropped. The two dusei came to crowd at her feet, giving her a living wall at her knees; and she held out her left hand to Niun, who settled on the deck beside her, elbow against the larger dus.

Duncan looked on them both: in his hazed senses he saw the modern control center become a hall for a priestess-queen, himself the stranger there. Melein gazed at him directly: behind her the starscreens showed a dust of light, and the colored telltales flashed in lazy sequence, hypnotically regular.

"Duncan," Melein said softly, "where is this ship going?"

He remembered that it was not always permitted to speak to her directly, though once he had been permitted: things were different now. He looked at Niun's veiled and uncommunicative face. "Tell the she'pan that *that* guides us," he answered, with a shrug toward the ovoid that rested beside them.

"I will speak to him," Melein said, and an anxious frown came over her face. "Explain. Explain, kel Duncan."

"Do you know," he asked her, "what it holds?"

"Do you?"

He shook his head. "No. Records. Navigational records. But not where we are going. Do you know?"

Her lovely face became like a mask, unreadable as Niun's, though unveiled. "Why are you alone with us? Might you not be wiser to have kept us apart from controls, kel Duncan?"

She trod the edges of questions with him. He fought his mind clear, gathered explanations, but she held out her hand to him, insisting, and there was nothing gracious but to take her long, slender fingers in his. The alien touch disturbed him, and he found himself against the dusei, a position of danger. "Sit, sit down," she bade him, for she must look up at him as he stood; and there was no place but the deck, against the bodies of the dusei, as Niun rested. "Are you too strange to us now?" she asked, taunting him.

He did as she asked, his knees finding the deck painful; he touched the dusei of necessity, and knew the trap, the contact with the beasts, the blurring flow of senses. He grew afraid, and the beasts knew it, stirring powerfully against him; he repressed the fear, and they settled.

"Once," said Melein to him, her voice distant and soft, "I said that we would find a ship and a way off Kesrith; I said that I must have the pan'en, and you were there to hear. Kel Duncan, are these things your gift, yours alone?"

Not naïve, this child-queen: she asked what she did not believe. He sensed depths opening at his feet. "Policy," he said, "does not want you in regul hands. You are free. No, it is not my gift; I didn't have it to give. Others—arranged these things. If you linger in regul space or human—you are done; this ship is not armed. But we have no escort now, she'pan. We are alone; and we will follow this tape to its end."

She was silent a moment. Duncan looked at Niun, found nothing of comfort, was not sure that he was believed in either quarter. Melein spoke in her own language; Niun answered in a monosyllable, but he did not turn his face or vary his expression. *Tsi'mri*, he heard: the mri word for outsider; and he was afraid.

"Do your kind hate you?" asked Melein. "Why are you aboard alone, kel Duncan?"

"To tend you— and the machinery. Someone must. She'pan, from *that*—from the object—scientists made our guidance tapes. We're locked on it, and there's nothing you or I can do to stop it. I will tend the ship; I will deliver you to your destination, whatever it is. And when I have done that, I will take the ship and meet my people and tell them that the mri want no more part of regul or human politics, and that the war is over, forever. Finished. This is why I'm aboard."

A troubled frown grew upon Melein's face as she gazed into his eyes. "I cannot read truth in you," she confessed, "tsi'mri that you are; and your eyes are not right."

"Medicines," Niun said in a low voice, the first word he had spoken without invitation. "They use them during transition."

The mri had none, refused medicines, even that: Niun's *they* acquired demeaning force, and Duncan felt the sting of it, felt the danger of it at the same moment. For the first time panic settled round him; the dusei jerked in alarm, and Niun rebuked them, steadied them with his hands.

"You do not know," said Melein then, "what your superiors have done to you, kel Duncan. How long are you given to return?"

"I don't know," he said.

"So long, so long a voyage. You should not be here. You should not have done this thing, kel Duncan."

"It's a long walk home, she'pan. We're across jump."

"This is a mri ship now. And where we go, no tsi'mri can go."

The dusei stirred, heaved up: Duncan started to rise, but Niun's hand seized his wrist, a pressure without strength, a warning without threat. "No," Niun said. The eyes above the veil were no longer hard. "No. Be quiet, Duncan."

The dusei had retreated into the recess to Melein's left, making sounds of alarm, small puffs of breath. Their small eyes glittered dangerously, but after a moment they settled, sat, still watching.

And quietly, in his own language, Niun spoke to Melein—received an answer and spoke again, urgently, as if he pleaded against her opinion. Duncan listened tensely, able only to catch the words *mri, Kesrith,* and *tsi'mri*—tsi'mri: as mri meant simply *the People*, the word for any other species was *not-people*. It was their thinking; he had known it long since. There was no reasoning against it.

Finally, with a few words, Melein rose, veiled her face and turned away, deliberately turning her back.

It was a chilling gesture. Duncan gathered himself to his feet, apprehensive; and Niun arose, using the cushion to steady himself, standing between him and the dusei.

"She has said," said Niun, "that I must not permit any stranger in her sight again. You are kel'en; I will fight you when I am able, or you may choose to stay with us and live as mri. You may choose."

He stared helplessly at Niun, even this made distant by the drug. "I didn't risk my neck getting you free only to kill one of you. No."

"You would not kill me," Niun said.

It set him off-balance. "I am not your enemy," he protested.

"Do you want to take service with the she'pan?"

"Yes."

He said it quickly; it was the only sane answer. When things were quiet, at some later time, then it would be the moment to reason with them, to explain why he must be set free with the ship: it was their own protection they considered.

But Niun remained still a moment, staring at him as if he suspected a lie in that consent.

"Niun," said Melein, her back still turned; Niun went to her, and they spoke in low voices. For a moment then Niun was still; the dusei shifted restlessly: one moaned and nosed at Niun's hand. He caressed it absently to silence, then came back to the side of the room where Duncan stood.

"Kel Duncan," he said, "the she'pan says that we are going *home*. We are going home."

It did not register for a moment—came then with a dull distant apprehension. "You called Kesrith home," Duncan said.

"And Nisren. Kel-truth. The she'pan knows. Duncan—" The eyes above the veil lost their impassivity. "Perhaps we are the last; perhaps there is nothing left; perhaps it will be too long a voyage. But we are going. And after this, I must forget; so must you. This is the she'pan's word, because nothing human can stay with us, not on such a voyage. The she'pan says that you have given the People a great gift; and for this service, you may keep your name, human though it is; but nothing more. We have gone from the sun into the Dark; and in the Dark, we forget, the whole of what we have been and seen and known, and we return to our ancestors. This is what you have entered, Duncan. If ever you stand on the homeworld of the People, you will be mri. Is this understood? Is this what you want?"

A dus crowded them, warm and urgent with emotion. Duncan felt a numbness; sensed, almost, Niun's anxiety. Violation of privacy, of self-control; he edged back and the dus shied off, then returned obstinately to its closeness. There was no lying to the dusei; none, eventually, to the mri. They would learn one day what humans meant to do to them, what he had aimed at their home: a second, deadlier gift. It was irony that they asked him to share it.

"It's what I want," he said, for he saw no other choice.

Niun frowned. "A mri," he said, "could not have chosen what you have chosen."

The distance that the drug lent was leaving, deserting him to cold reality. He heard what Niun said, and it twisted strangely, forebodingly in his mind. He looked at Melein's back, wondering whether she would now deign to notice him, since he had yielded to all their terms.

"Come," said Niun, gesturing to the door. "You have given up the ship. You do not belong here now."

"She cannot manage it," he protested, dismayed to think of Melein, desert-bred, regul-trained, setting hands on human-made machinery.

Niun's entire body stiffened; the frown reappeared. "Come," he said again. "Forget first how to question. You are only kel'en."

It was mad. It was, for the moment, necessary; Melein's ignorance could kill them, but she surely had sense enough to refrain from rashness. The ship could manage itself. It was a hazard less immediate than quarreling with Niun.

There were the dusei.

There was the plain fact that did he defeat the mri, he must kill him: and he had not broken with Stavros' orders, cut himself off from Kesrith, to finish the reguls' job for them. In time he could learn the mri enough to reason with them, wherever they were, mri world or regul.

He yielded, and with Niun, left the control center, the dusei in their wake. The door closed behind them, sealed: he heard the lock go into place.

Chapter Nine

Two warships, six rider-vessels.

Bai Hulagh Alagn-ni saw with satisfaction the difference that power made in the deportment of the humanfolk. They waited on the front steps of the Nom, two hands of human younglings to meet the caravan from the shuttle landing; and a number of regul younglings bringing four bright silver sleds. Hulagh spoke a curt instruction to his driver to draw up there, among the regul: some of the new personnel coming later in the caravan were skittish of humans yet, and Hulagh, despite his rank and the discomfort entailed, meant to be beforehand disembarking and wait upon the others. He himself had no fear of humans, and meant that none of the others should disgrace Alagn before them.

The car drew to a smooth halt. The hatch opened, admitting the familiar, acrid air of Kesrith: Hulagh snorted in distaste as it burned his nostrils—but it held a certain savor now, nonetheless.

He ignored the humans who peered at him in their curiosity; some reached out tentative hands to assist. His driver, Suth Horag-gi, urged them aside and with expert and efficient organization had the sled eased into position; carefully, carefully, Suth eased Hulagh's great weight up to his atrophied legs and swiftly down again in the indoors sled, a smoothness and gentleness that Hulagh had come greatly to value. he had come more and more to prize this youngling of the tiny doch of Hulagh; its comportment had been faultless in the delicate days at the station. He did not, of course, express this to Suth: it would spoil the youngling, whom he meant to train to further responsibilities.

Attendant not only to the first elder of Alagn, but to the first elder of the prime doch of the prime three of the regul: Suth did not know the good fortune to come. Hulagh smiled to himself, a gesture the humans would hardly recognize, a tightening of the musculature of his lower eyelids, a relaxation of his nostrils despite the biting air.

His long, careful maneuvering had succeeded.

Eight ships had come, a quarter the strength of doch Alagn, and others were waiting. They had come to discover the fate of their elder, delayed on Kesrith among humans and mri and long overdue. Humans had not apparently expected Alagn to react in such strength—as if Alagn could reasonably have done otherwise. Stavros had apparently failed to understand how much Alagn had committed here, in the presence of a prototype ship that was entrusted them by the high assembly of regul docha—now lost, twisted metal in the ruined port: a pang of fear disturbed Hulagh's satisfaction—but there was, in these anxious humans, the means to cover that loss and better the position of Alagn despite it.

It was evident in the faces of these human younglings, in the whole attitude of humans at the station, in communications with Stavros, that the humans did not want to fight. Hulagh had long believed that, and naturally applauded that common sense in the humans. On Kesrith, elders were committed, human ones and now three more regul, lesser elders of Alagn, in the portion of the caravan that was now beginning to disembark; it did not make sense to fight. Hulagh earnestly displayed this attitude by committing the elders of his own doch, and believed that it was safe. The humans could have begun battle at the appearance of the warships, at the first intimation that they were carriers for riders; but the humans had instead settled to talk, despite that they might have won: humans were fierce fighters, as evidenced by the fact that they had been able to meet the mri—with the advantage of numbers, to be sure, but regul could not have withstood the mri, and Hulagh privately acknowledged that fact. No, the humans did not want further conflict. After those first anxious days, Hulagh began sincerely to rely on the directness of bai Stavros, who avowed humans wanted the peace not only continued, but expanded.

There were surely, contained within that truth, deeper truths beneficial to Stavros and his private interests: Stavros, with a wisdom regul could respect, if not love, did not commit himself to one ally, but pursued many attachments, probing them for advantage.

There was, notably, the matter of the mri, whom Stavros still found of interest, through the agency of the allegedly mad youngling Duncan: the very thought caused Hulagh's skin to tighten. Mad, perhaps, but if the youngling were thus defective, then Stavros was mad to have reinstated him—and Hulagh did not believe that Stavros was mad.

A probe had gone out-system; the largest of the human warships had escorted the ship to the edge of the system, and returned home after a furious coded exchange with the ship and finally with Stavros. Hulagh regretted much that neither he nor his aides could understand that exchange, after which the warship and its rider had meekly returned to station, while the ship *Hannibal* had moved out to run escort for regul ships in their approach.

The ship with the mri aboard had left Kesrith immediately upon Stavros' being informed that regul ships were due; Duncan, after briefing with Stavros, had been sent to that ship with his belongings, such as remained from his original transfer: a permanent stay, then, the last vestige of his occupancy removed from the Nom, although he had been virtually residing on the ship. When regul presence in the system had been announced, the probe had left the station: Hulagh had learned this from his fellow elders.

Duncan, supposedly on the station, was not available, not to his most urgent request for the youngling, and humans were evasive.

Duncan's madness revolved around the mri, who were also—supposedly—at the station.

It was a regul kind of game. Hulagh's hearts labored whenever he let himself dwell on the mri; doubtless the humans knew his anxiety. It only remained to find out the nature of the bargain Stavros wished to strike with Alagn—for it was surely equally clear to the humans that he now had resources with which to bargain. Hulagh trusted the humans as he had never been able to trust the mri: he trusted well a human like Stavros, who reckoned profit as regul did, in power, in territory, in resources of metals and biostuffs—and in the protection of what was his. Such persons as Stavros Hulagh found comfortingly close to his own mind; and therefore he sought an early conference.

The last of the elders disembarked. Hulagh eased his sled about, awaiting them, a term in the acrid air for which he would pay throughout the day, with a dry throat and stinging nasal passages. Three elders with their attendant younglings: Sharn and Karag and Hurn, the latter a male; Sharn, female, fourth eldest of the doch; Karag, a recently sexed male and prone to the instabilities that the Change brought on young adults: Sharn's protégé, and probably current mate, Karag still had the smooth skin of a youngling and he had not yet acquired the bulk of Sharn or Hurn, certainly not Hulagh's prosperous dignity, but he still rated the use of a sled—the last settled by the attendant younglings. Hulagh watched, patient as the younglings fussed about the three adults and brought them on their way through the cluster of humans.

Hulagh was no longer alone, sole elder on Kesrith, surrounded only by younglings of limited experience and strange docha. His own were with him now, Alagn-ni, and his ships sat up at station, constantly manned, able by reason of proximity to the human craft and the station to prove a greater threat than ever they could in combat. The humans had allowed this; and this was another reason that Hulagh felt confident of the peace. He smiled to himself and turned, aimed the sled up the slight incline, Suth walking beside him, the humans giving way to admit him. He entered the warm, filtered atmosphere of the Nom at the head of a procession that awed the local younglings who stood inside to see it, and thoroughly satisfied his long-aggrieved pride.

"Stavros," he heard a human youngling inform Suth, observing regul protocol, "will see the bai immediately as requested."

"To the reverence bai Stavros," Hulagh intoned, when Suth had ceremoniously turned to him. "Now."

The meeting was not, as all previous meetings had been, in Stavros' small office, but in the formal conference hall; and Stavros had surrounded himself with uniformed younglings and a great deal of that immobility of countenance that in humans was evidence of a pricklish if not hostile mood. Hulagh, backed now by his three elders and an entourage of Alagn's younglings, looked about him and smiled human-fashion, far from disturbed at the new balance of powers that had doubtless troubled the humans.

"May we," Hulagh suggested at once, before seatings could become complicated, "dispense with superfluous younglings and speak in directness, reverence?"

Stavros turned his sled and directed: human younglings sorted themselves out by rank and some began to depart. Hulagh retained Suth, and each of the Alagn elders a personal attendant, the while the four humans who counted themselves adult arranged themselves in chairs surrounding Stavros' sled. Hulagh stared curiously at one of the four, on whom no trace of gray showed . . . this coloring he had thought indicative of human maturity, since other colorations did not seem to have bearing: he remained mildly suspicious that Stavros breached protocol, seating this one in the inner circle, but in his expansive mood, he did not find himself inclined to object. Elder he might be: Hulagh had never learned accurately to determine seniority among these beings, who sexed in infancy and varied chaotically in appearance on their way to maturity, and after. He anticipated questions from his elders, and to his embarrassment, he did not know the answers.

There was, by the younglings, the interminable serving of soi: necessary, for the journey had taxed the energies of everyone; there were the introductions: Hulagh absorbed the names and stations of the so-named elder humans and responded with the names of his own elders, who still seemed dazed by the rapidly shifting flood of alien sights and by exhaustion. But in the introductions, Hulagh found reason for exception, and fluttered his nostrils in a sigh of impatience.

"Bai Stavros," Hulagh said, "is there no representative from the bai of station?"

"It would be pointless," said Stavros, using the communications screen of the sled, for Hulagh had addressed him in regul language, and so Stavros responded. "Policy is determined here. It is carried out there. Bai Hulagh, if your elders are fluent, may we use human speech?"

Characteristic of the humans, whose learning resided not in their persons, but in written records, considerable time on Kesrith had not served to give these fluency in the regul tongue. They forgot. It had amused Hulagh that meetings were often recorded on tape, lest the human forget what they had said and what had been told them: doubtless this one was likewise being recorded. After another fashion, it did not amuse him at all, to reckon that every promise, every statement made by these creatures, relied on such poor memories. To state an untruth was a terrible thing for a regul, for what was once said could not be unlearned; but doubtless humans could unlearn anything they pleased, and sometimes forget what the facts were.

"My elders are not yet fluent," Hulagh said, and kept all trace of humor from his face as he added: "it will be instructive to them if you speak in human language; I will provide simultaneous translation on my screen."

"Appreciated," said Stavros aloud. "A pleasure to welcome your elders personally."

"We are pleased to be welcome." Hulagh set aside his empty cup and leaned back in the cushions, manipulating the keyboard to do as he had promised Stavros. "And we are pleased that our human friends were willing to interrupt their business to provide these welcoming courtesies. But true intent becomes obscured in much formality. We are not disputing docha, in need of such. You have not attacked; we have not attacked. We are pleased with the situation."

Such directness seemed to disturb the attendant humans. Stavros himself smiled, a taut, wary smile. "Good," he said. "We assure you again that we are most pleased with the prospect of wider dealings with doch Alagn and all regulkind."

"We are likewise anxious for such agreement. The mri, however, the mri remain an item of concern."

"They need not be."

"Because they are no longer at Kesrith?"

Stavros' brow lifted. It seemed a smile, perhaps; Hulagh watched the reaction carefully, decided otherwise. "We are working," said Stavros carefully, "to be able to assure the regul that there is no possible danger from the mri."

"I have inquired about the youngling Duncan," said Hulagh. "He is not available. The mri are off Kesrith. A ship has left. All these circumstances—perhaps unrelated—still seem to assume a distressing importance."

There was a long pause. Stavros' mouth worked in an expression that Hulagh could not successfully read, no more than the other: perplexity, perhaps, or displeasure.

"We are," said Stavros at last, "attempting to trace the extent of the mri. We have found a record which is pertinent. Bai Hulagh, the extent of the record is entirely disquieting."

Hulagh drew in air, held his breath a moment. Truth: he knew Stavros well enough to rely on it.

"Part of it," Stavros said, "may lie within regul space, but only part."

"Abandoned worlds," Hulagh said. He had neglected to translate in his distress: he amended his omission, saw shock register on the faces of his other elders. "Nisren, Guragen—but it is true that they have ranged far. A mri record, is it so?"

"They do write," said Stavros.

"Yes," said Hulagh. "No literature, no art, no science, no commerce; but I have been in the old edun—there, on the slopes. I have seen myself what may have been writings. But I cannot provide you translation, not readily."

"Numerical records, in great part. We have understood them well enough to be concerned. We are pursuing the question. It may prove of great concern to all regul. We are concerned about the size of what those records may show us. And about possible overlapping of our researches with regul territory. Marginal intrusion. Not troublesome to Alagn; but others—"

"Holn."

"Yes," said Stavros. "We are concerned about the path of that probe. Yet it had to be done."

Breath fluttered from Hulagh's nostrils; his hearts beat in disturbing rhythm. He was utterly aware of the frightened eyes of his elders upon him, reliant on his experience, for they had none to offer. He became agonizingly aware that he was faced with something that would have repercussions all the way to Mab, and there was no way to delay the issue or seek consultations.

Alagn had power to speak for the docha, had done so in negotiations with the humans before. Hulagh gathered himself, called for another drink of soi, and the other elders likewise took refreshment. He sipped at his, deep in thought, paused for a look at Sharn, whose counsel was welcome, if not informed; Sharn gave him a look that appreciated his perplexity, agreed with him. He was gratified in that. The other elders looked merely bewildered, and Karag did not well hide his distress.

"Bai Stavros," Hulagh said at last, interrupting a quiet consultation among the humans, "your . . . intrusion could be somewhat dangerous in terms of relations with the docha. However, with Alagn support, such an expedition might be authorized from here. The record of which you speak, I understand, extends farther than regul territory."

"Our understanding of your extent in certain areas is vague, but we believe so."

"Surely— our interests are similar here. We are not a warlike species. Surely you judged this when you launched the probe— and perhaps the great warship would have followed. Surely—" A thought struck Hulagh: his nostrils relaxed in astonishment. "You prepared that probe as an excuse. You let it ahead deliberately, to claim right of pursuit, to excuse yourself—a rebel mri craft. Am I right?"

Stavros did not answer, but looked at him warily: the faces of the others defied reading.

"Yet you held the warships back," Hulagh said. His hearts slipped into discordant rhythm. "For our consultation, bai Stavros?"

"It seemed useful."

"Indeed. Beware a misjudgment, reverence bai Stavros. A regul in home territory is much different from a regul in distant colonies. When a doch's survival is at stake—attitudes are very hard."

"We do not wish any incident. But neither can we let the possibilities raised by that record go uninvestigated. A mri refuge among Holn is only one such."

"We have similar interest," said Hulagh softly. "I will sanction passage of that warship—in a joint mission, with sharing of all data."

"An alliance."

"An alliance," said Hulagh, "for our mutual protection."

Chapter Ten

The human slept.

Niun, warm against the bodies of the dusei, his mind filled with the animal's peace, watched Duncan in the half-light of the star-screen, content to wait. There was in Duncan's quarters a second bed; he refused it, preferring the carpeted floor, the nearness of the dusei, the things that he had known in the Kel. He had slept enough; he was no more than drowsy now in the long twilit wait-ing, and he fought the impulse to slip back into half-sleep, for the first time finding acute pleasure in waking to this new world. He had his weapons again; he had the dusei for his strength; and most of all Melein was safe, and in possession of the pan'en and the ship.

Their ship.

He suspected they owed much to this human, shamefully much; but he was glad that Melein elected to take it, and to live. It was a measure of Melein's own gratitude that she bent somewhat, that she left the times of things in Niun's own hands; *when you think him fit*, she had said, and even permitted the ship's schedule to be adjusted so that they might enter a premature night cycle, which they themselves did not need: but Duncan needed the sleep, which he had denied himself in caring for them.

Elsewhere Melein surely rested, or worked quietly. The ship proceeded, needing nothing from them. They had far, impossibly far to travel. The reference star that shone wan and distant in the center of the screen was not their destination. They had only en-tered the fringe of the system, and would skim outward again, into transit.

And stars after stars there would be: so Melein had said.

They had made a second transit during the night, a space in which they were, and were not, and were again, and substances flowed like water. Niun had not panicked, neither this time nor the first, even though Duncan himself, experienced in such things, had wakened with a wild outcry and was sick after, sweating profusely and scarcely able to walk to the lab where he found the drugs that calmed him: they had thrown him into sleep at last; that still continued. And this, troubling as it was, Niun had tried not to see: this once, he allotted to the human's distraught condition. It was possible, he thought, that mri had some natural advantage in this state; or perhaps it was shame that kept a mri from yielding to such weakness. He did not know. Other shames he had suffered, at the hands of humans and regul, inflicted upon him; but this was his own body, his own senses, and of them he had control.

Their ship, their voyage, and the pan'en to guide them: it was the only condition under which living was worthwhile, that they ruled themselves, much as the fact of it still dazed him. He had not expected it, not though Melein had foreseen, had told him it would be so. He had not believed: Melein, who had been only sen Melein, his true sister—that was all that he had trusted in her: poor, houseless she'pan, he had thought of her, lost and powerless, and he had done what he could to fend for her.

But she had seen.

The greatest she'panei were said to have been foresighted, the greatest and holiest that had ever guided the People; and a feeling of awe possessed him when he realized that such was Melein, of one blood with him. Such kinship frightened him, to reckon that her heredity was also his, that there rested within himself something he did not understand, over which he had no power.

She was guiding them *home*.

The very concept was foreign to him: home—*a'ai sa-mri*, the beginnings of the People. He knew, as surely all mri had always known, that once there must have been a world other than the several home-worlds-of-convenience—despite that it was sung that the People were born of the Sun. All his life he had looked up only at the red disc of Arain, and, in the discipline of the Kel, in the concerns of his former life, he had never let his curiosity stray beyond that barrier of his childborn belief. It was a Mystery; and it was not pertinent to his caste.

Born of the Sun. Golden-skinned, the mri, bronze-haired and golden-eyed: it had never before occurred to him that within that song lay the intimation of a sun of a different hue, and that it explained more than the custom of the Kel, who were spacefarers by preference, who cast their dead into the fires of stars, that no dark earth might possess them.

He stared at the star that lay before them, wondering where they were, whether within regul space still or elsewhere. It was a place known to generations before Kesrith, to hands that had set the record of it within the pan'en; and here too the People had seen service. Regul space or not, it must have been so: the Kel would have hired to fight, as it had always been—mercenaries, by whose gold the People lived. He could not imagine anything else.

Stars beyond stars.

And from each in turn the People would have departed: so it was, in the Darks; it was unthinkable that they would have fragmented. All, all would have gone—and what might move them was beyond his imagining, save only that the vision of a she'pan would have led them. They either moved to another and nearby world, or they had entered a Dark; and in the Dark, in that voyage, they would have forgotten all that pertained to that abandoned star, to that former service; they had come to the next Sun, and another service; and thereafter returned to the Dark, and another forgetting, a cycle without end.

Until Kesrith, until they two began to come home, a voyage in which the era of service to regul, the two thousand years that he had believed was all of recorded time, became merely interlude.

> *From Dark beginning*
> *to Dark at ending,*

So the People sang, in the holiest of songs.

> *Between them a Sun,*
> *But after comes Dark,*
> *And in that Dark,*
> *One ending.*

Tens of times he had sung the ritual, the *Shon'jir*, the Song of Passings, chanted at births and deaths and beginnings and endings. To a kel'en, it had sung only of birth and death of individuals.

Understanding opened before him, dizzying in perspective. More stars awaited them, each considered by the kel-'ein of its age to be the Sun . . . each era considered the whole of recorded time . . . until they should come in their own backward voyaging—home, to the Sun itself.

To the beginning of the People.

To the hope, the faintest of hopes, that there others might remain: Niun took to him that hope, knowing that it would surely prove false—that after so many misfortunes that had befallen them, it was impossible that such good could remain: they two were the last children of the People, born to see the end of everything, *ath-ma'ai*, tomb-guardians not only to a she'pan, but to the species.

And yet they were free, and possessed a ship.

And perhaps—a religious feeling stirred in him, and a great fear—it was for something else that they had been born.

Niun caressed the dus' velvet-furred shoulder, gazing at the human whose face was touched by the white light of the screen. In drugged abandonment the man slept, after giving them the ship, and his life, and his person. Niun puzzled over this, troubled, reckoned all the words and acts that had ever passed between them, that he could have moved the human to such a desperate act. Against the wisdom of the People he had taken a prisoner; and this was the result of it—that Duncan had become attached to them, stubborn as the dusei, who simply chose a mri and settled with him or died of grief.

Human instincts surely did not run in that direction. For forty years the People had struggled to deal with humans, and suffered murder for it, kel'ein butchered by this species that fought only in masses and with distance-weapons. Forty years—and at the last, in human victory—came Duncan, who, ill-treated, brought the whole machinery of human mercy down upon them, who cast himself and his freedom into their hands for good measure.

Tsi'mri stupidity, Niun raged in his mind, wishing that he could separate himself from tsi'mri altogether.

Yet he remembered a long and terrible dream, in which Duncan had been a faithful presence—in which he had fought for his sanity along with his life, and Duncan had stayed by him.

Atonement?

Perhaps, Niun thought, what had possessed Duncan had seized on the rest of his kind; perhaps, after all, there was some strange tsi'mri sense of honor that could not abide what the regul had done—as if humans would not take a victory so ill-won; as if the ruin of the People made a diminution in the universe that even humans felt, and in fear for themselves they tried to make restitution.

Not for tsi'mri, such a voyage as they made: and yet if such ever had a claim on the mri, inextricably entangled with the affairs of the People, such was Duncan—from the time that he, himself, had held the human's life and missed the chance to take it.

Niun, he is tsi'mri, Melein had argued, *and whatever he has done, he does not belong, not in the Dark.*

Yet we take the dusei, he had said, *and they are of the Between, too; and shall we kill them, that trust us?*

Melein had frowned at that; the very thought was terrible, for the partnership between mri and dus was old as Kesrith. And at last she had turned her face away and yielded. *You cannot make a dus into a mri,* she had said last, *and I do not think you will succeed with a human either. You will only delay matters painfully; you will arm him against us and endanger us. But try, if your mind is set; make him mri, make him mri, or we must someday do a cruel and terrible thing.*

"Duncan," Niun said into the dark, saw Duncan's light-bathed face contract in reaction. "Duncan."

Eyes opened, wells of shadow in the dim light of the screen. Slowly, as if the drug still clouded his senses, the human sat up. He was naked to the waist, his strange furriness at odd contrast with his complexion. He bowed his head against his knee and ran his hand through his disordered hair, then looked at Niun.

"It is a reasonable hour," said Niun. "You do not look well, Duncan."

The human shrugged, by which Niun understood that his ill was of the heart as much as of the body; and this he could well understand. "There are things to be done," Niun said. "You have said that there are trade supplies aboard."

"Yes," Duncan said, a marginal lifting of his spirits, as if he had dreaded something more distasteful. "Food, clothing, metals, all that there was at the station, that was intended for mri trade. I figured it properly belonged to you."

"You most of all have need of clothing."

Duncan considered, and nodded in consent. He had been long enough with them to know that his naked face was an offense, and perhaps long enough to feel a decent shame. "I will see to it," he agreed.

"Do that first," said Niun. "Then bring food for the dusei, and for us both; but I will take the she'pan's to her."

"All right," Duncan said. Niun watched as the human gathered himself up and wrapped a robe about himself—blue, that was kath-color, and inappropriate for a man. Niun considered the incongruity of that—what vast and innocent differences lay between mri and human, and what a thing he had undertaken. He did not protest Duncan's dress, not now; there were other and more grievous matters.

Niun did not attempt to rise, not until Duncan had left the room, for he knew that it would be difficult, and shaming. With the dusei's help he managed it, and stood against the wall, hard-breathing, until his legs would bear him. He could not fight against the human and win, not yet; and Duncan knew it, knew and still declined to risk the dusei's anger, or to dispute against him, or to use his knowledge of the ship to trap them and regain control.

And he had undertaken to destroy the human.

When he has forgotten that he is human, Melein had said, *when he is mri, then I will see his face.*

Duncan had consented to it. Niun was dismayed by this, knew of a certainty that he himself would have died before accepting such conditions of humans. When other things had failed to kill him, this would have done so, from the heart outward.

And someday, when Duncan had become mri, then he would not be capable of bending again. This acquiescence of his was tsi'mri, and must be shed along with all the rest: the naive, child-like man who had attached himself to them would no longer exist.

Niun thought to himself that he would miss that man that they had known; and the very realization made him uneasy, that a tsi'mri should so have softened his mind and his heart. The worst acts, he told himself, must surely proceed from irresolution, from half-measures. Melein had feared what he proposed, had spoken against it with what he desperately hoped was not foresight. She had not forbidden him.

He went gingerly, on exhausted legs, into the bath, and looked on what things were there that belonged to Duncan. These must go, the clothing, the personal items, everything: when he was no longer reminded of humans by the things that surrounded him, then neither would Duncan be reminded.

And if change was impossible to the human, then best to know it soon: it was one thing to reshape, and another to destroy and leave nothing in its place. Mri that he was, Niun had not learned of his masters to be cruel, only to be pitiless, and to desire no pity.

He gathered up what of Duncan's belongings he could find and bore them into the lab, where he knew there was a disposal chute: he thrust them in, and felt a pang of shame for what he did, but it seemed wrong to compel Duncan to do this himself, surrendering what he had prized, a lessening of the man—and that he would not do.

And when that was done, Niun looked about him at the lab, at the cabinet from which Duncan had obtained his medicines, and resolved on other things.

The door would not yield to his hand: he drew his pistol and ruined the lock, and it yielded easily thereafter. Load after load of tsi'mri medicines and equipage he carried to the chute, and cast it out, while the dusei sat and watched with grave and glittering eyes.

And suddenly the beasts arose in alarm—shied aside from Duncan's presence in the doorway.

Niun, his hands full of the last of the medicines, thrust them within the chute and only then faced Duncan's anger, that had the dusei distraught and bristling.

"There is no need of such things," he said to Duncan.

Duncan had attempted to robe himself as mri: the boots and the *e'esin* he had managed, the inner robe; but the *siga*, the outer, he wore loose; and the veil he carried in his hand—he had never found the arranging of it easy. Face-naked, he showed his anguish, a despair that wounded.

"You have killed me," he said in a thin voice, and Niun felt the sting of that—less than certain, in that moment, of the honesty of what he had done, trusting that the human would not challenge, could not. The dusei moaned, crowding into the corner. A container crashed from a table under their weight.

"If your life is those medicines," said Niun, "then you cannot survive with us. You will survive. We do not need such things; you do not."

Duncan cursed him. Niun stiffened, set his face against such tsi'mri rage, and refused to be provoked.

"Understand," said Niun, "that you agreed. This is a mri ship, kel Duncan. You will learn to be mri, as a child of the Kath learns. I do not know any other way, only to teach you as I was taught. If you will not, then I will fight you. But understand, as all mri understand who enter the Kel, that kel-law works from the elder to the lesser to the least. You will hurt before you are done; so, once did I. And if you have it in you to be kel'en, you will survive. That is what my masters in the Kel once said to me, when I was of an age to enter the Kel. I saw twelve of my Kel who did not survive, who never took the *seta'al*, the scars of caste. It is possible that you will not survive. It is possible that you cannot become what I am. If I were convinced that you cannot, then I would not do what I have done."

The human quieted; the dusei snuffed loudly and rocked, still uneasy. But Duncan's naked face assumed a calm, untroubled look that was more the man they knew. "All right," he said. "But, Niun, I needed those medicines. I needed them."

Fear. Niun still felt it in the room.

And he was troubled after Duncan had gone away, whether he had in fact done murder. He had thought as mri, forgetting that alien flesh might indeed be incapable of what mri found possible.

And was it then wrong that aliens needed what mri law forbade?

It was not a kel-thought, not right for his caste to think or to wonder. He dared not even bring it to Melein in secret, knowing the thought beyond him and disrespectful to a young and less than certain she'pan, even from her kel'anth, senior of the Kel—such of a Kel as she possessed.

He hoped desperately that he had not killed Duncan.

And in that thought he realized clearly that he wanted Duncan to live, not alone for rightness' sake, but because two were a desolate sort of House, and because the silence in kel-hall could become very deep and very long.

He called the dusei to him, soothed them with his hands and his voice, and went to find where Duncan had gone.

Chapter Eleven

Four days.

Duncan held them as a blur in his mind, a moiled confusion out of which he remembered little of reason. He worked to fill his hours, exhausted himself deliberately to cast himself to sleep of nights without long thought, without dreams. Niun did nothing except to exercise, quietly and often: *I am not a bearer of burdens*, the mri had insisted stiffly, when Duncan suggested he might well exercise by assisting him; and the mri then compounded the affront by reminding him that the dusei wanted tending.

Neither am I, Duncan had retorted, and bit off the oaths that rose into his mouth: the mri were not tolerant; they would kill or die for small cause, and there was time later to reason with Niun, whose limbs' weakness doubtless fed his temper, and whose uncertainty about his total situation likely hardened his attitudes.

The dusei, in fact, did want tending; and after a suitable delay, Duncan went and saw to their wants—rewarded by their pleasure-impulse, he felt shame for having put them off in spite—and fled it, for he could not bear much of it.

It was not the last crossing of purposes with Niun; the mri asked things and insisted he should understand the mri language—understand he did, in some words, with gestures—and at times Niun affected not to understand until he used a mri expression, though the mri was fluent. *Starve, then*, he was tempted to say; and did not, for there was later for quarrels, and the dusei that hovered about were becoming unpleasant and upset, contributing to the situation. In the end, Niun had his way.

It made sense, Duncan thought late, upon his bed, while the mri chose the floor. Niun fought to keep what was his, a way and a language that had almost entirely perished. It was a quiet battle, waged against him, who had most helped them and now most threatened them. It was something against which guns and skill did not avail, but life and death, all the same. It was why they were here at all, why they had been unable to live among humans, why he had argued with Stavros to free them. There was no compromise possible for them. They could not bear with strangeness. A human could; a human could adapt, facile as the jo, who looked like sand or stone, and waited. He considered this, and considered the sleeping mri, who lay with his head against his dus, unveiled as he would not unveil to an enemy.

Jo-fashion, a human could change and change again; the mri would obstinately die: and therefore it was inevitable that Niun should have his way.

In the morning Duncan set about his routines, and utterly bit back objections with Niun, went so far as to ask what he would have done.

Niun's amber eyes swept the compartment; a long-fingered hand made an inclusive gesture. "*E'nai*," he said, "*i.*"—*Remove it all.* Duncan stared, drew a long breath, and considered the matter.

The ship grew cold in the passing days, the air gradually resembling Kesrith's dry chill. Duncan was glad of the warmth of the mri robes that he wore from the skin outward. He learned the veil and the manners of it; he learned words and courtesies and gestures, and abandoned his own.

Niun sensed, surely, how far he was pressed, the frustration that welled upward in him at times, and averted his face and resumed the veil when matters came too close to impasse. There would be silence for a time, and finally words again. Niun named the things of which he did not approve: comforts and furnishings of all sorts. Duncan acquiesced, yielded up such of his own belongings as still remained, for the attachment he had to them seemed distant in this place, faced with what misery lay ahead of him; and as for damage to the ship, that seemed insufficient revenge on those that had sent him here. He worked at it, bewildered at first by what Niun asked, then grimly pleased in it. He stripped the accessible compartments of all furnishings, disassembled the furniture and stored what parts were useful metals and materials, and cast the rest out the destruct chute. After that went all machinery the mri considered superfluous, medical and otherwise, and all goods in storage that were counted luxuries.

It was madness. Duncan abandoned himself to it, began in his own frustration to seek out things to cast away, destroying for the joy of it, making of the ship only a shell, in which he did not have to remember Stavros, or humanity, or any other thing that he had cast away to come here. The loss of everything dulled all sense of loss.

The labs were mostly stripped already, back at station: all that had been reckoned unnecessary to the mission had already been taken, and all that he would desperately have saved, Niun had already destroyed. Duncan finished the job, down to the cleats that had held the furnishings, chem-scrubbed the floors, the walls, rendering the place acceptable—for this largest compartment on the ship Niun had chosen for their own.

Thereafter Duncan slept on a pallet no thicker than a folded blanket, and wakened stiff and fell to coughing again in the chill air, so that he began to brood over his health, and thought desperately of the medicines that Niun had destroyed, for that and for other purposes.

But Niun looked at him with some concern, and tacitly forgot his objection to work, and took on himself that day the preparation of meals and the care of the dusei. Niun flourished in the chill, thin air—had lost that frail, tottering movement in his step, and ceased to tire so quickly.

"You rest," Niun wished him when he persisted in trying to keep his schedule; Duncan shrugged and avowed the machinery would not run without him, which it would; but he was panicked now at the thought of idleness, sitting endlessly in the shell that he had left of the labs, of the rest of the ship, without books— Niun had cast out the reading and the music tapes in his quarters—without any occupation for hands or mind.

And when he was forced, he returned to the lab, that featureless white room, and settled in the corner, where at least his pallet and Niun's and the joining of the walls gave him some feeling of location. There, as he would do late at night to fall asleep, he sat and added chains of figures, did complex calculations of imaginary navigation, anything to fill the hours—watched the unchanging starscreen that was the lab's only feature. There was for sound only the whisper of air in the ducts, the steady machine noise of the ship's inner workings.

And nothing.

Nothing.

Niun was long absent that day—with Melein, Duncan reckoned, in that part of the ship that was barred to him; even the dusei were gone, constantly attendant on Niun. In idleness Duncan found a bit of metal and made a design on the tiles next his pallet, and then, with a certain grim humor, made marks for the days that had passed, ship-time, desperately reckoning that there could come a time he would lose track of everything in this place.

Nine days, thus far. Even of this he was marginally uncertain.

He began a chain of figures, thrusting his mind away from the lattice-gaps he had begun to have in his memory, trying to lose himself in regularities.

Unlike the jo, he was not successfully camouflaging, he reckoned; even the jo, cast into this sterile cubicle, given nothing to pattern from, could not find a place. It would blacken like a wretched specimen he had seen in Boaz' lab, going through color change after color change until it settled on the most conspicuous of all—a method of suicide, perhaps, death wish.

He thrust his thoughts away from that, too, but the image kept returning, the black winged creature in the silver cage; himself, from godlike perspective, sitting in the corner of a white and featureless room.

Nine days.

The afternoon of the tenth, Niun came back earlier than previously, banished the dusei to the far corner of the room, and unveiled, settled crosslegged on the floor a little removed from Duncan and facing him.

"You sit too much," Niun said.

"I am resting," Duncan said with an edge of bitterness.

Niun held up two metal rods, slender, and no more than a hand's length. "You will learn a game," Niun said, not: *I will teach you*; not: *Would it please you?* Duncan frowned, considered taking offense: but that the grim mri had entertainments: this pricked his interest, promised comradeship, a chance to talk with

the kel'en as he had not been able to talk with him since the
desert.

And it promised something to fill the silence.

He bestirred himself on his pallet, assumed carefully the position the Niun held, crosslegged, hands on knees. Niun showed
him the grip he had on the end of the rod in his right hand.

"You must catch," said Niun, and spun the rod toward him.
Duncan caught it, startled, in his fist, not his fingers, and the butt
of it stung his palm.

The second followed, from Niun's left hand. Duncan caught it
and dropped it. Niun held up both hands empty.

"Both at once," Niun said.

It was difficult. It was exceedingly difficult. Duncan's work-
sore hands were less quick than Niun's slender fingers, that never
missed, that snatched the most awkward throws from midair, and
returned them always at the same angle and speed, singly until
Duncan could make the difficult catch, and then together.

"We call it *shon'ai*," said Niun. "*Shonau* is *pass*. In your language, then, the Passing game. It sings the People; each caste
plays in its own way." He spoke, and the rods flew back and forth
gently between them, Duncan's fingers growing more sure than
they had been. "There are three castes of the People: Kath and
Kel and Sen. We are of the Kel, we black-robes, we that fight; the
Sen is the yellow-robes, the scholars; and the white, the she'pan;
the Kath is the caste of women neither Kel nor Sen, the blue-
robes, and the children—they are Kath until they take caste."

Duncan missed. The rod stung his knee, clattered to the floor.
He rubbed the knee and then continued, back and forth, back and
forth in turn with Niun. It was hard to listen and concentrate on
the rods; in recklessness he tried to answer.

"Men," he said, "neither Kel nor Sen. What of them?"

The rhythm did not break. "They die," said Niun. "The ones
without skill to be Sen, without skill to be Kel, the ones with no
heart, die. Some die in the Game. We are playing as the Sen
plays, with wands. The Kel plays with weapons." The throws became harder, faster. "Easy, with two players. More difficult with
three. With larger circles, it grows most difficult. I played a circle
of ten. If the circle becomes much larger, it becomes again a matter of accidents, of chance."

The rods flew hard this time. Duncan flung his hands up to catch them, deflected one that could have injured his face, but could not catch it. It fell. The other he held. The rhythm ceased, broken.

"You are weak in the left hand," said Niun. "But you have the heart. Good. You will learn the skill before I begin to show you the *yin'ein*, the old weapons. The *zahen'ein*, the modern, you know as well as I; I have nothing there to teach you. But the *yin'ein*, one begins with *shon'ai*. Throw."

Duncan threw. Niun held up his hand, easily received the separate rods cast back to him—with one hand, sweeping them effortlessly from the air. Duncan blinked, dismayed at the skill of the mri, and measured his own.

"There is a time to rest," said Niun then. "I would not see you miss." He tucked the rods back into his belt. "It is time," he said, "that we begin to talk. I will not speak often in your language; I am ordered to forget it, and so must you. You know a few words of the mu'ara, the common speech; and even those you must forget, and stay to the hal'ari, the High Speech. It is the law of the Darks, that all the Between be forgotten, and the mu'ara that grows in the Between must die, too. So do not be confused. Sometimes there are two words for a thing, one mu'ara, one hal'ari, and you must forget even a mri word."

"Niun," Duncan protested, holding up a hand for delay. "I haven't enough words."

"You will learn. There will be time."

Duncan frowned, looked at the mri from under his brows, carefully approached what had already been refused. "How much time?"

Niun shrugged.

"Does the she'pan know?" Duncan asked.

The membrane flicked across Niun's eyes. "Your heart is still tsi'mri."

It was a mri kind of answer, maddening. Duncan traced the design he had scratched on the flooring, considering what he could do to reason with the mri; of a sudden Niun's hand stopped his. He jerked free, looked up in deep offense.

"Another matter," said Niun. "A kel'en neither reads nor writes."

"I do."

"Forget."

Duncan stared at him. Niun veiled himself and rose, an unbending upward that a few days ago he could not have done, a grace natural to a man who had spent his life sitting on the ground; but Duncan, in attempting to rise and face him, was less graceful.

"Listen," he said.

And a siren sounded.

It was in Duncan's consciousness a subtle moment before panic took over, raw fear. Transition was approaching; they had made a jump point. The dusei had learned. Their feelings washed about the room like a tide—fear, abhorrence.

"Yai!" Niun shouted at them, settling them. He walked to the doorway and took hold of the handgrip there. Duncan sought that on the other side of the room, feigning calm he did not feel; his gut twisted in dread of what was coming—and no drugs, nothing. It was Niun's cold, unmoved example that kept him from sinking to the floor to await it.

The siren stopped. In a moment a bell signaled imminent jump, automatic alarm triggered by the ship as the tape played toward its destination. They had not yet learned where they had been. The nameless yellow star still hung as only one among others in the field of the screen. No ships had come. Nothing.

Suddenly came that initial feeling of uncertainty, and walls, floor, time, matter, rippled and shredded. the mind underwent something irretrievable on the outflow, as the process reversed itself; but there remained an impression of inconceivable depth, of senses overstimulated. The walls rippled back into solidity. Hands felt. Breath and sight returned.

But the bell was still going, still warning of jump imminent.

"Something's wrong!" Duncan cried. He saw the look on Niun's face, fear, that was not accustomed there; and Niun shouted something at him that had to do with Melein—and ran.

The dus-feelings were flooding the room. The dissolution began again, rippling, stomach-wrenching, like a fall to death. Duncan clung where he was, wishing to lose consciousness, unable to do so. The room dissolved.

Reshaped.

The bell kept on and on, and the warping began a third time. Dus-flesh was about him, radiating terror. Duncan screamed, lost his grip and fell down among them, one with them, beast-mind, beast-sense, and the bells. Another time the rippling began, and faded back; and another; and another; and another.

He felt solidity about him, touch and sensations of light that were alien after the abysses he had voyaged. He cried out, and felt the dusei warm against him, their solid comfort, the mad irrationalities of their uncomprehending minds.

They were his anchor. They had held him, one with him. He gave up his humanity and gave way to them for a time, arm flung over a massive neck, receiving their warmth and comfort until he clearly realized what he yielded them, and cursed, and pushed them; then they withdrew, and he became aware of himself again.

Human, who had laid down with them, no more than they.

He hurled himself up and staggered to the doorway. His legs folded under him as he grasped the handhold, his fingers too weak to keep it. His stomach tried to evert itself, as if underfoot were sideways, but he had not the strength to heave up its contents, and grayed out.

He fell, sprawled, and realized it, still wanted to be sick and could not. He lay still a time, heaving with his effort to breathe, and the dusei crouched in the far corner, separate from him, giving him nothing but their fear.

Niun returned—after how long a time he knew not—sank down, bowed his veiled head wearily against his folded arms. Duncan lay still on his side, unwilling to chance more than breathing.

"Melein is well," Niun said in his own tongue: that much Duncan could understand; and something further he said, but Duncan could not put it together.

"What happened?" Duncan demanded to know, an effort that cost him much in sickness; but Niun only shrugged. "Niun, where are we?"

But Niun said nothing, perhaps unable to answer, or simply, mri-stubborn, pretending not to understand human language any more.

Duncan cursed him, and the effort knotted his stomach and heaved up the sickness at last. He could not move, even to move aside. After a long time Niun bestirred himself in what was surely disgust, and brought wet towels and cleaned the place and washed his face. The touch, the lifting of his head brought more dry heaving, and Niun let him alone thereafter, settling on the opposite side of the room just within his field of vision.

Came one of the dusei at last, nosing at him, urging at him with warmth. Duncan moved his limp hand and struck it. It reared aside with a cry of startlement and outrage, radiated such horrid confusion that he cried aloud. Across the room Niun rose to his feet.

And came the siren again; and the bell.

Dissolution.

Duncan did not seek the security of the wall, the illusion that he had some anchor. He let go. When it was over, he lay on the floor and retched and sobbed for breath, fingers spread on the unyielding flooring.

The dusei came back, urging their warm feelings at him. He began to gasp, unable to breathe, until something leaned on his chest and forced the air in, until Niun's hand gripped his shoulder and shook at him with bruising force, that dazed him and made him lose contact with the room again. He stared at the mri in utter blankness and sobbed.

He was composed again the next morning, a hard-fought composure, muscles of his limbs and belly still tending to spasm from the tension he could not force from them. He remembered with acute shame his collapse, how he had rested the remainder of yesterday—or the day before—tucked up in a ball in the corner, remembered tears pouring hotly down his face without emotion, without cause, only that he could not stop them.

This morning Niun stared at him, veiled amber eyes frowning as he offered a cup of soi into his trembling hand, steadying him so that he could drink it. The hot, bittersweet liquid rolled like oil into Duncan's unwilling stomach and lay there, taking some of the chill away. The tears started again, causeless. He drank slowly, holding the cup child-fashion in both hands, with tears sliding down his face. He looked into the mri's eyes and met there a cold reserve that recognized no kinship between them.

"I will help you walk," Niun said.

"No," he said with such force that the mri let him alone, rose and walked away, looked back once, then left, immune to the weakness that assailed him.

In that day even the dusei radiated distrust of him: crossing the room they would shy away from him, hating his presence; and Niun when he returned sat far across the room, soothing the troubled dusei and long staring at him.

With ship's night about them, they jumped once more, and a second time, and Duncan clung to his corner, clamped his jaws against sickness, and afterward was dazed, with vast gaps in his memory. In the morning he found the strength to stagger from his cramped refuge—to bathe, driven by self-disgust—finally to take some food into his aching stomach. But for the better part of the day he could not remember clearly.

Niun regarded him, frowning, waiting. Duncan thought distractedly, for him to die or to shake off the weakness; and Duncan felt the contempt like a tangible force, and bowed his head against his arms and brooded desperately, how he would wrest control from the tape before the malfunction killed them all, how he would take them to some random, lost refuge, where humanity could not find them.

But this he had no skill to do, and in his saner moments acknowledged it. The mri could survive, so long as the ship did. He began to think obsessively of suicide, and brooded upon it, and then remembered in his terrified and circular thoughts that the drugs were gone.

"Tsi'mri," Niun said of him finally, after standing and staring at him for a time.

Contempt burned in the mri's voice. The mri walked away, and the outrage of it gave Duncan strength to rise and fight his blurring senses. He was sick again immediately; he make it to the lavatory this time, blinked the tears from his eyes and washed his face and tried to control the tremor that ran through his limbs.

And came back into the living quarters and tried to walk across the naked center of it—halfway across before his senses turned inside out and he reeled off balance. He hurled himself for the wall, reaching wildly, found it and collapsed against it.

Niun stood watching. He had not known. Niun looked him up and down, face veiled.

"You were kel'en," Niun said then. "Now what are you?"

Duncan fought for words, found none that would come out. Niun went to his own pallet and sat down there, and Duncan sat where he was on the hard floor, wanting to rise and walk and give the lie to the mri. He could not. Niun's contempt gnawed at him. He began to reckon time again, how many days he had lost in this fashion, mindless and disoriented.

"A question," Duncan said in the hal'ari. "How many days—how many gone?"

He did not expect Niun to answer, was inwardly prepared for silence or spite. "Four," said Niun quietly. "Four since your illness."

"Help me," Duncan asked, forcing the words between his teeth. "Help me up."

Silently the mri arose, and came to him and took his arm, drew him to his feet and helped him walk, providing him an anchor that made it possible to move. Duncan fought his senses into order, trying to lie to them—persuaded Niun to guide him about the routines of maintenance in their sector, tried to do what he had been accustomed to do.

He rested, as best he could, muscles still taut; and began the next morning, and the next, and the next, with the determination that the next jump would not undo him.

It came, days hence; and this time Duncan stood fast by the handhold, fighting the sickness. Within a little time he tried to go to the hall, managed to walk, and returned again to his pallet, exhausted.

He might, he thought in increasing bitterness, have let the mri die; he might have had comfort, and safety; he hated Niun's ability to endure the jumps, that set of mind that could endure the phasing in and out without unraveling.

And Niun, whether sensing his bitterness or not, deigned to speak to him again—sat near him, engaged in one-sided conversation in the hal'ari, as if it mattered. At times he spoke chants, and insisted Duncan repeat them, learn them: Duncan listlessly complied, to have peace, to be let alone eventually, endless chains of names and begettings and words that meant nothing to him. He cared little—pitied the mri, finally, who poured his history, his myths, into such a failing vessel. He felt himself on the downward side of a curve, the battle won too late. He could no longer keep food down; his limbs grew weak; he grew thin as the mri, and more fragile.

"I am dying," he confided to Niun finally, when he had learned hal'ari enough for such a thought. Niun looked at him soberly and unveiled, as he would when he wished to speak personally; but Duncan did not drop veil, preferring its concealment.

"Do you wish to die?" Niun asked him, in a tone fully respectful of such a wish. For an instant Duncan was startled, apprehensive that the mri would help him to it on the spot: *Would you like a cup of water?* The tone would have been the same.

He searched up words with which to answer. "I want," he said, "to go with you. But I cannot eat. I cannot sleep. No, I do not want to die. But I am dying."

A frown furrowed Niun's brow. The eyes nictitated. He put out a slim, golden hand and touched Duncan's sleeve. It was a strange gesture, an act of pity, had he not better learned the mri.

"Do not die," Niun wished him earnestly.

Duncan almost wept, and managed not to.

"We shall play *shon'ai*," Niun said.

It was mad. Duncan would have refused, for his hands shook, and he knew that he would miss: it occurred to him that it was a way of granting him his death. But Niun's gentility promised otherwise, promised companionship, occupation for the long hours. One could not think of anything else, and play *shon'ai*.

By the side of a red star, for five days without a jump, they played at *shon'ai*, and spoke together, unveiled. There was a chant to the Game, and a rhythm of hands that made it yet more difficult to make the catch. Duncan learned it, and it ran through his brain even at the edge of sleep, numbing, possessing his whole mind; for the first time in uncounted nights he slept deeply, and in the morning he ate more than he had been able.

On the sixth day by that star, they played a more rapid game, and Duncan suffered a bone-bruise from a hit, and learned that Niun would not hold his hand with him any longer.

Twice more he was hit, once missing by nervousness and the second time by anger. Niun returned a cast with more skill than he could manage when he had thrown the mri a foul throw in temper for the first hit. Duncan absorbed the pain and learned that to lose concentration from fear or from anger was to suffer worse pain, and to lose the game. He cleared his mind, and played in earnest at *shon'ai*, still with wands, and not yet as the Kel played, with edged steel.

"Why," he asked Niun, when he had words enough to ask, "do you play to harm your brothers?"

"One plays *shon'ai*," said Niun, "to deserve to live, to feel the mind of the People. One throws. One receives. We play to deserve to live. We cast. Hands empty, we wait. And we learn to be strong."

There was a threshold of fear in the Game, the sure knowledge that there was a danger, that there was no mercy. One could be secure in it a time, while the pace stayed within the limits of one's skill, and then one realized that it was in earnest, and that the pace was increasing. Fear struck, and nerves failed, and the Game was lost, in pain.

Play, Niun advised him, *to deserve to live. Throw your life, kel'en, and catch it in your hands.*

He understood, and therein another understanding came to him, how the mri could take great joy in such a game.

And he understood for the first time the peculiar madness in which the mri could not only survive, but revel in the unnatural feel of the jumps, by which the ship hurled herself at apparent random from star to star.

Twice more they jumped, and Duncan stood still and waited as the bell rang and the dissolution began. He watched the mri, knew the mind of the kel'en who stood opposite him—knew how to let go and cast himself utterly to the rhythm of the Game, to go with the ship, and not to fear.

A wild laugh came to him on that second emergence, for the teaching of the Service had been *survive*, but that of the Game was something complexly alien, that careless madness that was the courage of the mri.

Kel'en.

He had shed something, something he once had valued; and as with the other possessions that he had cast into oblivion, the sense of loss was dim and distant.

Niun gazed at him, silently estimated, and he met that look directly, loss still nagging at him. One of the dusei, the lesser one, nosed his hand. He jerked it back, turned his face from Niun's critical stare, and went to the corner that was his—limbs steady, senses trying to deceive him and denied the power to do so.

He was not what Stavros had launched.

He sat on his pallet and stared at the scratched reckoning of days that he had begun, and that he had omitted to do. It was no longer the time that passed that mattered, but that which lay ahead, time enough that he could indeed forget.

Forget writing, forget human speech, forget Kesrith. There were gaps in his past, not alone in recent days, those fevered and terrible hours; there were others, that made strange and shifting patterns of all his memory, as if some things that he remembered were too strange to this ship, this long voyaging.

The Dark that Niun spoke of began to swallow such things up, as it lacked measure, and direction, and reason.

With the same edge of metal that had made the marks, he scratched through them, obliterating the record.

Chapter Twelve

The lost days multiplied into months. Duncan passed them in careful observance of maintenance schedules, stripped down units that did not need it and reassembled the machinery, only to keep busy—played *shon'ai* what time Niun would consent; memorized the meaningless chants of names, and constantly rehearsed in his mind what words he had recently gathered of the hal'ari, the while his hands found occupation in the game of knots that Niun taught him, or in the galleys, or in whatever work he could devise for the moment.

He learned metalwork, which was a craft appropriate to the Kel; and carving—made in plastic a blockish figure of a dus, for which he found no practical use in its beginning; and then purpose did come to him. "Give it to the she'pan," he said, when he had done it as well as possible; and pushed it into Niun's hands.

The mri had looked greatly distressed. "I will try," he had said, with perplexing seriousness, and arose at once and went, as if it were a matter of moment instead of a casual thing.

It was late before he returned; and he settled on the floor and set the little dus-figure between them on the mat. "She would not, kel Duncan."

No apology for the she'pan's hatefulness; it was impossible that Niun apologize for a decision of the she'pan. Understanding came, why Niun had hesitated even to try to take the gift to her, and after a moment heat began to rise to Duncan's face. He did not veil, but stared sullenly at the floor, at the unshapely and rejected little figure.

"So," he said with a shrug.

"It was bu'ina'anein—you invaded," Niun said.

"*Presumptuous*," Duncan translated, and the heat did not leave his face.

"It is not the time," said Niun.

"When will be?" Duncan asked sharply, heard the mri's soft intake of breath. Niun veiled himself in offense and rose.

Discarded, the little figure lay there for two days before Niun, in a mild tone of voice, and after fingering it for some little time, asked if he might have it.

Duncan shrugged. "Take it," he said, glad to have it gone.

It disappeared into the inner folds of Niun's robes. Niun rose and withdrew from the room. The dusei went, and returned, and went again, restless.

There was a line drawn in main-corridor, an invisible one. Duncan knew the places within the ship that he could go, and those that were barred to him, and he did not attempt the forbidden ones. It was not from the ship's workings that he was barred, so much as from Melein's presence; and Niun came and went there, but he could not.

Duncan went now, impelled by humanish obstinacy, curious where Niun had gone with the figure; and his steps grew less quick, and finally ceased at the corridor that he had not seen in uncounted days: around the bending of the passage as it was, he had not even infringed so far as to come this way—and the sight of it now cooled his anger and gave him pause.

The lights were out here, and faintly there was the reek of something musky that the filters had not entirely dispersed. A vast brown shape, and a second, sat in the shadows before an open doorway: the dusei—Niun's presence, he thought.

There was humanish stubbornness; and there was stubbornness mri-fashion, which he had also learned, which, in Niun, he respected.

There was the simple fact that, challenged, Niun would not back away.

But there were ways of pressing at the mri.

Silently, respectful of the barrier, Duncan gathered his robes between his knees and sank down crosslegged, there to wait. The dusei, shadows by the distant doorway, stood and snuffed the air nervously, pressing at him with their uncertainties. He would not

be driven. He did not move. In time, the lesser dus came halfway
and lay down facing him, head between its massive paws. When
he stayed still it rose up again, and halved that distance, and finally, much against his will, came and nosed at his leg.

"Yai!" he rebuked it softly. It settled, not quite touching,
sighed.

And from the doorway appeared a blacker shadow, that glittered here and there with metal.

Niun.

The mri stood still, waiting. Duncan gathered himself to his
feet and stood still, carefully at the demarcation.

It was not necessary to say overmuch with Niun—the mri observed him now, and after deliberation, beckoned him to come.

Duncan walked ahead into that shadow, the dus at his heels, as
Niun waited for him at the doorway; and human-wise he would
have questioned Niun, what manner of thing was here, what impulse suddenly admitted him to this place. But still in silence
Niun swept his hand to the left, directing his attention into the
room from which he had come.

Part of the crew's living quarters had been here. The musky
smell hung thick in this shadowy place, that was draped in black
cloth. The only light within was living flame, and it glistened on
the ovoid that rested at the far wall of the compartment, behind a
shadowed steel grating. Two conduits rose at the doorway, serving as pillars, narrowing the entry so that only one at a time might
pass.

"Go in," Niun's voice said softly at his back.

He felt the touch of Niun's hand between his shoulders, and
went forward, not wishing to, feeling his skin contract at the
shadow, the leaping flame so dangerous on the ship; the incense
was thick here, cloying. He had noticed it before, adhering to the
clothing of the mri, a scent he associated with them, thought even
natural to them, though he had missed it in the sterile labs.

Behind them the dusei breathed, unable to enter because of the
pillars.

And there was silence for some few moments.

"You have seen such a shrine before," Niun said in a low voice,
so that the prickling of his skin became intense. Duncan looked
half-about at the mri, heart pounding as he recalled Sil'athen, the

betrayal he had done. For a terrible moment he thought Niun knew; and then he persuaded himself that it was the first time he had come that the mri recalled to him, when he had come with permission, in their company.

"I remember," Duncan said thickly. "Is it for this you have kept me from this part of the ship? And why do you allow me here now?"

"Did I misunderstand? Did you not come seeking admittance?"

There was a stillness in Niun's voice that chilled, even yet. Duncan did not try to answer—looked away, where the pan'en rested behind its screen, at the flickering warm light, gold on silver.

Mri.

It had no echo now, this compartment, of the human voices that had once possessed it, no memory of the coarse jokes and warmer thoughts and impulses that had once governed here. It contained the pan'en. It was a mri place. It held age, and the memory of something he had done that he could not admit to them.

"In every edun of the People," Niun said, "has been a shrine, and the shrine is of the Pana. You see the screen. That is the place beyond which the Kel may not set foot. That which rests beyond is not for the Kel to question. It is a symbol, kel Duncan, of a truth. Understand, and remember."

"Why do you allow me here?"

"You are kel'en. Even the least kel'en has freedom of the outer shrine. But a kel'en who has touched the pan'en—who has crossed into the Sen-shrine—he is marked, kel Duncan. Do you remember the guardian of the shrine?"

Bones and black cloth, pitiful huddle of mortality within the shrine: memory came with a cold clarity.

"The lives of kel'ein," Niun said, "have been set to guard this; others that have carried it have died for that honor, holding secret its place, obeying the orders of a she'pan. But you did not know these things."

Duncan's heart sped. He looked warily at the mri. "No," he said, and wished himself out the door.

But Niun set his hand at his shoulder and moved him forward to the screen, there knelt, and Duncan sank down beside him. The screen was a darkness that cut the light and the shape of the pan'en into diamond fragments. Behind them the dusei fretted, barred from their presence.

There was silence. Duncan slowly let go his breath, understanding finally that there was no imminent threat. A long time Niun rested there, hands in his lap, facing the screen. Duncan did not dare turn his head to look at his face.

"Do you understand this place?" Niun asked of him finally, without moving.

"No," Duncan said. "And you have not taught me words enough to ask. What do you honor here?"

"First of Kel-caste was Sa'an."

". . . *Giver of laws,*" Duncan took up the chant in silence that Niun left, *"which was the service that he gave to Sarin the Mother. And the law of the Kel is one: to serve the she'pan . . ."*

"That is the *Kel'es-jir,*" Niun said. "The high songs each have a body, that is first learned; then from each major word comes a limb, that is another song. In the *e'atren-a* of Sa'an are twenty-one major words, that lead to other songs. That is one answer to your question: here kel'ein learn the high songs. Here the three castes meet together, though they keep to their places. Here the dead are laid before the presence of the Pana. Here we speak to the presence of Sa'an and the others who had given to the People, and we remember that we are their children." There was a long silence. "Sa'an was not your father. But bend yourself to kel-law and you may come here and be welcome. The kel-law I can teach you. But the things of the Pana, I cannot. They are for the she'pan to teach, when she will. It is a law that each caste teaches only what it best knows. The Kel is the Hand of the People. We are the Face of the People that outsiders see, and therefore we veil. And we do not bear the high knowledge, and we do not read the writings; we are the Face that is Turned Outward, and we hold nothing by which outsiders could learn us."

It explained much.

"Are all outsiders enemies?" Duncan asked.

"That is beyond kel-knowledge. The lives of the Kel are the living of the People. We were hired by the regul. It is sung that we have served as mercenaries, and those songs are very old, from before the regul. That is all I know."

And Niun made a gesture of respect and rose. Duncan gathered himself up and followed him out into the outer corridor, where the dusei waited. Pleasure feelings came strongly from them. Duncan bore it, trying to keep his senses clear, aware—fearfully aware—that his defenses were down, with the mri and with the dusei.

In kel-hall they shared a cup of soi. Niun seemed in an unusually communicative mood, and expressions played freely through his eyes, which could be dead as amber glass.

As if, Duncan thought, his seeking out the shrine had pleased Niun. It occurred to him that the long silences were lonely not only for himself, but perhaps for Niun too, who shared living space with a being more alien to him than the dusei, who could less understand him—and of whom Melein disapproved.

They talked, quietly, of what little was immediate, when they reckoned that jump might occur, and what was to be done on the morrow. There was a vast area of things they did not mention, that lay in past and future. There were things that Duncan, finding Niun inclined to talk, would have asked another human, things that he might have said—questions of the past, to know the man: *What was it—to live on Kesrith, when there were only regul and mri? Where did you come from? What women did you know? What did you want of life?* But Kesrith had to be forgotten; and so did the things that he himself remembered, human and forbidden to mention. The past was gone; the future was full of things that a kel'en must not ask, must not question, must not see, save in dim patterns—as beyond the screen.

Duncan finished his cup, set it aside, pushed at the dus that instantly sought to nose it.

"I will play you a round," said Niun.

Day after day, the Game, each day the same. The sameness became maddening. And on this day, with the memory of the shrine fresh in his mind, Duncan bit at his lip and weighed his life and gave another answer.

"With weapons," he said.

Niun's eyes nictitated, startlement. He considered, then from his belt drew the *av-tlen,* the little-sword, two hands in length. He laid that before him; and his pistol, that he put to the left, and apart; and the weighted cords, the *ka'islai,* that depended from his belt and seemed more ornament than weapon. And from an inner pocket of his belt he drew the small, hafted blades of the *as-ei,* with which the Kel played at *shon'ai.* All these things he laid on the mat between them, pistol on the left, and the *yin'ein,* the ancient weapons, on the right.

"There is missing the *av-kel,*" Niun said. "It is not necessary here."

The kel-sword: Duncan knew it, a blade three feet long and razor-edged; he had returned it to Niun, and it lay now wrapped in cloth, next Niun's pallet.

"You may touch them." Niun said; and as he gathered up the small blades of the *as-ei:* "Have a care of them. Of all these things, kel Duncan, have great care. *This*—" He gestured at the pistol. "With this I have no concern for you. But kel'ein who have played the Game from childhood—die. you are barely able to play the wands."

A chill, different fear crept over him in the handling of these small weapons, not panic-fear—he no longer entered the Game with that—but a cold reckoning that in all these arms was something alien, more personal and more demanding that he had yet calculated. He considered the skill of Niun, and mri reflexes, that quite simply seemed a deadly fraction quicker than human, and suddenly feared that he was not ready for such a contest, and that Niun waited for him to admit it.

"It seems," Duncan said, "that quite a few kel'ein might die in learning these."

"It is an honorable death."

He looked at the mri's naked face and sought some trace of humor there, found none.

"You are a kind," Niun said slowly, "that fights in groups. We are not. The guns, the *zahen'ein,* they are your way. You do not understand ours, I see that. And often, Duncan, often we tried to approach humankind; we thought that there might be honor in you. Perhaps there is. But you would not come alone to fight. Is this never done among humans? Or why is it, Duncan?"

Duncan found no answer, for there was a great sadness in the mri, so profound a sadness and bewilderment when he asked that—as if, had this one thing been understood, then so much else need not have happened.

"I am sorry," Duncan said, and found it pathetically little.

"What will you? Will you play?"

The grief still remained there. Of a sudden Duncan feared edged weapons with such feeling still in the air. He looked down at the small blades he held, cautiously attempted the proper grip on them nonetheless.

Niun's slender fingers reached, carefully adjusted his, then withdrew. The mri edged back to a proper interval.

"One blade at a time, Duncan."

He hesitated.

"That is no good," Niun said. "Throw."

The blade flew. Niun caught it. Gently it returned.

Duncan missed. it hit his chest and fell to his lap. He rubbed the sore spot over his heart and thought that it must be bleeding despite the robes.

He threw. Niun returned it. Awkwardly he caught the hilt, threw again: it came back, forth, back, forth, back—and his mind knew it for a weapon suddenly, and he froze, and a second time it caught him in the ribs. He gathered it from his lap and his hand was shaking. He cast.

Niun intercepted it, closed his hand on it and did not return it.

"I will keep playing," Duncan said.

"Later." Niun held up his hand for the other. Duncan returned it, and the mri slipped both back into his belt.

"I am not that badly hurt."

The mri's amber eyes regarded him soberly, reading him from shaking hands to his unveiled face. "Now you have realized that you will be hurt. So dó we all, kel Duncan. Think on it a time. Your heart is good. Your desire is good. Your self-knowledge is at fault. We will play again, sometimes with wands, sometimes with the blades. I will show you all that I know. But it is not all to be learned today. Let me see the injuries. I judged my throws carefully, but I could make a mistake."

Duncan frowned, opened the robe, found two minute punctures, one over his heart, one over his ribs, neither bruised, neither deep. "I suppose that I am the one more likely to make a mistake," he admitted. Niun regarded him soberly.

"True. You do not know how to hold your strength. I still must hold mine with you when we play at wands."

He regarded the mri with resentment.

"Not much," Niun conceded. "But I know your limit, and you do not know mine."

Duncan's jaw knotted. "What is the hal'ari for *arrogant*?"

Niun smiled. "*Ka'ani-nla.* But I am not, kel Duncan. If I were arrogant, you would have more than two small cuts: to use an opponent badly, that is arrogant. To press the Game beyond your own limits: that is stupidity. And you are not a stupid man, kel Duncan."

It was several moments before Duncan even attempted to answer. The dusei shifted weight restlessly.

"If I can make you angry," Niun said when he opened his mouth to speak, "I have passed your guard again. If I can make you angry, I have given you something to think about besides the Game. So my masters would say to me—often, because I myself was prone to that fault. The scars I have gained of it are more than two."

Duncan considered the mri, found it strange that after so long a time he learned something of Niun as a person, and not as mri. He considered the amusement that lurked just behind the amber eyes, and reckoned that he was intended to share that humor, that Niun instead of bristling had simply hurled back the throw that he had cast, as a man would with a man not his enemy.

"Tomorrow," Duncan said, "I will try the *as-ei* again."

Niun's face went sober, but there was pleasure in his gesture of assent. "Good." He absently extended a hand to fend off the dus that intruded on them: the beasts could not seem to resist intervening in any quiet conversation, wanting to touch, to be as close as possible.

But the dus, the lesser one, snarled an objection and Niun snatched his hand back quickly. The beast pushed roughly past him, and settled between them. An instant later it moved again, heaved its bulk nearer and nearer Duncan.

"It does that sometimes," Duncan said, alarmed by its behavior. There was a brush at his senses, affecting his heartbeat. The massive head thrust at his knee, and with a sigh the beast worked its way heavily against him, warm, beginning the pleasure sound. He lost himself in it a moment, then shuddered, and it stopped. He focused clearly, saw Niun sitting with his arm about the shoulder of the other, the larger dus.

"That is a shameless dus," Niun said, "that prefers tsi'mri."

He was, Duncan thought, vexed that the dus had snarled at him. Duncan endured the touch a moment more, knowing the attachment of the mri to the beasts, fearing to offend either by his complaint; but the touch at his senses was too much. A sudden shiver took him. "Get it away from me," he said suddenly; he feared to move, not knowing what afflicted the beast.

Niun frowned, carefully separated himself from the larger dus, put out his hand to touch that which lay against Duncan. It made a strange, plaintive sound, heaved the more closely against Duncan, hard-breathing. Niun, veilless already, took off the *zaidhe* that covered his mane—unwonted familiarity—leaned forward and shook hard at the animal. Duncan felt the strain of dus-feelings, of alienness. He tried to touch the beast himself with his hand, but it suddenly heaved away from him and shied off across the room, shaking its massive head and blowing puffs of air in irritation as it retreated.

"Tsi'mri," Niun judged, remaining kneeling where he was. "The dus feels something it cannot understand. It will not have me; it cannot have you. That is going to be a problem, Duncan. It is possible you cannot accept what it offers. But it can be dangerous if you will not accept it eventually. I cannot handle this one. There is a madness that comes on them if they cannot have what they want. They choose. We do not."

"I cannot touch that thing."

"You will have to."

"No."

Niun expelled a short breath, and rose and walked away, to stand staring at the starscreen, the dusty field that was all that changed in kel-hall. It was all there was to look at but a confused beast and a recalcitrant human. Duncan felt the accusation in that frozen black figure, total disappointment in him.

"Niun."

The mri turned, bare-faced, bare-headed, looked down on him.

"Do not call me tsi'mri," Duncan said.

"Do you say so?" Niun stiffened his back. "When the hal'ari comes easily from your mouth, when you play at the Game with weapons, when you can lie down to sleep and not fear the dusei, then I shall no longer call you tsi'mri. The beast will die, Duncan.

And the other will be alone, if the madness does not infect it, too."

Duncan looked at it, where it crouched in the corner. To have peace with Niun, he rose and nerved himself to approach it. Perversely, it would have none of him, but shied off and snarled. The dark eyes glittered at him, desiring what it could not find.

"Careful."

Niun was behind him. Duncan gave back gratefully, felt the mri's hand on his shoulder. The dus remained in its corner, and it did not seem the time to attempt anything with it.

"I will try," Duncan said.

"Slowly. Let it alone for now. Let be. There is no pressing them."

"I do not understand why it comes to me. I have tried to discourage it. Surely it understands I do not want it."

Niun shrugged. "I have felt its disturbance. I cannot answer you. No one knows why a dus chooses. I could not hold them both, that is all. It has no one else. And perhaps it feels in you the nature of a kel'en."

Duncan glanced at the dus, that had ceased to radiate hostility, and again at Niun, wondering whether he understood that in what the mri had said was an admission that he had won something.

That night, as they were settling to sleep on their pallets, Niun put away his weapons in the roll of cloth that contained all his personal possessions, and there, along with a curious knot of cord, was the ill-made figure of a dus, as if it were valued.

It pleased Duncan. He looked into the shadows at the living model that lay some distance from him, eyes glittering in the light of the starscreen, head between its paws, looking wistfully at him.

He whistled at it softly, an appeal ancient and human.

A soft puff of air distended the beast's nostrils. The small eyes wrinkled in what looked like anguished consideration.

But it stayed at a distance.

Chapter Thirteen

No longer gold-robed, but white, Melein. She had made herself new robes, had made herself a new home from the compartment nearest controls, plain and pleasant—one chair, hers, and mats for sitting, and upon the walls she had begun to write, great serpentines of gold and black and blue that filled the room she had taken for her own hall, that spread down the corridor outside in lively and strange contrast to the barren walls elsewhere. From her haven she had begun to take the ship, to make it home.

Out of her own mind she had resurrected the appearance of the lost edun, the House of the People. She had recalled the writings; and of her own skill and by her own labor she had done these things, this difficult and holy work.

Niun was awed when he saw it, each time that he came to attend her, and found her work advancing through the ship. He had not believed that she could have attained such knowledge. She was, before she was she'pan, youngest daughter of the House: Melein Zain-Abrin, Chosen of the she'pan Intel.

He had utterly lost the Melein he had known, his truesister, his comrade once of the Kel. The process had been a gradual one, advancing like the writings, act by act. He put from his mind the fact that they had been children of the Kath together, that they had played at being kel'ein in the high hills of Kesrith. Hers became the age and reverence of all she'panei. Her skills made her a stranger to him. Being merely kel'en, he could not read what she wrote, could not pierce the mysteries in which she suddenly spoke, and he knew to his confusion how vast the gulf was that had opened between them in the six years since they had both been of the Kel. The blue *seta'al* were cut and stained into her face as well as his, the proud marks of a warrior; but the hands were forbidden weapons now, and her bearing was the quiet reserve of the Sen. She did not go veiled. A Mother of an edun almost never veiled, her face always accessible to her children. Only in the presence of the profaning and the unacknowledgeable did she turn her face aside. She was alone: the gold-robed Sen should have been her servants; experienced warriors of the Kel should have been her Husbands; the eldest of the Kath should have brought bright-eyed children for her delight. He felt the inadequacy of everything he could do for her, at times with painful force.

"Niun." She smiled and touched his offered hand. He knelt by her chair—knelt, for the Kel did not use the luxury of furniture, no more than the ascetic Sen. His dus was near him, warm and solid. The little one, visitor, crowded near the she'pan's feet, adoring, dus-wise. A Sen-caste mind was said to be too complex, too cold for the dusei's taste. Niun did not know if this were true: it was strange that even when Melein had been of the Kel, no dus had ever sought her, a source of grief to her, and bitter envy of other kel'ein. Now she had none, would have none. The dus adored, but it did not come close with its mind—preferring even a human to Melein s'Intel, to the calculating power of a she'pan.

He bowed his head beneath her touch, looked up again. "I have brought Duncan," he said. "I have told him how to bear himself; I have warned him."

Melein inclined her head. "If you judge it time," she said, stroking the back of the dus that sat by her. "Bring him."

Niun looked up at her, to make one final appeal to her patience—to speak to her that he had known as a child; but he could not find that closeness with her. The disturbance passed to the dusei. His shook its head. He rose, pushed at the beast to make it move.

Duncan waited. Niun found him standing where he had left him, against the door on the other side of the corridor. "Come," he told the human, "and do not veil. You are not in a strange hall."

Duncan refastened the *mez* just beneath his chin, and came inside with him, hesitated in the middle of the room until Melein herself held out her hand in invitation, and showed him where he should sit, at her left hand, where the lesser dus rested.

Duncan went, fearing the dus, mortally afraid of that beast. Niun opened his mouth to protest, but he thought that he would shame Duncan if he did so, and make question of his fitness to be here. Carefully Duncan settled where he was asked; and Niun sat down in his own place at Melein's right, within arm's reach of Duncan and the other animal. He touched the smaller dus with his fingertips, felt it settled and was relieved at what he felt.

"Duncan," Melein said softly. "Kel Duncan. Niun avows you are able to understand the hal'ari."

"I miss words, she'pan, but I understand."

"But then, you did understand somewhat of the mu'ara before you came into our company."

"Yes. A few words."

"You must have worked very hard," she said. "Do you know how long you have been aboard?"

"No. I do not count the time anymore."

"Are you content, Duncan?"

"Yes," he said, which Niun heard and he held his breath, for he did not believe it. Duncan lied: it was a human thing to do.

It was wrong thing to have done.

"You know," said Melein, "that we are going home."

"Niun has told me."

"Did your people surmise that?"

Duncan did not answer. The question disturbed him greatly: Niun felt it through the dusei, a shock of fear.

"Our outward journey," Melein continued softly, "was long ago, before such ships as this were available to us, no such swift passage, no; and we delayed along the way that brought us to you, sometimes a thousand years or two. Usually there is time that the People in truth do forget, that in the Dark between suns there are generations born that are not taught the Pana, the Forbidden, the Holy, the Mysteries—and they step out onto a new earth, ignorant of all they are not told. But this time, this time, kel Duncan, we carry our living past with us, in your person; and though this is against every law, every wisdom of she'panei before me, so is this voyage different from other voyages and this Dark from other Darks. I have permitted you to remain with us. Did your people surmise, Duncan, that we are going home?"

There was a forbidden game the children of the Kath would play, the truth-game: touch the dus and try to lie. When the Mothers knew it, they forbade it, though the great beasts were tolerant of the children, and the children's innocent minds could not disturb the animals.

Find where I have hidden the stone.
Is it near? Is it far?
Touch the dus and try to lie.

But not among brothers, not within the Kel or the Sen. "Melein," Niun protested. "He fears the beast."

"He fears," she echoed harshly. "Tell me, Duncan, what they supposed of the record they put within this ship."

"That it might be—that it might be the location of mri bases."

The feeling in the air was like that before a storm, thick and close and unreal. The great dus shivered, lifted its head. "Be still," Niun whispered in its blunt ear, tugging at it to distract the beast.

"Ah," said Melein. "And humans have surely duplicated this record. They will have taken this gift that was in the pan'en, that rested within their hands. And to make us trust it, they gave us you."

The dus cried out suddenly, moved, both of them. It hurled Duncan aside, away—he rolled to the wall, sprawled at the impact and both dusei were on their feet, their panic tangible. "Yai!" Niun cried at his own, clapped his hands, struck it. It reacted, threw its weight against its lesser companion, and kept the confused dus at bay, constantly shifting to remain between it and him; and Niun flung himself to Duncan's side, forcing his dus to shield them both.

The panic crested, subsided. Duncan was on his knees, holding his arm against his body, shuddering convulsively; his face was white and beaded with sweat. Niun touched him, dragged the arm outward and pushed up the sleeve, exposing the ugly, swelling wound.

Dus-poison.

"You will not die of it," Niun told him, holding him, trying to ease the sickly shuddering that wracked the human. He was not sure that Duncan could understand him. Melein came, bent down, touched the wounded arm; but there was no pity in her, only cold curiosity.

The dusei crept back. The little one, abused, hung back and radiated distress, blood-feelings. The greater one nosed at Duncan, snorted and drew back, and the human flinched and cried aloud.

"You have hurt them both," Niun said to Melein, thinking that she would feel remorse for one or the other, the dus or the man.

"He is still tsi'mri," she said. "And Niun, he has lied to us from the beginning; I have known it; you have seen it."

"You do not know what you have done," said Niun. "He feared the dusei, feared this one most especially. How could you expect to get truth from him? The dus is hurt, Melein; I do not know how far."

"You forget yourself."

"She'pan," he said, bowed his head, but it did not appease her. He took Duncan's good arm and helped him to stand, and flung his arm about him, holding him on his feet. The human was in utter, deep shock. When Niun began to move, the dus came, and slowly, slowly they left the presence of the she'pan.

Sometimes the human fought his way out of the fever, became for a moment lucid; at such times he seemed to know where he was, and his eyes wandered his surroundings, where he lay against the dus, in the corner of the kel-hall. But it did not last. He could not hold, and retreated again into his delirium. Niun did not speak to him, did not brighten the lights too much; it was best to keep both man and dus as free of sensation as possible.

Finally, when by night-cycle there was no improvement, Niun went to Duncan, and, as a kath'en might undress a child, took from him his *mez* and *zaidhe,* and his robes too, so that he might take warmth from the dus. He bedded him between his own dus and the afflicted one, and covered him with a double blanket.

The poison was strong in him; and a bond had been forced between two creatures that had not been able to bear each other. The wound was a deep puncture, and Duncan had taken more venom from the hollow dewclaw than was good even for a mri who was accustomed to it. But the old ways said (and being kel'en, Niun did not know whether this was truth or fable) that a dus knew its man by this thereafter, that once the substance had gone into a man and he had lived, then he would nevermore be in danger from the venom or the anger of that particular dus, which would never part from him in life. This was not entirely so, for a man who handled dusei frequently received small scratches from the dewclaw; and occasionally deeper ones, which might make him fevered. But it was also true that a man not accustomed to a particular dus might react very strongly, even fatally, to a bad wound from it.

Melein had known better than what she had done: kel-trained and sen-trained, she knew dusei, and she knew that she was provoking the beast dangerously, worrying at Duncan, drawing panic from him. But like the other she'pan that he had served, Melein had coldness for a heart.

And Duncan, his naked skin exposed to the heat and the secretions of the dus' hot hide, its venom flowing in his veins, would adapt to the dus and the dus to him—if he did not die; or if the beast did not go *miuk,* into that madness that sometimes came on stressed dusei, that turned them killer. That was what Melein had risked, and knew it.

If the beast went, Niun did not know now whether he could prevent the human from going with it. He had heard of it happening: a mri dragged into insanity by a *miuk'ko* dus; he had not, he thanked the gods, seen it.

The warning siren sounded.

Niun looked frantically at the starscreen, and cursed in anguish. It was the worst of all possible times that they should prepare to transit.

The bell sounded. The dusei roused, terrified, and Duncan for his part simply flung his arms about his beast's neck and bowed his head and held on, lost, lost in the dus-fears and the mind of the beast.

Perhaps it protected him. They jumped, emerged, jumped again within half a night. The man and the dus clung together, and radiated such fear that the other dus could not stay by them.

It was said of the dusei that they had no memory for events, only for persons. And perhaps it was that which drew the human in, and provided a haven from which he would not emerge.

"Duncan," Niun said the next morning, and without pleading with him, held a cup to his lips and gave him water, for he was not a dus, to go without. He bathed the human's face with his fingertips.

"Give me my robe," Duncan said then softly, startling him, and he was glad, and drew the human away from the afflicted dus, helping him to stand. Duncan was very weak, the arm hot and swollen still; he had to be helped into his clothing, and when he was given the headcloth and veil, he veiled himself as if he earnestly wished its privacy.

"I will speak to the she'pan," Niun offered earnestly. "Duncan, I will speak to her."

The human drew a great breath, let it go with a shudder, and pushed away the dus that nosed at his leg. It nearly threw him with its great strength. He caught himself with Niun's offered hand, then pushed help aside a second time, stubborn in his isolation.

"But you are wrong," Duncan said, "and she was right." And when he had drawn another breath: "There are ships on our trail. My people. Warships. I lied, Niun. It was no gift. They have the same series of directions we do, and they will come on our heels. What they will do then, I do not know. I am not in their confidence. They put me aboard for the reason the she'pan guessed: to make you trust the gift, to learn things the tapes cannot tell, to get me and the information back if I could. I tore the ship out of their hands and ran. Tell her that. It is all that I know. And you can do what you like about it."

And he walked off, to the far side of the room, and curled up in the corner. The dus padded over, head hanging, and wearily flung its bulk down against him. Duncan put his arms about its neck and laid his head against it, and rested. His eyes were blank and weary, and held such a look of despair as Niun had never seen on any face.

"Bring him," Melein told him when he had reported the things Duncan had admitted.

"She'pan," he protested, "he has helped the People."

"Be silent," she answered. "Remember that you are kel'en, and kel'anth; and that you owe me some loyalty."

Right was on her side, the rightness of the mri, the rightness of their survival. He felt the impact of it, and bowed his head against her head and acknowledged it—and sat by in misery that evening while she began to question Duncan, and to draw forth from him all that he could tell.

It was in the guise of a common-meal, the first that they had held on the ship, a sad mockery. It lacked all fellowship, and the food was bitter in the mouth. Duncan hardly ate at all, but sat silent when he was not being directly questioned; the dusei were banished, and he had nothing, no one, not even—Niun thought wretchedly—his own companionship, for he must sit at the she'-pan's right, taking her part.

There was a temptation to them all to overindulge in the drink, the biting regul brew that filled the stores, *ashig,* fermented of the same source as soi. But at least, Niun thanked the gods, there was no *komal,* that had kept his last she'pan in thrall to drug-spawned dreams, illicit and shameful—dreams in which she had laid the plans that had launched them forth; dreams that were as guilty as ever Duncan was in ruining the People, in creating the danger they now knew followed them.

He saw again the arrogance of the she'pan who had no mercy for her own children.

But such a thing as that he dared not say to Melein, could not quarrel with her, whom he loved more than life and honor, over a tsi'mri who had tangled them in so much of evil. It was only when he looked at Duncan's face that it hurt, and the human's pain gnawed at him.

Each evening for four days they ate common-meal, and talked little, for most questions had been answered. There was during that time a chill in the she'pan's presence, and afterward a chill in kel-hall—weapons-practice cold and formal and careful, concerned more with rituals than with striking blows, with the traditions of combat rather than the actuality of it. At times there was such sickness in Duncan's eyes that Niun forbade him the *yin'ein,* and refused to practice with him at all.

Duncan had betrayed his own.

And there was no peace for such a man.

"Tsi'mri," Melein said of him in Duncan's absence, "and a traitor even to them, who shaped him blood and bone. How then should the People ever rely on him? This is a weak creature, Niun. You have proved that."

Niun considered him, and knew his own handiwork, and grieved for it.

The venom-fever left, but the misery did not: the dus, rejected by turns and grudgingly accepted, mourned and fretted; the man grew silent and inward, a sickness that could not be reached.

The ship departed that star, and jumped again and again.

Chapter Fourteen

They passed closed, this time, to the worlds of the system, dangerously close. For many days their course had been taking them for the yellow star and its worlds, until now the largest of the inner planets loomed before them, dominating the field of the screen in kel-hall.

Home? Niun wondered at first, and held his hope private in Melein's silence: if she knew, he reckoned, she would have told him. But as days passed a worried look settled on Melein; and often now she looked on the screens with fear in her eyes. It ceased to look as though they were hurtling toward the world—rather that the world filled their sky and was falling down on them, a half-world first, that lent Niun some hope they would hurtle just past it—terrifying, but an escape, all the same: but the disc began to rise in the scanner.

They were caught, going earthward like a mote in a burrower's sandpit: the image came unwelcomely to Niun as he sat by Melein's side and stared at the starscreen she had set in her own hall, to look constantly on the danger. He felt his own helplessness, a kel'en whose knowledge of ships was all theory; all his knowledge told him now was that everything was wrong, and that Melein, who likewise had never set hands to ship's controls, knew little more than he.

Perhaps, he thought, she knew the name of the world into which they were falling: but it was not going to stop them.

And the outrage of it grew in him—that they should die by mischance. For a time he awaited a miracle, from Melein, from some source, certain that the gods could not have directed them so far—only to this.

He waited on Melein; and she said nothing.

"You have two kel'ein," he reminded her at last, on the day that there was hardly any darkness left in the starscreen.

Still she said nothing.

"Ask him, Melein."

Her lips made a taut line.

He knew the stubbornness in her: they were of one blood. He set his own face. "Then let us fall into the world," he said, staring elsewhere. "Surely there is nothing that I know to do, and your mind is set."

There was long silence between them. Neither moved.

"It would assure," she said at last, "that one danger did not reach our destination. I have thought of that. But it would not stop the other. And in us is the knowledge of it."

Such a thought shook at his confidence. He felt diminished, who had thought only of their own survival, who have been forward with her. "I spoke out of turn," he said. "Doubtless you have weighed what we ought to do."

"Go ask him," she said.

He sat still for a moment, finding her shifts of mind as unsettling as transit, and his nerves taut-strung at the thought that the matter did indeed come down to Duncan.

Then he gathered himself up, called softly to his dus, and went.

Duncan sat, beneath the screen that held the scanner image, eternally whetting away at the blade of an *av-tlen* that he had made out of scrap metal: it was laser-cut and of a balance that Niun privately judged would never be true, but it kept Duncan's hands busy, and perhaps his mind, whatever darkness hovered in it. The dus lay near him, head between paws, eyes following the sweep of Duncan's hands.

"Duncan," Niun said. The noise of the steel kept its rhythm. "Duncan."

It stopped. Duncan looked up at him with that bleak hardness that had grown there day by day.

"The she'pan is concerned," Niun said, "about our near approach to this world."

Duncan's eyes remained cold. "Well, you do not need me. Or if you do, then you can find some means to work around me, can you not?"

"I respect your quarrel with us." Niun sank down on his heels, opened his hands in a gesture of offering. "But surely you know that there is no quarreling with the world that is drawing us into it. We will die, and you will have no satisfaction in that. As for your cause with us, I do not want to quarrel at all on this small ship, with the dusei in the middle of it. Listen to me, Duncan. I have done everything I know to give you an honorable way to put aside this grievance with us. But if you threaten the she'pan, then I will not be patient. And you are doing that."

Duncan went back to his task, sweeping steel against steel. Niun fought with his temper, knowing the result if he laid hands on the tsi-mri: a dus that was already precariously balanced on the verge of *miuk,* and the ship plummeting toward impact with a world—with some things indeed there was no quarreling. It was likely that the human was no more rational than the dus, affected by the ailing beast. If the dus went over the brink, then so did the mind that held knowledge of the ship.

Melein's handiwork. Niun clenched his arms about his knees and sought something to say that would touch the man.

"We are out of time, Duncan."

"If you cannot deal with this," Duncan said suddenly, "then you certainly could not land safely when you reach your home. I do not think you ever intended to be rid of me. You two seem to need me, and I think the she'pan has always suspected that. That was why she let you have your way. It was only a means of making me less an inconvenience than I would have been, a way of getting past my guard and getting from me what she wanted. I am not angry with you, Niun. You believed her. So did I. She had what she wanted. Only now I am needed again, am I?" The ring of steel continued, measured and hard. "Become like you. Become one of you. I know you tried. You armed me—but you never reckoned on the beast. Now you cannot deal with me so easily. It and I . . . make something new on this ship."

"You are wrong from the beginning," Niun said, cold to the heart at such thoughts in him. "There is an autopilot to bring us in. And the she'pan never lied to you, or to me. She cannot."

Duncan's eyes lifted suddenly to his, cynically amazed, and his hands fell idle. "Rely on that? Maybe regul automation is better than ours, but this is a human ship, and I would not trust my life to that if there were a choice. You could come down anywhere. And would you know how to engage it in the first place? Perhaps the she'pan is simply naïve. You do need me, kel Niun. You tell her that."

It had the sound of truth. Niun had no answer for it, shaken in his own confidence. There were things Melein could not reasonably know, things involving machines not made by the regul and motives of those not born of the People. Yet she proceeded on her Sight; he wished earnestly to believe in that.

"Come," he pleaded with Duncan.

"No," said Duncan, and fell to work again.

Niun rested unmoving, panic stirring in him. The rhythm became louder, steel on steel, metal clenched in taut, white-edged fingers. Duncan would not look up. A body's-length away, the dus stirred, moaned.

Niun thrust himself to his feet and stalked out of kel-hall, through the corridors, until he came again to Melein.

"He says he will not," Niun told her, and remained veiled.

She said nothing, but sat quietly and stared at the screen. Niun settled by her side, swept off *mez* and *zaidhe* and wadded them into a knot in his lap, head bowed.

Melein had no word for him, nothing. She was, he thought, finally reckoning with what she had wrought, and that reckoning was too late.

And by the middle of the night there was no more darkness left in the screen. The world took on frightening detail, brown patched with cloud swirls.

Suddenly a siren began, different from any that had sounded before, and the screens flashed red, a pulse terrifying in its implications.

Niun gathered himself to his knees, cast an anguished look at Melein, whose calm now seemed thinly drawn.

"Go to Duncan," she bade him. "Ask again."

He rose and went, covered his head, but did not trouble this time to veil himself: he went to plead with their enemy, and shame seemed useless in such a gesture.

The lights in kel-hall had dimmed: the screen, pulsing between the red of alarm and the white glare of the world, provided all the light, and Duncan sat, veilless, before it. There sounded still the measured scrape of metal, as if he had never ceased. Beside him lay the mass of the two dusei, that stirred and moved aside as Niun came and knelt before Duncan.

"If you know anything to do at this point," Niun said, "it would be well to do it. I believe we are falling quite rapidly."

Duncan rasped the edge one long stroke, his lips clamped into a taut line. A moment he considered, then laid aside his work and wiped his hands on his knees, looked up at the world that loomed in the pulsing screen. "I can try," he said equally enough, "from controls."

Niun stood up, waited for Duncan, who rose stiffly, then walked in with him through the ship. The dusei started to trail them. Niun forbade them with a sharp word, sealed a section door between, and brought Duncan into that section that belonged to the she'pan.

Melein met them there, in the corridor.

"He will try," said Niun.

She opened controls to them, and came in after, stood gravely by as Duncan settled himself into the cushion at the main panel.

Duncan paid them no further heed. He studied the screens, and touched control after control. A flood of telemetry coursed one stable screen. One after another the screens ceased their flashing and took on images of the world in garish colors.

"You are playing pointless games," said Melein.

Duncan looked half-about, back again. "I am. I have watched this world for some few days. It is puzzling. And it is still possible that the ship's defenses may take over when we reach the absolute limit: there are choices left, but for some reason it is not observing the safety margin, and the world's mass has anchored us, so that jump is impossible. Here." He took the cover off a shielded area of controls and simply pushed a button. Lights ran crazily over the boards. Immediately there was a perceptible alteration in course, the screens shifting rapidly. Duncan calmly replaced the cover. "An old ship, this, and it has run hard. A system failed. It should have reset itself now. It will avoid, then pull us back on course. I think that will solve the problem. But if there is an error in the tape that caused it to happen, why, we are dead."

He offered that with a cynical tone, and slowly rose, still looking at the scanners. "That world is dead," he said then. "And that is strange, given other things I read in scanning."

"You are mistaken," said Melein harshly. "Read your instruments again, tsi'mri. That is a world called Nhequuy and the star is Syr, and it is a spacefaring race that lives there and all about these regions, called the etrau."

"Look at the infrared. Look at the surface. No plants. No life. It's a dead world, she'pan, whatever your records tell you. This is a dead system. A spacefaring people would have come to investigate an intrusion this close to their homeworld. But none have. Not here, not anywhere we have been, have they? You could not have answered a challenge. You could not have reacted to their ships. You would have needed me for that, and you have not. World after world after world. And nothing. Why do you suppose, she'pan?"

Melein looked on him with shock in her unveiled face, a helpless anger. She did not answer, and Niun felt a chill creeping over his skin in her silence.

"The People are nomads," Duncan said, "mercenaries, hiring out whatever you have been. You have gone from star to star, seeking out wars, fighting for hire. And you have forgotten. You close each chamber after you, and forbid the Kel to remember. But what became of all your former employers, she'pan? Why is there no life where you have passed?"

Niun looked at the screens, at the deadness they displayed, at instruments he could not read—and looked to Melein, to hear her deny these things.

"Leave," she said. "Niun, take him back to kel-hall."

Duncan thrust back from the panel, swept a glance from her to Niun, and in the instant Niun hesitated, turned on his heel and walked out, striding rapidly down the corridor in the direction of kel-hall.

Niun stared at Melein. Her skin was pale, her eyes dilated: never had she looked so afraid, not even with regul and humans closing on them.

"She'pan?" he asked, still hoping.

"I do not know," she said. And she wept, for it was an admission a she'pan could not make. She sank down on the edge of a cushion and would not look at him.

He stayed, ventured finally to take her by the arms and draw her out of that place, back to her own hall, where the chatter of the machines could not accuse her. He settled her in her chair and knelt beside her, smoothed her golden mane as he had done when they were both only kath'dai'ein, and with his own black veil he dried her tears and saw her face restored to calm.

He knew that she was lost, that the machines were beyond her capacity; she knew that he knew; but he knelt at her knees and took her hands, and looked up at her clear-eyed, offering with all his heart.

"Rest," he urged her. "Rest. Even your mercies were well-guided. Is it not so that even the she'panei do not always know the Sight when it moves them? So I have heard, at least. You kept Duncan, and that was right to do. And be patient with him, for my sake be patient. I will deal with him."

"He sees what is plain to be seen. Niun, I do not know what we have done."

He thought of the dead worlds, and pushed the thought away. "We have done nothing. *We* have done nothing."

"We are heirs of the People."

"We do not know that his reckoning is right."

"Niun, Niun, he knows. Can you be so slow to understand what we have seen along the track of the People? Can there be so many worlds that have failed of themselves after we have passed?"

"I do not know," he said desperately. "I am only kel'en, Melein."

She touched his face, and he felt the comfort that she meant, apology for her words, and they did not speak for a time. Long ago—it seemed long ago, and impossibly far—he had sat by another she'pan. Intel of Edun Kesrithun, and leaned his head against the arm of her chair, and she had been content in her drugged dreams to touch, to know that he was there. So he did now, with Melein. Her hand restlessly stroked his mane, while she thought; and he sat still, unable to share, unable to imagine where her thoughts ran, save that they went into darkness, and into things of the Pana.

He heard her breath shudder at last between her teeth, and forebore to breathe, himself, fearful of her mood.

"Intel," she said at last, "still has her hand on us. The she'pan's kel'en: she held you by her until I wonder you did not go mad; and passed you to me—to see that her chosen successor succeeded not only to Edun Kesrithun, but to rule all the People. That Intel's choice survive. She would have waded to her aim through the blood of any that opposed her. She was *the* she'pan. Old—but age did not sanctify her, did not cleanse her of ambition or make her complacent. O gods, Niun, she was hard."

He could not answer. He remembered the scarred and gentle-eyed Mother of Kesrith, whose hands were tender and whose mind was most times fogged with drugs; but he knew that other Intel too. His stomach tightened as he recalled old angers, old resentments—Intel's possessive, adamantine stubbornness. She was dead. It was not right to cherish resentments against the dead.

"She would have taken ship," Melein said in a hollow voice, "and gods know what she would have done in leaving Kesrith. We no longer served regul; we were freed of our oath. She sent me to safety; I think she tried to follow. I will never know. I will never know so many things she had no time to teach me. She talked of return, of striking against the enemies of the People— ravings under the *komal*-dreams, when I would sit by her alone. The enemy. The enemy. She would have destroyed them, and then she would have taken us home. That was her great and improbable dream, that the Dark would be the last Dark, to take us home, for we were few already; and she was, perhaps, mad."

Niun could not bear to look at her, for it was true, and it was painful to them both.

"What shall we do?" he asked. "May the Kel ask permission to ask? What shall we do for ourselves?"

"I have no power to stop this ship. Would that I did. Duncan says that he cannot. I think that it is true. And he—"

There was long silence. Niun did not invade it, knowing it could bring no good; and at last Melein sighed.

"Duncan," she said heavily.

"I will keep him from your sight."

"You have given him the means to harm us."

"I will deal with him, she'pan."

She shook her head again, and wiped her eyes with her fingers.

The dusei came: Niun was aware of them before they appeared, looked and saw his own great beast, and welcomed it. It drew close in the wistful, abstracted manner of dusei, and sank down at Melein's feet, offering its mindless solace.

Afterward, when Melein breathed easier, Niun felt another presence. Astonished, he saw the lesser dus standing in the doorway. It also came, and lay down by its fellow.

Melein touched it; it offered no hostility to the hand that had caused its hurt. But somewhere else in the ship there would be pain for that touching. Niun thought on Duncan, of his bitter isolation, and wondered that his dus could have been drawn here, by her whom Duncan hated.

Unless he had brutally driven it away—or unless his thoughts had turned the dus in this direction.

"Go see to Duncan," Melein said finally.

Niun received back his veil from her hands and flung it over his shoulder, not bothering to wear it. He rose, and when his own dus would have followed him he bade it stay, for he wanted it by Melein, for her comfort.

And he found Duncan, as he had thought he would, back in kel-hall.

Duncan sat still in the artificial dawning, hands loose in his lap. Niun settled on his knees before him, and still Duncan did not look up. The human had veiled himself; Niun did not, offering his feelings openly to him.

"You have hurt us," Niun said. "Kel Duncan, is it not enough?"

Duncan lifted his face and stared toward the screen, where the world that had been called Nhequuy was no longer in view.

"Duncan. What else will you have of us?"

Duncan's dus was with Melein, touched and touching; he was betrayed. When his eyes shifted toward Niun there was no defense there, nothing but pain.

"I argued," said Duncan, "with my superiors, for your sake. I fought for you. And for what? Did she have an answer? She knew the world's name. What happened to it?"

"We do not know."

"And to the other worlds?"

"We do not know, Duncan."

"Killers," he said, his eyes fixed elsewhere. "Killers by nature."

Niun clenched his hands, that had gone chill. "*You* are with us, kel Duncan."

"I have often wondered why." His dark eyes returned to Niun's. Of a sudden he pulled the veil away, swept off the tasseled head-cloth, making evident his humanity. "Except that I am necessary."

"Yes. But I did not know that. We did not know it before."

It touched home, he thought; there was a small reaction of the eyes.

And then Duncan turned, a wild, distracted look on his face as he looked to the door.

Dus-feelings. Niun received them too, even before he heard the click of claws on tiling. Senses blurred. It was hard to remember what bitterness they had been about.

"*No!*" Duncan shouted as it came in. The beast shied and lifted a paw in threat, then dropped it and edged forward, head slightly averted. By degrees it came closer, settled, edged the final distance to Duncan's side. Duncan touched it, slid his arm about its neck. At the door appeared the other beast, that came quietly to Niun, lay down at his back. Niun soothed it with gentle touches, his heart pounding from the misery that radiated from the other— schism between man and dus: the very air ached with it.

"You are hurting it," Niun said. "Give way to it. Give it only a little."

"It and I have an accommodation. I do not push it and it does not push me. Only sometimes it comes too fast. It forgets where the line is."

"Dusei have no memories. There is only *now* with them."

"Fortunate animals," Duncan said hoarsely.

"Give way to it. You lose nothing."

Duncan shook his head. "I am not mri. And I cannot forget."

There was weariness in his voice; it trembled. For a moment there was again the man who had been long absent from them.

Niun reached out, pressed his arm in a gesture he would have offered a brother of the Kel. "Duncan, I have tried to help you. All that I could do, I have tried."

Duncan closed his eyes, opened them again; his fingers at the dus' neck lifted in a gesture of surrender. "I think that, at least, is the truth."

"We do not lie," he said. "There are the dusei. We cannot."

"I can understand that." Duncan pressed his lips together, a white line, relaxed again, his hand still caressing the dus.

"I would not play at *shon'ai* with a man in your mood," Niun said, baiting him, searching after hidden things. They had not, in fact, played in some time.

The dus began slowly to give forth its pleasure sound, relaxed to Duncan's fingers as Duncan eased his arm about its fat-rolled neck; it sighed, oblivious to past grief, delighting in present love.

The human pressed his brow to that thick skull, then turned his face to look at Niun. His eyes bore a bruised look, like one long without rest. "It has no happier a life than mine," Duncan said. "I cannot let it have what it wants, and it cannot make me over into a mri."

Niun drew a deep breath, tried to keep images from his mind. "I might destroy it," he said, hushed and quickly. The human, in contact with the beast, flinched, soothed the dus with his hands. Niun understood; he felt soiled even in offering—but sometimes it was necessary, when a dus, losing its kel'en, could not be controlled. This one had never gained the kel'en it wished.

"No," Duncan said at last. "No."

He pushed the animal away, and it rose and ambled over to the corner. There was peace in the feeling of the beasts. It was better than it had been.

"I would be pleased," said Niun, "if you would send to the she'pan your apology."

Duncan sat quietly for a moment, arms on knees. At last he nodded, changed the gesture for a mri one. "When she needs me," he said, "I will come. Tell her so."

"I will tell her."

"Tell her I am sorry."

"I will tell her that too."

Duncan looked at him for a moment, and then gathered himself up and stood looking at the dus. He gave a low whistle to it; it whuffed in interest and heaved itself up and came, followed to the corner where the pallets were.

And for a long time the human sat and worked over the dus, grooming it and soothing it, even talking to it, which seemed to please the beast. The dus settled, slept. In time, the man did.

Three days later the siren sounded, and they left Nhequuy and its sun. The next world was also without life.

Chapter Fifteen

Duncan turned from the screen that showed the stars and found his dus behind him—always, always the beast was with him, shadow, herald, partaker of every privacy of his life. He found no need to touch it. It sighed and settled against his back. He felt it content.

It was strange, when a pain ceased, that it would be gone some considerable time before it was missed.

And that when that pain was gone, it could not be accurately remembered.

Duncan had known in this place, in kel-hall, upon a certain instant, that he was no longer in pain: he had realized it, sitting here upon the floor; and he could remember the moment, the details, the place that the dus had been lying, the fact that Niun had been sitting exactly so, across the room—sewing, that day: odd occupation for a mri warrior, but Duncan had learned well enough that a man tended all his own necessities in the Kel—save food, that was taken in common.

Niun's face had been intent, the needle pursuing a steady rhythm. He had worked with skill, as Niun's slender hands knew so many skills. It would take years to learn the half of what Niun's native reflexes and the teaching of his masters had done for him.

Not an arrogant man, Niun: prideful, perhaps, but he never vaunted his abilities . . . save now and again when they practiced a passage of arms with the *yin'ein* that Duncan had made to match the beautiful old weapons that were Niun's. Then Niun was sometimes moved, perhaps from the sheer ennui of practicing with a man with whom he could not extend himself—to make a move so fast the eye could not follow it, so tiny and deft and subtle that Duncan hardly knew what had happened to him. Niun did such things, Duncan had noticed also, when he himself had almost settled into smugness in his practice with Niun. The mri subtly informed his student that he was still restraining himself.

Restraint.

It governed the kel'en's whole being.

And Niun's restraint made peace where there was none: extended to a human who provoked him, to dusei that at times grew restive and destructive in their confinement—extended even to Melein.

There was none of them, Duncan reflected with sudden grim humor, that wanted to disturb Niun, neither human, nor dusei, nor child-queen who relied on him.

It was Niun's peace that was on them.

The most efficient killers in all creation, Stavros had said of the mri.

He spoke of the Kel, of Niun's kind.

He had spoken before humankind even suspected the waste of stars that now surrounded them.

The record would be traced out, human ships tracking them to dead world after dead world; and there was no other conclusion that could occur to the Haveners manning those ships, but that they were tracing something monstrous to its source.

Duncan absently caressed the shoulder of his dus, thinking, as the same fearful thoughts had circled through his brain endlessly in the passing days—staring helplessly at Niun, whose imagination surely was sufficient to know what pursued them.

Yet there was no mention of this from Niun; and Melein, having asked her questions, asked nothing more; Niun went to her, but Duncan was not permitted, continuing in her disfavor.

The mri chose to ignore what pursued, to ask no further, to do nothing. Niun lived with him, slept beside him at night in apparent trust—and cultivated only the ancient skills of his kind, the weapons of ritual and duel, as if they could avail him at the end.

The *yin'ein,* ancient blades, against warships, against the likes of *Saber.*

Niun chose, advisedly.

An image came: night, and fire, and mri obstinacy. Duncan pushed it aside, and it came back again, recollection of mri stubbornness that would not surrender, that would not compromise, whose concept of *modern* was lapped in Darks and Betweens and the ways of tsi'mri who were only a moment in the experience of the People.

Modern weapons.

Duncan felt the taint of the word, the scorn implicit in the hal'ari, and hated the human in him that had been too blind to see.

The last battle of the People.

To meet it with modern weapons—if it came to that—that the People should come to a hopeless fight. . . .

Niun would not, then, plan to survive: the last mri would choose the things that made sense to his own logic, which was precisely what he was doing.

To seek his home.

To recover his ancient ways.

To be mri until the holocaust ended it.

It was all Niun could do, if he chose to think about it, save yield to tsi'mri. Duncan reckoned the depth of the mri's patience, that had borne with an outsider under such conditions—even Melein's, who endured Niun's tolerance of a tsi'mri, even that was considerable.

And Niun only practiced at duel with him, patiently, gently practiced, as if he could forget the nature of him.

The *yin'ein.* They were for Niun the only reasonable choice.

Duncan rested his arm on his knee and gnawed at his lip, felt the disturbance of the dus at his back and reached to settle it— guilty in his humanity, that troubled Niun. And yet the thought worried at him and would not let him go—that, human that he was, he could not do as Niun did.

That there were for him alternatives that Niun did not possess.

Perhaps, at the end, the mri would let him go.

Or expect him to lift arms against humankind. He tried to imagine it; and all that he could imagine in his hand was the service pistol that rested among his belongings—to deal large-scale death for his death: the inclination came on him. He could fight, cornered; he would wish to take a dozen of the lives, human or not, that would take his. But to take up the *yin'ein* . . . he was not mri enough.

There were means of fighting the mri would not use.

Human choices.

Slowly, slowly, shattered bits of what had been a SurTac began to sort themselves into order again.

"Niun," he said.

The mri was shaping a bit of metal into a thing that looked like an ornament. For several days he had been working at it, painstaking in his attention.

"*A?*" Niun answered.

"I have been thinking: we suffered one failure in instruments. If the she'pan would permit it, I would like to go back to controls, to test the instruments."

Niun stopped. A frown was on his face when he looked up. "I will ask the she'pan," he said.

"I would like," Duncan said, "to give her the benefit of what skills I do have."

"She will send if there is need."

"Niun, *ask her.*"

The frown deepened. The mri rested hands on his knees, his metalwork forgotten, then expelled a deep breath and gathered up his work again.

"I want peace with her," Duncan said. "Niun, I have done all that you have asked of me. I have tried to be one of you."

"Other things you have done," said Niun. "That is the problem."

"I am sorry for those things. I want them forgotten. Ask her to see me again, and I give you my word I will not offend against her. There is no peace on this ship without peace with her—and none with you."

For a moment Niun said nothing. Then he gave a long sigh. "She has waited for you to ask."

The mri still had power to surprise him. Duncan sat back in confusion, all his reckonings of them in disorder. "She will see me, then."

"Whenever you would decide to ask. Go and speak to her. The doors are not locked."

Duncan rested yet a moment, all impetus taken from him; and then he gathered himself to his feet and started for the door, the dus behind him.

"Duncan."

He turned.

"My brother of the Kel," said Niun softly, "in all regard for you—remember that I am the she'pan's hand, and that should you err with her—I must not tolerate it."

There was, for the moment, a ward-impulse in the room: the dus backed and its ears lay down. "No," said Duncan. It stopped. And he drew the *av-tlen* from his belt, and would have laid aside all his weapons. "Hold these if you suspect any such thing of me." It was demeaning to surrender weapons; Duncan offered, knowing this, and the mri flinched visibly.

"No," Niun said.

Duncan slid the blade back into place, and left, the dus walking behind him. Niun did not follow: the sting of that last exchange perhaps forbade, and his suspicion would worry at him the while. Duncan reckoned it, that although Niun slept by him, though he let down his guard to him in weapons-practice, to teach him, Melein's safety was another matter: the kel'en was deeply, deeply uneasy.

To admit a tsi'mri to the she'pan's presence, armed: it surely went against the mri's instincts.

But the doors had been unlocked.

The doors had always been unlocked, Duncan supposed suddenly; he had never thought to try them. Melein herself had slept with unlocked doors, trusting him; and that shocked him deeply, that the mri could be in that regard so careless with him.

And not careless.

Prisons, locked doors, things sealed, depriving a man of weapons—all these things went against mri nature. He had known it from the beginning in dealing with them: no prisoners, no capture—and even in the shrine, the pan'en was only screened off, not locked away.

Even controls, even that had always been accessible to him, any time that he had decided to walk where he had been told not to go; he might have quietly gone forward, sealed the doors, and held the ship—could, at this moment.

He did not.

He went to the door that was Melein's, to that dim hall, painted with symbols, vacant of all but a chair and the mats for sitting. He entered it, his steps loud on the tiles.

"She'pan," he called, and stood and waited: stood, for it was the she'pan who offered or did not offer, to sit. The dus settled heavily next to him, resting on its hindquarters—finally sank down to lay its head on the tiles. A sigh gusted from it.

And suddenly a light step sounded behind him. Duncan turned, faced the ghost-like figure in the shadow, white-robed and silent. He was not veiled. He was not sure whether this was polite or not, and glanced down to show his respect.

"Why are you here?" she asked.

"To beg your pardon," he said.

She answered nothing for a moment, only stared at him as if she waited for something further.

"Niun said," he added, "that you were willing to see me."

Her lips tautened. "You still have a tsi'mri's manners."

Anger came on him; but the statement was the simple truth. He smothered it and averted his eyes a second time to the floor. "She'pan," he said softly, "I beg your pardon."

"I give it," she said. "Come, sit down."

The tone was suddenly gracious; it threw him off his balance, and for an instant he stared at her, who moved and took her chair, expecting him to settle at her feet.

"By your leave," he said, remembering Niun, "I ought to go back. I think Niun wanted to follow me. Let me go and bring him."

A frown creased Melein's smooth brow. "That would reproach him, kel Duncan, if you let him know why. No. Stay. If there is peace in the House, he will know it; and if not, he will know that. And do not call him by his name to me; he is first in the Kel."

"I am sorry," he said, and came and sat at her feet, while the dus came and cast itself down between them. The beast was uneasy. He soothed it with his hand.

"Why," asked Melein, "have you been driven to come to me?"

The question struck him with confusion—rude and abrupt, she was, and able to read him. He shrugged, tried to think of something at the edge of the truth, and could not. "She'pan, I am a resource you have. And I wish that you would make use of what I know—while there is time."

The membrane flashed across her eyes, and the dus lifted its head. She leaned forward and soothed the beast, her fingers gently moving on its velvet fur. "And what do you know, kel Duncan, that so suddenly troubles you?"

"That I can get you home alive." He laid his hand on the dus, fearless to do so, and looked into the she'pan's golden eyes. "*He* has taught me; is not managing ships a part of the skill of a kel'en? If he will learn, I will teach him; and if not—then I will take what care of the ship I can do myself. His skill is with the *yin'ein,* and mine never will approach his—but this I can do, this one thing. My gift to you, she'pan, and worth a great deal to you when you reach your home."

"Do you bargain?"

"No. There is no *if* in it. A gift, that is all."

Her fingers did not cease to stroke the dus' warm hide. Her eyes lifted again to his. "Are you *my* kel'en, kel Duncan?"

Breath failed him an instant. The hal'ari, the kel-law had begun to flow in his mind like blood in his veins: the question stood, yes or no, and there was no going back afterward.

"Yes," he said, and the word almost failed of sound.

Her slim fingers slipped to his, took his broad and human hand. "Will you not turn on us, as you turn on your own kind?"

The dus moved at his shock: he held it, soothed it with both hands, and looked up after a moment at Melein's clear eyes.

"No," she judged, answering her own question, and how, or of what source he did not know. Her sureness disturbed him.

"I have touched a human," she said, "and I did not, just then."

It chilled. He held to the dus, drawing on its warmth, and stared at her.

"What do you seek to do?" she asked.

"Give me access to controls. Let me maintain the machinery, do what is needful. We went wrong once. We cannot risk it again."

He expected refusal, expected long days, months of argument before he could win that of her.

But controls, he thought, had never been locked. And Melein's amber eyes lowered, by that silent gesture giving permission. She lifted her hand toward the door.

He hesitated, then gathered himself to his feet, made an awkward gesture of courtesy to her, and went.

She followed. He heard her soft footfalls behind the dus. And when he settled at the console in the brightly lit control room, she stood at his shoulder and watched: he could see her white-robed reflection in the screens that showed the starfields.

He began running the checks he desired, dismissing Melein's presence from his concerns. He had feared, since last he was dismissed from controls, that the ship was not capable of running so long and hard a voyage under total automatic; but to his relief everything checked out clean, system after system, nothing failed, no hairbreadth errors that could ruin them, losing them forever in this chartless space.

"It is good," he told Melein.

"You feared something particular?"

"Only neglect," he said, "she'pan."

She stood beside him, occasionally seeming to watch the reflection of his face as he glanced sometimes to that of hers. He was content to be where he was, doing what his hands well remembered: he ran through things that he had already done, only to have the extra time, until she grew weary of standing and departed his shoulder to sit at the second man's post across the console.

Lonely, perhaps, interested in what he did: he recalled that she was not ignorant of such machinery, only of that human-made, and he dared not try too much in her presence. She surely knew that he was repeating operations.

He took the chance.

Elapsed time, he asked of the records-storage.

It flashed back refusal. *No record.*

Other details he asked. *No record. No record,* it answered.

Something cold and hard swelled in his throat. Carefully he checked the status of the navigational tapes, whether retrace was available, to bring him home again.

Classified, the screen flashed at him.

He stopped, mindful of the auto-destruct linked into the tape mechanism. Suspicion crept horridly through his recollections.

We want nothing coming home with you by accident.

Stavros' words.

Sweat trickled down his side. He felt it prickling on his face, wiped the edge of his hand across his mouth and tried to disguise the gesture. Melein still sat beside him.

The dus came nearer, moved between them, close to the delicate instruments. "Get out of there," Duncan wished it. It only lay down.

"Kel'en," said Melein, "what do you see that troubles you?"

He moistened his lips, shifted his eyes to her. "She'pan—we have found no life . . . I have lost count of the worlds, and we have found no life. What makes you think that your homeworld will be different?"

Her face became unreadable. "Do you find reason there, kel'en, to think we shall not?"

"I have found reason here . . . to believe that this ship is locked against me. She'pan, when that tape runs to its end, it may have no navigational memory left."

Amber eyes flickered. She sat still with her hands folded in her lap. "Did you plan to leave?"

"We may not be able to run. We will have no other options, she'pan."

"We never did."

He drew in his breath, wiped at the moisture that had gone cold on his cheek, and let the breath go again. Her calm was unshakable, thoroughly rational: *Shon'ai* . . . the throw was cast, for them—by birth. It was like Niun with his weapons.

"She'pan," he said quietly, "you have named each world as we have passed. Do you know the number that we have yet to see?"

She nodded in the fashion of the People, a tilt of the head to the left. "Before we reach homeworld," she said, "Mlara and Sha, and Hlar and Sa'a-no-kli'i."

"Four," he said, stunned at the sudden knowledge of an end. "Have you told—?"

"I have told him." She leaned forward, her arms twined on her white-robed knees. "Kel Duncan, your ships will come. They are coming."

"Yes."

"You have chosen your service."

"Yes," he said. "With the People, she'pan." And when she still stared at him, troubled by his treachery: "On their side, she'pan, there are so many kel'ein one will not be missed. But on the side of the People, there is only one—twice that, with me. Humankind will not miss one kel'en."

Melein's eyes held to his, painfully intense. "Your mathematics is without reproach, kel Duncan."

"She'pan," he said softly, moved by the gratitude he realized in her.

She rose, and left.

Committed the ship to him.

He sat still a moment, finding everything that he had sought under his hands, and suddenly a burden on him that he had not thought to bear. Had he intended betrayal, he did not think he could commit it now; and to do to them again what he had done on Kesrith, even to save their lives—

That was not an act of love, but of selfishness . . . here, and hereafter. He knew them too well to believe it for their own good.

He scanned the banks of instruments, that hid their horrid secrets, programs locked from his tampering, things triggered perhaps from the moment he had violated orders and thrown them prematurely onto taped running.

Or perhaps—as SurTacs had been expended before—it was planned from the beginning, that *Fox* would not come home, save as a rider to *Saber*.

There was the pan'en, and the record in that; but under *Saber*'s firepower, *Fox* was nothing . . . and it was not impossible that the navigational computer would go down as the tape expired, crippling them.

He reached for the board again, plied the keys repeatedly, receiving over and over again *No Record* and *Classified*.

And at last he gave over trying, and pushed himself to his feet, reached absently for the dus that crowded wistfully against him, sensing his distress and trying to distract him from it.

Four worlds.

A day, or more than a month: the span between jumps was irregular.

The time seemed suddenly very short.

Chapter Sixteen

Mlara and Sha and Hlar and Sa'a-no-kli'i.

Niun watched them pass, lifeless as they were, with an excitement in his blood that the somber sights could not wholly kill.

They jumped again, and just after ship's noon there appeared a new star centered in the field.

"This is home," said Melein softly, when they gathered in the she'pan's hall to see it with her. "This is the Sun."

In the hal'ari, it was Na'i'in.

Niun looked upon it, a mere pinprick of light at the distance from which they entered the system, and agonized that it would be so long a journey yet. Na'i'in. The Sun.

And the World, that was Kutath.

"By your leave," Duncan murmured, "—I had better go to controls."

They all went, even the dusei, into the small control room.

And there was something eerie in the darkness of that section of the panels that had been most active. Duncan stood and looked at it a moment, then settled in at controls, called forth activity elsewhere, but not in that crippled section.

Niun left the she'pan's side to stand at the panel to Duncan's right: little enough he knew of the instruments, save only what Duncan had shown him—but he had knowledge enough to be sure there was something amiss.

"The navigational computer," Duncan said. "Gone."

"You can bring us in," Niun said without doubt.

Duncan nodded. His hands moved on the boards, and the screens built patterns, built structures about a point that was Na'i'in.

"We are on course," he said. "We have no starflight navigation, that is all."

It was not of concern. Long after the she'pan had returned to her own hall, Niun still stayed by Duncan, sitting in the cushion across the console, watching the operations that Duncan undertook.

It was five days before Kutath itself took shape before them, third out from Na'i'in . . . Kutath. Duncan guided them, present at controls surely more than reason called for: he took his meals in this room, and entered kel-hall only to wash and to take a little sleep in night-cycle. Restless he would go back before the night was done, and Niun knew where to find him.

Nothing required his presence at controls.

There were no alarms, nothing.

It was, Niun began to reckon with growing despair, the same as the others. Melein surely made her own estimation of the lasting silence, and Duncan did, and none spoke it aloud.

No ships.

No reaction.

The sixth day there were the first clear images of the world, and Melein came to controls to look at them. Niun set his hand upon hers, silent offering.

It was a red world and lifeless.

Old. Very, very old.

Duncan cut the image off the screens. There was agony in his face when he looked at them both, as if he thought himself to blame. But Niun drew a deep breath and let it go, surrendering to what he had known all his life.

That they were, after all, the last-born.

Somewhere in the ship the dusei moaned, gathering in the grief that was sent them.

"The voyage of the People," said Melein, "has been very, very long. If we are the last, still we will go home. Take us there, Duncan."

"Yes," Duncan said simply, and bowed his head and turned to the boards so that he did not have to look on their faces. Niun found it difficult to breathe, a great tightness about his heart, as when he had seen the People die on Kesrith; but it was an old grief, and already mourned. He stood still while Melein went her way back to her hall.

Then he went apart, unto himself, and sat down with his dus, and wept, as the Kel could not weep.

"Why should we be sorrowful?" asked Melein, when they had met again that evening, for their first common-meal in many days, and their last, before landing. "We always knew that we were the last. For a time we believed otherwise, and we were happier, but it is only the same truth that has always been. We should still be glad. We have come home. We have seen what was our beginning, and that is a fit ending."

This was something the human could not understand. He simply shook his head as he would do in pain, and his dus nosed at him, disconsolate.

But Niun inclined himself wholly to Melein's thoughts: they were true. There were far worse things than what lay before them: there was Kesrith; there were humans, and regul.

"Do not grieve for us," Niun said to Duncan, and touched his sleeve. "We are where we wish to be."

"I will get back to controls," Duncan said, and flung himself to his feet, veiled himself and left their company without asking permission or looking back. His dus trailed after him, radiating distress.

"He can do nothing there," said Melein with a shrug. "But it comforts him."

"Our Duncan," said Niun, "will not let go. He is obsessed with blame."

"For us?"

Niun shrugged, pressed his lips together, looked aside.

She put out her hand and touched his face, recalled his attention, regarding him sadly. "I have known that it was possible, that it might have been too long. Niun, there have been above eighty Darks, and in each more than one generation has passed; and there have been above eighty Betweens, and the most of them have lasted above a thousand years."

He attempted a deprecating laugh, a shake of his head: it did not come out as a laugh. "I can reckon that in distance—but not in years. Twenty years is long for a kel'en. I cannot reckon a thousand."

She bent and pressed her lips to his brow. "Niun, the accounting is no matter. It is beyond my reckoning too."

That night, and the night after, Niun slept sitting, his head against her chair. Melein did not ask it. He simply did not want to leave her. And when Duncan came from his lonely watch for what few hours of true sleep he sought, he curled up against his dus in the corner—here, and not in kel-hall. It was not a time that any of them wanted to be alone. The loneliness of Kutath itself was overwhelming.

On the eighth day Kutath swung beneath them, filling all the screen in the she'pan's hall—angry, arid, scarred with its age.

And Duncan came to the she'pan's presence, burst in like a gust of wind and swept off *mez* and *zaidhe* to show his face: it was aglow.

"Life!" he said. "The scan shows it. She'pan, Niun—your world is not dead."

For an instant neither of them moved.

And of a sudden Melein struck her hands together and thanked the several gods; and only then Niun dared to draw breath and hope.

Behind Duncan, Melein went to controls, and Niun followed after, with the dusei padding behind them and blowing great puffs of excitement. Melein settled on the arm of the cushion and Niun leaned beside her, the while Duncan tried to make clear to them what his search had found, showing them the screens and the figures and all the chattering flow of data that meant life.

Life of machines; and very, very scant, the evidence of growing things.

"It looks like Kesrith from space," said Duncan softly, and sent a chill over Niun's flesh, for often enough the old she'pan had called Kesrith the forge that would prepare the People . . . for all that would lie before them. "The dusei," said Duncan, "should fare well enough there."

"One moon," Niun read the screen, remembering with homesickness the two that had coursed the skies of Kesrith; remembering his hills, and the familiar places that he had hunted before humans came.

This world of their ancestors would hold its own secrets, its own graces and beauties, and its own dangers.

And humans—soon enough.

"Duncan," said Melein, "take us down."

Chapter Seventeen

Kutath.

Duncan inhaled the air that blew into the hatch, the first breath off the surface of the world, cold and thin, faintly scented. He looked beyond the hatch at the red and amber sands, at the ridge of distant, rounded mountains, at a sun sullen-hued and distorted in its sky.

And he did not go down. This was for the mri, to go first onto their native soil. He stood in the ship and watched them descend the ramp, Melein first, and Niun after her—children returned to their ancient mother. They looked about them, their eyes surely seeing things in a different way than his might, their senses finding something familiar in the touch of Kutath's gravity, the flavor of its air—something that must call to their blood and senses and say *this is home.*

Sad for them if it did not, if the People had indeed voyaged too long, and lost everything for which they had come. He did not think they had; he had seen the look in Niun's eyes when they beheld the world beyond the hatch.

He felt his own throat tight, his muscles trembling with the terrible chill of the world, and with anxiety. If he felt anything clearly, it was a sense of loss—and he did not know why. He had succeeded for them, had brought them home, and down safely, and yet there was a sadness on him.

It was not all he had done, that service for the People.

Across the system a beacon pulsed, a marker on the path incoming ships would use; and on Kutath, the ship itself now served as a beacon. Silent the pulse was, but it was going now . . . would go on so long as power remained in the ship—and that would be beyond their brief lifespans.

Friendship, friendship, the ship cried at the heavens, and did human ships care to inquire of that signal or the other, there was more.

He had not confessed this to Niun or Melein. He did not think they would approve any gesture toward tsi'mri, and therefore he did not ask their approval.

He saw the dusei go, whuffing and sniffing the air as they edged their turned-toed way down the ramp—rolling with fat from their long, well-fed inactivity on the ship, sleek and shining under the wan sun. They reached the sand and rolled in delight, shaking clouds of red powder from their velvet hides when they rose up again. The greater one towered up on his hind legs, came down, playing, puffing a cloud of dust at the mri, and Niun scolded him off.

The beasts went their own way then, circling out, exploring their new world. They would allow no danger to come to the mri without rasing alarm about it, and their present manner was one of great ease. Unharmed by the wind of the ship, a clump of blue-green pipes grew nearby. The dusei destroyed it, munching the plants with evident relish. Their digestion could handle anything, even most poisons; there was no concern for that.

Where plants grew, there was surely water, be it ever so scant. Duncan looked on that sparse growth with satisfaction, with pride, for he had found them a place where life existed in this otherwise barren land, had put their little ship down within reach of water—

And close also to the power source that scan detected.

There was no reaction to their presence, none in their descent, none now. The ship's instruments still scanned the skies, ready to trip the sirens and warn them to cover, but the skies remained vacant . . . both desired and undesired, that hush that prevailed.

He felt the pleasure-feelings of the dusei, lotus-balm, and yielded.

Almost timidly he came down the ramp, feeling out of place and strange, and approached the mri silently, hoping that they would not take offense at his presence: well as he knew Niun, he felt him capable of that, toward a tsi'mri.

"She'pan," he heard Niun say softly, and she turned and noticed him, and reached out her hand to him. They put their arms about him as they would a brother, and Duncan felt an impulse to tears that a man who would be kel'en could not shed. He bowed his head for a moment, and felt their warmth near him. There was a healthy wind blowing, whipping at their robes. He put his arms about them too, feeling on the one side the fragility that was Melein and on the other the lean strength of Niun; and themselves alien, beast-warm, and savoring the chill that set him shivering.

The dusei roved the area more and more widely, emitting their hunting moans, that would frighten anything with ears to hear.

And they looked about them, and save for the ship's alien presence, there was nothing but the earth and sky: flat in one direction, and beyond that flatness at the sky's edge lay mountains, rounded and eroded by time; and in the other direction the land fell away into apricot haze misted with purples, showing a naked depth that drew at the eye and disturbed the senses—no mere valley, but an edge to the very world, a distance that extended to the horizon and blended into the sky; and it reached up arms of cliffs that were red and bright where they were nearest and faded into the ambiguous sky at the far horizon.

Duncan breathed an exclamation in his own tongue, forbidden, but the mri did not seem to notice. He had seen the chasm from above, had brought them down near it because it seemed the best place—easier to descend than to ascend, he had thought when choosing the highlands landing, but he had kept them far from the edge. From above it had seemed perilous enough; but here, themselves reduced to mortal perspective, it gaped into depths so great it faded into haze at the bottom, in terraces and slopes and shelves, eroded points and mounts . . . and distantly, apricot-silver, shone what might be a lake, a drying arm of what had been a sea.

A salt lake, it would surely be, and dead: minerals and salts would have gathered there for aeons, as they had in Kesrith's shallow, drying seas.

They stood still for some time, looking about them at the world, until even the mri began to shiver from the cold.

"We must find that source of power you spoke of," said Melein. "We must see if there are others."

"You are close," said Duncan, and lifted his arm in the direction he knew it to be. "I brought you down as near as I dared."

"Nothing responded to your attempts to contact."

"Nothing," Duncan said, and shivered.

"We must put on another layer of robes," said Niun. "We must have a sled packed with stores. We will range out so far as we can—shall we not, she'pan?—and see what there is to be seen."

"Yes," said Melein. "We shall see."

Duncan started to turn away, to do what would be necessary, and finding no better time he hesitated, pulled aside the veil he had assumed for warmth. "She'pan," he said. "It would be better—that I should stay with the ship."

"We will not come back," said Melein.

Duncan looked from one to the other of them, found pain in Niun's eyes, realized suddenly the reason for that sense of loss.

"It is necessary," Duncan said, "that I take the ship—to stand guard for you, she'pan. I will not leave this sun. I will stay. But it is possible that I may be able to stop them."

"The markers that you have left . . . Are they for that?"

Shock coursed through him, the realization that Melein had not been deceived.

"Yes," he said, hoarse. "To let them know that here are friends. And it may be that they will listen."

"Then you will not take the ship," she said. "What message you have left is enough. If they will not regard that, then there is nothing further to be said. The ship carries no weapons."

"I could talk with them."

"They would take you back," she said.

It was truth. He stared at her, chilled to the bone by the wind that rocked at them.

"You could not fight," she said, and looked about at the wide horizon, lifted her arm toward it. "If they would seek us out in all of this, then they would not listen to you; and if they would not, then that is well. Come with us, kel Duncan."

"She'pan," he said softly, accepting.

And he turned and ascended the ramp.

There were supplies to find: Niun named what was needed, and together they bolted aluminum tubing into what passed very well for a sled. They loaded it into the cargo lift, and secured on it what stores Niun chose: water containers, food, and the light mats that were for sleeping; aluminum rods for shelter, and thermal sheets—tsi'mri luxury that they were, yet even Niun found the cold outside persuasive.

They chose spare clothing, and a change of boots; and wore a second *siga* over the first.

And last and most important of all they visited the shrine of the pan'en, and Niun gathered the ovoid reverently into his arms and bore it down to the sled, settling it into the place that was prepared for it.

"Take us down," Melein said.

Duncan pressed the switch and the cargo lift settled slowly groundward, to let them step off onto the red sands.

It was already late afternoon.

Behind them, the cargo lift ascended, crashed into place again, with a sound alien in all this desert, and there was no sound after but the wind. The mri began to walk, never looking back; but once, twice, a third time, Duncan could not bear it, and glanced over his shoulder. The ship's vast bulk dwindled behind them. It assumed a strange, frozen quality as it diminished, sheened in the apricot light, blending with the land: no light, no motion, no sound.

Then a rise of the land came between and it passed from view. Duncan felt a sudden pang of desolation, felt the touch of the mri garments, that had become natural to him, felt the keen cold of the wind, that he had desired, and was still conscious that he was alone. They walked toward the sun—toward the source of activity that the instruments had detected, and the thought occurred to him that did they find others, his companions would be hard put to account for his presence with them.

That there could come a time when his presence would prove more than inconvenient for Niun and Melein.

It was a bad way to end, alone, and different.

It struck him that in his madness he had changed places with those he pitied, and sorriest of all, he did not believe that Niun would willingly desert him.

Na'i'in set, providing them a ruddy twilight that flung the dying sea into hazy limbo, a great and terrifying chasm on their left, with spires upthrust through the haze as if they had no foundation. They rested in the beginning of that sunset, double-robed against the chill and still warm from walking, and shared a meal together. The dusei, that they had thought would have come at the scent of food on the wind, did not appear. Niun looked often during that rest, scanning their backtrail, and Duncan looked also, and fretted after the missing beasts.

"They are of a world no less hard," Niun said finally, "and they are likely ranging out in search of their own meal."

But he frowned and still watched the horizon.

And a strange thing began to happen as the sun declined. Through the gentle haze in the air, mountains leaped into being that had not been visible before, and the land grew and extended before them, developing new limits with the sun behind the hills.

On the shores of the dying sea rose towers and slender spires, only a shade darker than the apricot sky.

"Ah!" breathed Melein, rising; and they two rose up and stood gazing at that horizon, at the mirage-like city that hung before them. It remained distinct only for a few moments, and then faded into shadow as the rim of Na'i'in slipped beneath the horizon and brought them dusk.

"That was surely what the instruments sensed," said Duncan.

"Something is alive there."

"Perhaps," said Niun. Surely he yearned to believe so, but he evinced no hope, no anxiousness. He accepted the worst first: he had constantly done so; it seemed to keep the mri sane, in a history that held little but destructions.

Melein settled again to her mat on the sand, and locked her arms about her knees and said nothing at all.

"It could be very far," Duncan said.

"If it is the source of what you scanned?" Niun asked.

Duncan shrugged. "A day or so."

Niun frowned, slipped the *mez* lower to expose most of his face. "Tell me truth: are you able to make such a walk?"

Duncan nodded, mri-fashion. "The air is thin, but not beyond my limits. Mostly the cold troubles me."

"Wrap yourself. I think that we will rest in this place tonight."

"Niun, I will not be a burden on you."

Niun considered this, nodded finally. "Mri are not bearers of burdens," he said, which Duncan took for kel humor, and the precise truth. He grinned, and Niun did likewise, a sudden and startling gesture, quickly gone.

The veils were replaced. Duncan settled to rest in a thermal sheet with rather more peace at heart than he knew was rational under the circumstances. In the chill air, the blanket and the robes together made a comfortably warm rest, deliciously so. Overhead, the stars, strangely few in a clear sky, observed no familiar patterns. He made up his own, a triangle, a serpent, and a man with a great dus at his heels. The effort exhausted his fading mind, and he slept, to wake with Niun shaking his shoulder and advising him he must keep his turn at watch: the dusei had not yet returned.

He sat wrapped in warmth the remaining part of the night, gazing at the horizon that was made strange by the growth of pipes atop the plainsward ridge, watching in solitude the rise of Na'i'in over their backtrail, a heart-filling beauty.

It was more than a fair trade, he thought.

As the light grew, the mri began to stir; they took a morning meal, leisurely in their preparations, content to say little and to gaze often about them.

And on the rising wind came a strange, distant note that made them stop in the attitudes of the instant, and listen; and then Niun and Melein laughed aloud, relieved.

The dusei were a-hunt, and nearby.

They packed up, and loaded the sled: Duncan drew it. Niun, kel'anth, senior of the Kel, could not take such work while there was another to do it; this had long been the order of things, and Duncan assumed it without question. But the mri watched him, and at the first rise they approached, Niun silently set his hand on the rope and disengaged him from it, looping it across his own shoulder.

It was not hard work for the mri, for the land was relatively flat and the powdery red sand glided easily under the metal runners. The chill that made their breaths hang in frosty puffs in the dawn grew less and less, until by mid-morning both Niun and Melein shed their extra robes and walked in apparent comfort.

During a rest stop, one of the dusei appeared on the horizon, stood for a time, and the other joined it. Ever and again the beasts put in an appearance and as quickly vanished; they had been gone some time in this last absence. Duncan willed his back, concerned for it and distressed at its irrational behavior, but it came only halfway and stopped. It looked different; he would not have recognized it, but that there were only two on all Kutath, and the larger one was still hanging back at the crest of the slope. Both looked different.

Leaner. The sleek look was gone, overnight.

The dus swung about suddenly and joined its partner on the ridge. Both went over that low rolling of the land; Duncan watched to see them reappear going away, and blinked, for it seemed impossible that something so large could vanish so thoroughly in so flat a land.

"What is the matter with them?" he asked of Niun; the mri shrugged and resumed his course behind Melein, meaning, Duncan supposed, that Niun did not know.

And soon after, as their course brought them near some of the blue-green pipe, Niun cut a bit of it with his *av-tlen* and watched it fill with water in the uncut portion.

"I would not sample that," Duncan said uneasily.

But the mri took a little into his mouth, a very little, and spat it out again in a moment. "Not so bad," he said. "Sweet. Possibly the pulp is edible. We shall see if I sicken from it. The dusei did not think so."

This was a mystery still, that there could be communication of such precise nature between dus and man; but Duncan remembered the feeling they had had in the first discovery of the plants—an intense pleasure.

Niun did not sicken. After midday he sampled a bit more, and by evening pronounced it acceptable. Duncan tasted, and it was sweet like sugared fruit, and pleasant and cold. Melein took some last of all, after camp was made and after it was clear that neither mri nor human had taken harm of it.

The sun slipped to the rim of the chasm and shredded into ribbons, lingering for a last moment. Their city returned amid the haze.

It was large; it was firmly grounded on the earth, and no floating mirage. The towers were distinctly touched by the light before it vanished.

"It is written in the pan'en," Melein said softly, "that there was a city of towers—yellow-towered Ar-ehon. Other cities are named there: Zohain, Tho'e'i-shai and Le'a'haen. The sea was Sha'it, and the plains had their names, too."

There was the wind, and the whisper of the sand grains moving. It was all that moved, save themselves, who came as strangers, and one of them strange indeed.

But Melein named them names, and Kutath acquired substance about them, terrible as it was in its desolation. Niun and Melein talked together, laughed somewhat in all that stillness, but the stillness settled into the bones, and stopped the breath, and Duncan found difficulty in moving for a moment until Niun touched his wrist and asked him a question that he must, in embarrassment, beg the mri to repeat.

"Duncan?" Niun asked then, sensing the disturbance in him.

"It is nothing," Duncan said, and wished for the dus back, to no avail. He gazed beyond the mri into the darkening chasm of the dying sea, and wondered that they could laugh in such a place.

And that Melein in her mind saw the vast waters that had lapped and surged in that nakedness: that more than anything else thrust home to him the span of time that these two mri had crossed.

Niun pressed his arm and withdrew, wrapped himself in his blanket and lay down to sleep, as Melein likewise settled for the night.

Duncan took the watch, wrapped in his thermal sheet and warm in the air that frosted his breath. The moon was aloft, gibbous. A wisp of high clouds appeared in the north, not enough to obscure the stars.

He felt the presence of the dus once. It did not come close, but it was there, somewhere near them, reassurance.

Chapter Eighteen

Sharn, trembling with weakness, pressed the button that brought the food dispenser within reach. A slight inclination of her body brought her mouth against it, and for a time she was content to drink and to let the warmth flow into her belly. The tube already increased the flow of nutrient into her veins, but the long food deprivation had psychological effects that no tube-feeding could diminish.

About her, on the bridge of *Shirug,* a double hand of younglings slept, still deep in the hibernation in which they had spent major portions of the long voyage. Only Suth and a Geleg youngling named Melek had remained awake throughout, save for the brief sleeps into which jump cast them. Suth was fully awake already, and made haste to approach Sharn, dutiful in concern for the elder to whom it belonged, bai Hulagh's lending.

"May I serve?" Suth asked hoarsely. Fever-brightness glittered in Suth's eyes. The bony plating of his cheeks was white-edged and cloudy, an unhealthful sign. Sharn saw the suffering of the youngling, who had endured so long a voyage fully awake, and in a rare courtesy, offered Suth the same dispenser which she was using. Suth flushed dark in pleasure and took it hungrily, consumed food in great noisy gulps that surely brought strength to his tottering limbs—then returned it to her, worship in his eyes.

"Awaken the others," she bade Suth then, and the youngling moved at once to obey.

Mission tape stood at zero.

They had arrived.

A quick look at scan showed the human ship riding close at hand, but the humans would hardly be organized yet. Often during the voyage Sharn had awakened for consultation with Suth, and each time she had known the humans slower than regul in coming to focus after jump: drugs; they had not the biological advantage of hibernation. Some few were operating, but they were still hazed. This was known; the mri, who needed neither hibernation nor drugs, had always been able to take advantage of it.

And about them lay the mri home system.

That thought sent chills through Sharn's blood and set her two hearts pumping almost out of time. From her remote console, she called up new plottings, activated her instruments, and sent the ship easing away from the human escort while they were still dazed. Automatic challenge sounded on the instruments, a human computer advising her that she was breaking pattern. She ignored it and increased speed in real space.

She was bound for the inner planets. Behind her, humans stirred to wakefulness, and sent her furious demands to return. She ignored them. She was ally, not subject, and felt no obligation to their commands. About her, the younglings stirred to life again under the ministrations of the skillful youngling provided her by the bai—a measure of his esteem, this lending of his personal attendant: Sharn reckoned dizzyingly of her own possible favor, as well as her own present dangers.

"We will serve as probe," she sent the angered humans at last, deigning to reply. "It is needful, human allies, that we quickly learn what manner of armed threat we face, and *Shirug* has sufficient mobility to evade."

It was not the regul habit to go first.

But regul interests were at stake. Dead world after dead world: the incredible record of devastation enforced what decisions had been made on Kesrith. Doch-survival was personal survival, and more than that . . . incredible in itself . . . there was consciousness of threat against the regul species, that no regul had ever had to reckon.

Behind her, visible on the screens, the human ship seemed to fragment. *Saber* shed her riders, the little in-system fighter *Santiago* and the harmless probe *Flower*. Neither warships nor probe had the star-capable flexibility of *Shirug*, medium-sized and heavily armed, capable of evading directly out of the system and back again, capable of near-world maneuvers which would prove disaster for vast and fragile *Saber,* that was all shielding and fire-power.

The humans were not happy. *Saber* gathered speed and her riders stayed with her. It was not pursuit. Sharn was nervous for a time, and snapped pettishly at her recovering younglings, but she determined at last that the humans were not going to take measures against her, not with all of them in reach of the mri. Their threats, had they issued them, would have made no difference. Sharn had her orders from Hulagh, and while she distrusted the Alagn elder's sometimes youngling-impulsive decisiveness, she also trusted his knowledge and experience, which was a hundred twelve years longer than hers.

In particular, Hulagh knew humans, and evidently had confidence that the peace which was in force would not be breached, not even if regul pressed it hard. This was a distasteful course. Regul were not fighters; their aggressiveness was verbal and theoretical. Sharn would have felt far more secure had she a mri aboard to handle such irrational processes as evasion and combat. Random action was something at which mri excelled. But of course they were facing mri, and the unaccustomed prospect of fighting against mri disturbed her to the depth.

Destroy.

Destroy and leave the humans to mop up the untidiness. Regul knew how to use the lesser races. Regul decided; the lesser species simply coped with the situation . . . and Hulagh in his experience found that the humans would do precisely that.

A beacon-pulse came faintly: hearts pounding, Sharn adjusted the pickup and amplified.

Friendship, it said. *Friendship.*

In human language.

Treachery.

Just such a thing had Hulagh feared, that the mri, who had left regul employ, would hire again. There was a human named Duncan, a contact with the mri, who worked to that end.

Sharn sighted on the source of the signal, fired. It ceased.

Human voices chattered at her in a few moments, seeking to know why she had fired. They had not, then, picked up the signal.

"Debris," Sharn answered. Regul did not lie; neither did they always tell the truth.

The answer yes, perhaps, accepted. There was no comment.

Shirug's lead widened. It was possible she had the advantage of speed. Possibly the human craft were content to let her probe the inner system defenses, taking her at her word, reasoning no further into it. She doubted that. She had confidence rather in *Shirug*'s speed: strike-and-run, that was the ship's build—*Saber*'s was that of a carrier, stand-and-fight. Doubtless the insystem fighter, *Santiago,* was the speed in the combination, and it was no threat to *Shirug. Flower* was not even considerable in that reckoning.

Sharn dismissed concern for them: Hulagh's information was accurate as it had been consistently accurate. *Shirug,* stripped of riders according to their operating agreement, still had the advantage in everything but shielding and firepower.

She gave whole attention to that matter and allotted the chatter of humans to Suth's attention thereafter. There was the matter of locating the world itself, of reaching it first.

Destroy, and leave the humans to cope with what followed.

Chapter Nineteen

It was painful to stop, with the city in view, so close, so tantaliz-ingly close—but the night was on them, and Niun saw that Dun-can was laboring: his breath came audibly now. And at last Melein paused, and with a sliding glance toward Duncan that was for Niun alone, signaled her intent to halt.

"Best we rest here the night," she said.

Duncan accepted the decision without so much as a glance, and they spread the mats for sitting on the cold sand and watched the sun go down. Its rays tinted the city spires against the hills.

"I am sorry," Duncan said suddenly.

Niun looked at him; Duncan remained veiled, not out of reti-cence, he thought, but that the air hurt him less that way. He felt the mood behind that veil, an apartness that was itself a wound.

"*Sov-kela,*" Niun hailed him softly, kel-brother, the gentlest word of affection but truebrother. "Come sit close to us. It is cold."

It was less cold for them, but Duncan came, and seemed cheered by it, and perhaps more comfortable, for his body heat was less than theirs. They two leaned together, back to back, lack-ing any other rest. Even Melein finally deigned to use Niun's knee for her back. They said nothing, only gazed at the city that was sunk in dark now, and at the stars, fewer than those in skies he had known . . . so that he wondered if they lay at the very rim of the galaxy, first-born perhaps, as Duncan's folk came from in-ward.

A long, long journey, that of the People inward. He almost wished that this trek last forever, that they might forever walk to-ward the city, still with hope, and not know what truth lay there.

And yet Duncan had claimed to have detected power use in that place.

Niun bit at his lip and shifted his weight, so that everyone shifted uncomfortably, and was aware, subtly, of that which had suddenly disturbed him.

Dus-presence.

"They are back," he said softly. "Yes," said Duncan after a moment.

Sand scuffed. There was a whuffing sound. Eventually the beasts appeared, heads lowered, absent-mindedly looking this way and that as if at this last moment they could not recall what they were doing there.

And this time they did not shy off, but came within reach. Melein moved aside and Niun and Duncan accepted the beasts that sought them.

Pleasure thoughts. Niun caressed the massive head that thrust at his ribs and ran his hand over a body gone rough-coated and thin, every rib pronounced.

"It is changed," Duncan exclaimed. "Niun, both of them are thinner. Could they have had young?"

"No one has ever decided whether a dus is he or she." Niun fretted at the change in them—was nettled, too, that Duncan should seize what thought he had half-shaped, Duncan, who was new to the beasts. "Some have said they are both. But the People have never seen this change in them. We have never," he added truthfully, "seen young dusei."

"It is possible," said Melein, "that there are no young dusei, not as we know young. Nothing survives where they come from that is born helpless."

Niun stood up and looked all about the moonlit land, but dusei could well conceal themselves, and if there were young thereabouts, he could not find them. But when he sat down again, the head of his dus in his lap, he had still a feeling of unease about the beast.

"It is dangerous," said Duncan, "to loose a new species on a world, particularly one so fragile as this."

Duncan spoke. Niun had a thought, and for love, forbore to say it.

And suddenly Duncan bowed his head, and there was discomfort in the dus-feelings.

"This is so," said Melein gently, "but we should feel lonely without them."

Duncan looked at her in silence, and finally put his arms about his beast's neck, and bowed his head and rested. Niun made place for Melein between them, and they slept, all slept for the first time since the ship, for the dusei were with them to guard them, and they had the body warmth of the beasts for their comfort.

Dusei multiplied, begat other dusei, that were born adult and filled the world until all Kutath belonged to them, and they filled the streets of the dead cities and had no need of mri.

Niun wakened, disturbed at once by the dus thoughts that edged upon the nightmare, aware of sweat cold on his face, of the others likewise disturbed . . . perplexed, perhaps, what had wakened them. Duncan looked round at the hills, as if some night wanderer might have come nigh them.

"It is nothing," Niun said.

He did not admit to the dream; the fright was still with him. He had never in his life felt exposed to the dusei, only sharing. Human presence: it was something that Duncan's presence had fostered, suspicion, where none had existed.

Dusei, he reminded himself, *have no memories.* For these two dusei, Kesrith no longer existed. They would never recall it until they saw it again, and that would be never. Persons and places: that was all that stayed in their thick skulls . . . and for them now there was only Kutath. They were native, by that token, one with the land, sooner than they.

Niun closed his eyes again, shamed by the dream that he was sure at least Melein suspected, though she might falsely blame it on Duncan, and feel herself fouled to have shared a human's night fears, dus-borne. The beast sent comfort now. Niun took it, and relaxed into that warmth, denying the fear.

The dus would not in any wise remember.

They made no great haste on the morrow: they knew Duncan's limit in the thin air, and would not press him harder.

And they were cautious; they followed the rolls of the land in their approach, and, dus-wise, appeared no plainer to the city than they must.

But the nearer they came, the less useful such precaution seemed.

Old, old. Niun saw clearly what he had suspected: spires in ruins, unrepaired, the sordidness of decay about the whole place. None of them spoke of it; it was not a thing that they wanted to admit.

At the last they abandoned caution. The wind that had tugged at them gently for days suddenly swelled, kicking up sand in a veil that itself was enough to screen them, and the force of it exhausted them. The dusei went with nostrils pressed close and heads lowered, snorting now and again and doubtless questioning the sanity of them that insisted on moving. Niun's eyes burned despite the protection of the membrane, and he lowered the visor of the *zaidhe* as Duncan had done from the first that the sand had begun to blow; Melein lowered the gauzy inner veil of her head-cloth, the *sarahe,* that covered all her face and made of her a featureless figure of white, as they were of black.

Under other circumstances, prudence would have driven them to shelter: there were places that offered it; but they kept walking, slowly, and took turn and turn about with the stubborn sled.

Sand flowed in rivers through the streets of the city. They went like ghosts into the ruins, and their tracks vanished behind them as they walked. Spires towered above them, indistinct beyond rusty streamers of dust, save where outlined by the sun that pierced the murk; and the wind howled with a demon-voice down the narrow ways, rattling sand against their visors.

Spires and cylinders spanned by arches, squarish cylinders looming against the sand-veiled sun . . . no such buildings had stood in Niun's memory, anywhere. He gazed round at them and found nothing familiar, nothing that said to him, *Here dwelled the People.* Fear settled over him, a deep depression of soul.

For a time they had to rest, sheltered in the shell of a broken spire, oppressed by the noise of the wind outside. Duncan coughed, a shallow, tired sound, that ceased finally when he was persuaded to take a little of their water; and he doubled the veil over his face, which did for him what the gods in their wisdom had done for the mri, helping him breathe in the fine dust.

But of the city, of what they saw, none of them spoke. They rested, and when they could, they set out into the storm again, Duncan taking his own turn at the sled, that by turns hissed over sand and grated over stone: burden that it was, they would not leave what it bore. There was no question of it.

Melein led them, tending toward the center of the city, that was the direction that Niun himself would have chosen: to the heart of the maze of streets, for always in the center were the sacred places, the shrines, and always to the right of center stood the *e'ed su-shepani,* the she'pan's tower access. In any mri construction in all creation a mri knew his way: so it had been, surely, when there had been cities.

The dusei vanished again. Niun looked about and they were gone, though he could still feel their touch. Duncan turned a blind, black-masked face in the same direction, then faced again the way that Melein led and flung his weight against the ropes. The squeal of runners on naked stone shrilled above the roar of the wind, diminished as they went on sand again.

And the spires thinned, and they entered a great square.

There stood the edun, the House that they had sought . . . slanted walls, four towers with a common base: the House that they had known had been of earth, squat and rough . . . but this was of saffron stone, veiled with the sand-haze, and arches joined its upper portions, an awesome mass, making of all his memories something crude and small . . . the song, of which his age was the echo.

"Gods," Niun breathed, to know what the People had once been capable of creating.

Here would be the Shrine, if one existed; here would be the heart of the People, if any lived. "Come," Melein urged them.

With difficulty they began that ascent to its doors: Duncan labored with the sled, and Niun lent a hand to the rope and helped him. The doors were open before them: Melein's white figure entered the dark first, and Niun deserted Duncan, alarmed at her rashness.

The dark inside held no threat; it was quieter there, and the clouds of sand and dust did not pursue them far inside. In that dim light from the open door, Melein folded back her veil and settled it over her mane; Niun lifted his visor and went back to help Duncan, who had gained the doorway; the squeal of the sled's runners sounded briefly as they drew inside. The sound echoed off shadowed walls and vaulted ceiling.

"Guard your eyes," Melein said.

Niun turned, saw her reach for a panel at the doorway: light blazed, cold and sudden. The membrane's reaction was instantaneous, and even through the hazing Niun saw black traceries on the walls that soared over them: writings, like and unlike what Melein had made, stark and angular and powerful. An exclamation broke from Melein's own lips, awe at what she had uncovered.

"The hall floors are clean," Duncan remarked strangely, wiping dusty tears from his face, leaving smears behind. Niun looked down the corridors that radiated out from this hall, and saw that the dust stopped at the margin of this room: the way beyond lay clean and polished. A prickling stirred the nape of Niun's neck, like dus-sense. The place should have filled him with hope. It was rather apprehension, a consciousness of being alien in this hall. He wondered where the dusei were, why they had gone, and wished the beasts beside them now.

"Come," said Melein. She spoke in a hushed tone, and still her voice echoed. "Bring the pan'en. You will have to carry it."

They unbound it from the sled, and Niun gave it carefully into Duncan's arms—one burden that he would have been honored to bear, but it came to him that his place was to defend it, and he could not do that with his arms hindered. "Can you bear it, sov-kela?" he asked, for it was heavy and strangely balanced, and Duncan breathed audibly; but Duncan tilted his head mri-wise, avowing he could, and they went soft-footed after Melein, into the lighted and polished halls.

The shrine of the House must lie between kel-access and sen-. The Kel, the guardians of the door, the Face that was Turned Outward, always came first; then the shrine, the Holy; and then the sen-access, the tower of the Mind of the People, the Face that was Turned Inward, the Veilless. Such a shrine there was indeed, a small, shadowed room, where the lamps were cold and the glass of the vessels had gone iridescent with age.

"Ai," Melein grieved, and touched the corroded bronze of the screen of the Pana. Niun averted his eyes, for he saw only dark beyond, nothing remaining in the Holy.

They retreated quickly from that place, gathered up Duncan, who waited at the door, shy of entering there; and yet by his troubled look Niun thought he understood: that had there been any of the People here, the House shrine would have held fire. Niun touched the chill surface of the pan'en as they walked, reaffirmation, a cleansing after the desolation in the shrine.

Yet there were the lights, the cold, clean light; their steps echoed on immaculate tiles, though dust lay thick everywhere outside. The place lived. It drew power from some source. Melein paused at yet another panel, and light came to other hallways . . . the recess of the sen-tower, and on the right, that which had been the tower of some long-dead she'pan.

And most bitter of all, the access to the kath-tower, that mocked them with its emptiness.

"There could be defenses," Duncan said.

"That is so," said Melein.

But she turned then and began to climb the ramp of the sen-tower, where kel'ein might not follow. Niun stood helpless, anxious until she paused and nodded a summons to him, permission to trespass.

Duncan came after him, bearing the pan'en, hard-breathing; and slowly they ascended the curving ramp, past blockish markings that were like the signs of the old edun, but machine-precise and strange.

More lights: the final access to sen-hall gave way before them, and they entered behind Melein into a vast chamber that echoed to their steps. It was naked. There were no carpets, no cushions, nothing save a corroded brass dinner service that sat on a saffron stone shelf. It looked as if a touch would destroy it: corrosion made lacery of it.

But there was no trace of dust, nothing, save on that shelf, where it lay thick as one would expect for such age.

Melein continued on, through farther doorways, into territory that was surely familiar to one six years a sen'e'en; and again she paused to bid them stay with her, to see things that had been eternally forbidden the Kel. Perhaps, Niun thought sadly, it no longer mattered.

Lights flared to her touch. Machinery lay before them, a vast room of machinery—bank upon bank: like the shrine at Sil'athen it was, but far larger. Niun delayed, awestruck, then committed himself unbidden to stay at her back. She did not forbid, and Duncan followed.

Computers, monitoring boards: some portions of the assemblage he compared to the boards of the ship; and some he could not at all recognize. The walls were stark white, with five symbols blazoned above the center of the panels, tall as a man's widest reach. In gleaming, incorruptible metal they were shaped, like the metal of the pan'en that they bore.

"*An-ehon*," Melein said aloud, and the sound rang like a thunderclap into that long silence.

The machinery blazed to life, activated with a suddenness that made Niun flinch in spite of himself, and he heard the beginnings of an outcry from Duncan, one immediately stifled. The human stood beside him, knelt to set the pan'en down, and rose again, hand on his pistol.

"I am receiving," said a deep and soulless voice. "Proceed."

By the name of the city Melein had called it: Niun's skin prickled, first at the realization that he had seen a symbol and heard it named, a forbidden thing . . . and then that such a creation had answered them. He saw Melein herself take a step back, her hand at her heart.

"An-ehon," she addressed the machine, and the very floor seemed to pulse in time with the throb of the lights. It was indeed the city that spoke to them, and it had used the hal'ari, the High Language, that was echoed unchanged throughout all of mri time, "An-ehon, where are your people?"

A brighter flurry of lights ran the boards.

"Unknown," the machine pronounced at last.

Melein drew a deep breath—stood still for several moments in which Niun did not dare to move. "An-ehon," she said then, "we are your people. We have returned. We are descended from the People of An-ehon and from Zohain and Tho'ei'i-shai and Le'a'haen. Do you know these names?"

C. J. Cherryh

There was again a flurry of lights and sounds, extreme agitation in the machine. Niun took a step forward, put a cautioning hand toward Melein, but she stood firmly, disregarding him. Bank after bank in the farthest reaches of the hall flared to life: section after section illumined itself.

"We are present," said another voice. "I am Zohain."

"State your name, visitor," said An-ehon's deeper voice. "Please state your names. I see one who is not of the People. Please state your authority to invoke us, visitor."

"I am Melein s'Intel Zain-Abrin, she'pan of the People that went out from Kutath."

The lights pulsed, in increasing unison. "I am An-ehon. I am at the orders of the she'pan of the People. Zohain and Tho'e'i-shai and Le'a'haen are speaking through me. I perceive others. I perceive one of the not-People."

"They are here with my permission."

The lights pulsed, all in unison now. "May An-ehon ask permission to ask?" the machine began, the ritual courtesy of one who would question a she'pan; and the source of it sent cold over Niun's skin.

"Ask."

"What is this person of the not-People? Shall we accept it, she'pan?"

"Accept him. He is Duncan-without-a-Mother. He comes from the Dark. This, of the People, is Niun s'Intel Zain-Abrin, kel'anth of my Kel; this other is a shadow-who-sits-at-our-door."

"Other shadows have entered the city with you."

"The dusei are likewise shadows in our house."

"There was a ship which we permitted to land."

"It brought us."

"There is a signal which it gives, not in the language of the People."

"An-ehon, let it continue."

"She'pan," it responded.

"There are none of the People in your limits?"

"No."

"Do any remain, An-ehon?"

"Rephrase."

"Do any others of the People survive, An-ehon?"

"Yes, she'pan. Many live."

The answer struck; it went uncomprehended for several heart-beats, for Niun had waited for *no*. Yes. Yes, many, *many, MANY*!

"She'pan," Niun exclaimed, and tears stung his eyes. He stood still, nonetheless, and breathed deeply to drive the weakness from him, felt Duncan's hand on his shoulder, offering whatever moved the human, and after a moment he was aware of that, too. Gladness, he thought; Duncan was glad for them. He was touched by this, and at the same time annoyed by the human contact.

Human.

Before he had heard An-ehon speak, he had had no resentment for Duncan's humanity; before he had known that there were others, he had not felt the difference in them so keenly.

Shame touched him, that he should go before others of the People, drawing this with them—self-interest shame and dishonorable, and hurtful. Perhaps Duncan even sensed it. Niun lifted his arm, set it likewise on Duncan's shoulder, pressed with his fingers.

"Sov-kela," he said in a low voice.

The human did not speak. Perhaps he likewise found nothing to say.

"An-ehon," Melein addressed the machine, "where are they now?"

A graphic flashed to a central screen: dots flashed.

Ten, twenty sites. The globe shaped, turned in the viewer, and there were others.

"There were no power readings for those sites," Duncan murmured. Niun tightened his hand, warning him to silence.

Melein turned to them, hands open in dismissal. "Go. Wait below."

Perhaps it was because of Duncan; more likely it was that here began sen-matters that the Kel had no business to overhear.

The People survived.

Melein would guide them: the thought came suddenly that he would have need of all the skill that his masters had taught him—that first thing in finding the People, it would be necessary to kill: and this was a bitterness more than such killing ever had been.

"Come," he said to Duncan. He bent to take the pan'en into his own arms, trusting their safety now to the city, that obeyed Melein.

"No," Melein said. "Leave it."

He did so, brought Duncan out and down again, where they had left their other belongings; and there they prepared to wait.

Night came on them. From sen-tower there was no stir; Niun sat and fretted at Melein's long silence, and Duncan did not venture conversation with him. Once, restless, he left the human to watch and climbed up to kel-hall: there was only emptiness there, vaster by far than the earth-walled kel-hall he had known. There were pictures, maps, painted there, age-faded, showing a world that had ceased to be, and the sight depressed him.

He left the place, anxious for Duncan, alone in main hall, and started down the winding ramp. A chittering, mechanical thing darted behind him . . . he whirled and caught at his pistol, but it was only an automaton, a cleaner such as regul had employed. It answered what kept the place clean, or what did repairs to keep the ancient machinery running.

He shrugged, half a shiver, and descended to Duncan—startled the human, who settled back again, distressed and relieved at once.

"I wish the dusei would come back," Duncan said.

"Yes," Niun agreed. They were limited without the animals. They dared not leave the outer door unguarded. He looked in that direction, where there was only night, and then began to search through their packs. "I am going to take the she'pan up some food. I do not think we will be moving tonight. And mind, there are some small machines about. I think they are harmless. Do not damage one."

"It comes to me," Duncan said softly, "that An-ehon could be dangerous if it chose to be."

"It comes to me too."

"It said . . . that it *permitted* the ship to land. That means it could have prevented it."

Niun drew a slow breath and let it go, gathered up the packet of food and a flask, the while Duncan's words nagged at him. The human had learned well how to keep his thoughts from his face;

he could no longer read him with absolute success. The implications disturbed him; it was not the landing of their own ship that Duncan was thinking of.

Others.

The humans that would come.

Such a thought Duncan offered to him.

He rose and went without looking back, climbed the way to sen-hall, thoughts of treachery moiling in him: and not treachery, if Duncan were Melein's.

What *was* the man?

He entered cautiously into the outer hall of the Sen, called out aloud, for the door was left open; he could hear the voice of the machine, drowning his words, perhaps.

But Melein came. Her eyes were shadowed and held a dazed look. Her weariness frightened him.

"I have brought you food," he said.

She gathered the offering into her hands. "Thank you," she said, and turned way, walked slowly back into that room. He lingered, and saw what he ought not, the pan'en open, and filled with leaves of gold . . . saw the pulse of lights welcome Melein, mortal flesh conversing with machines that were cities. She stood, and light bathed her white-robed figure until it blazed blue-white like a star. The packet of food tumbled from her loose hand, rolled. The flask slipped from the other and struck the floor without a sound. She did not seem to notice.

"Melein!" he cried, and started forward.

She turned, held out her hands, forbidding, panic on her face. Blue light broke across his vision: he flung himself back, crashed to the floor, half dazed.

Voices echoed, and one was Melein's. He gathered himself to one knee as she reached him, touched him: he gained his feet, though his heart still hammered from the shock that had passed through him.

"He is well?" asked the voice of An-ehon. "He is well?"

"Yes," Melein said.

"Come away," Niun urged her. "Come away; leave this thing, at least until the morning. What is time to this machine? Come away from it, and rest."

"I shall eat and rest here," she said. Her hands caressed his arm, withdrew as she stepped back from him, retreating into the room with the machine. "Do not try to come here."

"I fear this thing."

"It should be feared," she lingered to say, and her eyes held ineffable weariness. "We are not alone. We are not alone, Niun. We will find the People. Look at yourself, she'pan's-kel'en."

"Where shall we find them, and when, she'pan? Does it know?"

"There have been wars. The seas have dried; the People have diminished and fought among themselves; cities are abandoned for want of water. Only machines remain here: An-ehon says that it teaches the she'panei that come here, to learn of it. Go away. I do not know it all. And I must. It learns of me too; it will share the knowledge with all the Cities of the People, and perhaps, with that One it calls the Living City. I do not know, I cannot grasp what the connection is among the cities. But I hold An-ehon. It listens to me. And by it I will hold Kutath."

"I am," he said, dazed by the temerity of such a vision, "the she'pan's Hand."

"Look to Duncan."

"Yes," he said; and accepted her gesture of dismissal and left, still feeling in his bones the ache that the machine's weapon had left; dazed he was still, and much that she had said wandered his mind without a tether to hold it . . . only that Melein meant to fight, and that therefore she would need him.

A'ani. Challenge. She'panei did not share: the she'pan served by the most skillful kel'en, survived.

Melein prepared herself.

He returned in silence to the hall below, curled up in the corner, massaging his aching arms and reckoning in troubled thoughts that there was killing to be done.

"Is she all right?" Duncan intruded into his silence, unwelcome.

"She will not leave. She is talking to it, with *them*. She speaks of wars, kel Duncan."

"Is that remarkable for the People?"

Niun looked at him, prepared to be angry, and realized that it was a failure of words. "Wars. Mri wars. Wars-with-distance-weapons." He resorted to the forbidden mu'ara, and Duncan seemed then to understand him, and fell quickly silent.

"Would that the dusei would come," Niun declared suddenly, wrenching his thoughts from such prospects; and in his restlessness he went to the door and ventured to call to them, that lilting call that sometimes, only sometimes, could summon them.

It did not work this time. There was no answer this night, nor the next.

But on the third, while Melein remained shut in sen-tower, and they fretted in their isolation below, there came a familiar breathing and rattle of claws on the steps outside, and that peculiar pressure at the senses that heralded the dusei.

It was the first night that they two dared sleep soundly, warm next their beasts and sure that they would be warned if danger came on them.

It was Melein that came; a clap of her hands startled them and the beasts together, wakened them in dismay that she, though one of them, had found them sleeping.

"Come," she said; and when they had both gained their feet and stood ready to do her bidding: "The People are near. An-ehon has lit a beacon for them. They are coming."

Chapter Twenty

The storm days past had left banks of sand heaped in the city, high dunes that made unreal shapes in the light that whipped about the square.

Duncan looked back at the source, a beacon from the edun's crest that flashed powerfully in the still-dark sky, a summons to any that might be within sight of the city.

And the People would come to that summoning.

They took nothing with them: the pan'en, the sled, everything they owned was left in the edun. If they fared well, they would return; if not, they had no further need. There was, he suspected, though Niun had not spoken overmuch of their chances, no question of flight, whatever happened.

The dusei were disturbed, the more so as they neared the city's limits. Niun scattered them with a sharp command; it was not a situation for dus-feelings. The beasts left them, and vanished quickly into the dark and the ruins.

"Should I not go also?" Duncan asked.

The mri both looked at him. "No," said Niun. "No," Melein echoed, as if such an offering offended them.

And in the dawning, on the sand ridge facing the city, appeared a line of black.

Kel'ein.

The Face that is Turned Outward.

"*Shon'ai*," Niun said softly, *Shon'ai sa'jiran,* the mot ran. The cast is made: no recalling it. "She'pan, will you wait, or will you come?"

"I will walk with you . . . lest there be some over-anxious

kel'en on the other side. There are still she'panei. We will see if there is still respect for law."

And in the first light of Na'i'in, the black line advanced, a single column. They walked to meet it, the three of them, and there were no words.

The column stopped, and a pair of kel-ein detached themselves and came forward.

Melein stopped. "Come," Niun said to Duncan.

They walked without her. "Keep silent," Niun said, "and keep to my left flank."

And at speaking-distance, only barely, the strange kel'ein stopped; and hailed them. It was a mu'ara, and not a word of it could Duncan understand, but only *she'pan.*

"Among the People," Niun shouted back, "is the hal'ari forgotten?"

The two strangers came forward still further, and paused: Duncan felt their eyes on him, on what of his face was not veiled. They knew something amiss; he felt it in that too-close scrutiny.

"What do you bring?" the elder asked Niun, and it was the hal'ari. "What is this, kel'en?"

Niun said nothing.

The stranger's eyes went beyond Niun, distant, and came back again. "Here is Sochil's land. Whatever you are, advise your she'-pan so, and seek her grace to go away. We do not want this meeting."

"A ship has touched your lands," Niun said.

There was silence from the other side. They knew, and were perturbed: it did not need dusei to feel that in the air.

"We are of Melein s'Intel," said Niun.

"I am Hlil s'Sochil," said the younger, slipping hand into belt in a threatening posture. "And you, stranger?"

"I am daithon Niun s'Intel Zain-Abrin, kel'anth of the Kel of Melein."

Hlil at once adopted a quieter posture, made a slight gesture of respect. He and his elder companion were clad in coarse, faded black; but they were adorned with many *j'tai,* honors that glittered and winked in the cold sun—and the weapons they bore were the *yin'ein,* worn and businesslike.

"I am Merai s'Elil Kov-Nelan," said the elder. "Daithon and kel'anth of Kel of Edun An-ehon. What shall we say to our she'-pan, kel'anth?"

"Say that it is challenge."

There was a moment's silence. Merai's eyes went to Duncan, worrying at a presence that did not belong; worrying, Duncan thought, at questions that he would ask if he could. They knew of the ship; and Merai's amber eyes were filled with apprehension.

But suddenly Merai inclined his head and walked off, he and Hlil together.

"They sense something wrong in me," Duncan said.

"Their she'pan will come. It is a question for her now. Stand still; fold your hands behind you. Do nothing you are not bidden to do."

So they stood, with the wind fluttering gently at their robes and blowing a fine sifting off the surface of sand. A tread disturbed the silence after a time; Melein joined them.

"Her name is Sochil," Niun said without looking about her. "We have advised her kel'anth of your intentions."

She said nothing, but waited.

And in utter silence the People came, the kel'ein first, ranging themselves in a circle about them, rank upon rank, so that had they intended flight there was no retreat. Duncan stood stone-still as his companions, as did the hostile Kel, and felt the stares that were fixed on him, on them all, for surely there was strangeness even in Niun and Melein, the fineness of their clothing, the za-hen'ein that they bore with the yin'ein, the different style of the zaidhe, with its dark plastic visor and careful folding, while their own were mere squares and twists of cloth, and their veils were twisted into the headcloths, and not fastened to the metal band that theirs had. Hems were ragged, sleeves frayed. Their weapon hilts were in bone and lacquered fiber, while those of Niun were of brass and gold and cho-silk wrappings: Duncan thought even his own finer than those these strangers bore.

A figure of awe among them, Niun: Duncan did not know the name that Niun had called himself—daithon was like a word for son, but different; but he reckoned suddenly that the kinsman of a she'pan ranked nigh the she'pan herself.

And himself, Duncan-without-a-Mother. He began to wonder what would become of himself—and what this talk was of challenge. He had no skill. He could not take up the *yin'ein* against the likes of these. He did not know what Niun expected him to do.

Do nothing you are not bidden to do. He knew the mri well enough to believe Niun literally. There were lives in the balance.

Gold robes appeared beyond the black. There stood the Sen, the scholars of the People; and they came veilless, old and young, male and female, lacking the *seta'al* for the most part, though some few bore them, the blue kel-scars. The Sen posed themselves among the Kel, arms folded, waiting.

But when Melein stepped forward, the sen'ein veiled, and turned aside. And through their midst came an old, white-robed woman.

Sochil, she'pan. Her robes were black-bordered, while Melein's were entirely white. She bore no *seta'al,* though Melein did. She came forward and stopped, facing Melein.

"I am Sochil, she'pan of the ja'anom mri. You are out of your proper territory, she'pan."

"This city," said Melein, "is the city of my ancestors. It is mine."

"Go away from my lands. Go unharmed. This is neutral ground. No one can claim An-ehon. There can be no challenge here."

"I am Melein, she'pan of all the People; and I have come home, Sochil."

Sochil's lips trembled. Her face was seamed with the sun and the weather. Her eyes searched Melein, and the tremor persisted. "You are mad. She'pan of the People? You are more than mad. How many of us will you kill?"

"The People went out from the World; and I am she'pan of all that went out and all that have returned, and of all the cities that sent us. I challenge, Sochil."

Sochil's eyes flickered as the membrane went across them, and her hands went up in a warding gesture. "Cursed be you," she cried, and veiled, and retreated among her Sen.

"You are challenged," Melein said in a loud voice. "Either yield me your children, she'pan of the ja'anom mri, or I will take them."

The she'pan withdrew without answering, and her Kel formed a wall protecting her. None moved. None spoke. A misery crept into taut muscles. The side of the body turned to the wind grew chill and then numb.

And came kel'anth Merai, and two kel'ein, one male, one female.

"She'pan," said Merai, making a gesture of respect before Melein. "I am kel'anth Merai s'Elil Kov-Nelan. The she'pan offers you two kel'ein."

Melein set her arms in an attitude of shock and scorn. "Will she bargain? Then let her give me half her people."

The kel'anth's face betrayed nothing; but the young kel'ein at his side looked dismayed. "I will tell her," the kel'anth said, and tore himself away and retreated into the black ranks that protected Sochil.

"She will not accept," Melein predicted, a whisper to Niun, almost lost in the wind.

It was a long wait. At last the kel'ein gave way, and Sochil herself returned. She was veiled, and she stood with her hands tucked into the wide sleeves of her robes.

"Go away," Sochil said softly then. "I ask you go away and let my children be. What have you to do with them?"

"I see them houseless, she'pan. I will give them a house."

There was a pause. At last Sochil swept her arm at the land. "I see you destitute, fine she'pan with your elegant robes. I see you with no land, no Kel, no Kath, no Sen. Two kel'ein, and nothing more. But you will take my children and give them a house."

"I shall."

"This," said Sochil, stabbing a gesture at Duncan, "is *this* called of the People where you have been? Is this the reward of my Kel when it defeats your kel'anth? What is this that you bring to us, dressed in a kel'en's robes? Let us see its face."

Niun's hand went to his belt, warning.

"You demean yourself," Melein said. "And all this is without point, she'pan. I have told you what I want and what I will do. I will settle your people in a house, either half or all, as you will. And I will go and take clan after clan, until I have all. I am she'-pan of the People, and I will have your children, half now, all later. But if you will give half, I will take them and withdraw challenge."

"It cannot be done. The high plains cities have no water. Stranger-she'pan, you are mad. You do not understand. We cannot build; we cannot take the elee way. We are enough for the land, and it for us. You will kill us."

"Ask An-ehon that was your teacher, Sochil, and learn that it is possible."

"You dream. Daughter of my ancestors, you dream."

"No," said Melein. "Mother of the ja'anom, you are a bad dream that the People have dreamed, and I will make a house for your children."

"You will kill them. I will not let you have them."

"Will you divide, she'pan, or will you challenge?"

There were tears in Sochil's eyes, that ran down and dampened her veil. She looked on Niun fearfully, and on Melein again. "He is very young. You are both very young, and in strange company. The gods know that you do not know what you are doing. How can I divide my children?—She'pan, they are terrified of you."

"Answer."

Sochil's head went back. Her glistening eyes nictitated and shed their tears, and she turned her back and stalked off.

Her people stood silent. They might have done something, Duncan thought, might have shown her support. But Melein would claim them; they would remain Sochil's only if Sochil would return challenge.

Sochil stopped in her retreat, among the ranks of her Kel, turned suddenly. "*A'ani!*" she cried. It was challenge.

Melein turned to Niun, and carefully he shed the belt of the *za-hen'ein,* handed the modern weapons to Duncan; then with a bow to Melein, he turned and walked forward.

Likewise did Merai s'Elil.

Duncan stood still, the belt a weight in his hands. Melein laid her hand on his sleeve. "Kel Duncan: you understand . . . you must not interfere."

And she veiled herself and walked away through the enemy kel'ein, and likewise did Sochil, in her wake. The wall of kel'ein reformed behind them.

There was silence, save for the whistling of the wind.

In the center of the circle and Niun and Merai took up their positions, facing one another at fencers' distance and a half. Each gathered a handful of sand and cast it on the wind.

Then the *av'ein-kel,* the great-swords, whispered from sheaths.

A pass, in which they exchanged position; the blades flashed, rang lightly against each other, rested. A second pass: and kel Merai stopped, and seemed simply to forget where he was; and fell. The blade had not seemed to touch him.

But darkness spread over the sand beneath him.

Niun bent and gathered dust on his fingers, and smeared it across his brow . . . began, as if there were nothing else in the world, as if there were no watching ring of strangers, to cleanse his blade with a second handful of sand.

Then he straightened, sheathed the *av-kel,* stood still.

For a time there was only the flutter of robes in the wind. Then came a wail from the People beyond the ranks of the Kel.

Duncan stood still, lost; he saw, he heard, he watched the shifting of ranks: Niun also left him. He was forgotten in the confusion.

Men bore away the dead kel'anth, quietly, toward the desert. Soon enough came kel'ein bearing a bundle wrapped in white, and that shook Duncan's confidence: Sochil, he thought, hoping that he was right. How she had died, by whose hand, he had no means to tell. Many kel'ein attended that corpse away. Others spread black tents and made a camp.

And the wan sun sank, and the wind grew cold; Duncan stood, in twilight, at the camp's edge, and watched the return of the burial parties . . . sank down to sit finally, for his legs grew numb and he had no more strength to stand in the cold and the wind.

There was a breathing near him: soft-footed, the dusei, when they chose to be. He felt them, and they came and nosed at him, identifying him. One ventured away; he called it back, Niun's dus. It came and settled uneasily with him. He was glad of their presence, less lonely with them, less afraid.

And after full dark he saw a tall shadow come out of the camp, and saw the gleam of moonlight on bronze-hilted weapons and on the *zaidhe's* visor, and knew Niun even at great distance.

He rose. Niun beckoned, and he came, the dusei padding behind him.

There was no explanation, nothing. The dusei caught Niun's mood, that was still tense. They walked, they and the beasts, into the midst of the strange camp, into the largest of the tents.

Black-robes filled it, heads and bodies alike swathed in kel-cloth, veiled and expressionless; at one side was a small cluster of the eldest gold-robes, unveiled, and one ancient blue-robe, that sudden surmise told Duncan would be the kath'anth, senior of the Kath.

And one white, veilless figure seated at the end, that was Melein.

Golden skins, golden, membraned eyes, all alike—and only the beasts and himself were alien. Duncan walked the aisle Niun and the beasts made toward Melein, his heart beating in a lost, forlorn terror, for the dusei gathered the tension they felt and cast it back to him, and he forbade it to swell to rage: no enemies these, not now.

Nor friendly to him.

The dusei came to Melein's hand before they turned, as Niun took his place by her side and Duncan took the shadowed place behind her; the beasts began to pace back and forth, back and forth, eyeing the crowd with hostility scarcely contained.

"Yai!" Niun forbade them. The little one half-reared and came down again slowly, no play this time. The company did not flinch, but waves of fear were intense in their midst. The dusei snorted and came and settled between Niun and Duncan.

Hlil s'Sochil, in the front rank of the Kel, rose and unveiled; so did others. Hlil came bringing a handful of small gold objects, offered them into Niun's hands, and Niun unveiled and took them, bowed; there was an easier feeling in the company then.

J'tai. Honor medals—Merai's. Duncan listened, watched, as there came two kel'e'ein, a woman of years and another younger: to each Niun surrendered one of the *j'tai*—kinswomen of Merai, they were, proud and fierce: they touched Niun's hands, and bowed, and walked away, to settle again among their comrades.

More veils were put aside, all the Kel, eventually, yielding their faces to the sight of the Mother that had taken them.

Duncan kept his own, ashamed of his strangeness in this company, and hating his shame for it.

Kel'ein came, nine of them, old and young, to press the hand of Melein to their brows and give their names: Husbands, they proclaimed themselves, of Sochil.

"I accept you," Melein said, after all had done; and then she rose and touched Niun's arm. "This is born of a birth with me, and he is the she'pan's kel'en, and kel'anth over my Kel. Will any challenge?"

There was an inclining of heads, and no challenge.

And to Duncan's dismay, Melein took his hand, bringing him forward.

"There are no veils, Duncan," she whispered.

He dropped his, and even kel-discipline could not prevent the looks of shock.

"This is kel Duncan. Duncan-without-a-Mother. He is a friend of the People. That is my word. None will touch him."

Again heads inclined, less readily. Released, Duncan retreated into the shadows again and stood next the dusei. Challenge: if it came, Niun must answer it, would answer it. He was not competent for his own defense among them, Duncan-without-a-Mother, the man with no beginnings.

"And listen to me now," Melein said softly, settling again to her chair, the only furniture in the tent. "Listen and I will open a Dark to the understanding of my companions; tell me where you remember. These are the things that I know:

"That from this world came mri and elee and surai and kalath, and in the passing of years, the elee took the surai and kalath, and the mri lived in the shadow of the elee . . .

"That since An-ehon has stood, mri and elee knew the same cities, and shared . . .

"That the elee built and the mri defended.

"That as the sun faded and wealth declined, the ships went out. They were slow, those ships, but with them the mri took worlds. There was wealth . . .

"And war. *Zahen'ein* wars. Strangers' wars."

"This is so," said the Sen, and the Kel and the kath'anth murmured in astonishment.

"We would have made the folk of Kutath masters. The elee rejected us. Some mri rejected us. We continued the war. Whether we won or not, I do not know. Some of us stayed and some of us parted this world. Slow ships, and ages. Sometimes we fought. We took service with strangers eighty and more times. What we have seen in our returning . . . the track of People that went out, ja-anom, is desolation.

"We came home. We thought that we were the last, and we are not. Eighty-three Darks. Eighty-three. We are all that survive, of all the millions that went out."

"Ai," the People murmured, and eyes mirrored struggle to understand.

The eldest sen'en arose then, a man bent with age. "We have known Darks. That into which you went was one. That in which we remained was another. Tsi'mri came. We did not fall to them, and they did not come back. We had strength then, but it faded. No tsi'mri came again. And the cities died, and in the last years even the elee fought, elee against elee. It was a burden-bearer's war, and wasteful. We had a she'pan then named Gar'ai. She led us out into the mountains, where the elee could not live. Even then some of the People denied her Sight and would not come, and stayed in the elee cities, and died, fighting for bearers-of-burdens. Now the elee are fading, and we are strong. That is because we cannot be held in the hand. We are the land's wind, she'pan; we go and we come and the land is enough for us. We ask you, do not lead us back. There is no water enough for cities. The land will not bear it. We will perish if we leave it."

Melein was silent for a long moment, then swept a glance about the assembly. "From a land like this came we. We do not fold our hands and wait to die. That is not what the she'pan of my birth taught."

The words stung like a blow. Kel'ein straightened, and the sen'anth looked confused, and the kath'anth sat twisting her hands in her lap.

"Tsi'mri are following us," Melein said. "Armed."

The dusei surged to their feet. Duncan moved for them flung his arms about them both, whispering to them.

"What have you brought us?" cried the sen'anth.

"A thing that must be faced," Melein snapped, and bodies froze in the attitudes that they then occupied. "We are mri! We were attacked and challenged, and will this remnant deny that you are also mri, and that I am she'pan of this edun, and of all the People?"

"Kel'anth," breathed an old kel'en, "ask permission to ask . . . who, and when, and with what arms."

"I answer," said Niun. "The People have another chance. Another life. *Life* is coming across this desert of dead worlds. We have it in our wake, and it can be seized!"

Duncan heard, and clenched his fists the tighter on the dusei's loose skin, close to shivering in the fever-warmth of the tent. They had forgotten him. Their eyes were on Niun, on the stranger-kel'anth, on a she'pan that promised and threatened them.

Hope.

It glittered in the golden eyes of the black-robed Kel, ventured timidly into the calculating faces of the Sen. Only the old kath'en looked afraid.

"An-ehon has given me its records," Melein said. "I have poured into An-ehon and into all the cities linked with him the sum of all that the People have gathered in our wanderings. We are armed, my children. We are armed. We were the last, my kel'anth and I. No more. No more. A last time the Kel goes out, and this time we are not for hire. This time we take no pay. This time is for ourselves."

"*Ai-e!*" cried one of the Kel, a shout that stirred the others and tightened on Duncan's heart. Dus-feelings washed about him, confused, threatening for his sake, stirred for Niun's.

Kel'ein came to their feet with a deafening shout, and the sen'ein folded their arms and stood too, stern eyes gleaming with calculation; and lastly the kath'anth rose, and tears flowed on her face.

Tears for the children, Duncan thought, and something welled up in his throat too.

"Strike the tents," Melein shouted. "We will rest a time in the city, recover what we have left there, ask questions of each other. Strike the tents."

The tent began to clear, rapidly; there were shouts in the mu'ara of the ja'anom, orders conveyed.

And Niun stood watching their backs, and when Melein had walked out into the night, Duncan rose and followed with him, the dusei padding after.

Melein went apart from them, among the Sen. It was not a place for kel'ein. Duncan stood shivering in the chill wind and at last Niun drew him over to a clear space where they could watch the tents come down, where they could breathe easily.

The dusei crowded close to them, disturbed.

"Do not worry for yourself," Niun said to him suddenly.

"I do not."

"The killing," said Niun, "was bitter."

And he settled on the sand where they stood, with a mri's disregard for furniture. Duncan knelt down beside him, watched as Niun drew from his robes a folded cloth that held the *j'tai* that he had received of Merai's death, watched as Niun began to knot them to the belt that should hold them, so that their cords let them hang freely in his robes.

Complicated knots. Mri knots. Niun's slender fingers wove designs he had not yet mastered, meanings he had not yet learned, intricacies for intricacy's sake.

He tried to think only of that, to shut from his mind what he had seen in the tent, the shout that still echoed in his ears, hundreds of voices lifted, and himself the enemy.

About them appeared blue-robes, striking the tent of assembly, the oldest boys and girls taking the poles down, bearing the brunt of the work, and the women and middle-years children aiding. Only the littlest children in their mothers' arms sometimes raised a whimper in all the confusion, and the little ones that could walk finally slipped discipline and began a game of tag among their busy elders, uncomprehending what changes had turned their world upside down.

"The Face that Smiles," said Niun of them. "Ah, Duncan, it is good to see."

A cold closed about Duncan, a foreboding heavy as the she'-pan's alleged Sight . . . the children's voices in the dark as the tent came down, laughter . . .

The towers that had fallen on Kesrith . . .

"Let me go back," Duncan said suddenly. "Niun, ask the she'-pan. Now, tonight, let me go back to the ship."

The mri turned, looked at him, a piercing and wondering look. "Fear of us?"

"*For you.* For them."

"You left your markers. The she'pan has already said that it was enough. She gave you her word on the matter. If you go back, they will take you back, and we will not permit that."

"Am I a prisoner?"

Niun's eyes nictitated. "You are kel'en of this Kel, and we will not give you away. Do you wish to go back?"

For a moment Duncan could not answer. The children shouted, laughed aloud, and he winced at the sound. "I am of this Kel," he said at last. "And I could serve it best there."

"That is for the she'pan to decide, and she has already decided. If she wishes to send you, she will send."

"Better that. I am not wanted here. And I could be of use there."

"I would die a death myself if harm came to you. Stay close by me. No kel'en that has won the *seta'al* would challenge you, but the unscarred might . . . and no unscarred will trespass with me. Put such thoughts out of your mind. Your place is here, not there."

"It is not because I would run from them that I ask. It is because of what I hear. Because you have not learned of all that you have seen. Dead worlds, Niun."

"Sov-kela," said Niun, and his voice was edged, "have care."

"You are preparing to fight."

"We are mri."

The beast beside him stirred. Duncan held to it, his blood pounding in his ears. "The survival of the species."

"Yes," said Niun.

"For that, you would—do what, Niun?"

"Everything."

There was long silence.

"Will you," asked Niun, "seek to go back to them?"

"I am at the she'pan's orders," he said at last. "With my own kind, I can be damned no more than I am. Only listen to me sometimes. Is it revenge you want?"

The mri's nostrils flared, rapid breathing, and his hands moved over the dus' velvet skin, long-fingered and oddly graceful. "Species survival. To gather the People. To have our homeworld. To be mri."

He was answered. The human in him would not understand it; but kel-law did . . . to be the sum of all things the mri had ever been, and that meant to be bound by nothing.

No agreements, no conditions, no promises.

And if it pleased the mri to strike, they would strike, for mri reasons.

Peace was four words in the hal'ari. There was *ai'a,* that was self-peace, being right with one's place; and *an'edi,* that was house-peace, that rested on the she'pan; and there was *kuta'i,* that was the tranquility of nature; and there was *sa'ahan,* that was the tranquility of strength.

Treaty-peace was a mu'ara word, and the mu'ara lay in the past, with the regul, that had broken it.

Melein had killed for power, would kill, repeatedly, to unite the People.

Would take the elee, their former allies.

Would take Kutath.

We will have ships, he could hear her saying in her heart.

And they knew the way, to Arain, to human and regul space.

It was not revenge they sought, nothing so human, but peace— *sa'ahan*-peace, that could only exist in a mri universe.

No compromise.

"Come," said Niun. "They are almost done. We will be moving now."

Chapter Twenty-One

The house murmured with voices, adults' and children's. The People stared about them, curious at this place that only sen'ein had seen for so many hundreds of years . . . marveling at the lights, the powers of it—and, mri-fashion, unamazed by them. The forces were there; they were to be used. Many things were not for Kath or Kel to understand, but to use, with permission.

And the Shrine held light again: lights were lit by Melein's own hands, and the pan'en was brought and set there behind the corroded screens, to be moved when they moved, to be reverenced by the House while they stayed. There were chants spoken, the Shon'jir of the mri that had gone out from Kutath; and the An'jir of the mri that stayed on homeworld.

> *We are they that went not out:*
> *   landwalkers, sky-watchers;*
> *We are they that went not out:*
> *   world-holders, faith-keepers;*
> *We are they that went not out:*
> *   and beautiful our morning;*
> *We are they that went not out:*
> *   and beautiful our night.*

The rhythmic words haunted the air: the long night, Duncan thought, standing at Niun's side . . . a folk that had waited their end on dying Kutath.

Until Melein.

The songs sank away; the hall was still; the People went their ways.

There was kel-hall.

A long spiral up, a shadowed hall thrown into sudden light . . . the Kel spread carpets that had been the floors of their tents, still sandy: the cleaners skittered about in the outer hall, but stayed from their presence.

The Kel settled, made a circle. There was time for curiosity, then, in the privacy of the hall. Eyes wandered over Niun, over the dusei, over Duncan most of all.

"He will be welcomed," Niun said suddenly and harshly, answering unspoken thoughts.

There were frowns, but no words. Duncan swept a glance about the circle, meeting golden eyes that locked with his and did not flinch—without love, without trust, but without, he thought, outright hate. One by one he met such stares, let them look their fill; and he would have taken off the *zaidhe* too, and let them see the rest of his alienness; but to do so was demeaning, and insulting if offered in anger, a reproach to them. They could not ask it; it was the depth of insult.

A cup was passed, to Niun first, and to Duncan: water, of the blue pipe, in a brass cup. Duncan wet his lips with it, and passed it to Hlil, who was next. Hlil hesitated just the barest instant, as he might if he were expected to drink after the dusei; and then the kel'en touched his lips to it and passed it on.

One after the other drank in peace, even the kel'e'ein, the two kinswomen of Merai. There were no refusals.

Then Niun laid his longsword in Duncan's lap, and in curious and elaborate ceremony, all kel'ein likewise drew, and the *av'ein-kel,* Duncan's as well, passed from man and woman about the circle until each held his own again.

Then each spoke his name in full, one after the other. Some had names of both parents; some had only Sochil's; and Duncan, glancing down, gave his, Duncan-without-a-Mother, feeling curiously lost among these folk who knew what they were.

"The kel-ritual," said Niun when that had been done, "is still the same."

It pleased them, perhaps, to know that this was true; there was gestured agreement.

"You will teach us," said Niun, "the mu'ara of homeworld."

"Aye," said Hlil readily.

There was a long silence.

"One part of the ritual that I know," said Niun, "I do not hear."

Hlil bit his lip . . . a man of scars more than the *seta'al*, Hlil s'Sochil, rough-faced for a mri, who were slender and fine-boned. "Our Kath—our Kath is frightened of this—" Hlil stopped short of *tsi'mri*, and glanced full at Duncan.

"Do you," Niun asked in a hard voice, "wish to make a formal statement of this?"

"We are concerned," Hlil said, glancing down.

"We."

"Kel'anth," said Hlil, scarcely audible, "it is your right, and his."

"No," Duncan said softly, but Niun affected not to hear; Niun looked about him, waiting.

"The Kath will make you welcome," said one of the old kel'e'ein.

"The Kath will make you welcome," others echoed then, and last of all, Hlil.

"So," said Niun, and arose—waited for Duncan, while others stayed seated, and Duncan sought any other point but the eyes that stared at them.

The dusei would have come. Niun forbade.

And the two of them went alone from kel-hall, and down the ramp. It was late, in the last part of the night. Duncan felt cold, and dreaded the meeting to which they went: the Kath, the women and the children of the House, and—perhaps, he hoped, only ceremony, only ritual, in which he could remain silent and unnoticed.

They ascended kath-tower; the kath'anth met them at the door. Silently she led them within, where exhausted children sprawled on their mats and carpets, and some few of the older ones, male and female, sleepless in the excitement of the night, stared at them from the shadows.

They came to a door in a narrow hall: "Go in," the kath'anth said to Duncan; he did, and found it spread with carpets, and nothing more. The door closed; Niun and the kath'anth had left him there, in that dim chamber, lit with an oil lamp.

He settled then, in a corner, apprehensive at the first, and conscious finally that he was cold and sleepy, and that perhaps the kath'ein would abhor him and would not come at all. It was a bitter thought; but it was better than the trouble that he foresaw. He wished only to be let alone, and perhaps to sleep the night out, and not to be questioned after.

And the door opened.

A blue-robe stepped inside, bearing a small tray of food and drink; the door closed without her effort, and she brought the offering—knelt down to set it before him, and the cups rattled loudly on the tray. She wore no veil, not even on her mane; she was of about his years, and from what he could see of her downcast face in the lamplight, she was lovely.

Tears rolled down her cheeks, forced by a blink.

"Were you made to come?" he asked.

"No, kel'en." She lifted her face, and gentle as it was, there was stubborn pride in it. "It is my time, and I did not decline it."

He thought of it, of trying to deal with her, and the coldness stayed in him. "It would be bitter. Would it offend the Kath if we only sat and talked?"

Golden eyes wandered his face, through a sheen of tears. The membrane flashed, clearing them.

"Would it offend?" he asked again.

Pride. Mri honor. He saw the war in her eyes, suspecting offense, suspecting kindness. He had seen that wariness often enough in Niun's eyes.

"No," she agreed, smoothing her skirts; and after a moment she tilted her head and firmed her chin. "My son will call you father, all the same."

"I do not understand."

She looked puzzled, as much as he. "I mean that I shall not make it public what you wish. My son's name is Ka'aros, and he has five years. It is a courtesy, do you not understand?"

"Are we—permanent?"

She laughed outright despite herself, and her laugh was gentle and the sudden touch of her hand on his was pleasant. "Kel'en, kel'en . . . no. My son has twenty-three fathers." Her face grew sober again, and wistfully so. "I shall make you comfortable at least. Will you sleep, kel'en?"

He nodded mri-fashion, bewildered and weary and finding this offer the least burdensome. Her gentle fingers eased the *zaidhe* from him, and she stared in shock at the manner of his hair that, although he had let it grow shoulder-length, mri-fashion, was not the coarse bronze mane of her kind. She touched it, unbound by the formalities of kel-caste, tugged a lock between her fingers, discovered the shape of his ears and was amazed by that.

And from the covered wooden dish on her tray she took a fragrant damp cloth, and carefully, carefully bathed his face and hands—it was easement for the sandburns and the sunburn; and he loosed his robes at her insistence, and lay down, her knees for his pillow. She spread his robes over him and softly caressed his brow, so that he felt distant from all the world, and it was very easy to let go.

He did not wish to: treacheries occurred to him, murder—he strove to stay awake, not to show his distrust, but all the same, not to slip beyond awareness what passed.

But he did drift for a moment, and wakened in her arms, safe. He caressed her cradling arm, slowly, sleepily, until he looked into her golden eyes and remembered that he had promised not to touch her.

He took his hand away.

She bent and touched her lips to his brow, and this disturbed him.

"If I came back another night," he said, for the time was short, and there suddenly seemed a thousand things he wished to know of the Kath—of this kath'en, who was gracious to a tsi'mri, "if I came back again, could I ask for you?"

"Any kel'en may ask."

"May *I* ask?"

She understood then, and looked embarrassed, and distressed— and he understood, and forced a smile.

"I shall not ask," he said.

"It would be shameless of me to say that you might."

Then he was utterly confused, and lay staring up at her.

A soft, lilting call rang out somewhere in kath-hall.

"It is morning," she said, and began to seek to leave. She arose when he sat up, and started for the door.

"I do not know your name," he said, getting to his feet—human courtesy.

"Kel'en, it is Sa'er."

And she performed a graceful gesture of respect and left him.

He regretted, then, that he had declined . . . regretted, with a curious sense of anticipation . . . that perhaps, on some other night, things would be different.

Sa'er: it was like the word for morning. It was appropriate.

His thoughts wrenched back to Elag/Haven, to rough and careless times, and next Sa'er, the memory was ugly.

One did not, he knew in all the principles of kel-law, hurt a kath'en, either child or woman. There was in him a deep certainty that he had done in this meeting what was right to do.

And there was in him increasing belief that she would not, as she had said, breach confidence; would not make little of him with others; would not come next time with tears, but with a smile for him.

Cheerful in that thought, he settled to the carpets and put his boots on, gathered his robes about him, and his belts and weapons, that he had put aside: rising, he put them to rights; and put on the *zaidhe,* that was more essential to modesty than the robes; but the *mez* he flung across his throat and over his shoulder.

Then he went out into the hall, and flushed hot with sudden embarrassment, for there was Niun, at the same moment, and he hoped that kel reticence would prevent questions.

The mri, he thought, looked well-content.

"Was it well with you?" Niun asked.

He nodded.

"Come," said Niun. "There is a courtesy to be done."

Kath-hall looked different under day-phase lighting. The mats were cleared away, and the children scurried about madly at their coming, ran each to a kath'en, and with amazing swiftness a line formed, guiding them to the door.

First was the kath'anth, who stood alone, and took Niun's hands together and smiled at him. "Tell the Kel that we do not understand the machines in this place, but there will be dinner."

"Perhaps I could assist with the machines," Duncan suggested when the kath'anth took his hands in turn; and the kath'anth laughed, and so did Niun, and all the kath'ein that heard.

"He or I might," Niun said, covering his embarrassment with grace. "We have many skills, he and I."

"If the Kel would deign," said the kath'anth.

"Send when we are needed," said Niun.

And they passed from her to the line of kath'ein; Niun went first and gravely took the hands of a certain kath'en, bowed to her and took the hands of her little daughter and performed the same ritual.

Duncan understood then, and went to Sa'er, and did the same; and took the hand of her son as the boy offered his, wrist to wrist as men touched.

"He is kel Duncan," said Sa'er to her son, and to Duncan: "He is Ka'aros."

The child stared, wide-eyed with a child's honesty, and did not return Duncan's shy smile. Sa'er nudged the boy. "Sir," he said, and the membrane flicked across his eyes. He did not yet have the adult's mane: his was short and revealed his ears, that were tipped with a little curl of transparent down.

"Good day," said Sa'er, and smiled at him.

"Good day," he wished her; and joined Niun, who waited at the door. Silence reigned in the hall. They left, and then he heard a murmuring of voices after them, knowing that questions were being asked.

"I liked her," he confessed to Niun. And then further confession: "We did nothing."

Niun shrugged, and put on his veil. "It is important that a man have good report of the Kath. The kath'en was more than gracious in the parting. Had you offended her, she would have made that known, and that would have hurt you sorely in the House."

"I was surprised that you took me there."

"I had no choice. It is always done. I could not bring you into the Kel like a kel'e'en, without this night."

Duncan tucked in his own veil, and breathed easier to know himself well-acquitted. "Doubtless you were worried."

"You are kel'en; you have learned to think as we think. I am surprised that you chose a resting-night. It was wise. And," he added, "if you send the kath'en the *ka'islai,* and she does not return them, then you must go and fetch them."

"Is that how it is done?"

Niun laughed, a soft breath. "So I have heard. I myself am naïve in such matters."

They came to main hall, and Duncan went behind Niun as he paid his morning respects at the shrine; he stood silently there, thinking strangely of a place in his childhood, sensing in another part of his thoughts a dus that was fretting and impatient, confined in kel-hall.

And of a sudden came the machine-voice, An-ehon, deep and thundering through all the halls, through stone and flesh:

Alarm . . . alarm . . . ALARM.

He froze, dazed, as Niun thrust past him. "Stay here!" Niun shouted at him, and rushed for sen-hall access, where a kel'en had no business to be. Duncan stopped in mid-step—cast about left and right, saw other kel'ein rushing down from kel-tower; and there were kath'ein; and Melein herself, descending from the tower of the she'pan, seeking sen-access at a near-run amid the frightened questions that were thrown at her.

"Let me come!" Duncan cried at her, overtaking her, and she did not forbid him. He followed her up, up into sen-hall, where alarmed sen'ein boiled about like disturbed insects, gold about Niun's black, who stood before An-ehon's flickering lights—who questioned it, and obtained screens lighted with pictures the rudest kel'en could understand: the desert, and a dying glow in a rising cloud on the far horizon.

The ship.

Melein thrust her way through the sen'ein, that crowded from her path, and the while she laid hands on the panels her eyes were for the screens. Duncan tried to follow her, but the sen'ein caught at him, thrust out their hands in his path, forbidding.

"Strike was made from orbit," An-ehon droned, the while the mad alarm dinned from another channel.

"Strike back," Melein ordered.

"*No!*" Duncan shouted at her. But An-ehon's flicker-swift reaction showed a line of retaliation plotted, intersecting orbit.

Lines flashed rapidly, perspectives shifting.

"Unsuccessful," An-ehon droned.

And the panels all flared, and the air filled with sound that began too deep to hear and finished like thunder. The floor, the very foundations shook.

"Attack has been returned," said An-ehon. "Shields have held."

"Stop it," Duncan shouted, pushed sen'ein brutally aside and broke through to Melein, stopped when Niun himself thrust a hand in his way. "Listen to me. That will be a class-one warship up there. You cannot beat it from earthside. We have no ship now, no way out—do not answer fire. They can make a cinder of this world. Let me call them, let me contact them, she'pan."

Melein's eyes were terrible as they met his: suspicion, anger . . . in that moment he was alien, and close to the edge of her rage.

The thunder came again. The mri held their sensitive ears, and Melein shouted another order for attack.

"Target is passing out of range," An-ehon said when the noise had faded. "Soon coming up over Zohain. Zohain will attack."

"You cannot fight it," Duncan shouted at them, and seized Niun's arm, received from the mri a look that matched Melein's. "Niun, make her see. Your shielding will not go on holding. Let me call them."

"You see what good your signal from the ship did," said Niun. "That is their answer to your signal of friendship. That is their word on it."

"Zohain has fallen," said An-ehon. "Shields did not hold. I am receiving alarm from Le'a'haen . . . There is another attack approaching this zone. Alarm . . . alarm . . . ALARM . . . ALARM . . ."

"Get your people out!" Duncan shouted at them.

Terror was written in the eyes of Melein and Niun, nightmare repeated: the floor shook. There was a rumbling crash outside the edun.

"Go!" Melein cried. "The hills, seek the hills!"

But she did not, nor Niun, while the Sen broke for the door, for outside, abandoning possessions, everything. Even over the sounds of An-ehon cries could be heard elsewhere in the edun.

"Get out, get out—both of you," Duncan pleaded. "Wait for a break in the attack and get out of here. Let me try with the machine."

Melein turned to Niun, ignoring him. "Kel'anth, lead your people." And before Niun could move, she looked up at the banks that were An-ehon. "Continue to fight. Destroy the invaders."

"This city is holding," droned the machine. "Outer structures may be drained of shielding to protect the edun complex. When this city falls, there are others. We are coordinating defenses. We are under multiple attack. We advise immediate evacuation. We advise the she'pan to secure her person. Preservation of her person is of overriding importance."

"I am leaving," Melein said; and to Duncan, for Niun had gone: "Come. Haste."

He thrust past her, to the console. "An-ehon," he said, "give me communication—"

"Do not permit it!" Melein shouted, and the machine struck, a force that lit the air and hurled him numb and cold against the floor.

He saw her robes pass him, and she was running, running, down the center of sen-hall, with the floor shuddering under renewed attack . . . it shook beneath him, and he tried repeatedly to gather his numbed limbs under him.

The floor bucked.

"Alarm . . . ALARM . . . ALARMLLL . . ." cried An-ehon.

He rolled his head, dragged a shoulder over, saw areas of the banks going dark.

And the floor shook again, and the lights began dimming.

There was a time of quiet.

He found it possible finally to move his legs, arms, to drag himself up, and he staggered through littered sen-hall into the winding corridor down to main hall. A great shadow met him there, his dus, that almost threw him off his feet in the pressure of its body: he used it then, leaning on it, and staggered past the litter that confused the hall, and out into the light, the open city—there began to see the dead, old sen'ein, children of the Kath—a kel'en, crushed by a toppling wall.

He found Sa'er, a huddled shape in blue at the bottom of the ramp, a golden hand clenched about a stone, a face open-eyed and dusty with the sand of Kutath.

"Ka'aros!" he called with all the strength in him, remembering her son, and there was no answer.

The People's trail was marked with dead, the old, the fragile, the young: all that was gentle, he thought, everything.

He heard a sound of thunder, looked up and saw a flash, a mote of light. Something operating in-atmosphere. He expected, even while he ran with all the speed that was in him, the white flash that would kill him, as he left the protective zone.

But it went over the horizon. The sound died.

Beyond the city, beyond the pitiful ruin, there stretched a line of figures, alive and moving. He made haste to follow, desperate, exhausted. The dus moved with him, blood-feelings stirred in it, that caught up his rage and fear and cast it back amplified.

He overtook the last of the column finally, his throat dry, his lungs wracked with coughing. Blood poured from his nose and tasted salt-coppery in his mouth.

"The kel'anth?" he asked. A narrow-eyed kel'e'en pointed toward the head of the column. "The she'pan?" he asked again. "Is she well?"

"Yes," one said, as if to answer him at all were contamination.

He kept moving at more than their pace, seeing the column's head, passed kel'ein that carried kath-children, and kath'ein that carried infants, and kel'ein that supported old ones of any caste, though few enough of the old were left them.

They went toward the mountains, that promised concealment, as they were pitifully exposed on this bare, naked sand. He saw the line extended over the roll of the land, and it seemed yet impossibly far, beyond his strength at the pace he tried. He paused, cut a bit of pipe that was left as a stub from someone else's cutting, a prize that was seen by others too, and he offered them of his, but none would deign to touch it. Leaving the rest to them, he sucked the water from a sliver and managed simply to keep his feet under him and to stay with the middle of the column—outside it, for he felt their hatred, the looks that the Sen cast him.

He had betrayed himself before the Sen; they knew, they had seen the nature of him, and whence he was they guessed . . . if not what. They could not know the reason that they were attacked, but that they were mri, and that the tsi'mri invaded, and they were dying at such hands as his.

No attack came on them. He was not amazed by it, for there was little inclination for a large orbiting craft to waste its energies on so small a target as they made. But the city came under periodic fire. They could look back and see it, the shields flaring rainbow colors under the rainless sun, and the whole of the city settling into increasing ruin. The city that had stood dreamlike against the setting sun itself glowed and died like embers, and the towers were down, and ugliness settled over it.

"A-ei," mourned an old kath'en. "A-ei."

And the children wept fretfully, and were hushed.

The Sen shook their heads, and there were tears on the faces of the old ones.

From the Kel there were no tears, only looks that burned, that raged. Duncan turned his face from them, and kept moving at such times as the column rested, until at last he had sight of Melein's white robes, and he knew the tall kel'en by her, with the dus.

They were well; that was enough to know, to take from him some of the anguish. He kept them in sight for the rest of that day, and when they at last paused at evenfall, he came to them.

Niun knew his presence. The dus went first, and Niun turned, looking for his approach.

Duncan settled quietly near them.

"You are all right?" Niun asked him.

He nodded.

Melein turned her face from him. "Doubtless," she said finally, "your wish was good, Duncan; I believe that. But it was useless."

"She'pan," he murmured with a gesture of reverence, grateful even for that; he forbore to argue with her: among so many dead, argument had no place.

Niun offered him a bit of pipe. He showed his, and declined, and with his *av-tlen,* cut off a bit of it that was sickly sweet in his mouth. There was a knot at his stomach that would not go away.

A cry went up from the Kel. Hands pointed. What looked like a shooting star went over, and descended toward the horizon.

"Landing," Duncan murmured, "near where the ship was. There will be a search now."

"Let them come into the mountains looking," said Niun.

Duncan put a hand to his stomach, and coughed, and wiped his eyes of the pain-tears. He found himself shaking.

He also knew what had to be done.

He rested. In time he made excuse, a modest sort of shrug that denoted a man on private business, and rose and moved away from the column; the dus followed him. He was afraid. He tried to keep that feeling down, for the dus could transmit that. He saw the desert before him, and felt the weakness of his own limbs, and the terror came close to overwhelming him, but he had no other options.

The dus suddenly sent a ward-impulse, turned.

He looked back, saw the other dus.

There was a black shadow a distance to the side of it. Duncan froze, remembering that Niun, like him, had a gun.

Niun walked across the sand toward him, a black shape in the dark. The wind fluttered at his robes, the moon winked on the brass of the *yin'ein* and the plastic of the visor, and on the *j'tai* that he had gained. The great dus walked at his side, turn-toed, head down.

"Yai," Duncan cautioned his, made it sit beside him.

Niun stopped at talking distance, set hand in belt, a warning. "You have strayed the column widely, sov-kela."

Duncan nodded over his shoulder, toward the horizon. "Let me go."

"To rejoin them?"

"I still serve the she'pan."

Niun looked at him long and closely, and finally dropped his veil. Duncan did the same, wiped at the blood that began to dry on his lips.

"What will you do?" Niun asked.

"Make them listen."

Niun made a gesture that spoke of hopelessness. "It has already failed. You throw yourself away."

"Take the People to safety. Let me try this. Trust me in this, Niun."

"We will not surrender."

"I know that. I will tell them so."

Niun looked down. His slender fingers worked at one of the several belts. He freed one of the *j'tai,* came toward Duncan, stood and patiently knotted the thong in a complicated knot.

Duncan looked at it when he had done, found a strange and delicate leaf, one of the three *j'tai* that Niun had had from Kesrith.

"It was given me by one of my masters, a man named Palazi, who had it from a world named Guragen. Trees grew there. For luck, he said. Good-bye, Duncan."

He gave his hand.

Duncan gave his. "Good-bye, Niun."

And the mri turned from him, and walked away, the one dus following.

Duncan watched him meet the shadow, and vanish, and himself turned and started on the course that he had plotted, the sand and rocks distorted in his vision for a time. He resumed the veil, grateful for the warmth of the beast that walked beside him.

Chapter Twenty-Two

Beast mind, beast sense. It protected. Duncan inhaled the cold air carefully and staggered as he came down the gentle rise—an ankle almost twisted: death in the flats. He took his warning from that and rested, leaned against the dus as he settled to the cold sands and let the fatigue flow from his joints. A little of the blue-green pipe remained in his belt-pouch. He drew his *av-tlen* and cut a bit of it, chewed at it and felt its healing sweetness ease his throat.

It was madness to have tried it, he had to realize in the burning days, madness to have imagined that he could make the wreckage in time, that they would have stayed where there was no life.

But there was no choice. He was nothing among the People, but a problem that Niun did not need, an issue over which he might have to kill; a problem to Melein, who must explain him.

He served the she'pan.

There was no question of this in him now: if he walked and found nothing, still it only proved that his own efforts were worth nothing, as those of An-ehon had been nothing, and the burden passed: the she'pan had other kel'ein.

He gathered himself and began to walk again, staggered as the dus suddenly lurched against him with a snarl. He blinked in dull amazement as a cloud of sand puffed up from the side of a rock and something ran beneath the sand, not like a burrower's fluttering broad mantle, but something lithe and narrow that—like the burrower—dug a small pit, a funnel of sand.

"Yai," he called hoarsely, restraining the dus, that would have gone for it and dug it into the light with its long venomed claws. Whatever was there, he did not know the size of it, or its dangers.

He caught the hunt-sense from the dus, put it down with his own will, and they skirted the area, climbed up the near ridge. When he looked down, he saw all the area dotted with such small pits. There was regularity about them, like points on concentric circles. They formed a configuration wide enough to embrace a dus.

"Come," he wished the beast, and they moved, the dus giving small, dissatisfied whuffs, still desiring to go back.

But of other presence there had been no sign. There was the cold and the wind and the streaming light of Na'i'in; there was the track of their own passing swiftly obliterated by the wind, and once, only once, a tall black figure on a dunecrest.

One of the kel'ein, an outrunner of the People, another band, perhaps, insolently letting himself be seen. Duncan had felt exposed at that, felt his lack of skill with the *yin'ein* . . . the unknown under the sand did not frighten him half so much as the thought of encounter with others.

—Of encountering a she'pan other than Melein. It was, he thought, a mri sort of fear—a hesitance to break out of that familiarity which was Melein's law. With that fear, with mri canniness, he kept to the low places, the sides, the concealments available in the land, and his eyes, dimmed by his lowered visor, carefully scanned the naked horizons when he must again venture across the flat.

The great rift of the lost sea came into view at noontime. He looked away into that hazy depth where sand ribboned off into the chasm in wind-driven falls, and lost his sense of height and depth in such dimensions. But scanning the horizon, he knew where he was, that was not far from the place he sought.

He kept moving, and by now the lack of solid food had his stomach knotting. The ache in his side was a constant presence, and that in his chest beat in time with the ebb and flow of his life.

Dus.

He felt it, and looked up as if someone had called his name. *Niun?* he wondered, looking about him, and yet did not believe it. Niun was with the People; he would not have deserted Melein, or those in his charge. There were the Kath and the Sen, that could not make such a trek as he had made, kel'en and unencumbered.

Yet the dus-feeling was there.

Left. Right. He scanned those horizons, stroked the velvet rolls of flesh on the neck of his own beast, sent question to its mind. Ward-impulse went out from it.

No illusion, then.

With his nape hairs prickling he kept moving, constantly aware of that weight against his senses.

Brother-presence.

Dus-brother.

The dus beside him began to sing a song of contentment, of harmony, that stole the pain and stole his senses, until he realized that he had walked far and no longer knew the way he walked.

No, he projected at it, *no, no, no.* He thought of the ship, thought of it again and again, and desired, urged toward it.

Affirmation.

And threat.

Darkness came then, sudden and soft and deep, and full of menace, claws that tore and fangs that bit and over it all a presence that would not let him go. He came to awareness again still walking, shivering periodically in the dry, cold wind. His hands and arms were sandburned and bloody, so that he knew that he had fallen hard at some time and not known.

Ship, he thought at the beast.

Hostile senses surrounded him. He cried out at the dark and it thrust itself across his path, stopping him. He stood shuddering as it rubbed round his legs, vast, heavy creature that circled him and wove a pattern of steps.

Others came, two, five, six dusei, a third the size of the one that wove him protection. He shuddered in horror as they came near and surrounded him, as one after another they reared up man-tall and came down again, making the sand fly in clouds.

There was a storm-feeling in the air, a sense charged and heavy with menace.

Storm-friends, the mri called them, the great brothers of the cold wind.

And none such had been known on arid Kutath, no such monsters had this world known.

They have come here of their own purpose, Duncan thought suddenly, cold, and frightened. He remembered them entering the ship, remembered them, whose hearts he had never reached, living with them on the long voyage.

A refuge from humans, from regul. They had fled their world. They chose a new one, the escape that had lain open for them, that he had provided.

Closer they came, and his dus radiated darkness. Bodies touched, and a numbing pulse filled the air, rumbling like a wind-sound or like earthquake. They circled, all circled, touching. Duncan flung himself to his knees and put his arms about the neck of his beast, stopping it, feeling the nose of a stranger-dus at the nape of his neck, smelling the hot breath of the beast, heat that wrapped and stifled him.

Ship, he remembered to think at them, and cast the disaster of An-ehon with his mind, the towers of Kesrith falling. Pleasure came back, appalling him.

No! he cried, silently and aloud. They fled back from him.

He cast them images of waterless waste, of a sun dying, of dusei wasting in desolation.

Their anger flooded at him, and his own beast shuddered, and drew back. It fled, and he could not hold it.

He was alone, desolate and blind. Suddenly he did not know direction or world-sense. His senses were clear, ice-clear, and yet he was cut off and without that inner direction that he had known so long.

"Come back," he cried at the dus that lingered.

He cast it edun-pictures, of water flowing, of Kesrith's storms, and ships coming and going. Whether it received on this level he did not know. He cast it desire, desperate desire, and the image of the ship.

There was a touch, tentative, not the warding impulse.

"Come," he called it aloud, held out his hands to it. He cast it fellowship, mri-wise—together, man and dus.

Life, he cast it.

There was hesitance. The warding impulse lashed fear across his senses, and he would not accept it. *Life,* he insisted.

It came. All about him he felt warding impulse, strong and full of terrors, such that the sweat broke out on him and dried at once in the wind. But his dus was there. It began to walk with him, warding with all its might.

Traitor to its kind. Traitor human and traitor dus. He had corrupted it, and it served him, went with him, began to be as he was.

Fear cast darkness about them and the afternoon sun seemed dimmer for a time; and then the others were gone, and there appeared finally black dots along a distant ridge, watching.

Children of Kutath, these dusei, flesh of the flesh that had come from Kesrith, and partaking not at all of it.

Only the old one remembered—not events, but person, remembered him, and stayed.

By late afternoon the wind began rising, little gusts at first that skirled the sand off the dune crests and swept out in great streamers over the dead sea chasm. Then came the flurries of sand that rode on battering force, that made walking difficult, that rattled off the protective visor and made Duncan again wrap the *mez* doubled about his face. The dus itself walked half-blind, teartrails running down its face. It moaned plaintively, and in sudden temper reared up, shook itself, blew dust and settled again to walk against the wind.

The others appeared from time to time, walking the ridges, keeping their pace. They appeared as dark shadows in the curtain of sand that rode the wind, materialized as now a head and now less, or a retreating flank. What they sent was still hostile, and full of blood.

Duncan's beast growled and shook its head, and they kept moving, though it seemed by now his limbs were hung with lead and his muscles laced with fire. He coughed, and blood came, and he became conscious of the weight of the weapons that he bore, weapons that were useless where he was bound, and more useless still were he dead, but he would not give them up. He clenched in one hand the sole *j'tal* he wore, and remembered the man that had given it, and would not be less.

Su-she'pani kel'en. The she'pan's kel'en.

Pain lanced up his leg. He fell, cast down by the treacherous turn of stone, carefully gathered himself up again and leaned on the dus. The leg was not injured. He tried to suck at the wound the stone had made on his hand, but his mouth was dry and he could not. There was no pipe hereabouts. He hoarded what moisture he had and chose not to use the little supply that remained to him, not yet.

And one of the lesser dusei came close to him, reared up so that his own interposed its body. There was a whuffing of great lungs, and the lesser backed off.

Ship, he thought suddenly, and for no reason.

Desire.

There was no warding impulse from the stranger. He felt only direction, sensed presence.

He called to his dus, softly, from a throat that had almost forgotten sound, and went, felt a presence at his left side, a warm breathing on the hand that hung beside him.

Doubly attended now he went. Another was with them, thought of destination, desired what they desired.

Men.

Shapes wandered his subconscious. Memory, no. Some elsewhere saw, cast vision, guided him. He knew this.

Shapes obscured in sand, a half-dome. Jaws closed on his hand, gently, gently . . . he realized that he was down, and that the dus urged him. He gathered himself up again and started moving, staggered as his boot hit something buried and something whipped at the leather, but it did not penetrate, and whipped sinuously away in the amber murk. Dus-feelings raged at it, and ignored it thereafter, preferring his company.

Night was on them, storm-night and world-night, friendly to them, hiding them. He knew the ship near, stumbled on pieces of it, bits of wreckage, bits of heat-fused sand, before its alien hulk took shape in the ribbons of sand, and he saw the havoc that had been made there.

And a half-dome, squat half-ovoid on stilts, the red wink of lights beaconing through the murk.

Dusei ringed him, all of them; fear-desire-fear, they sent.

"Yai!" he cried at them, voice lost in the wind. But his stayed, plodded its turn-toed way beside him as he walked toward that place, that alien shape on Kutath's dead seashore.

He knew it as he came near, vast and blind as it was, knew the patterning of its lights—

And for an instant he did not know how to name it.

Flower.

The word for it came back, shifting from reality to reality.

"*Flower,*" he hailed it, a cracked and unrecognizable voice in the living wind. "*Flower*—open your hatch."

But nothing responded. He gathered up a fist-sized stone and threw it against the hull, and another, and nothing answered. The storm grew, and he knew that he had soon to seek shelter.

And then he saw the sweep of a scanner eye, and light followed it, fixing him and the dus together in its beam. The beast shied and protested. He flung his arm up to shield his visored eyes, and stood still, mind flung back to another night when he had stood with this dus in the lights, before guns.

There was long silence.

"*Flower!*" he cried.

The lights stayed fixed. He stood swaying in the gusts of wind, and held one hand firm against the dus' back so that the beast would stand.

Suddenly the hatch parted and the ramp shot down, invitation.

He walked toward it, set foot on the ringing metal, and the dus stayed beside him. He lifted his hands, lest they mistake, and moved slowly.

"Boz," he said.

It was strange to see her, the gray suddenly more pronounced in her hair, reminding him of time that had passed. He was conscious of the guns that surrounded him, of men that held rifles trained on him and on the dus. He took off the *mez* and *zaidhe,* so that they might know him. He smoothed his hair, that he had let grow; there was the stubble of beard on his face, that no mri would have. He felt naked before them, before Boaz and Luiz. He looked at their faces, saw dismay mirrored in their eyes.

"We've contacted *Saber,*" Luiz said. "They want to see you."

He saw the hardness in their looks: he had run, taken the enemy side; this, not even Boaz was prepared to understand.

And they had seen the mri track, the desert of stars.

"I will go," he said.

"Put off the weapons," said Luiz, "and put the dus outside."

"No," he said quietly. "You would have to take those, and the beast stays with me."

It was clear that there were men prepared to move on him. He stood quietly, felt the dus' ward impulse, and the fear that was thick in the room.

"There are arguments you could make in your defense," Boaz said. "None of them are worth anything if you make trouble now. Sten, what side are you playing?"

He thought a moment. Human language came with difficulty, a strange, déjà-vu reference in which he knew how to function, but distantly, distantly. There were ideas that refused clear shaping. "I won't draw my weapons unless I'm touched," he said. "Let *Saber* decide. Take me there. *Peace.*" He found the word he had lost for a time. "It's peace I bring if they'll have it."

"We'll consult," said Luiz.

"We can lift and consult later. Time is short."

Boaz nodded slowly. Luiz looked at her and agreed. Orders were passed with gestures, and a man left.

"Where are the others?" Luiz asked.

Duncan did not answer. Slowly, carefully, lest they misinterpret any move, he began to resume the *zaidhe,* which made him more comfortable. And while Luiz and Boaz consulted together, he put back the veil, and adjusted it to the formal position. The dus stood beside him, and the men with guns remained in their places.

But elsewhere in the ship came the sound of machinery at work—preparation for lift, he thought, and panic assailed him. He was a prisoner; they had him back, and doors had closed that he could not pass.

Warning lights began to flash in the overhead. He looked about apprehensively as another three regulars came into the compartment, rifles leveled at him, and Luiz left.

"Sit down," Boaz advised him. "Sit down over there and steady that beast for lift. Will it stay put?"

"Yes." He retreated to the cushioned bench and settled there, leaned forward to keep his hand on the dus that sat at his feet.

Boaz delayed, looking down at him: blonde, plump Boaz, who had grown thinner and grayer, whose face had acquired frown lines—wondering now, he thought, and not understanding.

"You speak with an accent," she said.

He shrugged. Perhaps it was true.

The warning siren sounded. They were approaching lift. Boaz went to the opposite side of the room, to the bench there; the regulars with their guns clustered there, weapons carefully across laps. The dus lay down at Duncan's feet, as the stress began, flattening itself to bear it.

The lift was hard, reckless. Duncan felt sweat breaking from him and his head spinning as they lofted. The dus sent fear . . . afraid, Duncan thought, of these men with guns. The fear turned his hands cold, and yet the heat of the compartment was stifling.

It was long before they broke from the force of lift, before new orientation took over and it was possible to move again. Duncan sat still, not willing to provoke them by attempting to rise. He desired nothing of them. Boaz sat still and stared at him.

"Stavros did this to you," she said finally, with a look of pity.

Again he shrugged, and kept his eyes unfixed and elsewhere, lost in waiting.

"Sten," she said.

He looked at her, distressed, knowing that she wanted response of him, and it was not there. "He is dead," he said finally, to make her understand.

There was pain in her eyes: comprehension, perhaps.

"I feel no bitterness," he said, "Boz."

She bit at her lips and sat white-faced, staring at him.

Luiz called; there was an exchange not audible to him, and the regulars stood by with lowered guns, kept them constantly trained on him. He sat and stroked the dus and soothed it.

The guards sweated visibly. To confront a disturbed dus took something from a man. They were steady. There was no panic. Boaz sat and mopped at her face.

"We're some little time from rendezvous," she said. "Do you want some water or something to eat?"

It was the first offering of such. A slight hesitation still occurred to him, consciousness that there was obligation involved, had they been mri.

Here too, obligation.

"If it is set before me," he said, "free, I will take it."

It was. Boaz ordered, and a guard set a paper cup of water within reach on the bench, and a sandwich wrapped in plastics.

He took the water, held it under the *mez* to sip at it slowly. It was ice-cold and strange after days on the desert water: antiseptic.

Likewise he tore off bits of the sandwich with his fingers and ate, without removing his veil. He would not give his face for their curiosity. He had no strength to sit and trade hate with them, and the veil saved questions. His hands shook, all the same. He tried to prevent it, but it was weakness: he had been too long without more than the pipe for nourishment. His stomach rebelled at more than a few bites. He wrapped the remainder in the plastic again and tucked it into his belt-pouch, saving it against need.

And he folded his hands and waited. He was tired, inexpressibly tired. In the long monotony of approach he wished to sleep, and did so, eyes shut, hands folded, knowing that the dus watched balefully those others that occupied the compartment, watching him.

Boaz came and went. Luiz came and offered—a sincere offer, Duncan reckoned—to give him treatment for the cough that sometimes wracked him.

"No," he said softly. "Thank you, no."

The answer silenced Luiz, as he had silenced Boaz. He was relieved to be let alone, and breathed quietly. He stared at the man in command of the regulars—knew that one's mind without the help of the dus, the cool mistrust, the almost-hate that would let the human kill. Dead eyes, unlike the liveliness of the mri among brothers: Havener, who had seen evils in plenty. There was a burn scar on one cheek, that the man had not had repaired. A line man, by that, no rear-lines officer. He had respect for this one.

And the man, perhaps, estimated him. Eyes locked, clashed. *Renegade,* that was the thought that went visibly through the man's gaze; it wondered, but it did not forgive. Such a man Duncan well understood.

This man he would kill first if they laid hands on him. The dus would care for the others.

Let them not touch me, he thought then, over and over, for he remembered why he had come, and what was hazarded on his life; but still outwardly he kept that quiet that he had maintained, hands folded, eyes unfocused, sometimes closed. There was need for the moment only of rest.

At last came maneuvering for dock, and the gentle collision. Neither Boaz nor Luiz had been there for some time . . . consulting, doubtless, with higher authority.

And Luiz nodded toward the door.

"You will have to leave your weapons," Luiz said. "That is the simplest way; otherwise they'll force it, and we'd rather not have that."

Duncan rose, weighed the situation, finally loosed the belt of the *yin'ein* and the lesser one of the *zahen'ein,* turned and laid them on the bench he had quitted.

"Boz," he said, "you bring them for me. I will be needing them."

She moved to gather them up, did so carefully.

"And the dus stays," Luiz said.

"That is wise," he said; he had not wanted the beast thrown into the stress of things to come. "It will stay here. Have you made all your conditions?"

Luiz nodded, and the guards took positions to escort him out. He felt strangely light without his weapons. He paused, looked at the dus, spoke to it, and it moaned and settled unhappily, head on paws. He looked back at Boaz. "I would not let anyone try to touch him if I were you," He said.

And he went with the guard.

Saber's polished metal corridors rang with the sound of doors sealing and unsealing. Duncan waited as another detachment of regulars arranged itself to take charge of him.

And little as he had given notice to these professionals, he gave it to the freckled man that commanded the group from *Saber.*

"Galey," he said.

The regular looked at him, tried to stiffen his back, turned it into a shrug. "I got this because I knew you. Sir, come along. The admiral will see you. Let's keep this quiet, all right?"

"I came here to see him," Duncan said. Galey looked relieved.

"You all right? You walked in, they said. You're coming in of your own accord?"

Duncan nodded, mri-wise. "Yes," he amended. "Of my choice."

"I have to search you."

Duncan considered it, considered Galey, who had no choice, and nodded consent, stood with his arms wide while Galey performed the cursory search himself. When Galey was done, he rearranged his robes and stood still.

"I've got a uniform might fit," Galey said.

"No."

Galey looked taken aback at that. He nodded at the others. They started to move, and Duncan went beside Galey, but there were rifles before and rifles at his back.

A taint was in the air, an old and familiar smell, dank and musky. *Humanity,* Duncan thought; but there was an edge of it he had not noticed on the other ship.

Regul.

Duncan stopped. A rifle prodded his back. He drew a full breath of the tainted air and started walking again, keeping with Galey.

The office door was open; he turned where he knew he must, and Galey went with him into the office, into the admiral's presence.

Koch occupied the desk chair.

And beside him was a regul, sled-bound. Duncan looked into that bony countenance with his heart slamming against his ribs: the feeling was reciprocated. The regul's nostrils snapped shut.

"Ally, sir?" Duncan asked of Koch, before he had been invited to speak, before anyone had spoken.

"Sharn Alagn-ni." The admiral's eyes were dark and narrow as the regul's. His white, close-shaven head was balder than it had been, his face thinner and harder. "Sit down, SurTac."

Duncan sat, on the chair at the corner of the desk, leaned back and stared from Koch to the regul. "Am I going to have to give my report in front of a stranger?"

"An ally. This is a joint command."

Pieces sorted into order. "An ally," Duncan said, looking full at Sharn, "who tried to kill us and who destroyed my ship."

The regul hissed. "Bai Koch, this is a mri. This is nothing of yours. It speaks for its own purposes, this youngling-without-a-nest. We have seen the way these mri have passed, the places without life. We have seen their work. This impressionable youngling has been impressed by them, and it is theirs."

"I left beacons," Duncan said, looking at Koch, "to explain. Did you read them? Did anyone listen to my messages before you started firing—or did someone get to them first?"

Koch's eyes flickered, no more than that. Darker color came to Sharn's rough skin.

"I told you in those messages that the mri were inclined to friendship. That we reached agreement."

Sharn hissed suddenly: the color fled. "Treachery."

"In both our houses," Duncan said. "Bai Sharn, I was sent to approach the mri—as you were surely sent to stop me. We may be the only ones in this room who really understand each other."

"You are doing yourself no good," said Koch.

Duncan shrugged. "Am I right about the beacons? Was it Sharn who chose to move against the cities?"

"We were fired on," Koch said.

"From my ship? Was it not the regul that came in first?"

Koch was silent.

"You have done murder," Duncan said. "The mri would have chosen to talk; but you let the regul come in ahead of you. Defenses have been triggered. The mri no longer have control of them. You are fighting against machines. And when you stop, they will stop. If you go on, you will wipe out a planet."

"That might be the safest course."

Duncan retreated to a distant cold place within himself, continued to stare at the admiral. "*Flower* witnesses what you do. What you do here will be told; and it will change humankind. Perhaps you don't understand that, but it will change you if you do this. You will put the finishing touch on the desert of stars that you have traveled. You will be the monsters."

"Nonsense."

"You know what I mean. *Flower* is your conscience. Stavros—whoever sent them—did right. There will be witnesses. The lieutenant here—others in your crew—they will be witnesses. You are warring against a dying people, killing an ancient, ancient world." His eyes wandered to Sharn, who sat with nose-slits completely closed. "And you likewise. Bai Sharn, do you think that you want humanity without the mri? Think on checks and balances. Look at your present allies. Either without the other is dangerous to regul. Do not think that humankind loves you. Look at me, bai Sharn."

The bai's nostrils fluttered rapidly. "Kill this youngling. Be rid of it and its counsels, bai Koch. It is poisonous."

Duncan looked back to Koch, to the cold and level stare that refused to be ruffled by him or by Sharn, and of a sudden, thinking of humans again, he knew this one too: Havener, full of hate. A mri could not hold such opinions as ran in Koch: a mri had allegiance to a she'pan, and a she'pan considered for the ages.

"You want to kill them," he said to Koch. "And you are thinking perhaps that you will hold me here as a source of information. I will tell you what I know. But I would prefer to tell you without the presence of the bai."

He had set Koch at disadvantage. Koch had to dismiss Sharn or keep her, and either was a decision.

"Do your explaining to the security chief," Koch said. "The report will reach me."

"I will say nothing to them," Duncan said.

Koch sat and stared at him, and perhaps believed him. Red flooded his face and stayed there; a vein beat at his temple. "What is it you have to say, then?"

"First, that when I am done, I am leaving. I have left the Service. I am second to the kel'anth of the mri. If you hold me, that is your choice, but I am no longer under orders of Stavros or of your service."

"You are a deserter."

Duncan released a gentle breath. "I was set aboard a mri ship to learn them. I was thrown away. The she'pan gathered me up again."

Koch was silent a long time. Finally he opened his desk, drew out a sheet of paper, slid it across the desk. Duncan reached for it, finding the blockish print strange to his eyes.

Code numbers. One was his. *Credentials, special liaison Sten X Duncan; detached from Service 9/4/21 mission code Prober. Authorization code Phoenix, limitations encoded file SS-DS-34. By my authority, this date, George T. Stavros, governor, Kesrith Zone.*

Duncan looked up.

"Your authorizations," said Koch, "are for mediation—at my discretion. Your defection was anticipated."

Duncan folded the paper, carefully, put it into his belt, and all the while rage was building in him. He smothered the impulses. *If I can make you angry,* Niun had said once, *I have passed your guard again. I have given you something to think about besides the Game.*

He looked at Sharn, whose nostrils trembled, whose bony lips were clamped shut.

"If there is no further firing," said Koch, "we will cease fire."

"That relieves my mind," Duncan said from that same cold distance.

"And we will land, and establish that things are permanently settled."

"I will arrange cease-fire. Set me on-world again."

"Do not," said Sharn. "The bai will take a harsh view of any accommodation with these creatures."

"Do you," Duncan asked cynically, "fear a mri's memory?"

Sharn's nostrils snapped shut and color came and went in her skin. Her fingers moved on her console, rapidly, and still she stared at them both.

"Mri can adapt to non-mri," Duncan said. "I am living proof that it is possible."

Koch's dark eyes wandered over him. "Drop the veil, SurTac."

Duncan did so, stared at the man naked-faced.

"You do not find it easy," Koch said.

"I have not passed far enough that you can't deal with me. I am what Stavros, perhaps, intended. I am useful to you. I can get a she'pan of the People to talk, and that is more than you could win by any other means."

"You can spare a day. Firing has stopped, while we maintain distance. You will debrief."

"Yes. I will talk to Boaz."

"She is not qualified."

"More than your security people, she is qualified. Her work makes her qualified. I will talk to her. She can understand what I say. They wouldn't. They would try to interpret."

"One of the security personnel will be there. He will suggest questions."

"I will answer what I think proper. I will not help you locate the mri."

"You know, then, where their headquarters are."

Duncan smiled. "Rock and sand, dune and flats. That is where you will have to find them. Nothing else will you get from me."

"We will find you again when we want you."

"I will be easy to find. Just send *Flower* to the same landing site and wait. I will come, eventually."

Koch gnawed at his lip. "You can deliver a settlement in this?"

"Yes."

"I distrust your confidence."

"They will listen to me. I speak to them in their own language."

"Doubtless you do. Go do your talking to Boaz."

"I want a shuttlecraft ready."

Koch frowned.

"I will need it," Duncan said. "Or arrange me transport your own way. I would advise sending me back relatively quickly. The mri will not be easy to find. It may take some time."

Koch swore softly. "Boaz can have ten hours of you. Go on. Dismissed."

Duncan veiled himself and rose, folded his arms and made the slight inclination of the head that was respect.

And among the guard that had remained at the door, he started out.

A squat shadow was there. He hurled himself back. A regul hand closed on his arm with crushing strength. The regul shrilled at him, and he twisted in that grip; a blade burned his ribs, passing across them.

Security moved. Human bodies interceded, and the regul lost balance, went down, dragging Duncan with him. Galey's boot slammed down repeatedly on the regul's wrist, trying to shake the knife loose.

Duncan wrenched over, ripped a pistol from its owner's holster and turned. Men reached for him, hurled themselves for him.

Sharn.

The regul's dark eyes showed white round the edges, terror. Duncan fired, went loose as the guard's seized him, let them have the pistol easily.

He had removed the People's enemy. The others, the younglings, were nothing. He drew a deep breath as the guards set him on his feet, and regarded the collapsed bulk in the sled with a sober regret.

And Koch was on his feet, red-faced, nostrils white-edged.

"I serve the she'pan of the People," Duncan said quietly, refusing to struggle in the hands that held him. "I have done an execution. Now do yours or let me go and serve both our interests. The regul know what I am. They will not be surprised. You know this. I can give you that peace with Kutath now."

In the corner the regul youngling, released, disarmed, crept to the side of the sled. A curious bubbling sound came from it, regul grief. Dark eyes stared up at Duncan. He ignored it.

"Go," said Koch. The anger on his face had somewhat subsided. There was a curious calculation in his eyes. He looked at the guard, at Galey. "He will go with you. Don't set hands on him."

Duncan shook his arms free, adjusted his robes, walked from the room, passing through a confused knot of regul younglings that gathered outside. One, more adult than youngling, stared at him with nostrils flaring and shutting in extreme agitation, darted behind another as he passed.

Quietly, without a glance at the humans who lined the corridor to stare, Duncan passed back to *Flower*.

"What are you going to do now?" Boaz asked after long silence.

Duncan looked at the tape. Boaz turned it off. He sat crosslegged on the large chair, elbows on knees, not choosing the floor in deference to Boaz.

"What I said. Absolutely what I said."

"Reason with mri?"

"You yourself don't think it's possible."

"You're the expert," she said. "Tell me."

"It's possible, Boz. It's possible. On mri terms."

"After murder."

He blinked slowly. He was veiled. He was not comfortable among them, even here, even in conditions of hospitality. "I did what had to be done. No other could have done it."

"Revenge?"

"Practicality."

"They do not hold resentment toward the regul, you say."

"They have forgotten the regul. It is a Dark ago. I have wiped the present slate clean. It is over, Boz. Clean."

"And your hands?"

"No regret."

She was silent a time, and whatever she would have said, she did not say. It was like a veil upon her eyes, that sudden distance in them. "Yes. I imagine there is not."

"There was a woman whom the regul caused to be killed. She was not the only one."

"I am glad there is that much left in you."

"It was not for her that I killed the regul."

Boz went silent on him again. There was less and less that remained possible to say.

"I will remember the other Sten Duncan," she said at last.

"He is the only one you will understand."

She rose, gathered up his weapons from the counter, gave them back to him. "Galey is going to fly you down. He asked to. I think he has delusions that he knows you. The dus is shut in the hatchway."

"Yes." He knew where the dus was. It knew his presence too, and remained calm. He buckled on the weapons, familiar weight, touched the *j'tal* that was his, straightening the belts. "I'd like to be away now."

"It's arranged. There's a signal beacon provided to a kit they want you to carry. They want you to use it when you can provide them a meeting."

"I will need a while." He walked to the door, stopped, and thought of unveiling, of giving that one gesture to what had been a friend.

He did not feel it welcome.

He went out among the guards that waited, and did not look back.

And with the dus beside him he descended to the shuttle bay, accepted from security the kit that they provided; he left the guards there and walked the ramp to the ship, the first moment that he had been free of them.

He entered and went through to controls, where Galey waited.

Brave man, Galey. Duncan looked at him critically as the man rose to meet him, giving place to the dus that crowded between. *Afraid:* he felt that in the dus-feelings; but something else had driven Galey to be present despite that.

Loyalty?

He did not know to what, or why, or how he could have stirred that in a man he hardly knew . . . only that they two had walked Sil'athen—that this man, too, had known the outback of Kesrith, as few of his kind had seen it.

He gave his hand to Galey, human-fashion, and Galey's hand was damp.

"Got some idea where you want to go?"

"Let me out by the ship, at *Flower*'s recent landing site. I'll manage."

"Sir," Galey said.

He settled into his place at controls; Duncan took the seat beside him, buckled in while the dus wedged itself in firmly, anchoring itself: spacewise, the beast.

Lights flared. Duncan watched Galey's intent face, green-dyed in the light of the instruments. The port opened and the shuttle flung itself outward, toward the world.

"High polar," Duncan advised. "Defenses are still active."

"We know the route," said Galey. "We've used it."

And thereafter was little to say. The ground rushed up at them, became mountains and dunes over which the shuttle flew with decreasing speed.

There was the sea chasm, their guide home. The dus, feeling braver now, stood up and braced itself on four legs. Duncan soothed it with his fingers, and it began to rumble its pleasure sound, picking up that which was in his mind.

The shuttle settled, touched, rested. The hatch opened.

The cold, thin air of Kutath came to him. He freed himself of the harness and stood up, took his hand from the dus as he gathered up his kit and walked back to the hatch. He heard Galey's rise behind him, paused and looked back at him.

"You're all right?" Galey asked strangely.

"Yes." He took about his face the extra lap of the veil that made the change in air more bearable, and gazed again at the wilderness that lay beyond the hatch. He started forward, down the ramp, and the dus padded at his heels, down to the sand, that had the comfortable feeling of reality after the world above.

Home.

He set his face toward the sea chasm, a false direction first. He would take the true one when light faded, when he was sure that there were none to watch him. He would bury the kit in the rocks there against future need, not trusting to bring any human gift among the mri; his weapons also he would strip and examine, distrusting what had been out of his hands among them. They would not trace him.

The she'pan's service. The wild, fresh land. He inhaled the wind, and only when he had come a considerable distance did it begin to worry at him that he had not heard the shuttle lift.

He looked back and saw a small figure standing in the hatchway, watching him.

He turned and kept walking, and finally heard it go.

It passed over. He looked up, saw the shuttle bend a turn as if in salute, and depart.

BOOK THREE

KUTATH

Chapter One

There was chaos about the docking bay; Galey observed it as he was coming in, heard it, a chatter of instructions in his ear, warning him to keep his distance. He held the shuttle parked a little removed from the warship, watching kilometer-long *Saber* disgorge a trio of small craft. Blips showed on his tracking screen, an image supplied him by *Saber*-com, from *Saber's* view of things. One blip was himself; one other was blue and likewise human— that had to be *Santiago* . . . *Saber* had deployed the insystem fighter between itself and the red blip that was *Shirug*.

The outgoing blips were likewise red: regul shuttles in tight formation. Galey read the situation uneasily and kept his eye to the steady flow of information on the screen. There was one dead regul to be disposed of: that was likely what was in progress out there . . . the late bai Sharn Alagn-ni, ferried out to her own ship for whatever ceremony the regul observed with their dead. Sharn: ally, as all regul were allies according to the treaties . . . according to the agreement which had brought a human and a regul warship into orbit about this barren world, this home base of the mri. Regul made Galey's skin crawl. It was a reaction he did not speak aloud: promotions in the service were politics, and politics called regul friendlies.

Mri, now, mri were near human-looking, whatever the insides of them might be like. Galey hated them with a different dutiful hate. He was Havener, of a world lost and retaken in the mri wars. Parents, a brother, cousins—had vanished into the chaos of that war-torn world and never surfaced again. It was a remote kind of grief, rehearsed guiltily in every other scene of slaughter he had witnessed, but he could not recover the intensity of it. His kin were lost, in the sense of not found, misplaced in the war and gone: dead or alive, nor knowing for sure. He had not been home when the strike came, and in the years after, the service had become home, *Lancet, Saber, Santiago,* whatever ship received his papers, wherever his current ship took him, live or die. Mri were like that. Just soldiers behind their black robes and veils. Nothing personal. He had a friend who had gone mri . . . he had seen a different look on him after the years of absence, disdainful, remote; there was something heart-chilling in standing close to a man in that black garb, something intimidating in gazing close at hand into a face of which only the eyes were visible—amazing how much of expression depended on the rest of the face, concealed behind black cloth. But for all of that, a human could understand them.

Regul . . . regul had hired the ships, the weapons, the mri themselves, and planned, and named the strikes, and profited from them. Forty years of war, bought by regul. An investment . . . Galey sounded the words out in his mind, distastefully. Po-li-cy. Cash on the table. Big folk, the regul, who sat fat and safe, who made the decisions and put out the cash, sending their mri mercenaries out to war. Humans and mri killed each other, and the wise old regul, reckoning a forty-year war nothing against their centuries-long lifespans, and reckoning the tally of gain and loss—kept the war going just so long as it profited them.

In the same way the regul turned up on the human side during the cleanup—had turned on their own mercenaries, slaughtering them and the mri's civilian population without warning. That was the mri's final payoff for serving regul. A simple change of policy: regul knew the right moment to move. And, truth be told, everything human breathed a sigh of relief to know the mri were gone, and that someone else had pulled the trigger.

Regul came now, having tracked the last two survivors of the mri who had served them, to their homeworld, to Kutath, the far, far origin of their kind. Regul had rushed ahead to destroy a peace message from Kutath before humans could hear it, had fired on a quiet world and elicited answering fire before humans understood the situation. More mri were dead down there. The last remnants of dying cities were shot to ruin; the last of a dying species were made fugitives on their own world . . . the last place, the very last, that mri existed.

Something tight and unpleasant welled up in Galey's throat when he thought of that. Somehow it was Haven again, and civs getting killed. He had come very far to feel something finally. It was ironic that he felt it for the enemy, that deep-down sickness at the belly that came of seeing an unequal contest.

It would have been that kind of blind, helpless death for his own kin. It gave him nightmares now, after so many years. No fighting back; a city under fire from orbit; no ships; no hope: folk armed with handguns and knives against orbital strike.

Everything dead, and no way out.

There was a little drift in his position. It had been minor, but the shuttles were still in his path and he had to maintain a while longer. He corrected a fraction. Sweat was running down his sides. He tried to stop thinking, tried to concentrate on his instruments for a time. There was no reason for uneasiness. The feeling simply grew. And in time the thoughts crept back again. His eyes traveled inexorably and unwillingly toward the outward view. Kutath's dying surface was barely in his visual field. The rest was stars, fewer than he ever liked to see. He sweated. He had never been in a place where the goblins got to him so thoroughly, those ancient human ghosts that tagged after a man in the deep. They dogged him, kept, as proper ghosts should, just behind him . . . gone when he would look.

Look back, they whispered against his nape, stirring the hairs, *Look again.*

The stars hung infinite in his drifting view, as deep down as up, as far on left as on right; and a near star, Na'i'in, the mri called it, which would make even *Saber* a mote of dust beside it. All, all those little lights which were suns, and some cloudy aggregates of suns, themselves reduced to dust motes by distance which reached out from himself, who was the center of the universe, and then not—an insignificance, less than the mote of a world, far less than a sun, infinitely less than the vast galaxies, and the distance, the cold, deep distance that never stopped, forever.

Move it, he thought at the ships which held him off. He wanted in, wanted *in,* like a boy running for his front door and warmth and light, with the goblins at his back. It had never gotten to him, not like this.

The mri had a word for it: the Dark. Scientists said so. Anyone who had traveled the wild places in little ships had to have a word for it. Except maybe regul, who could not imagine, only remember.

Mri felt it. He understood beings who could feel it.

He worked his hands on the controls, heard the chatter in his ear, the thin lifeline of a voice from *Saber,* proving constantly his species was real, however far they sat now from friendly, trafficked space.

Real. Alive. Men existed somewhere. Somewhere there were human worlds, less than dust motes in the deep, but living. And that somehow affirmed his own reality.

Was it this, he wondered, for the two mri, last of all their company . . . who had run this long, desperate course home? *Their* little mote was dying, an old world under an old sun, and what fragile life of their kind survived here, regul refused to leave alive. Was it such a feeling, that had made *home* more urgent for them than survival—to come in out of the Dark, even to die?

He began to shiver, catching a moving dot of light among all the others. *Shirug.* The regul shuttles were too far and too small to see now. It had to be regul *Shirug,* catching the sun.

"NAS-12, come on in," *Saber*-com said. "Shuttle NAS-12, come on in."

He kicked the vessel into slow life and eased onward, resisting the temptation to close the interval with a wasteful burst of power. There was time. The bay was all his.

"Priority, NAS-12."

They gave him leave to move. His heart started thudding with a heavier and heavier weight of premonition. His hands moved, throwing the little ship over into rightwise alignment and hurtling it at *Saber* with furious haste.

"Sir," the intercom announced, "Lt. Comdr. James Galey."

Adm. Koch scribbled a note on the screen, hit FILE and disposed of one piece of business, touched the intercom key in silent affirmative. A second screen showed the busy command center: Capt. Zahadi was taking care of matters there at least; and Comdr.

Silverman in *Santiago* was currently linked to Zahadi, keeping a wary eye over the world's horizon. Details were all Zahadi's, until they touched policy. Policy began here, in this office.

Galey arrived, a sandy-haired, freckled man who had begun to have lines in his face. Galey looked distressed—ought to be, summoned directly to this office for debriefing. The eyes flicked to the corner, where a high-ranking regul had lately died; Koch did not miss it, returning the offered courtesies.

"Sir," Galey said.

"You set SurTac Duncan downworld in good order?"

"Yes, sir. No trouble."

"You volunteered for that flight."

Galey was masked in courtesies. The face failed to react to that probe, only the eyes, and that but slightly, betraying nothing.

"Want you to sit down," Koch said. "Relax. Do it."

The man looked about him, found the only chair available, drew it over and sat on the edge of it. Koch waited. Galey dutifully eased himself back and positioned his arms. Sweat was standing on Galey's face, which might be from change of temperature and might not. Careers rose and fell in this office.

"Why?" Koch pursued him. "The man walks into this office wearing mri robes, asks for a cease-fire, then guns down a ranking regul ally. Security says he's gone entirely mri, inside and out. Science department agrees. You imagined some long-ago acquaintance, is that it? You volunteered to ferry him back—why? To talk with him? To satisfy yourself of something? What?"

"I—worked with him once. And I'd flown guide for *Flower's* landing, sir; I happened to know the route."

"So do others."

"Yes, sir."

"You worked with him—on Kesrith."

"One mission, sir."

"Know him well?"

"No, sir. No one did. He's SurTac."

The specials, the Surface Tactical operatives, were remote from the regul military, in all ways remote: peculiar rank, peculiar authorities, the habit of independence and irreverence for protocol. Koch shook his head, frowned, wondering if that was, even years ago, sufficient explanation for Sten Duncan. Governor Stavros,

back in Kesrith Zone, had trusted this wildness, enough to hand
Duncan two mri prisoners and their captured navigational records.
It had paid the dividend Stavros had reckoned: they were here, at
the mri home world; and Duncan, with the mri contacts no one
had ever been able to establish, came suing for peace. . . .

Then shot a regul in the same interview, bai Sharn, commander
of *Shirug,* lieutenant to humanity's highest placed ally among
regul, and all plans were off.

I have done an execution, Duncan had said. *The regul know
what I am. They will not be surprised. You know this. I can give
you peace with Kutath now.*

Mri arrogance. Duncan had been acutely uncomfortable, asked
for a moment to drop the veil with which he covered his face.

"You worked with the man," Koch said, regarding Galey
steadily. "You had time to exchange a few words with him in getting him back to Kutath. Impressions? Do you know him at all
now?"

"Yes," Galey said. "It's what he was, back on Kesrith. Only it
wasn't—wasn't all the same. Now and again it's there, the way he
was; and then . . . not. But—"

"But you think you know him. —You . . . were in the desert together back at Kesrith, recovered the records out of that shrine . . .
had a little regul trouble then on the way back, all true?"

"Yes, sir."

"Hate the regul?"

"No love for them, sir."

"Hate the mri?"

"No love there either, sir."

"And SurTac Duncan?"

"Friend, sir."

Koch nodded slowly. "You know the pack he was given has a
tracer."

"I don't think that will last long."

"You warned him?"

"No, sir, didn't know. But he's not anxious to have us find the
mri at all; I don't think he'll let it happen."

"Maybe he won't. But then maybe his mri don't want him
speaking for them. Maybe he told the truth and maybe he didn't.
There are weapons on that world worth reckoning with."

"Wouldn't know, sir."

"Your first run down there, you took damage."

"Some. Shaken about. What I hear, it's old stuff. I didn't see anything to say different; no fields, no life, no ships. Nothing, either time. Only ruins. That's what I hear it was."

"Less than that down there now."

"Yes, sir."

A dying world, cities decayed and empty, machines drawing solar power to live: armaments returning fire with mechanical lack of passion; and the mri themselves. . . .

Rock and sand, Duncan had said, *dune and flats. The mri will not be easy to find.*

If it's true, Koch thought. *If—there are no ships in their control, and if all the cities are machine life only.*

"You think they pose no threat to us," Koch said.

"Wouldn't know that either, sir."

There was a feeling of cold at Koch's gut. It lived there, sometimes small, sometimes—when he thought of the voyage behind them—larger. It grew when he thought of the hundred twenty-odd worlds at their backs, a swath which marked the trail mri had followed out from Kutath to Kesrith, a trail eons old at the beginning and recent at the farther end, in human space, where the mri had been massacred. Before that, along that strip—all worlds were scoured of life . . . more than desert: dead.

Mri hired themselves for mercenaries. Presumably they had done so more than once, until the regul turned on them and ended them.

Ended a progress across the galaxy which left no life in its wake, a hundred twenty-odd systems which by all statistical process should have held life, which might have supported intelligent species.

Void, if they had ever been there . . . gone, without memory, even to know what they had been, why the mri had passed there, or what they had sought in passing.

Only Kesrith survived, trail's end.

I have done an execution, Duncan had said, black-robed, mri to the heart of him. And: *The regul know what I am.*

"Bai Sharn," Koch said, "is being transported back to her ship. There *is* no regul authority with us now; the rest are only

younglings. They can probably handle *Shirug* competently
enough, but nothing more, without some adult to direct them.
That puts things wholly into our laps. *We* deal with the mri, if
Duncan can get their holy she'pan to come in and talk peace. *We*
run operations up here. And if we misread signals, we don't get
any second chance. If we get ourselves ambushed, if we die
here—then the next thing human space *and* regul may know is
more mri arriving, to take up the track the others left at Kesrith,
and this time, this time with a grudge. The thing we've seen . . .
continued. Is that understood, out among the crew?"

"Yes, sir," Galey said hoarsely. "Don't know whether they
know about the regul, but the other, yes, it's something I think
everybody reckons."

"You don't want to make a mistake in judgment, do you? You
don't want to make a mistake on the side of friendship and botch
a report. You wouldn't hold back information you could get out of
SurTac Duncan. You understand how high the stakes are . . . and
what an error could do down there."

"Yes, sir."

"I'm sending *Flower* and the science staff back down. Dr. Luiz
and Boaz are friends of his. He'll talk with them, trust them, as
far as he likely trusts any human now. I have need of someone
else, potentially. What we want is a substitute for a SurTac, someone who can operate in that kind of terrain." He watched the apprehension grow, and a twinge of pity came on him. "Our options
are limited. We have pilots we could better risk. You're rated for
Santiago, and you know your value . . . don't have to tell you that.
But it's not a matter of skill in that department. It's the land, and a
sense of things—you understand what I'm saying."

"Sir—"

"I want you first of all *reserved.* Just prep. We keep our options
open. Maybe things will work out with mri contact. If not . . . you
have a good rapport with the civs, don't you?"

"I've been in and out of the ship more than most, maybe."

"They know you."

"Yes, sir."

"In some things down there, that could be valuable; and you've
been in the desert."

"Yes, sir," the answer came faintly.

"I want you available, whenever and wherever SurTac Duncan comes into contact with us; I want you available—if he doesn't. Willing?"

"Yes, sir."

"You'll have some semblance of an office, whatever scan materials we come up with, original and interpreted. Whatever you think you need." Koch delayed a moment more, pursed his lips in thought. "It took Duncan some few days to get from the mri to groundbase; allow—ten, eleven days. That's the margin. Understood?"

It was; it very much was, Koch reckoned. He had a sour taste in his mouth for the necessity.

One covered all the possibilities.

A private office: that was status. Someone had put a card on the door, the temporary sort: LT COMDR JAMES R GALEY, RECON & OPERATIONS. Galey keyed open the lock, turned on the light, finding a bare efficiency setup, barren walls, down to the rivets; and a desk and a comp terminal. He settled in behind the desk, shifted uncomfortably in the unfamiliar chair, keyed in library.

ORDERS: the machine interrupted him with its own program. He signaled acceptance. SELECT COMPATIBLE CREW OF THREE AND RESERVE CREW, GROUND OPERATIONS, REPORT CHOICE ADM SOONEST.

He leaned back, hands sweating. He little liked the prospect of taking himself down there; the matter of selecting others for a high-risk operation was even less to his taste.

He made up a demanding qualifications list and started search through personnel. Comp denied having any personnel with drylands experience. He erased that requirement and started through the others, erased yet another requirement and ran it again, with the sense of desperation he began to understand that Koch shared.

They were Haveners on this mission, and for all the several world-patches on his sleeve, won on this ship, there was nothing they had met like this save Kesrith itself; there was no time at which they had relied on themselves and not on their machines. *Saber* had not been chosen for this mission: it had gone because it was available. As for experience with mri—none of them had had that, save at long range.

Devastation from orbit: that had been their function until now. Now there was the barest hope this would not be the case. He was not given to personal enthusiasm in his assignments; but this one—a means of avoiding slaughter—that possibility occurred to him.

Or the possibility of being the one to call down holocaust: that was the other face of the matter.

He did not sleep well. He sat by day and pored over what data they could give him, the scan their orbiting eyes could gather, the monotone reports of comp that no contact had been made.

Flower descended to the surface. Data returned from that source. Day by day, there was no reply from Duncan, no sighting of mri.

He received word from the admiral's office: SELECTIONS RATIFIED. SHIBO, KADARIN, LANE: MAIN MISSION. HARRIS, NORTH, BRIGHT, MAGEE: BACKUP. PROCEED.

The days crawled past, measured in the piecing of maps and vexing lapses in ground-space communication as Na'i'in's storms crept like plague across its sickly face. He took what information *Saber*'s mapping department would give him, prowled Supply, thinking.

The office became papered with charts, a composite of the world, overlaid in plastics, red-inked at those sites identified in scan, mri cities, potential targets.

He talked with the crew, gave them warning. There was still the chance that the whole project would be scrubbed, that by some miracle *Flower* would call up contact, declaring peace a reality, the matter solved, the mri willing to deal.

The hope ebbed, hourly.

Chapter Two

Windshift had begun, that which each evening attended the cooling of the land, and Hlil tucked his black robes the more closely about him as he rested on his heels, scanning the dunes, taking breath after his long walking.

The tribe was not far now, tucked down just over the slope by the rim, where the land fell away in days' marches of terraces and cliffs, and the sea chasms gaped, empty in this last age of the world. Sencaste said that even that void would fill, ultimately, the sands off the high flats drifting as they did in sandfalls and curtains off the windy edges, to the far, hazy depths. Somewhere out there was the bottom of the world, where all motion stopped, forever; and that null-place grew, yearly, eating away at the world. The chasms girdled the earth; but they were finite, and there were no more mountains, for they had all worn away to nubs. It was a place, this site near the rims, where one could look into time, and back from it; it quieted the soul, reminded one of eternity, in this moment that one could not look into the skies without dreading some movement, or reckoning with alien presence.

The ruins of An-ehon lay just over the horizon to the north, to remind them of that power, which had made them fugitives in their own land, robbed of tents, of belongings, of every least thing but what they had worn the morning of the calamity. There was the bitterness of looking about the camp, and missing so many, so very many, so that at every turn, one would think of one of the lost as if that one were in camp, and then realize, and shiver. He was kel'en, of the warrior caste; death was his province, and it was permitted him to grieve, but he did not. There was a dull bewilderment in that part of him which ought by rights to be touched. In recent days he felt outnumbered by the dead, as if all the countless who had gone into the Dark in the slow ages of the sea's dying ought rather to mourn the living. He did not comprehend the causes of things. Being kel'en, he neither read nor wrote, held nothing of the wisdom of sen-caste, which sat at the feet of a she'pan alien to this world and learned. He knew only the use of his weapons, and the kel-law, those things which were proper for a kel'en to know.

It had become appropriate to know things beyond Kutath; he tried, at least. The Kel was the caste which veiled, the Face that Looked Outward. That Outward had become more than the next rising of the land; it was outsiders and ships and a manner of fighting which the ages had made only memory on Kutath, and pride and the Holy the Kel defended forbade that he should flinch from facing it, since it came.

They had a kel'anth, the gods defend them! who had come out of that Dark; they had a she'pan who had taken them from the gentle she'pan who had Mothered the tribe before her . . . young and scarred with the kel-scars on her face; fit, he thought, that the she'-pan of this age should bear kel-marks, which testified she once had been of Kel-caste, had once attained skill with weapons. A she'pan of a colder, fiercer stamp, this Melein s'Intel; no Mother to play with the children of the Kath as their own Sochil had done, to spend more time with the gentle Kath than with Sen-caste, to love rather than to be wise. Melein was a chill wind, a breath out of the Dark; and as for her kel'anth, her warrior-leader. . . .

Him, Hlil almost hated, not for the dead in An-ehon, which might be just; but for the kel'anth he had killed to take the tribe. It was a selfish hate, and Hlil resisted it; such resentments demeaned Merai, who had lost challenge to this Niun s'Intel. Merai had died, in fact, because gentle Sochil had turned fierce when challenged: fear, perhaps; or a mother's bewildered rage, that a stranger-she'pan demanded her children of her, to lead them where she did not know.

So Merai was dead; and Sochil, dead. Of Merai's kinship there was only his sister left; of his tribe there was a fugitive remnant; and the Honors which Merai had won in this life, a stranger possessed.

Even Hlil . . . this stranger had gained, for kel-law set the victor in the stead of the vanquished, to the last of his kin debts and blood debts and place debts. Hlil was second to Niun s'Intel as he

had been second to Merai. He sat by this stranger in the Kel, tolerated proximity to the strange beast which was Niun's shadow,
bore with the grief which haunted the kel'anth's acts . . . which
could not, he was persuaded, be distraction for the slaughter of a
People the kel'anth had not had time to know—but which more
attended the disappearance of the kel'anth's other alien shadow,
which walked on two feet.

That the kel'anth at least grieved . . . it was a mortality which
bridged one alienness between them, him and his new kel'anth.
They shared something, at least; if not love . . . loss.

Hlil gathered up a sandy pebble from the crumbling ridge on
which he rested, cast it at a tiny pattern in the sands downslope. It hit
true, and a nest of spiny arms whipped up to enfold the suspected
prey. Sand-star. He had suspected so. His hunting was not so desperate that he must bring *that* to the women and children of Kath. It
wriggled away, a disturbance through the sand, and he let it. A pair
of serpents, a fat darter, a stone's weight of game; he had no cause to
be ashamed of his day's effort, and there was a stand of pipe growing within the camp, so that they had no desperate need of moisture,
certainly not the bitter fluid of the star. It nestled into safety next to
some rocks, spread its arms wide again, a pattern of depressions in
the sand. He did not torment it further; it was off the track so, and
offered no threat. Kel-law forbade excess.

And in time, with the sun's lowering, kel'ein came. Hlil sat his
place, sentinel to the homecoming path, and marked them in, as
he had known by the fact that this post was vacant, that none had
come in before him. They saw him as they passed, lifted hands in
salute; he knew their names and put a knot in the cords at his belt
for each—knew them veiled as they were, by their manners and
their stature and simply by their way of walking, for they were his
own from boyhood. Had there been one of higher rank than he
that one would have come and relieved him of this post, to take
up the tally; there was none, so he stayed, as they entered the
perimeter of the secure area of the camp.

They came in groups as the sun touched the horizon, appearing
like mirages out of the land, so well they judged their time, to
meet at homecoming after hunting apart all day: black-robed, like
drifting shadows, they passed in the amber twilight, while the sun
stained the rocks and touched the hazy depths of the sea basins,

going down over the far, invisible rim as if it vanished in midair, drawing out shadows.

The knots filled one cord and another and another, until all the tale was told but two.

Hlil looked eastward, and of certainty, at the mid of sunfall, there came Ras. He need not have worried, he told himself. Ras would not be careless, not she—kel'e'en of the Kel's second highest rank. No reasoning with her, nothing but ordering her outright, and he could not, even if it were wise.

Ras s'Sochil Kov-Nelan. Merai's truesister.

Of that too, Niun had robbed him. They had been a trio, Hlil and Merai and Ras, in happier days; and he had dreamed dreams beyond his probabilities. He was skilled: that was his claim to place; he had had Merai's friendship; and because of that—he had been always near Ras. He had taught her, being older; had gamed with her and with Merai; had watched her every day of her life . . . and watched her harden since Merai's death. Her mother, Nelan, had been one of those who failed to come out of An-ehon; of that Ras said nothing. Ras laughed and spoke and moved, took meals with the Kel and went through all the motions of life; but she was not Ras as he had known her. She followed Niun s'Intel, as once, as a kath-child, she had followed him; where Niun walked, she was shadow; where he rested, she waited. It was a kind of madness, a game lacking humor or sense; but they were all a little mad, who survived An-ehon and served the she'pan Melein.

Ras arrived, in her own time, paused on the path below the rocks—began, wearily, to climb up to him. When she had done so, she sank down on the flat stone beside him, arms dropped loosely over her knees, her body heaving with her breaths.

"Did you hunt well?" he asked, although he knew what game she hunted.

"A couple of darters." It was not, for her, good. And it was a long walk that brought Ras back out of breath.

Hlil looked out, and in the darkening east, there were two dots on the horizon. The kel'anth and the beast, strung far apart.

"East," Ras said beside him, finding breath to speak. "Always east, along the same track. He would have brought back no game at all, but the beast routs things out for him. He delays only to gather it, and he takes long steps, this kel'anth of ours."

"Ras," he objected.

"He knows I am there."

He gathered up another stone, rolled it between his fingers. Ras simply rested, catching her breath.

"Why?" he said finally. "Ras—let him be. Anger serves no purpose; it dies unless you go on nursing it."

"And you do not."

"I am the kel'anth's second."

"So you were," she said, which was a heart-shot; and a moment later she looked on him with something like her old fondness. "You can be. I envy you."

"I have no love for him."

She accepted that offering in silence. Her fingers stole, as they would, to one of the many Honors which hung from her belts. Merai's death gift, that one, from Niun's hand.

"We cannot challenge him," she said. "Law forbids, if it were revenge for Merai; but there are other causes. Just causes."

"Stop thinking of it."

"He is very good. If I challenged him, he would kill me."

"Do not," he said, his heart clenched.

"You want to live," she accused him. And when he did not deny it: "Do you know how many generations of Kel-birth lie behind me?"

"More than mine," he said bitterly, heat risen already to his face: his plain birth was a thing of which he was deeply conscious.

"Eighteen," she said. "Eighteen generations. It comes to me, Hlil, that here I sit, last of a line that produced kel'ein and she'-panei. Last. They are dead, all the rest; gods, and they would never understand such times as these. I look around me; I think—maybe I do not belong here; maybe I should go too, end it. And I think of my brother. Merai saw it standing in front of him—saw just the edge of the horizon waiting for us. And I think . . . he *died,* Hlil. He was not himself against this stranger; he missed a blow he could have turned. I know he could have turned it. Why? For fear? That was not Merai. It was not. So what do I believe? That he stepped aside—that he let himself die? And why so? At one word from these strangers that they are the Promised, the Voyagers-out? Could he stand in the way of such a thing?"

Hlil swallowed heavily, "Do not ask me what he thought."

"I ask myself. He could not see ahead. And then I think: *I see.* I am here. I am my brother's eyes. Gods, gods, he died knowing it was for a thing he would never see or understand. To clear the way, because he was set where this man had to stand. And I am desperate to see— Truth, Hlil: this kel'anth of ours will live under my witness; and if he cannot bear that, if he feels guilt, it is his guilt, let him bear it; and if he turns and strikes me—you will know. And what you do about that—I leave in your lap, Hlil-my-brother."

"Ras—"

"I leave it there, I say."

They sat still, staring alike at the shadowing land.

The beast arrived far in advance, a great warm-blooded animal, down-furred, pug-nosed and massive. Its feet turned in when it walked, its head wandered from side to side close to the ground as if it had lost something and forgotten what it was. It was probably nearsighted. Ras hissed a soft sound of distaste when it came up the rise toward them. Hlil felt a crawling at his gut whenever it was by him, for the length of those claws (venomed, the kel'anth had warned them) and the power of those sloping shoulders argued its way wherever it went, and something in the creatures set nerves on edge when they were disturbed. It came now, nosed wetly at each of them. Ras cursed it and pushed it, and Hlil set his hand at the side of its head and heaved to turn it aside, for all that those great jaws could take the hand entire. It moved, rebuffed finally. It put fear into him, and no beast Kutath had bred had ever done that; it consumed, gods, it surely must: it rolled with fat and moisture. On hungrier days Hlil had looked at it resentfully . . . but the thought of eating warm-blooded flesh nauseated him, like cannibalism.

Another gift of the kel'anth, this creature.

"Go on," he said to Ras. And when she delayed still: "Go on back."

She muttered soft agreement and rose, slipped away down the rocks, vanished into the shadows.

The beast made to follow her, snorted and came back again, nosed about and found the sand-star with uncanny accuracy. The star had not a chance. The beast—dus, its name was—lay down with the tendrils wrapped about one massive paw and ate with noisy relish. The sound became a rumbling, mind-dulling, pervasive.

Contentment weighted Hlil's limbs, at odds with the distress that tugged at him from another direction. It was as if he grew two minds, one warring with the other. The dus—he connected the sensations, the slow purring, felt his senses dulled. . . .

"No!" he said.

It stopped, a silence like sudden nakedness, devoid of warmth. Small, glittering eyes lifted to him.

"Go away," he told it. It did not. He sat and watched Niun come, weary and limping more than a man should from a day's ordinary hunting. He ought to walk down to the path, signaling to the kel'anth that he might simply take the way into camp, being the last.

He did not. He sat still, let Niun walk up the stony walk to her perch among the rocks.

"Is someone still out?" Niun asked, hard-breathing and in a manner of some concern.

The accent with which he spoke was also different; they had in common only the hal'ari, the high tongue, preserved changeless in the city-machines, and the kel'anth struggled badly in what he had learned of the mu'ara, the tribe speech.

"No," Hlil said, rising, ignoring the kel'anth's vexation. "You are last; I will walk down with you."

The beast rose up, shambled out to rub against Niun as he started down; Hlil walked as close to it as he must.

"You walked far," Hlil said.

"Ai," Niun muttered as he walked, evading him.

"So did Ras."

That stopped him. Niun turned a veiled face toward him, looking up on the shadowed slope. "Your sending?"

"No."

"She wants a quarrel—does she not, kel Hlil?"

"Perhaps. Perhaps she is only curious where you go . . . daily."

"That too, it may be. I beg you—intervene."

That was not the answer he had expected to provoke. He slipped his hands into the back of his belt, far from his weapons, evidencing reluctance for quarrel. "I beg *you*, kel'anth . . . bear with her."

"I do," he said. "What more can I do?"

Hlil regarded him, the alien fineness of him, the familiar Honors which winked among his robes: easy to hate—this too-fine, too-skilled stranger. The dus laid its ears back and rumbled an ominous sound, stilled as Niun touched it.

"Ras and I," Hlil said, "have little more to say to each other. You speak to her if you like. I cannot."

The kel'anth did not answer him—turned and picked his way to the bottom, walked onto the sandy track toward camp, the great dus ambling along behind him. "Yai!" he snapped at it then, and it fell back, turned aside from the trail into camp: it rarely did come in.

Hlil followed, seething with resentment, as if the kel'anth abandoned him equally with the beast . . . followed the kel'-anth's straight figure in among the shadows of overhanging cliffs, and out into light again . . . the rim itself suddenly on the left hand, a dizzying drop to the cut which gave them refuge from the kel'anth's enemies aloft.

"Tell the sentry we are in," Niun turned to bid him. "Here, I will take your pouch."

The dismissal further angered him. He shed the pouch containing his day's take into the kel'anth's outstretched hand and left the trail, going up into the high rocks.

It was a reasonable order. Had Merai ordered, he would have felt no least resentment; he argued so with himself, through the heat of anger. *To claim my hunting for yours?* he wondered, a petty suspicion, when in fact the kel'anth did him a great courtesy, to offer to bear his burden that little distance: rank forbade. It was always like that between them, that bitterness underlay whatever dealings they had one with the other, that they could not speak the simplest words without offense; that they could not take loyalty for granted between them, which they ought to be able to do, for the tribe's sake.

It was Ras, who committed slow suicide . . . Ras' eyes were on him too, surrogate for Merai.

It had been so when Merai was alive, that Merai's was the greater soul, the higher-tempered, the quicker—a great prince of the People, kel Merai; and he was only Hlil s'Sochil, born of Kath-caste and no special father—no shame, but no great distinction; no particular grace, nor handsomeness—weapons-scars had not improved him in that; never quickness of tongue. Only skill, and stubborn adherence to the kel-law and what seemed right.

Those two things had never diverged, save now.

Niun hesitated at the bottom, in the shadows, staring into the camp. Ras was not waiting for him. He had thought she might be; she had, then, gone her way to Kel. Mad she was, but not enough to discommode herself, sitting out in the dark. He summoned a little of that cold-bloodedness of hers and slung the two pouches of game over his shoulder, walked his unhurried course in the shadow of the cliffs.

It was a place which offered at least the hope of concealment from humans, this deep maze of eroded overhangs . . . a stream course, perhaps, while water had flowed the high plain and seas had surged from rim to rim of the great basins. The cut ran down and down the vast terraces, more and more steeply, to lose itself in the evening murk. Between these cliffs was a sandy floor, dangerous at the rimside, the seam of a sandslip running a good stone's throw up the center; farther along the sands were stable. Infrequent gusts carried clouds of sand down into the cut, making veils necessary even for children on windy days. It was no comfort, but it was shelter of a sort, a bad place in storm, on which account the seniors of the Kel had objected; but he had overridden them. They had experienced fire; they knew the theory of machines and strike from orbit; but they still did not realize how thorough an enemy's scan might be. There were deep places within the maze, decent separation for the castes, Sen to the north, with the she'pan; Kel to the south, nearest the entry, to protect it, if it were a question of enemies who dared face them; and farthest back, deepest, the Kath, the child-rearers and children: the strongest place of all for the children, of whom they had lost most in An-ehon, in the ruin of the city.

One strike from above, only one, and they were done. He much feared so.

He turned in at the shelter which served for kel-hall, walked deep within. The glitter of weapon hilts and Honors pierced the gloom, shadowy faces showed in the light of oilwood flame. One came to him, a kel'en who had not yet won the kel-scars: Taz, his name was; on such as he fell the burden of all labor in the Kel.

Niun slung the game pouches into his hand. "Mine and Hlil's. Carry it to Kath."

His eyes located Ras, inevitably, among those who stood to welcome him. He slid his glance aside from her and the others, unveiled and turned to make the token respect to the empty shrine, the three stones piled in symbol of the Holy, which they had lost in their flight. The whole place smelled of oilwood, the fiber of which served for incense.

The others had settled at his dismissal; he walked among them, sank down nearest the small fire which served them. On a square of leather which served them for a common-bowl, was supper, an *ab'aak* Kath had contrived out of other days' hunting—the pulp of pipe and whatever flesh could be spared: more pipe than meat, truth be told, and done without salt or utensils or other amenities. They had fared worse, and better. He ate, in the others' silence.

Hlil returned, sat with him, took his own share. There was idle talk finally, a muttering of small matters, the sort of things passed among folk who had spent all their lives in each other's company, but self-consciously, in the hal'ari and not in the more natural tribe speech. It faltered. Constantly there was a silence ready to enfold them, as every evening. Niun sat staring into the fire, letting the chatter flow through him, about him, unparticipant. He scarcely knew their names, let alone those of the dead, who figured all too often in their rememberings; old jokes were lost on him; too much had to be explained. In truth his mind was elsewhere, and perhaps they knew it.

He remembered, when he let himself. Memory was where his own Kel lived; his House; his friends and companions. He remembered the ship: that was most vivid. Reminiscence could become a disease with him, and he did not permit it often, for even the most unpleasant things involved the familiar, and home, and past pains were duller. Wise, he thought, that the law of the People had commanded them to forget, in each between-worlds voyage . . . even to cease to speak the language or think the old thoughts. To go into the Dark was to return to the center of things, where only the hal'ari was spoken, where worlds were not important, where no past existed, or future.

Even on Kutath it was done, the deliberate forgetting, by all but the scholars of Sen-caste. It was, he suspected, the sanity of a

THE FADED SUN: KUTATH   531

world so very old. Sen remembered, No kel'en might, save in the chants of legends, of which he was one.

> *The Ships which went out,*
> they sang of his kind,
> *With the World at their backs . . .*

The noise of their voices oppressed him as silence. He looked up, realizing his lapse, looked about him, at Hlil, and the several survivors of the first rank of the Kel, the Husbands of the she'pan.

"We—" he said, and silence fell, flowing to the rearmost ranks. "We should consider a matter. Our supplies . . . in An-ehon. And what we do next."

"Send us," a young kel'en exclaimed from the middle ranks, and voices seconded him. "Aye," another said. "Day by day, we could bring them out, if we hunt that way."

"No," he said shortly. "It is not that simple. Listen to me. Putting a limb of the Kel into An-ehon . . . gods know what we could stir up. Ships may have landed there. The place may be watched, and not alone with eyes. Rubble may have buried what is left . . . no knowing; and if we go to the open land again—chances are we will be seen. What hit An-ehon could come down on us when we have only canvas over our heads. We need the supplies; I am sick of seeing Kath struggle to make do with what little we have. And I agree with you, we are pressing luck staying here. But I prefer rock between us and them for now. I am thinking of moving up into the hills."

"Not our range," objected Seras, eldest of the Husbands.

"Then we take it," he said in a small and bitter voice.

The fusion of tribes, the merging of Holies . . . oil and water. It was trouble; he saw their faces, and it was the hardness he expected to see.

You cannot hold this tribe well, they were thinking. *What power have you to hold two at once?*

"The she'pan's word?" Seras asked.

That too was challenge.

"I have not talked with her. I am going to."

"So," said Seras.

There was silence after that, no murmur of suggestions, no expressions of opinion. Their faces, alike scarred with the kel-scars, regarded him, waited on him, set as stone. He considered asking again for their free discussion, reckoned that he would have only silence for answer. He brushed at his robes, gathered himself up and walked through their midst as they rose, perforce, a respect which might be omitted, which they never omitted, which began, to him, to have the flavor of mockery.

They would do their talking after he was gone, he reckoned. Hlil and Seras and the rest of the Husbands led them, in truth; him they only obeyed. He veiled himself, walked out along the narrow trail which followed the curving of the cliffs in the dark, back farther in the cliffs where in places not even starshine reached. A sandfall sheeted down, daily building at a large cone of sand with a constant, hissing whisper. He walked between it and the cliff, ducked his head from the windblown particles. He missed the dus, which probably hunted somewhere above, in the rocks: well that it had not come in with him, this night, with resentments smoldering in the Kel.

And on that thought he looked back, half expecting Ras to be there. She was not.

At the sharp bend of the cliff he walked across the open center, past the stand of pipe, which rose at an assortment of angles, its greater segments thick as a man's waist. Good fortune that it grew here, making far easier their existence with its reliable moisture; it was the only good fortune they had to their account.

Faint light showed in Sen's retreat. Gold-robes who sat in contemplation at the entry looked up in mild inquiry, scrambled up in haste when they recognized him, and stood aside in respect for the kel-first. He walked farther, into the shadow and lamplight of the inner sanctuary, disturbing more of them from their evening's meditations. He unveiled out of respect to their elders, and one went ahead while he waited, to ask permission, and returned with a gesture bidding him pass.

He rounded the turning, into the last secrecy, where a few gold-robes sat about the piled stones which served Melein for her chair of office, in this little recess which served as the she'pan's hall, primitive and far from the honor she was due. Her robes were white, her face always unveiled: Mother, the tribe ought to call her, and she'pan, keeper-of-Mysteries, the Holy.

Truesister, Niun thought of her, with a longing toward that companionship they had once had. Often as he had seen her in the white robes and surrounded by sen'ein, he could not forget kinship.

She motioned dismissal of the others, summoning him; he bowed his head and waited as the sen'ein passed, murmured courtesy to the sen'anth, old Sathas—received back a grumbled acknowledgment, but that was Sathas' way with everyone.

"Come," Melein said.

He did so, took the offered place at her feet.

"You look tired," she said.

He shrugged.

"You have some trouble?"

"She'pan—Kel does not admit this is a safe place to be."

"So. Are not others worse?"

That was a drawing question; impatience. "Others require taking. But perhaps that is what we have to do."

"Kel agrees?"

"Kel offers no opinion."

"Ah."

"The Holy, the things we lost in the city. . . . I think by now if there were ships we would have seen them. Give me leave to go in. I think we can get them out. And for the rest—maybe it is not something in which Kel should have an opinion."

"You have begun to stop waiting."

He looked up at her, made a small gesture of helplessness, disturbed more than he wanted her to see. "I know the old kel'ein say weather change is a little distance off yet . . . on the average of years. But we ought to prepare our choices. This cut will be headed for the basins when the wind starts up; I believe that. We have to do something; I have been trying to think what. Chance is lying heavier and heavier on our shoulders."

"You have talked with the Kel."

He shrugged uncomfortably. "I have told them."

"And they have no opinion."

"None they voiced."

"So." She seemed to stare past him, her eyes focused on something on the ground beyond him, her face half in shadow, gold-lit by the oilwood flames. At last her eyes flickered, the membrane passing twice before them, betraying some inner emotion.

"Which way would you go?" she asked. "Down, into the basins? They tell me tribes range there too, that the air is warmer and moisture more plentiful; we would find larger tribes, likely, or smaller ranges. You would win challenge. I have no doubt that you would. Your skill to theirs—is far more than they would want to meet: nine years with the finest masters of the Kel—I have no dread of that at all. We could, yes. Even seize upon a Holy to venerate, take their supplies, if our own are lost . . . the gods forbid. And what more?"

"I am kel'en; how should I know?"

"You were never without opinions in all your life."

"Say that I find no better hope in them."

"You are missing one of your *j'tai*."

His hand went to his chest belt before he caught her meaning, touched the vacant place among his Honors.

"It was one of your first," she pursued him. "A golden leaf, a *leaf,* on Kutath. Surely it would not have dropped away and you not notice it. I have—for many days."

"Duncan has it." It was no confession; she knew: he knew now she always had.

"We do not discuss a kel'en who left without my blessing."

"He went with mine," he said.

"Did he? Even the kel'ein of this tribe consult me; even with the example of you and Duncan before them. I have waited for you to come to me to tell me. And I have waited for you to come to speak for the Kel. And you do neither, even now. Why?"

He met her eyes, no easy matter.

"Niun," she murmured, "Niun, how have we come to such a pass, he and you and I? You taught him to be mri, and yet he could defy my orders; and now you follow after him. Is that the trouble I hear from the Kel? That they know where your heart is?"

"Perhaps it is," he said faintly. "Or that theirs is constantly with Merai."

"Because you constantly push them away."

There was a long silence after.

"I do not think so," he said.

"But that is part of it."

"Yes. Probably that is part of it."

"Duncan went back," she said, "of his own choice. Was it not so?"

"He did not go *back*. He went to the humans, yes, but he did not go back. He still serves the People."

"So you believed . . . or you would never have given him your blessing. And have you talked of this with the Kel?"

"No."

"Humans would surely not let him go again, if he even lived to reach them."

"He *has* reached them." Niun made a gesture which included An-ehon, northward, the wide sky above the rocks. "There have been no ships, no more attacks. She'pan, I know that he has reached them, and they have heard him."

"Heard him say *what?*"

That struck him dumb, for all his faith in Duncan did not bridge that gap of realities, that could span what was mri and what was human with a request to go away.

"And you talk of regaining the means to move," she said. "So I have thought in that direction too, but perhaps with different aims. You always hunt eastward. I have heard so."

He nodded, without looking at her.

"You hope to stay close hereabouts," she said. "Or to move east, perhaps. Do you hope, even after so many days—that he will find us?"

"Some such thing."

"I shall send Hlil to An-ehon," she said. "He may arrange his own particulars; he may take whatever of the Kel he needs, and a hand of sen'ein."

"Without me."

"You have other business. To find Duncan."

On two thoughts his heart leaped up and crashed down again. "Gods, go off with the Kel in one place and yourself left with no sufficient guard—"

"I have waited," Melein said, as if she had not heard him. "First, to know how long this silence in the heavens would last. We need what is in An-ehon, yes; a hand of days or more: Hlil will need a little time in the city, and more returning if they are successful, and carrying their limit. But alone, with no burden at all—I daresay you could search even to the landing site and reach us again here in that time."

"Possibly," he said. "But—"

"I have weighed things for myself. I doubt you will succeed; Duncan surely went with his dus, and if it were still with him, he could have found us by now . . . if he were coming. But I loved him too, our Duncan. Take it at that value, and find him if you can; or find that we have lost him, one or the other. And then set your mind on what you have to do for this tribe."

"You need not send me, not to satisfy *me*."

"Lose no time." She bent, took his face between her hands, kissed his brow, delayed to look at him. "It may be, if you are too late getting back—you will not find us here. There are other cities, other choices."

"Gods, and no more defense there than we had in An-ehon. You know, you know what humans can do—"

"Go. Get moving."

She let him go, and he rose up, bent to press a farewell kiss to her cheek. His hand touched hers, fingers held a moment, panic beating in him. He was skilled enough to fend challenge from her; Hlil was; she was parting with both of them.

"My blessing," she whispered at him. He went, quickly, past the wondering eyes of the sen'ein, averting his face from their stares. He was halfway back to the Kel before he recalled the veil.

And suddenly, by the sandfall, a shadow startled him, kel-black and somber. Ras. He finished tucking the veil in place, met her. "Ras?" He acknowledged her courteously, attempting comradeship.

But she said no word. She never did. She walked behind him, a coldness at his back.

Silence fell in Kel, at his coming. They waited, a ring of black, of gold-limned faces. He came among them and through their midst with Ras in his wake as far as the ring of the second rank; they stayed seated when he motioned them to do so. He dropped to his knees nearest the lights, across from Hlil; and he removed both veil and headcloth, *mez* and *zaidhe,* in token of humility, of request.

"Kel'ein," he said in that silence. "Yes—at least to the matter of recovering our belongings from the city." He leaned his hands on his knees and drew breath, gazing at their shadowed faces, row on row, to the limits of the recess. "Hlil will be in charge of that party; Hlil, surely the she'pan will give you some advice in that matter. If not, seek it of her."

"Aye," Hlil muttered with a quizzical look on his broad face.

"I warn you this much: be wary. A kel'en should go in ahead, searching for any traces of landing. There could be machines set to sense your presence, very small. Anything that does not seem to belong there—O gods, kel Hlil, be suspicious, of every small thing. And if you should see ships aloft, do not lead them; go astray, lose them, until the wind has blotted your trail. They do not depend on eyes, but on instruments."

"You refuse leading, kel'anth?"

"I am sent elsewhere." His heart set itself to beating painfully. "Kel Seras, be in charge over the Kel that stays in camp; Hlil, I have said. Good evening to you."

They did not question him; he desperately did not invite it. He rose, gathered up an empty pouch for food, slipped on the headcloth again and veiled himself.

And turned to face kel Ras, who had risen among the others, whose cold face was veilless, eyes hard above the kel-scars. "Ras," he said in a voice he wanted to carry no farther than it had to. "Ras, in this—go with Hlil."

"If Hlil wills," she said likewise quietly; but in the silence of the Kel it surely carried. It was more reasonable in her than he had expected, which itself made him suspect some tangled motive.

"Thank you," he said, and started away, through their midst.

"Kel'anth," Hlil called out; and when he stopped and looked back: "Will you take nothing with you?"

"Kath and Sen will be short of hunters. The dus and I will manage."

"That beast—"

"—cares for me," he said, knowing their disapproval of it. "Life and honors."

Hlil omitted any wish to him in return. Only Ras came and with irony watched him out onto the path. She did not follow. He looked back to be sure, and once again; and then put her from his concerns and walked on, the long corridor outward.

He alarmed the sentry, coming out at such an hour. He gave the signal, a low whistle, and passed, hearing the kel'en high in the rocks settle back to his place.

Dus, he called when he had reached the outside, the level of the plain.

It was there. He kept walking and felt it before he heard it, a heavy shape moving among the rocks, a whuff of breath suddenly at his heels as he passed a boulder. He sensed disturbance in it, an echo of his own troubled mind, and tried to calm himself, as a man must who walked with dusei.

He took the way he had taken daily, from which he had come this same evening. He was footsore even in starting out; day after day he had pushed himself farther than he ought. Sense said he should rest now; but he could do that on the journey, when he must. Time was precious—life itself, if one ran out of it.

And anxiously as he walked he scanned all the heavens, to be sure that they were empty of watchers, gazed over all the flat horizons, the rounded hills. The night-bound desolation dismayed him, starker than it was by day. Dead stars above. And enemies.

A soft surge of strength came into him then, beast-blank: dus mind, offered to his need. It wished to comfort, brushing against him in its waddling stride.

He took the gift, bearing eastward.

The place where their own ship had landed: that was surely where Duncan had gone, to the first place humans would have come in trying to locate them. He walked steadily—did not dismiss the dus from his side to hunt, not now: he needed it by him to find a safe way, exhausted as he was, for the open sands held ugly surprises.

It made him no complaints. Dusei were night walkers by preference. It tossed its massive head and ranged either at his side or a little ahead of him, snuffing the wind, panting a little at times from the pace he set.

Duncan . . . had never been able to match his stride. Always he had had to shorten his steps when Duncan was by him; and the very air of Kutath was hostile to a human's lungs. It was madness that Duncan had ventured this desert alone.

The chance was—he admitted it to himself—that the odds had overtaken Duncan, coming back, if not going. Only one thing Duncan had had in his favor, that he might have been mri enough to handle: the company of his dus.

Find it, he willed his own, casting it the image. Dusei, it was said, had no memory for events, only for persons and places. He shaped Duncan for it; he shaped the other dus, so long its companion. *Find them; hunt.*

Whether it understood clearly or not he could not tell; on the following day it began to radiate something in answer, which prickled at the nape and tightened the skin behind his ears.

Friend, he shaped.

It tossed its head and kept casting about anxiously, making occasional puffs of breath. Its general tendency was eastward, but it had no track, no more than in all the other treks they had made, only a vague, persistent nervousness.

He slept by snatches, day or night, whenever he could go no farther, curled up against the dus's warmth until he could regain his strength. He was by now out onto the wide flat, where the land went on forever, save for the rim and the void beyond, world's edge. He drove himself, not madly, as one who did not know his limits, but as one who did, and thought he might pass them by a margin.

He caught a darter or two in his path, and for all he hated raw flesh, he ate, and shared with the dus, which persisted in its distress.

And finally he looked back, at the west, where the sun set with a shadow on it, amber and red and darker tones.

Not moisture-bearing cloud, not on Kutath.

Dust across the sun.

He stared at it, and beside him the dus flicked its ears uneasily and moaned.

Chapter Three

The weather had held steady for days, out of Kutath's eternally cloudless sky, but the west bore a murkiness this dawn which boded trouble.

And the back trail . . . daylight showed nothing, no hint of movement.

Duncan kept moving, looking frequently over his shoulder; it was the land's deceptive roll, a trick of the eye—on his side for once. He made what time he could, looking to the storm with hope.

Cover, he desperately needed.

And again and again he sought the presence of his dus. The beast ranged out at times, hunting, perhaps, exercising a little fear-warding on those who followed, kel'ein, strangers. He was full of dread whenever it was parted from him, that it might try to attack his pursuers, that they might kill it.

Here, he ordered it, but it did not touch his mind, so that he went alone, blind in that sense he needed. He walked steadily . . . cut off a bit of the blue pipe which he carried among his other supplies, and slipped it into his mouth beneath the veils. Doubled, he wore them, like the robes, for although he had become acclimated, he had no business carrying the smallish pack he bore, no business doing anything that taxed his breathing. *We are not bearers of burdens,* mri were wont to say, disdaining manual labor and any who would perform it; and he had long since understood the common sense in that attitude, in which a mri kel'en walked the land with no more burden than his weapons, often taking not so much as a canteen, where no free water existed. He pushed himself too hard. He knew it, in the rawness of his throat, the headaches which half blinded him. He played just beyond the convenient reach of his mri shadows—curious, he reckoned them, keeping an eye on a stranger, and it was not to his advantage to increase the pace. He kept himself constantly alert to the horizons and the sand underfoot, stayed to sandstone shelves and domes where he could, not alone to avoid leaving tracks, but to avoid the dangers of the sand. *Mez* and *zaidhe,* veil and visored headcloth, and the several layers of the kel-robes: these he had chosen, although others had been offered; and a pistol and the ancient *yin'ein,* the weapons-of-honor . . . these he had by similar choice. He reckoned he might try a shot to dissuade his followers, but firing *at* them . . . all the kel-law abhorred such a thing; he had more than the robes to mark him mri, and he would not.

The dust began to kick up in discernible clouds, wave fronts borne on the wind. The sand ran in moving serpentines like water across the broad shelf of sandstone which he followed.

He turned his head yet again, half-blinded by the sand, lowered his visor against the dust.

And when he looked back again before him there was a black figure on the northwest horizon, nearer by far than he had expected, and in a different quarter.

Panic tugged at him, bidding him swing away south, and perhaps that was what they wanted him to do. He glanced to that horizon and saw nothing but naked land and naked, sand-fouled sky. There was an incline: his eye had learned to pick variations out of the vast samenesses, the incredible flat expanses. Ambush was possible there.

He bore west, summoning his dus with all his might, apprehensive now of every quarter of the horizon. They might cut him off to question him; and even a stone's-throw sight of him would tell them he did not belong here, that some connection might be made between ships and destroyed cities and a stranger-kel'en.

Only the dusei, if they had not killed them, his own and the wild ones which was its offspring, might set fear enough into them, sendings of nameless dread.

But time would come when that fear itself drove them to attack, for kel'ein were trained to caution, not cowardice. They would fight the fear as readily as they would an enemy.

His heartbeat hammered in his temples; there came times when he walked blind, sight blurred, numbed by want of air. He dared not, as he wanted desperately to do—abandon the pack. They would come on it, know by the alien things of it that here was a mystery they could not leave unsolved. A sand-laden gust rocked him, rattled off his lowered visor, stinging his hands, the only part of his flesh exposed. He leaned into it, hands tucked into the wide sleeves of his robes. The battering gusts made him stagger, and after a time he was less and less sure that he remained true to west. The rock underfoot was uneven, and dipped and rose, misguiding him when he needed to catch his balance.

Dus, he sent, desperate, cursing it for its tendency to be elsewhere when it was most needed. The wind blasted body heat away from him, weakened his limbs. He began to be afraid, wondering whether to take shelter for fear of the wind itself, or to keep walking, trying to lose his pursuers while the wind erased tracks and obscured vision.

He slipped suddenly, rock peeling under his feet; he hit soft sand, caught his balance, tried to retreat onto the sandstone shelf, but it had run out. He tried vision without the visor, a mistake; he lowered it again, and in that little time he stopped to clear his eyes his limbs were chilled to the bone, shaking so that it tore his joints.

He was blind and out on open sand; and of a sudden he began to be very much afraid, that he was making wrong choices, that he should have stayed on the rock surface. It was not panic fear, only deep dread; he kept moving, into the wind, the only means he had of determining west.

Fear grew. He looked behind him and the bleared eye of Na'i'in showed through the storm and the visor like the ghost of a sun, wan and sickly hued. In all the world there was neither up nor down, neither horizon nor sand underfoot, only the sun strong enough to penetrate the murk. He swung about again, sucked dusty air through the veils, weary with the battering. If he went down, he thought, he would die.

"Dus," he muttered aloud, wishing, pleading it back to him. The wind drowned all sound, the demon voice becoming an element in itself. His knees tottered under him, his joints wearied from the slipping sand and the force of the gusts, until at last he slipped to his knees and hunched away from the wind, fumbling with shaking hands after the bit of pipe he carried. His fingers were stiff; he bit the piece instead of using the knife, stuffed the rest back. His mouth was so dry it stuck, and his eyes stung with the dryness. "Dus," he murmured again, despairing.

A curious paralysis had settled on him, the cessation of pain. The wind vibrated into his very bones, masked every other sound, and became no-sound. He had no more force at his back; sand was piling up there, sheltering him, making an arc about him, drifting into his lap.

And fear—grew. Sweat prickled on his skin, sucked dry before it could run. He began to think of something creeping up on him, something better adapted than he to the wind and storm—it seeped into him, so that slowly he moved, stirred himself, thrust himself to his feet and staggered farther against the wind. Panic drove him, a dread so strong he tore his knees with his driving strides.

Dus-fear, not his own: he recognized it suddenly; not his own beast, but another, and near. It drew on the images of the rational mind, shaped itself. Ha-dus, wild one, wild-born, of the tame pair the mri had brought here . . . and dangerous without his own to fend it back.

He moved; it was all he could do.

And suddenly a shadow came at him on the other side.

He snatched at the shortsword, staggering aside—knew suddenly, recognized it.

His dus. It materialized out of the murk, pressed against him, and he sank down with its great body between him and the wind. It wove this way and that between him and the gusts; and another shape and another joined it, slope-shouldered, massive, weaving him a circle of protection. He knew his own, flung his arms about its hot, fat-rolled neck, and the beast heaved itself down beside him, five hundred kilos of velvet-furred devotion, venom-clawed, radiating a ward-impulse that meant business.

The other dusei, the wild ones, settled about him so that among the three he was warm and sheltered from the wind. Sand built up about them too, but each time they rose and shook it off, their great strength untroubled by the effort. He lay against the shoulder of his own, breathing in great gasps—found strength enough

to finally shrug out of the pack, to fumble out packets of dried
food. He put bits in his mouth, sipped at the canteen, holding
water there to moisten them, and finally gained control enough to
chew and swallow.

His dus nudged at him, begging; he offered it a piece of dried
meat. The massive head pushed at his hand, flat face inclined; the
prehensile upper lip picked the tidbit off so delicately he felt nothing but the hot breath on his hand. The other dusei crowded him,
and for one and then the other he offered the remainder, in either
hand, fingers carefully out of the way, for the jaws could crush
bone. The bits vanished as daintily as the other. He tucked down
again, hands within sleeves, conscious of vibration, first from his
own dus and then from the others, pleasure-sound, inaudible in
the shriek of the wind. Eyes shut, ears down, nostrils opening
only slightly, filtering through fringed internal hairs and membranes, the dusei were not suffering in the least.

Duncan snugged down between, wiped what he reckoned was a
trace of blood from his nose and bit himself off another bit of
pipe, as safe as any man could be in Kutath's wild, companioned
by such as these.

Chapter Four

The younglings huddled, muttered in hissing whispers. Occasionally one looked up, shifted weight uncomfortably.

Suth loathed them, once companions. They came near the bed when they must, offering food rich and elaborate. They trembled until it was accepted. They mourned one elder on the ship; another was in the making. Suth Horag-gi clenched degh's bony lips and groaned in the agony of Change.

Suth: *it*, neuter until the hormonal shifts had begun to course hot and cold through degh's body, until appetite increased and temper shortened to the verge of madness. The ship *Shirug* moved far apart from human ships orbiting Kutath, and ignored inquiries. There was the Wrapping of the departed elder; there was mourning; there was *ag-arhd,* the Consuming. These were secret things, in which Suth felt an instinctive vulnerability. Degh was not capable of full function in degh's hormone-tormented state, moving toward Change. Humans inquired, offered help, doubtless deviously motivated, hoping to learn enough to gain control . . . offered regret, soliciting information in the process. Degh commanded degh's attendants to silence.

Degh ate. Already the pallor of youngling skin was diminishing, and each move freed tissue-thin sheets of former skin, exposing elder-dark new skin beneath, a complete skin change twice since the Consuming. Suth was sore, sensitive new skin like a bleeding wound. The joints of degh's facial plates ached, aggravated by the need to eat, to drink, constantly. Degh burned with fever, heightened metabolism, and most of all those parts which had not yet determined function burned, swollen, maddening with pain.

A youngling ventured near with *mul,* water-soaked, to ease the skin. Suth suffered it, sucking on a straw from a mug of soi, occasionally reaching to a platter for a sweet.

Suddenly there was pain, and Suth screamed and flung the platter and struck. Something cracked, and when the grayness cleared, other younglings were bearing away the dead one and cleaning up the spilled sweetmeats. Suth hissed satisfaction, annoyance departed. Another took up the washing, more carefully.

"Report," Suth breathed, clenching degh's hand about a new mug of soi. Degh sucked at it, looked at the frightened younglings. "Witless, the news: report."

"Favor, Honored, there is no report available; storm is covering the land."

"Storm."

"A vast and violent storm. Honored, 687.78 *koingh* across. We attempted to penetrate it, but at this range, and with the dust—"

Suth breathed a sigh of weary pleasure. "Perhaps the human Duncan will die."

"Perhaps, Honored."

Degh wished this earnestly. This human had killed the reverence bai Sharn, in command of *Shirug.* Human elders on *Saber* had then dismissed this Duncan as if this act were inconsiderable to them. Degh had been only youngling then, neuter, confused, horrified by the death as all the younglings had been horrified.

Now degh yearned toward the death of this human; it was anomaly, perverted; it no longer knew what it was, this Sten Duncan. It had killed younglings, it and its mri allies, and now it killed an elder. Its kind excused this . . . threatened now even to treat with mri, through this mri-imprinted youngling. The very thought set Suth's hearts to hammering and made degh short of breath.

Forty-three years the mercenary Kel had served regul against humans, and now at war's end came a new arrangement to trouble regulkind: mri, intriguing with humans.

Adult authority was desperately needed in this crisis, a mind to make decisions on which the survival of other elders might rest, back at Kesrith, even on homeworld itself. Sharn was dead; elder Hulagh was years removed, on Kesrith. Someone had to make the decisions.

The pain. . . .

"Honored, Honored, be easy," a youngling murmured, sponging gently with the *mul.* Suth panted and strove to rise, fell back again, amazed at the feel of degh's own body, the increase in girth. The bony carapace which covered the face ached maddeningly. Degh closed degh's eyes and breathed in great gasps, aching in degh's lower belly until the pain was intolerable.

"Degh is in crisis," a youngling moaned. "Days, days of this; it must end, it must end, or degh will die."

"Silence!" degh shouted, and shouting helped; the pain ebbed somewhat. Muscles contracted. The hearts sped and the temperature rose.

It was true. Degh was in deep trouble. Degh had served bai Hulagh, male, and approached Impression; degh had looked to the time of Change, knowing degh's future gender with smug certainty, female to Hulagh's male . . . ambition, to mate the Eldest of great doch Alagn: security, and vast power.

But to Suth's lasting dismay there had been transfer; Suth, most honored of Hulagh's youngling attendants, passed as special favor to bai Sharn, who undertook a mission on which but one elder could be risked: Sharn, female, on a voyage years in length. Maleness tempted; Sharn herself was very high in doch Alagn.

Sharn, female, fourth eldest of one of the greatest of the docha, and murdered by a deranged human youngling.

Degh had been Impressed in witnessing that incomprehensible act. To replace bai Sharn . . . to *be* Sharn . . . that desire came with the Consuming.

And degh could not complete the Change, poised between, for days neither Hulagh's nor Sharn's, neither female nor male.

Degh screamed aloud and cursed the human who had done this thing, who allied with mri and tried to lure others of his species after. A hundred twenty-three stars, a hundred twenty-three . . . dead . . . lifeless . . . systems. And even after seeing the deadly track the mri had cut through the galaxy . . . humans approached these killers and spoke of peace.

Degh must live. Species demanded. *Life* demanded. More than personal ambition, more than doch, than the chance of elevating degh's little doch of Horag, allying to powerful Alagn at its highest levels: these things were motivation . . . but this touched something at depth Suth had never felt, which perhaps no regul had ever had to feel, for no regul had ever confronted such a possibility, death on such a scale. Degh must live, generate, produce lives to deal with this threat, innumerable lives.

There came another touch at degh's body, faint, tremulous. It was Nagn, an older youngling. And it tore back with a shriek of dismay.

"Honored," it cried, "I burn!"

It had happened: next eldest had gone prematurely into Change. Suth cried out with relief and shut degh's eyes.

The pain moved lower. Muscle contractions began at last, fever increasing, skin sloughing and peeling. The younglings brought food, and bathed deghn, and applied unguents to the swollen parts.

Scarcely supported by the younglings, the Honored Nagn moved again to degh's side, touched, shuddering in degh's own pain.

The choice was Suth's. Suth's body was making it. The swelling continued as one vestigial set of organs was absorbed, and the other began, in convulsive heaves of Suth's body, to press down into the membrane covering the aperture . . . descended, evident as it would never be henceforth save in mating.

"Male!" a youngling declared.

Nature's logic. Suth smiled, a tightening of the muscles beneath his eyes, and this despite the pain. Elsewhere Nagn writhed in the throes of Change, but Nagn's choice was set, and swifter. Tiag cried out in agony, and Morkhug, the hysteria of Change settling upon all the eldest.

The pain ebbed in time. Suth moved, supported by younglings. Never again would he stand long unaided. His bulk, already increased by his appetite, would increase twice more. His legs, once strong, would atrophy until little muscle lay under the abundant fat, although his arms, constantly exercised by the operation of the prosthetic supports, would remain strong. Senses would dim hereafter, save for sight. The mind dominated. Regul memory was instant and indelible; he would live, barring accident or murder, for three hundred years more, remembering every chance moment and every minute detail to which he paid attention.

He had lived to be adult, and only thirty percent of regul did so; he was, by virtue of being the first adult on the ship, remote from others of greater age . . . an elder, in command of *Shirug* and of whatever other adults matured; only one percent of regul reached such status.

And by the Change which had come on him he could not now meet his old bai Hulagh as mate . . . but as a rival of another doch. He was senior to Nagn and Tiag and Morkhug, who were Alagn, and therefore this great Alagn ship, the pride of the doch, became Horag territory. Hulagh of Alagn had miscalculated, reckoning every eventuality but Sharn's premature death and a Horag sexing ahead of the others. Suth smiled.

Then he looked on the three who were in the throes of Change, . . . on Nagn, who was flushing with the swift completion of agonies which had held him for days.

"Out!" he shouted at the other younglings.

They fled. He struck at those who supported him, and they joined the others in flight. He could not long stand, but sank down on his weakened legs, panting.

"Honor, reverend Nagn," he said.

"Honor, bai Suth." She struggled to sit. He had deprived her of younglings to help her, but she was female and would always be more mobile than he save in the final stage of carrying.

And she had not near attained his dignity of bulk, nor suffered the several skin changes. Those were, for her, only beginning.

"Favor," said Suth, "Nagn Alagn-ni."

"Favor, Suth Horag-gi."

She came to him, the order of their age of Change, although it was established by mere moments. He mated her, with dispatch and twice, for honor to her precedence of the others. She was next eldest and would hold that rank while he held the ship. He moved then, necessity, and mated the other two, which likely would produce no young, but which would Impress them with more haste, painful as it was for them. He would mate them until all three were with as many young as they could carry. These were his officers; it was economical, his maleness. There was need of rapid reproduction of Horag young: eldest claimed all young in any mating. As other younglings aboard *Shirug* sexed, they would sex under his Impress, female.

Horag young would increase on the ship at first by the factor of the litters these three would bear; and more, with more females. Had he sexed female as he had first tended, the Alagn youngling Nagn would have sexed male in complement, and the next two would have sexed randomly, with himself bearing three to five young as female, some by Nagn, some by any other young male that might develop, and though he could claim such young as Horag, as female he could make only a small nest of Horag young on an otherwise Alagn ship.

It was indeed nature's logic—and politics—but Suth was smug in it, suffused with a feeling of power and rightness after his long suffering. There would be a new order on this ship, *his* ship. And for Horag to succeed in an operation where great Alagn had failed miserably. . . . Ambitions occurred to him, incredible in scope.

"It is not necessary," he said, "that humans know we exist."

"No," Nagn agreed, "but until they realize we have an elder on this ship, they will be continuing on their own course of action. They will do what pleases them without consulting us."

"If all witnesses die," said Suth, "—there is no event."

"Eldest?"

"We are far from human bases; we can do what pleases us."

"Strike at elders?"

"Secure ourselves."

Nagn considered this, her nostrils flaring and shutting in agitation. Finally they remained open. "With their rider ship and their probe as well, they have mobility we do not."

"Mri could even the balance."

"Even mri have some memory, eldest. They will not hire to us."

"On that world, Nagn Alagn-ni, there is power. It struck back at our ship; we experienced it and we know the sites of it. If both mri and human witnesses perish—then regul worlds are freed of an inestimable danger; and humans can ask questions—but regul need give no answers."

Nagn grinned, a slow relaxation of her jaws and a narrowing of her eyes.

Chapter Five

Yet again the beasts shifted position, not to be buried, shaking the sand off with a vengeance. The gale had fallen off markedly, and Na'i'in shone brighter this morning than it had yesterday noon. Duncan stumbled to his feet, muscles aching. He had slept finally, when the dusei no longer roused so often; and he was stiff, the more so that the great beasts had pressed on him and leaned on him: instinct, he reckoned, to keep his chilling body up to their fever warmth. They milled about now, blew and sneezed wetly, clearing their noses. Duncan shivered, folding his arms about him, for the cold wind threatened to steal what warmth he had gathered.

Time to move. Anxiety settled on him as he realized he could see horizon through the curtain-like gusts; if he could see, so could others, and he had lingered too long. He should have been on his way in the night, when the sand had ceased to come so heavily; he should have realized, and instead he had settled down to sleep.

Stupidity, his mri brother had been wont to tell him on other occasions, *is not an honorable death.*

"Hai," he murmured to the dusei, gathered up his pack, shrugged into it, started off, with a protest of every muscle in his body, making what haste he could.

He took a little more of the dried food, with a last bite of the pipe, and that was breakfast, to quiet his hunger pangs. The dusei tried to cajole their share, and he gave to his own, but when he offered to the others, his began a rumbling that boded trouble.

He at once flung the handful wide, and the two stranger dusei paused, themselves rumbling threats, letting the pace separate them. After a moment they lowered their heads and took the food, and the curtaining sand began to come between. The storm-night was over, truces broken. His heart still beat rapidly from the close call, the injudiciousness of his own dus to start a quarrel while he had his hand full of something the others wanted. He glanced back; one of them stood up on its hind legs, a towering shadow, threatening their backs; but his own whuffed disgust and plodded on, having evidently dismissed the seriousness of the threat. His was tame only in the sense it wanted to stay with him, which dusei had done with the mri of Kesrith for two thousand years, coming in out of their native hills, choosing only kel-caste, bonding lifelong; and not even the mri knew why. Kath'ein had no need and sen'ein minds were too complex and cold for the dusei's taste: so the mri said. But for some mad reason, this one had chosen a human—its only existing choice, perhaps, when mri on Kesrith had perished.

He had a dread of it someday departing his side, deserting him for the species it preferred; truth be told, that parting would be painful beyond bearing, and lonely after, incredibly lonely. He needed it, he suspected, with a crippled need a kel'en of the mri might never have. And perhaps the dus knew it.

He walked, his hand on the beast's back, looked over his shoulder. The other two were only the dimmest shadows now. They would choose, perhaps, other kel'ein. . . . He hoped not the kel'ein who followed him now; that was a dread thought.

His rumbled with pleasure, blowing at the sand occasionally, shambling along at his pace, turning its face as much as might be from the wind.

But after a time that pleasure-sound died, and something else came into its mood, a pricklish anxiety.

The skin contracted between his shoulders. He looked back, searching for shadows in the amber haze—coughed, blind for a moment.

The dus had stopped too, began that weaving which accompanied ward-impulse, back and forth, back and forth between him and some presence not far distant.

"Hush," he bade it, dropped to his knees to fling his arms about its neck and distract it, for a determined pursuer could use that impulse to locate them.

A mri who pursued . . . could well do that.

The impulse and the weaving stopped; the beast stood still and shivered against him, and he scrambled up and started it moving again, facing the wind, blind intermittently in the gusts, and with the beast's disturbance sawing at his nerves like primal fear.

The land did not permit mistakes. He had made one, this morning, out of weakness.

Turn, he thought, and meet his pursuers, plead that he carried a message that might mean life or death for all the mri?

One look at his habit and his weapons and his human-brown eyes . . . would be enough. Mri—meant the People; outsiders and higher beasts were tsi'mri: not-People. He and the dus were equal in their eyes; it was built into the hal'ari that way, and no logic could argue without words to use.

It was a stranger behind him, no one of the tribe he knew: they would have showed themselves long since if that were the case; there was more than curiosity involved, if pursuit continued after the storm. He was sure of it now, with a gut-deep knowledge that he was in serious trouble.

Kel'ein did not walk far alone, not by choice. There was a tribe somewhere about, and a Kel which had set itself to trail an invader.

Hlil stopped with the sand-veiled shadow of the city before him, sank down on his heels on the windward side of a low dune and surveyed the altered outlines of the ruin tsi'mri had left.

An-ehon. *His* city. He had never lived in it; but it was his by heritage. He had come here in the journeyings which attended the accession of a she'pan, when he was very young; had sat within walls while the Sen closed themselves within the Holy and the Mother gained the last secrets she had to know, which were within the precious records of the city.

No more. It was over, the hundred thousand years of history of this place—ended, in his sight, in an instant. He had seen the towers falling, comrades slain on right and on left of him, and for so long as he lived he would carry that nightmare with him.

What he had to do now . . . was more than recover the tents, the Things, which concerned only life; it was to retake the Holy, and that . . . that filled him with fear. The stranger-she'pan had laid hands on him, giving him commission to handle what he must: perhaps she had the right to do so. He was not even certain of that. An-ehon was destroyed, the means of teaching she'panei gone with it, and they must trust this stranger, who claimed to hold in herself the great secrets. It was all they had, forever, save what rested here.

Merai, he had thought more than once on this journey, with even the elements turning on them, *Merai, o gods, what should I do?*

He did so now, thinking of the city before them, of the tribe— gods, of the tribe, pent within that narrow cut and the sand moving. In his mind was a vision of them being overwhelmed in it by sandfalls, or the sandslip building all down the cut, gravity bearing them in a powdery slide into the basin, a fall which turned his stomach to contemplate.

He had sent five hands of kel'ein back when the storm began, to aid if they could. That far he went against the she'pan's plans, dividing his force. Perhaps she would forgive; perhaps she would curse, damning him, cutting him off from the tribe for disobedience. That was well enough, he thought, tears welling up in his throat, if only it saved the rest of the children. There was following orders and there was sanity; and the gods witness he tried to choose aright . . . to obey and to disobey at once.

Sand slipped near him. Ras had caught up with him, came over the crest and slid down to a crouch at his side. In a moment more came Desai, third-rank kel'en, blind in one eye, but the one that saw, saw keenly: a quiet man and steady, and after him came Merin, a Husband, and the boy Taz . . . an unscarred, who had begged with all his heart to come. There were others, elsewhere, lost in the rolls of the land and the gusting wind. He took to heart what the kel'anth had said of ambushes and ships, and kept his forces scattered.

He waited a moment, letting the others take their breaths, for beyond this point was little concealment. Then he rose up, started down the trough, keeping to the low places where possible, while his companions strayed along after him at their own rate, making no grouped target for the distance-weapons of tsi-mri.

But when they neared the buildings and crossed the track by which they had fled the city, and came upon the first of the dead, anger welled up in him, and he paused. Black-robe: this had been a kel'en. He gazed at the partially buried robes, the mummy made of days in the drying winds, ravaged by predators: they must have held feast in An-ehon.

The others overtook him; he walked on without looking at them. Ahead were the shells of towers, geometries obscured in sand, horizonless amber in which near buildings were distinct even to the cracks in their walls and the distant ones hove up as shadows. And everywhere the dead.

"This was Ehan," Desai said of the next they came to; and "Rias," said Merin of another, for the Honors these dead wore could still distinguish them, when wind and dryness had made them all alike.

From time to time they spoke names of those they saw among the passages between the ruined buildings; and the dead were not only kel'ein, but old sen'ein, gold-robes, scholars, whose drying skulls had held so much of the wisdom of the People; young and old, male and female, they lay in some places one upon the other, folk that they had known all their lives; among them were the bodies of kath'ein, blue-robes, the saddest and most terrible—the child-rearers and children. Walls had fallen, quick and cruel death; in other places the dead seemed without wound at all. There were the old whose bronze manes were dark and streaked with age; many, many of their number, who had not been strong enough to bear the running; and in many a place a kel'en's black-robed body lay vainly sheltering some child or old one.

Name after name, a litany of the dead: kath Edis, one of his own kath-mates, and four children, two of whom might be his own: that hit him hard; and sen'ein, wise old Rosin; and kel Dom: they had come into the Kel the same year. He did not want to look, and must, imposing horrors over brighter memories.

And the others, who had lost closer kin, Kel-born, who had kin to lose: Taz, who mourned trueparents and sister and all his uncles; and Ras—Ras passed no body but that she did not look to see.

"Haste," he said, having his fill of grieving. But Ras trailed last, disobedient, still searching, almost lost to them in the murk.

He said nothing to that: matters were thin enough between them. But he looked at no more dead; and the others grew wise, and did not, either, staying close with him. Chance was, he thought, that they could run head-on into members of their own party, if they were not careful in this murk, come up against friends primed to expect distance-weapons and primed to attack . . . an insanity: he had no liking at all for this kind of slipping about.

Suddenly the square lay before them, vast, ribboned with blowing sand which made small dunes about the bodies which lay thicker here than elsewhere in the city. At the far side hove up the great Edun, the House of the People, Edun An-ehon, sad in surrounding ruin. It was mostly intact, the four towers, slanting together, forming a truncated pyramid. The doorway gaped darkly open upon steps which ran down into the square. The stone of the edun was pitted and scarred as the other buildings; great cracks showed in the saffron walls, but this place which had been the center of the attack had also held the strongest defense, and it had survived best of any structure in the city. Hope welled up in him, hope of success, of doing quickly what they had come to do and getting away safely.

He moved and the others followed, on a course avoiding the open square, taking their cover where they could find it among the shattered buildings and the blowing sand. Finally he broke away at a run, up the long steps, toward that ominous dark within, hard-breathing with the effort and thinking that at any moment fire might blast out at him.

It did not. He slid through the doorway and inside, against the wall, where dust slipped like oil beneath his feet, where was silence but for the wind outside and the arriving footsteps of the others. They entered and stopped, all of them listening a moment. There was no sound but the wind outside.

"Get a light going," he bade Taz. The boy fumbled in the pouch he carried and knelt, working hastily to set fire in the oilwood fiber he had brought. Ras arrived, last of them. "Stay out there," Hlil ordered her, "visible; others will be coming soon."

"Aye," she said, and slipped back out again into the cold wind, a miserable post, but no worse than the dark inside.

The flame kindled; Taz shielded it with his body and lit a knot of fiber impaled on an oilwood wand. They all, he, Merin, and Desai, kept bodies between the fire and the draft from the door.

Merin lit other knots and passed them about. Outside, Ras' low voice reported no sight of the others.

Hlil took his light and walked on. The inner halls echoed to the least step. Cracks marred the walls, ran, visible once eyes had adjusted to the dim light, about the higher walls and ceilings, marring the holy writings there.

The entry of kel-tower was clear, and that of Sen, the she'pan's tower and Kath . . . affording hope of access to their belongings. But when he looked toward the shrine his heart sank, for that area of the ceiling sagged, and the pillars which guarded that access were damaged. He felt of them and stone crumbled at his least touch on the cracks.

He had to know; he went farther into the shrine, thrust his light-wand into a cracked wall and passed farther still.

"Hlil," Merin protested, behind him.

He hesitated, and even as he stopped a sifting of plaster hit his shoulders and dimmed the light.

"Go back," he bade Merin and the others. "Stand clear."

The Holy was there, that which they venerated and the Holy of the Voyagers; his knees were weak with dread of the great forbidden; but in his mind was the hazard of losing them once for all, these things which were more than the city and more than all their lives combined.

He moved inward; the others disobeyed and followed: he heard them, saw the lights moving with him, casting triple shadows of himself and the pillars and the inner screen.

Beyond that—the stranger-she'pan had given him her blessing to go: *that first,* she had bidden him. He was shaking unashamedly as he put out a hand and moved the screen aside.

A tiny box of green bronze; figures of corroding metal and gold; a small carven dus and a shining oval case as large as a child: together they were the Pana, the Mysteries, on which he looked, on which no kel'en ought ever to look. He thrust out a hand almost numb, gathered up the smallest objects and thrust them, cold and comfortless, within the breast of his robes. He passed the box to Merin, whose hands did not want to receive it. Last he reached for the shining ovoid, snatched it to him in a sifting of dust and falling plaster. It was incredibly heavy for its size, staggered him, hit a support in a cascade of plaster and fragments.

He stumbled back at the limit of his balance, hit the steadying hands of Desai who snatched him farther, outside, as dust rolled out at them and they sprawled, shaken by the rumble of falling masonry. It stopped.

"Sir?" Taz's voice called.

"We are well enough," Hlil answered, holding the pan'en to him, bowed over it, though the chill seemed to flow from it into his bones. Other hands helped him rise with it: the light of the door showed in a shaft of dust, and the figures of Taz and Ras within it, casting shadows. He carried his burden to the doorway, past them and out into the light and the storm, knelt down and laid the pan'en and the other objects on the top of the steps. Merin added the ancient box, stripped off his veil to shield the Holy objects . . . so did he, and Ras and Desai too. He looked up into the faces of the others, which were stark with dread for what they had in hand. He looked from one to the other, chilled with a sense of separation . . . for kel'ein died, having touched a pan'en: such was the law. Or if they lived, then forever after they were known by it: *pan'ai-khan,* somewhere between Holy and accursed.

"I have dispensation," he said. "I give it you."

They crouched down, huddled together, he and the others, protecting the Holy as if it were something living and fragile, that wanted mortal flesh between it and the elements.

The boy Taz was not with them.

"Taz—are you well?" Hlil shouted into the dark.

"I am keeping the fire," the boy said. "Kel-second, the dust is very thick, but there is no more falling."

"The gods defend us," Hlil muttered, conscious of what he had his hand on, that burned him with its cold. "Only let it hold a little while longer."

Duncan paused, where a scoured ridge of sandstone offered a moment's shelter from the wind, flung his arms about the thick neck of the dus and lowered his head out of the force of the gusts. He coughed, rackingly; his head ached and his senses hazed. The storm seemed to suck oxygen away from him. He uncapped the canteen and washed his mouth, for the membranes were so dry they felt like paper. . . . He swallowed but a capful. He stayed a moment, until his head stopped spinning and his lungs stopped hurting, then he found the moral force to stand and move again.

There was a bright spot in the world, which was the sun; in the worst gusts it was still all that could be seen. The dus moved, guiding him in his moments of blindness.

Then something else grew into reality, tall shadows like trees, branched close to the trunk and rising straight up again, gaunt giants. Pipe. He went toward it, consumed with the desire for the sweet pulp which could relieve his pain and his thirst better than water. The dus lumbered along by him, willingly hurrying; and the shadows took on more and more of substance against amber sky and amber earth.

Dead. No living plants but pale, desiccated fiber materialized before him, strands ripped loose, blowing in the wind, a ghostly forest of dead trunks. He touched the blowing strands, drew his *av-tlen* to probe the trunk closest, to try whether there might be life and moisture at the core.

And suddenly he received something from the dus, warning-sense, which slammed panic into him.

He moved, ran, the beast loping along with him. He cursed himself for the most basic of errors: *Think with the land* the mri had tried to teach him: *Use it; flow with it; be it.* He had found a point in the blankness. He had been nowhere until he had found a point, the rocks, the stand of dead plants. He was nowhere and could not be located until he made himself somewhere.

And childlike, he had gone from point to point. The dus was no protection: it betrayed him.

Think with the land, the Niun had said. *Never challenge beyond your capacity; one does not challenge the* jo *in hiding or the burrower in waiting.*

Or a mri in his own land.

He stopped, faced about, blind in the dust, the shortsword clenched in his fist. Cowardice reminded him he was tsi-mri, counseled to take up the gun and be ready with it. He came to save mri lives; it was the worst selfishness to die, rather than to break kel-law.

Niun would.

He sucked down mouthfuls of air and scanned the area around about, with only a scatter of the great plants visible through the dust. The dus hovered close, rumbling warnings. He willed it silent, flexed his fingers on the hilt.

The dus shied off from the left; he faced that way, heart pounding as the slim shadow of a kel'en materialized out of the wind.

"What tribe?" that one shouted.

"The ja'anom," he shouted back, his voice breaking with hoarseness. He stilled the dus with a touch of his hand; and in utter hubris: "You are in the range of the ja'anom. Why?"

There was a moment's silence. The dus backed, rumbling threat.

"I am Rhian s'Tafa Mar-Eddin, kel-anth and daithon of the hao'nath. And your geography is at fault."

His own name was called for. They proceeded toward challenge by the appointed steps. It was nightmare, a game of rules and precise ritual. He took a steadying breath and returned his *avtlen* to its sheath with his best flourish, emptying his hands. He kept them at his sides, not in his belt, as Rhian had his. He wanted no fight.

"Evidently the fault is mine," he said. "Your permission to go, kel'anth."

"You give me no name. You have no face. What is that by you?"

"Come with me," Duncan said, trying the most desperate course. "Ask of my she'pan."

"Ships have come. There was fire over the city."

"Ask of my she'pan."

"Who are you?"

The dus roared and rushed; pain hit his arm even as he saw the mri flung aside. "No!" Duncan shouted as the dus spun again to strike. The dus did not; the mri did not move; Duncan reached to the numb place on his arm and felt the hot seep of moisture.

Two heartbeats and it had happened. He trembled, blank for the instant, knowing what had hit, the palm-blades, the *as-ei*, worn in the belt. The dus's attack, the mri's reflex—both too quick to unravel: dusei read *intent*.

He shuddered, staggered to the dus and found the other blade, imbedded in the shoulder . . . fatal to a man, no serious thing to the dus's thick muscle. He was shaking all over . . . shock, he

thought; he had to move. It was a kel'anth who lay there, a whole
Kel hereabouts . . .

He leaned above the prostrate form, still shaking, put out a
hand to probe for life, his right one tucked to him. Life—there
was; but the kel'en had dus venom in him, and sand already covered the edges of his robes. Duncan gasped breath on his own,
started away—cursed and shook his head and came back, seized
the robes and tugged and struggled the inert form to the stand of
pipe, left him sitting there.

"Dus," he called hoarsely, turned, veered off into the wind
again, running, the dus moving with lumbering haste at his side.

They would follow; he believed that beyond question. Blood
feud if the kel'anth died and someone to tell the tale of him if he
did not. He coughed and kept running, sucked in dust with the air
despite the veils, slowing when he could no longer keep from
doubling with pain. Dus-sense prickled about him, either the animal's alarm or its sense of a new enemy. He held his injured arm
to him, running a little, walking when he could not run, making
what speed he could.

Two mistakes on his own; the dus had accounted for the third.

"Storm is diminishing," the voice from *Flower* reported. "No
chance yet to assess conditions outside."

"Don't," Koch said, passed a hand reflexively over the stubble
on his head. "Don't risk personnel, in any limited visibility."

"We have our own operations to pursue." *Flower's* exec was
Emil Luiz, chief surgeon, civ and doggedly so. "We know our
limitations. We have measurements to take."

"We copy," Koch muttered. The civs were indeed under his
command, but they were trouble and doubly so since they were
the potential link to the SurTac. "We are dispatching *Santiago* to a
survey pattern. We wish you to observe unusual cautions for the
duration. Please do not disperse crew or scientific personnel on
outside research. Keep everyone within easy jump of the ship,
and no key personnel out of reach of stations. This is a serious
matter, Dr. Luiz. We fully sympathize with your need to gather information, but we do not wish to have to abandon personnel onworld in case of trouble. Understood?"

"We will not disperse personnel outside during your operation. We copy very clearly."

"Your estimation of mission survival down there?"

There was long silence. "Obviously natives survive such storms."

"Unsheltered?"

"We don't know where he is, do we?"

Koch tapped his stylus nervously against the desk. "Code twelve," he cautioned the civ; they used scramble as standard procedure, but there was a nakedness, sending information back and forth after this fashion. He misliked it entirely.

"We suggest further patience," Luiz said. "Anything will have been delayed in this storm."

"We copy," Koch said.

"We request an answer," Luiz said. "*Flower* staff recommends further patience."

"Recommendation noted, sir."

"Admiral, we request you take official note of that recommendation. We ask you cease flights down there. These are clearly reconnaissance and they're provocative. Our personal safety is at stake and so are our hopes of peaceful contact. You may trigger something, and we are in the middle. Please discontinue any military operations down here. Do you copy that, sir?"

Koch's heart was speeding. He held his silence a moment, reached and coded a number onto his desk console. The answer flashed back to his screen, negative.

"We will look into the matter," Koch said. "Please code twelve that and wait shuttled reply."

Now there was silence for a few beats on the other end.

"We copy," Luiz said.

"Any other message, *Flower?* We're moving out of your range. *Santiago* should be in position soon to serve as relay and cover. Ending transmission."

"We copy. Ending transmission."

The artificial voices and crawl of transcription across the second screen ceased. Koch wiped sweat from his upper lip and punched in Silverman of *Santiago.* The insystem fighter was in link at the moment, riding attached to *Saber's* flank as she had ridden into the system. "Commander, Koch here. Report person-ally, soonest."

He received immediate acknowledgment. With matters as they were, key personnel kept communicators on their persons con-stantly.

He punched up security next, Del Degas. The man was in the next office and available, there as soon as four doors could open.

"Sir."

"Someone's overflying *Flower's* scan down there. Who?"

Degas's thin face went tauter still. "We have no missions downworld right now."

"I know that. What about our allies?"

"I'll find out what I can."

"Del—if they're regul . . . theoretically younglings can't take that kind of initiative. If someone's data is wrong on that point, if *Shirug* can function in their hands—that's a problem. Theoreti-cally those shuttles the agreement allows them—aren't armed."

"Like ours," Degas said softly.

"Want *Santiago* out there where she has a view, Del; scan oper-ations have to be subordinated to that for the time being. They won't let us inside; we do what we can."

Regul could not lie; that was the general belief. Their indelible memories made lying a danger to their sanity. So the scientists said.

Likewise regul were legalists. To deal with them it was neces-sary to consider every word of every oral agreement, and to reckon all the possible omissions and interpretations. Regul mem-ory was adequate for that kind of labyrinthine reckoning. Human memory was not.

Degas nodded slowly. "Try again to open contact?"

"Don't. Not yet. I don't want them alarmed. *Santiago's* maneu-vering is enough."

"And if they're not regul doing those overflights?"

"I consider that possibility too."

"And act on it?"

Koch frowned, Del Degas had his private anxiousness in that matter. Conviction, perhaps . . . or revenge. A man who had lost both sons and a wife to mri might harbor either.

"The SurTac," Degas pursued uninvited, "is a deserter. That may have been planned by the office that sent him; but his attitudes are not a calculation; the attitude that dumped that tracer and the transmitter into the canyons . . . was not carelessness. His behavior is clear; he's not human; he's mri; he *says* there are no mri ships. But the psychological alteration he must have undergone, years alone with them on that ship. . . . Those who think they know him may recognize a role he's playing, if he's playing at being SurTac Duncan."

Duncan had refused to debrief to security, only willing to talk to *Flower* staff, with Degas to frame the essential questions and take notes. Degas had been outraged at the order that permitted it.

"The SurTac is a fanatic," Degas said. "And like all such, he's capable of convoluted reasoning in support of his cause. There's also the possibility he saw only what the mri wanted him to see. I strongly urge an attempt to get direct observation down there. Military observation. Galey's mission—"

"Will not be diverted to that purpose."

"Another, then."

"Do you want an objection to policy put on record? Is that what you're asking?"

Degas drew a deep breath, looked down at the floor and up again in silent offense. They had grown too familiar, he with Degas; neighbors, card players; a man had to develop some human associations on a voyage years in duration. They were not of the same branch of the service. He had found Degas' quick mind a stimulation to his own. Now there were entanglements.

"We don't use Galey," Koch said. He considered a moment, weighing the options. "The regul matter first; it may not be youngling shyness that keeps them over-horizon from us. If they can operate, they have powerful motivation for revenge. That's a motive you're not reckoning."

"Assuming human motives. That may be error."

"Who's our regul expert now?" It had been Aldin, Koch recalled. Aldin was dead: old age, like *Saber's* former captain, like the translations chief. Repeated jump stresses took it out of a man, put strain on old hearts. "Who's carrying that department?"

"Dr. Boaz is Xen head."

Boaz, Duncan's friend, the mri expert. Koch bit at his lip. "I'll not pull her up. She's important down there."

Degas shrugged. "Dr. Simeon Averson specialized in language under Aldin; ran the classification system for library on Kesrith. He would be the likely authority in the field after Aldin and Boaz."

The man's knowledge of the unbreachable intricacies of *Flower's* departments did not surprise him. Del Degas was a collector of details. Pent in a closed system of humanity for the years of the voyage, he doubtless had turned his talents to the cataloging of everyone aboard. Koch dimly recalled the little man in question. He tried to call on *Flower* personnel as little as possible, disliking civs operating underfoot, delving into military records and files. Kesrith's civilian governor had saddled him with *Flower,* and Mel Aldin had once been useful in the early stages of the mission, conducting crew briefings and studies, settling matters of protocol between regul elder and humans unused to regul. But the years of voyage had passed; things had found a certain routine, and Aldin had diminished in necessity and visibility. *Flower* held its own privacies.

"You'll want him shuttled up?" Degas asked.

"Do it." Koch leaned back impatiently, rocked in his chair. "Galey moves down: Harris. Two shuttles. Every time we drop a rock into that pond we risk stirring something up. I don't like it. We don't know that machinery's dead. We'll draw ourselves a little back. I don't want us a sitting target."

"I can have armaments moduled in, and scan; a very short delay. As well have several shuttles downworld as two. While we're making one ripple in the pond, so to speak, we might as well take utmost advantage of it. Your operation with Galey might benefit by the information."

Koch expelled a slow breath. A long voyage, a mind like Degas' . . . security had gone incestuous in the long confinement. "Everything," he said, "every minute detail of those flight plans will be cleared with this office." He tapped the stylus against the desk, looked at Degas, turned and keyed an order into the console.

Chapter Six

Others came, across the square, up the steps, shadows out of the storm. Hlil gathered himself up to meet them. "It is safe," he said to kel Dias, who commanded them, and looked beyond her to the ones who followed, sen'ein. He set his face, assumed the assurance he did not feel, met the eyes of the gold-robes who were veiled against wind and dust. "I secured the Pana first; that was my instruction."

They inclined their heads, accepting this, which comforted him. They took charge of the Holy, one spreading his own robes to cover it, for the kel-veils blew and fluttered in the wind.

He left them and went inside with the others, where Taz began to share his light, where knot after knot of fiber flared into life. "Haste," he urged them, "but walk lightly; there has been one collapse in here already."

They moved, no running, but swiftly. He watched them scatter with their several leaders, one group to Kel, one to Kath, one to Sen, and another to the storerooms, and two to the she'pan's tower, so that in a brief time all the building whispered to soft, quick steps, the comings and goings of those who had come to loot the House of all that was their own.

"Go," he murmured distractedly, finding Taz still by him. "If there are any proper lamps at hand, get light in that middle corridor. The rubble is unstable enough without someone falling."

"Aye, sir," the youth exclaimed, and made haste about it.

Even now some were beginning to come down with burdens, stumbling in the dark, having to choose between light and two hands to steady their loads. Hlil stationed himself to guide them to the point where they could see the doorway; the flow began to be a steady to and fro. There was no science in their plundering that he could see; he forbore to complain of it. In their haste and dread of collapse they snatched what they could, as much as they could.

Taz managed lights, two proper lamps, set in the area of the fallen shrine; and to Hlil's vast relief the essential things began to appear, the heavy burden of the tents, the irreplaceable metal poles, wrapped meticulously in twisted and braided fiber; their vessels, their stores of food and oil; a sled of offworld metal; lastly hundreds of rolled mats, the personal possessions of the tribe.

And two sen'ein came inside, gathered up one of the lamps from the hall, passed out of sight into the entry of sen-hall.

He disliked that. He walked a few steps in that direction, fretting with the responsibility he bore for them, and his lack of authority where it regarded sen-matters. He stared anxiously after them, then turned for the door, where a diminishing trickle of kel'ein tended. Shouts drifted down from the heights of the edun, that they had gotten all of it, to the very last.

Hlil walked out onto the steps and into the particle-laden wind, where the two sen'ein who had remained with the Pana struggled to load the Holy onto the sled, padding it with rolled mats below and above. Merin and Dias and Ras had charge, directing the division of goods into bearable portions. They were not going to leave any portion of it if they could help.

He stood idle, fretting with the matter, prevented by rank from lending a hand to it. Perhaps, he thought, they should all have gone back to the relief of the tribe in the storm; or perhaps he should never have divided his force, and should have trusted the she'pan and kel Seras to do the necessary. The load was no easier for the driving wind; and it was a long trek back.

Yet there seemed some lessening in the storm. Excessive optimism, perhaps; the wind would diminish for a time and then return with double force. He could see the top of the ruined building nearest, of many of the buildings, which he had not been able to do when they came.

And the dead, revealed in their numbers, stretching in a line from the bottom of the steps to the far side of the square. Those he had to look on too.

"We might bury them, sir," said a young voice. He looked to his left, at Taz. The boy had lost all his kin in the rout. All.

"No. We have strength for what we do, barely that."

"Aye," Taz said . . . scarless, no one yet in the Kel; but he had great grace, and Hlil was grateful for that.

"Forgive, kel Taz."

"Sir," Taz said quietly, and turned away, for a few moments finding something essential to do with the packing.

It was that way with many of them. The Kel-born had lost most, knowing their kin in certainty. He looked on Ras, who labored with the others, and hoped, seeing that energy in her, that there might be some healing worked.

He could set his hand to none of the work; he paced back inside, restless, saw the last kel'ein returning from the storerooms. "Do not take the lamps yet," he bade them. "Ros, wait here; we have two still up in sen-tower."

"Aye," the one of them said. Hlil walked out again with the other, counting them, counting those outside, making sure he had all their whereabouts. They were all there. He reassured himself, stood in the cold with arms folded, watching while the readied bundles were carried down the steps, piled there, a little to the side of a heap of the dead.

"Ras," one of those at the bottom called up. The kel'en gazed down at that pitiful tangle of black and lifted his face upward. *"Kel Ras—"*

O gods, Hlil thought, cursing that man.

Ras left the others at the top and walked down the steps, no haste, no show of dread. Hlil watched, and after a moment followed. It was Nelan s'Elil who lay there; there was no doubting it. He stood by as Ras knelt by the body of her truemother, watched Ras take from among the dusty black robes the beautiful sword which had been that of Kov her father. The *j'tai,* Ras did not touch, the Honors which her truemother had won in her life; those passed only in defeat, and Nelan had never suffered that.

"Ras," he said. She sat still, the sword across her lap, the wind settling sand in the folds of her robes. No one moved, not she, not kel Tos'an who had summoned her. "Ras," he said again.

She straightened, rising, turned her unveiled face toward him, the sword gathered to her breast. There was no expression; to a friend even a kel'e'en might have shown something. He was consumed with the need to get her away from this place.

"Go back," he said. "We cannot attend to one lost, and not others. Duty, Ras."

She took the fastenings of the sword in hand, carefully unhooked her own and replaced it, laid what was hers against Nelan's body.

And walked away, to stand supervising the others, having spoken no word to him.

He walked away too, up the steps, not looking back, cast a naked-faced scowl at kel'ein who had paused in their work. There was a hasty return to it. He reached the top, started to turn and look down.

And suddenly, from inside, a snap of power, a flare of lights.

Everyone stopped in that instant; and there was a heart-stopping rumble.

"Run!" he shouted; they moved, raced ahead of a cloud which billowed out from the door. But the full collapse did not follow.

The two young sen'ein outside started back up the steps running. "No!" he forbade them, and went himself, paused in the doorway, in the choking dust. "All of you," he shouted back, "stay out."

He tucked the tail of the *zaidhe* across his face for a veil, entered the white cloud which the wind whipped away as rapidly as it poured forth. Somewhere inside one cold light shone undamaged, giving no help in the swirling dust: no light of theirs, but a powered lamp.

The whole center had given way. He looked at the ceiling, waded farther through the rubble, disturbing nothing he could avoid, the membrane of his eyes flicking regularly to clear the dust and sending involuntary tears to the outer corner of his eyes.

At one such clearing he saw what he had feared to see, a white-dusted bundle of black amid the rubble.

"Ros," he called, but there was no answer, no pulse to his touch, which came away wet-fingered. He looked up, heartsick, at the ruined ceiling where electric light cast a blinding haze, saw, to his left, sen-hall's access, likewise alight.

"Sen Kadas," he shouted, and obtained only echoes and the steady sifting of plaster.

He left the kel'en's body, entered the access, coughing in the dust. Cracks were everywhere in the spiral corridor. Bits of the wall crumbled to his touch. He trod carefully, ascended to sen-hall itself. The window there had given way, admitting daylight in a huge crack through which the wind swirled patterns of dust.

And beyond . . . lights gleamed through a farther doorway.

"Sen Kadas," he called. "Sen Otha?"

There was no response. He ventured in, within a room of row upon row of machinery . . . knew what he was seeing, which was the City itself, the mind, which had taught she'panei and sen'ein time out of mind. This too was a Holy, a Mystery not for a kel'en's sight. He walked farther, stopped as he realized the cracks which ran everywhere, the ruin which had plunged down through the very core of the tower, taking machinery and masonry, everything.

"Sen'ein," he called.

Light pulsed, a white light which glared down at him from the machine. He looked up at it, blinking in that blinding radiance.

"Who?" a voice thundered.

"Hlil s'Sochil," he answered it, trembling creeping through him.

"What is your authorization?"

"From the she'pan Melein s'Intel."

Lights flared, points of red and amber visible through the white glare, from somewhere beyond it.

"Where is the she'pan?" it asked.

He retreated from it in dread; the light died. With all his heart he would have fled this place, but two of his company were lost. He crept aside to the walls, trod the vast aisles of machinery amid the lights. More lights were being added constantly, places which had been dark coming alive, like something stirring to renewed power.

"Sen'ein," he called hoarsely.

Suddenly the floor slipped underfoot, a tiny jolt, that penetrated to his heart. He edged back.

And gazing down into the rubbled collapse at the core, he saw what ended hope of the sen'ein, gold cloth in the slide, amid blocks larger than a man. He could not reach them; there was no means—no need.

"Gods," he muttered, sick at heart, and, reckoning the disrespect of that here, shuddered and turned away.

"I am receiving," An-ehon thundered. The white eye of the machine flared. "Who?"

He fled it, walking softly, quickly as he could—gained the doorway into the sen-hall and kept going, breathless, into the spiraling passage down.

A shadow met him in the turning: one-eyed Desai, who had not followed orders. He grasped the kel'en's arm, grateful for that living presence.

"Haste," he said, turning Desai about; they descended together, past the ruin at the bottom, and out, out into the anxious gathering at the door. Hlil drew breath there, coughed, wiped his face with a sleeve which was powdered white with dust.

"Away," he ordered them. "Get these things away from the edun. There is nothing we can do here. Lately-dead have no more claim than the others."

They obeyed, with small murmurings of grief. He disregarded proprieties and took burdens himself, took up one at the bottom of the steps, for kel Ros, while the remaining sen'ein prepared to draw the sled holding the Pana alone.

"Move out," he ordered them, watched them all form file and begin the journey. Ras passed him, lost in some thought of her own, bearing a burden too heavy for her; but most did. He gazed on her with a personal misery which dulled itself in other things, anxiety for all his charges. Nothing which he had touched had gone right. They had lost lives, had lost sen'ein—helpless even to bury the lost ones.

His leading.

He looked back, last of those who left the city, blinked in the wind—turned from the ruin which was not the city he wished to remember.

Three lives lost; and the tribe itself—it was not certain that anyone survived there to need the things they had gathered. It was his decision to go on, his decision now, to take all that was theirs when they might have halved the weight and abandoned the possessions of the dead.

He understood one rule, that waste was death; that what one gave the desert it never gave back, to world's end.

He did what he knew to do, which was to yield nothing.

*   *   *

The bleeding had started again. The wound sealed and broke open again by turns, whenever the slope of the land put him to effort. Duncan clenched the arm against his body and tried to move it as little as possible in his walking. A cough urged at him, and that was worse—much worse, if that set in. He tried desperately to pace his breathing, tasting copper in his mouth, the sky occasionally acquiring dark edges in his sight. He was followed; he knew that he was, and the slow rolls of the eternal flat gave him and them cover. He sought no landmarks, but the sun's last light, a spot of lurid flame in the west, tainted with the thinning dust.

The dus beside him radiated occasional surges of flight impulse and of anger, confused as he, driven. Occasionally small life rippled the sand ahead, clearing their path, a surreal illusion of animate sands.

And one did not. He stepped into yielding sand, cords whipping up his leg. He snatched out his shortsword and hacked at the strands . . . sand-star, a smallish one, else it had been up to his face: they grew that large. This one recoiled, wounded; and the dus ate it, the while he stumbled on his way, half-running a few steps in sickened panic. Whether it had gotten above the boot or not, his flesh was too numb to feel. He walked with the blade in hand after that, finding the hilt comfort in the approach of dark. He ought to take the visor up, he reckoned, before he stumbled into worse; but the sand still blew, and when he tried it for a time his eyes stung so he was as blind without as with. He lowered it again to save himself the misery, and trusted to the beast and to the sword.

The sun sank its last portion beyond the horizon and it was night indeed; whether stars shone or not, whether the dust had cleared that much he could not tell.

He rested in the beginning of the dark; he must. After the tightness had relaxed from his chest and his head pounded less severely he began with dull stubbornness to gather himself up, reckoning that if he were to go on living he had no choice about it.

And suddenly the dus sent him strong, clear warning, an apprehension like a chill wind on their backtrail. *Come,* he sent it, and started to move at all the pace he could.

Madness, to begin a race with mri. He had lost it already. Better sense by far to turn and fight: they would give him the grace of one-at-a-time.

And that was worth nothing if one lost in the first encounter. He gasped breath and tried to hit a steady pace.

Abruptly the dus deserted him, headed off at a tangent to the left. Panic breathed at his shoulders; he turned with it, staying with the beast, having lost control of it. It was taking him to the attack, into it; he felt the wildness surge into his brain—and sud-denly—fragments.

It hit from all sides, dus-sense, all about him.

The others.

They had come. His skin contracted in the rage they sent; they had made a trap, the dusei. A fierceness settled into his bones, an alien anger—danger, danger, *danger*—

A dus reared up out of the dark in front of him, higher than his head; he shied from it, spun, met a kel'en a sword's length from him.

He flung his sword up, low; steel turned the blade as the kel'en closed with him, shadow and hard muscle and a dus-carried wash of familiarity that stopped him cold. A hard hand seized his arm and hurled him back.

Niun.

He gasped breath, struggled for mental balance, spun left in the sudden awareness of others on them, dus-sense warning them.

"Who are they?" Niun asked him, shortsword likewise in his hand. "What have you stirred?"

"Another tribe." He gasped for air, shifted his grip on his hilt as he tried to make figures out of the darkness about them. Dusei were at their backs, more than their own two. He drew a shaken breath and lifted his visor, made out a dim movement in the dark before them.

"Who are you?" Niun shouted out.

"The hao'nath," the answer came back, male and hoarse. "Who are you?"

"Kel'anth of the ja'anom. Get off my trail, hao'nath! You have no rights here."

There was long silence.

And then there was nothing, neither shadow nor response. Dussense went out like a lamp flame, and Duncan shivered convulsively, gasped for the air that suddenly seemed more abundant.

Steel hissed into sheath. Niun tugged down his veil, giving his face to him; Duncan sheathed his sword and did the same, and Niun offered him his open hands.

Duncan embraced him awkwardly, aware of his own chill and the mri's fever-warmth, his own filthiness and the mri's fastidious cleanliness.

"Move," Niun said, taking him by the shoulder and pushing him; he did so, and about them the shadows of dusei gave way, scattered, save his own and the great dus which was Niun's. He struggled to keep Niun's pace, no arguments or breath wasted. That was trouble at their backs, only gone back to report; Niun's long strides carried them off southerly, to rougher land—broke at times into a run, which he matched for a while. It ended in his coughing, doubled up, trying only to walk.

Niun kept him moving, down a gentle roll of the land, an ill dream of pain and dus-sense, until his knees began to buckle under him in the sand and he sank down before a joint should tear and lame him.

Niun dropped to his heels beside him, a hand on his shoulder, and the dusei, his and the other, made a wall about them. "Sovkela?" Niun asked of him: my-brother-of-the-Kel? He caught his breath somewhat and gripped Niun's arm in return.

"I reached them. Niun, I have been up there, in the ships."

Niun was silent a moment; disturbance jolted through the dus sense. "I believed," Niun said, "you had gotten through when there were no more attacks; but—not that you would have gone among them. And they let you go. They let you go again."

"Regul have come," Duncan said, and felt the shock fed back to him. The membrane flashed across Niun's eyes. A human might have cried aloud, so intense that feeling was.

"Regul and not humans?"

"Both."

"Allied," Niun said. Anger fed through. Despair.

"No more firing. Regul did the firing; humans have realized by now . . . Niun, they have listened. The she'pan—they sent a message. She can contact them. Talk with them."

Again the membrane flashed across. Duncan shivered in that feeling.

"Have you taken hire?" Niun asked. It was a reasonable question, without rancor. The Kel was mercenary.

"I take no hire."

The dusei caught that feeling too, and wove them together. Niun reached out and caught the wrong arm, let it go at his flinching . . . rubbed at the blood on his fingertips.

"I thought," Duncan said, "I could reason with someone. The hao'nath kel'anth came up on me. He knew something was wrong. Knew it; and he or the dus moved before I did."

"Dead?"

"I left him against the pipestalks; dus poison, broken bones or not—I stayed to keep him out of the sand: no more than that."

"Gods," Niun spat. He faced him away, took the pack from him, hooked a strap over his own shoulder and started them moving. Duncan blinked, blear-eyed with relief at having that weight gone, and tried to keep his pace, staggering somewhat in the loose sand. Niun delayed and flung a fever-hot arm about him, hurrying him.

"What are they likely to do?"

"I would challenge," Niun said. "But that would suit them. It is the tribe that is in danger now."

"Melein—"

"I do not know." Niun pulled at him, for all his efforts to keep stride. "Gods know who is with the she'pan at the moment. I am here; Hlil, in the city . . . The hao'nath have gone back to their own she'pan; they will not challenge the kel'anth of a tribe without her consent, not if she is available. . . . But they will not stop that long. If—" He caught his breath. "If they take us here, I can challenge, aye, but one after the other. The meeting of she'panei . . . is different. The she'pan is our protection; we are hers."

He said nothing else, hard-breathing with a human burden. Duncan took his own weight, cupped the veil to his mouth with his hand to warm the air, went blindly, by sound, by dus-sense, at last with Niun dragging at him.

They found a place to rest finally, hard ground, a ridge which stretched a stone's cast along the sands. Duncan flung himself down in an aching knot and fumbled anxiously after the canteen, trying to ease his swollen throat . . . offered to Niun, who drank and put it away. The dusei crowded as close to them as possible as if themselves seeking comfort, and for the time at least there was no intimation of pursuers. Duncan leaned against his dus, his sides heaving harder than those of the beast, wiped at his nose beneath the veils and wanted nothing more than to lie still and breathe, but Niun disturbed him to see to his wound, soaked a strip torn from his veil in the saliva of his dus and bandaged it. Duncan did not question; it felt better, at least.

"These tsi'mri in the ships," Niun said. "You know them?"

"I know them."

"You talked with them—a very long time."

"No. A day and a night."

"You walk slowly, then."

"Far out of my way. Not to be followed; and I walk slowly, yes."

"Ai." Niun sat still a moment, nudged finally at the pack he had carried. It was question.

"Food." Duncan reached for it, to show him. Niun caught his wrist, released it.

"Your word is enough."

Duncan took it all the same, opened it and pulled out an opened packet of dried meat. He put a bit in his mouth, tugging the veil aside, offered the packet to Niun. "Tsi-mri, you would say. But if they were offering—I took. Food. Water. Nothing else."

Niun accepted it, tucked a large piece into his mouth, put the packet into his own pouch; and by that small action Duncan realized what he had perceived in deeper senses, that Niun himself was almost spent, quick-tiring . . . hungry, it might be. That struck panic into him. He had thought the tribe a reachable walk away. If what they had yet to face had undone Niun, then for himself—

He chewed and forced the tough bits down a throat almost too raw to swallow. "Listen to me. I will tell you what happened. Best both of us should know. The beacons I left when we landed . . . to say that there was no reason of attack—regul came in first, took out the beacons and our ship; humans never heard the message. Regul were determined they should not."

Niun's eyes had locked on his, intent.

"Regul attacked," Duncan said, "and city defenses fired back; humans came in and were caught in it, and believed the regul; but now they know . . . that they were used by the regul, and they do not like it. The regul elder tried to silence me; I killed her. Her younglings are disorganized and humans are in command up there. They are warned how they were misled."

The membrane flashed.

"I told them, Niun, I told them plainly I no longer take their orders, that I am kel'en. They sent me with a message to the she'-pan: come and talk. They want assurance there will be no striking at human worlds."

"They ask *her*."

"Or someone who would be her voice. They are reasoning beings, Niun."

Niun considered that in silence. There was—perhaps—a desire in Niun's expression that he would never have shown a human.

"The landing site," Duncan urged at him. "They will be waiting there for an answer. An end to this, a way out."

"The hao'nath," Niun said hollowly. "Gods, the hao'nath."

"I do not think," Duncan said, "that humans will go outside that ship. At least—not recklessly."

"Sov-kela—the comings and goings of ships, the firing over An-ehon—are the tribes deaf and blind, that they should ignore such things? They are gathering, that is what is happening. And every tribe on the face of the world that has seen cities attacked or passings in the skies—will look to its defenses. An-ehon is in ruins; other cities may not be. And now the hao'nath know it centers on this plain; and that its name is ja'anom."

City armament. Duncan bit at his lip, reckoning what in his dazed flight he had never reckoned . . . that some city in the hands of a desert she'pan might strike at warships.

That through the city computers, messages could pass from zone to zone with the speed of comp transmission, not the migration of tribes.

He had rejected everything, everything security might have tampered with: cast gear into the basins, kept only food and water, only the things he could assure himself were safe and light enough to carry. He made a tent of his hands over his mouth, a habit, that warmed the air, and stared bleakly into the dark before him.

"Your thought?" Niun asked.

"Go back; get to that ship—you and I. Put machines on our own side. And I know we cannot."

"We cannot," Niun said.

Duncan considered, drew his limbs up, leaned against the dus to push himself to his feet. Niun gathered up the pack and also rose, offered a hand for support. Duncan ignored it. "I cannot walk fast," he said. "But long—I can manage. If you have to break off and leave me, do that. I have kept ahead this far."

Niun said nothing to that; it was something that might have to be done: he knew so. He doubled the veil over his lower face, left the visor up, for the wind had slacked somewhat: there were stars visible, the first sky he had seen in days.

And after a time of walking: "How far?" he asked.

"Would that I knew," Niun said. A moment more passed. They were out on open sand now, an occasional burrower rippling aside from the dusei's warding. "Cast the she'pan for the dusei. The storm, sov-kela . . . I am worried. I know they will not have stayed where I left them; they cannot have done that."

"The tents—"

"They are without them."

Duncan drew in a breath, thinking of the old, the children, sick at heart. He shaped Melein for the dusei, with all his force. He received back nothing identifiable before them, only the sense of something ugly at their backs.

"I sensed you," Niun said. "And trouble. I thought to turn back in the storm; but there was no getting there in time to help anything . . . and this . . . the dus gave me no rest. Well it did not. Even the wild ones. I have never felt the like, sov-kela."

"They are out there," Duncan said. "Still. They met me on the way." An insane memory came back, an attempt to reach them, to show them *life*, and choices. Survival or desolation. He shuddered, staggered, felt something of his own dus, a fierceness that blurred the senses. Both beasts caught it. Somewhere across the flat a cry wailed down the wind, dus.

Melein, Duncan insisted.

Their own beasts kept on as they were heading; it could be answer; it could be incomprehension. They had no choice but to go with them.

Chapter Seven

Luiz appeared in the doorway of *Flower's* lab offices, leaned there, his seamed face set in worry. "Shuttle's down," he said. "Two of them. They're coming in pairs."

"The dispatch is nearly ready." Boaz made a few quick notes, sorted, clipped, gathered her materials into the pouch and sealed the coded lock: Security procedures, foreign to her. She found the whole arrangement distasteful. In her fifty-odd years she had had time to learn deep resentment for the military. Most of her life had been wartime, the forty-three-year mri wars. Her researches as a scientist had been appropriated to the war in distant offices; on *Flower* they had been directly seized. She had to her credit the deciement of mri records which had led them here, which had led to the destruction of mri cities, and the death of children; and she grieved over that. A pacifist, she had done the mri more harm with pick and brush and camera than all of *Saber's* firepower and all the ships humans had ever launched; she believed so; and she had had no choice—had none now that she was reduced to writing reports for security, reckonings of yet another species for military use.

She had had illusions once, of the importance of her freedom to investigate, the tradeoff of knowledge for knowledge, for a position in which she, having knowledge, could sway the makers of policy; there had been a time she had believed she could say no.

She put the pouch into Luiz's hands, looked beyond him to the other men who had come into the lab: Averson, Sim Averson, a balding fellow who walked as though he might break. He came, and she offered her hand to him. Three years Averson had worked aboard *Flower* before the Kesrithi mission, which made him one of the seniors of the present staff, a sour, fretsome fellow who took his work in Cultures and his library more seriously than breathing, and lived for the increase of data and systems to his personal credit in libraries back home. Averson had taken naturally to specialization in regul, as slow and methodical as they, pleased with the mountains of statistics which regul tended to accumulate. He had taken over Aldin's office with a sour intimation of satisfaction, as if Aldin's death had been fate's personal favor to him . . . appropriated Aldin's notes and materials and immersed himself in more cataloging. It likely did not occur to Averson now that the military might have interests wider than specific questions, that what he did might have moral implications . . . or if it did, it did so at a distance outside Averson's more vivid concerns. He looked now only annoyed, roused out of his habits and his habitation and his work.

"Be careful," Boaz urged him. "Sim, something's wrong up there."

Dark eyes blinked up at her, somewhat distantly. Averson had grown into the habit of looking down. He shrugged his bowed shoulders. "What can we do? When they ask, we come, however inconvenient it happens to be. My tapes, my programs, everything disarranged. I told them. Of course it's wrong. I'll be a week putting things in order. Can I explain this to them? No. No. Security has no comprehension."

"Sim, I mean that there's something wrong with the regul."

Averson's brow fractured into different wrinkles, distant recognition of a fact both germane and foreign to his research: he was slow of habit, but not slow-witted.

"I queried about the overflights," Luiz said. He folded his arms and set his back more firmly against the doorframe . . . his knees troubled him; he had gotten old, had Luiz, fragile as Averson. . . . *We have all grown old,* Boaz thought desperately. *None of us will live to reach humanity again, not with all our functions intact. I will be near sixty, Luiz seventy-five if he makes it through the jumps again: Koch seventy at least; and some of us are dead, like Aldin.* "Koch went silent on me in a hurry. Now he wants you up there. And files on the regul. Boz is right. Something's astir up there with our allies."

Averson blinked slowly. "Metamorphosis. We reckoned . . . a longer time required."

"Stress conditions," Luiz surmised.

"Possibly." Averson chewed at his fingernail and frowned, staring at nothing in particular the while he followed some train of thought.

"Sim," Boaz said, "Sim, watch out for security."

Averson blinked at her, drawn back from his musing.

"Don't trust them," Boaz said. "Don't trust what they do with what we give them. Think. *Think* before you tell them something . . . how ignorant men could interpret it, what they could do with it. They aren't objective. We daren't trust that. People want statistics to justify what they *want* to do. That's the only reason we've ever asked."

"Boz," Luiz protested, with a meaningful glance at the intercom. *Flower's* operations staff was all military.

"So what do I care? What can I lose? Promotion? Assignments in the future? None of us are going to be fit for another after this one; and it's dead certain they're limited on replacements for us."

"Influence, Boz."

"What have we been able to influence? Between *Saber* and the regul, invaluable sites have been blasted to rubble, the greatest cities of the world in ruins, an intelligent species maybe reduced beyond viability . . . and we observe, we take notes . . . and our notes provide information so that regul and mri can kill each other. And maybe we can join in. Duncan took his own way out. I look at this and suddenly I begin to understand him. He at least—"

A shadow fell in the corridor doorway. Boaz stopped. It was Galey, from *Saber,* with another man. Vague surprise struck her, that Galey should have come down: an old acquaintance, this man . . . a freckled young man when he had set out from Kesrith, full of promise; a man in his thirties now, with a perpetually worried look. Youth to man to senior by the time he could get back to human space again, Boaz thought; mortality was on them all. The thought began to obsess her.

"Dr. Averson?" Galey inquired, came with the black man into the main lab. He proffered Luiz a cassette, had it signed for, passed the tab to his dark companion. "Lt. Harris," Galey identified the other. "Running shuttle up for Dr. Averson. Orders explain matters. Myself and my crew, we're staying on down here; cassette explains that too, I think, by your leave, sir, doctor."

There was a moment's cold silence.

"What's going on up there?" Boaz asked.

"Don't know," Galey said, and avoided her eyes. "Sir?" he said to Averson. "We have a limited access here. Better move as quickly as possible."

Luiz handed over the dispatch, received a signature in turn, from Harris.

"Suppose," Boaz said, "you see him settled, Mr. Galey."

Galey gave her that perplexed stare he could use; she did not relent. "Doctor," he murmured, and took his leave with Harris, shepherding Averson along with them in some haste.

"My tapes," Averson was saying. "My records—"

The door closed.

"Blast!" Boaz spat, and sat down.

"There's no help for it," Luiz said.

"His whole life," Boaz murmured, shaking her head; and when Luiz looked puzzlement at her: "Theirs, mine, yours. Spent on this thing. More than just the years. We can go home. But to what? What's the chance Stavros is still governor on Kesrith? No, new policies, a new governor—the whole situation years without our input. And what do we bring back? What do we tell them about what we've seen out here, a track of dead worlds—saying *what?* No one's asking the right questions, Emil. Not we, not the regul . . . no one's asking the right questions."

Luiz wrapped his thin arms about him and stared at the floor. "We can't get out there to ask the questions."

"And now we've got the military."

"We're vulnerable here; *That's* what's on my mind. Boz, whatever's afoot, I'm going to request all but essential personnel shuttled up. Fifty-eight people is too many to risk down here."

"No!" She thrust herself to her feet. "*Flower* has to stay here, right here; we have to make it clear to them we're staying."

"We have to wait for Duncan as long as there's hope of waiting. That's our purpose; our only purpose. The Xen department has to understand that. There's no chance of doing more than that, and there's sure none of making gestures of principle with fifty-eight lives. Forget it, Boz."

"And when that fails?" She stalked to the door, looked back at him. "We'll lose the mri, you know that. How do we win, in a waiting game with regul?"

"We apply pressure . . . quietly. It's all we can do."

"And can't they figure that out? It's their game. Our generations are a fraction of theirs. Our whole lifespans are nothing to their three centuries. If you're right, if there is an adult developing among them, they can even out-populate us in the long run. And if there isn't one now, there will be, sooner or later, this year or the next. Sooner or later, *Saber* will give up and pull us out. We're mortal, Emil. We think in terms of week and months. The regul will get the mri in the end. Do you see *Saber* tying itself up here for longer than a few months? And do you think regul wouldn't wait fifty out of their three hundred years to have their own way with the mri? And we can't. Fifty years . . . and we're all dead."

Luiz gazed at her, his dark eyes shrouded in wrinkled lids, his mouth pressed to a fine line. "Don't you go on me, Boz. We've lost too many to that kind of thinking. I won't hear you start it."

"Four suicides and six on trank? It's Galey's sort who go that route . . . the young, who had illusions of a life after this mission is over. You and I, we're too old for that. We at least have a past to look back on. They don't. Only the jumps. And more of them to face on the way home. The drugs may not last; we were handing out doubled doses at the end. And what after that? You tell me what that voyage will be like *with no drugs*."

"We'll find something."

"We can *try*." She made a shrug that was half a shiver. "This world, Emil, the age, the *age* of it—one vast tomb; the seas dried up, the cities frozen and waiting for the sun to go out—and all space about empty of life. Dear God, what is it to be young among such sights as these? It's bad enough to be old."

Luiz came and took her by the arms, gathered her to him, and she held to him until the shivers stopped.

"Emil," she said, "promise me something. Talk to the staff. Let me talk to them. We can hold *Flower* here, right where we sit, with all her staff. No lessening the stakes, no making it easier for them, regul or human."

"We can't. We can't make gestures, Boz. Can't. I don't know what Koch has in mind up there or down here, but we can't cripple our own side by making independent moves. We have to protect our people and we have to be ready to lift on the instant the orders come. We're the other star-capable ship and we've no right to gamble with it."

"We've no right not to."

"I can't listen to you."

"Won't." Boaz turned aside, drew a long breath, glanced back again. "And what answer does Koch have for us?"

Luiz drew the cassette from his pocket, stared at it as at something poisonous. "I'll lay bets what answer he has; that those overflights aren't ours."

"Play it," Boaz said. She closed the door. "Let's both hear it."

He looked doubtful, frowning, but after a moment walked around her desk to push it into the player.

Gibberish filled the screens, codes, authorizations, *Saber's* emblem. Boaz came and sat on the edge of the desk near Luiz, arms folded, heart beating hard with tension.

"*. . . request Xen staff cooperation with military mission,*" the tape meandered to its point, "*in on-site recon if this should prove necessary. Your base is base for this operation; request your staff conduct advance briefings prior to start of mission. Mission head is Lt. Comdr. James R. Galey. All decisions mission Code Dante to be made by Comdr. Galey, including final selection among* Flower *staff volunteers for mission slot. Suggest staff member D. Tensio. Your full cooperation in this matter urgently pleaded. Mission is recon only, stress, recon only, effort to comprehend nature of civilization and establish character of city installations. Failure of* Flower *cooperation will jeopardize search for alternative solutions.*"

She flung herself off the desk edge and started for the door.

"Boz," Luiz called after her.

She stopped. The tape had run out.

"Boz," Luiz said, his wrinkles drawn into lines of anguish. "You're fifty-two years old. There's no way you could keep up with those young men."

She looked down at herself, at a plump body that resisted diets, that ached with bad arches and wheezed when she had to carry equipment in standard gee. She had not been good to herself in her life: too much of sitting at desks, too much of reading, too much of postponing.

And the sum of her life rested in the freckled hands of a whip-cord young soldier with no sense what he was about.

"I'm going," she said. "Emil, I'm going to talk to young Mr. Galey and he's going to listen."

"Jeopardize the operation for your personal satisfaction."

She turned a furious look on him, took a breath and drew herself up to her small height. "I'm going to give them the best they can get, Emil, that's what; because I know more than Damon Tensio or Sim Averson or any three of the assistants put together. Say otherwise."

He did not. Perhaps, she thought halfway down the corridor at as fast a pace as she could manage—

She glanced back, half-expecting to see him in the doorway. He was. He nodded to her slowly—too old himself, she realized; he knew her mind, knew to the bottom of his heart. He would be down the hall ahead of her if he could.

She nodded, a tautness in her throat, turned and went hunting Galey.

Harris kicked in the engines, took a cursory glance at the instruments, his mind wandering to *Saber*, to a hot cup of coffee; and to the next day off-duty, which was the reward of a downworld flight. Last of all he cast a glance to his right, at the little man who fussed nervously with the restraints.

"They're all right," Harris said. Groundling, this Dr. Averson, a dedicated groundling. He decided, humanely, to make the lift as gentle as possible; the man had some years on him. Averson blinked round-eyed at him, the sweat already broken out on his brow. Harris diverted his attention again to the instruments, advised *Flower* bridge of his status, began slow lift.

The shuttle responded with a leisurely solidity. He watched the altimeter, leveled gradually at 6,000 m and banked to come about for their run.

"We're turning," Averson said; and when he gave no answer: "We're turning." Averson raised his voice well over the noise of the engines. "We never turned. What's the matter?"

"We're coming about, sir," Harris said, adjusted the plug in his left ear to be sure he could hear warnings over Averson's clamor. He set the scan to audio alarm, wide-range. "Shuttles handle different than *Flower*. We're just heading where we should be."

They came to course. The desert slipped under them by slow degrees, with the indigo to pink shadings of the sky above and the bronze to red tones of the desert, the great chasm which might once have been a sea—passed the area of the recent storm and across the chasm. Scan clicked away the whole route, the instruments moduled into cargo. They crossed no cities this way and made no provocations. It was a tame run, toward a gentle parting with Kutath's pull. He relaxed finally as Averson settled down; the man took enough interest to lean toward the port and look down, though with a visible flinching.

Quiet. Sand and sky and quiet. Harris let go a breath, settled for the long run out.

Suddenly a tone went off in his ear and he flicked a glance at the screen, his heart slamming in panic. He accelerated on the instant and their relation to the blips altered in a series of pulses as Averson howled outrage.

He angled for evasion and the howl became a choked gasp.

"Something's on our tail," he said. "Check your belts." The latter was something to take Averson's mind off their situation. He was calculating, glancing from screen to instruments. Two blips, coming up at his underbelly.

He veered again. The blips were in position to fire on the rise, could; might; he felt it in his gut. He increased the climb rate and the ship's boards flashed distress at him.

For the first time the bogies separated, shifting position and altitude. His heart went into his throat and he flipped the cover off the armscomp, ready. "Hang on," he yelled at Averson, and punched com, breaking his ordered silence. "Any human ship, NAS-6; we've got a sighting."

He banked violently and dropped; and Averson's scream echoed in his ear. The bogey whipped by and a screen flared; they had been fired on. He completed his roll and nosed up again as rapidly as the ship could bear.

"Get us help!" Averson cried.

THE FADED SUN: KUTATH 587

"Isn't any." He punched com again, hoping for someone to relay to *Saber*. "Got two bogeys here. Does anybody read?"

The pulse in his ear increased, nearing. He whipped off at an angle that wrung a shriek from Averson, climbing for very life, trying at the same time to get an image on his screen. The sky turned pink and indigo, the pulses died, went offscreen. In a little more the indigo deepened and they were still accelerating, running for what speed and altitude they could attain: the sound of the engines changed as systems began to convert.

Averson was sick. Harris reached over and ripped a bag out of storage and gave it to him. For some little time there was the quiet sound of retching, which did no kindness to his own stomach.

"Water in the bottle there," Harris said. And fervently: "Don't spill anything. We're going null before long." He devoted his attention the while to the vacant scan, to making sure all the recorders were in order. He heard Averson scrabbling about after the water, the spasm seeming to have passed. His own stomach kept heaving in sympathy. "Disposal to your right."

Dayside was under them, and *Saber* was over the horizon. The instruments had nothing, not a flicker. Harris calculated. Somewhere on this side of the world lay regul *Shirug,* beyond their scan; and somewhere downworld were cities with weapons which could strike at craft in orbit, if they once obtained a fix on so small a vessel as themselves.

Or if they had it already.

Averson snatched at another bag, dry-heaved for a time. They were in a queasy wallowing at the moment. Harris gave them visual stability with the world, wiped at the sweat that coursed his face, trying to reckon where *Shirug* might be. He had a dread of her coming up in forward scan, and the bogeys coming up under him again.

"Going to go back on course," he said to no one in particular. "At least that way downworld isn't so likely to have a shot at us."

Averson said nothing. Harris reoriented and Kutath's angry surface swung under their forward scan.

There was no reaction anywhere. A slow tremor came into Harris's muscles, a knee that wanted to jerk against his will. He reckoned that somewhere over the horizon *Saber* would grow concerned when they failed schedule, that somewhere near them *Santiago* must be on the prowl over dayside, regul-watching.

Then a tone sounded in his ear and a blip appeared on the edge of the screen, on and off. He kept his eye on it, his pulse pounding so that it almost obscured his audio. He did not tell Averson. It was of no use yet. He considered another dive into atmosphere. Maybe, he thought, that was what he was being encouraged to do. There had been two of them.

The sweat ran, the single blip grew no closer, and he wiped at his lip and tried to reckon his chances of being allowed to go his way. He could find himself up against some outrunner for *Shirug*, against which he was a gnat-sized irritant.

"How much longer?" Averson asked him.

"Don't know, sir. Just stay quiet. Got a problem here to recalculate."

There was no way it avoided having him in scan, traveling so neatly at the edge of his own.

Suddenly it disappeared out of range.

That gave him no feeling of safety. It was back there; there could be any number back there.

The ruddy surface of the world slipped under their bow and whitened to polar frost. Ahead was the terminator.

Be there, he entreated. *Saber, Saber, for the love of God, be there.*

Averson fumbled after something in his pocket, a bottle of pills. He shook one out and put it into his mouth. He was looking gray.

"Things are going all right," Harris lied. "Relax, sir."

"We're alive," Averson muttered.

"Yes, sir, we are."

And a blip appeared at three o'clock of the scope, coming up fast. The pulse erupted in his ear, faster and faster, deepening as the instruments gauged size: it was big.

A screen flared, a computer flashed demands to his comp. Hasty pulses flurried across, coded; he punched in, braced for recognition or for fire.

"Shuttle NAS-6," a human voice said, "this is *Santiago*."

He punched com, weak with relief. "This is NAS-6. Two bogeys downworld, fire on their side, coming in with a bogey on my tail."

"Affirmative, NAS-6, we copy. Correct course our heading. Proceed to *Saber*."

He made the adjustments, recalled Averson, looked into the round-eyed face and nodded confirmation of the hope he saw there.

They crept farther into night, within the protective cloak of *Santiago's* scan. He had *Santiago's* scope on-screen now; it showed reassuringly clear, all but human shuttles and a friendly blip that was *Saber*.

Harris shifted footing uncomfortably, received the nod that sent him into the admiral's office . . . stood there, staring down at the hero of Elag/Haven and of Adavan, at the balding visage which up till now he had never had to face alone.

The formalities were short and on his own part unsteady. "Averson?" the admiral asked him, and his voice was grim.

"Meds have him, sir. A little shaken up."

"Close?"

"Close, sir."

"Security will have your tapes running now. Sit *down*, lieutenant. Did you get a clear image on your attackers?"

Harris sank into the offered chair, looked up again into that lean, ruddy face. "No, sir. I never managed it. Tried, sir. Not big, not quick on high gee maneuvers; had me, if they could or wanted, . . . harassment or just too slow, maybe."

"You're suggesting by that remark that they could have been regul?"

Harris said nothing for the moment. A mistake, a mistake in that opinion: he reckoned where that led; and swallowed bile. "I couldn't be a hundred percent sure of anything. They were about that size; they shied off from high gee turns and climbs. I've flown against mri. Mri feel different. Fast. Apt to outguess you and crosscut your moves." He silenced himself, embarrassed before a man who had been in it before he was born, who sat regarding him with cold calculation. Koch would know, all the same.

The impression would make sense to a man who had flown against both.

"I'll view the tapes," Koch said. Harris reassured himself with that, desperately relieved to believe someone else would be counter-checking his observations. "Did you," Koch asked, "have your armscomp engaged?"

"Yes, sir."

"Maneuver to fire?"

"No, sir; they came up at my belly and I zigged and got out without firing."

Koch nodded. It might be approval of his actions or simply introspection. Koch leaned aside to key something into the desk console. There was delay; finally a response lit the screen, but Harris could not read it at his angle.

"Dr. Averson's under process in sick bay," Koch said; and Harris reckoned that hereafter would be complaints. He was caught in the vise, civ and military. Someone gave the orders and the complaints ended up on his record. "Meds indicate he came through in good shape," Koch said, "but they're going to keep him a little while. We'll be talking with him. Did he have any comment on the scanning pass?"

"Said nothing, sir. Wasn't much to see."

"And the ships?"

"Don't think he observed much, sir."

"Point of origin?"

"From my view, east and low, veered to my heading and tailed."

Koch nodded slowly, leaned back. "I appreciate the job, lieutenant. That will be all. Dismissed."

"Sir." He rose, saluted, left, his knees still wobbling in carrying him past the secretary in the front office and down the corridor outside. There would be other flights, he suspected so; backup or not, there would be use found for him. He had beaten the odds in the war, and the war was supposed to be over. He had believed so. Every human alive had believed so.

He took the turn down to the prep room, half seeing the scatter of men and women who were ordinary about the place, preferring this company until he had his nerves steady again. It was the unofficial center for preflight meetings and for beating the goblins after; it had hot coffee around the clock, an automat, and human company that made no demands—a clutter of zone charts on the walls, unofficially scrawled with notes—*home,* one wit had scrawled on a system chart, with an arrow spiraling forlornly off the board—a screen linked to scanning; tables and hard chairs, lockers for personal gear.

He wandered over to the coffee dispenser and filled a cup, stirred ersatz cream into it, suddenly aware of silence in the room. A group of men and women were clustered about the center table, some standing, some seated. . . . He looked that way, found no one looking at him directly, and wondered if he was the subject of the rumor. James, Montoya, Hale, Suonava—he knew them . . . too well for such silence.

He ventured among them, stubborn and uncomfortable, and Suonava moved a foot out of a seat for him: his rumpled blues and their crisp ones marked which had priorities at table in this room without rank. He sank into the chair and took a sip of his coffee.

The silence persisted. No one moved, some seated, some standing. He set the cup down, looked about him.

"Something wrong?"

"NAS-10's failed rendezvous," one said. "Van is missing down there."

His heart began that slip toward panic, the same as it had when the ships turned up in scan. He took a drink of coffee, hands shaking, set it down, his fingers still curled around the warmth. He knew Van. Experienced at Haven. One of the best. He looked for others who had flown out with him, on his tail and Galey's. There was no one else; likely they were still tied up in security's triplicate-copy debriefing . . . if they had returned.

"Any details?" he asked them.

"Never showed, that's all," Montoya said. "Everyone else is in; should have come in ahead of you that went to *Flower.* But Van didn't show."

"There's bogeys out there," Harris muttered, guilty at contributing to the rumor mill that operated out of this room; it would be traced; there would be a reprimand for it. But these people were flying out into that range next. Lives rode on such rumors; apprehension made reflex quicker.

"Mri," Suonava spat. "Mri!"

Harris brought his head up. "Didn't say that," he insisted, forcing the words. And because he was already committed: "And I don't think so. The feel was wrong. I don't think so."

There was silence after, sober-faced men and women settling about the table. No one spoke. It would be all over the ship by the next watch, on *Santiago* by the next. Harris did not plead for discretion. Suddenly advancements and careers shifted into small perspective.

"That doesn't leave us in a good spot," Montoya said, "does it?"

"Quiet," Hayes muttered.

Cups were refilled, one after the other retreating to the dispenser and returning. Pilots settled back at the table and drank their coffee, grim-faced. No one said much. Harris stared into the lights reflecting off the coffee, thinking and rethinking.

It was a joyous sight, the appearance of a kel'en standing high among the rocks near the camp. Hlil flung up an arm and waved, and the sentry gave out a cry taken up by others. The very rocks seemed to come alive, first with black figures, and then with gold and blue. The weary column hastened, finding new strength in galled limbs and aching backs, as brothers and sisters of the Kel hurried out to their aid, as even blue-clad children came running to lend their hands, shouting for delight.

Only the sen'ein who drew the Pana accepted no help until others of the Sen could reach them to take the labor from them. And Hlil, freed of his burden by another kel'en, walked beside them up into the camp. Where the Pana went there went a silence in respect, a pause, a gesture of reverence, before celebration broke out again.

But all was quiet when they drew near the center of the open-air camp, where the she'pan waited, conspicuous in her white robes, seated on a flat stone. The sen'ein who drew the sled on which the Pana rested stopped it before her, and Hlil watched with a tautness in his throat as she lifted her eyes from that to him.

"Kel-second," she said. He came, half-veiled as he was, dropped to his knees in the sand before her and sat back.

"There are three dead," he said in a calm, clear voice that carried in the silence about them. "Sen Otha, sen Kadas, kel Ros. At An-ehon . . . a collapse killed them. The edun is in ruin."

Her eyes lowered to the Pana, lifted yet again. "Who recovered it?"

"I," he said, "for any harm that attaches." He removed the headcloth, for all that there were children present. "Merin and Desai and Ras—by my asking."

"And the power in the city . . . live or dead, after the collapse?"

"Live," he said. "I saw: forgive."

"How far alive?"

For all the dignity kel-law taught him, his gesture was uncertain, a helpless attempt to recall what he had tried to wipe from his mind. He built back what he had seen, shut his eyes an instant, recalled with the meticulous care with which he had been trained to retain images. "Each row . . . some lights, mostly red, some gold; generally two hands of lights; more, the third row of machines. It spoke; I gave it my name and yours; it called for you."

She said nothing for the moment. He stared into her face . . . young and cold and scarred with kel-scars. A curse, he thought, that would be her gift to him. A chance for her to be rid of him, who was of the old order.

"Was the Pana damaged, kel Hlil?"

"No."

"You sent back half the force you took. We here thank you for that. We are without deaths in this camp because you sent us strength enough to shelter us. We could hardly have kept the sand clear without that help."

He blinked at her confused, realizing dimly that this was honest, that this cold young she'pan offered him praise.

"*J'tai* are owed you," she said. "Every one." She bent forward, kissed his brow, took his hands and rose, making him rise.

"She'pan," he murmured, and stepped back to let others through. One by one, to the very last and least, she took hands and kissed them, and there were bewildered looks on the faces of more than one of the Kel, for she had no reputation for such gestures.

Only Ras hung back, and when she was too obviously the last:
"The kel'anth is not back," Ras said to his hearing and that of too
many others. "Where is he, she'pan? I ask permission to ask."

"Not back yet," said Melein.

And Ras simply turned her back and walked away.

"Ras," Hlil hissed after her, his heart sinking; he hesitated between going after her and staying to plead with the she'pan, who
must reprimand the rudeness; someone must. It could not be ignored. It was on him, kel-second, and he stood helpless.

But Melein turned her face away as if not to notice Ras's leaving. "Make camp," she said into that deathly silence . . . clapped
her hands with a sharp and commanding energy. "Hai! Do it!"

"Move!" kel Seras called out, and clapped his hands, an echo
of hers. Kath'ein called to children and sen'ein joined kel'ein in
helping Kath divide the loads they had brought.

Hlil stood still, caught the she'pan's eyes as she glanced back
across an intervening distance. Her calm face considered him for
a moment, face-naked as he was, and turned from him.

There was canvas overhead this night, the brightness of lamps,
the comfort of mats spread on the ground, in the place of the cold
sand and rocks which had been their bed; enough to eat, and
warmth besides closeness of bodies. But most of all . . . the Pana.
Melein kept it by her—once opened, to be sure that the precious
leaves within were intact. She had her chair, robes for her lap, and
outside, evident in laughter—happiness in the camp, after all past
sorrows.

Concerning Niun, she refused to give way to fear; there had
been the storm, and the desert and Niun's mission kept no schedules. He could fend for himself no less than those born to this
land; she convinced herself so.

She sat, throned in her chair, the pan'en beside her, veiled
again. She reached out her hand and touched it from moment to
moment, this object which had come with her all her long journey and which contained all the voyage of those before. She
feared . . . not personally, unless it was a fear rooted in her pride,
an unwillingness to fail when millennia of lives rested on her
shoulders. It was a burden which might drive her mad if she allowed herself to dwell on that. Kel-training had given her the gift

of thinking of the day as well as of the ages, as Sen thought. It was said that she'panei—the great and true ones—acted in subconscious foreknowledge, that the power of the Mystery flowed through their fingers and the shapings that they shaped were irresistible—that they sat at the hinge-point of space and time. From such a point—events flowed about one, and all who stood nearest. Time was not, as Kel and Kath perceived, like beads on a string, event and event and event, from which Darks could sever them, breaking the string. There was only the Now, which extended and embraced all the Past which she contained and the pan'en contained, and all the past which had brought Kutath to this moment; and all the future toward which she led.

She was not single, but universal; she inhaled the all and breathed it through her pores. She Saw, and directed, and it was therefore necessary to do very little, for from the Center, threads ran far. It was that, to believe in one's own Sight. There was no anger, for nothing could cross her. There was no true pride, for she was all-containing.

And at other moments she left that vision, suspecting her own sanity. She was kath Melein, kel Melein, sen Melein, who desired most of all to shed the burden and take only the black robes of Kel . . . to have freedom, to take up arms, to strike at what should offend her honor and to walk the land empty of past and future.

Years in voyaging, and, but for an occasional hour . . . quite, quite alone, to study and meditate on the pan'en. One's meditations could become convoluted and bordering madness.

Did she'panei truly believe the Sight? Or was it pretense? She did not know; she had become she'pan in the People's dying . . . last, quite lost; and her own she'pan had not prepared her . . . had herself been on the edge of madness.

If she entertained one keen fear, it was that: that she was similarly flawed, that she was heir to madness, that the ancestors who had gone out had spent themselves and the World's life to no sane purpose—or that the Sight had perverted itself, and had brought her home as the logical end of things, the mad she'pan of a mad species, to destroy.

"She'pan."

A shadow moved, gold-robed as it entered the light. Sathas, sen'anth. She blinked and lifted her hand, permission; and the aged sen'en came and sat at her feet. She had called the anth'ein, the seniors-of-caste; she drew a deep breath, regarded Sathas with quiet speculation.

New to his post: none of the original anth'ein had survived the march out of An-ehon, save if one counted Niun; the tribe was crippled by that loss of experience. But of all castes, Sen was the rock on which she stood.

"Sathas," she said softly, "how goes it?"

"Surely you mean to ask us that."

"I ask of the tribe, Sathas."

He frowned . . . kel-scarred like herself, one of very few of this Sen who had come up through that caste as she had; and she treasured him for that, that core of common sense that came of kel-training. Wind and sun and years had made of his face a mask in which the eyes alone were quick and alive, the planes of his countenance creased with a thousand lines.

"As she'pan . . . or as Mother?"

It was well-cast. She lowered her eyes and declined answer, looked up and saw the kath'anth and Hlil in the parting of the curtains. "Come," she bade them.

The kath'anth seated herself, inclined her head in respect: Anthil, a fiftyish kath'en, and never, perhaps, beautiful; but the weathering of years had given her the placidity that kath-ein attained. Young Hlil s'Sochil—quite otherwise, she thought; he would have a face like Sathas' some day, all grimness.

That it was Hlil, and not Niun . . . she tried not to think on that.

"She'pan," they murmured greeting.

"Anth'ein," she responded, folding her hands in her lap. "Can we move camp tomorrow?"

Heads inclined at once, although there was no happiness in the face of the kath'anth, and that of kel Hlil was as impassive as one could look for in a kel'en.

"Understand," she said, "not . . . back to your own range; but to a place I choose. We have come home; there are old debts; a service to discharge."

Membranes flickered in the eyes of the kath'anth and of Hlil, disturbance. "The Kel," Hlil said hoarsely, "asks permission to ask."

"We have lost An-ehon, kel-second; but what you saw there confirms what I hope, that we are not without resources. There is a city beyond the hills, youngest of cities, one never linked to us in the attack . . . nor ever one of our own."

"Elee," Hlil murmured, shock plain in his unveiled face.

"The city Ele'et," said sen Sathas. "Sen agrees with the she'pan in this undertaking. We may perish. We do as we must."

"She'pan," Hlil murmured faintly.

"Elee were our first service," Melein pursued him. "Is not the return . . . appropriate? Of the races which came of this world, are we two not the last? And in the trouble that attends us—I think it an appropriate direction. I have consulted Sen, yes. Long since." She flicked a glance at Anthil. "I have seen Kath withered in the House of my birth, kath'ein and children lost by my own she'pan, who killed them in the forging that shaped my generation, on a world too harsh for them . . . but not so harsh as Kutath itself. You are stronger, Kath. But ask, and I will part you from the tribe, give you into some shelter and set kel'ein to guard you."

"No," the kath'anth exclaimed at once.

"Think on it before answering," Melein said.

"We go," the kath'anth said, a voice gentle as befitted her; and unyielding. "I shall ask; but I know Kath's answer."

That pleased her. She inclined her head, accepting—glanced at Hlil. Not unthought, that she appealed to Kath before Kel: the others were true anth'ein, no surrogates; and the others knew their authority. "Kel-second," she said, "do you understand now . . . what the matter is before you? My own kel'anth—we came of such a struggle, he and I: of tsi'mri, and ships, and the serving of a service. It has been a long time, has it not, for this Kel? Nigh a hundred thousand years you have served to the service of living, of surviving the winds, of providing for Kath and Sen . . . and perhaps . . . of waiting. Do you hear me, kel Hlil? The world has tsi'mri over its head . . . and you, for the moment, wield the Kel; you are my Hand . . . and the People have need. I may be the last age, kel-second. Can you lead if you must . . . even into the Dark?"

The membrane flicked rapidly across his eyes; the kel-marks stood stark upon his face. Such distress was for her to see; he did not give her the blankness that was for strangers.

"I beg the she'pan put kel Seras in my place."

"He is experienced," she agreed, and felt pain for this man, that he should make such a retreat . . . fear, perhaps, She met his eyes and a curious sense came on her that something very tough rested at the core of this kel'en. "No," she said. "I ask you: why did kel'anth Merai s'Elil set you to be kel-second?"

Hlil looked down at his hands, which were like himself, unlovely. "I was his friend, she'pan, that is all."

"Why?" she returned him; and when he looked up, plainly confounded: "Do you not think, kel-second, that it had something to do with yourself?"

That was a heart-shot, she saw it. After a moment he bowed his head and lifted it again. "Then I have to report," he said in a still voice, "that we are missing one of the Kel. That kel Ras—is not in camp. Should we do something in that matter, she'pan?"

She let go a slow breath, looked on the man and read pain. The eyes met hers, quite steady and miserable.

"I shall not ask what the Kel would do," she said. "You would judge harshly because you want not to. I am afflicted with an unruly Kel; can I heal it with impatience? Perhaps I should be concerned; but I am more concerned for those who remain. Let her go if she will; or return. I do not forbid. And as for the matter at hand," she said, going placidly about the matter of orders and looking instead at Anthil, "we abandon nothing, except by Kath's discretion, I do not urge it. Some of the least kel'ein can walk burdened, and some of the lesser sen'ein too. Settle that within your own caste. Divide the property of the dead according to kinship and need. I trust the Kel can bear another trek?"

"Aye," Hlil said quietly, earnestly. Sathas and Anthil added soft assent.

"Then at dawn," she said, dismissing them with a gesture. They rose, pressed her hands in courtesy. Only Hlil held a moment more, looked at her as if he would speak . . . and did not.

They withdrew. She leaned back in her chair, touched at the pan'en, stared before her with an unfocused gaze on the lamps.

To manage others . . . had a bitter taste in the mouth, a taint of Intel, her own she'pan, who had known how to seize her children and wring the hearts out of them, who could choose one to live and one to die, who could use, and move, and wield lives like an edged blade.

So she had sent Niun; and in cold realization of necessity, selected another weapon, for its hour.

Only Ras. . . . She attempted, consciously, to use Sight, to know whether she was a danger or no: and Sight failed her, a vast blankness all about the name of Ras s'Sochil.

The vision was at times not comfort enough; when she doubted it altogether, it was far less.

Chapter Eight

They were still there. Duncan rolled aside on the dune face and turned his head to regard Niun, who still rested on his belly and his forearms, though he too had slid down somewhat. The beasts rested down in the trough, needing nothing of vision to tell them where their enemies were, spread wide about the horizon of dunes under a morning sun.

"Yai!" Duncan said hoarsely, stopping that impulse, lest their followers use it to track to them.

"We need to keep moving," Niun said. "When you can."

Duncan considered it, lay there, content to breathe. Food nauseated him; but he accepted the dried strip of meat Niun offered him while they waited. He thrust it into his mouth and finally chewed it and choked it down his raw throat. Things tasted of blood and copper, even the air he breathed. There were frequent moments when he lost vision, or when his knees threatened to bend the wrong way in walking the uneven ground. His head pounded. Alone, he would have burrowed into the first stony cover he could find and prepared to fight if hiding failed; Niun would make other choices, that would get him killed.

"Much farther?" he asked.

"Some," Niun said. "Tonight, maybe."

Duncan lay still and considered that, which was better than he had thought. "And then what? You fight duel? You have walked twice their distance."

"So," Niun said. "But it remains what I said: that between she'-panei . . . the challenge is single; must be. If we started the matter here, we would have bloodfeud, and no end of challenges." He drew a short breath, himself near panting. "Hai, and their kel'anth may not be with them; in that case challenge falls to their kel-second. That can only be in our favor."

Niun was very good. So, Duncan reckoned, might others be.

"Do you want to go on from here?" Duncan said. "They do not have us always in sight; if I walk over your tracks you might be a good way back to—"

Dusei stirred below, uncomfortable. "No," Niun said. He touched his own face, where the veil crossed his cheeks and the blue edge of the kel-scars was visible. "You are unscarred; no kel'en should challenge you; but alone—gods know what they would do."

"That is my difficulty, is it not?"

By the look in Niun's eyes it was not.

"Aye," Duncan said. Much, Niun had taught him aboard the ship, much is mind; what one will, one can. He had survived jump without drugs, as mri did, and that was called a physical difference. He sucked air slowly, measuring his breaths, warming the air through his hands, finally gathered himself up off the face of the dune and started moving. Niun swiftly overtook him, and the dusei, shambling along at a better pace than they had been making.

"Do not overdo it," Niun said.

He slacked a little, went blind to his surroundings and concentrated on breathing and pace and the little bit of sand about them. Until night. He reckoned he might last that long.

It was back, the human ship *Santiago,* despite all maneuvers to shake it. Bai Suth glared at the image of it, which was, even against *Shirug's* vast teardrop shape, a threat. An elder human commanded *Santiago,* bai Silverman. Were there only human younglings in question, *Shirug* might dispose of that nuisance and argue the point with bai Koch later, in confidence that human anger would not ascend to a hostile move against *Shirug* itself: humans had three ships: regul, one. It was a clear question of proportional damage.

The fighter simply maintained orbit, observing. The shuttles sown into atmosphere during the evasive maneuver could not return without another such. They performed maneuvers frequently, whether or not shuttles were going; and each brought *Shirug* closer than Suth liked to come to the planet. There was no means to lose the human craft: a hard run and a threat toward jump might keep *Santiago* from their vicinity for days, but in fact all the fighter needed do was to sit at the objective, orbiting Kutath close-in, and all elusive maneuvers came to naught. The fighter was far more maneuverable in close planetary orbit than was *Shirug,* being able to cut lower and get out again, as *Shirug* possessed similar advantage over giant *Saber,* and therefore *Saber* had the ultimate advantage while it had *Santiago,* a two-point flexibility which made eluding them nigh impossible.

To remove that ship—permanently—might well be worth the hazards of human reaction, if that reaction could be understood in advance.

No doubt remained at least that humans had decided an adult existed among regul. Suth fretted with disappointment that this realization had come sooner than he would have wished, but it did give them added safety—assuming elder status meant what it should to human minds.

But elder status had not at all protected bai Sharn from death. It might be argued that the youngling Duncan was thoroughly mri, and that what Duncan did, did not speak for humans; it might even be argued that Duncan was mad, and therefore apt to any act. But the fact remained that humans had not shown sufficient disturbance at Duncan's act of elder-murder. Distress . . . of course that was not to be anticipated; Sharn's death was a political convenience to humans, and they could only be pleased at the opportunity which fell into their hands . . . but the lack of emotional disturbance in the presence of a dead elder, the cold haste in which they had been ejected from the ship and sent back to *Shirug,* in which they must wait a day on the release of their elder's body—that was a reaction without sane emotion, a void where some emotion ought to exist and failed. Suth turned this circumstance over and over in his mind, day by day, smothering his own anger in an increasing preoccupation with this illogic. A reaction existed in regul which—perhaps—humans did not feel at all. This insensitivity had vast implications, and Suth felt keenly the lack of experience which was his. What he had once heard, what he had once seen, what things had impinged on his life or what he had studied, every minute detail, he recalled unshakably.

Humans, he had observed, recalled things in time-ahead. *Imagination,* they called this trait; and since they committed the insanity of remembering the future—Suth had been tempted to laughter when he first comprehended this insanity—the whole species was apt to irrational actions. The future, not existing, was remembered by each individual differently, and therefore they were apt to do individually irrational things. It was terrifying to know this tendency in one's allies—and worse yet not to know it, and not to know how it operated.

They might do anything. The mri suffered from similar future-memory. Presumably two such species even thought they comprehended one another . . . if two species' future-memories could possibly coincide in any points; and *that* possibility threatened to unbalance a sane mind.

This was one most profound difference between regul and human, that regul remembered only the past, which was observable and accurate as those who remembered it. Humans accustomed to the factual instabilities of their perceptions, even *lied,* which was to give deliberate inaccuracy to memory, past or future. They existed in complete flux; their memories periodically purged themselves of facts: this was perhaps a necessary reflex in a species which remembered things that had not yet happened and which falsified what had occurred or might occur.

Disrespect of temporal order; this was the sum of it. Anything might alter in them, past, present, future. They *forgot,* and wrote things on paper to remember them; but they might not always write the truth; and the possibility that they might accurately *imagine* the truth . . . Suth backed his mind from that precipice, refusing the leap.

Humans had not experienced disorientation in the killing of a regul reverend with the accumulated experience of nearly three hundred years. It was as if they could *forget* all this information, not valuing it—perhaps because they could change whatever they pleased, or *imagine* backward as well as forward.

And it evidently did not matter to them whether they remembered accurately; it did not disorganize the species, who were accustomed to divergency in future-memory, and therefore—perhaps—cared nothing for divergence in past-memory.

How did they view the present? Did it likewise shift about?

Could they likewise *forget* the killing of a human elder, if it was not useful to remember it?

If he could reach a correct conclusion, it would be of great value in determining policy.

He sat now, in his sled, which supported his increasing bulk and provided him, on rails and wheels, swift transport about the spiraling corridors of *Shirug,* if he needed it. In fact there was little need for him to stir from his office, and he did so seldom. Every control on the ship was accessible directly or indirectly from his sled console. Only actual flight operations demanded more meticulous attention to incoming data than he could conveniently handle, and a nervous clutch of Alagn younglings attended the controls constantly. He had killed several for inattention . . . and also because they were older Alagn younglings, and there was the remote chance of one of them sexing male, once the immediate hysteria of Change had eased on the ship, and while the fact of his command was still new to the crew.

The younglings who survived his tempers had improved markedly in efficiency, working feverishly whether or not his eye was immediately on them; this was to the good of the ship. They learned; he would Impress them, so that even years hence he would have no rivals.

Therefore he was prepared to deal with humans. He had absolute power on his own ship, and he was calmer about entering the maze of regul-human relations that he might have been.

Therefore he allowed himself to contemplate confrontation.

He keyed the position of *Santiago* to the screen on the panel of his sled, and widened the schematic to include the latest plotting of the position of *Saber,* over the horizon. *Flower* was a third dot, below, on Kutath's surface. There were four other points, two human shuttles aloft, two regul shuttles left on Kutath: younglings, expendables.

He stared in prolonged speculation at the screen, his nostrils flaring and shutting in dislike as he sorted all past action to determine present ones, combining and recombining pieces like a stoneworker, seeking those which made coherent structure.

A light flashed on his board, signaling someone wishing his personal attention. He cleared the screen and received a notation from Nagn: *Urgent. Direct-contact, favor.*

He flashed back his permission. "Door," he shouted at the youngling who kept the anteroom, and it stirred out in haste: Ragh, its name was, clever and zealous and mightily fearful.

The other doorway opened. Not one but three sleds arrived, Nagn and Tiag and Morkhug, with attendants and commotion. Ragh showed them through, directed the other attendants, stumped this way and that offering drink, murmuring anxious courtesies.

"Out!" Suth snapped; Ragh daringly slipped a cup into his hand and fled with all possible speed, herding the other younglings into the anteroom. "Report," Suth asked of his mates. "What is the urgency?"

"Important news," Nagn said. "Favor, reverence bai: analysis of the new tapes indicates a resurgence of power in the sites."

Suth hissed softly, delayed for a drink to stabilize the out-of-phase beating of his hearts. "Details."

"Scant, reverence. The readings are faint. More might be done . . . but the likelihood of triggering fire with *Shirug* in range. . . ."

The hearts tended apart, and then toward unity. "Mri with weapons. This can be demonstrated in plain data. Mri with weapons."

"Every site," Nagn said in a low voice. She keyed a graphic to their screens, the world rotating, sites lighting, all edging on the great chasms. "Concentrated life signs indicate moisture in the depths of the basins; what is there, is patently available for use at such sites. Life requirements are available to a technology advanced sufficiently to draw the water up. The area out of which the youngling Duncan appeared . . ." The graphic reversed its revolution and narrowed in field. ". . . possesses more than one such site."

"Old," Suth murmured, staring at the distance between the diminished water sources and the city sites. It was shattering constantly to realize how old. Data available in home space had indicated the mri to be a young species, and regul oldest of all—regul, who had risen on the cycles of famines and the dread of famines, to seek resources outward, warless, with errorless passing of knowledge from one generation to the next. But not the oldest. Far from oldest. Millions of years lay even in the decay of Kutath.

Of mri who, like humans . . . *forgot.*

Data existed in such cities, recorded as *forgetting* species must record such things: a treasury of eons, knowledge of all these regions of space, records of the dead worlds which the mri had killed, of all this aged, alien species had done and known and been. To destroy this knowledge. . . .

The very thought sent a wave of revulsion through him, almost unbearable in intensity. It was the death of elders. It was murder. He sucked air, his hearts paining him. Sharn had committed such destruction, without understanding what she did. He was cursed to know. But what was down there was knowledge inaccessible to regul, in language mri had never given regul to learn, of experiences which had to make sense only to mri—or to those who could speak the language, who could become mri.

A human could. Duncan spoke the mri tongue, and assumed the robes and the manners and the thoughts of mri. A human *forgot* his own way, and crossed that boundary which regul in two thousand years had not crossed nor wished to.

Humans would gain access to such knowledge with the fall of the mri world, or with the peaceful accommodation they sought with it. They would possess the experience of millions of years which would be recorded down there. Would become . . .

. . . mri. Imitating, as Duncan so facilely imitated. The model was before them, in the youngling Duncan.

To let this happen . . . to allow to exist information which regul could not use, and allow it into the hands of a species which could *forget* its own nature and assume that of another . . . or which already shared tendencies which mri had—

"Eldest?" Nagn murmured. "Eldest?"

"We have a difficulty, bai Nagn. One which affects policy. Heed: I shall tell you a thing. Once . . . in the memory of doch Horag, a dispute of Horag elders was to be resolved by the combat of mri kel'ein. And one kel'en said that he sought this particular combat gladly, because he understood that the other Horag elder had abused her mri mercenary. Yet the first mri killed the second."

"That is mad," said Tiag.

"Not so. The regul who lost the challenge, lost territory and younglings and influence. Thus the dead mri was avenged powerfully, and his killer was indeed his avenger as he had purposed to be. Mri are fully capable of understanding revenge. And they do not value survival above status as humans do."

"Their lives are short by nature," Morkhug said with contempt. "And they *forget* what they are told."

"Do not reckon that they lack wit, mate-of-mine. Errors have been made on this account, serious errors."

"There is a human with them, reverence. He is the dangerous one. He has made them dangerous, as they were not before his coming among them. Humans are capable of some memory functions, if only on paper and tape. Remove this one human and the mri are disorganized."

"No," Suth said flatly. "No. Sharn and doch Alagn erred, because Alagn never employed mri directly and did not understand them. Alagn came from homespace . . . as you do. But Horag doch has employed mri in the colonies, for two thousand years. *I remember.*"

This silenced them all, Alagn-born that they were; they were tied now to Horag, and lifted their faces to him, respectfully expecting enlightenment.

"I shall share my knowledge," he promised them, "as it becomes needful. Alagn erred. Bai Hulagh Alagn-ni of Kesrith failed to ask into the experience of his predecessors. Therefore Alagn does not remember. I do not make that error of omission. If any of you has pertinent information or acquires it, I order you to give it to me at once."

One after the other they solemnly confessed ignorance of mri.

"Attend," said Suth with a pleased hiss. "It is necessary to touch that mri characteristic I named."

"This is not Kesrith," Nagn said. "Bai—"

"Does a question occur to you?"

"There are cities. Machines. Do mri construct such things? Have mri ever constructed such elaborate things themselves? This is not consonant with observation."

"Mri have always worked . . . among themselves, or for their own benefit. They would not lift a pebble at our bidding; but to house themselves, yes, they have built their own edunei, and they handle complex machinery—expertly. Does Alagn estimate the mri edun on Kesrith was built by regul? Does Alagn not know that kel'ein have handled regul ships—with controls designed for regul minds and memory, which humans have greatest difficulty grasping? Alagn has failed to observe, until now. I congratulate you, bai Nagn, at least on an appropriate question."

The three Alagn-ni fretted in visible discomfiture.

"Further question," Suth pursued. "As this is the mri home-world—we accept human reckoning this is so—do associational structures here operate as they did in mri for hire far from the authorities of this world? It will not be wise to make simplistic conclusions based on data from Kesrith. Facts too soon recorded are sometimes imperfect."

"But," Tiag said, her nostrils fluttering still under the sting of sarcasm, "this is an armed world, reverence. Facts not swiftly enough recorded are not available for our defense, reverence bai."

Suth swelled in pique, not overmuch. Logical that Tiag had sexed as she had; she had always had a brusqueness that disturbed. "Physically, bai Tiag, we could launch further fire into those sites. But humans are onworld; humans must perceive the origin of the threat clearly as mri. We are within range of human ships as well as mri cities." In exaggerated lack of haste he reached for the sled-console, sipped at his cooling cup from one hand while he keyed in library functions with the other. He obtained memory-films, meant to chronicle the mri wars for any youngling which might be born on board; and he smiled, having obtained what he sought. Editing them on the spot was a simple matter, ordering the machine to duplicate, beginning and ending at certain points, and to arrange scenes into desirable sequence.

Human faces showed on the screen: Duncan's face. The mri slaughter at Elag lay tangled in smoking ruin; the towers of Nisren's edun fell in fire and human troops rushed across a field strewn with mri dead; human warships hovered above mri ruins.

He composed, sent the result to the others, watched their faces conceive excitement.

"We do not speak the mri tongue," he said, "but these powered sites surely have the facilities to receive simple transmissions. And demonstration speaks all tongues."

"Bai," Nagn murmured.

"We have ten shuttles. Several can be dropped; we reserve four for maneuverings where humans can keep them in sight. The ones sent down are at very high risk. But I tell you this for your information, honored mates: these mri . . . all the laughter regul have indulged in over species whose memory is lost without their paper . . . and these humans too. . . . Does it occur to you that in the Alagn debacle at Kesrith, these aforesaid humans gathered up a great deal of regul paper and tapes? The library was lost. Your great Alagn bai Hulagh salvaged machines and ships and lives of younglings and let the library fall into human hands; a minor loss, so long as the minds which contained that—doubtless trivial—information were packed onto ships and sent back to home space and safety, true? Or perhaps Hulagh would have fired the library before leaving . . . if he had had time. Observe this youngling Duncan, observe how exactly he imitates mri. A minor loss, a poor colonial library on a mining colony? Regul lost nothing; but humans gained. Did humans much fret for the loss of the machines Hulagh lifted off? No. But humans swarmed over that library in the first days of Kesrith's occupation like insects over corruption. Does no conclusion yet occur to you?"

"We erred," Nagn said after a moment, her nostril edges showing pallor. "Reverence, why have we failed to note such things?"

"Because, Nagn Alagn-ni, the bai of your doch lacked experience, for all his years; so did Sharn. I have realized it. This question has occurred to me; but even as a youngling I possessed something great Alagn did not have—experience of non-regul. You were insulated, safe, in home space. Horag is colonial. We dealt with mri, with humans, with mri beasts. We gained models against which to compare actions. You have lacked such models. Your comprehensions are wise within your limitations, but there are other species in the universe . . . and Horag has been dealing with them for two thousand years."

"Mri and dusei and humans," Tiag exclaimed in disgust. "What can they discover that some regul has not already discovered and remembered the first time?"

"Lackwit, observe what Nagn has correctly observed and think! What would humans do with the records of our own homeworld? And what world is this before us?"

"The mri homeworld," Morkhug said. "Cities, storehouses of data—"

"To which this Duncan has already gained access," said Suth. "Mri . . . value revenge. The revenge they owe Alagn is considerable, and I do not want that inheritance. But that is not the only cause for which we should fear. Of how many years might be the experience logged in cities which were built to surround seas which are no longer there?"

"Mri," said Tiag, attempting scorn, but her nostrils kept dilating.

"Mri with ships," said Nagn, "who made the desert of stars as far as our own space, and turned back only when they ran out of lives. And humans, who keep their memories only on paper, gather the memories of this place. Millions of years, Tiag."

"But we cannot destroy it," Tiag moaned.

"Mri," Suth said, "and incomprehensible to us. Valueless to us, in a language we cannot read. But do you observe, mates-of-mine, that the mri mind and the human . . . are compatible?"

"What shall we do, then, bai?"

"What do we do with irrationalities? We remove them from the present. Alien minds are able to bridge these irrationalities. The reflexes of *forgetting* are not all detriment, to my observation. We cannot operate by such absorptions. Already we are troubled by impossible combinations of concepts. We talk in paradoxes when we carry on any lengthy discourse with humans. We have walked into a morass. We do not extricate ourselves by swallowing mud. Remove it: that is what has to be done. It is not the weapons which are the danger; it is not the feud with mri, it is the combination, mates-of-mine, the *combination,* this absorptive tendency in our allies . . . with what we have seen in coming here. How did we first involve ourselves with humans at first hand? A human named Stavros imitated our ways. How did mri involve themselves with humans? A human named Duncan imitated theirs so successfully he has been transformed. This is beyond courtesy. This is a mechanism. This is a biological mechanism by which this species survives. There is one human, in each instance, there is one human who walks from among them, who allows himself to become Impressed, who *becomes* the enemy . . . who then bridges the gap, and gains knowledge. One sacrifice. One transformation. Who of us, who of the mri, is able to become human? Can you, Tiag? Can you define, having observed Stavros and Duncan and Koch, even what *is* human?"

Tiag shuddered visibly, eyes rolling aside.

"We shall never be quit of humans," Suth said bitterly. "By Alagn's grievous error, we let them inside. But we can see to it that what belongs to this world . . . stays here. Ends here. And we can go back to home space and give our information and observations to regulkind, without mri in the equation. We can cut off this branch, so that there is no hazard at least from this source: we can focus human attention here, where it can no longer profit them, and buy us time."

"We have one ship," Morkhug protested. "One to their three. How can we deal with them?"

"More of Alagn's negotiation. We should initiate a new negotiation. My presence gives us that option, being of different doch. We should see to the arrangement of advantages, maneuver as best we can." He set his cup aside, empty, stared grimly at the three of them. Carrying, all three; the young could not come to term in any reasonable time to be of assistance: they had not the time of years, but time as humans reckoned it, and actions had to be undertaken . . . quickly.

The tribe was not there. Niun felt it from the time that they passed the great rounded rock which had been his landmark returning from many a hunt . . . and where once he had felt a sense of occupancy—there was nothing from the dusei, only that feeling which nagged at their shoulders, warning that their pursuers were, if anything, nearer.

They had made good time, the best that Duncan could do, from nooning till now, that the sun began its midair vanishing out over the basins, and shadows were beginning to fade. Duncan kept the pace still, his breathing loud and raw. At times Niun caught him walking with eyes shut: he was doing so now, and Niun took his arm and guided him, breaking rapport with the dus, wishing to shed none of his despair on Duncan. He tried it again in the shadows' deepening . . . shaped again what he sought of the dusei, received back nothing comforting, no sense of friendly presence. There was a prickling of something else as they neared the rocks, a sense which might come of one of the ha-dusei, remote, disturbed.

Melein had warned him: other cities, she had said. Other choices. Hlil had gotten back; must have.

And somewhere they must find a place to rest, a place for Duncan. They had entered into a trap, a triangle of land with the rim on one side, the chasm of the cut on the other, and the enemy behind them, on the third. The dusei had led them here; they had followed, hoping and blind, reliant on them.

Still that blankness: dusine obsession, perhaps, with what followed . . . they were notoriously single-minded. But the dread grew in him, that the emptiness might be death, might be that Hlil had failed, that the storm had been too much for them. Dusei could not comprehend death, minds that would not respond; a bewildered persistence even without answer.

"Sov-kela," he said finally, himself hoarse with exertion. "They have moved on."

Duncan did not falter, did not answer. Some emotion came back through the dusei, a kind of panic, quickly smothered.

"We . . . go across the cut," Niun said. "We know where they are not; and the dusei probably mean . . . we should keep going south. The cut goes half a day's march around its farther end; a long diversion for our followers . . . a cautious approach this way, to go down . . . where they could meet trouble. Where I know the ground and they do not. Stay with me. Stay with me."

"Aye," Duncan said, a sound hardly recognizable.

Colors began to fade from the land. In the treacherous last light they entered the trail itself, passed under the place where a sentry should have challenged them. Sand had filled here, unreadable in the constant gentle wind, a thick blanket which lay knee-deep over the old trail, half burying rocks which had once stood clear. The dusei gave neither alarm nor sense of contact, shambling along before them.

Suddenly the way opened to the terrible vista of the sand-slip, which admitted the last amber light upon a sand-surface widened and seamed much farther than it once had been. "Yai!" Niun exclaimed, willing the dusei to stay close to them, giddy even to contemplate that fall and tormented with an abiding fear, that the dusei had brought them here because they had no other track, because there was nothing farther, and the others were lost, down that, down *there.*

Duncan breathed an exclamation beside him, a choked sound; Niun reached back, flung an arm about him, guided his unsteady steps as they came down along the edge of the cliffs. The least breath might set it into motion again, might rip loose not only that unstable surface but reach far back into the canyon.

He and Duncan walked the edge of the cliffs, the dusei throwing their heads in mistrust of this place . . . by instinct or some knowledge gleaned of his mind, they hugged the cliffs as well, shouldering against the rock, rolling nervous eyes on that outer surface.

They reached the place which had belonged to Kel, and within was nothing but shadow, sand filled halfway up to the roof of the recess. Beyond that the sandfall continued, pouring down onto what was now the face of the slip, having lost much of the cone which it had built up before. They crossed under the whispering fall and back and back in the canyon, where it had begun to be night, where the seam of the slip did not reach.

"Now," Niun said. "We cross here. No delicacy and no delay; it goes or it does not."

He sent stern command to the dusei and seized Duncan by the arm, and such as they could, they ran, crossing the stone's-throw of sand. There was a natural slipping underfoot, no more than that; and the rocks loomed before them, received them into safety. Duncan stumbled and caught himself against the rocks, moved when Niun seized him and pulled him on, up, into the tangle of rocks and wind-carved stone. The dusei climbed, no natural activity for them, with a clatter of stone and scratching of claws, and Niun clambered after, up and up where there had been an ascent from the far side.

And halfway up, a shelf, a tilting slab, hardly more than a dus' width. The beasts went on climbing, sending down small rocks; Niun stopped there, tucked up in a cramped position, dragged Duncan as much onto the ledge as he could. Duncan coughed, a racking, heaving cough, lay face down and curled somewhat; and Niun crouched there listening, his hand on Duncan's heaving shoulder.

The dusei reached the top, perhaps to move on, perhaps to wait; Niun willed them to wait, felt Duncan's breathing ease at last to deep gasps and finally to a quick, shallow pace. There was no bed but the cold stone, no place but this to rest. In his mind Niun hoped their pursuers would try the cut in the dark—one grand slide to oblivion for that carelessness, going into that place not knowing it was there. Or if they came around it, they would go some distance out of their way, some far distance. There was time to rest, enough, at least, to give Duncan a little ease.

Melein, he cast out toward his dus, hoping, desperately hoping. There was nothing, but only that remote unease that had begun this day and continued. He dared not yield to sleep; tired as he was, he might go on sleeping, until the moment he found himself surrounded by hao'nath.

He did sleep, came awake with a guilty jerk, an attempt to focus his eyes on the stars, to know how long. The moon was up. For a moment it seemed a star moved, and his strained eyes blinked and lost it: illusion, he persuaded himself. There was still a star there, stable and twinkling with dust. He watched that patch of visible heavens until he found his eyes closing again, despite numbed limbs and the misery of a point of rock in his back; Duncan's back moved evenly under his hand. He stayed still a long time, finally moved his hand and shook at Duncan, as reluctantly as he would have struck him.

"Move," he said. "We have to move."

Duncan tried, almost slipped off the ledge in trying to push himself up to his knees; Niun seized him by his Honors-belt and steadied him, moved his own stiffened limbs and pulled, secured a better grip on him. Somewhere above them the dusei stirred out of a sleep, and vague alarm prickled through the air, a re-reckoning of positions. The enemy had a new direction . . . going around the cut, Niun reckoned.

Where Melein might have gone, to be set in their path before he might.

He climbed, hauling Duncan's faltering steps higher with him, bracing himself and struggling by turns. At last the upper rocks were about them, and a sandy ridge, a last hard climb. Duncan hung on him and made it, carried his own weight then, though bent and stumbling. The dusei met them there, comfort in the dark and the moonlight; and before them stretched another flat, and the low southern hills.

A land with no more limits than the one they had just passed from; and no sight of a camp, nothing.

"Come," he urged Duncan, against complaints Duncan had not voiced. He caught Duncan's sleeve, gentle guidance, started walking, a slower pace than before. It was almost the worse for rest; aches settled into bones, rawness into his throat: Duncan's hoarse breathing and occasional coughs caught at his own nerves, and at times he hesitated in a step as if his joints yielded, minute pauses, one upon the next.

And suddenly there was sense of presence, familiar presence, home, home, home.

"They are out there," Niun exclaimed. "Sov-kela, do you feel it?"

"Yes." The voice was nothing like Duncan's. It managed joy. "I do."

And out of some reserve of strength he widened his steps, struggled the harder, a hand cupped to his mouth, attempt to warm the air.

Rounded domes of rock existed here and there, knobs of sandstone wind-smoothed, sometimes hollowed into bowls or flattened into tear shapes. A skirl of sand ran along the ground, a wind for once at their backs, helping and not tormenting, for all that it was cold; and a lightening began in the east, the first apricot seam of dawn.

Dus-sense persisted, a muddle of confusions, urging them south, unease in one quarter and another, as if the evil had fragmented and scattered; there was hope amid it; and a darkness that was nearest of all, a void, a shielded spot in the network.

It acquired substance.

There was a stone, a roughness in the land: dus, perhaps . . . a ha-dus might have such a feel, nonparticipant; might look so, a lump of shadow in the dawn.

The shape straightened, black-robed, weapons and Honors aglitter in the uncertain light. Niun stopped; Duncan did. And suddenly dus-sense took hold of that other mind, a muddle of distress before it closed itself off again.

"Ras," Niun murmured. He started walking again, Duncan beside him. The dusei reached the kel'e'en and edged back, growling.

"Ja'anom," Duncan breathed.

"Aye," Niun said. He walked closer than stranger's-distance to her; it was no place for raising voices.

"You found him," Ras said.

"Where is the rest of the tribe?"

She lifted a robed arm south-southeast, as they were bearing.

"Are they well?" Niun asked, bitter at having to ask.

"When I left."

Duncan made a faltering move and sat down, bowed over. Ras spared him a cold glance. Niun swallowed pride and knelt down by him, fended off the dus that wanted close to him, then let it, for the warmth was comfort to Duncan. Niun leaned his hands against his own knees, to rest, the reassurance of Ras' message coiling uncertainly in his belly. He put aside the rest of his reserve and looked up at Ras. "All safe?"

"Kel Ros, sen Otha, sen Kadas . . . dead."

He let it go, bowed his head, too weary to go into prolonged questioning with Ras. He had not known the sen-ein; Ros had been a quiet man, even for a kel'en; he had never known him either.

Ras settled with a rustling of cloth, kel-sword across her knees to lean on.

"There are others out there," Niun said at last. "Hao'nath. They have been following some few days."

If that perturbed Ras she did not show it.

"Did Hlil send you?" he asked.

"No."

The old feeling returned, that tautness at the gut that assailed him whenever Ras turned up in his path, or behind him. Brother and sister was the obligation between them; it was mockery. For a moment the hao'nath themselves seemed warmer.

"Come," he said. "Duncan, can you?"

Duncan moved and tried. Niun rose and took his arm, lifting him up, and at the unsteadiness he felt, slipped an arm about him, started in the direction the dus-sense indicated.

Ras walked beside him this time, a shielded blankness in the dus-sense. Mri of Kesrith had learned that inner veil, living among dusei; Ras had, of loathing or of necessity, ignoring even a warding-impulse to stay with him.

The light brought detail to the land, the rounded hills, the limitless flat, the shadowy gape of the cut they had passed.

There was nothing in all of it that indicated a camp.

The preparations had that cold and lonely feeling which always came of dawn hours and broken routines. Galey meddled with his personal gear while the three regs with him did the same, and all of them waited on Boaz.

Ben Shibo, Moshe Kadarin, Ed Lane, two legitimate regs and Lane, who was more tech than not, in armscomp. Shibo was backup pilot; Kadarin he had picked for a combination of reasons the others shared, the several world-patches on his sleeve, a personnel file that indicated an absence of hatreds, a phlegmatic acceptance of close contact with regul.

They took to Boaz's presence the same way: quietly, keeping misgivings to themselves.

At present the misgivings were his own, a fretting at the delay, wondering if at the last moment Luiz might not confound them all by interposing his own orders.

But at length she came, Luiz trailing anxiously in her wake. She had a clutter of gear with her, photographic and otherwise; and Galey objected to nothing—it was civ business and none of his. She paused to press a kiss on the old surgeon's cheek, and Galey turned his head, feeling oddly intrusive between these two. "Load aboard," he told the others; Kadarin and Lane gathered up the gear and went out. Shibo delayed to offer a hand for Boaz's gear.

"No," she said, adjusting the straps. Fiftyish, stout to the extent she could not fit into one of their flight suits, she wore an insulated jacket and breeches that in no wise made her slighter. Her crown of gray-blonde braids lent her a curious dignity. She looked at him, questioning. "Out," he said. She paused for another look at Luiz and went.

The question had occurred to him more than once, how much *Saber* knew, whether Luiz had communicated to Koch precisely

which civ had been included. There was at the back of his mind a
doubt on that point, the suspicion that he was ultimately responsible, and that Koch would lay matters to his account. Boaz was not
expendable.

So what good, she had cornered him, *what good is some assistant of mine with good legs and no comprehension of what he's
seeing? What's known of mri customs is my work; what's known
of the mri writings I broke in the first place. You need me to get
the answers you're going for. I'm your safety out there.*

He wanted her, trusted her attitudes that did not want holocaust.
He offered his own hand to Luiz, forbore the question and walked
out, after the others.

Cold, thin air. Without the breathers for the short trip between
hatch and shuttle, they were all panting by the time they had the
shuttle hatch closed, and settled into the cheerless, cramped interior. Galey took his place at controls, gave them light other than
what came in from outside, started up the engines.

He cast a look back and to the side of him, found nothing but
calm faces in the greenish glow . . . wondered if Boaz was afraid:
no less than the rest of them, he reckoned.

He cleared with *Flower* and started lift, disturbing the sand. He
did not seek any great altitude; the ground ripped past in the
dawning, a blur of infrequent irregularities in the sands. Eventually the chasm gaped beneath them and he banked and dropped.
He passed no orders, kept scan audio in his ear, and Shibo, beside
him, watched as intently.

They went for the nearest of the sites; and it was the safest approach in his calculation, the best approach to that site potentially
ready and hostile . . . to fly below rim level. Dizzying perspective
opened before them in the dawn, rocks blurring past on the left.
Air currents jerked at them. In places sand torrented off the
heights before them, cables and ribbons of sand which fell kilometers down to the bottom of the sea chasm . . . stained with sun
colors. Rounded peaks rose disembodied out of the chasm haze.

And nearer and nearer they came to the city, to that point at
which he had designated on their charts a limit to air approach.

His hands sweated; no one had spoken a word for the duration
of the flight. He gathered a little altitude, peering over the rim and
hoping to live through the probe.

"No fire," Lane breathed at his shoulder . . . for confirmation, perhaps, that they were still alive.

The ruins were in sight now; he slipped over the plateau, settled down, shut down the engines.

No one seemed to breathe for the moment.

"Out," Galey said, freeing himself of the restraints. There was no question, no hesitation, no sorting of gear: all of that on their part was already done. They went for the exit and scrambled down, himself last, to secure the ship. After that there was the ping of metal cooling, the whisper of the sand and the wind, nothing more. They shouldered the burden of breather-tanks, pulled up the masks which rasped with their breaths, adjusted equipment.

And walked, an easy pace, heavily booted against the denizens of the sands. Breathing seemed easier out of the vulnerable vicinity of the ship.

Boaz meddled with a pocket, fished out black and gold cloth which fluttered lightly in the breeze. "Suggest you adopt the black," she said. Galey took one, and the other three did, while Boaz tied the conspicuous gold to her arm.

"Black is Kel," he said, "and gold is scholars."

"Noncombatant. If they respect that, you've a chance in an encounter."

"Because of you."

"It's something they might at least question."

It was something, at least. There was the city before them, a far, far walk, and a lonely one. They were smaller targets apart from the ship, less deserving of the great weapons of the city.

Most of all was the cold, the knife-sharp air, and an abiding consciousness that they had no help but themselves.

Mri did not take prisoners. Humanity had learned that long ago.

Chapter Nine

The tents were in sight, appearing out of the evening and a roll of the land, and there was still no forcing. Duncan tried, and had soon to sink down and rest all the same, senses completely grayed for the moment, so that all he felt was his dus and the touch of its hot velvet body.

More came, then: dus-carried . . . Niun's presence, the cold blankness that was Ras Kov-Nelan. It was one with the sickness that throbbed in his temples, that muddle of anxiousness and cold.

"Go on," Duncan said after a moment. "Am I a child, that I cannot walk to what I can see? You go on. Send someone out for me if you must."

Niun paid no heed to him. He moved his numb hands over the shoulder of the dus, his vision clearing finally. Niun was kneeling near him, Ras standing. Somewhere was consciousness of what they sought; somewhere was the sense of their pursuers, anger and desire, an element in which he had moved for uncounted time, that gnawed persistently at them, far, far east and north, dus-carried.

"Duncan," Niun urged at him.

Unjust, that they would not let him walk his own way, in his own time; he began to reason like a child, and knew it, at some remote distance from his own intelligence. Niun seized his arm and pulled him up, and he stayed on his feet, moved when they did, reckoning to make it this time. He shut his eyes and simply followed dus-impulse, lost to it for a time, feeling occasionally Niun's touch when he would falter. The coppery taste of blood grew more pronounced. He coughed, and the moisture began to trickle inward, so that he wove in his steps and began to shake in his joints ... frightened, mortally frightened. A knee gave, and Niun had him before he fell, keeping him on his feet. There was a touch at his other side, likewise holding him. He bent and coughed and cleared his senses, dully aware of both of them, aware of dus-sense, that was roused and angry.

Kel'ein. Ahead of them, between them and the camp in the dusk, appeared a shadow like fluid rolling across the land. It moved out toward them. Dus-feelings moiled in the air like the scent of storm. *"Yai!"* Niun rebuked them both, and stilled it. "Send them away, Duncan. Send them off."

It was hard. It was like yielding up a part of him. He dismissed the dus, felt suddenly cold, and clearer minded. The beasts strayed off a distance. He took more of his own weight, looking at that line of kel'ein who stopped before them, recognized the one who walked forward, saw sudden yielding in the line which flowed about them and included them. Hlil. He remembered the name as the kel'en tugged the veil down.

"She is well?" Niun asked.

"Well," Hlil answered, and it dimly occurred to Duncan that *she* was Melein. "Ras," Hlil said then, acknowledging her presence with a curious prickle of coldness in that tone. And for only a moment the kel'en stared directly at him, no more warmly.

"Hlil," Niun said, "there are hao'nath—" He pointed northerly. "Within this range, and with blood between us, it may be. Let the Kel keep an eye to that direction."

"Aye," Hlil said in that same still tone.

Niun shed the pack he had borne so far into the hands of a young kel'en, reached and took Duncan again by the sleeve, urging him to walk. Duncan did so. His vision blurred, cleared again. There was silence about them, not so much as a whisper from the Kel as they walked back toward the tents that now shone light-through-black in the gathering dark.

There was a stir as they reached the tents, other castes venturing out to see, kath'ein veilless and solemn, gathering children to them as they saw what had returned to them ... sen'ein too, who whispered together.

They went to the greatest of the tents ... realization struck him: the she'pan; he had that before him, need of wit and sense and whatever eloquence he could summon.

Warmth hit their faces like a wall as they swept within: warmth and gold light of lamps lit the antechamber of the tent, and the smell of incense choked him. They paused there, and beyond the veil which shrouded the center light gleamed on ovoid metal, a shimmer through gauze.

The pan'en. They had gotten it back. He was numbly relieved that among their other possessions they had gained this again, this most precious thing to them. Niun paid it respect; and respect to the Mystery he reverenced. He thought that he ought, but it was not something Niun had shown him fully, this last and most secret aspect of the People. He stood back instead, intimidated by the fervor of the others, made a token gesture toward removing his veil as they had unveiled before the Holy, but he kept his head down and his alien face inconspicuous.

Then Niun came and took his arm, drawing him through the curtain at their right, into the huge area of assembly, among the others.

Gold sen-cloth was the drapery; and golden the lamplight; gold-robed sen'ein made a bow about the single white figure which was Melein. She took her chair as the shadow of the Kel flowed about the walls to left and right; and a few older kath'ein insinuated themselves next Sen like a touch of bright sky. Duncan tried to walk steadily through the parting ranks without Niun's hand, which hovered at his elbow. Manners came back to him, recollection of courtesies which had to be paid, things told him by kel-law, though he had never been so much the center of matters.

Niun went beyond the place he should, took Melein's hands, kissed her brow and was kissed in return, whispered low words which had to do with hao'nath and strangers. Her amber eyes flicked once with distress, and she inclined her head.

"So,"she said in a low voice, "that will come as it will." Very slightly her hands moved, beckoning.

Duncan came the few steps forward, settled to his knees as Niun did, head bowed; and because he did not come with favor, he reached and swept off the *zaidhe* in humility, baring his shoulder-length hair, so unlike a mri's bronze mane. Unshaven, bloody about the nose . . . he even stank, and knew it. Humans smelled differently; he had always been careful of cleanliness and of shaving. He felt a nakedness in this exposure he had never felt in his life.

"Kel Duncan," Melein said softly.

"She'pan," he breathed, head down, hands clenched upon the veil and headcloth in his lap. The calm control of her voice made silence in which there was scarcely even the rustle of cloth in the assembly. His temples pounded, and his throat was tight.

"Where was your permission to leave us, kel'en?"

"No permission." His voice broke. A cough prickled at his throat and he tried to swallow it, succeeded with difficulty, his eyes watering.

"And you have been—"

"To the ships, she'pan. Into them."

For the first time there was a breath of protest from the gathering. Melein lifted her hand and it died at once.

"Kel'en?" she prompted him.

"Three ships," Duncan pursued past the obstruction in his throat. "Regul have come with the humans; regul did the firing on you and on the city. I killed their elder. No more . . . no more regul."

The membrane betrayed disturbance. Melein understood him if no others could. "How was this done, kel Duncan?"

"The regul was aboard one of the human ships . . . attacked when I had finished speaking to the human kel'anth. I killed her. Regul have no leader now. Humans . . . never received my message; now, now they have listened. They are offended by the regul; they asked me to bear word to you—" The name of what he was to say slipped him, untranslatable in the hal'ari. He had composed it . . . lifted a shaking hand to his brow, tried in humiliation and panic to organize what he had prepared to say. Niun moved; he brushed off the hand and stared up at Melein. "No attack; no . . . wish for attack, if the People assure humans likewise."

There was no sound but anger gathered on naked faces about the she'pan, and on Melein's cold face a frown appeared.

"What have mri to say to tsi'mri?"

It was inevitably the attitude. Millennia of contempt for outsiders, for other species. The hal'ari had four words for peace, and none of them meant or imagined what humans hoped for; one of them was sinister: the obliteration of potential threat. He found both hands shaking visibly, the bitter taste of defeat in his mouth, and the tang of blood.

"Kel Duncan—the Sen will consider the matter you have brought to council. Your effort has great value. The People thank you."

He did not hear it clearly. Perhaps others in the gathering did not; there was no stir, no move. Then it dawned on him that she had not outright rejected the offer of conference . . . more, that she leaned forward, took his filthy, rough face between her hands, and kissed him on the brow as one of her own. Her fingers pressed something into his hand, a little medallion of gold, a *j'tal* of service.

There was a muttering in the assembly at that. And then he shamed himself thoroughly, for when she drew back from him and he sat staring at what he held in his hand, the tears slipped his control, and he had no veil to hide them. He put the Honor within the breast of his robe, trying not to show his face, trying to swallow the pain in his throat.

And coughed; blood stained the hand he put to his mouth and nose. There was a great deal of it. He began shaking again, and heard a murmur of distress as he lost control of his limbs. Niun seized him, held him hard against his trembling.

He was able, after a moment, to be helped to his feet—to walk, at least to the outside of the tent, into the cold night air. Niun held him. So did another. He heard his dus nearby in the dark, moaning with distress, wanting him. He shook free and tried a few steps, not knowing where he was going, save to the dus, and then he had to reach for support. Someone caught him.

"Help me," he heard Niun say in anger. *"Help me!"*

Eventually he felt another touch. He struggled to bear his own weight, and then coughing came on him again and he forgot everything else.

Niun ate, only a token amount, from the common dish. He had no hunger, and allowed others his share. He sat now, unveiled, his hands in his lap, and stared across the tent to the Kel to the corner where Duncan lay with his dus, propped sitting against the beast, unconscious as he was, for he bled inside, and might strangle. He was no lovely sight, was Duncan, and there were many in the Kel who cast furtive looks at him, hoping, likely, for his death.

For the end of both of them, it might be, if their enemies called them out in the morning. It was a dire thing, the merging of two tribes; they had not wanted it . . . but perhaps many existed in this tribe who would count it better to accept that, and gain another kel'anth, another she'pan. He ought to clear his mind, to take food, to sleep, against such an event; he knew these things clearly.

He made attempt, and the food stuck in his throat; he swallowed that, and no more, sitting still again.

There came a slow silence in the Kel. Movements grew quieter and less. Voices hushed. No hand now reached for the bowls; no one spoke. He knew that they were staring at him, and eventually he grew as quiet within as without, remote from his pain.

Challenge me, he wished certain of them, not excluding Ras. *I will kill, and enjoy the killing.*

"Kel'anth," Hlil said.

Niun paid no attention to him.

Hlil sat silent a moment, offended, doubtless; and finally Hlil leaned closer to the fen'anth Seras, who sat next him; and then to Desai. There was some muttering together, and Niun removed his mind from all of it, letting them do what they would, reckoning that it would come to him when it was ready.

He rose instead, and withdrew to Duncan's side, sat down there, against the dus. The beast rumbled its sorrow and nosed at him, as if begging solace or help. Duncan breathed with a slow bubbling sound, and his eyes were open a slit, but they were glazed, dimly reflecting the lamplight.

The others resumed their meal, but for a small cluster about Hlil who withdrew together to talk in the opposite corner of Kel-tent, and for Ras, who came and sat down against one of the great poles, her face no more angry, only very weary, eyes shadowed.

She had, at the last, helped; he was mortally surprised for that . . . practicality, perhaps, that Duncan slowed them too much. He had long since ceased to try to account for what Ras did. He watched the others in their group, and anger moiled in him for that; he remembered the dus and stilled it . . . put a hand on Duncan's shoulder and pressed slightly, obtained a blink of the eyes.

"I know you are there," Duncan said, a faint, congested voice. "Stop worrying. Is there word yet—about the hao'nath?"

"No sign of them. Do not worry for it."

"Dus thinks they are still out there."

"Doubtless they are. But they have to think about it now."

"More . . . more than one. Back . . . side . . . front. . . ." Coughing threatened again. Niun tightened his hand.

"Save this for later."

Duncan's strange eyes blinked, and tears fell from inner corners, mixed with the dirt and the blood, trailing slowly into the hair of his face. "Ai, you are worried, are you? So am I. There are many . . . Dusei, maybe."

"You are not making sense, sov-kela."

"Life. I tried to show them life. I think they understood."

"Dusei?"

There was movement; a sudden apprehension came into Duncan's eyes, focused beyond him. Niun turned on one knee as a shadow fell on them, a wall of black robes about them. The dus stirred; but those foremost moved to kneel, restoring a little of the lamplight, and Niun moved his hand ashamedly from his weapons. Hlil—Desai, Seras, and young Taz. Niun frowned, thrust out his hand in confusion when Taz set a smoldering bowl near Duncan.

"The smoke will help," Seras said.

It was some portion of the oil-wood, which they used for lamp fuel, a greasy smoke with the cloying sweetness of some other herb added. Niun held his hand from striking it away at once, distracted between the harm it might do and his failure to have comprehended their honest intent. He settled his hand on Duncan's shoulder instead, with the other hand poised to refuse their further intervention.

"Kel'anth," said Hlil coldly, "we know some things you do not. We were born on this world."

Duncan feebly reached for the smoldering bowl. Taz edged it closer and Duncan inhaled the smoke fully. It was true. Niun felt his own raw throat eased by the oily warmth. The smoke offended the dus, which turned its great head the other way with a deep whuff of displeasure, but of a sudden the beast caught up feelings utterly naked and wove them all together uninvited, Kutathi mri and Kesrithi.

"Yai!" Niun rebuked it, and faces averted slightly one from the other in embarrassment. He looked on Duncan, who breathed deeply of the fumes, and then gazed at Hlil until Hlil looked up at him.

"S'sochil," Niun said very quietly, "I thank you; I should have said that; forgive."

"Ai," Hlil muttered, and soured the moment with a scowl and a gesture of contempt toward Duncan.

There was an explosive breath at the door. Niun looked about, saw his own dus, which had decided at last to come in out of the dark, drawn by some inner impulse. Kel'ein moved out of its path in haste as it came across the mats, head down and seemingly preoccupied; and when it had come to him, it nosed at him and sank down against Duncan's beast.

Niun rested an arm on its shoulder, tugged at its ear to distract it, lest it reach his mind and Hlil's together. For a long moment he stared at Hlil's scarred, unlovely face, fearing that the dus did indeed broadcast what moved in him. Or perhaps it came from both sides, that longing: even one who knew dusei could not always tell. Beside him Duncan rested, breathing in larger breaths, as if the smoke had taken the pain away.

Niun loosed one of his own Honors, offered it, his hand nigh trembling. He thought surely that Hlil would reject it, offending and offended; but he was obliged to the offering.

"For what service?" Hlil asked.

"That I find the tribe . . . well in your keeping. You and Seras . . . if you would."

Hlil did take; and Seras too . . . of the Honors which had been Merai's, which were his to give away; of the friend for whom, Niun thought with a sudden pang, Hlil would always grieve. It surged through the dusei unasked, the desolation and the loneliness.

"We have watchers out," Hlil said. "You did not seek this, with the hao'nath. This was not your purpose."

"No," Niun said, dismayed to realize how things had fit such a thought. "You do not know me, kel Hlil, to have wondered that."

Hlil's eyes wandered briefly to Duncan, up again.

"They tracked him," Niun said.

"They have come to the cities," Hlil said. "So should we . . . if we had not already. Kel'anth—it will not stop with the hao'nath. You understand that. Word will spread . . . of this . . . stranger with us."

"I know," he said.

Hlil nodded, glanced down, rose, excusing himself as if there were nothing more he could say; so, one by one, did the others. Taz lingered last, silently produced a small handful of dried roots and pale fiber from the breast of his robe, along with a small leather sack.

"Sir," Taz said, laying it beside the pot. "I can find more, if need be: Kath surely has to spare."

The boy went away. Niun started to speak to Duncan, to ask if he was comfortable; and looked, and saw Duncan's eyes shut and his breathing eased.

He leaned against the dus, with the knot that had been so long at his belly somewhat less taut, watching all the Kel settle for the night, each to their mats that composed the flooring of the tent. The lamps were put out, all but the one that hung nearest them, and the little bowl of smoldering fibers curled up smoke about them.

Only Ras remained, sitting; she stirred finally, and he reckoned that she too would seek her mat and sleep; but she returned after a moment, a shadow in the haze of smoke and the lamps, came close and knelt down by them with something in her arms, a roll of matting, which she set down by him.

"What is it?" he asked of her. "Kel Ras?"

She said nothing . . . withdrew to the shadows, lay down finally and seemed to sleep.

He drew the matting into his lap, unrolled it, uncovering the *cho*-silk bindings of his longsword, the coarser work of Duncan's, left behind in An-ehon. He bit his lip, fingered the ancient work of the hilt, drew the fine steel a little distance from the leather sheath, eased it back again. It was precious to him, the solitary vanity of his possessions: he had counted it lost.

Challenge, he thought, to hold what he had taken. *It will not stop,* Hlil had said, *with the hao'nath.*

Time after time, while Kutath bled its strength out, and tsi'mri waited for answers.

He laid the swords beside him, settled back again. In the quiet which had settled, Duncan's breath still bubbled, and now and again he stirred and coughed and blotted at his mouth with the soiled veil. But much of the time he did sleep, and at last the bubbling ceased.

At that sudden silence Niun roused anxiously—but Duncan's chest rose and fell with peaceful regularity, and the blood which stained his lip was dried.

He rested his eyes a time then—jerked awake at a whisper of cloth by him, saw the boy Taz kneeling and feeding more of the fiber into the bowl.

"I shall wake, sir," Taz said.

He was dazed somewhat, and ungracious—simply looked at Duncan, whose breathing remained eased and regular, and let his head down again against the shoulder of the dus, moved his slitted eyes over all the Kel, that made huddled heaps in the darkness—shut them again.

The lamp gave feeble light for study; Melein turned in her hands the golden and fragile leaf from the casing of the pan'en, laid it on her knee and drew another forth, replacing the first in sequence. She canted it to the light and the lamp picked out the graven letters like hairline fire. She read, as for years and years before this she had read, the record of the People's travels. They were incomplete. Nigh on a hundred thousand years the record stretched; in so blindingly swift a few years they had come back, she and Niun and Duncan. There would come a time when she would write her own entry into the leaves of gold, the last of the People of the Voyage, the last statement, the seal.

And she shivered sometimes, thinking of that.

The hand which held the tablet lowered to her lap. She gazed at the flickering lamp, thinking, centered in the Now.

Where do I go? That was determined.

What do I do? That too, she knew.

But other questions she did not. Some of them extended to human space and regul, and dead worlds; some of them centered

on Kutath itself, on the past in which mri had known another service. And they were one question.

A touch descended on her shoulder. She drew herself back, and
shivered, looking into the gentle face of Kilis, the young sen'e'en
who attended her, whose hands robed and disrobed her, and
whose young eyes witnessed all her life.

"She'pan—the Council of the Sen is waiting. You sent for
them, she'pan."

She smiled at that, for at times the dreaming was too strong; it
was not so for her, at least—not often. "I will see them," she said,
and carefully gathered the leaf of gold from her lap, slipped it into
the casing with the others.

The curtains stirred and the Council entered, the first and second ranks of the Sen, to settle on the mats before her. Most were
very old, older than kel'ein tended to live, hollow-cheeked and
wrinkled; but there was among them Tinas, who had a kel'e'en's
robustness about her, and kel-scars slanting across her cheeks.
Foremost among them, Sathas also bore the scars, sen'anth; grimness on him was a habit, but more than one face was frowning
this night.

"Has the Sen questions?"

"You appreciate our present danger," Sathas said. "It is what
we warned you, she'pan."

"Indeed."

"It does not disturb you."

"It disturbs me. I would wish otherwise. But that is not ours to
choose. Is that your question?"

"The she'pan knows our questions. And they are all tsi'mri."

"We have choices, sen'anth, and kel Duncan has given them to
us."

"Did you send him out?"

She looked into the guarded offense of Sathas' eyes and tautly
smiled, opened her hand palm up. "He is self-guiding. I let him
go."

Eyes flashed, nictitating with inner passion.

"You seriously consider this offer they have made?" asked
Sathas.

"It is a matter we will consider . . . for the worth in it. You do
not care for his presence, doubtless. But he has brought us

choices; and knowledge of what hangs above our heads; he comprehends them . . . and serves the People. His life has value. You understand me."

"We understand."

"And dislike it."

"We are your only weapon, she'pan, and you are ours. Do you turn aside?"

"From our course? No. No, trust me in this, sen'ein. *I am not yet done.*"

No one spoke. For a moment eyes glittered hard with speculations. *Believe me:* it was Intel who spoke, her old she'pan . . . who could persuade when reason counseled otherwise, with a voice which had wrapped silken cords about herself when she was younger; she had learned it, wielded it . . . consciously.

Perhaps all she'panei had had such arts; she did not know. It was the nature of she'panei that they never met, save the one by whose death one rose.

It was true that Intel had controlled her children when they would have rebelled, and persuaded elders who had power in their own selves: that half-mad force in her that chilled the spine and held the eye when the eye would gladly turn away . . . that followed after, so that even out of her presence the most cynical reason had no power to utterly shatter that argument.

Intel still held her; and she . . . held them.

Chapter Ten

The chief of security was back again, to trouble the labs. Averson blinked and focused on him, this dark man so persistent in his patrols. He glanced likewise at the collection of papers beside him on the desk, made a nervous snatch toward them as Degas gathered one up and looked at it.

"You've made progress with the regul transmissions?" Degas asked. "There's some urgency about it."

"It's—" Averson held out his hand for the paper and received it back. Degas favored him with a sardonic smile as he shuffled it back into order. "It's couched in idiom, not code. It might be clear if we understood Nurag."

"Nurag."

"Homeworld has bearing on language," Averson answered shortly, and experienced a little uneasiness as Degas sat down on the edge of the desk facing him. Degas put down cassettes, click, click, click, on the desk top before him.

"There's a great deal going on, Dr. Averson. Our time is escaping us. The onworld mission has decided to go . . . prudently or not rests elsewhere; they've moved out, to whatever they may find. And they may stir something up. There's always that chance. Now we have a request for permission for a regul shuttle to go down and sit with *Flower*."

Averson gnawed at his lips.

"The admiral is stalling," Degas said.

Perhaps he was supposed to make some observation on this. He did not like the thought of regul in *Flower*'s neighborhood; he did not reckon what to do about it.

"The admiral," said Degas, "understands from your reports and your advisements that the regul may move in with or without our permission."

"They may," Averson allowed. "They would reckon we would not move to stop them."

"This:" Degas reached across the desk to the spot directly in front of his hands, tapped it with his forefinger. The man was dark in manner, dark in dress, but for the weapons and the badges; he glittered with them, like kel'ein, Averson thought, much like them. "This, Dr. Averson: you've paralyzed us with your yes and no. You've said nothing, except that there's no action to be taken. Wait, you say; and what is your general feeling on the regul? Where are your opinions?"

"I can't, I've told you. I can't pronounce with any surety—"

"Your *guess,* doctor."

"But without supporting data—"

"Your guess, doctor. It's more valuable than most men's studied opinion."

"No," Averson said. "It's more dangerous."

"Give it."

"I—find it possible . . . that there is more than one adult. One to remain here, one . . . on that ship they want to send down. Logically, you see—they don't function without elder direction. You think there are regul ships down there now; I agree. But no elder. I think they would like to get one down there if they could."

Degas's breath hissed softly between his teeth.

"The hydra's head," Averson said. Degas looked at him with no evidence of comprehension. "An old story," Averson said. "Not the star-snake . . . the old one. Cut off the head and two more take its place. Kill a regul elder and more than one metamorphoses to take its place. Shock . . . some biological trigger. . . ."

Degas frowned the more deeply.

"One thing that bothers me," Averson said. "How do they learn?"

"A question for the science department," Degas said, rising. "Solve that one on your off time. What about the rest of the data I gave you? What about the transmissions?"

"No," Averson said. "Listen to me. It's an important question. They don't write everything down."

Degas shrugged in impatience. "I'm sure that's solved somehow."

"No. *No!* Listen to me. They *remember* . . . they remember. Eidetic memory. What died with bai Sharn . . . is forever lost to them. They have to lose something in the transitions. Young regul metamorphosing and taking over adult function by themselves and without outside influence, without the supporting information of their docha-structures and adults—"

"The easier to deal with them. There's no reason for panic."

Averson shook his head, despairing. "Not necessarily easier. You want guesses, good Colonel Degas. I shall give you guesses. That we have here regul without home ties, regul without past, regul who can't imagine what they're missing, regul more likely than any others to act as regul don't act; and that is dangerous, sir. A spur, a splinter of Nurag maybe; maybe of Kesrith, maybe that. On Kesrith, regul *attacked,* and these young regul *learned* that. They overcame mri. It became reality. The psychology of the eidetic mind . . . is different. That's why you asked me up here, is it not, to tell you these things? Those ships that attacked us on the way up here weren't mri; they were regul."

"Prove it."

Averson made a helpless gesture. He was confused in the motivations of this man, so supremely stubborn. He understood regul, and failed with this member of his own species, and suddenly he doubted everything, even what he knew he understood.

Degas leaned again toward him, laid his hand on all the papers in the stack. "Prove it, when none of our analyses could. By *what* do you know? Point it out to me."

"The action is consistent with the pattern. It makes a larger pattern."

"Show me."

Averson shook his head helplessly.

"I have a tight schedule, doctor. Explain it to one of my aides when you think of it. But in the meantime, I have to work on *all* the possibilities. The cassettes, doctor, come from a downed ship and the one that recovered the recorder. A man died down there. How does that fit your patterns?"

"I've told you, if you would listen."

"I'll listen when there's consistency in your advice." Degas gathered up one of the cassettes. "Landscan. Can you handle this or do we shuttle it down to *Flower*?"·

"I'm not qualified. Wait. Wait, I—would like to look at it before you send it on."

"Inconvenient, to have the science staff split here and there. You say that you can't handle it expertly; someone downworld can. I'll have your affidavit on that. You'll record it."

"If you wish."

"Now." Degas ripped paper off a pad, shoved it across the desk at him, put a stylus down by it. "Write that."

"Now?" Averson took a deep breath, mustered his anger. "I am also a busy man, colonel. You could wait."

"Write it."

He did not like Degas. The man was forceful and unpleasant. Capitulation would get him out of the lab. Averson picked up the stylus. *Suggest transfer of landscan tape to more affected department,* he wrote, and looked up. "I have some notes of my own I'll want to send down when this goes."

"If they make the shuttle, fine." Degas tapped the paper. "Sign it. Write 'Urgent.'"

"I will not be bullied."

"Sign it."

Averson blinked and looked up in shock, blinked again, thinking of things going on outside his comprehension, of motives in this man which intended things outside his own interests.

"I should consult with the admiral," Averson protested.

"Do your job. If you can't do it, pass it to those who can. Sign the paper. Note it as I told you. The shuttle will have it down within the hour."

"Excuses for more flights."

"Sign it."

"I'm right, aren't I?"

Degas put his hands framing his and leaned on them, gazing into his face at short range. "Do you know what happens if security is hamstrung, Dr. Averson? Do you comprehend your personal hazard? We have a shuttle down there poking about old sites and weapons, and ships loose we *don't* have identified; science department is giving us cautions we already understand. We want information. We're in orbit in range of ground-based weapons. Do you comprehend that? Sign it. And put 'Urgent' on it."

Averson did so, his hand shaking. He did not understand security's function in this. He understood personal threat. Degas collected the note and the cassette.

"Thank you," Degas said with great niceity.

And walked out.

Averson clenched his hands together, finding them sweating. Such men had had great power in the days of the mri wars. Some evidently thought that they still did.

This one did, where they sat, with the mri below and the regul above, and themselves neatly in the middle.

He reached for the pad and dashed off another note:

> Emil: Boaz was right. Security is involved in this, something maybe personal or political. I don't figure it out. Watch for the regul. Don't let them into the ship. Please, be careful. All of you be careful. And send Danny up here if you can spare him.
>
> I begin to understand things. I can't make these soldiers comprehend simple logic.
>
> Sim.

He folded the paper in all directions, put it into an envelope, and sealed it. *Luiz,* he wrote on it, *Personal Mail.*

And then he sat holding it on his lap and doubting where it would finally go.

The cassettes. He suddenly regretted the loss of the landscan tape, the tiny morsel of information now denied him. He manipulated the new data into the player on the desk, rapid-scanned it.

It told partial tales. All the mosaic was not there. Bioscan. He read it with an amateur's eye, split screens, readouts, instruments he did not know. What he did told him only of an intermittent vegetation, more than they had yet seen.

With fevered haste he rejected that tape and pushed in the second. It made even less sense to him, ship's instruments or some such, data with symbols of fields outside his specialization: physics, numbers that made no sense at all except that they might be electrical or some such power symbols.

A man dead, Degas had said. There was a pilot lost; he had heard that, a man named Van. The flow of data rippled past, with a man's death in it, and told him nothing. They took landscan, of which he could have made at least a modicum of sensible interpretation, and left him this jargon . . . in payment for his signature. It was the signature security had wanted, to get another shuttle launched, a ship down there, nothing more than that. They had made games of him and he had let them. Perhaps what motivated them really was locked in these incomprehensible records . . . and Degas placed them in his hands for mockery.

They must not even need interpretation of the data . . . or they would have taken it all.

Harris: he thought of the pilot Harris, one man he knew on the ship who had some expertise in shuttles and the kind of scan they were carrying, who at least might know what field these strange notations came of. He cut off the tape with a jab of his finger, punched in ship's communications.

Com answered, a young voice.

"This is Dr, Simeon Averson down in lab. Request you locate one Lt. Harris, pilot, and ask him to come to my lab as soon as possible."

"Yes, sir."

He thanked com, broke connection and leaned back, gnawing at his knuckle.

And in a moment the screen activated again. "Dr. Averson," said a different and female voice.

"Yes."

"Dr. Averson, this is Lt. McCray, security. Col. Degas's regards, sir, but your last request violates lines of operations."

"What request?"

"For communications with the military arm, sir. Regulations make it necessary to deny that interview. Lt. Harris is on other assignment."

"You mean he's not on the ship?"

"He's on other assignment, sir."

"Thank you." He broke connection, clenched his hands a second time.

And after a moment he snatched up a pertinent handful of his notes, his notebook, and the tapes, stalked across to the door and opened it.

There was a young man in AlSec uniform just outside, not precisely watching—or moving, or with reasonable business in the otherwise deserted corridor.

Averson retreated inside and closed the door between them, feeling a prickling of sweat, a pounding of his heart which was not good for him. He walked back to the desk and sat down, slammed his notebook at the cassettes and the papers down, fumbled in his breast pocket for the bottle of pills. He took one and slowly the pounding subsided.

Then he stabbed at the console and obtained com again. "This is Averson. Get me the admiral."

"That has to go through channels, sir."

"*Put* it through channels."

There was prolonged silence, without image.

"Dr. Averson," Degas's voice came suddenly over the unit. "Do I detect dissatisfaction with something?"

Averson sucked in his breath, let it out again. "Put me through to the admiral, sir. Now."

The silence again. His heart beat harder and harder. He was Havener. In the war, such men had had power there. Absolute power. He had learned so.

"Now," Averson repeated.

More silence.

"That comes by appointment," Degas said. "I will make that appointment for you."

"This moment."

"I will meet you at the admiral's office. If there is some question regarding security operations, it will be necessary."

The heartbeat became painful again, even more than in the terror of the flight up.

"I trust you won't be needing transfer back downworld," Degas said blandly. "Flights are very much more hazardous than they were when you came up. I would not risk it."

"No," Averson said, short of breath.

"Perhaps you have come up with some new advice. I would like to hear it."

"A complaint. A complaint about security's bullying tactics. I want that man taken off my door. I want access to anyone I choose. I want contact with the admiral."

"In short, the whole ship should arrange itself and its operations to accommodate you. Dr. Averson, I have tried to be helpful."

"You have taken away data I could use."

"A copy will be sent you. But I have your statement that you aren't qualified in that area. Precisely what direction are your researches taking now, Dr. Averson? The admiral will want to know."

"I object to this intimidation and harassment."

"Stay there, Dr. Averson."

Panic set in. He sat still, hearing the connection broken, sat still with the realization that there was no contact he could make past this man; nowhere he might go without encountering the man in the corridor. Sensibly he suspected that no violence would be done him if he tried to leave, but he was not a physical man; he flinched from the possibility of unpleasantness and confrontations, which touched on his medical condition. He dared not, could not, would not.

He had to sit and wait.

And eventually the man arrived, closed the door and crossed the room to him, quiet and looking ever so much more conciliatory than needed be.

"We have a misunderstanding," Degas said. "We should clear that up."

"You should get that man off my door."

"There *is* no man out there."

Averson drew in his breath. "I object," he said, "to being intimidated."

"You are free to object—as I am free to state otherwise."

"What is the matter with you?" Averson cried. "Are we on opposite sides?"

"Opposite sides of opinion, perhaps." Degas settled again on the edge of the desk, towering over him. "We are both men of conscience, doctor. You have an opinion colored by panic. Mine rests on convictions of practicality. A pattern, you say. Have you *met* mri, doctor? Have you dealt with the agent who became mri?"

"We are all Haveners. All of us—remember . . . but—"

"Some interests here want to throw over alliance with the regul for protection of the mri. Do you understand that?"

He blinked, realized his mouth was open and closed it. The matter of politics began to come clear to him. "I—don't see where it is . . . No. Breaking up the regul alliance is insanity."

"And unnecessary."

"Unnecessary, yes." He lifted a hand and wiped perspiration from his upper lip, gazed up at Degas, who backed off from him a few paces.

"You do not counsel this," Degas said.

"No. It's possible to deal with the regul. I know this; I would never say otherwise. It is possible to deal with them. But dangerous . . . dangerous under present conditions."

"Do you really understand the situation, doctor? Certain interests are pro-mri. Why they have taken this position . . . leave that to them to answer. It is a very dangerous position. The mission onworld, the personnel on that mission—the mission leader, your own Dr. Boaz, if you will forgive me, who is with them . . . are predisposed to find the mri nonaggressive, to counsel us into an approach to them. Regul do not threaten us; *regul* are not an aggressive species. Regul don't pose the primary threat. Do you agree: they don't pose the primary threat?"

"We're in a dangerous position here. You yourself said—"

"But the mass of mankind, back home . . . a threat to them?"

"No. No danger from regul. No possible danger."

"Do you see what these well-meaning influences would have you do? And what the result will be? From which species is the real threat of conflict, doctor?"

"I—see what you're saying. But—"

"Application of humanitarian principles. But Cultures above all ought to see through our moralistic impulses. We're talking about a species of killers, Dr. Averson, a species that lives by killing, parasites on the wars of any available power, who cultivate wars as regul cultivate trade. We may lose the regul here. And save what we'll regret. You understand me?"

"I—"

"I suggest, Dr. Averson, that these are points worth considering. Those reports you make should be carefully considered for effect on policy at high levels. We have new data from the surface, a disturbing resurgence in the destroyed sites. The mri do not offer to contact us. So we send a peace mission stirring into the ruins. We have allies taking on independent operations thanks to these changes in our policy and the killing of their leader by a mri agent. . . . You can't interpret their intention . . . or won't. How do we proceed? Do you have answers? Or do we let the situation go others' way?"

Averson sat and sweated and slowly, after considering, wadded up the envelope in his hand, put it into his pocket under Degas's stare. "You found life in the old sites and the mission went anyway."

"We learned it this morning. We don't have direct contact with the mission . . . can't reach them without endangering everything."

"Can't call them back?"

"Officially," Degas said in a low voice, leaning close to touch a finger before him, "not without blowing what we're doing wide open to the regul, among other things. And how do regul take that? What reaction could we anticipate? You should appreciate the significance of your own reports, doctor. They set directions. You should understand that."

"I do not intend to set directions."

"You're in that position. What do you say about the regul? I should have hoped your peculiar insights into their culture would have balanced . . . other interests in Cultures. What do you say?"

"We should not lose them, no. We should not let that happen."

"Make it clear, then." Degas leaned there with both hands. "We have dissenting views. We need this in writing, in recommendations with practical application, or we slip toward another line of policy. We're sitting up here blind, over active weapons. We're protecting mri at the expense of all we've gained by the treaties. We're alienating a species from whom the gains could be enormous. I suggest, Dr. Averson, that you and I have a long conference on these matters."

"I will—talk about it."

"Now," Degas said.

Chapter Eleven

Someone stirred close by; Niun drew a sudden breath, lifted his head, remembering Duncan with a slight panic. . . . He looked toward him and found him sleeping.

Kel Ras was sitting on her heels just the other side of him, veiled, staring at him in the shadow, leaning on the sword which rested across her knees. "They are out there," she said. "Kel'anth, I really think you should come and see."

The Kel had begun to rouse at the whispering. Hlil was there, and Seras and Desai and Merin, the youth Taz, Dias, others. A chill came over him, a profound sense of loneliness. He gazed down at Duncan, who remained oblivious to what passed, quietly disengaged himself from the dusei, a separation which had its own feeling of chill, physical and mental.

Whatever befell, they might leave Duncan in peace, at least until he was stronger; he was kel'en and some ja'anom might take that as a matter of honor. For himself and Melein. . . .

He gathered himself to his feet, shook off the concern that urged at him, bent again to gather up his sword and slung it to his shoulder. He walked outside into the beginnings of dawn, with Ras and Hlil and Desai close to him.

"Has anyone advised the she'pan?" he asked, and when no one answered he sent Desai with a gesture in that direction. It was necessary to think of no more concerns, to settle his mind for what had to be met and what had to be done. He had no feeling of comrades at his side, rather that of witnesses at his back, and the loneliness persisted.

There was no possibility yet of seeing clearly what had come. Halflight tricked the eye, made the land out to be flat when it was not. A thousand enemies could be hidden in that gentle rolling of the sands. They walked out to the rear of Kel, and Ras lifted her arm silently toward the northeast, where a faint hint of rocks marred the smoothness of the land.

No one was in sight now, and that was perhaps another of the land's illusions.

Kel'ein joined them out of Kath, rousing out in some haste; and kath'ein came in haste with bowls of offering to the Kel. The word had spread through all the camp by now; sein'ein came, but the children were held in Kath, concealed.

A kath'en he knew brought a bowl to him, offered; he recalled another morning, when there had been the illusion of safety, and love with this gentle, plain-faced kath'en. "Anaras," he murmured her name, and took the bowl from her hands, ate a very little, gave it back, lonelier than before. He was afraid; it was not an accustomed sensation.

The kath'en withdrew; all that caste did, having no place in what might come. Sen remained, and turning, he saw Melein's pale figure among them, caught her eye. She had no word for him, only a nod of affirmation, a beckoned permission. He went to her and she touched lips to his brow, received his kiss in return; and from that dismissal he went out, past the tents, with all the Kel at his back.

They stopped after a space; and he walked as far again alone, stopped on the verge of a long slope, facing the open and seemingly empty land. It was cold in the wind, which swept unhindered across the land.

He had not been wise, after running so long, not to have spent all the night before in the indulgence of his own needs, forgetting Duncan; but he could not have done so, could not have rested— went at least with clear conscience for the things that he had done. He veiled himself, as one must facing strangers, as all the Kel was veiled. He put aside Niun s'Intel, slipped from himself into the Law, into the she'pan's hands, and the tribe's, and the gods'.

He waited.

The city depressed, the crumbling aisles of stone, the sad corpses, the alleys resounding to their footsteps and the rasp of the breathers, the whisper of the wind. Galey kept an eye to the buildings, the hollow shells which seemed long untouched by any living. It was such a place and such an hour as made him glad of the weapon under his hand and several armed companions about him, Boaz the only one of them who carried no weapons.

It was at once relief and discouragement, that there was no stir from the place, neither the attack they had dreaded nor the approach they had hoped. Nothing. Wind and sand and shells of ruins.

And the dead.

There were only kel'ein corpses at the first, black-robed; then others, gold-robes and blue, and children. The blues were without exception women and children, and babes in arms. Boaz stood over a cluster of sad husks and shook her head and swore. Shibo touched at a kel'en's body with his foot, not roughly, but in distaste.

"There's nothing alive here," Boaz said. She was hard-breathing despite the mask, overburdened with the equipment and her own weight; she hitched the breather tank to another place on her shoulder and drew a gasping breath. "I think they'd have buried them if they could have."

"But it was inhabited," Galey said. "Duncan maintained the cities were empty." The suspicion that in other particulars Duncan's data might have inaccuracies in it . . . filled him with a whole array of apprehensions, a cowardice that wanted to go running back to the ship, pull offworld and declare failure, so that guns could blast at each other at a distance where humans had advantage. Another part of him said no . . . looked at dead civs and children and turned sick inside. Kadarin, Lane, Shibo . . . what they felt he had no idea but he suspected it was something the same.

"Isn't saying," Boaz said, walking farther among the dead, "that the city was inhabited. Just that people were killed here. Children were killed here. Duncan's mri. I think we've found them . . . just the way he said. He talked about dead cities; he'd seen one, been there . . . with the mri. He talked about a woman who died; and the children . . . he'd seen that too."

"He talked about machines," said the tech Lane, a young man, and worried-looking. "Live ones."

"I don't doubt," said Boaz, "We'll find that here too." She paused again in the crossing of two alleys, with the sand skirling about her feet, looked about her, looked back, made a gesture indicating the way she wanted them to go.

"Come on," Galey said to the others, who from time to time laid nervous hands on their weapons as they passed the darkened entries, the alien geometries of arches which led into ruin, or nowhere. *Walk like mri,* Boaz had advised them. *Keep your hands away from guns.* It was not easy, to trust to that in such a place.

A black line materialized out of the slow swell of the land opposite their own, grew distinct, stopped. Niun stood still, his legs numb with fatigue, waiting, silent declaration of the resolution of the ja'anom. The enemy had come, waited now for bright day. Sun-born, legend said of the People; the hao'nath had not chosen to move upon them by night. Neither would he, given choice. To face an enemy of one's own inclinations . . . had an eerie, homely feeling about it.

Dus-sense played at the back of his mind. The beast was quiet, far from him . . . would stay there. It had an instinct that would not intrude on a fight on equal terms, like mri, who would not attack in masses. It knew. It drank in the whole essence of the camp and gave it to him, drank in the presence of the enemy and fed him that too, threads complex and indefinable, a second dimension of their reality, so that the world seemed the same when it stopped, only faded somewhat, less intense, less bright.

He banished it, wishing his mind to himself.

The light grew, colors became fully distinct. In the east the sun blazed full.

And with it other shapes took form, a new line of kel'ein, separate from the others, and apart from them. Niun's heart skipped a beat in alarm. Had it been his native Kel at his back he might have turned, might have betrayed some emotion; they were not, and he did not. He moved his eyes slowly, and saw with a slight turning of his head that there were yet others, a third Kel ranged to the south.

They had been herded. Runners must have gone, signals passed, messages exchanged among she'panei. Three tribes were set against them. Three kel'anthein . . . to challenge.

One by one or all at once; he had his option. He saw the trap, and the warmth drained from his limbs as he thought on Melein, who would die when he fell . . . flooded back again with anger when he thought of all that had been sacrificed to bring them this far, and to lose . . . to lose now—

A figure separated from the others before him; he knew the beginning of it then: the hao'anth came first. Another began to come out from among the tribe to the east; and another separated himself in the south. He detached his mind, drew quiet breaths, began to prepare himself.

Suddenly a line appeared at the extreme south; and another figure moved forward . . . a fourth tribe; and another at north northeast, a fifth.

They knew . . . all knew . . . that strangers had come among them, and where those strangers might be found. Niun felt again the prickling touch of his dus, the beast growing alarmed, full of blood-feelings.

No, he sent it furiously. He detached his sword, the *av-kel,* and held it in his hands crosswise, plain warning to those who came toward him from five directions . . . perhaps more still; he did not turn his head and utterly abandon his dignity. If they came also at his back, they must at least do him the grace of moving around to face him. Heat suffused his face, that he had let this happen and not known it; that he had run so blindly with dusei warning him persistently of outlying presence, that Duncan in his ravings had felt it, and he had not conceived the truth.

That his own kind did this to him, repudiating all that he was, all that they had come to offer, blind to all but difference. . . . There was no talking with them under these circumstances: they could read well enough that the kel'anth of this Kel stood by himself, that not a person at his back would move to assist him.

He could see all the five at once now: tribal names, he thought, that he should have known, were he mri of this world. . . . Black-veiled, glittering with Honors which meant lives and challenges . . . they preserved decent interval from each other, separate in tribe, neither crossing the other's space. Perhaps they bore instructions from their she'panei already, as he did from Melein: that would shorten matters. They risked much, all of them: absorption . . . for what tribes he took before dying himself, the kel'anth who killed him would possess, and those she'panei die . . . a measure of their desperation and their outrage, that they combined to take such risk.

Near enough now for hailing. He did not, nor go out to them; it was his option to stand still, and he had had enough of walking these last days. His back felt naked enough without separating himself so far from his own tents.

There was movement behind him. It startled him . . . one shameful instant he tensed, thinking of ultimate treachery, tsi'mri; steps approached him, solitary. *Duncan,* he thought, his heart pounding with despair . . . he turned his head slightly as a kel'en came to stand by him on his left.

Hlil. The shock of it destroyed his self-possession; the membrane flicked when Hlil looked at him straightly; and beyond Hlil, Seras came . . . too old, Niun thought anxiously: a Master of weapons, but too old for this. It was an act of courage more than to help to him. Steps stirred the sand on his right, and he looked that way . . . saw to his shock that it was Ras, her eyes cold as ever; suicidal, he reckoned. They were four now. Suddenly there was another, their fifth: kel Merin of the Husbands, whom he hardly knew.

That changed the complexion of the matter. He turned again toward the five who came to challenge, his heart beating faster and faster, from wild surmises that this was somehow a trap, arranged, between his own and them; to surmises that for some mad reason these kel'ein came to defend his hold on the ja'anom. He could challenge all at once, take the strongest himself, use these four at least as a delay until he could turn his hand to the next.

They would die doing that; there was no sane reason for them to preserve the ja'anom for his possession.

The five halted before them, individually.

"Kel'anth of the ja'anom!" the central one shouted. "We are the ja'ari, the ka'anomin, the patha, the mari, the hao'nath! I am kel'anth Tian s'Edri Des-Paran daithenon, of she'pan Edri of the ja'ari. We hear reports of landings; and I ask: does the Kel'anth of the ja'anom have an answer?"

"Kel'anth of the ja'anom!" shouted the one farthest right. "I am kel'anth Rhian s'Tafa Mar-Eddin, daithenon, of the she'pan Tafa of the hao'nath. And my question you well know."

There was silence after. They had spoken in the hal'ari, not the mu'ara of tribes: and that the kel'anth of the hao'nath was alive to protest in person . . . here was a stubborn man.

"Kel'anthein! I am kel'anth Niun s'Intel Zain-Abrin, daithenon, of she'pan Melein of the ja'anom and of all the People." He drew in a second great breath, clenched the sword tightly in his fists. "I am kel'anth of the Voyagers, of those who went out from the world; heir of An-ehon and Le'a'haen, of Zohain and Tho'e'i-shai; kel'anth of the Kel of the People. Hand of the she'pan of the Mysteries; for she'pan Melein I took the ja'anom, and in her name I defend it if challenged, or challenge if she so decides. The path we take is our path, and I defend her right to walk it. Be warned!"

They stood still a moment. Somewhere the dus stirred, troubling, and he willed it silent.

A rustling of cloth and steps approached behind him, a breath of holy incense, a wisp of white robes in the corner of his eye that he dared not turn from his enemies.

Melein.

"Kel'anth of the ja'anom!" shouted Rhian of the hao'nath. "Ask your she'pan for a message and we will bear it."

Any word of enemies must, by custom, pass through him. "Tell them," Melein shouted back in her own voice. "Call your she'panei here. Call them *here.*"

More dead lay in the great square, corpses becoming barriers to sand which drifted in waves across the pavings, the scale of everything reduced by the great edun which towered even in ruin. "Straight through the center," Galey said in a low voice, and led the way for them. Boaz insisted it was the sane thing, that mri would not attack from ambush if the approach were direct: she had that information from Duncan.

Forty years humans had been fighting mri, and all experience denied that theory: mri had fired from ambush; had done precisely—the realization hit him with sudden irony—what humans had done. No human had ever walked plainly up to mri. He recalled stories of mri who had advanced alone against humans, berserkers, shot to rags. Of a sudden things fit, and sickened him.

And the dead . . . everywhere—alien; but dead infants were tragedy in any reckoning. Here a woman had fallen, her arms spread wide to shield a trio of children, covering them with her robes as if that could save them; here one of the warriors had died, bearing a blue-clad infant in his arms; or a pair of the gold-robes, embraced and tucked up still sitting, as if the flight had become too much for them and they had resigned themselves to die; an older child, whose mummified body preserved the gesture of an outstretched hand across the sandy stones, reaching toward what might have been its mother.

Alien and not. Regul had killed them; or perhaps he had. It was Haven, and Kiluwa, and Asgard, and Talos, and all the evils they had done to each other. It was world's end, and earnestly he wished for some stir of life within these ruins, some relief from such things.

The steps hove up before them; he kept walking, hands at his side, toward the dark inside. He knew of edunei, these places that served mri for fortresses and what else no one knew. Shrines. Holy places. Homes. No one understood. Forty years and no one understood. Forty years and no one had understood that the warrior Kel was not the whole of the mri culture; no one had known that there was Kath or Sen, that two-thirds of the mri population were strictly noncombatant.

The place afflicted all of them. From time to time the regs had stared at some sight worse than the others, stared longer than they might from curiosity, shook their heads. They were born to the war; anyone under forty could say that, but this was not a thing they had had to see first hand.

No one spoke. Boaz paused at the top of the steps to take a picture of the way they had come, of the square with its dead. Then the dark of the interior took them in, and their footsteps and the suck and hiss of the breathers echoed in great depth.

Galey took his torch in hand and switched it on, played it over the rubble which blocked most of the accesses to the towers. "Hey!" he shouted, trying the direct approach to the uttermost; and winced at the echoes.

"Left tower," Boaz said.

"Place is like to fall in on us," Galey objected, but he went, the others with them, into the left-hand access, up a spiraling passage dark before their light and dark after, a place for ambushes if any existed anywhere in the city.

Light shone at the top; the great room there had a split wall; and beyond, through another doorway—he walked in that direction, to anticipate Boaz, who was sure to go without their protection. His heart beat fearfully as he saw the rows of machines. He had seen the like before, on Kesrith.

"Shrine," he said aloud.

Boaz paused in the doorway and looked back at him, advanced again carefully. The whole center of the floor was gone, a pile of rubble and twisted steel.

And lights burned on the panels, far into the dark.

"Don't touch anything," Lane said. The tech pushed himself to the fore, looked about him, pulled Shibo and Kadarin aside from a circle marked on the flooring. Galey's own foot had crossed that line. He took it back.

"Weapons,"Lane said, "very likely controlled from here."

And the last word was choked into hush, for there was a gleam of light from above, the circle suddenly drowned in glare.

"An-hi?" a mechanical voice thundered. Boaz shook her head in panic, denying understanding; it asked again, more complexly, and again and again and again.

Weapons, Galey thought in sick terror. *O God, the ships up there . . . We've triggered it.*

Lane moved, thrust himself into the circle, into the light that bathed him in white unreality. He looked up at the source of it, at screens that flared with mri writings.

"Hne'mi!" he cried at it: *Friend!* It was one of the only words they knew.

It hurled words back, complex and then simple, repeating, repeating, repeating.

And struck. Lane sprawled, still, glaze-eyed from the instant he hit the floor. "No fire!" Galey cried, seeing a gun in Shibo's hand. Every board was alight, the screens alive, and the light flaring blue. Boaz reached for Lane's outflung hand . . . changed her mind and drew back; all of them froze. Galey shifted a glance toward the door, to Shibo and Kadarin, whose faces were stark with fright, to Boaz, whose face was fixed toward the machine, the white light turning her to shadow and silver—to Lane, who was quite, quite dead.

Eventually there was silence again. The light faded. Galey chanced a quick move, herding the two men, dragging at Boaz. They all ran, into the sunlight of the room outside, with the machine flaring to life again, thundering its questions.

"Go," he urged them. "Get out of here." He hastened them to the access, down, into the lower hall. They pelted across it, a flight close to panic; he seized at Kadarin and stopped when they reached the open air, listening.

There was only the sunlight and the square, unchanged. They stood there, their breaths hissing into the breathers, their eyes mutually distraught.

"We couldn't help him," Galey said. "There's nothing to be done for him. We get out of this—we come back for him."

They accepted that . . . seemed to.

"It was what Duncan said," Boaz broke the silence after a moment. "Machines. What he described."

There had been no firing aloft, no hostile act from the city. The holocaust had come close to them, but it had not happened. It waited, perhaps, on orders. Mri orders. Perhaps that was what it had asked of them.

Who are you?

What am I to do?

An idiot power seeking instruction.

"If there's a link between the cities," Galey said, "we may just have sent a message."

Shibo and Kadarin said nothing, only looked at Boaz, at plump, fragile Boaz, who had become their source of sanity: a mri world, and they needed mri answers.

"I'd say that's likely," she agreed. "Maybe it has; but they haven't fired yet."

"And we get out of here," Galey said. "Now."

He strode down the steps, the others behind him, past a knot of kel'ein corpses, out across the open square. His mistake, his responsibility. It had been a brave act on Lane's part, to try to deal with the machine. He could have done something; he was not sure what . . . pulled Lane out, it might have been.

"Mr. Galey," Boaz said, her breath wheezing in her mask; she pulled it down a moment, gasped as they walked. "We have *nothing* to report. We can't go back with this."

He said nothing for a long space of walking, trying to think in the interval, to draw his mind back from Lane and onto next matters. He stopped when they had cleared the square, among the ruined buildings, looked at the face of Shibo and Kadarin. "We get back to the shuttle," he said. "We try another site."

"Sir," said Kadarin, "no argument, but what could we have done that we didn't? What can we do with a thing like that? Mri maybe, but that thing—"

"I got another worry," said Shibo, "what happens when we try to move that shuttle with that thing stirred up."

"Mri," Boaz said, "are in open country; Duncan gave us truth in what he told us. We should take the rest of it—look for mri, not the machines."

"We're near enough the rim," Galey said, "I'll slide for it and stay low, and that's the best we can do. We've got no help but that. But we can't go off cross-country. We've got our corridors set up, Boz, to get us from one point to the other without crossing what we figure for defense zones, and that doesn't give us much space in this region for any search. But I figure we keep this mission going; another site, maybe—in better condition." He looked at the ground, hands in pockets, a cold knot in his belly, looked up at them after a moment. "I reckon not to include Lane in the report; it goes quick, no space for explaining; they have enough excuse for canceling us off this business and going some other route. If I were Lane I wouldn't want that. That's my feeling on it; that we keep trying."

"While we do," Boaz said, looking straight at the others, "we hold out hope of another solution. Of stopping what we've seen here. We go back . . . and what else are they going to do? We stay out here; just by that we prove there's hope in an approach to these people. We remove *fear* . . . and we bring sanity to this situation."

The two regs nodded. Galey did, reckoning plainly it was court martial. "Come on," he said. "It's a long walk."

                              *   *   *

It took time, that the she'panei should come from their tribes to that sandy slope; some were very old, and all reluctant. Niun stood still, aching from the long strain of standing, watching with a sense of unreality five white-robed figures advancing from separate points of the horizon, each accompanied by her kel'anth and several sen'ein.

Melein started forward eventually, to meet them on equal ground at the bottom of the slope. He walked with her, slowly, with sen'anth Sathas joining them. He offered no words; if she wanted to speak, she would. Doubtless her mind was as full as his; doubtless she had some clear intention in this madness. He hoped that this was the case.

To challenge them all, perhaps, after giving them her ultimatum. So she had done with the she'pan of the ja'anom.

They stopped; the others came to them, as close as warriors might come to one another, a stone's easy toss: such also was the distance for she'panei in the rare instance that they must meet. Kel'ein remained veiled; she'panei and sen'ein met without, elder faces, masked in years. One by one they named themselves, Tafa of the hao'nath; Edri of the ja'ari; Hetha'in of the patha; Nef of the mari; Uthan of the ka'anomin. Tafa and Hetha'in bore the kelscars, and only Nef was as young as middle years.

"Your kel'anth has used powerful names," said Tafa, when the naming came to Melein herself. "What do you use?"

"I am Melein s'Intel, Melein not-of-the-ja'anom, out of Edun Kesrithun of the last standing-place of the Voyagers, heir of the cities of Kutath and of the edunei of Nisren, of Elag called Haven, and of Kesrith. For names I begin with Parvet'a, who led us out, and who began the line of which we two are born; and I say that we are home, she'panei. Ja'anom met us and would not acknowledge my claim. I took the ja'anom."

Eyes nictitated. There was not a glance or a word among them.

"Will you challenge?" Melein asked. "Or will you hear?"

There was the sound of the wind whipping at their robes, the whisper of sand moving. Nothing more.

"I need kel'ein," Melein said, "the service of forty hands of kel'ein from each Kel; lend them. Such as survive I shall send back again with Honors which those who did not go will envy."

"*Where* will you take them?" asked Hetha'in. "To what manner of conflict, and for what purpose? You have brought us attack, and tsi'mri, and the wasting of our cities. Where will you take them?"

"I am the foretold," Melein said. "And I call on you for your children and their strength, for the purpose for which we went out in the beginning, and I shall build you a House, she'panei."

There were small movements, a glancing from one to the other, who ought never to look to one another, who were never united.

"We have trailed a tsi'mri among you," Tafa said.

"That you have," Melein answered her. "See, and trust your Sight, she'panei; by the Mystery of the Mysteries, by the Seeing . . . give me kel'ein who have the courage to fight this fight and sen'ein to witness and record it in your shrines."

"With tsi'mri?" cried Tafa. "With walking-beasts?"

"By them you know that I am not Kutathi; and by that you know what I am, Tafa of the hao'nath. See! We are at a point, she'panei, of deciding. Our ship is gone; our enemies are many; of the millions who went out, my kel'anth and I are the last alive. We two—made it home, and do you by your suspicion destroy us, who have survived all that tsi'mri have done? Sit down and die, she'panei; or give me the forces I need."

Tafa of the hao'nath turned her back, walked away and stopped by her kel'anth. A coldness settled at Niun's belly. For a moment he had hoped . . . that five she'panei who could unite against an intruder could see farther than most.

The kel'anth of the hao'nath walked forward: Rhian s'Tafa; Niun moved out to meet him, met the eyes above the veil, of an older man than he, and worn with hurt and dus-poison and the march that had worn them both. There was nothing of hate there now, only regret. There had been such in Merai's eyes when they had met, that sorrow. He wished to protest; it was double sui-cide, Tafa's madness . . . but in challenge they were held even from speaking.

The kel'ein of two tribes should ring them about, shield the other castes from such a sight; here kel'anthein did that office, too few to do more than make the token of a ring.

They drew, together, a long hiss of steel; Rhian's blade lifted to guard; he lifted his own, waited, slipped his mind into hand and blade, nothingness and now.

A pass; he turned it and returned, cautiously; countered and re-turned. He was not touched; Rhian was not. The blades had breathed upon each other, no more. This was a Master, this Rhian. Another pass and turn, a flutter of black cloth, cut loose; his eyes and mind were for the blade alone; a fourth pass: he saw a chance and a trap, evaded it.

"Stop!"

Tafa's sharp command; they paused, alike poised on guard. He thought of treachery, of the insanity of trusting strangers. But not tsi'mri: mri. Eyes amber as his own regarded him steadily beyond the two blades.

"Kel'anth of the hao'nath," Tafa cried. "Disengage!"

Niun stayed still as the kel'anth retreated the one pace which took them out of sword's-distance. "Disengage," Melein bade him. "The hao'nath have asked."

He stepped his pace back, stood until the hao'nath kel'anth had sheathed his sword; then he ran his own into sheath, steadily enough for all the tautness of his nerves. It was challenger's pre-rogative, to stop the contest without a death; challenge then might be returned from the other side, without mercy.

It dawned on him slowly that he had won, that this man had gotten out alive, and he was glad of that, for his bravery. He did not relax. They might all try his measure, one after the other. He tried to subdue the pulse which hammered in his veins; one thing to fight well; the greater matter was discipline, not to be shaken by any tactic, fair or foul.

"We lend you your two hundred," Tafa said, "and our kel'anth with them. You might demand more; but this we offer."

There was a moment's silence. "Acceptable," Melein said. The breath left Niun's lungs no more swiftly, but the pounding of his heart filled his ears.

"And we lend," said the she'pan of the patha, "our kel'anth and two hundred to stay if they bring fair report of you. We cannot sit under one tent, she'pan; but let our kel'anthein do so, and bring us word again what they have seen, whether to do what you ask or to challenge. This is fair, in our thinking."

"So," said mari and ja'ari almost at one breath.

"We ka'anomin are out of Edun Zohain, far out of our range. Our allegiance is to the ma'an mri, but we agree unless the ma'an send to recall us. For a hand of days let them observe; and that long we will wait for answer."

"Agreeable," said Melein, and other heads bowed. "A hand of days or less. Life and Honors."

She turned away; the other she'panei did so, with their sen'ein. Kel'anthein remained a moment, covering the retreat.

Niun cast a glance at Rhian. A bit of cloth lay on the sand; his, Rhian's, he was not sure. He took down his veil and gave his face to the kel'anthein lately strangers, feeling naked and strange in doing so . . . glanced from face to face as they did the same, memorizing them, the fierce handsomeness of Rhian of the hao'nath; the plainness of Tian of the ja'ari; Kedras of the patha was one of the youngest, his mouth marked with a scar from edge to chin; mari's Elan was broad-faced and elder; but oldest of the lot was Kalis of the ka'anomin, her eyes shadowed by sun-frown and the kel'scars faded with years.

He turned to follow after Melein, and they went their separate ways for the time. He looked up at the slight rise on which his own Kel waited, before the tents, where the four who had come to his support still stood . . . for the tribe's sake, he persuaded himself in clearer reason: for pride of the ja'anom and its Holy, that they would not have merged with another tribe in defeat, though much the same distress would attach to merging as the consequence of winning. It was pride. Ras's line in particular . . . had long defended the ja'anom. It was duty to her dead brother. He understood that. And Hlil was kel-second and Seras fen'anth, and Merin a friend of Hlil's. They had their reasons; and their reasons had been fortunate for him and for Melein; he took even that with gratitude.

He walked among them, spared a nod of thanks to either side as they closed behind him and the black ranks of the Kel flowed back into the camp, where anxious kath'ein and sen'ein waited to know the fate of the tribe, clustering about Melein.

"There is agreement," Melein said aloud, so that all might hear. "They will send kel'anthein into our Council; and they may lend us help. Challenge was declined."

It was as if the whole camp together drew breath and let it go again . . . no vast relief, perhaps; they still sat in the possession of a stranger, led to strange purposes. But the ja'anom still existed as a tribe, and would go on existing.

His dus ventured out of kel-tent, radiating disturbance. Niun met it and touched it, tolerating its interference as he stood for a moment staring after the figure of Melein, who retreated among the Sen.

Reaction settled on him like a breath of cold wind. He turned away, the dus trailing him, went into the tent of the Kel, dull to the looks which surrounded him . . . missed the four to whom he owed some expression of spoken gratitude; perhaps, he thought, they turned away from it. He did not seek them out, to force it on them. He went instead to Duncan's side, settled there, concerned that Duncan slept still, unmoved from the shoulder of his dus, his face peaceful as death in the faint light which reached them from the wind vents.

Niun touched the beast, recoiled from the numbing blankness the dus contained, nothingness, void that drank in sense. His own settled down, apart from that touch, and he leaned against it, unwilling to invade that quiet the dus had made for Duncan. He rested cross-legged, hands in his lap, bowed his head and tried to rest a little.

Footsteps disturbed the matting near him. He looked up as Hlil crouched down by him and tugged his veil down.

"You took no wound."

"No," he said. "I thank you, kel Hlil."

"Kel-second belonged there. For the tribe."

"Aye," he agreed. It was clearly so. "Where is Ras?"

"Wherever she wills to be. I am not consulted in her wanderings." Hlil looked down at Duncan, frowning. Niun looked and found Duncan's eyes open a slit, regarding them both; he watched Hlil reach and touch his sleeve as if touching him at all were no easy thing. "The sight of him will be trouble," Hlil said, "with the other kel'anthein."

Niun moved his own hand to Duncan's shoulder, lest Hlil's cold touch should disturb him; he felt contact with the dus, which had the same leadenness as before, mind-dulling if he permitted. Duncan was conscious, but only partially aware.

"They are coming now," Hlil said to him. "Watch has them in view. I do not think since the parting . . . such a thing has ever happened in the world." His eyes strayed back to Duncan, glanced to him again. "He is yours; no stranger will touch him. But best surely if he is not the first thing they see."

Duncan blinked; perhaps he had heard.

"No," Niun said. "Bring them here when they reach camp."

Hlil frowned.

"Let them see me as I am," Niun said. "I make no pretenses otherwise."

"This is not yourself," Hlil exclaimed. "You are not—not what the eye of strangers will see here. You are not this."

The outcry both angered and touched his heart. "Then you do not know me. Look again, Hlil, and do not make me what I am not. This is my brother; and the beast is a part of my mind. I am not Kutathi, and I am not Merai. Bring them here, I say."

"Aye," Hlil said, and rose up and walked away in evident distress.

They came, eventually, a soft stirring outside, a whisper of robes . . . kel'anthein of the five tribes with each several companions, sixteen in all, a blackness in Hlil's wake; and Hlil returned to sit by him and by Duncan.

Niun moved his upturned hand, offering them place on the mats. They sat down and unveiled; the tent stirred behind them with the arrival of ja'anom kel'ein, for it was the business of all of them, this opening of the tent to strangers.

Niun put out a hand to the dusei, one and the other, soothed them, deliberate demonstration . . . let them all look on him and them as long as they would, Rhian most of all, whose face betrayed nothing. After a moment Niun reached to his brow and swept off the headcloth in a gesture of humility, equaling their disadvantage on strange ground.

"I welcome you," he said. "I warn you against strong passions; the beasts sense them and spread them if you are not wary of what they do; bid them stop and they will do so. Sometimes one can be deceived by them into feeling their anger; or strangers share what strangers would rather not. The Kel from which I came knew such things, valued them, learned to veil the heart from them; and what hurt they have done, lay to my account: I brought them. They are as devoted companions as they are enemies: Rhian s'Tafa, it was a moment's misfortune and confusion: I beg your pardon for it."

The others, perhaps, did not understand. The hao'nath's eyes met his with direct force, slid deliberately to Duncan's sleeping form.

"He is ja'anom," Niun answered that look.

There was long and heavy silence. The dusei stirred, and Niun quieted them with a touch, his heart pounding with dread, for they could lose it all upon this man's pride.

"This came from the alien ships," Rhian said. "We tracked it. And you met with it. And that is a question I ask, kel'anth of the ja'anom."

"I am Duncan-without-a-Mother." The hoarse voice startled them all, and Niun looked, found Duncan's eyes slitted open. "I came on a *mri* ship; but I had gone to speak with the tsi'mri, to ask them what they wanted here."

"Sov-kela." Niun silenced him with a touch, glanced up at Rhian. "But it is truth, all the same. He does not lie."

"What is he?" asked Kalis.

"Mri," Niun said. "But once he was human."

What the dusei picked up disturbed, brought a shifting of bodies in instinctive discomfort all about the tent.

"It is a matter among us," Hlil said, "with respect, kel'anth of the ka'anomin of Zohain."

There was long silence.

"He is sickly," said Rhian with a wave of his hand.

"I shall mend," Duncan said, which he had the right to say, passed off in so contemptuous a manner; but it was desperately rash. Niun put out his hand, silencing further indiscretions; all the same he felt a touch of satisfaction for that answer.

And Rhian's haggard face showed just the slightest flicker of expression: not outright rage, then, or he would have been as blank as newlaid sand. "So be it," Rhian said. "We discuss that matter later."

"Doubtless," said Kalis of the ka'anomin, "we are different; gods, how not? Some we accept, at least while we observe. But what have you brought us? We have seen the coming and going of ships. The hao'nath say that An-ehon is totally ruins. We do not know the fate of Zohain. This is not the first coming of tsi'mri to this world, but, gods! never did mri bring them."

"Of the People who went out," Niun said, "we are the last; we were murdered by tsi'mri who bought our service, not by Duncan's kind. And they come to finish us here. Bring them, no. But that is the she'pan's matter, not mine. Share food and fire with us; share Kath if it pleases you; they will take honor of you. For the rest, suspend judgment."

"When will the she'pan speak to us?" asked Elan of the mari.

"I do not know. I truly do not know. She will send. We will lodge you until then."

"Your tent cannot hold us," said Kedras of the patha.

"We will do it somehow. If each caste yields a little canvas we can run cord between our poles and Sen."

"Possible," Kedras said, resting hands on knees. There was a small silence, and Kedras hissed a short breath. "Gods, all under one canvas."

"In the Kel of my birth," Niun said slowly, "we fought at the hire of tsi'mri; and went from world to world on tsi'mri ships; and it was done, that kel'ein onworld were sheltered by strange she'panei and edunei not of their birth, until their hire took them away again. Perhaps it was so on Kutath once, in the days of the great cities."

"This Kel does not remember," Kedras confessed, and others moved their heads—no.

"We will bring our kel'ein," said Tian of the ja'ari. "Perhaps each of us can spare a little of canvas."

Others assented.

"Kel'anthein," Niun gave them murmured courtesy, watched as they rose and departed, filing out of the tent, as all about them, ja'anom rose in courtesy, settled again. Hlil followed them out, gathering a band of kel'ein to serve what needed be done.

Niun sat still a moment, replaced the headcloth, sat staring at the empty doorway.

"Strangers," Duncan said beside him, and he realized that of all that had changed, Duncan knew none of it. "More than hao'nath."

"I will tell you later. Rest, be still. All is better than it was."

He rubbed at the dus's shoulder to soothe it, looked out over the faces of his kel, at eyes which were fixed on him in strange concentration . . . with distress, it might be; or simple bewilderment. Ras was there; she had come in, and Seras, and Merin. There was a curious thing in the air, a sense of madness that quivered through the dus-sense; so a man might feel with his feet on the rimsands.

"Deal with them as with our own," he said to them. He put off the kel-sword, laid it again on the matting, looked up as Taz appeared with a bowl which he offered, a small portion of liquid, a delicacy reserved for honor, and for those in need. "Kath sends," Taz told him; and he drank, though he would rather have yielded it to Duncan, who needed it more. He gave the bowl back, thought on kath Anaras, thought that this evening would be well spent in Kath, where he might take pleasure, and ease. Rhian's skill had made him think on dying, and Kath was a place to forget such thoughts. He had much neglected them, owed Anaras courtesy which he had never paid. She was fortunate, her child had survived the flight, but the kel'anth had never come a second time to her.

Tonight there were strangers in camp, and duty, and he could not. He shut his eyes, exhaled, opened them again. "I will return it," he said.

"Sir," Taz objected; it was not custom.

He rose up, taking the small bowl with him, and walked out.

Chapter Twelve

Luiz stared at the screen, the message tape looping over and over again.

DUNCAN INFO CONFIRMED ON SITE ONE, the message ran tersely. DANTE PROCEEDING NEW SITE HOPING FURTHER DATA.

No way to contact them; mission Dante went its own way. That any message had come meant they had gone aloft again, messaged from one of the so-reckoned safe corridors, and flitted gnat-like to the next choice of sites.

Boz, he thought with a shake of his head; the muscles of his mouth attempted a smile as he reckoned her happiness . . . let loose in such treasuries with camera and notebook and recorder; she would be in agony if the soldiers hastened her on too soon.

Salve to the soul, for all she had given up in leaving Kesrith.

Reparations. To save something. The smile faded into heartsickness. Guilt drove her. Would kill her. The young men would keep going—had to—she would break her heart out there in the dunes, climbing where young men went.

But she had won something. INFO CONFIRMED, the message ran.

He reached for a pad and stylus. *Tight transmission Saber,* he wrote for the ComTech, and transcribed the message in full, with transmission time.

There was another thing on his desk, which had not given him such relief. CAUTION: READINGS INDICATE LIFE RESURGENCE IN THE CITIES. POWER THERE RESTORED. MAINTAIN SHIP FLIGHT STANDBY.

And with it another shuttled dispatch: ADVISE YOU ALLIED MISSION DEMANDING LANDING: SITUATION DELICATE.

He turned from his desk and handed the slip to Brown, who was *Flower*'s pilot. "Transmit," he said.

"Sir," Brown said, as if he would object.

"Do it."

Brown left to do so. It would go quickly. *Santiago* hovered over them in this crisis like a bird over eggs.

He stared at the repeating message, scowling. He would gladly get the two current messages to Boaz if it were possible. It was not. They were on their own. Presumably they knew about the power in the sites . . . and if so they neglected to mention it; neglected to warn them of potential hazard.

He bit his lip, reckoning Boaz's persuasive powers, wondered with a small and uneasy suspicion—how much else Galey's mission neglected. A deliberately optimistic message; a biased message. He sent no comment with it, guilty by silence.

Saber, he reasoned, could draw its own conclusions.

The prep room remained a haven of sanity. *Saber*'s pulse went through it, this place where all had casual access, where a sharp eye might pick up what was developing, what missions went, what missions came in; and a sharp ear hear any rumor that was drifting about. Harris came by routine, in the unease that went with no missions and the lack of contact with Galey. He sat in the rhythm of the room, a frantic pace of outgoing and incoming flights, shuttles which kept their senses extended over the world's horizons . . . gamed sometimes among friends, among the others who were bound to this assignment, who came, as he did, to sit and drink and watch the scan and the boards and say to themselves, *not now, not this watch, not yet.*

Harris filled his cup from the dispenser, used his rations card to get a cellopack of dried fruit, pocketed it while he made his usual nervous pass by the flight boards.

Regul, someone had scrawled on the margin of the clear plastic which overlay the system chart; and with it an eye.

Home, it had said once; but some zealot officer had erased that.

There were two ships out besides *Santiago;* that was normal. Four names on the present flight list; four more going up next. Good enough; it was all routine.

He walked next to the status board, found the point that was *Flower,* isolated as it ought to be. He sipped at the coffee and strayed back to the table, to sit and wait as he spent his days waiting. He activated the library function, propped his feet up, drank his coffee, and found himself four pages into the book he was reading, with no comprehension of it. He stared at it, heard others coming in, looked. It was the next group out, come in for prep.

"How'd it go last night?" one gibed at him; he gave a placid shrug, smug with a memory he was not going to have public, watched as they collected their flight gear from the lockers. The outward blips had made their slow way back on the scan; the outgoing team had it timed to a nicety.

Two men entered the room: North and Magee, two of his own. He moved his feet and offered them the place, while the other team walked out and on their way to the hangar deck. North went to make his own pass by the boards and charts.

And of a sudden all status on scan was arrested; the ships stayed where they were. Harris rose to his feet; so did Magee. The ships began to turn, four neat and simultaneous changes of position, oriented to different quarters, two proceeding back the way they had come, two moving wide.

The screen adjusted to wider field. Red blips were proceeding out from the larger red ship.

"Here it comes," Magee muttered. There was a cold in the air. Harris swallowed and watched. The red blips tracked not toward the world, but headed toward themselves.

The screen flashed letters: CODE GREEN.

"Going to board," North said. They knew the routine. An aisle was established from the bay to the quarantine areas near command. Regul quarters were there for use when they must be. Areas not meant for regul were put under security yellow, which meant cardlock for everyone needing passage into and out of sections.

Bile rose into Harris's throat. He swore softly.

"Guess we got our allies back," North said.

"That regul expert," Magee said. "That's what he brought us. That Averson got us *regul*."

Koch sipped at the obligatory cup of soi, stared levelly at the regul delegation and his own staff, who sat disposed about the room, the regul adult in his sled and the inevitable younglings squatting on the carpet beside . . . not much difference between standing and sitting for their short legs. Degas, Averson, and two aides: two opinions he truly wanted at hand and two live bodies more to balance the odds in the room; protocol: there had to be youngling figures so that regul knew by contrast whom to respect.

"Reverence," said the newly adult Suth, gape-mouthed and grinning affably. "A pleasure that we are able to deal sensibly after crisis."

"Bai Suth." Koch stared at the regul sidelong, finding difficulty to believe that he had known this individual regul before, that what bulked so large in the sled had been one of the relatively slim servitors. There was not even facial similarity. Plates had broadened and ridged; skin had thickened and coarsened into sagging folds. The metamorphosis had been radical considering the elapsed time; and yet this one had not attained the late Sharn's bulk and roughness. "We are pleased," Koch pursued, "if this meeting can prove productive; our good wishes to you in your new office."

Nostrils flared; the smile became a hiss. Experts called that laughter. "There have been misunderstandings, reverence bai Koch. One, for instance, between subordinates. . . ."

"You refer, perhaps, to my missing ship."

Eyes flickered; no, that was not what the bai had meant, but he covered with a widening of the grin. "I refer to matters between ourselves and your ship *Flower,* to which we have asked access. I seriously urge that we arrange closer cooperation . . . for mutual safety."

"You have not answered my question, bai."

The nostrils shut. That was anger. "Youngling matters and not at all productive. Are we responsible for ships which come and go without our knowledge or the courtesy of consulting us? I would prefer to continue this meeting; but if we persist in raising extraneous matters—"

"You persist, bai, in ignoring data which has been given you repeatedly: that our species is adult at a considerably earlier age than regul. We do not slaughter our younglings; we do not consider hazard to ships flown by *young adults of our species* . . . to be a minor matter."

"I repeat: I would prefer to continue this meeting."

It was there, on the table, toss them out or abandon the issue. Koch considered, scowled. "Then I think that you have answered my question all the same, bai Suth."

"No. I have ignored it, reverence bai. Assumptions between species are hazardous. I return to the previous matter under objection. You have interfered with our operations and seem offended that we want to enter yours."

"Your own bid likely to interfere with ours; you will not have our leave to approach *Flower*, take our strongest warning of that. Any ship that approaches will not be safe."

"Impasse."

"Impasse, bai Suth."

The regul shifted his weight in his sled, slowly finished off his soi, wished more of it of a youngling servitor which panted about immediately to satisfy him. "Bai Koch," Suth said when he had received the cup, "it is a matter of concern to us, this widening gap in our cooperation. We find difficulty reasoning in the unfortunate absence of the bai Sharn and the bai doctor Aldin, who had established useful rapport—" He rolled his eyes toward Averson, gaped a smile. "But we rejoice in the new elevation of this person to your councils, reverend bai doctor Averson." The eyes took in Degas, lingered there, rolled back again, the whites vanishing. "We are appreciative of any move toward understandings. We are allies. You agree. We cannot pursue differences and remain allies; I suggest we pursue cooperation. I have not mentioned the murder of an elder. I have not mentioned the discourtesy in treatment of bai Sharn's body. I have not mentioned the collapse of firm contracts between us. And I do not think it productive to mention these things. But if certain things are raised between us, rest assured that these other things can be objected . . . justly objected, now and in the future of our two species. We have, you are aware, long memory. But let us pass over these matters. Indeed, let us pass over them. Give me the benefit of your imagination, reverence bai. How will the mri respond to the situation you have posed?"

Koch did not let his face react. *What situation?* he wondered, not sure how much was known to them. "We hope for peaceful settlement with them, bai Suth."

"Indeed. Regul experience counsels that this is a vain expectation."

"Our experience counsels otherwise."

"Ah, then you are relying on records. Records from mri?"

"Of many situations, bai. Human records."

"Our experience of mri is two thousand years long; and it argues against yours, of recent duration. Mri are intractable and inflexible. Certain words are beyond their understanding. *Negotiation* is one such. The concept does not exist with them. Observed fact, bai. Where concept does not exist . . . how does action?"

Koch considered this, not alone of mri . . . glanced at Averson and back at Suth. "A question you have evaded, reverence: do you have a mri expert among you?"

The mouth gaped at once into a hiss, amusement. "He sits among you, bai Koch. I am that expert. I am, you may mark for your memory, a colonial of doch Horag. Horag has employed mri as guards for most of the two thousand years in question. Doch Alagn misled you; they were amateurs and newcomers, and you believed them expert. My adulthood has put into authority . . . a true expert in these matters. And a new doch. You are very prudent to inquire."

"Are you fluent in their language too?"

"There are two languages. I sorrow, bai, but the languages of mri were always a point of stubbornness with them. They persisted in coercing the regul language into their sluggish memories and speaking it badly."

"Meaning that they would not permit outsiders to become fluent."

"Meaning whatever that means within their mental process, reverence. These leaps of analysis are perhaps a natural human process, or you are withholding data. It means what the mri wish it to mean; we are patently not mri, neither you nor I. Are you withholding data?"

"No. No, bai Suth." Koch reflected on that matter, staring at the bai, nodded finally. "You are an authority on mri. Without access to their thought processes."

Nostrils shut and flared in rapid succession. "I contain information, bai, but without it you may deal in errors and experimentations at hazard of life. I tell you that we have never been able to translate the concept of negotiation into the mri understanding; and that should be marked for memory. I tell you that at any time a mri was hired to fight, there was no deviation from that path; he would kill or be killed and no offer would sway him. Trade concepts are not in their minds, reverence bai. They hired out their mercenaries, but *hired* is our word for the process and *mercenary* is your word. We deal in regul and human words; what do *they* think?"

"The bai is right," Averson interjected. "There is no exactitude between species. Regul *hocht* and our *mercenary* aren't the same either."

Nostrils expanded. Koch watched and wondered how much of his own expression the bai had learned to read. "You've come here for some specific purpose, bai. Perhaps we could have some definition of that."

"Understanding. Mutual protection."

"We do not desert our allies, if you are concerned."

That hit the intended mark; the flutter was clearly visible. "Bai, we are delighted to know that. There is of course reason that the mri should bear a grudge against us. And how will you deal with that matter in this peaceful solution you seek?"

"We will not desert our allies."

"Mri do not back up, as regul do not forget."

"Mri forget; perhaps regul can back up."

Again the flutter of emotion. "Meaning, bai Koch?"

"That mri may be persuaded to forget this act of yours at Kesrith if they have assurance that regul will not act against them here."

"Your leaps of process bewilder me, bai Koch. I have been led to understand that forgetting is not a precise act."

"We use it with many meanings, bai Suth."

Suth's nostrils heaved and flared. Suth's great fist banged the re-emptied cup against the sled and the youngling nearest raced in stumbling steps to fill and return it. Suth drank in great gulps, seeming in physical difficulty.

"Forgive us," Koch said. "Have we disturbed you?"

"I am disturbed, indeed I am disturbed." Suth drank heavily, set the cup down on his sled's rim. "I perceive great threat based on real experience and my allies leap like insects from one precarious point to the next."

"We are constantly monitoring the situation. We do not believe the threat is immediate. Information indicates we are dealing with a declined and nomadic group."

"Nomads: unstable persons."

"A stable but mobile community." He reflected on the difficulty of translating *that* to a species which regarded the least walking as agony. "They have no arms or transport sufficient to damage us. The cities are purely automated fire."

Suth's nostrils flared and shut, flared again. "Do not be angry, human bai. But can mri lie? This is a human possibility. Is it also mri? Does your experience or your imagination . . . judge?"

"We don't know."

"Ah. Do you imagine?"

"We don't have sufficient data."

"Data for imagining."

"It does take some, bai Suth. We operate at present on the premise that they can." He considered a moment, made the thrust. "In our experience, bai Suth . . . even regul can be dishonest."

"Dishonest, not honest, not . . . truthful."

"What is truth, bai Suth?"

Nostrils closed. "According to fact."

Koch nodded slowly. "I perceive something of your thinking, then.—Is there, Dr. Averson, a regul word for *honest?*"

"In business, the word *alch* . . . meaning evenly balanced advantage or observation, or something like. Value for value, we say."

"Mutual profit," Suth said. "We can spend much time at these comparative exercises, reverence. Favor, consider our position in orbit about this world. We are in range of these cities, which you imagine to be safe. I strongly urge a reconsideration."

"What would the regul wish?"

"Negation of the hazard here."

"Ethical considerations forbid. Or is that another word that doesn't translate?"

There was a silence from the other side. Koch looked at Averson. Averson muttered a regul word.

"We understand," said Suth. "We also respond to instincts."

"Sir," said Degas, "I think abstracts are in the way."

"Yes," said Suth, and grinned broadly.

Koch frowned at Degas, nodded slowly. "So the bai is concerned for our safety and that of home space. So are we."

"How much time, bai Koch, how much time? This youngling Duncan . . . how much have you given him?"

"A human matter, bai."

"We are allies."

"We are waiting."

"Humans walk very quickly. This youngling has taken far more days than needed to reach *Flower* after the attack. This evidences misfortune . . . or lack of cooperation on the part of this youngling. True?"

"Do you have information on him, bai?"

"No. Nor do you. Fact?"

"We simply wait."

"How long do you wait?"

"Does it matter?"

"Mri have had time to prepare response, bai Koch. Does this seem wise, to afford them this? They have weapons."

"Perhaps. Perhaps not."

"You balance all home space on this *perhaps,* bai."

"We are aware of the hazard."

"If they fire—"

"We adjust policy."

Suth clamped his bony lips shut, exhaled long and softly. "We are your allies. We, we are not a fighting people. We are your very safe neighbors, rich in trade, in mutual profit. And will you trade us for mri? Go home, bai. Leave this matter to us if your instincts forbid you to settle it. You know that we do not lie. We have no interest in hiring mri."

"It isn't likely that you could, is it, reverence?"

"The situation does not make agreement likely."

"Doubtless not. Nor was the fact that bai Sharn destroyed peace messages from them and deliberately deceived us."

"The messages themselves were deceptive."

"I thought regul did not hypothesize."

"We do not leap across dataless voids. The intent of the messages was to delay your response and encourage your near approach to the world without firing. You are alive; you might now be dead. Consider this hypothesis, bai."

"We do, in all aspects."

"How long will you wait on this youngling?"

"Our patience is not yet exhausted."

"We remain, then, in danger. The dead worlds: think on them; and what if there is a mri fleet loose; and what if it comes on us here?"

"Regul imagination?"

"We make hypotheses based on data and experience. Both indicate mri are apt to wild actions which do not take into account their personal survival. We suggest you set *Saber* a little farther out in the system; one of our two ships can hover over *Flower* for its safety since you insist on its remaining on the surface; one of us can scan the other side of the world. We have not been sharing data. I suggest we do so, to our mutual benefit."

"We at least have a basis for discussion."

Suth let go a great breath. "So, indeed, I invite the human bai to my ship."

"No."

"Basis?"

"Nature of human patterns of command, bai; I have to stay near my own machines. We're not as highly automated."

Suth's nostrils puffed. Whether he believed this or whether a regul could doubt a plain declaration . . . remained uncertain.

"Compromise," Suth said. "We discuss through channels. We may also consider opening channels between *Flower* and our own onworld mission."

"You do have an onworld mission."

"Why not, reverend ally? Why should we not? A closer cooperation, I say."

Koch frowned. "I shall take it under advisement, bai Suth. I think we are at that point.—*What* regul activity onworld?"

"When we have *Flower* data, we shall give you ours."

"When we have yours we will consider the matter."

"Simultaneous exchange?"

That put it untidily fair. Koch felt the burden on himself, denied it with a hissed breath the regul might understand. "What might you have? Scan data? Our own is highly efficient."

"You have more?"

"Might." Regul feared not knowing, Averson had advised him; it seemed valid, for Suth showed discomfiture at that suggestion.

"Neither of us knows what the other has," Suth said.

"I will consult with my own staff, bai Suth. Doubtless you will want to consult with yours."

Suth's nostrils puffed back and forth, back and forth. Suddenly the grin reappeared. "Excellent, reverence bai. Soon, another conference, in which we hope specific proposals.—Younglings, move. Your favor, bai."

"Favor, reverence." Koch leaned elbows on his desk, stared at the flurry of motion as the massive sled trundled toward the door and the waiting escort, and the younglings hastened after. Koch shifted a glance toward their own two superfluous aides, dismissing them to join the group outside. They understood and went without oral command.

The regul left a musty scent behind them. They had gotten it cleared out of the ship and it was back again. Koch had not begun by hating it, but it produced now a tautness in his gut, memories of tense encounters and regul smiles.

He slid a glance to Degas as the door closed, pushed away the cooling cup of soi, the taste of which he associated with the smell. Degas offered nothing, discreetly blank. He looked at Averson.

"Advice," he said.

"My advice." Averson wiped at his mouth and felt after some object in his pocket, patted it as if to be sure it was there. "I have given it, sir."

"Your opinion on what you just heard."

Averson moistened his lips. "The maneuverings of their ship . . . this forward and back, forward and back, the eluding of watch: this is what I said . . . bluff. They have a word for it, somewhere between status and assertion. They are here to assert themselves after their crisis."

"Or they're screening some operation. They're very anxious to have us move."

"Assertion. Ask more than you can get; provoke and study the reaction."

"That can get men killed down there, doctor. Or worse."

"This is a new doch, this Horag. A new power. A totally new entity in control. They're distressed by this silence on our part; they lost an elder here, and that confounded all bargains, because that elder was replaced by a different doch entirely. They deal only in memory; and the murder of an elder . . . they remember vividly. They need some current reaction from us, some approach, some substance against which they can plan policy. Remember that they can't imagine, sir. And we don't know what Horag remembers."

"What difference?" Koch asked impatiently. "They were all on one ship."

"A lot of difference, sir. A great deal of knowledge was lost with Sharn. This youngling comes out of a different pool of knowledge. His entire reality is different."

"I leave that to the psych lads. My question is what specifically will he do? What is he likely to do in the matter with *Flower*?"

Averson's hands were visibly trembling. He extracted a bottle of pills from his pocket. . . . Koch stared at the performance critically; jump-stress, maybe. There were younger men in that condition among them.

"You have to give them data to convince them of cooperation," Averson said. "But no, sir, they haven't gone down there because your threat is believed. They believe the line you've drawn." Averson tucked the pill into his mouth, put the bottle away, an annoyingly meticulous process with shaking hands. "If they fear too much they could also leave this star. Break down the whole treaty arrangement by going back to home space and reporting a human-mri alliance. Fact is, we don't know that mri and humans are the only sapient life regul are in contact with. We don't know that any exist. We don't know anything about what lies inside or the other side of regul space. And we know this one direction, where all the worlds but this one are dead; and we need to get back, sir. If no one gets back—who'll tell it?"

Koch leaned chin on his locked hands and frowned. There were things not spread to Averson's level . . . that *Saber* might not be the sole mission; that Kesrith would send out another, and another . . . desperate to have an answer. The way to the mri homeworld was the mri's secret, and humanity's, and regul . . . when *Shirug* reached home . . . their secret too. And if a human

marker were not in place broadcasting peace to ships which
came . . . human ships would move in with force. It might take
time; second missions might go world by world, years upon years
in searching dead worlds: they had followed mri, quick and desperate. But come they would, if humans feared enough, if men
and equipment sufficed to hurl out here.

"Dr. Averson, . . . I appreciate your effort. I'd appreciate a written analysis of the transcript for our files. Things have a way of
coming clear when they're written. If you would do that."

"Yes, sir," Averson replied. He looked much calmer, looked left
at Degas as if to learn whether this was dismissal.

"Good day, doctor," Koch said, waited patiently as Averson
made his awkward and slow retreat, with backward glances as
though he would gladly have stayed.

"Opinion," Koch said to Degas.

Degas locked his hands across his belly, relaxed in his chair.
"Cautious credence. I share your apprehensions about the bai; but
there is merit in their position and in their offers."

"I reckon they've read the scan also. They know those cities are
live again; that's what's brought them running. The question is
whether they know about Galey."

"Possibly. Possibly not," Degas said. "Our strong warning has
had some effect, I believe."

"On *Flower*'s safety, yes. We still haven't accounted for their
own operation, and the only possible motive their mission can
have is provocation."

"Observation."

"Possibly."

"They aren't physically capable of getting into the sites.
Chances are they suspect some operation like Galey's. We might
calm them by feeding them Galey's reports openly; but I doubt
they would put much weight on them."

"Because their decision is already firm."

Degas frowned; by his face he wanted to say something, finally
gestured and did so. "Sir, I would suggest that we're also operating under subconscious bias."

"Meaning?"

"The regul are repulsive, aren't they? No one likes them; the
crew shies from them. It's an emotional reaction, I'm afraid.

There's nothing lovely about them. But the fact is, the regul are nonviolent. They are safe neighbors. Of course the mri are appealing; humans find their absolutisms attractive. They have instincts that almost overlap our own . . . or seem to; they're handsome to human eyes. But they're dangerous, sir; the most cold-blooded killers ever let loose. Incompatible with all other life. We learned that over forty bloody years. Regul don't look noble; they aren't, by our rules; they'll cheat, given the chance . . . but in terms of property, not weapons. They would be good neighbors. We *can* understand them. Their instincts overlap ours too; and we don't like to look at that. Not nearly so attractive as the mri. But the end result of regul civilization is trade and commerce spread over all their territories. And we've had a first-hand look at the result of mri civilization too . . . the dead worlds."

Koch made a face. It was truth, though something in it was sour in his belly. "But it's rather like what Duncan said, isn't it, Del—that we shape ourselves by what we do here. We become . . . what we do here."

Degas's face went flat and cold. He shook his head. "If we kill here, . . . we stop them. We stop them flat. It's our doing; it doesn't go any farther than that. We have to take the responsibility."

"And *we* become the killers we kill to stop, eh? Paradox, isn't it? We can sneak out of here regul-fashion and let the regul become the killers; or do our own killing, and how will regul look on us then, a species that looks like the mri, that could do what the mri did? Another paradox. What's the human answer to this situation?"

"Side with the peaceful side," Degas said too quickly, like a man with his mind long made up. "Blow this place."

Koch sat and stared at him, thinking that the connection of those two ideas was not half so mad as might be. Not here. Not with mri.

"Pull up Galey's mission," Degas urged him. "And *Flower* too. You can't entirely stop the regul from prodding about down there. Regul do that, keep pushing a situation. Humans can deal with that. Mri . . ."

"You're still taking for granted mri control those weapons."

"I don't believe the possibility ought to be excluded on the basis of Galey's report. There's still only one answer when it comes down to who we want for neighbors. And preserving the mri is—"

Degas did not finish that. Koch sat back. "I propose you this, Del: regul are good traders. If we do what they don't like, they'll still come back and bargain again. We can do what we want here . . . and they'll have to negotiate from that point, not a point of their choosing."

Degas seemed to consider, slowly and at length. "Possibly. If there are no alternatives for them. Or if they don't reach some instinctual limit as a result of something we do . . . like a mri alliance."

"They're likely to hire more mercenaries. Humans, maybe; a lot of our people are trained for war, Del; a lot are rootless, and some are hungry. Does that make regul such safe neighbors?"

A second and deeper frown from Degas. "I figure that's more trouble for the regul than they want; they don't take to human ways easily, not at depth. The mri never let the regul know them; and maybe that's how they tolerated each other so long. We may be more open than the regul like. But that doesn't change my advice. We can't stay here forever. Can't. I recommend we take the responsibility and get the ugly business over with."

"No."

"Then land a force if those cities are dead and you trust this report. Go in on foot and wipe out these deserted cities, destroy their automations and their power sources. Propose that to the regul for a compromise."

"Reckoning—"

"That if the regul are right, the mri will resist with everything they have; we'll throw it back at them doubled, and be done with this. And if they're wrong and those sites aren't used, then what harm would the destruction of power sources do . . . to declined and nomadic people? Let the mri exist. That's the humane solution you asked. One the regul could accept; it's reasonable; one we could accept; it's moral. Give the mri what they need to live; let them live out their natural decline. Charity is well enough at that point."

Koch considered it, rocked back and forth, weighed the possibilities. It began to make sense. It was, by all they knew, something that the regul could accept. He considered it further, staring at Degas's tense and earnest face. "You wouldn't have discussed that with Averson?"

"No. But I'm sure he could give you some sort of analysis of regul reaction, before putting it to them."

"*Flower* might accept it. Might."

"Possibly," Degas said, his eyes glittering.

"I want Averson's opinion on it. Put it to him, as from yourself. Have it written up and on my desk as soon as possible."

"Sir," Degas said with uncharacteristic zeal.

To be back in the safety of *Shirug* . . . Suth breathed a sigh of profound relief as he eased his sled free of the shuttle's confines, entered the landing bay. His youngling attendants puffed about in their own concerns, the securing of the ship. Suth locked into the nearest rail connection and punched the code of his own office.

Automation locked in, high priority. The sled shot into motion, whisking round the turns and through dark interstices of sled-passages, out into brief bright glimpses of foot corridors. Freight sleds went by with a shock air, dead-stopped at intersections as, in his case, even other adult-sleds must stop. Sunk in his cushions he accepted the accelerations, his two hearts compensating for the shifting stresses. His blunt fingers punched in a summons, and he received acknowledgment that his staff was on its way.

They were already in his offices when he braked at the door, disengaged, and trundled through the anteroom and into his own territory. Morkhug's youngling proffered him soi. He drank gratefully, having suffered depletion of his strength in this shifting about.

"Report," he asked of his three mates, who waited on him.

"The two shuttles have dropped," Nagn announced with evident satisfaction.

"Observed by any?"

"Questionable, reverence; they are at least down intact."

Suth settled back, cup in hand, vastly relieved. "Flexibility," he pronounced with a hiss. "My own operations were not without success. They are stalling, these humans. They have been set off balance by our demands, and they are talking."

"The supplies with the shuttles," said Morkhug, "will extend the life of the younglings onworld by ten days. We are considering the feasibility of recovery. We cannot afford to lose the machinery if we remain here and protract this situation."

Suth drank and reflected on the matter. In eight days, panic would begin to set in among the younglings onworld, water for the humidifiers running short; and food . . . in increasing anxiety they would eat. They had oversupplied food in relation to water: better shortage of anything but food; the presence of it would satisfy them toward the terminal stages if no provision could be made to rescue them. Fear of hunger brought madness, irrational action. It was necessary that that reaction be staved off as long as possible.

Expendables: the younglings downworld knew it as these present here did. It was the eternal hope of younglings that efficiency would win favor and spare one from dying . . . the deep-rooted desire to feed and placate the governing elders, to be constantly reassured about one's status. Recipient of such attentions and no longer bound by them, Suth settled into remote consideration of alternatives.

Deal with humans and thereby win access to supply food to the mission?

Koch's reasoning nagged at him, blind, humanish obstinacy.

Regarding forgetting . . . *We use it with many meanings, bai Suth.*

Precise forgetting?

The deliberate expunging of data?

One could alter one's reality and all time to come. Was this linked to future-memory and imagination?

Suth shuddered.

"Food," Melek breathed anxiously, tearing at the wrappings of the supply packets; its fingers were all but numb: the cold crept in everywhere, despite the wrappings with which they swathed themselves, and the biodome which, with its flooring and translucent walls, attempted to provide them some measure of moving space in their base. Four shuttles clustered about the dome, dimly visible in the dawning, where basin haze made the daybreak the hue of milk, where the shadow of a seamount drifted disembodied and lavender above the haze. All of them avoided that exterior view whenever possible; the flatnesses, they were not so bad; but

he barren sand, the eternal emptiness, the color of the earth, the
alienness of it . . . these were terrible. The regular thudding of the
compressor measured their existence within the air-supported
dome. The air was supposed to be heated, but the nights, the
dreadful nights, when the sun sank and vanished in mid-sky . . .
brought chill; and fearsome writhings disturbed the floor of the
biodome, the life of Kutath, seeking moisture, seeking warmth;
they wore footgear when they must go out to the ships, hastened,
shuddering at the slithering whips and cables which attempted to
impede them and to invade their suits and their doorways.

Now two more lostlings were sent among them. Melek chewed
at the concentrates, its trembling somewhat abated; its comrade
Pegagh sat munching on soi nuts, the while the newcomers settled
in among them. Magd and Hab their names were, Alagn like Pegagh. Melek, of Geleg doch, regarded them all with suspicion, its
double hearts laboring in the dull dread that they were to be held
here too long, that the calculations it had made were inaccurate,
and it was not valued and honored for being of another doch than
Alagn . . . quite the contrary. Melek did not speak such things,
certainly not to them; and made no complaints, as Pegagh did not:
one never knew in what ear such complaints would be dropped
should they survive. There was a swelling in Melek's throat that
made swallowing difficult in such contemplations. They flew
their missions precisely as told; they beamed Eldest's tape over
the wide flat nothingness.

They hoped, forlornly, to be taken home and fed and comforted.

Now they were four.

There were ten shuttles in all; and four of them sat here. Two
more coming down could not carry supplies sufficient to make
the trip worthwhile: they would then be six marooned down
here . . . a matter of diminishing returns. There would be no more
supplies. Melek made the calculations with interior panic.

Perform.

Obey orders precisely.

Hope for favor and life.

It was all they had.

Chapter Thirteen

Duncan looked a sorry sight under any circumstances. Stripped naked and in daylight he was sadder still, scrubbing away at himself with handfuls of sand to take the blood and grime away. Niun worked at his own person, the two of them alone on the edge of camp where the slight rolling of the land gave them a measure of privacy and the wind blew clear. He rubbed dust into his mane and shook it until the dust was gone, scrubbed his skin until it stung and then quickly sought the warmth of clean robes, shivering in the wind.

Duncan managed the same for himself, although his hair-coated skin would not shed the sand so easily and the hair of his head was prone to retain the dust. Still he labored fastidiously at it, sitting somewhat sheltered from the wind, and his stress-thinned limbs shivered so that Niun took concern for him and held his robes between him and the treacheries of the breeze.

"Come, you are clean enough. Will you not make haste about it? My arms tire."

Duncan stood and shrugged into the robes, shivered convulsively, and fastened the inner robe with its cloth belt, the while Niun sat down again on the side of the slope to work his boots on.

Duncan coughed a little, smothered it. Niun looked up anxiously. Duncan ignored the matter and sat down again, began with a little oil and the blade of one *as-en*, to scrape away at the hair on his face. Niun regarded the process with furtive glances. It was a matter of meticulous care with Duncan, and a difference between them which Duncan sought assiduously to hide, which humans in general did, for Niun supposed that all had this tendency, and that all cared for it as Duncan did, not the hair of the body but that of the face: a tsi'mri observance he continued as compatible with mri, perhaps, or simply that the veil was the one portion of clothing a kel'en could not maintain in the camp.

And Niun deliberately sought privacy for Duncan to attend to his person, so that the newcomers should not see the differences of his body. He was vaguely ashamed at this deception, although Duncan freely consented in it. He remained uncertain whether Duncan did so out of shame of his own structure, or out of some consideration for him, not to embarrass him. Niun greatly suspected the latter . . . but asking Duncan why—that required delving into tsi'mri thoughts. It had been more comfortable to ignore the matter, and to provide Duncan that measure of privacy, the two of them.

Duncan lived, and that was enough at the moment. He was wan and thin and slow in his movements as an old man, but alive, and without the bleeding this bright morning. It was a good thing in a man, that he wake with a sudden concern for his appearance and his cleanliness, and an evidence of impatience with his own condition. It was a good thing.

This morning there seemed much of good in the world.

The dusei were out and away, lost somewhere in the haze of the amber morning . . . presumably hunting as they should be, and not out troubling the camps which lay over the horizons on all sides of them. The stranger-kel'en had settled into camp, in a makeshift patchwork of three shades of canvas on ropes between sen-tent and Kel. There was a quiet there, sensible mri folk who were not going to provoke quarrels in stupidity, as sensibly silent and observing as folk were who knew they might be set to kill, and who could profit from understanding as much as possible and seeing clearly and without passion. Their own she'panei directed them to take orders within the camp; they did so, adapting to strangeness with the confidence that came of knowing their own tribes relied on them for eyes and ears . . . the Face-Turned-Outward of their she'panei. Even the ja'anom were unwontedly reasonable, for all Duncan's presence among them. It would not last; but it was, for the moment, good.

In the camp children of the Kath played, laughing aloud and having the energy at last to skip and run. They had caught a snake this dawn, unfortunate creature which had strayed in seeking the

camp's moisture. Nothing ventured into camp wily enough to escape the sharp-eyed children, who added it triumphantly to the
common pot. They teased and played at pranks, amusing even the
sober strangers.

And that laughter, reaching them, was a comfort to the heart
more than all others.

"Why the face?" Niun asked in sudden recklessness.

Duncan looked up, wet a finger in his mouth, touched a bleeding spot on his chin. He seemed perplexed by the question, but
quite unoffended.

"Why the face and not—" Niun made a gesture vaguely including his own body.

Duncan grinned, a shocking expression in his gaunt, half-
tanned face, which was brown about the eyes and not elsewhere.
More, he laughed silently. "It would take a long time. Should I?"

That was not the sober reaction Niun had expected. He found
himself embarrassed, frowned and touched his brow. "Here is
mri, sov-kela. The outside is a veil, like the other veil. You and I
are alike enough."

Duncan went sober indeed, and seemed to understand him.

"My brother," Niun said, "pleases *himself* by this. For them—"
He gestured widely toward the mingled camp and all the camps
about.

Duncan shrugged. "*Should* I remove it all?"

"Gods," Niun muttered, "no."

And Duncan confounded him by an inward smile, a nod. "I
hear you."

"My brother is perverse as a dus."

"And similarly coated."

Niun hissed, high exasperation, and found himself compelled
to laugh because Duncan could so deftly lead him.

Human laughter; it was at times irreverent of most serious
things; but that Duncan retained his sense of balance, that was a
knowledge cleansing as a draft of wind.

"Gods, gods, I have missed you."

And that for some reason brought a touch of pain to Duncan's
face, a shadow of a sorrow.

That question too he would have liked to ask, and for his peace
and Duncan's . . . declined.

Duncan sat down and pulled on his boots, gave a deep breath when he had done and rose shakily, belted on his weapons and his Honors. Niun stood and resumed the visored headcloth and Duncan did likewise, until there was only the difference of the face and Duncan's lesser stature between them.

"You think—" Duncan said then, as if it were something which had been biding speaking a long time. "You think these stranger-kel'ein would go back with us to the ship?"

"That is not for Kel to say."

"The she'pan said that she would consider. What is she considering?"

"The Sen deliberates." Niun felt exposed in the hedging, ashamed; there were times that Duncan could meet a stare with the look of a kath'en and the steadiness of a kel-Master. "Did I not teach you patience, without questions?"

"They have been deliberating the second day now."

"Sov-kela."

"Aye," Duncan answered him, glancing away. Niun made a bundle of the clothing they had shed, knotted it and rose again; he set his other hand on Duncan's shoulder, turning him back toward the main aisle of the camp, and Duncan for all his disquiet reached and took the cord of the bundle, carrying the burden with a courtesy automatic as one born to it. Niun regarded that, and felt the more uncomfortable himself.

"Do you doubt the she'pan?" Niun asked. "Do you think she would not do the best thing?"

"There are thoughts I cannot say in the hal'ari, that I am not good enough to say." They walked slowly, boots crunching on the wind-scoured sand beside their outward footprints, already wind-dimmed. "If you would hear—if you would remember human language for a small moment, and let me say in human terms—"

"Veil," Niun cut him off. "Do not breathe the wind. Manners do not apply to the sick."

Duncan did so, and was silent.

"You had years on the ship to talk to us," Niun said. "*You* are the speech you would make, and it is already well-made." He took a pass of the veil across his own mouth, for courtesy between them, not to make Duncan conspicuous, and mindfully shortened his long strides. "It is all said, Duncan."

The morning haze fell kindly about the tents, touching them al
with the tranquility of the hour. Even the black fabric of kel-ten
and the patchwork tent adjoining had a little of gold on thei
coarse surface; and gold stained the paler hue of that of the
she'pan and of the others. The trampled center of the camp wa
alive with blue-robes, goings and comings of the children, wome
working by Kath in the morning light, cookfires burning. But o
gold there was none; and of black-robed figures but one, and tha
one vanished into the main kel-tent as they approached; other
came out then, jamming the doorway, and sudden apprehensio
gathered at Niun's belly, the morning dimmed . . . he opened hi
mouth to warn Duncan and did not. Duncan was wise on his own
and some things were too evil to suspect aloud.

They walked as close to the doorway as they might with the
Kel blocking their way. Hlil was there in the center of matters
unveiled; some were and others were not.

"The she'pan has called half-council," Hlil said. "Ours an
theirs together."

It had come, then. Niun dismissed his worse suspicions with
profound shame. "Aye," he told Hlil and started away with him a
once. But a few steps away he delayed, still with that vile feelin
crawling at his belly. He looked back and caught Duncan's eye
who stared after him.

"The dusei," he said to Duncan. "It concerns me . . . where the
are. You might call them."

If you need them, he meant. He thought that Duncan took hi
meaning; that sort of glance went between them, and there was
touch of apprehension in Duncan's eyes, but no panic.

He turned then and went with Hlil.

Kel'ein settled about the doorway, showing no disposition t
enter the tent . . . ja'anom, but not all ja'anom: kel'ein of the othe
Kels hovered about the edges, and more and more arrived
strolling up casually. The door was blocked, inconvenient t
reach, and it was dark inside, lacking witnesses. Duncan settle
on the sand in their midst, his back to the tent, the black bulk o
which served to shelter him and them from the slight wind. H
kept his head bowed, doing as Niun had suggested, thinking o
the dusei, but when time passed in the quiet and extraneous con

versation of those near him, he dismissed his more vivid fears and
glanced furtively at the ja'anom, wondering if he understood anything at all of what game they were playing. One was old Peras, a
quiet one and civil to him; he could not think evil of him. There
was Taz . . . Taz's unwontedly expressionless face gave him no
comfort; he had never seen the boy but that he was alive and
alight to every need about him, and he was withdrawn now,
watching. And Ras . . . Ras and Niun did not agree: he had sensed
this thoroughly, even without the dusei. She came now and settled
slightly behind him, so that she could see him and not otherwise.

Silence fell in the group. Most withdrew inside, strangers as
well as ja'anom, not into their proper tent; and that was unwonted. Others stayed sitting. Duncan glanced down rather than
appear to question this movement, reckoning silence the best
course. Niun needed no trouble of his making; trouble there was
already, and he reckoned that a portion of it had maneuvered to
take him in. He knew names more than Peras and Taz and Ras,
but few more; there were ja'anom whose names and reasons he
ought to know, and did not, so short a time he had been among
them before. If they had helped him live now, it was out of some
sense of honor, or something that Niun had the power to make
them do; not for love: he had no illusions of that.

The kel'en on his right touched his sleeve.

"Tsi'mri," that one said, but as if it were fact, not a calculated
insult, "you say nothing."

He looked up perforce, met the unveiled face of that man and
of others, young and old, male and female. None of them showed
expression. All those left had the kel-scars, the *seta'al,* time-
faded on the faces of some, new and bright on others. "Perhaps
there are some who do not wish me well. What do you wish,
kel'ein?"

Silent glances went from one to the other, and Duncan followed these exchanges with anxiety he did not allow to his face.

"You are wise," said a kel'a'en, "always to keep to someone's
shadow."

Duncan felt the wind, felt his back naked without Niun, and
bowed his head to them, which was all his recourse.

"We see what is toward," another said. "Best you sit here."

He cast a look toward the aisle, toward the she'pan's tent, into which Niun had vanished, and all that he could see was a wall of stranger-kel'ein, listening silently on the fringes. Almost he rose to walk away from them all, to go settle at the she'pan's door in safety, but a grip on his sleeve advised him otherwise before he could make the move. He looked back at them. An old kel'e'en touched the scars on her face, mark of a skill he lacked. "You are *tsi'seta*. Who would challenge *you* but another unscarred? And there are none such here."

"What is happening?" Duncan demanded of them, knowing that they meant something by this, and not knowing even who ranked highest in this complex of skill and birth and seniority of mingled tribes. He scanned from face to face, lost and betraying it . . . settled last on old Peras, whose lean, seamed face indicated at least reverence owed, and whose eyes perhaps showed something of sympathy. "What is happening? The Council . . . is that it?"

"Tsi'mri kel'en, there is division in the camp. Yonder stand other tribes; ours and others come and go. They ask us questions. And while you sit here with us in this circle—there is no one free to make a mistake."

That disparaged him; it was also the kind of insult any without rank in the Kel had to accept as a matter of course.

"Sir," he murmured humbly, which was always the right answer to a warrior who had won the *seta'al*, from one who had not.

"Kel'en," Peras responded, which was more courtesy than an elder needed use.

"He speaks well," said one of the out-tribesmen, settling near. "It is remarkable."

Others behind him nodded, and one laughed a breath. "This is a wonder," that one said, "to sit and talk with a tsi'mri."

The word, Duncan reflected placidly, studying his hands in his lap, also applied to the dusei.

"He is mannered," another said.

The old kel'en reached and touched at his sleeve. "Veil, kel'en. The air does you harm; there is courtesy and there is stupidity."

He inclined his head in thanks and did so, headcloth and twice-lapped veil.

And now and again in the silence which followed, he glanced in the direction of the she'pan's tent, for one by one the standing kel'eun settled; he was anxious, for himself and for what manner of maneuvering might have encompassed Niun as well and for what passed in Council among those who had power . . . all that he had tried to do, all that he had paid his life for, and now he could not even merit to sit at the door to hear judgment passed on his offering to them. He sat, in their long silence, and fretted, aware finally of another presence responding to his distress.

It came padding across the sand toward them, his dus, anxious and hasty. He felt it; and it sensed hostility, and its presence loomed dark and ominous.

He glanced about him with a gesture of appeal, to ja'anom and to the others. "Do not hate," he wished them.

That was like asking the wind to stop; but heads nodded after a moment. The dus came, worked quietly among them, wended its stubborn way to his back, dislodging Ras a little space. He cherished that warmth against him where Ras had been. And in the long silence that followed that shifting about, he drew from his belt the weighted cords, the *ka'islai,* and began to knot them in the star-mandala.

It was the *islan* of Pattern, which imposed order on confusion. It was the most complex he knew, which in his learning fingers would take long to complete.

He was, after a dogged fashion, committing an insolence. He was better in the *islai* than some who had the kel-scars; he had had long practice, on the ship, in idleness. He meant to defy them, for all it was unwise. He did not even look up . . . feeling their eyes on him, who aped their ways; felt a grating at his nerves, the shifting of his dus. Ras had her hand on it, which few dared.

He kept his mind to his pattern, refusing to be distracted even by that.

"Kel'en," said Peras.

"Ai?"

"Council deliberations can be quite tedious. Do you play *shon'ai?*"

His heart began to beat rapidly. The Game of the People was one thing played among friends; he thought were Niun at hand to hear that he would be on his feet in outrage. He carefully stripped out the complex knots and looped the *ka'islai* again to his belt. "I am mri," he said softly, "for all you protest it. Yes, I play the Game."

There were soft hisses, reaction to his almost-insolence. Old Peras took from his belt the *as-ei,* the palm-blades.

"I will play partner to kel Duncan," Peras said.

In the Game, Niun had taught him, one's life relied on seating. When strong player sat opposite weak or when grudges and alliances seated themselves out of balance in the circle, someone could die. There was only the partnering of the players at one's elbows to counsel an enemy across the circle not to throw foul. Strong beside weak was a protection, if weak were wise where he sent his own casts.

He had learned paired, only the Game of Two, patternless save for the pattern of the throws themselves, high and low.

They began to form a circle of six, with the others to witness. Duncan took comfort, for it was gentle Dias, Peras's truemate, who took the place opposing him in the circle, and those who flanked her were young, lesser in skill than some. But then kel Ras bent down and touched the sleeve of Dias. Some words passed in low voices and short dispute, and Ras, of the second rank of the Kel, replaced kel Dias of the fourth, facing him and Peras.

And suddenly Duncan minded himself what Niun had always told him of death by stupidity.

They would kill him if they wished. He suddenly realized that he did not know the limits of his skill. He had played only Niun, and Niun was his friend.

Ras . . . was no one's. At Duncan's left there was another substitution, an old kel'en, on whom the scars were well-weathered.

The dus drew back a little, rested head on paws, puffed slightly and followed all this insanity with darting moves of its eyes.

The Game; it was a means of passing time, as Peras had said. An amusement.

But the Kel amused themselves with blades, and amusements were sometimes—even unintended—to the death.

They gave their names, those Duncan did not know well; one did not play with strangers save in challenge. Duncan dropped his veil, for it was no friendly act to play veiled. There was hazard enough without that.

Kel Peras began, being eldest . . . threw to Ras. Hands struck thighs, the rhythm of the Game; and on the name-beat of the unspoken rhyme, the blades spun across the circle again.

They played about him, from man to man and woman to man and youth to youth, back and forth, weaving patterns which became established, excluding him, a Game of Five, oddly seated. Mri fingers, slim and golden and marginally quicker than human, snatched spinning steel from the air and hurled it on at the next name-beat.

At no time did he relax, knowing that the rhythm could increase in tempo and that some impulse might send the blades spinning his way, from the youths, from Ras, any of those three.

Suddenly he had warning, a flicker of the membrane as Ras stared at him. Next time: he nodded, almost unnerved by her warning, whether courtesy or reflex.

The blades spun to her, shining in the sun, and she snatched them, waited the beat and hurled them at the steady time of the Game, no deception or change of pace.

He made the catch, hurled them left of her in his time, to a young kel'en. Now a new lacery began, which wove itself star-patterned like the *islan,* the mandala of the Game, the Game of Six, as each Game was different by every factor in it.

The pattern varied, and beside him kel Peras laughed, catching the treachery of Ras: the blades, missed, might have killed; Ras' eyes danced with amber merriment, and the blades came back at her, cunningly thrown, low-and-high. She cast them again to Peras, left-slant; he threw to her, again left; back to elder Da'on, right; and he threw to young Eran and he to young Sethan.

Tempo altered, making again a safer rhythm, the moment's sport among Masters tamed again, beating slower for lesser players.

It came back, from Ras to himself; he caught, and threw to the youngest, Sethan, tacit recognition of his status.

It returned, evenly paced; he cast back; it went to Da'on on his left, to Ras, to Peras—

And stopped. Peras signaling halt. The rhythm of the hands ceased. Duncan drew a great breath, suddenly coughed from the chill air and realized that that reflex a moment ago might have killed him.

"Veil," Da'on advised him. He did so, holding the cloth to his mouth and nose until the chill left his lungs. The dus edged up to him, settled against his back, offering him its warmth.

"An unscarred," said Da'on, "should never play the Six."

"No, kel'en," he agreed. "But when a scarred asks, an unscarred obeys."

Breaths hissed softly between teeth. Heads nodded.

"You play the Game," Peras said, "in all senses. That is well, human kel'en."

He leaned against the dus, caressed its neck, for his heart was still pounding and the dus shivered in reaction.

The tent flap stirred. Another kel'en came out and sat down on the sand, out of the wind. He looked up and two more followed, and four and three, not all of their own Kel. The black assembly widened, veils dropped, so that he felt he should take his own down, and did so, trying to breathe carefully.

He must not be afraid. The dus would catch it up and cast it to them. He must not be angry. The dus would rouse and they would sense that too. The mri of Kutath could not veil their emotions, not generally. He received a touch of resentment, and some rarer things warmer, pure curiosity. It was not attack, not yet. He soothed the dus with his touch, himself master of it and not the other way about, making it feel what he wished it to feel, quiet, quiet.

Shon'ai, the mri of Kesrith said: the Game-throw is made.

No calling it back, no mending it now.

Shon'ai: it is cast!

Throw your life, kel'en; and deserve to live, for joy of the Game.

They had been there all along, and more came now, until all in the kel-tents must be there, and he was the center of it.

"Tell us," said Peras, "kel'en-who-has-shared-in-Kath, make us all to understand this thing of ships and enemies."

He cast an anguished glance toward the she'pan's tent, hoping against hope to see Niun and the others, some indication even that the Council might be near an end, that he might delay. It was a vain hope.

"Shall an unscarred of this kel know more," asked Peras, "than the seniors of it, who sit in Council? Things are out of balance here, young kel'en of the ja'anom. That is one disease here. Remedy it."

"I am from the other side of a Dark," he protested, "and I am forbidden to remember."

"So is this brother I have gained for my brother," said Ras in a harsh voice, "who calls you brother to him. We are by that . . . *kin,* are we not? Answer. We kel'ein, are we not the Face that Looks Outward? Our eyes are used to the Dark. And the trouble has come here, to us, has it not, tsi'mri brother? Has the she'pan silenced you on that matter—or is it for your own sake you keep your secrets, ai? What arrangement did you and my brother-by-death have, that he knew where to find you?"

A muscle jerked in his face. He fought for control. "Hlil arranged this."

"Hlil would not," she said. "I. My kindred. *I* ask."

He gazed at her, kel'e'en of the second rank; daithe, kin of the last kel'anth and blood-tied to no knowing how many kindreds. A chill settled into him.

"I hear you," he said, understanding. He bowed his head then, soothing the restive dus with the touch of his fingers . . . felt her touch against the other side of it, so that the animal shivered.

It was a mutual trap, that contact. There were no lies possible, no half-truths. He laid his hand firmly against the beast.

And yielded, point by point.

Chapter Fourteen

"There have been arguments," the she'pan conceded, facing the Council. Niun sat nearest her, cross-legged on the mats, no Husband, but the she'pan's own kel'en, and kel'anth at once, doubly owning that place of honor. The Husbands of ja'anom sat ranged nearest, and the several highest of the five tribes settled by them, a black mass. The ja'anom kath'anth was there, Anthil; and the whole ja'anom Sen, in a golden mass, beneath the lamps which they used in Council even in daytime. Sen'anth Sathas was foremost of them, but there were sen'ein of the five stranger-tribes there too, who had come in yestereve with the kel'ein.

"There have been strong dissensions," Melein continued, "within the ja'anom . . . for the losses we have suffered, for the choices we face. But Sen has agreed in my choices. Is it not so, sen'anth?"

"So," Sathas echoed, "Sen has consented."

"Not easy, to come home. The pan'en which is holy to us . . . what can it mean to you? A curiosity, full of strange names and things which never happened to you? And the holy relics of your wanderings on Kutath . . . how shall my kel'anth and I understand them? We struggle to do so, you with us and we with you. We of the Voyagers, we who went out . . . we want a place to stand; and you who stayed to guard Kutath so many millennia ago—perhaps you look about you and hate us, that we were voyaged out at all. Is that not part of it? Is that not a little part, that you blame us two, that of all Kutath sacrificed . . . we are all that have come home, all who will ever come home?" Her eyes moved to the Kel, traveled down to Niun. "Or is it perhaps for what we brought home with us, for what we call one of us?"

Niun glanced down. "Perhaps. It is many things, she'pan, but both may be so."

"And the ja'anom Kath?"

"Kath," said Anthil's soft voice, "blames no one. We only mourn the children, she'pan; those lost and those to come."

"And the songs you have taught those children over the ages . . . look for what, kath'anth? For the returning of those who went out when the world was younger and water flowed?"

"Some songs—hoped for that."

"When our ancestors were one," Melein said, "not alone the tribes, but yourselves and my ancestors . . . that was a great age of the world; and there had been many before. The cities were standing, already old, built on the ruins of others, and our ancestors walked on the dust of a thousand thousand civilizations and forgotten races. The four races who walked the world at the beginning of that age dwindled to two, and them you know. After so long there was building again: elee cities were standing, already old, built on the ruins of others, green of an old, old plant that the sands had long buried . . . but its roots were deep and it stood in the winds again. It was the last of everything that nourished it; it took from all else, so that it was the last greening . . . mri saw this: and we who had loved the land . . . knew. We built . . . the great edunei; and the great machines of the elee we appropriated to our own purposes.

"We and the elee," Melein's voice continued, low and vibrant. "We knew, and they wanted only what had always been. *Shon'ai!* we cast ourselves—to chance and the great Dark. *'Go out,'* we advised the elee, in the world's bright hour. *'We have risen on all the world's strength; now we go out, shon'ai! now . . . for the world's wind is at our backs, and we feel it.'*

"*'Go then,'* said the elee, for all they hated such an idea and pleased themselves to turn their faces away. We went and we brought greater and greater things, bringing them comfort, so that for an age the elee were very content, seeing the chance of more and more comfort and long life. We went further: we took stars for the elee, in slow years of voyaging, and brought knowledge.

"But the elee began to be afraid. They feared the Dark and hated anything strange. They wanted only Kutath, and to live with their comforts and their cities and to use up the wealth we could bring. They cared only for that. They let the stars go.

"And they let us go. They put us increasingly out of their thoughts. Had they been able, they would have sealed us up on this world.

"Some of us . . . stayed; you held this world for mri; you entered on a holy trust, to save the standing place from which we launched, to save the precious things and to honor the service that we served.

"Hard for us . . . to keep our ways, in our slow voyaging, always out of touch with the visible, the physical Kutath. We had to keep it in our hearts, and yet to protect the knowledge of it: only she'panei and Sen of the voyagers were permitted to remember; Kath and Kel knew only the ships . . . or between the Darks . . . the hundred twenty-five homeworlds-of-convenience. Aye," she said when Niun looked up at her in stark bewilderment. "They were *ours. Ours,* our homes, Niun.

"And hard for you who stayed behind," she said, "—to live with the visible, among the monuments, with Kutath a reality about you—and to keep contact with the invisible, with the dream.

"When we must, we moved on, shedding each world's taint, renewing ourselves like something born always new, young again and strong: we kept nothing of the Betweens. We boarded our ships and Kutath was born anew aboard them, the old language, the ways, the ancient knowledge during generations of voyage.

"When calamity fell here, you had no means to veil what resulted: the sights—were before you. You lived in the visible and looked to the promise . . . so long, so very long.

"To go on believing . . . and clinging to old ways . . . when elee mocked them; to teach the young the promise . . . which they might never see, while the seas sank further, and the world had no more strength for a new beginning, and the elee interest only in the moment. To remember skills which had passed beyond use; to sing the old chants; to look for hope, when all the sights about you counseled that the world was ending, and that there was no sane hope that this year or the next thousand years would bring what millennia before did not.

"Hardest, surely, when ships did come . . . when after centuries of waiting . . . ships came down on you—not ours—and then the elee wanted protection; then they surely wanted what they had cast from them. The world was laid waste and mri and elee were slaughtered, the land ruined so that even the enemy fled it. Enemy . . . it was the collapse of the empire which we had made; it was the last tremor of a dying power, in which the elee had refused to involve themselves, which had gone its own way; and that power died and their worlds with them perhaps. At least they did not come again.

"After that, what was there left, but to live narrowly, to find elee fighting among themselves for water and for less substantial things? Some mri took hire in these wars; some left the promise and involved themselves in the immediate and the visible. But the she'pan Gar'ai s'Hana, may her name live to all castes so long as there are mri to sing it—led a retreat from the cities and the wars, into the open land. I know her," Melein added, and there seemed not a breath in Council, the while tears flowed openly down her face, across the kel-scars. "I know such a she'pan, to do the unreasonable, and to lead others where she would fear to send even one. She foresaw, perhaps, the death of the children and the elders, of all the vulnerable ones; and for what? For what hope? To exist, and wait, singing the old songs, while the mountains wore away.

"And we Voyagers . . .

"We served—other services. Darks intervened. To my sorrow, the passing of the she'panate of the Voyagers to me was in calamity, the massacre of us all on a world named Kesrith. Some things my she'pan had no time to teach me. Most of all—the reason *why,* the reason why we went out at all, and why after so many, many ages . . . we never returned. The reason why at least . . . the she'pan who prepared me for the she'panate . . . had decided it was time to turn the People homeward."

There was disturbance in the Kel. Niun glanced that way with a forbidding frown and unfocused his eyes and stared through them, his heart leaden within him, the confirmation of doubts he had held from the beginning.

"Is it this," Melein pursued, "for which we were met with doubt? That dreams are better than what we can touch? That Niun and I are the too-mortal flesh of a great hope? That the dream brought you destruction, and the death of friends and children, and tsi'mri, as it was in the world's worst hour?

"Why did my she'pan refuse the offer the tsi'mri of our last service made, of a green and living world, and choose instead Kesrith, which was desolation? The Forge of the People, she named it, and gave the Sen no other answer. Why did she speak even before the danger came on us . . . of leaving the service that we served, which was to regul and against humans; and why was her mind set toward this homecoming?

"It might have been the diminishing of our numbers: we were very few when the regul decided to betray us and kill us, in the knowledge that they could no longer control us.

"It might have been that my she'pan was mad; there were some who believed so, even among her children.

"And do you think that I was not afraid, when I took up the robes, when I knew that I was charged to come home, and that I had not been told the last secret, the great *why* of all the she'panei before me. I tell you that I was greatly afraid.

"I gained the pan'en for my guide; and in the beginning I believed blindly, reading the record it holds, that guided our ship . . . the way that the People had passed, viewing world after world which our ancestors had known, and thinking them beautiful."

"She'pan," Niun objected, a breath, a pain which wrung at him.

"But they were all dead." Her voice faltered and steadied. "Dead worlds, every one. And do you think then that I was not afraid?

"I walked this world. I found the place, the very city from which most of my ancestors came . . . for we kept our chants and our lineages. And after all that time, I have found my own: the ja'anom are my far, far kindred, An-ehon's children; as are you all, even ka'anomin of Zohain . . . blood-kin to me. I spoke with the city; and with the Sen of the ja'anom, and with the sen'ein who have come from other tribes . . . and I know; I know the nature of the promise, and most of all what turned us homeward . . . in *ships, in ships*, my distant children, which cross the great Darks in an eye's blinking.

"Enemies have followed us. They have destroyed our ship and our city, but to destroy us, no, the gods forbid and the Mystery forbids. Tsi'mri do as they will. We—Niun and I—we have *done* what we set out to do. The dream is true. We have it in our hands. Tsi'mri are here, within reach of our hands, and nothing in a hundred thousand years . . . has promised such as we bring you."

It was back, that fierceness of her first night among the ja'anom; it glittered in the eyes of the Kel, ja'anom and stranger alike; even in the eyes of the Sen, and shone in the mild face of the kath'anth. Of this the shameful flight had cheated them, driving them hunted across their own land; of this they had been frustrated, hiding and cowering from tsi'mri weapons, not alone in these days but in earlier days and on other worlds, dying helpless and uncomprehending of purpose. They were suddenly Melein's, hers, clenched in her fist.

This hope . . . *within reach,* Melein had said.

Duncan.

A great cold washed over Niun, realization why Melein had been willing to cast even himself from her hand in the chance of finding Duncan, why she had remained silent while the tribe fell apart in quarrel, and had no answer—until she could find Duncan again, knowing full well where he had gone, as she had known about the messages to humans which Duncan had tried to send, which the regul had destroyed.

O my brother, he mourned, but grief stayed from his face, the habit of the Kel, that there was no link between heart and countenance, not before the adversary.

"Kel'anth," said kel Seras of the Husbands, "say to the she'pan that she is our Mother and that the ja'anom Kel is with her, heart and hand."

"And that we hear," said the kel'anth Rhian, "a message we are anxious to bear to our she'panei."

"Aye," muttered other kel'anthein.

This should have given him the most profound, the uttermost joy. It did not. He looked up into Melein's eyes, glad that there was no dus by them, to catch up the she'pan's inexorable and calculating coldness and hurl it into him, keener than any blade. "You hear," he echoed hoarsely. "And in all matters . . . I am the she'pan's Hand."

"Kel'anth," she said, "the message which came to us from tsi'mri, that we should come and speak with them . . . tell me, kel'anth of the ja'anom, what will tsi'mri do if we should fail that rendezvous they ask? Will they attack?"

"Am I tsi'mri, to answer what they will do?"

"Your knowledge of them is best of all but Duncan's. What will they do if their expectations are thwarted? What would kel Duncan have done, when he was human?"

He glanced down, lest the membrane betray his disturbance. "I would expect of a human . . . first, distress; puzzlement that things did not agree with his hopes; then anger. But—humans are more likely to come probing at us than to launch devastating attack, unless cornered. Regul . . . regul are another species; and they are up there too; and that is different. Duncan believes humans are restraining them—but humans reckon patience from moment to moment, and a day is soon to them. That is what I dread, that their patience is too short even to comprehend how slowly a man must walk in this land. They live with machines, and expect everything to come quickly."

"And once challenge has been made?"

Niun sat still, eyes unfocused, seeing a place he was forbidden to recall, fire and night, ships lacing back and forth above ruin. "Humans fight in masses; so do regul, no single combat. The People lost thousands before we learned this fact and the thinking behind it. *But*—" He struck his palm upon the floor, looked suddenly at Kel and Sen. "But they make other replies. Duncan is one. When it was all over, when regul had effectively finished us and humans had fought us to our ruin . . . Duncan came alone, as none of them had ever come alone to our challenges; and handed us himself, and struggled for us, gave us the ship in which we came here. Ask him why. He has no idea that he can express. Instinct? A response of his kind? He did not know the answer when he was human. Now he is mri. Perhaps he remembers enough that Council might call him, ask him why, or how humans think. Ask *him*."

"No," Melein said softly. "No. Can mri give a tsi'mri kind of answer? We are ourselves, kel'anth. Do not look so deeply into the Dark that you lose your balance."

He caught his breath, looked up at her, his heart beating against his ribs.

*   *   *

The dus stirred. Duncan caught up something, vast sorrow, and stopped in mid-word, looked about at the Kel and shivered in a sudden breeze.

Others gathered it up without understanding it. Duncan looked toward the door of the she'pan's tent, knowing direction, and a great fear bore down upon him.

"Kel'en," said Peras, and Peras in leaning forward touched the dus. The spilling of emotions touched him too, and the veteran's eyes nictitated, amazed and chagrined.

"What is wrong?" asked old Da'on. "Peras?"

The feeling faded, like something passing out of focus. It was hard to imagine that it had been there. Duncan stroked the velvet fur with both his hands, bowed against it, lifted his face again.

"The tsi'mri called *regul,*" kel Ras prompted him.

"Dead," Duncan said hoarsely. "I killed her. She stirred her younglings to attack, and I killed her and gave the matter over to humans. Only—" He found himself saying more than he wanted to and ceased, but the dus betrayed him, gathering up feelings and weaving them together, himself and his hearers, himself and Ras who sat against the beast. A dread was on him and they shared it, perhaps without knowing why.

"O my brothers." It was the idiom of the hal'ari, and he meant it in that moment. "The Dark is very wide out there, and all about this world, there is no life, none at all. They have seen it. And they are afraid."

"We move on," said Melein, "as we have been moving. I will say no more of it; I do not bind myself with words; I do as the Now asks. Tell your she'panei we move with the dawn. A double hand of Kel'ein will hunt outward from our column to feed us. If any she'pan will draw back and not lend to me, I do not permit: I challenge. If any will challenge me, well, there is honor in that, and if she will take up my robes and stand where I stand, that is well. But I do not believe the gods will permit me to fall; I shall absorb that tribe and take them for my children. The gods have not preserved me through so much to fall in tribal rivalry. If any she'pan will lend me her children in my need, I shall write her in the Holy's last table, and in the beginning of the new; and the mri who stood with me, living and dead, will mark a new beginning in the songs of their line. All things begin and end from this coming day. When I have done what I will, I shall give their children back to them with gratitude and Honors: the law prevents us of the White from standing face to face . . . but apart, we are each a point strength on Kutath's wide face. I am she'pan'anth, she'pan-senior of the Voyagers . . . she'pan'anth of all mri; and I have need. Say that to them. Is there question?"

Silence hung in the air, trembling with force.

"Go," she said, a whisper like a sword's slash. "And come back to me."

It was a moment before bodies stirred, before any had the temerity to move . . . and in a thick silence the Kel stood, the kath'anth withdrawing first in the precedence of leaving. Kel'ein waited. Niun moved, realizing it was on him, and walked out into the forechamber of the tent where the Shrine was, paid shaken homage to the Holy, wishing to gather up the threads of all that had been cast him, that drank up reason and made madmen of them all.

But others swarmed about him, a dark and fearsome presence, the blackness of Kel, his own and others', crowding the Shrine and the door out of which Sen must come. It was chaos, and he stifled in it, moved for the door and daylight, to disperse them by his leaving, but a hand caught his arm, familiarity none of them ventured with him.

"Kel'anth," said Hlil.

He resisted, but Hlil was determined. "Kel'ein?" he asked, without moving or looking particularly at any of them. "Kel'an-thein?"

The hand tightened with force. "Aye," Hlil said. "You never give us your face, even when the veil is down. You have your secrets. But what the she'pan has finally said, kel'anth, we have waited to hear, and others have. She has the Seeing, is it not so?"

"That may be so," Niun said hoarsely. "I have sometimes thought so."

"You are kin to her."

"Was."

"*They* are here, other kel'anthein, other tribes; you are kel'anth to us, and we know your manner. You go out of the fingers like sand, Niun: s'Intel; you have no face, even to us, as the wind has none. We have watched you, silent with the strangers when you ought to speak, brooding over that tsi'mri, apart. We understand the she'pan. Perhaps we even understand you . . . but how can they? You are her Hand. And what she gains, you bid fair to cast away."

"That may be," he said, finding breath difficult. He no more looked at them than before. "If that is so, then I deserve blame for it."

"What *is* in you, kel'anth?"

"Let go of me, Hlil."

"Once, reach out your hand and take up this Kel. Or what will they go back and say? That the kel'anth preferred other company?"

He understood the gist of it then, set his face and glared at Hlil. "Ah. My orthodoxy. That I defended kel Duncan. That is at issue."

"Answer."

"I was taught kel-law; we kept it strictly in my House. I cannot read or write and I never knew the Mysteries. Two thousand years bounded all I knew. But my House fell. My Kel died. I have carried the pan'en of the Voyagers in my own hands and crossed in my life all the Darks that ever were. Shall I shed this on you all? One kel'en was with me throughout; one kel'en knows the law that I knew and the songs as my Kel sang them, and saw what I have seen. I am arrogant, yes. I have all the faults you think I have. And you pick a poor time to quarrel with me, Hlil, kel-second."

He would have torn away; Hlil's hand clenched tighter still. "I hear you," Hlil said. "Long since, I have heard you. Now someone else does."

Heat crept to his face, resentment toward Hlil, toward witnesses of this humiliation. Then he thought: *before my own Kel it would not shame me to say.* And secondly: *my own Kel.* This was. *They* were.

"Forgive me," he said. He let the restraint from his face, even to Rhian of the hao'nath, and the others, and it was worse to him than stripping naked. "Forgive me for offense." He recited apology docilely, like a child . . . knew that there would be murmuring when they were out of hearing. That too was just. He pressed

Hlil's shoulder, felt the hand drop from his arm, turned from that quieted company to the outside, his eyes nictitating from the sudden sunlight. They cleared, and he saw the gathering by the tent of the Kel, the whole mass of them there, shoulder to shoulder.

His heart constricted.

"Duncan," he breathed aloud, and hastened, strode across the sand with strides which left the others who had followed him, met the mass of kel'ein about the tent and parted them, his and theirs, thrust his way ungently through their midst, foreseeing everything in shambles, bloodfeud, all ties unraveled.

And stopped, seeing most seated about the center, the whole mingled Kel, and Duncan in the midst of all, sitting with Ras against his dus's broad shoulder and talking peaceably to all of them.

He shut his eyes an instant and caught what the beast held, that was the essence of Duncan, a quiet thing, and strong, with the stubbornness of the dusei themselves.

And love, and profound desire for those about him.

Duncan felt his presence and looked up, rose anxiously and stood there staring at him, casting question, question, question like the beating of a panicked heart.

Niun came to him, kel'ein moving aside to give place to him and the kel'ein who came after him.

"Sov-kela," Niun said, catching him by the arm and drawing him aside from those centermost. "I was worried for you and I find you entertaining the whole Kel."

"Is it all right?" Duncan asked him. "Did it go all right?"

The question stopped him cold. What Duncan asked and what they had arrived at in Council were two different matters. The dus came between, forcing its way. Niun recoiled in his thoughts, blank to it, quickly enough, he hoped. Then the second dus made its appearance, unfelt until it came within sight around the tent corner. And all about them were listening. He set his hand on Duncan's shoulder. "Get in out of the wind, sov-kela."

Duncan went, unquestioning. Niun looked about at the others, the faces that expected answer of him, wondering the same things. "Ask of your own," he said. "We move in the morning. It would be presumption of me to wish that you will all be with us. But I do. And for my own Kel . . . give me a very little time—I ask this."

There was a murmuring. He walked through them, and into the tent, and no one followed, only the dusei. There was no one inside, but only Duncan, in the dim light of the wind vents overhead.

"I should not have asked you in public," Duncan said.

"Do not fret for it. It was all right."

"I know," said Duncan in that same faint voice, "that something is wrong. Something went wrong. But not with them and you. Am I mistaken?"

O gods, Niun thought *how much did you feel?* The dusei were there; Duncan had a talent with them . . . let them have too much, received back more than mri had ever gotten. *His nature,* he thought, *that he reserves nothing.*

"Where is your service?" he asked of Duncan.

"With the she'pan."

"And if we fight?"

"You cannot fight!" Duncan lowered his voice in mid-breath at Niun's warning, made a gesture of helpless appeal. "You know the odds; you know, if they do not. You have no hope at all. Do you want another Kesrith?"

"If we fight—are you mri?"

"Yes," Duncan said after a moment.

"You could not be mistaken."

"No."

Niun opened his arms, embraced him, set him back at arm's-length, staring into his anguished eyes. "Sov-kela—if you are wrong, we will break your heart."

"What did they decide?"

"It was always decided. A mri way. Do you hear me? The she'pan has already determined what way she will lead; and perhaps she will use what you have given her . . . but not—not as you gave it."

"I hear you." The dusei crowded near, moaning, shied off again. Duncan caught a breath and made a gesture as he would when he was without a word, let the breath go and the gesture fall, helpless. His dus came to him and he caressed its thick neck as if that were the most absorbing task in the world. "You choose your own way," he said finally. "If I have interfered, it was because I hoped there was a way the mri could survive and keep their own way. If I was wrong, it was tsi'mri taint, perhaps, a fondness for survival."

"No. You do not understand. I am not asking whether you can *die* with us. I am talking about the she'pan's order. Your honor . . . is it mri?"

Duncan stared at him, his face stark in the dim light, and for a moment frightened. The fear passed. "I warned them. I told them."

"If they are as you once were . . . can they have believed a plain warning?"

"Some likely not. But I gave it, all the same."

There was a stirring next the walls, the soft murmur of voices, diminishing; the stranger-kel'ein were departing the patchwork tent. Niun walked to the outside doorway, looked on the ja'anom who waited, solemn and quiet, Hlil foremost among them. He beckoned, and they came, settling into council in absolute quiet. Duncan would have sought last rank, but Niun signed to him and cleared a place near him, not by rank, but in a place where those concerned in council business might be set out of their order.

"Is there any matter," he asked, "that passed out there . . . that was not resolved?"

No one spoke. But after a moment there was a stir from the second rank, and heads turned as Ras stood up. She excused herself through first rank and came to center, and in disquiet Niun stood up, and Duncan. Ras came to Duncan and embraced him, and after that to Niun, as one would with an unscarred on his first day in Kel. "I swore to be first," she said.

Others came, Peras and Dseai and Hlil and Merin; Dias and Seras and all of them from first rank to last, first Duncan and then himself, in strange and quiet courtesy; to the first he was numb, and toward the last, beginning to comprehend it not as irony, but as something given from the heart. They all settled in their places, even Duncan, and the dusei by him; and he was left staring at them with heat risen to his face and a dazed lack of grace.

After a moment he sat down, hands in lap, stared at them for some moments more before he could recover his wits or reason the tautness from his throat.

"The matter before council," he managed finally in a voice which sounded distant in his own ears. "You asked to know it."

Chapter Fifteen

No life existed here either. Boaz stared at the city from wind-sore eyes—the damaged streets, the sand-choked alleys, and hope began to ebb. Her heart pounded in her ears with the steady strain; joints ached as from long fever, and popped with sharp little pains when the sand made the going hard. The boys wanted to carry the necessary pack; she refused that stubbornly, for they had their own. Her breath rasped in her throat and came too short through the hissing mask: if she could have shed anything, irrationally, it would be that rattling tank at her shoulder, and the mask that seemed more restraint on breathing than aid, but it was life. She turned the valve from time to time, shot a little oxygen in; it made her light-headed and her throat hurt. She blamed that and not the air and the cold.

There were at least no dead; they were spared that, at least. There was no sign that mri had visited here since the seas fled. But there had been fire from this place: regul and human fire had pinpointed to areas which had fired, finding their targets by that means. Something was alive here, but not—she began to be sure—not flesh and blood. Not the mri they had needed to find.

Galey stopped ahead of her, slung his pack off and sat down on a fallen stone, arms slack between his knees; rest stop: Boaz was glad of it, and sat down, Kadarin next to her. There were three; by Galey's decision, since Lane's death—they sat themselves on strict schedule, and left Shibo with the ship, to monitor com . . . and, Boaz suspected, to get word back if they met trouble. They were out of room for recklessness. Shibo was the other pilot . . . capable of leaving them. Had those orders in certain contingencies, she suspected. Galey had not said. It was, perhaps, salve for a soldier's conscience—that truth might get back if they did not.

"Got to be close to the central square," Galey said. "Or my direction's off."

She nodded. Galey and Kadarin looked terrible, faces lined with Kutath's cruel dryness, red-marked with the masks . . . cracked lips, eyes red like sick animals'. Nails broken to the quick and skin at joints galled and cracked and crusted. Mri robes made sense, she reckoned: no way she could have persuaded the military, but mri who wore loose robes and exposed scarcely their eyes to this torment . . . had more sense than they. She would have given much for the thickness of those coarse robes between her and the wind, which buried their feet in sand even while they sat. She thought of Duncan, who had walked this land on mri terms . . . and come in strangely more whole than they: recalled the face, gaunt and changed, and narrow-eyed, smooth, as if humankind were burned out of it, and wrung out with the moisture; and placid, as if expressions were waste.

There had been a touch of the mri. Here—save for the edunei—things did not agree together. She looked about her, at stones, which had a touch of lavenders amid the apricot dust of afternoon . . . at streets and buildings. What it might have been in its prime, this great city . . . her expert eye filled in, missing angles, shaping with the remembered fragments of the saffron-hued city of so many dead: alien arches, bizarre geometries, delicate symmetry of threes.

Threes, she thought, a preponderance of triangles. Three castes. The silhouette of the edunei. The three-way intersection of streets. Buildings of slanting walls and ground-plans which made sensible geometry if the wings were divided triangularly. She shivered, recognizing an underlying geometry of alien perceptions, another thing than underlay the dualities that underlay human architecture, human relationships, human sex, either-or, up and down, black and white, duality of alternatives. The minds which built this had thought otherwise, had seen differently.

Never the right questions, she thought with a tightness at her stomach.

In any situation . . . were there *three* alternatives?

And the great edunei: always the edunei, where mri had lived in human/regul space . . . never such streets, such buildings, asprawl in triangular multiplications. Mri had used the edunei: huge ones, by report, far greater than Kesrith . . . and those were dimmest echoes of the edun of the saffron city: mud-walled echoes. Residences, presumably here as there.

And what were these outer buildings, this disorderly sprawl centering about the edun?

The triangularity was the same. The flavor was not. The logic was not. The life within the self-contained edunei . . . and in this sprawl . . . could not be the same.

"Not mri," she said aloud. "The makers of this . . . were not mri." And when Galey and Kadarin gazed at her as if she had lost her reason: "It's not the ruins we need. Duncan was right all the way in the other city; and in this one . . . no dead. Deserted, as he said. I advise we get back to that shuttle. Out in the land. There are the ship's lights . . . by night they'd be quite visible."

"Boz," Galey said, "what are you talking about, not mri?"

"Didn't Duncan tell us the truth once? And again . . . here: these cities are not where we find the mri. What *is* mri is in those machines, and we can't get at it; and what's out here in these streets is of no use to us. These buildings—are no use. We're already taking one chance, staying out here. Take a further. Go all the way. Find the mri; there may be something here we can't afford to find, whoever made the outer city. A logic we can't deal with. A language we know nothing of."

Galey stared at her, and cast a glance about the buildings, his masked face contracting in a grimace of distress. Perhaps even to his eyes things fell into new order; he had that kind of look, that of a man seeing something he had not.

"What are we into?" he asked. "Boz, are you sure?"

"I'm sure of nothing. But I suggest we take our chances on the known quantity. That if we go looking long enough . . . we might turn up something that doesn't follow the rules we know, even what little we know. And what do we do then?"

"What do we do with the mri?"

"We get a contact. We try the names we know. We get back into the range of Duncan's mri and we turn on the lights."

Galey's eyes slid aside to Kadarin, back again. "That totally breaks with the orders I have."

"I know that."

"We rest here the night; we'll go back tomorrow morning, if that's what we're going to do."

"Now." She shivered with the thought. "My old bones don't like the thought of a night walk; but how much time can we have? If we delay here, then we're giving up time; and if it comes to waiting—on the mri . . . then time is the only thing we have to use, isn't it?"

Galey sat still a long moment, staring at nothing in particular. Finally he looked at Kadarin. "You have a word in this."

"What works," Kadarin said. "What works and gets us home with it done."

"It's on my head," Galey said. "Say that I ordered you, all the way."

"Kel'anth," Dias whispered. "Watch says they are coming."

Niun sprang up from morning meal and excused himself through the Kel which scattered for their weapons. He walked along beside kel Dias, out into the dark before dawn and a stiff wind out of the south; his kel-sword he had with him, and his dus determined to follow, inanimate and living accouterments. He tucked his veil into place and felt somewhere not far from him the other dus, and Duncan, heard running steps this way and that through the camp, messengers dispatched to the other tents, to advise them of outsider approach. Hlil came up beside him, matched his pace. Ahead of him the watch stirred out, from the seeming of a rock on the crest of the eastward dune, a robed kel'en unfolding to stand and point mutely toward the east, to the dim showing of dunes in the starlight.

The Kel spread out along the crest facing that darkness, where the hint of shadow moved far, far off. Niun found himself, as he ought to be, the center of the line, with Hlil at his right hand and the dus at his left. Duncan was not far from him . . . he and his dus had no right to stand so near center; he turned his head to see, and found him by Ras, in second-rank, orderly and with second-rank distributed evenly as they ought, accepting of that presence . . . second-rank's business, he reckoned, disturbed—turned his face again to the dark and waited, the dus which touched him beginning a vibrating song, incongruous here, this overconfidence. It sang against him, such that only those nearest might hear at all, so deeply that it shuddered into bone and flesh, numbing, soothing. For a moment there was awareness of the mate a few paces behind; of Duncan, anxious; and Ras, a bleeding shadow; of Melein awake in another tent and an exultation so fierce it pulsed in the ears; of sen'ein calm, kath'ein love, the sleeping peace of children . . . camps and kel'ein scattered around about them, far across the dunes. Farther still, dus-sense, contact with others . . .

He shuddered suddenly, disrupted the gnosis, pulled out of it from deeper than he had ever fallen within it. Duncan's manner with them . . . no restraint. No barriers. The song reached to others, to sweep them in also. "Yai!" he said. It stopped, and the dus threw its head, brushing against him. There *were* others out there, beyond the dark and the shadow which had taken on distinction on the opposing crest, that flowed down it, weapons and Honors aglitter in the starlight.

Hao'nath: that was apparent by the direction of them; and by the way they came, their intent was plain, for warriors walked long-striding, with hands loose, at random intervals and not by order.

"Ai," someone murmured nearby, the whole Kel relaxing; a current of joy ran through the dusei like a strong wind.

Other masses appeared on the horizon, signaled by the first breaking of daylight, the appointed time. One in the east, one southeast, and north . . . perhaps.

The hao'nath were coming upslope now, hastening somewhat in the nearness of the camp. Rhian s'Tafa led them, center to center, and Niun came out to meet him, unveiled as Rhian unveiled, embraced the older kel'anth gladly. The Kels mingled, kel'ein who had come to know each others' faces, finding each other again with a relief strangely like a homecoming, for veils were down and hands outstretched.

There was for the moment lack of order; and in such chaos Niun turned, looked for Duncan, who had likewise unveiled, conspicuous among the others as the dus by him. He turned and looked back down the slope, and saw others coming as the hao'-nath had come, easily and without hostility, the second and the third tribes, with the fourth now a shadow against the coming dawn.

"They are coming too," he said to Hlil, overjoyed, and at a sudden and cold impulse from the dus by him he turned again, toward Duncan, abruptly as if a hand had caught his shoulder.

Rhian had paused there, only looking at Duncan and Duncan at him, and Niun cuffed at the dus to stop that unease from building . . . but Rhian turned his back to walk away.

"I am not sick," Duncan said, audible to all about them. "Sir."

Rhian turned again, and Niun's heart lurched, for all he approved that answer, for all he had some faith in the hao'nath himself. Rhian tilted his head, looked Duncan up and down, and the beast by him as well.

"You are unscarred," Rhian said, which settled any matter of challenge between them, but not of right and wrong.

"My inexperience loosed my fear; and fear loosed the beast," Duncan said. "My profound apology, sir."

Again there was long silence, for a kel'anth's pride was at stake. "You ran well," Rhian said, "kel'en." And he turned his back again, the while a murmur came about him . . . *ai-ai-ai,* that was relief and deprecation at once, Kutathi applause, as for a good joke in kel-tent, as to say it had not been so serious. Rhian shrugged and smiled grimly, touched one of his own folk and touched the hand of a kel'e'en—truemate, she might be.

Duncan stared after him soberly, as if he well knew what a chill wind had brushed him.

And suddenly the ja'ari were among them, with Tian s'Edri at their head; they had met with Kalis of the ka'anomin of Zohain and her band and theirs had joined in the madness of companionship on the way, poured among them like a black wind out of the dawn, glad to find the hao'nath ahead of them. Niun and Hlil and Rhian met the two kel'anthein, and stood atop the crest to watch the arrival of yet another group who came as the others, in haste and gladly.

"Mari," said kel Tian, who had come in nearest them. And soon another black mass had joined them, and Elan of the mari was among them, to embrace and be embraced.

"Last but the patha," Tian said, but the excitement now quickly faded, and Niun gazed out toward the lightening horizon with increasing unease. There was no sign of the fifth tribe. Quiet began to settle over the mingled Kel, until all eyes were on that vacant expanse of sand and sky.

Eventually there was total quiet, and where had been confusion, the line began to expand itself along the crest, the mood gone grim.

Light came full enough for colors, an amber and apricot dawn which flung hills into relief. "Perhaps," said Elan, "they hope for us to walk to them." And there was a murmuring at that from Tian and Rhian.

Then there was something, a darkness moving, a shadow. A few pointed, but no one spoke after that, not the long while it took for folk to walk so far, not during the intervals in which the comers were out of sight in the rolls of the land.

They vanished a last time, and reappeared on the crest facing, a huge number, nigh five hundred kel'ein, and hastening down the slope in friendly disorder.

Breaths and laughter burst from the Kel at once. "Ai, the patha cannot tell the hour," a ja'ari exclaimed, and a current of soft laughter ran the line, so that Niun himself laughed for relief and others did. It was the sort of tag that might live in a Kel for decades, the kind of gibe that a man might spend effort living down. The patha came up the slope out of breath, and met that tag to their faces, but it was not only Kedras of the patha but a second kel'anth, a young kel'en and few in Honors.

"I am Mada s'Kafai Sek-Mada," the kel'anth proclaimed himself. "Of the path'andim eastward, second sept of the patha, and here by the summons of the patha to the summoning of the she'-pan'anth. Where is the kel'anth Niun s'Intel?"

"They are late," Niun said to the others, "but they multiply." Laughter broke out, in which the patha themselves could join, and Niun embraced Mada after Kedras, looked about him in the dawning at the sight of more than fifteen hundred kel'ein, a number more than he had ever seen of his own kind in all his life, more than most kel'anthein he had heard of had ever had about them, save the very greatest and most desperate struggles. The weight of it settled on him like a weight of years.

"Come," he bade them all, "into camp."

He walked through the line, which folded itself inward and spilled after him among the tents, where the kel-ein left in camp joined them, where kath'ein and children came out to stare wide-eyed at such a sight, and sen'ein bowed greeting.

Melein waited in the dawning, veilless and with her eyes shining. "My ja'anom," she hailed them, "and my borrowed children." She held out hands, and Niun came and kissed her, received her kiss in turn; and after him the other kel'anthein, the six, each a kiss; and then all, all the others for at least a touch upon the hand, a brushing contact. "She is so young," murmured a path'andim, in Niun's hearing, and then realized who heard and bowed his head and made quick withdrawal.

"Strike camp!" Melein called aloud, and kath'ein, both women and children moved to obey. "Lend hand to them!" Niun bade the ja'anom Kel, and other kel'anthein called out the same, to the confounding of the Kath and the order of things. Baggage was hastened out, tents billowed down to be sectioned and the poles laid separate. The Holy was carried out among the sen'ein, shrouded in veils; and silence went where it passed, to that place which should be Sen's on the march. Children ran this way and that, awed by strangers, darting nervously among them on their errands for Kath.

And Duncan labored with them, beside Taz and other unscarred, until Niun passed by them and quietly took Duncan by the sleeve.

Duncan came aside with him, the dusei plodding shadow-wise at their heels. "Carry yourself today," Niun bade him. "That is all."

"I cannot walk empty-handed," Duncan said.

"Did you play the Six?"

"Aye," Duncan admitted, with a guilty look.

"So. You are not last-rank. And you walk empty."

The line was forming. They could not, now, walk together; rank separated them; she'pan'anth, Melein named herself, she'pan of she'panei, and he had kel'anthein for companions, on the march and in whatever came.

"What am I?" Duncan asked him.

"Walk with last for now; the pace is easier. Do not press yourself, sov-kela." He touched his shoulder, walked away toward the place he should hold. Duncan did not follow.

*   *   *

"Two of them," Kadarin breathed, and confirmed what Galey feared he saw: two ships, not one, a double gleaming in the haze and the sun and the desolation.

They were due a rest, overdue it. "Come on," Galey said, slipping an arm about Boaz's stout waist. She was limping, staggering, breathing heavier than was good for anyone. He expected her to object and curse him off, but this time she did not, for whatever help he was, with his height. Kadarin locked an arm about her from the other side and from that moment they made better time, nigh carrying Boaz between, until they were panting as hard as she.

Regul, he kept thinking, recalling another nightmare in the Kesrithi highlands, a ship unguarded, regul swarming about it.

Shibo. Alone there. Alone with whatever had landed next him. They were all vulnerable . . . no retreat but the desert, no help but the sidearms he and Kadarin had, against an armed shuttlecraft.

He grimaced and strained his eyes to resolve the outlines, hoped, by what he saw, and kept quiet.

"Think that's one of ours," Kadarin gasped after a moment.

He kept moving, with Boaz struggling between them, breaths rasping in sometime unison, hers and theirs. His eyes began to confirm it, the other ship a copy of their own. He had a cold knot at his gut all the same. It was trouble; it could not be otherwise.

Recall: that was likeliest, a decision to pull the mission out.

Or disaster elsewhere. . . .

The possibilities sorted and re-sorted themselves in agonizing lack of variety. He had a man dead, neglected in his report; he had lost credibility by that. He had no success to claim, nothing, save Boaz's eloquence: and against distant orders . . . there was no appeal.

He tightened his arm about her, trying whether she needed to stop, whether they were hurting her. "Stop?" he asked her.

She shook her head and kept walking.

No hatch opened in advance of their coming . . . ought not: they wasted no comfort to the winds. They limped up to a blind and closed wall. No need at the last to hail them—machinery engaged, and the ramp and lock welcomed them, too small to afford them access all at once. Kadarin climbed up, Boaz next, himself last.

Two men were waiting for them. Shibo. Another, black against
the light from the port. Galey pulled the breather-mask down,
sought to guide Boaz to a cushion, but she was not willing to sit.
She stood, braced against a cushion in the dark, seat-jammed
space.

"Harris, sir," the other said. "Orders from upstairs."

Gene Harris. Galey gathered himself a breath and sank down
into the co-pilot's cushion, tried to adjust his eyes to the daylight
as Harris slipped a paper into his hand. Kadarin leaned past,
switched on an overhead light. He rubbed his eyes and tried to
focus on it, past a throbbing head and hands that wanted to shake,
blurring the letters.

Mission codes and authorizations. Koch's office.

*Cooperative rapprochments with allies are underway at highest
levels. Agreements have been reached regarding a mutually acceptable solution to the future threat of mri retaliations . . .* There
was more.

"What are they wanting?" Boaz interrupted his reading.

"We're ordered to destroy the machines."

"The computers?"

He spread the paper on his knee, read aloud. " '. . . ordered to
use successful techniques of access to effect demolition of high
tech installations and power sources, beyond any remote possibility of repair. Allies have—applauded—this operation and will
make on-site inspections at the termination of your phase of operations. Request utmost dispatch in execution of this order. Probe
Flower will remain onworld outside estimated limit of fire of city
sites. Orbiting craft will not be in position to receive or relay messages. Exercise extreme caution in this operation regarding safety
of crew and equipment. Your knowledge is unique and valuable.
Luiz will be your contact during this operation should mission-
abort prove necessary. Re-stress extreme priority this mission,
crucial to entire operation. Urge extreme caution regarding—possible allied operations onworld out of contact with allied high
command. Do not provoke allied observers. Use personal discretion regarding sequence of operations and necessary evasions in
event weapons are triggered. Shuttle two and crew under your
command. Transport civilian aide to ground command if feasible,
your discretion.' "

There was a harsh oath from Boaz.

Galey folded the paper, slid it into the clip by the seat, sat still a moment. "How many with you?" he asked Harris.

"Magee and North; we opted Bright out to get cargo in."

"Demolitions?"

Harris nodded. "Enough, at least to start."

Galey ventured a look toward Boaz, toward a face gone old, red-marked with the breather-mask, her gray-blonde braids wind-shredded. Agony was in her eyes. Kadarin rested a hand on her shoulder, his own face saying nothing.

"We lost Mike Lane," Galey said. "A mistake with those machines. They have defenses."

There was silence. He ran a hand through his knotted hair, haunted still by Boaz's eyes. His heart labored like something trapped.

"They're going to take everything we've done," she said, "and use that to destroy the sites. To wipe out their past and their power sources. They take *that* on themselves."

No one spoke. A muscle in Boaz's cheek jerked convulsively.

"And mri aren't the only ones involved. You don't know. You don't know what you've got your hand to."

He shook his head.

"Refuse the order."

He considered it . . . actually considered it. It was madness. Harris's presence—brought sense back. "Can't," he said. "They've got us, you understand. They can blow the world under us if we don't do this. You, all of us, we're expendable in a going operation, in a policy they've got set. It's better than losing them, isn't it? It's better than killing kids."

"To kill their past? Isn't that the other face of it?"

There was an oppression in the narrow cabin, a difficulty in breathing. Boaz's anger filled it, stifled, strangled.

"No choice." He reached out toward Harris, made a weary gesture toward a cushion; his neck ached too much looking up. "Sit down."

Harris did. "We run the doctor back to base?"

Galey lifted a hand before Boaz could spit out the next word. "She's ours," he said. "She goes back only if she wants."

"She doesn't," Boaz said.

"She doesn't." Galey drew a deep breath, wiped at his blurred eyes, looked from one to the other of them. "We penetrate the sites; that's easy; we carry the stuff in on our backs, set it, the margin we know, walk out, get the ship clear . . . nothing easier. Chances are we'll trigger something that will blow us all. I figure if *Saber* says there's no one in position for relays, that means they and the regul are backing off for fear of a holocaust down here. We're in the furnace. *Flower's* safe, maybe; you understand that, Boz: you'd have a better chance on the ship; and maybe there's nothing more you can do out here."

She shook her head.

"Got a message for you," Harris told her, fished it from his pocket, a crumpled envelope.

"Luiz," Boaz said without having to read the name. She opened it, read it, lips taut. " 'My blessing,' " she said in a small voice. "That's all it says." She rubbed at her cheek, wadded the paper and pocketed it. "Who does this profit? Answer me that, Mr. Galey?"

"The mri themselves. They live."

"Excluding that doubtful premise."

"I'm not sure I follow."

"Our command ship is backing off. We've got a regul operation onworld. Whose benefit?"

He sat there with an increasing pulse, adding that up. "I'm sure that's been calculated at higher levels than this one."

"Don't give me 'calculated.' The admiral's been taking advice from Sim Averson and he can't see past his papers."

"Boz—"

She said nothing more. He gnawed at his lip and looked at Harris. "You stay on standby, here. If we go out there afoot, I want to be sure we don't have any regul prying about here."

"How do we stop them?" Harris asked.

"Shoot," he said, reckoning on protest from Boaz; he knew her principles. She said nothing. "You and Boaz stay here; if we get any regul contact, I want her by a com set in a hurry. And you listen to her, Gene. She doesn't carry guns. Doesn't approve. She knows regul. If she calls strike, she'll have reason. You monitor everything that moves; make sure Boz understands the limits of our scan and how long it takes to react. And if she says go, go to kill. Agreed?"

Harris nodded without a qualm evident. "You're going back?"

"Better," he said. He rose up in the narrow confines, rubbed his beard-rough face, wishing at least for the luxury of washing; could not. He took a drink from the dispenser and started gathering supplies from the locker, replenishing what they had used out of the kits. Kadarin did the same, and Harris went with Shibo to gather up the demolitions supplies.

He let them; that gave a little time for rest. When it was all ready he gave Boaz a squeeze of the hand and walked out down the ramp, with Kadarin, and Shibo, and Harris's man Magee. He pulled the breathing mask up and started them moving. He was cold already; his feet were numb, beyond hurting. He could have sent Harris.

Could have.

Duncan was lost. He admitted that now. Lost: dead, or lost, with the mri. There was no hope, no miracle, only this ugly act that was better than other choices.

Their past, Boaz had called it, killing the past. He looked about him; reckoned there was for this barren, dying world . . . little else left.

He shook his head, set his eyes on the city whose name he did not even know, and walked.

Pillars rose, spires of the same hue as the hills against which they stood, such that they might have been made by nature . . . but they were baroque and identical, and there were others round about them in the distance, marching off toward the south; there was beyond that a jewel-gleam, a shining the eyes could not resolve.

Ele'et.

Duncan gazed on it in sometime view beyond the shoulders of kel'ein before him . . . he was lost among them, a head shorter than most, when all his life among humans he had been tall; as for all his thinness now, he was still wider-boned than they, broader of hand, of foot, of shoulder: different, anomaly among them. And mingled with other thoughts was unease, the thought that they faced something more difficult still.

"The People served the elee," he said to Taz, who walked hard by him, with a burden slung to his shoulder. "Do you know what they look like?"

"I have not seen one," Taz said. And after a space more: "They are tsi'mri," which dismissed interest in them.

He said no more then, having enough to do only to walk, with the veils wrapped thickly about nose and mouth, and his joints remembering the pain of the long trek before. He had the dus by him, and through it, sometime sense of Niun, which comforted him.

He was afraid; it came down to that.

Why they were going to this place, what they hoped to have of the race which lived there, which—perhaps had resources uninvolved in the catastrophe, weapons. . . . he had no clear imagination. To fight, Niun had said. He had given them the breath of a chance to do so, that much; had killed the regul: that much.

They rested—had done so several times during the day, for it was Kath's pace which dictated their progress; and this time a ripple of orders went down the line: *make camp.*

Kel'ein muttered surprise, gathered themselves up from the places where they had settled, to aid Kath. Duncan began to, and remembered orders, and sat still, by the dus, his arm across it. Unease would not leave him. Dus-sense, the realization came on him; the beast itself was stirred. They were making camp as if all were well, and the dus-sense had the discomfort of a cliff's edge, a dizziness, a profound sense of strangeness.

Niun would know; would be aware of it. He rose up, ignored in the confusion of assembling canvas and the assembling of the tall poles, wended his way among them, his way blocked by a little child who looked up at him and blinked in shock, scrambled aside from him and the beast at once.

He stared that way, distracted, disturbed, walked past this kel'en and the other in search of Niun, following dus-sense. There were others out there, shadows, following them, following them and him since the ship, all these days of walking, the young of his dus and Niun's, ha-dusei, wild. They sought. They were scattered, the senses on which their own dusei drew, eyes and ears ranging wide of their own.

His.

And they were coming in.

Niun was there, near the site of sen-tent, which was billowing in the pull of the ropes; kel'anthein were about him, and it was not a time for an unscarred to speak to him. *Niun,* he cast through the dus-sense, turned at the dark impulse of another mind.

Ras. He reached out, touched her sleeve, met her veiled face and distracted stare, began to ask her to go to Niun.

Ras. It was Ras. The dus-sense leaped through the touch. He stopped speaking and Ras looked away, following the direction that he himself sensed. "They are coming in," he said. "Kel Ras—they are coming in."

"For days—" she answered hoarsely, "for days it has been there. It will not let be. Since the time I went back from the tribe—it has been there."

The storm feeling grew, acquired other direction, another essence, male. And another.

Another still. Duncan looked, saw dusei on the sandy ridge nearest, coming down toward the camp.

"Gods!" Ras muttered. Her voice trembled; she would have backed away; he felt the tremor in his own muscles.

"It wants," he said. "There is no stopping it."

"I will kill it!"

"It has two brains, two hearts and there is a madness comes on them when they are rebuffed. Believe me, sometimes it touches the kel'en too. *Shon'ai* . . . let go. Let go, Ras. You are in its mind already. You have been."

"Drive it back."

He felt his heart laboring as it would with his own in distress, human pulse and mri and dus dragged into synch. His and Ras's and Niun's; whose else there was no knowing.

"Are you afraid?" he asked of Ras. There was nothing that might sting more.

She walked from him, through anxious, silent kel'ein, for the whole company had gone still and turned eyes toward the beasts. He walked after, heart still pounding, watched from the edge of camp as Ras went out among them, as one of the four made for her, personal nightmare: kill it she could not; it would be a knife against her own flesh.

Not hate: he understood that, which he had sensed already . . . that the signature of Ras was something else again, a stone-steadiness, a stubbornness—devotion. The stranger-dus reared up, towering above her, came down with a puff of dust and a warding-impulse which shivered through his own beast.

Then another thing, that sent dizziness through him, as dus and kel'e'en touched, as she knelt down and put her arms about the dus's neck. Power, dus-mind and mri, a thing dangerous and disciplined. Mri scattered as other dusei came in; children fled for Kath. Other bonds were forged, and he knew as his own dus had touched these minds before. . . . Hlil; the boy Taz, who was a desire so deep it shuddered through the camp; and Rhian, who feared, and stopped fearing.

"Yai!" Duncan exclaimed, dropped to his knees and hugged the beast by him, trying to shut it off, mri minds, and dusei. It would not go, not for long, slow moments. He hung still against the beast, aware finally of it nosing at him, gentle pushes that were not, to a man, gentle. He choked down nausea, free finally, of what still lodged in memory, of knowing too much, and too well, and all the veils being down.

Niun was there, as dazed as he—mri, and stable. Duncan rose to his feet, walked, aching from the convulsion of his muscles, and the dus went beside him. There was a silence everywhere, kel'ein and all the others staring at him, at them, who were also there, who assembled with Niun at center. Rhian was there, a mind he had felt all too long as hunter; Hlil, Ras; and unscarred Taz, dazed and frightened to be dragged into commonality with kel'anthein.

They met, met eyes. Duncan felt his heartbeat even yet tending from his own normal pace, struck at his dus and stopped it. Heat rose to his face, consciousness that he knew strangers as he knew Niun, was known by them.

"I am sorry," Taz murmured, as if it were his fault a dus had chosen him.

"No one answers where dusei are concerned," Niun said. "They choose. They find something alike in us—gods know what."

"They sense the strangers," Duncan said thickly. "They are here—to protect. There is another one still wild, still out here. Why . . . I do not sense. Their own business, it may be."

"We are going into the city," Niun said. "Kath and all but a few hands of sen'ein stay in camp, with a guard. They have taken service."

Duncan looked from him, to the white figure of Melein among the Sen, and beyond, to the pillar-sentinels of the elee.

Attack. He realized that of a sudden.

Alignments made sense suddenly, mri and tsi'mri, to draw the line and set all enemies across it. Mri had no allies.

"Did you not understand?" Niun asked. "We take this place."

The dusei had realized it . . . had come to take sides, as they had chosen on Kesrith.

With mri. With several in particular, who had something in common.

Madness, perhaps; Duncan reckoned so.

Chapter Sixteen

The ships were indeed retreating. Suth studied the screens, smiled, keyed a signal to his own crew.

Shirug began to move, a slow withdrawal from the world, keeping *Santiago* and *Saber* constantly in scan.

And on screen, bai Degas waited. "We have begun," Suth advised the human bai. "As agreed, we will keep to pattern with each other. And our communications will remain linked to yours, reverend bai Degas."

"I am instantly available in any emergency."

"Favor, bai." Suth gaped a grin; he liked this human, after a fashion. There was a pleasantness about him in sharp contrast to the others, a sense of solidity in his reactions.

And for that reason he was to be feared: not dull, this bai Del Degas-si, not at all dull-witted. He retained things very well for a human.

"I shall turn contact over to a youngling now," Suth said. "Our profound gratitude for this cooperation."

"Favor reverence," the human replied in lisping approximation of that courtesy. Suth grinned dutifully, shut off the contact for his own screen and leaned back in his sled.

Behind him the other sleds moved, entering his field of vision.

Nagn, Tiag, Morkhug.

There was no elation, no exultation. It was not a time for such.

"Keep in close contact with this office," Suth said. "When you sleep, do so in the presence of one of us four being awake. All channels are to be strictly monitored by some one of us."

"This dismantling of mri sites," said Nagn, "is *said* to be progressing. Human information is not always accurate."

"*Lie,* Nagn. The word is *lie.* Humans deceive in false statements as well as actions; but we work with this particular action . . . indeed, we work with it."

Morkhug puffed her nostrils uneasily. "I still dislike it. One threat gone: the mri sites; and I do not see the human advantage in this."

"Unless they lie," Nagn said.

"Impoverished mri," said Tiag, "must take service with someone. Or die, of starvation."

"Question," said Nagn. "Do humans assume they will take service with them?"

Suth hissed. It was insanity, that regul adults sat here contemplating trues and maybe-trues regarding human minds. They learned. They all began to think in mad terms of shifting realities. He gathered a stylus from the board before him, held it between his palms and rolled it. "Observe, mates-of-mine, the flat face of the stylus. Where does it exist? Has it a place as it spins?"

"In fractional instants," Nagn said.

"Analogy," said Suth. "A model for imagination. I have found one. The place faces all directions for an instant, a blur of motion. Human minds are and are not so many faces that they seem ready to move in any direction. They are composite realities. They apparently face all directions simultaneously. This is human motive." He laid the stylus down. "They are facing us and the mri simultaneously."

"But action," said Tiag. "They cannot act in all directions forever."

"They act for themselves. What is of value to them?"

"Survival," said Nagn.

"Knowledge," Suth said. "They *state* that they are destroying the sites."

Nostrils flared and shut in rapid alternation.

"I accept no data from humans," Suth continued, feeling the palpitation of his hearts. "Mates-of-mine, among *forgetful* species, this is the only sanity. Among species which *imagine,* this is the only alternative. I have set a sane course. I made appropriate motions by human request, to avoid unprofitable developments. Humans state that they are destroying the sites: potentially true. They omit to state that they are gathering knowledge. We know that they are using the elders of *Flower* as additional personnel. They have stated so, and if this is a lie, I do not find motive in it."

"We are letting them destroy armaments we had counted useful to us," Morkhug objected.

"No," said Suth. "We do not do that. Our base . . . will not do that."

"Nothing, sir."

Luiz leaned against the side of the cushion to the right of Brown and shook his head sorrowfully. Brown's eyes stared back at him with a bruised look . . . the man had not left this bridge, not he nor any of the rest of the military crew—had rather bedded down here near controls; the night shift was sleeping on pallets over against the storage lockers, and everyone kept movements quiet for their sakes. They had a full crew, with everyone awake; half on turn and turn about; and the men had given more than duty, monitoring scan, helping science staff with the rapid filing of data, the breakdown of delicate instruments and equipment, frantic storing of whatever might be damaged in a violent lift. There was no panic aboard; fear . . . that was an abiding guest.

They were alone, for the first time truly alone, save for—intermittently, a shuttle closer to Kutath than the big warships dared be; and Galey's mission, down with them.

They hoped, at least. There was no contact with Galey. Harris's mission could find them—if they were following the agreed sequence of sites; and the next thing they could look for was either holocaust or a progress report.

That they would delay to bring Boaz back . . . that, if it rested with her, they would not. Luiz scanned the master chart which plastered the pinup board . . . lingered on second site, where at best reckoning, she was. Eleven major targets. Even the young men had to come in for relief, somewhere in that world-spanning chain of targets; and then she would. He hoped so.

If nothing went wrong before then.

"I don't expect word," Brown murmured, evidently reckoning he was obliged to say something. "Takes a while, to get there, to lay plans, a lot of things, sir. Could be quite a while."

It was, he reckoned, a kindly attempt at comfort; he felt none.

* * *

Beyond the pillars of carved stone, the city Ele'et sat, a fantastical combination of glass and stone, aglow in the fading light. Kel'ein murmured with wonder; and Niun gazed on it thinking on his youth, on evenings spent in the hills above a regul city, looking on lights in the twilight, and dreaming dreams of ships and voyages and war, and Honors to win.

He looked on Melein, who walked among the Sen who had come with them, for all his wishing otherwise. She had no words, none, but she had simply set out with them, and what *she* would, she did. The Holy reposed in safety; she and her sen'ein, fifteen including Sathas himself, walked in the blackness of more than a thousand kel'ein, and said nothing of how they should take this place.

He had not far to reach for companions: they were near as the dusei, moving here and there throughout the column; he summoned, and they came, those not by him already, even to Taz, who was devastated by his fortunes. "Stay close," he bade them all, and at Duncan especially he looked. "You have the other gun, sov-kela; and I would you stay nearer the she'pan. These are tsi'mri."

"Aye," Duncan murmured. The incongruity did not draw a flicker from him. They were two, Niun thought, who had known the old war, on different sides as they were; who knew the Kesrithi law—distance-weapons for those who would use them: the mercenary Kel had lost its compunction in such matters.

"They must know we are here," said Hlil.

"Doubtless," Niun said.

Nearness made the rocks of the hills take on strange form in the sunset, twisted shapes, joined by aisles of stone and glass; shapes shaped by hands, he realized of a sudden, the whole face of the hills hewn into abstract geometries, as the pillars had been hewn, with glass facing the intervals: hills, whole domes of rock the size of edunei . . . carved in elaborations the north side of which the sand-laden winds had eroded, and the size—the size of it . . . only a tenth part was alight.

"Gods," he murmured, for suddenly their number seemed very small, and the sky leaden and full of enemies.

Ward-impulse prickled in the air; something started in the sand before them, and another. Soon a whole cloud of burrowers fled in distress, and the sands rippled beyond that. It was as if the very sands hereabouts lived, writhing like the mutilated stones.

Water. Outspill from the city.

And dus-sense grew more and more disturbed. "Do not loose it," he bade those about him. "You understand me. The beasts are not to be loosed."

There was murmured agreement.

"Nor the Kel," said Melein, startling them. "Take me this city. Do not destroy it. Do not kill until you must."

"Go to the center," he wished Melein. "You must have care."

To his amazement she did so, without demur. He drew breath, surveyed the place before them, which balked them with a maze of walls and no streets, nothing of accesses, nothing of pattern.

He led them straight on as the wind would blow, with contempt for their barriers and their building and the logic of their structures. He led them to a great face of glass, which showed within a hallway, and carven stones, and great carven boulders rising out of the very floor, prisoned and changed in this tsi'mri place.

He drew his gun, unfired in years, and with wide contempt, burned an access. That fell ponderously, that shattered with a crash that woke the echoes and scattered glass among the carven stones. Warmth came out at them, and moisture-bearing air.

They walked within, glass ground under their boots, the dusei snorting at the prick of slivers which let blood. His own let out a hunting moan that echoed eerily through the vast halls, and found direction, guiding them all. He kept his gun in hand, and with a wave of his arm sent a flood of kel'ein the width of the hall, to find out all sides, all recesses of the carved monuments. They were beyond the glass now, and the floor echoed to their tread, itself patterned in mad designs.

And figures stood at the end of the hall, glittering with color, gods, the colors! As one they stopped, staring at hues of green and deep blue and bright colors which had no name, none that he knew—the robes of mri-like folk who had no color, paler even than Duncan's pallor, whose manes were white and long and shamelessly naked, the whole of their whiteness bejeweled and patterned.

He had walked alone into a regul city, which shared nothing at all with mri. He had the face for this, and walked ahead, with the dus beside him and comrades about him, wondering what they would do, whether challenge, whether panic and bring forth weapons.

They ran.

Weapons ripped from sheaths with one thousand-voiced rasp of steel. "No!" he said. "But keep your weapons in hand."

He kept walking, calmly enough. They passed one archway and entered another, and into a tangle of carved stone that mimicked pipe roots, or some mad dream. Screaming began, wails, the fall of a city which had not yet struck a blow.

The steps of the great edun lay ahead, brown-hued in a lavender city, simplicity amid the maze. Galey drew in an insufficient breath through the trickle-flow of the breather, made the climb ahead of the others . . . staggering from weariness, but made it, into this sanctuary from the winds.

They brought their own lights and used them, not touching any that the place itself might have, for fear of alerting the guard systems, such as there might be. Galey looked about him at writing on the walls, at the wholeness of what the other edun had been, at a place untouched in the disaster.

"Appreciate what you're seeing," he said hoarsely, distorted in the mask. "This is a holy place to them; it's their history and their home; it's their Earth and these are its shrines. And we kill them. Remember that."

The faces of Harris's two men stared back at him, masked and demonic in the lamps' glow, eyes betraying shock. Only Kadarin . . . Kadarin, who had been with Boaz . . . he understood.

"No one ought to kill something," he said, "and not know it." He pressed the mask tighter against his face, sucked air and turned away toward the access of the machine hall . . . what must be so if the edunei were as identical as Boaz said, leading toward the tower.

And in the core of that tower must be the power accesses; structurally, it was the only place to expect them. A slender stem, which might be severed; but well-sheathed. Such a tower had stood in the other edun though all else had suffered severe damage.

"Got to get at the core in there," he said, laying a hand on the wall. "Simple job, I figure. We have a power source to worry about, maybe a lot of them. But the brain's up there, and this is the spinal cord. Isn't any coordination available without that. We blow these, and we can send cleanup teams out later, to do the job on anything left; without these, there's no danger to orbiting ships, so we reckon. You hunt those other towers. I don't think you'll find much; but we make—"

Something scuttled across the floor, a dart of silver; North ripped out a gun and Galey seized his arm, his eyes making the object clear in the next instant as mechanical, a silver dome. It wandered aimlessly, came toward them, passed blindly as they stepped aside, sucking up dust.

"Maintenance," Kadarin said in a shaken voice.

"Move out," Galey said. "Don't touch any switches and don't fire at anything. Alert this thing and we'll all be sorry."

They parted in the directions he indicated to them, moving quickly, a rippling of lights and shadows. Dark then, as they probed the towers one by one, steps echoing high up in the building, descending again, all but the machine tower, where they assembled finally.

"Nothing," Kadarin said. "Just service machinery." The others agreed.

"Then set the charges at the stem of the second tower, at every level, and assume it's shielded. —Kadarin. Come with me."

Kadarin hastened after him, quietly, up into the spiral of the machine tower. They moved with caution, the light casting into reality only a portion of the spiral at a time and darkness following as swiftly after.

It opened upon a room eerily like the other place, the same grill-worked window, identical as if one mind, one architect had conceived it. But this one was whole, lacking the crack, as if some all powerful hand had healed it.

They walked with soft steps to the room beyond, found what had been in the other place. Galey cut off his light and motioned Kadarin to do the same, not wishing to provide any photosensitive alarm among the banks of machinery with a fatal stimulus.

"Could be a high-threshold audio alarm," he whispered. "Lane set it off when he crossed that circle there on the floor. Avoid it.

We set charges on every bank and make the least sound possible. Then we get out of here. A quarter-hour trigger. Right?"

"Sits right over the core," said Kadarin. "Core's right under this first unit here."

"Likely."

Galey moved in, set that charge himself, trod carefully down the aisles, Kadarin a gliding shadow as fast-moving as he.

They tripped a maintenance robot. It shot out of an aisle, a red telltale glowing on its side, jerked about, stopped, moved off on its own business.

And in feverish haste Galey fixed the last charge, walked back to the door, met Kadarin there. "Go!" he hissed.

They still walked, quietly, across the hall outside, entered the spiral descent, and ran it, met the others below.

"Done, sir," he heard. He motioned them to move, and they crossed the foyer at a dead run, ran down the steps outside, were still running as they crossed the courtyard and took shelter in an alley among the lavender buildings, leaning there, their breathing harsh and hollow in the breathers, interspersed with hissing jets of oxygen.

It should not blow with great violence. The mind should go, the automations fail, whatever regulation the power sources needed likewise go. Quiet oblivion, likely noncontaminating power which would simply stop.

Suddenly it happened; the building disjointed itself on the left side, a dissolution with fire in the joints; a collapse, a sound which started with a dull clap and became a vibration in the bones. Galey flinched without willing it, every muscle taut, a sickness clutching at his belly as the collapse became an up-welling of dust, and the dust began to swell outward, carried away from them by the wind.

It comes, he thought, expecting at any moment the flare of weaponry to protect the city, that might annihilate the shuttles, annihilate them, wake the world to war.

It did not.

The dust settled, some of it drifting aloft. There was silence. Behind him North swore softly.

"We're alive," Galey muttered, finding that remarkable. They still could not see the place clearly where the edun had stood, only that there was a great deal of dust, and that the tower was completely down.

"No way those machines do anything again," said Kadarin. "We got it, sir, and no one's dead."

His muscles wanted to shake. He gathered himself up, shot a considerable jolt of oxygen into his breather and fought lightheadedness. Another thing dawned on him, as it had during the walk to the site: that they were not alone in this land.

"We just sent up a considerable signal," he said. "We'd better set better time getting back to the shuttles than we set getting here."

There was no argument at that. They had fought mri in the wars; and the tendency of mri to ignore their own casualties was legend. Four men with handguns was no deterrent; they had not Boaz's yellow scarf with them, not on this walk.

And he reckoned that with that thought at his heels he might last to the ships.

Elee clustered among their monuments. Chattering in tremulous voices, tall, pale bodies over-weighted in robes crusted with jewels and embroideries, manes . . . incredible manes, like white silk . . . flowing before the shoulders and halfway down the back, trimmed square or braided, on some making the ears naked, immodesty that sent a rush of heat to a mri face. Niun held up his hand, with more vast corridors before them and more elee scattered here and there about them and beyond; the Kel halted, and the elee nearest clung together in dread.

"You," Niun said, pointing at one tall enough to be male, and at least not Kath: the robes masked bodies and faces were alike, delicate. "You, come and speak."

The white face showed its terror, and hands clung to companions. The elee hesitated, and came with small steps like a frightened child for all his tall stature. It was strange face, mri-like, white even to the lips, and eyes of pale blue, shaded blue around the lids. Paint, Niun decided. It was paint. It livened the eyes, made their expression gentle and vulnerable.

"Go away," the elee said in a faint voice, much-accented.

Niun almost laughed. "Where is your Mother?" he asked, expecting a flare of defiance at least at this question. But the elee slid a glance toward the farther corridor for answer, and at that all the Kel murmured in disgust. "Walk with us," Niun said, and when the elee tensed as if to flee: *"We take no prisoners.* Walk with us."

The elee looked in one moment apt to break with terror, and in the next assumed a smile, made a graceful gesture of his long hands and offered them the way ahead.

Niun looked at his comrades, looked at Melein, who had veiled herself in this place of tsi'mri. "Ask his name," she said.

"Mother-of-mri, it is Illatai."

Weapons moved. Tsi'mri did not speak to her, save in peril of their lives; but she bade them stay, looked at Niun. "Tell this Il-latai he must take us to the she'pan of elee."

Illatai glanced about him, at his folk who stood staring, and there was consternation in his face, the smile threatening to fade. The dusei stirred and moaned.

Tsi'mri, Niun thought, who even after so long, did not know mri. He considered, took the delicate sleeve of Illatai by its edge, and led him; the graceful man went with them, looked from one to the other with smiles for all they were veiled, nor did his eyes miss the beasts, nor the smile change. Niun let him go and let him walk as he would.

It was dream and nightmare, the halls of carven boulders and glass lit from glass structures of jewel colors, which light stained the floor of patterned stone and dyed the white manes and skins of elee and profaned Melein's robes too. There was no word from the Kel, none, for here were tsi'mri, and they were too proud; but elee talked behind their delicate hands and shrank from their presence, hiding themselves behind their monuments and their pillars of living stone and their jewel lamps. Here were columns rising to the ceiling, serpents wrought in gold, which crept up carven rocks and held the ceiling up, or crawled across it, writhing from this side to the other.

And beyond an archway of glass, and moisture-misted doors, a place where plants grew rife, and water flowed on stone walls and broke off glass panes. Plants bloomed, in warmth and mist. Vines hung thick, and fruit ripened, lush and full of moisture. "Gods," someone said in the ja'anom mu'ara. It was on them all, the daz-

zlement of such wealth; *this,* Niun thought, *this was Kutath once,
before the seas fled.*

And more practical things: "Pumps," Duncan muttered very
low. That must be so, that they had sunk deep as the basins to
draw up such plenty.

More glass, panels and screens, prism colors: he remembered
rainbows, which Kesrith had had and Kutath had forgotten. Doors
yielded to the forceless hands of Illatai; his smile persisted, his
moving was neither quick nor slow, but fluid as the water streams.
Beyond the doors more elee clustered, and here gathered to bar
the way, creatures delicate as lizards, whose robes seemed of
greater weight than themselves, more alive than they, figured
with—he realized it now—flowers, and beasts, and serpents.

Beautiful, he could not but think so. Beautiful as humans were
not. He stopped, and the Kel stopped, before the white out-thrust
hands, the frightened eyes which threatened nothing and pleaded
defenselessness.

So also Illatai, who hovered between, as if to beg reason of
either side.

"We shall go through," Melein said. "Say that to them."

"No," said Illatai. "Send. I shall carry messages."

Niun scowled at that, signed at Hlil, and toward one of the delicate lights. Steel flashed, and crystal shards tumbled in ruin. The
elee cried out in dismay, as out of one throat, and ward-impulse
from the dusei began to build like storm.

"We go through," Niun said, and the elee stood still, clustered
still before the doors. Blades were ready. Rhian and Elan were
among the first to advance, and the elee simply shut their eyes.

"Do not," Niun said suddenly. "Move them."

It was not to anyone's taste, to lay hands on men and women
who had chosen suicide. But lesser kel'ein performed that task,
simply moving the elee aside; and as for Illatai, he turned his
beautiful eyes on them all and gestured diffidently toward the
inner hall.

The hall beyond blazed with gold, with colors, with the green
of living things; and one elee there was in silver and gold, and
one in gold and one in silver, amid others in colored robes: a gasp
attended their entry, and elee tried ineffectually to prevent them,

thrusting white hands before edged steel: they bled as red as mri and humans.

"No!" cried an aged voice, and the one in gold and silver held up her hands and forbade her defenders. The gold and the silver stayed close by her, the gold male, the silver young and female, who seated themselves in chairs as the eldest did, whose unity tugged unpleasantly at the senses: chairs, as if they were all of such rank. The bright-robed younger folk clustered behind them.

"Who speaks?" Niun asked.

"She is Mother," said Illatai softly, making a bow and gestures to either side. "Abotai. And mother-second, Hali. And Husband-first, T'hesfila. You speak to them, mri prince."

He looked back in profound disturbance, such that the dusei caught it. An order like their own; and not: a Mother who was not alone, who—he suspected—was not chaste. Melein folded her hands, unperturbed. "Among elee," Melein said as if she spoke in private council, "they have different manners. Abotai: you understand why I have come."

"To take service," the old elee said, and a frown came on her face. "You have thrown the world into chaos, and now you come to take service. Do so. Rid us of this trouble you have brought."

Melein glanced about her, cast a look at the elee, walked to one of the monuments and traced the delicate carving of a stone flower which bloomed out of living stone. "Tell the bearers-of-burdens, kel'anth of the ja'anom, that her existence is very fragile. And that An'ehon is in ruins; likely ruin belts the world, into cities beyond the basins. Tsi'mri have come from outside. And doubtless she knows this. This delicate place . . . stands; it did not link itself to An-ehon in the hour of attack, no. It was apart. Protected."

"Did the elee hear?" Niun asked coldly, though by the flickering of the membrane in the elee's eyes he knew that they were understood.

"Do you not know me?" Melein asked.

"I know you," the elee Abotai said, her old voice quavering with anger.

"And yet you let me in?"

"I had no choice," the elee acknowledged hoarsely. "I beg you, send your war away. It has no place here."

"Eighty thousands of years . . ." Melein murmured. "Eighty thousand years of voyaging . . . and to hear that we should go away. You are of persistent mind, Mother of elee."

"You will ruin us," the mother-second cried.

"Listen," said Abotai, and made a trembling gesture to her companions. "Show them. Show them."

A young elee moved, stirred several others into motion, a glittering of jewels, a nodding of white heads so swiftly moving that Niun clenched his hand on his gun and watched well where hands were. Light and colors flared, an entire jeweled wall parting upon a screen which came alive with images . . . black, and fire . . . dead mri, a tangled field of corpses, an edun in ruins; an edun fell in fire, and figures ran, swarming like corruption over the dead. . . .

—came closer, showing naked human faces.

—changed again, ships over ruins, and Kesrithi landscape.

And a human face dominated the screen, young and familiar to them. The Kel went rigid, and dus-sense lashed out. "No," Duncan said beside him, and Niun set a hand on his shoulder. "No. This is nothing humans have sent."

"Regul," Niun said, loudly enough for Melein, and the possibilities set a great dread into him. Melein's face had lost all humor.

"Open your machines to me," she said.

"No," the elee she'pan said. "Go fight from the dead cities."

"We have not come to go away at your bidding. If we fight, we will begin here."

The old she'pan's lips trembled. After a moment she rose up, and the mother-second and the Husband with her. She made a move of her hand; elee opened farther doors, and Niun gazed in amazement at a machine like and unlike that of An-ehon . . . like, for it had the same form; and unlike, for it was almost lost in ornament, in precious metal embellishments, in glass, in jewels.

"Come," said Melein to the few of the Sen who had come with them; they walked alone into that place, and the she'pan of the elee sought to follow.

"No," said Niun quickly, gestured, and kel'anthein moved at once to sweep their own contingents this way and that about the hall of the she'pan of the elee, setting their own bodies and their weapons, between the elee and the machine that was Ele'et.

"It will kill you," Abotai cried. "Our machine does not speak the hal'ari."

Melein turned, small and white against that metal complexity, walked back within the doorway. "Will it? Then you remind me of something even I had forgotten, Mother-of-elee: that elee know how to lie."

There was silence.

"Let her come," Melein said. "You may all come."

Niun hesitated, made a slight sign to the others, walked with Duncan and Hlil and Ras into that place; with Kalis and Mada and Rhian keeping close guard upon what elee strayed in and others holding the room behind.

Melein stepped within the white area of the floor, bathed at once in light that set her robes agleam; and Niun's heart clenched in him at the meaningless words that came.

"Na mri," she answered it, and again: "Le'a'haen! An-ehon! Zohain! Tho'e'i-shai!" Banks began to light, all but one. "A'on! Ti'a'ma-ka! Kha'o!" More flared into life, and there was an outcry of consternation from the elee present. Melein's voice continued, a roll call which set banks alight from one end to the other of the vast hall . . . the cities, Niun realized with a stirring of the hair at his nape: she was summoning the minds of the cities all about the world, names he had heard her name and names he had not—dead witnesses, the past springing to life about them, the guardians of the World.

And with every bank but two alight, with the thunder of machinery working, Melein spun in a swirl of white robes and pointed the finger at the she'pan Abotai with the blaze of triumph in her eyes.

"*Ai*, tell me now, Mother-of-elee, that I have no claim, tell me now that this place is yours, Mother of wars, Devourer of life! Now take the machine from me, elee!"

The elee stepped forward, stopped, at the edge of the light, her white face and white mane and metal robes agleam with it.

"The machines," Melein continued, her arm outstretched, "hold what I have given them, assume the pattern I built, as it was, as it *was*, elee she'pan. It holds the past of Kutath and the past of my own kindred, not, elee she'pan, not of Kutath; the Mysteries of those-who-went-out are within the net as well, my working; and it speaks the hal'ari, elee she'pan."

"Ele'et!" the elee cried.

"I am here," the machine responded, but it answered in the hal'ari, and the elee seemed shaken by that.

"Duncan," Melein said.

There was silence then, save for the machines. "Sov-kela," Niun murmured, touched Duncan's arm, received a distressed look, to which he nodded, indicating the circle to which he was summoned. "Leave the dus, sov-kela, for its sake."

Duncan entered the circle, and the dus stayed. "I am here," he said.

"This is the shadow-who-sits-at-our-door," the machine answered. "An-ehon remembers."

"Kel Duncan," Melein said. "Are you mine?"

"Yes, she'pan."

"I have need of a ship, kel'en. From here, it would be possible for you to contact humans. Do you think they will come to your request?"

"To take it?"

"That you will do for me too."

There was a moment's silence. There were five of them who felt that pain; and Niun swallowed heavily, trying to remain in contact. Duncan nodded assent; Melein reached to the board nearest and made some adjustment, looked back again.

"You have only to speak," she said. "An-ehon, give kel Duncan access for a transmission."

"He has access."

There was a moment when Duncan stood still, as if paralyzed; dus-sense purged itself, grew clear.

"SurTac Sten Duncan code Phoenix to any human ship, please respond."

He had spoken the human tongue. Niun understood; Melein would; there were no others, and the Kel and the elee shifted nervously. Duncan repeated his message, again and again.

"Flower *here*," a human voice returned. *"Duncan, we copy; what's your location?"*

And another voice, supplanting it, female: *"Duncan, this is Boaz. Where are you?"*

Duncan looked at Melein; she nodded slightly.

"Shuttle one, this is Flower." It was a different voice, older. *"Boz, don't jeopardize your position: keep silence. You may draw fire."*

"Tell them otherwise," Melein said.

"This is Duncan. The cities will not fire, if you do not provoke it. I can give you my location. Boaz, is a shuttle out?"

"We have two. Galey's down here; you know him, Sten. We'll come in if you'll let us. No firing. Where are you?"

"Terms," the voice from Flower cut in. *"What guarantee of safety? Duncan, are you speaking under threat?"*

"Your name is Emil Luiz, sir, and if I were under threat I would not give you a correct answer. —Boz, from the ruins nearest Flower, *southeast to some low hills; you'll see pillars, Boz, and a city within the rocks. Do you know that site?"*

"We can find it. We'll be there, Duncan. Be patient with us."

"Understood, Boz. You'll be safe to land. You only."

"Cease," said Melein.

"Transmission ceased," the machine echoed.

"Aliens," Abotai hissed. "You deal with aliens."

Duncan pulled his veil aside, and there was a void in the dus-sense; a cry went up from the elee, for it was the face of the image. He seemed not to regard it, but looked at Melein. "Is there else," he asked, "she'pan?"

"When they come," she answered.

"Aye," Duncan said, and the void persisted, a gap and a darkness where Duncan had been. A touch fell on Niun's shoulder; it was Hlil. He felt all of them, Ras, Rhian, Taz. Only Duncan was not there, for all that Duncan returned to him, and looked nakedly into his eyes, and stood among them.

"Veil yourself," Niun said, "sov-kela."

Duncan did so, and he and his beast went aside, into the other room, among the others who waited.

They rested . . . must, finally. Galey sucked in great breaths from the mask, bowed over, uninterested in the rations the others passed among them. A drink of water, that he took, and bowed down with his head against his arms. His knees ached and his temples pounded. He rubbed at eyes which ran tears that never stopped.

More such to go: the city of the mri dead . . . that one next, he reckoned.

"Sir," Kadarin said. And when he responded lethargically: *"Sir . . ."*

He looked up, rose, as the others scrambled to their feet. There was a ship coming. He stared at it, blank, and terrified; and there was no place to go, no concealment in the vast flat: it was coming low.

One of their own. He blinked, no less disquieted, heard the same realization on the lips of Magee and Kadarin.

It was coming for them, coming in fast.

"Treachery," Nagn hissed, her color gone white around the nostrils.

Suth sat still, his hearts quite out of phase, stared at the screens on which shuttles and *Santiago* were moving dots, all his calculations amiss.

"Bai," Morkhug pleaded.

Suth faced his sled about. His attendant crouched in the corner, attempting invisibility. Suth considered, regarding his mates who looked to him for decision . . . suddenly keyed in the control center, where a contact to *Saber*-com was maintained continuously.

"Bai Koch," he requested of his own younglings, and slowly calmed his breathing, suppressed the racing heartbeats with reason. The human face suddenly filled his screen: Koch, indeed: Suth knew him by the ruddiness and white, clipped hair.

"Bai Suth?" the human bai asked.

"You are undertaking operations without consultation, bai, contrary to agreement."

"No operations; maneuver. As you have an observer near the world, as you have received transmission, as we have. We are moving more reliable monitoring into position. We confess surprise, bai Suth; we are not yet ready to address policy."

"What action are you taking, bai?"

"Meditating on the matter, bai Suth."

"What is your installation onworld doing?"

A hesitation. "What is yours doing?"

"We are not in contact. They are pursuing previous instruction. Doubtless they will not act beyond those instructions."

"Ours likewise, bai Suth."

Suth sucked air. "Is your intention to accept this offered contact, reverend ally?"

There was a second hesitation. "Yes," Koch said.

Suth's hearts left synch again. "We . . . urge the bai to enter urgent consultations with us."

"Most assuredly. You are welcome aboard."

"We also . . . must contact our onworld mission."

Koch's face remained impassive. There was a slight flaring of his nostrils; what this meant in a human was disputable.

"We advise you," Koch said, "to stay clear of Kutath; we do not mean to have lives endangered. We should take very seriously any approach to Kutath, bai Suth."

"We wish to send a shuttle to your ship."

"I have said that you are welcome."

"I am entering arrangements. Favor, bai Koch, maintain a full flow of data to our offices."

"Agreed."

"Favor."

"Favor," Koch murmured in turn, and faded.

Suth sucked a deep breath, puffed it out with a flutter of his nostrils. "They wish me aboard."

"Bai?" Tiag mourned, visibly disturbed.

"Secure ship," Suth said. And when they delayed in confusion: "Leave onworld to onworld; secure the ship. *Saber* . . . is *here*."

"Enough," said Melek in horror; Magd killed the message which played over and over in the recorder. There was the thump of the pumps in the silence, the furtive scratching of some night-wandering crawler at the plastic dome.

They were alone, they two, senior. They had killed their assistants, a grim matter of economics. They hungered almost constantly in their terror; and Magd looked on Melek with continual fear. It was next, when it came to seniority.

"There is a way out," said Melek.

"I am listening." Magd's belly hurt. It really existed on short rations, pampering Melek, beginning to die slowly in the hope of living longer. Its skin flaked; its joints were whitening. More than anything it desired to please; its thoughts were nightmare, of hunger on the one hand, being refused survival by the elder Suth if it dared leave its post; of slaughter at Melek's hand, merciful and more immediate. It could not think. It wanted life, clung to hope, scrabbled after this one, that Melek itself offered.

"Orders," Melek said, "require we observe and find this youngling Duncan. That we stir up the mri and destroy this youngling if we find it. This is our way out. Listen . . . *listen*, youngest! Will this message have gone out and *Shirug* not know? Is not our time shortened here? They will send us orders; we finish here; we *finish*. Then we can come back; then Eldest will welcome us and make us favorites, feed us of his own cup. Both . . . both of us. If we do this for him. If we finish."

Magd had no inner confidence. Magd's hearts labored and its mouth was dry, its tongue sticking to the membranes, so that water and soi were the only coherent desires. Magd knew the trap: that yielding food to Melek, Magd was no longer strong enough to resist, no longer keen-witted.

"Yes," it said, desperate, paid anxious attention as Melek brought up charts on their screens.

"Here," Melek said, indicating a place near hills. "This is the place. We must be ready; we must work out all the details. You will lead in, youngest."

"Yes," it said again.

It would have agreed to any instruction.

Chapter Seventeen

It was an hour for sleeping. Perhaps some within the elee city did so, but none within the hall of the elee she'pan, nor anywhere about it. Niun sat still, at the feet of Melein, his dus and his companions by him, while certain kel'ein, mostly hao'anth and ja'ari, walked the corridors of the city, wandering by twos and by threes, to observe the things which passed among the elee. None offered them violence. None challenged them, or alarm would have been raised in the halls of Ele'et, and blood would have flowed: it did not; and the most part of the Kel sat quietly in attendance on the she'pan.

"You must call them back," said Abotai of the kel'ein who ranged the city corridors. "They must not—must not harm Ele'et."

"They do not," Melein said softly, and stilled any protest of Sen or Kel with an uplifted and gently lowered hand. "And we go where we will."

"Understand . . ." Abotai's lips trembled, and she held the hand of the Husband who sat beside her. "More than lives . . . these precious things, she'pan of the mri."

"What things?"

Abotai gestured about her, at the hall full of carved stones, flowers in jade, ornate work over every exposed finger's-length of surface, works in glass, statues in the likeness of elee and mri and lost races and beasts long forgotten, whether myth or truth. "Of all Kutath has made, of beauty, of eternal things . . . they are here. Look—look, mri she'pan." Abotai slipped from her ornate robes a pin, passed it to the youth Illatai, who sat in a chair near her. He leaped up to bring it, but Niun gestured abruptly and intercepted

it. It was a translucent green stone, the likeness of a flower even
to veins within the leaves, and a drop of moisture on a petal. He
handled it most carefully, and passed it to Melein.

"It is very beautiful," Melein said, and passed it back at once
the same route it had come. "So are live ones. What is that to
me?"

"It is an elee's life," said Abotai. "A sculptor spent his life to
perfect that flower. Everything you touch . . . even to the stonework under your feet . . . is the life of an elee, a perfection. Ele'et
is a storehouse of all the millions of years of the meaning of Kutath, not alone of elee. *You* are here, wrought in stone, written in
records, as we are."

"You are generous, then. A manner of pan'en, a holy thing. We
shall tread lightly on it, this stonework. But we care nothing for
it."

"It is all here," said Abotai. "All the goodness of the past. All
perfection. Saved."

"For whom?" Melein whispered. "When the sun fades and the
last lake of the last sea is drunk, and the sand is level . . . for
whom, mother of elee?"

"For the Dark," said Abotai. "When the Dark comes . . . and all
the world is gone . . . these things will stand. They will be here.
After us."

"For whom?" Melein said yet again. "When the power fades,
when there is not even a lizard left to crawl upon your beautiful
stones—what is the good?"

"The stones will be here."

"The wind will erode them and the sand will take them."

"Buried, they will survive any wind that blows."

"Will it matter?"

"They will exist."

Niun drew in his breath, and there was a murmuring in the Kel.

"Is that the end," asked Melein, "of all the races and the civilizations, and the dreams of the world, to be able to leave a few
stones buried beneath the sands, to tell the Dark that we were
here? Leave us out of your pan'en, she'pan of elee. We want no
part of it. Consumer of the world's substance, was it this, was it
this for which you ate all the world and let the ships go . . . to
leave a few stones to say that you were here?"

"And what gift do you leave?" Abotai pointed to the kel'en by serpent pillar, at Duncan. "*That,* and the beasts? Aliens, to come ere and see these things, and steal them, or destroy them?"

Duncan had looked up, and for a moment, a brief moment, he as back with them, a touch of pain in the dus-sense.

"He," said Melein in a still voice, "is more to Kutath than you, r your children, or the fine trinkets you have made to amuse the ark. You gave me a flower in stone to touch, and it was the life f an elee. Duncan, kel'en, shadow-at-my-door . . . come here. ome here to me."

No, Niun pleaded with her in his mind, for Duncan had borne nough, had more yet to bear; but Duncan rose up and came, and at down again at Melein's feet, his dus settling disconsolately gainst him. Melein set her hand on his shoulder, kept it there, hile Duncan lowered his head. "He is not for your touching," Melein said. "But he is *our* gathering, elee she'pan, and far more recious than your stone flower."

"Abomination!"

"There are builders and there are movers, mother of elee; and n the great Dark—the builders have only their stones." She ouched Duncan's shoulder, rested her hand there. "We went out, o find a way for all to follow. The great slow ships in which gen-rations were born and died . . . took Kutath as far as our genera-ons could reach; there was no hope, so few the ships, so many ose left behind, on a world with no means left for ships—your oing, elee. But the ships of humans, that leap the Darks so linding-swift—one such, only one: and perhaps eyes will live at will *see* these pretty stones of yours. And desire them. And catter them, perhaps, that all the universe will wonder at the ands that made them."

"No," Abotai hissed.

"Then close your eyes, mother of elee. You are bound to see ings you will not like at all. We do not serve to your service any ore. And first, a ship, ai, kel'en-my-brother's-brother?"

Duncan looked up. The edge of his veil was damp and his eyes lmed. "Aye," he said.

She bent and kissed his brow. "Our Duncan," she murmured, nd whispered: "If lives of humans come into our hands, take or

give: I pass them to you. I do not ask more of you than the Peopl
need. And you will not do less."

"She'pan," he replied.

Time passed, that the elee murmured together in the edges c
the hall, that elee brought food and drink, and offered to them; bu
they were not guests, and would not take. Elee ate and drank
those of the People that hungered drew what they needed of thei
own supplies, and if cups of water tempted them, pride forbade
and the law. They took nothing, not one.

And suddenly it came, the machine voice out of the other hal
advising them of movement in the skies of Kutath. Melein spran
up, all the People rising. "Stay," she bade them, and went wit
Sen only; and in the frightened whispers of the elee, the Kel se
tled back again.

"It has come," Niun said, hearing from the other room the ad
visement that it moved their way. He reached out, touched Dun
can's sleeve. "Sov-kela?"

The void in the dus-sense filled, slowly, remarkably calm.

"We ought to go out there," Duncan said. "Not have them com
in among elee; no knowing what could result of that. I should b
out there, myself."

"So," Niun agreed.

"And you. If you would."

"I shall ask that," Niun said. Other dus-sense came to them
Taz, anxious and concerned; Rhian, who moved to join them an
sank down on his heels, silent, solid.

Ras came. "Are you well?" she asked, touching at Duncan'
arm; and Duncan murmured that he was. Strange, Niun thought
that there was affinity between these two, but there was; and Hl
drew near, who had no love of tsi'mri things . . . but he had los
his distaste regarding Duncan. Taz moved to them. *Always s*
Niun thought, *on Kesrith, that we and the beasts sat together; on
never wondered there, whose was the need.* There was a numb
ness, a blessed lack of pain, the slow song of dusei—then distur
bance, a sense of distance, of looking heavenward.

"The wild one," Duncan murmured. "It warns us. We have t
go out now. We have to go."

"Not all," Niun said. "You and I. A few hands of others. I wan
some dusei left here, for safety." He rose up, hastened unbidde

o the machine hall, stood there an instant until Melein turned her
ace to him.

"I set it in your hands," she said, "and Duncan's. They are com-
ng in."

Elee watched them in their passage through the halls. The
kel'ein ignored elee in their haste, hands empty of weapons; and
Duncan spared them only an anxious glance, white, blue-eyed
aces which stared at them forlornly and listlessly and perhaps . . .
perhaps had self enough left to worry for their own brief lives and
not for their treasure. He shuddered at them. They shrank away in
equal terror whenever a kel'en brushed close to them.

And when it was clear they meant to go out, a frightened group
of the jewel-robed citizens held up hands to stop them, hastening
o show them a door that they might use, well-hidden in a trio of
carved and living stones.

"They are jealous of their glass walls," said one-eyed Desai,
when they were out in the dark and free. There was a muttering of
laughter, for mri hated barriers, borders, and locked doors. The
way that they had come in, letting the wind into the halls . . . that
was a satisfaction to them, mri humor, equally grim.

Dawn had begun; it was a logical time for meetings, and the
logical place was before them, the wide expanse of sand between
the city and the carved pillars: room enough there for landings.
Duncan walked, and Niun stayed beside him, with the others at
his back, nothing questioning. The sand ahead writhed and rippled with life which fled the ward impulse of their two dusei. And
when they had come most of the distance he stopped to wait.

Niun stood close, having moved between him and the wind.
Desai did so from the other side, setting a hand upon his shoulder;
and the ja'anom, for they were mostly ja'anom in the company,
stood as close as they might, as if to shelter him, caring for him as
for a child. He was always colder than they, and they seemed to
realize his tendency to chill.

Sometimes, Niun had taught him early, a kel'en might find
himself regretting friendships out-of-House, caught in a tangle of
obligations and debts: best never to form them. When one did,
there was one clear law, one service above other services, and that

was the she'pan's will; if one was mri, one believed that. There were two lights in the sky, brightening steadily out of the north.

"Shuttle's aboard, bay one," the secretary reported.

Koch took note of it, impatient, more interested in the flow of data from *Santiago,* which had moved closer to Kutath, within the critical limit. Regul visitors aboard were not to his taste; not now. They were here and they had to be welcomed. Averson would be coming up at any moment, to handle interpretation where needed. He had prepared information to satisfy regul curiosity and quiet their fears. Degas was scanning what further materials Averson planned to send the allies to be sure they were clean and clear of sensitive items. That was a hasty job, and critical. And it had to be ready; with regul on the ship, they were out of time.

He reached for the panel, coded in Degas's office.

And suddenly alarm lights flashed red.

"Sir," the bridge cut through. "Damage to landing bay one."

He stabbed the reply button, ignoring other lights which began to flash on his board, an urgent pulse from Degas's channel, the muffled babble of information from the operations contact. "The regul shuttle? Was it involved?"

"Yes, sir; we don't know details, we don't get com down there; the whole bay is breached. Casualties undetermined. Cause undetermined. Crash team is on its way, and med and security. The section sealed."

"Sir," Zahadi's voice overrode. "*Shirug* is moving our way."

Panic slammed into him. *Fire,* instinct advised him, xenophobic; politics was more cautious. "Get in touch with them," he said. "Advise them keep clear. Advise them we're doing what we can with the shuttle and they're to stay back."

A moment passed. He opened contact with Degas. "Take charge in-ship," he said, and broke off. His eyes were on scan, where each sweep jumped them nearer. There was a tiny blip out of *Shirug*'s front, a shuttle, flea-sized between the warships.

They were not stopping.

"Bai," said a regul voice suddenly. "This is youngling Ragh, favor, bai. What is the situation? What has happened to the shuttle? What is the extent of damage?"

"Stand off, *Shirug*. Stand off at once. We don't know what has happened down there yet. We do not permit any closer approach. Stand off or expect strong action."

"Were there deaths, bai Koch? What of casualties?"

Koch darted a glance aside to scan, stabbed in a code for *Santiago*. RECALL. RECALL. CODE RED. "We are determining that now, youngling. Who is in command of *Shirug*? Was bai Suth on that shuttle?"

There was silence from the other end. The regul were at the limits of their shield; if they came closer, *Shirug* itself would penetrate that critical perimeter; it was fire or permit approach. The shuttle was already inside it.

Peace or war, on a word, an act.

"Sir." It was Degas, breaking through on red-channel. "Sir—"

"Back us off!" Koch ordered Zahadi. *"Up shields!"*

They hit maneuver without warning. Lights flashed everywhere on the boards.

"We don't have full shielding," Zahadi's voice returned. "The damage in bay one—"

There was a shudder in *Saber*'s framework. Scan flicked to another image, pulsing warning. The shuttle within their perimeter was coming at the base line, at their kilometer-long midsection.

"Fire on the shuttle," Koch ordered. "Fire!" And then a second look at rapidly altering scan.

All the instruments jumped; a shock quivered through frame and hull like the blow of a fist.

"Hit," command relayed. "Damage—"

"Localize command!" Koch shouted into com, handing it to Zahadi entirely. He reached for the desk, for the restraint.

Scan went out.

Suddenly pressure hit, and red dissolved to white like the tearing of a film.

They were dead. He had time to know that.

The ships came in, one, and the other of them, in close sequence. The Kel regarded this with no outward show of emotion . . . this their first close sight of ships, and strangers who had struck at An-ehon, at them, and killed kin of theirs.

Two ships. They had expected one.

"Let me go out alone," Duncan asked, received in reply a pres sure of Niun's hand on his shoulder.

"When they are in full sight," Niun said, "then whatever yo will. In this, you say what should be, sov-kela."

The hatch of the first was opening. Men came down, with black scarves tied on their blue sleeves—strange combination to m eyes; and masks which made them fearsome, like machines; las came a familiar woman, small and broad and wearing a gol scarf.

"Ai," muttered the kel'ein at one breath, for none sent ou sen'ein to a prospective quarrel; it was a good sign.

"She is Boaz," Duncan said, "sen-second. I know her."

He touched his dus, to bid it stay, walked forward on his own The second ship had opened its hatch, and a black man stoo alone in the hatchway; he did not know him, only the two: Boaz and the man by her, whose tangled reddish hair he recognized de spite the masks.

"Boz," he said in meeting. "Galey."

"Duncan," Boaz said, and drew down her mask to speak breathing the thin air. "Do we get the meeting we came for?"

"Come with me; bring all your company with you."

"We leave a guard," Galey said.

"No," Duncan said softly. "You do not. Lock no door to a mri That is the way of things."

"Do it," Boaz said.

"Boz—"

"You can't have it by human rules," said Duncan. "Maybe yo can speak to the she'pan; I will do as much as I can in that regard and likely you can; but an argument will diminish your chances Come. Don't delay here."

"Trust them?" Galey asked.

"You might," Duncan said, "if you could explain your meanin to them. A mri is himself; trust that. It's all you will get. *Shon'ai* they say: cast and catch. You cannot play the Game with a close fist. And you lock no doors to them; they never will with you. It' important to realize that. Come. Come with me."

"It's what we came for," Boaz said to Galey and the two me with him. "Haven't we taken worse chances, with less assur ance?"

Galey nodded after a moment. "Do you want our guns?"

"No. Just come. Keep your hands off them. And if you know any names among them . . . be wary of using them."

"Niun is here?" Boaz asked. "And the she'pan?"

"Expect no recognition. Likely he would not remember at all. He is not grateful for human help; and some of it was not help, Boz. You know what was done to him. Do not presume any gratitude or any grudge. Come."

"Harris!" Galey shouted across to the other ship. "All of us out. Come on out and leave the hatch open."

There was some hesitation at that; they came down finally, and the hatch stayed open . . . three men in that group.

Duncan turned and led them across the sand to the black line of the Kel. There was neither welcome nor threat. Hands stayed visible and at sides.

"He is Niun s'Intel," Duncan said to Boaz at that meeting. "Kel'anth of the ja'anom tribe and of the she'pan Melein. The city is elee, but you have nothing to do with them. The kel'anth understands all that you say; don't expect him to admit to human speech: it's enough he comes out here to meet you."

"Offer him and the she'pan my respect and my thanks for meeting us," Boaz said. "We appreciate his courtesy."

Niun inclined his head, but in the same moment kel'ein moved out toward the ships. "Hey," Galey exclaimed in outrage, and two of his men moved hands to weapons.

"No!" Duncan said sharply; and before Galey could object further, for mri hands were equally poised, and quicker: "You have lost them, Galey. Let it be. You can fight challenge: that is what they offer. Or I don't doubt you could walk away into the desert, with your weapons and provisions. *Owning* things, except what one can wear . . . this is not their reckoning. If you have a point, it is much wiser to come in and talk about it."

Galey slid a look at Boaz. She nodded, and Galey signed his companions to let be.

"The machines," Duncan said in the hal'ari, "belong to their authorities. They feel offended, but they were sent to talk, and they agree to come and do that."

"Is that translation?" Niun asked dryly, who had understood every word. "They are very eloquent."

"I know these two," Duncan said, "Boaz and Galey, and they have known you. They feel some obligation to reason on that account."

Niun's eyes flickered, memory, perhaps, of a long nightmare. "And these others?"

"If Galey chose them, they are sensible. And if Boaz is here, it is her choosing. The mri have no better friend among humans."

"Ai," Niun said, and with a darting glance toward the human company: "Walk with us," he said in the human tongue. "We ask."

"Sir," Boaz murmured, glancing down in courtesy, and gestured the others to come.

There was an easier feeling as they walked along, amber eyes which acquired expression, which frankly admitted curiosity. They had not gone far before whispers began to be passed in the Kel, remarking on their varied looks and statures and their clothing and their manners, which, for all it was not courtesy, was a step toward it: mri would discuss a man long before approaching him.

Easier, Duncan thought, moved, *that they have become used to me;* for one said: *Our Duncan knows them,* as if that settled some essential question.

They neared the city, and the open doors. Then Duncan recalled the elee, and that matter, opened his mouth to explain.

Suddenly there was an impulse from the dusei, a vague disturbance. He stopped; Niun did, likewise troubled . . . looked skyward at the same instant Duncan felt the same impulse. The whole Kel had paused, looked, whether by curiosity to them or that they also felt it, the darting apprehension.

"Duncan?" Boaz asked.

"Niun," Duncan said, a sinking feeling in his gut. "Something's moving in. It's not the she'pan's alarm. It's out there. The outwalker sees it."

"Tsi'mri trick," Niun exclaimed.

"What is it?" Boaz asked louder, and then stopped, for there were visible now two dots in the sky, eastward, for all eyes to see.

"Regul," Galey breathed, which needed no translation. "O God, *they're* downworld too. Duncan, the ships . . . the ships . . . caught on the ground—"

"Go!" Niun shouted suddenly, and pushed at Galey, toward the shuttles. Galey ran, nothing questioning; the black man spun about unhindered and ran too; and the others after, all but Boaz, for Duncan seized her arm. "Desai!" Niun shouted. "Run tell the kel'ein let them go at once—*run,* kel'en!"

He gripped Boaz's arm too hard; he realized it and pressed her hand instead, held it for comfort. He might have gone . . . *he* . . . but the hal'ari was between him and such ships, hands not in practice, mind divorced from such realities. He watched; it was nightmare, the slowness with which frightened humans could run in advance of oncoming ships. The two stranger ships were distinguishable now, coming fast. Desai sped to the kel'ein by the ships in advance of the humans; and the kel'ein let them through, Galey's to the nearest and the black man and his crew to the second, the kel'ein already running back as the hatches sealed one after another. The ships were obscured for a moment in their own dust . . .

. . . lifted.

"Ai!" the Kel exclaimed, sensing the import of that race for the sky; the ships streaked up, aloft.

"They have made it," Duncan said past the tautness in his throat. He realized the grip of Boaz's hand on his cold fingers, saw the ships roll and evade, the oncoming craft veering aside.

One human ship headed for them in pursuit; the other kept climbing, up and up, and beyond sight.

"He's going for help," Boaz cried. "Duncan, they're not ours, I swear they're not; and he's after help. Tell them that."

"Truth?" Niun asked.

"Boaz believes it," Duncan answered. "And she could well know."

Niun spun about suddenly, gestured the kel'ein toward the doors of Ele'et. "Come. Quickly!"

They moved, Boaz panting into her mask; Duncan seized her arm and belt and dragged her along; kel Merin took her other arm, and they entered the city corridors, past wide-eyed elee faces, nigh running, which mri did not do.

Dus-sense enveloped them, Boaz's fright, Niun's pain, his own . . . it was one. They had too many enemies, and too little of time. The odds had come down on them.

Came suddenly a shriek of air and the hall beyond exploded in shards of rock and glass.

They were hit. Something had gotten through.

"Run!" Niun shouted. They plunged through wind-borne smoke and over glass and blood-soaked elee bodies, for Melein and the rest of the Kel sat trapped at the heart of it.

"She'pan!" Rhian exclaimed at the shock, but Melein stood firm within the circle of light, staring up at the screens, trying to stay with the flow of data which poured out from Ele'et, and the voice which reached out to them, as desperate as the voice about her.

"She'pan," it said through Ele'et's voice, sexless, magnified, human. "She'pan, are you there? Do you hear?"

"I hear," she replied.

". . . under fire. Requesting . . . the firing. . . ."

"Repeat," she said steadily, for all that the foundations of Ele'et quaked, and glass shattered. "This attack is not our doing, human sen'anth."

""Regul," the voice returned, audible for the moment. "Do you understand that? Regul warship. . . ."

"This is Harris," another cut in on the frequency. "I'll get him. Galey's gone for—"

"There was abrupt silence. "Harris?" the human voice pursued.

A light vanished from the screen. Fire shook them.

"Strike at the aircraft," Melein said. "Ele'et, strike!"

It vanished. The screen was empty.

"Regul fire," the human voice continued, appealing to her. "Orbiting . . . if you have weapons . . . them. . . ." The voice went out in prolonged disruption.

She looked about her, at anxious faces, at ruin in the hall beyond, shattered pillars, broken glass and carvings. "Return fire!" she called to the machines. "All cities, return fire to any ship which fires at us."

It would destroy the cities; there was no hope; she knew it.

"Not in range," the remorseless voice of Ele'et replied. "Seeking target."

"It is your doing," Abotai wailed, from without the circle. "Pull us out! Pull us out of the network! Ele'et is worth a thousand of the other cities. Bate the power and hide us."

"It is irony," Melein said. "You are honored to become warriors in the world's last age; and you avoided it so zealously until now."

"Ele'et!" Abotai cried, and lunged forward into the light, at her. Melein sprang aside, startled, looked up at the flash of a firearm in an elee hand . . . moved, kel-quick.

Kel Mada sprang for it; his body took the shot; and an instant later the sweep of a path'andim sword cut the elee Illatai half asunder. Abotai screamed, and Melein spun on her heel at the sting of something from back to arm; struck, with a shout of anger, and Abotai sprawled in her jeweled robes, neck broken.

Elee screamed in anguish; some fled; some struck blows with glass shards. And Hlil and Ras and Dias were instant with a fence of blades. Dusei launched themselves. What elee were within reach of those paws died worse than the others.

A section of the board went out, a city dead.

And by that dead panel, the Husband and the she'pan-second died. Kalis of the ka'anomin killed them, and the several elee who had fled, armed, into that corner.

"Coming up on target," the city Ele'et droned. "Priorities: shields or fire?"

"Shields," Melein said at once. She had killed; white-robed, she had struck in anger; she was dazed by that enormity—at the touch of sen'ein, who seized up her arm and tried to stanch her wound she realized that blood was running freely off her fingers. And beyond the hedge of kel'ein were others . . . Niun was back; and Duncan; and with them a strange small woman. Melein stared at her, at success and failure at once, while the city rocked with fire which sent the sound of breaking glass everywhere at once. She flinched, as they all did, despite dignity, stood still again as a sen'en bound her arm.

"Your ship is under fire," Melein said to the human who wore sen-color. "I have spoken with your sen'anth. They accuse regul; two ships lifted from here; I permitted. But one was destroyed."

"We are holding the way open," Niun said, came to her, took
her good hand. "Come. Please, let us get you out of this place
while there is time."

She hesitated, reason persuading her that he was right; and if
there was Sight, he was wrong. She leaned upon it, that inward
turning which she had constantly distrusted.

Intel's kind of madness, she thought; it had launched them in
the beginning, a she'pan's vision.

"Come!" Niun pleaded with her. "If this can be fought, humans
are fighting it. For once, we cannot."

"We can," she insisted, but reckoning the cost. She turned from
him, and from the sne'ein, looked up at the machine. "Ele'et. Location of the enemy. Show me."

Screens leapt to life. She saw the world, and a point above it
which flashed in alarm, another point, stationary, a third, indistinct.

"Fire on ships which fire at Kutath."

"They have passed this range," Ele'et said. "Coming up over
Le'a'haen. La'a'haen priorities: shields or fire?"

"Fire," Melein said. The membrane hazed her eyes a moment,
cleared again. She watched the steady advance of the enemy.

In time another set of lights began to flicker on the boards.

There was nothing for the moment, only the dark and the stars
and change-over. Galey struggled with suit-fastenings, locked on
his helmet; it was an exhausting exercise in the tight space of the
shuttle, trying the while to keep an eye to scan.

"Not getting anything," Shibo muttered, fussing with com with
one hand and working at his helmet with the other.

There was, ominously, something on scan.

It was *Santiago,* by its size; and it gave no answer to hailing.

"Where's *Saber*?" Kadarin asked. "What's going on, that
Saber's not up here doing something? They wouldn't have let
regul through to us."

"Didn't let them, I'm thinking." Galey freed both hands, kicked
in full toward the silent object in scan. Computer signal raised
nothing. "No more com," he said. "Hold it. Let's give no one anything we can help. All we have for protection is being too small to
spot."

They had visual finally, stark shadow and stark metal-glare in the light of Na'i'in. It was *Santiago,* hard to recognize, for the black shadow was in the wrong places on its hull, and it was rolling very slowly, describing its own peculiar dance about the globe of Kutath.

"Dead," Shibo whispered through the suitcom. "O God, we're up here with nothing. *Santiago, Saber* . . . both gone."

"Not our regul allies," Kadarin said, a thin, cold sound. "They're here, I'm betting, somewhere around the curve. Pounding the surface into rubble. And *Flower* . . . *Flower*'s all we've got can get us home."

"What do we do?" Shibo asked. "Sir?—We dive back down there?"

Galey took several quick breaths, trying to think, with nausea heaving at his stomach. "The regul have to be close in," he said. "If *Shirug*'s firing on the surface, they have to be close in as they can get; and they don't like to do that." The silver and black hulk of *Santiago* filled all their view now; he put the shuttle under comp, to match with its roll. From the others there was not a word, only careful breathing hissing over the suitcoms. It was an ugly operation, matching the tumbling hulk; comp did most of it. He jerked control back again at the last, contacted the flat plane aft with a jolt and grappled, trying not to look out the ports or at the screens which tumbled and spun with them.

"We're going in?" Kadarin asked. "Its armscomp can't have lasted."

"Easy," Galey muttered, his mind too muddled for argument. He applied power carefully, biting blood from his lips as the shuttle strained to control the derelict, sliding and grating metal on metal. It began to have its effect, a gradual stability, easing over to come level in the concealment of shadowside.

"We got us a ship," Shibo muttered. "And what, sir?"

"Hang to it," Galey said. He heaved himself out of the cushion and slung hand over hand aft, toward the hatch. "I'm going in to see if the E-system's active. If I can move her, we'll see."

"What are *we* supposed to do?"

"Aim her; keep her straight at them."

Shibo's voice and Kadarin's exclaimed protest; he did not stop, did not argue orders; it was not a thing that bore thinking, what there was left for them to do.

Shirug was due over that horizon sooner or later, downworld from them.

He was acrophobic, always had been, mildly. He seized a hand-jet from the locker, vented himself out the lock, looking steadily at *Santiago*'s surface and not the stars, nor Kutath. There was no need to use the lock for entry; the gaping hull afforded access. The big ships were never meant to land, fragile compared to the tough downworld probes and the shuttle-workhorses: she had blown badly. The blackness inside was absolute, and his light showed barren ruin . . . no bodies, no gee, no power, no atmosphere, dead metal. He used the handjet in total dark, walls and bulkheads and hazards careening insanely past in the momentary contact of his suit lamp . . . fended a jagged edge of metal with his boot, bounced a wall in his haste, hurled himself through a hatchway and against another hatch. He used manual, and it opened, without the blast of atmosphere he had braced for. There was void, gaping ruin here too: the bridge had blown. Comp was down; the cold had got it. One light still showed, a red eye in the dark, on a panel at the right.

"Got some life," he sent back into the static. "E-light's lit. Think I can get her moving. You ungrapple when I do. Get yourselves downworld."

There was faint acknowledgment. He eased over to the panel. His stomach kept trying to heave and he swallowed repeatedly, sweating in the suit and cold at the same time. He found the whole progress of it like a bad dream; kept thinking traitor thoughts of taking them all and diving downworld to live: they did not know, in fact, whether *Flower* herself survived, whether the whole exercise had any use at all for anyone, any use.

Only he was *Santiago*'s sometime pilot; she was his ship, and there was no one else.

Think job by job, he urged himself, held the handgrip. With a punch at the glowing button, other lights flickered in, an emergency-powered trickle of life in the vital systems.

Waiting: that was hardest. He held still, staring at the panel and trying not to think at all.

"You need help?" a thin voice came, lifeline to reality. "Sir?"

"Stay put, you copy? You see if you can't line us up real carefully when they show; I don't know what I have for directionals: you're my guidance. And don't you miss. Or hang on too long. I'll do what I can for myself."

There was prolongedsilence.

"Shibo, you copy?"

"I copy clear, sir. We'll do it."

And a moment later: "We got a ship in scan, sir. Think it's *Shirug*."

A small anomaly fixed to the flat surface of a dead ship, a hulk which had been gently rolling: he hoped the regul were paying more attention, for a few moments, to Kutath. He imagined the angles for himself, the curvature of the world, the likely course of the regul over the major sites. Hoped . . . hoped, that it was not for nothing.

That was the hardest thing: that he would never know.

He looked out, holding the handgrip, letting his body drift until he could see the stars beyond the rent . . . the vast deep. He suffered the old inside-out wrench, the down-up-sideways of the senses trying to remember which way was which. It was a trick of the mind, human stubbornness. He knew with a curiously certain sense which way Kutath lay; goblin whispers urged at him, stirring at his neck.

Down . . . as far as a man could fall.

There was a shifting of the stars which attended movement, a fine adjustment.

"Now," Kadarin's voice hissed. "God help us."

He pushed the main thrust in, and *Santiago* started to move in earnest, with the emergency systems full. It was meant for pulling a crippled ship out of proximity to some mass; it was good for one long run.

"Closing," Kadarin's voice said. "Straight as she bears, sir."

"Cast off!" he shouted into com, sick at heart. "Cast *off!*"

Fire flung the bridge into blinding white. He reckoned he had done what he could, scrambled hand over hand for the gaping hole forward, one desperate chance.

A black wall blotted out the stars before him. It was *Shirug*.

Fire hit again, flung him back, drifting, with cold spreading through his legs.

"Evade!" Suth screamed into the unit, felt the wrench as *Shirug* made an abrupt maneuver.

"Fire does not stop them," the youngling voice of command wailed, breaking in panic. "They do not react—"

There was impact. It grated, rang through the whole of the vast teardrop; the sled-console went chaotic.

"Eldest!" Nagn cried; and Tiag and Morkhug tried to break through on their channels, drowned in static.

"Leave orbit!" Suth ordered. "Witless, leave orbit!"

There was no response. There was a lightness, a feeling that the least movement would unbalance things, his own great bulk, the sled itself, for all it was locked down.

"Command!" he ordered. Across the room the youngling Ragh, ghastly in its pallor, attempted to reach him, holding to furnishings which were fixed in place.

"Command!"

Nothing responded.

"See to it," he bade Nagn. Fearfully she detached from safety, trundled across the carpet, disappeared from his vision. Ragh reached him, held to the sled, moaning.

Gravity was not what it had been. Suth sat very still, his hearts persistently out of phase; there was sudden silence, the air circulation cut off.

Eventually the lights dimmed. He punched buttons frantically and received only chaos.

"Youngling!" he cried, but Ragh had sunk down by him, huddled down in a ball, out of his reach. "Youngling!" he kept shouting and punched buttons until he knew that no one would answer.

Then he began in his terror to go to sleep, to slow his pulse deliberately, shutting down, for there was a strange sensation of descent, whether truth or madness he had no experience to know. He wished not to know.

For a considerable time they would descend, as the orbit decayed.

All but a last handful of lights went out on the boards. Niun watched, crouched, his arms about his knees, in this dimmed hall which they held at the cost of lives. Duncan was by him, the dusei, and the others of his comrades of the several tribes. The doors were guarded, that to this room and that of the one beyond, all that they did hold securely, for the elee found courage to fight when their treasures were threatened, and no few of them had distance-weapons.

Melein turned from the machines, in the dimming of the world's cities, of Ele'et itself; signaled wearily. Young kel'ein hastened to bring her a chair and she settled into it, bowed her head, her injured arm tucked against her, a silence in which none dared intrude.

The woman Boaz was there, sitting in the corner where elee dead had lain . . . and mri, until kel'ein had carried out all the dead which profaned the she'pan's presence. An elee robe sheltered the human, for she was beyond youth by some few years, and very tired, and the air was, for a human, cold. Niun had ordered that himself, the plundering of a dead elee, of which they had numerous.

Outside was dark, night fallen . . . dark in the hallways of broken glass and shattered monuments, where elee scurried about gathering possessions, furtive scavengers, armed with distance-weapons, in which they had no great skill, but then, the weapons needed little. Some of them had come into mri hands. *Honor does not forbid,* Niun had told his Kel plainly. *If tsi'mri fire them at you, fire back, and do it better.*

They learned aim very quickly; and practiced on injudicious intruders.

More such fire came from outside. The sen'ein Boaz lowered her head into her hands, looked up when it was done. "Is there no talking with them out there? Could I try?"

"Tsi'mri," Niun muttered.

"Tsi'mri," Boaz echoed him. "Is there no talking—ever—with you?"

"Boz," Duncan said, "be still. Don't argue."

"I'm asking them something. I want an answer. I want to know why they don't want to reason . . . why a hundred twenty-three worlds are dead out there, and this one has to be added to the list. I want to know why. You face regul, and you take on the elee and us too. Why?"

Niun frowned, anger hot in him; he took a moment, to gather self-control.

"I answer you," Melein said, startling him. "You ask me, sen Boaz. Of the dead worlds?"

"Why?" Boaz asked, undaunted when she should have been. "Why? What could make a reasonable species do such a thing?"

Niun would have spoken, but Melein lifted her hand, preventing. "You were at Kesrith, sen'e'en?"

"Yes. I was there."

"What happened there . . . to the mri?"

"Regul . . . turned on you; we had nothing to do with—"

"Why did regul do this thing, when regul do not fight?"

"For fear."

"That we would go away?"

Boaz grew quiet, thought proceeding in her dark and human eyes. "That they couldn't control you any longer; that you . . . might go to us. That you were too dangerous—to leave loose at the end of the war, not obeying them."

"Ah," said Melein. "And when the People have served, sen Boaz, always we ask a place to stand, where only our feet and theirs walk; when the agreement is gone, we go—The dead worlds, sen Boaz, . . . were *ours*. You have seen Kesrith. In Kesrith—we defended while we could; at Nisren—we might have left regul service, and did not, to our great sadness—I suspect, because we had no means to rescue a thing . . . very precious to us. We used regul; we took a new homeworld. Nisren is a dead world; Kesrith is almost so. Who made them dead? We? You are the killers of worlds. Among the hundred twenty-three . . . are many Nisrens, many Kesriths. And you have come to make another."

There was profound silence. Of those who could have understood, there were three, but dus-sense translated something of it, that sat in the anguished eyes of Boaz, of Duncan.

"We have lost the shields," Melein said in the hal'ari. "We might survive another pass here; the living rock is over us here, and more stubborn than stones that hands have set. But I think of the camp, of Kath and Sen. We cannot send a messenger to them from here, through the elee; and any who tries to reach us will be murdered in their treachery. I weary of this place. The rocks outside can shelter us. And reaching them . . . cannot be too difficult, with the walls broken out. We will go there. We will learn whether our Kath and Sen survives. And you other tribes, go, if you will, but I ask otherwise."

"Let us," said kel Rhian, "send messengers each to our own tribes, to know how they fare. But the hao'nath stay."

"So do the ka'anomin," said old Kalis. Other kel'anthein nodded, Elan and Tian and Kedras.

"What for our dead?" asked the path'andim second. They mourned their kel'anth Mada, and no few of their number, for in their rage at the elee, they had been forward in the defense. "They will be butchered by elee hands."

"Can the ja'anom dictate to any?" Niun asked. "We go with weapons in our hands and as quickly as we can, to protect the she'pan. We do not quit serving when we are dead; for me, if I fall, I am glad if the elee waste their strength on me, and if my brothers save what I would save if I lived."

"Ai," muttered the path'andim. "We hear."

"Ai," the murmur ran the room. Niun stood up, and Duncan, and all the others, sen Boaz last, and uncertainly.

"We are leaving the city," Duncan translated for her.

"Our ships will come," Boaz insisted, looking from him to Melein. "We should wait *here*. They will come and help, she'pan."

"Then we should be alive when they come," said Melein, honoring her with a touch of her hand. "Come with us, sen Boaz. Walk with our Sen."

She opened her mouth as if she would dispute; and closed it, bowed her head. When they prepared to go out, she wrapped her elee cloak about her and adjusted her mask, and set herself where other sen'ein put themselves, inward of the Kel, with Melein.

Swords came out, a whisper of steel. For his part, Niun drew both gun and kel-sword; so did Duncan; and those who possessed elee weapons held them ready. They walked quietly into the next room, where path'andim and the patha of Kedras held the door.

"They are massed out there," the patha second said softly, "all in hiding. Behind the pillars, behind the rocks both small and large. Some of the dead are not dead, to our reckoning, but wounded who fear to move."

"Ai," Niun said, taking that danger into account. "Then we make sure of them."

"We are at your back," said Rhian. "We follow ja'anom lead."

"Aye," said Kalis. "I am senior and I say so." There was a whispered agreement of other voices.

"Then follow," Niun said. He moved, first kel'anth, first to go, with the others at his back. He laid down fire and fire came back: someone by him fell, and his dus screamed rage and scrambled forward into that dark hall with a pace he could scarcely match on the polished floors. He fired where he saw fire; by his side was another with a gun, and another dus: Duncan, Duncan was by him, a kel'en well-accustomed to this manner of fight.

The dusei hit glass, breached the walls into the moisture of the gardens, admitting the Kel; elee fired from cover there and then fled. More fire came from the door beyond, and of a sudden one of the dusei roared with pain and lunged forward, gone berserk, a madness the others caught, and the youth Taz with them. Taz plunged ahead, riddled with elee fire, and took several elee in the sweep of his blade before more shots brought him down.

"Yai!" Duncan shouted at the dusei, bidding for sanity . . . Ras took a hurt: *they* felt it; and Taz's maddened dus plunged into elee like the storm wind. Niun went after it, holstered the failing gun and hewed with the sword whatever opposed him, foremost of a wedge which broke and reformed around the monuments, the carven stones, the statures, sweeping the hall of life.

There were exits; they did not take them . . . rushed, killing, as the dusei killed, after Taz's beast, for its kel'en was dead, and it was mad. Dus-sense filled the halls, the elee fled, screaming, abandoning weapons, casting off the weight of their jeweled robes, whatever hindered them; the Kel ran over broken glass and pools of blood and the jeweled fabric of elee garments.

"Out!" Niun cried, trying to break from the madness, that felt like desertion. The dus was dying; it wanted . . . *wanted,* followed the essence of Taz into the Dark, and drew the living Kel after.

He stopped, buffeted by bodies of his own kel'ein, seized at them, turned them for the open air, for the nearest breach in the walls, and out into the clean wind and across the sands. Dusei joined them. They ceased running outside, walked, with the dusei among them. Niun walked backward a moment, taking count . . .

saw the white form of Melein; felt Duncan safe, and all the others
dus-linked, all alike filled with horror for the beast which still
pursued its crazed way apart from them, ranging the shattered
halls of Ele'et, screaming its anguish and killing. Sen Boaz was
with them, half-carried by two kel'ein, her elee robes stained with
dark gouts of blood, but none of it, seemingly, her own. Melein's
white was stained with more blood, as all of them reeked of it.
They walked, a space apart from the city, up a slope to the carven
rocks of the hills, where the hurt and the old might sink down and
breathe in safety, ringed about by weapons.

The dusei crowded together; they who were linked with them
did so, and Niun sank down among the others and held to his
beast, its blood on him, for it was burned and glass-cut and shuddering in its misery.

Of a sudden there was a break, a cessation of hurt, like storm
lifted.

"It is dead," Duncan said hoarsely, and Ras and Hlil and Rhian
of the hao'nath held close to their dusei, shivering with them.

"Mi'uk," Niun said. "Dus-madness. It almost took us all into
the Dark. Gods . . . gods . . . gods."

His mind cleared, still numb, remote. He pushed himself to his
feet, the few steps to Melein's side, to kneel and take her hand,
frightened for her state of mind; but the calm came from her to
him, a slight pressure of her fingers, a steadfast look. "What
loss?" she asked him.

"Kel Taz; his dus—" He looked about him in the dark, questioning with his look . . . heard names others murmured, of those
left behind.

Dias was lost, and Desai. He bit his lip, sorrowing for him in
particular. A double hand of the ja'anom had perished; four hands
plus two of the path'andim including the kel'anth Mada; one hand
three of the patha; Kalis of the ka'anomin and two hands of her
kel'ein; a hand three of the ja'ari; two hands one of the mari; four
hands two of the hao'nath.

"My blessing on them," Melein said, looking suddenly very
tired, and drawing her wounded arm more closely to her side.
"Now we must see how the camp fared."

"Better than here," said a voice, very young and female. There
was a stirring from the hindmost ranks near the rocks, and an un-

scarred, veilless, worked her way through in haste. She knelt
down by Melein and bowed for her touch . . . looked up as Melein
lifted her head with her fingers.

"You are—"

"Kel Tuas, Mother. Kel Seras sent us, when the fire stopped;
it came near, but never hit the camp; I do not think it hit it since.
I ran and hid in the rocks, to see what I could learn: my truebrother . . . went in. And I do not think by what I saw—"

"He did not reach us," Melein said.

"I thought that was so," Tuas said very faintly. "I have
waited—some little time. May I carry word to Seras, Mother, that
you are safe?"

Melein took her face in her hands and kissed her on the brow.
"Are you able, kel'e'en?"

"Aye, Mother."

"Then run."

The kel'e'en sprang up and returned the kiss, turned in blind
haste; but Niun caught her arm, took an Honor from his own
robes and pressed it into her cold hand. "Kel'anth," she murmured. She was ja'anom; he recalled her now, an innocent like
Taz. The tribe was vital; it lost lives and gained them again in the
young.

"Run," he said. "Life and honors, kel Tuas."

"Sir," she breathed, and parted their company, passed the ranks
of those gathered about, serpent-quick. She was not the only messenger sped; others ran out, through the hills, shadows, young and
swift of foot.

And those of them who remained, settled, reassured for what
small news they had, that Ele'et had drawn the fire and the camps
gone unscathed. They caught their breath, began to bind up
wounds: Niun felt a growing ache in his lower arm, and found a
bad slash, which Duncan bound for him. Ras had taken a wound
in the shoulder, and Hlil attended it; Rhian had taken a minor hurt
on his arm; there was hardly a kel'en in all the company entirely
unscathed, and the dusei moaned and keened piteously with their
own hurts, burns and lacerated paws. None of them would die,
neither dus nor kel'en. Dusei licked at their own wounds assiduously, and at wounds of kel'ein where they might. Niun accepted
it for his own, and it helped the pain.

Sen Boaz sat among them. "Are you hurt?" Duncan inquired of her, but she denied it, sat bowed, breathing great gasps from her mask, her elee robe wrapped about her and glittering with precious stones in the starlight.

And it was not the only such robe in sight.

"Look," said Rhian of the hao'nath, pointing toward the city, where elee stirred forth, pale faces and white manes and jeweled robes showing clearly in the dark among the huge rocks about which Ele'et had its shape.

"Let them come," kel Kedras said, "if they have gone entirely mad. I weary of elee."

"Aye," a number of voices agreed, and Niun himself sat with the blood pounding in his temples and an anger for the dead they had lost.

But the elee below wandered the near vicinity of their city as if dazed, and some of them were small: children. The anger of the Kel fell when they realized that, and the air grew calmer. Kel'ein talked then, grimly, but not of killing.

Niun bowed his head against his dus and felt all the aches in his body; and those of the dus; and those of the others. There were moments when dus-sense had no comfort to give, when the beasts needed, more than gave; and he comforted it such as he could, with a gentle touch and what calm of mind he could lend.

"They do not come," he said at last to Duncan. "Neither regul nor humans. Gods, I do not know, sov-kela; I think—" He did not dare to voice despair; the Kel was about them. He slid a glance instead to the human sen'e'en. "She says they will come; but she does not know. Ai!" he said sharply, looking up, and all the company looked heavenward. For a moment he both hoped and feared.

A star fell in the west, over the basins.

That was all.

"They will come," Melein said.

"Aye," they all murmured, as if hoping could make it so.

Duncan settled down, and Ras, and Rhian and Hlil; he did, and laid his head against the shoulder of his dus, for warmth, and for comfort of it. The dusei made a knot, all touching, spreading warmth even beyond their circle.

Only the lightness, the shyness which had been Taz s'Sochil was gone from them. Somewhere up in the hills was the wild one, the only wild one.

There should be one, Niun thought, one which went apart.

"Ai," someone murmured, toward the dawning, and *Ai!* came the cry from the height where the sentries sat.

The whole Kel came awake, and Niun scrambled to his feet as the dusei surged up, among the others. Melein stood, and the sen'ein, and the human Boaz, last and with difficulty . . . eyes lifted toward the skies.

It began as a light, a brightening star overhead, that became a shape, and a thunder in the heavens.

"Flower!" Boaz cried; and if the Kel did not know the name, they saw the joy. *"Ai,"* they cried softly, and excitement coursed through the dusei.

The elee below had seen it. Some which had come out to spend the night at the edge of the ruin fled indoors again. Others ran for the rocks, their fine robes and white manes flitting as a pallor in the dawn.

Then *Flower* came down, ponderous, ungainly, settling near the city; it extended its strange stilt legs and crouched down to the sand like some great beast. The dusei backed around behind the shelter of the line of the Kel and moaned distress, snorting in dislike of the wind it raised.

The sound fell away; the wind ceased, and the whole ship crouched lower and lower, opened its hatch and let down the ramp.

Waited.

"Let me go down to them," Boaz asked.

There was silence.

"If we say 'go,'" Melein said finally, "you enter your ship and go away—and in what state are we, sen Boaz? Without ships, without the city machines, without anything but the sand. Humans would understand our thought . . . at least in this."

"You want to bargain?"

There was another silence, longer than the first. Niun bit at his lips until he tasted blood, heat risen to his face for the shame that mri should face such a question.

"No," Melein said. "Go down. Send us out a kel'en who will fight challenge for your ship."

"We don't do things that way," Boaz protested. "We can't."

"So." Melein folded her hands before her. "Go down, then. Do what you can."

The sen'e'en looked uncertain, began to walk away, with more than one backward glance at the beginning, and then none at all, hastening down the slope.

"They are tsi'mri," Duncan said out of turn. "You should not have given her up; she would have stayed. Call her back."

"Go to them yourself," Melein said in a faint voice, "if you see more clearly than I. But I think she is much like you, kel Duncan. Is she not?"

He stood still.

And after a little time the sen'e'en Boaz did, halfway down the slope to the ship. She looked back at them, then turned to the ship again, cried out strange words, what might be a name.

In time a man appeared in the hatch, came out, and down the ramp. Boaz walked toward him. Others came out, in the blue of the human kel'ein.

They stood in the open a time, and talked together, Boaz, a man who looked to be very old, and two like those who had been with the kel'en Galey.

Then they turned, with Boaz and the old one arm in arm, and began to walk up the hill, toward the People, bringing no weapons at all.

Chapter Eighteen

Boaz came. Duncan was glad of that, on this last morning . . . that it was Boaz who came out to them.

He ceased his work, which was the carrying of very light stones, for the edun which should stand on the plain of the elee pillars, in this place where the game was abundant and elee machinery still provided water. He went out from the rest, dusted his hands on the black fabric of his robes, weaponless but for his small arms, as the mingled Kel generally went unburdened in this place of meeting. Ja'anom, hao'nath, ja'ari, ka'anomin, mari, patha and path'andim; and now homa'an, kesrit, biha'i; and tes'ua and i'osa, up out of the depths of the great western basin, three days' hard climb . . . all the tribes within reach lent a few hands of kel'ein to this madness, this new edun on an old, old world; and to the she'pan'anth Melein, the she'pan of the Promised.

Even elee, who could not leave their ruins, who languished in the sun and found the winds too harsh for their eyes and their delicate skins . . . labored in their own cause, retreating by day to shelter, coming out to work by night, peopling the plain with strange stones, statues, likenesses of themselves, setting their precious monuments out in the wind and under the eyes of mri and humans, as if to offer them to the elements, or to strangers, or simply to affirm that elee existed. They did not come near the tents of mri or the edun; would not; never would, likely; but they buiit, that being their way.

Six hands of days: the edun walls stood now high as a kel'en's head. They began to build ramps of sand to ease the work, for it would someday rise high as that of An-ehon, to stand on a plain of statues, a fortress against the Dark.

"Boz," he greeted her as she came, and they walked together, khaki clothing and kel-black, casting disparate shadows. His dus moved in, nudged at Boaz, and she spared a caress for it, stopped, gazing at the work.

"Galey should have seen this," she said.

"I will tell you a thing," he said, "not for your records: that among things in the Pana of the mri, in the tables . . . there are three human names. His is one." He folded his hands behind him, walked farther with her, past the lines of children of the Kath, who carried their loads of sand for the ramps. "Yours is another."

She said nothing for a space. Beyond them, the tents of the camp were set, shelter until the edun should rise, and that was their direction.

"Sten. Come back with us."

"No."

"You could argue the mri's case . . . much better than I. Have you thought of that?"

"The she'pan forbids."

"Is that final for you?"

"Boz," he said, and stopped. He loosed his veil, which kel'ein still would not, before humans . . . met the passing shock in her eyes, for the scars on his face, which had had time to heal. And perhaps she understood; there was that look too. "Between friends," he said, "there is no veil. Truth, Boz: I'm grateful she refused."

"You'll be alone."

He smiled. "No. Only if I left." He started again toward the tents, put down a hand to touch the dus which crowded close to his left as they walked. "You'll do well for the People. I trust that."

"We're going to set markers up there; you'll not be bothered by visitors until we can get through."

"Human visitors, at least."

"Regul didn't get the tapes, only the chance to tag us, and that information died here so far as they're concerned, along with their chance. I don't think, I truly don't think human authorities are going to make free of mri data where regul are concerned. It was unique circumstance that brought them with us. It won't be repeated."

"We will hope not." He veiled himself again, half-veil, for they walked among the tents, among kath'ein and children. They were expected at the tent of the she'pan; sen'ein and kel'ein waited there, and walked in behind them, through the curtain.

Melein sat there, with a few of the sen'ein about her; and with Niun, and Hlil, and Seras, with two more of the dusei.

Hlil rose as they walked in, inclined his head.

"You do not have his service," Melein said to Boaz, "but he will be under your orders as regards his presence on your ship. He is my Hand reached out to humans. He is Hlil s'Sochil, kel-second; and the beast that is Hlil's: it goes with him too."

"We thank you," Boaz said, "for sending him. We will do all we can to make him welcome."

"Kel Hlil," Melein said, kissed him and received his kiss, dismissal; and from that distance: "Good-bye, sen Boaz."

It was dismissal. Formalities between mri and tsi'mri were always scant. Boaz gave him one look, a touch of the hand, walked away alone, and Hlil summoned his dus to him, paused to embrace Niun, and walked after.

Only beyond him he paused yet again, at the curtain, to look on a certain kel'e'en. "Life and honors," he bade Ras, lingered a scant moment, walked on, with wounding in the dus-sense. By Melein's side, Niun gathered himself to his feet. But Hlil had gone, with brief reverence to the Holy.

"Permission," Ras said, a thin, faint voice. "She'pan."

"You ask a question, kel Ras?"

"I ask to go."

"It is not," said Melein, "a walk to the rim and back. And do you serve the People, kel'e'en—or why do you go?"

"To see," she said; and after a long moment: "We are old friends, she'pan, Hlil and I. And I ask to go."

"Come here," Melein said; and when she had done so, took her hand. "You know all that Hlil knows. You can agree with my mind. You can do what I have bidden Hlil do."

"Aye," Ras said.

Melein drew her down, kissed her, was kissed in turn, let her go, with a nod toward the door. "Haste," she said.

Ras went, her dus after her, with a respect to the Holy and a quiet pace: she would surely have no difficulty overtaking a small, plump human.

Melein sank back in her chair, looked at Niun, looked out at Duncan, and suddenly at other kel'ein, with a quick frown. "Ask among all the Kels," she said. "Quickly: whether there is not one in all this camp, a kel'e'en who will go with them, that they can have a House. Kel Ras is right; they ought not to be alone among strangers."

It was the kel'e'en Tuas who went, who went striding out to the human ship in the last hour before their parting, and the camp turned out to wish her well; paused again in its labor when the ship *Flower* lifted, to watch it until it was out of sight.

"They will see Kesrith," Niun murmured, that night before they slept, in Kel-tent.

"Would you have gone?" Duncan asked. "Have you not had enough of voyaging?"

"A part of my heart went." Niun sank down on his arm, and Duncan did, and the dusei settled each at their backs. There was now besides them, only Rhian's, in the hao'nath camp, and the wild one, somewhere in the far north. "I have wondered," Niun said, "why the dusei chose . . . why ourselves, why Rhian, why Ras and Hlil, and Taz. I thought it might be for your sake, sov-kela; you have always had a strange way with them. But look you—look you: they chose those who would go out. Who would meet strangeness. Who would look longest and deepest into the Dark. That is how they always chose. I think that is so."

Duncan did not answer for a moment . . . gazed at the dus, at him. "No more. Only we hold it off here. Long enough."

"We wait," Niun said. "And we hold it off."

It was a larger city, after so many years: sprawling buildings and domes and covered avenues in the place of regul order. The scent of the wind was the same: acrid and abrasive; and the light . . . the red light of Arain. It must have rained that morning. Puddles stood at the curb before the Nom, and Boaz stopped a moment to stare about her, to reckon with change.

The three kel'ein with her did not make evident their curiosity. Doubtless they were curious, but they were under witness, and did not show it. It was much from them, that they all came, leaving the dusei on the ship . . . her asking.

Governor Stavros was dead, years ago; she had learned that even while *Flower* was inward bound. And there were changes more than the buildings.

"Come," she bade her companions, noting sourly the escort of military personnel which formed for them, with guns and formalities; she had her own, she reflected with grim humor. They walked through the doors of the Nom and into the once-remembered corridors, into a reception of officials, outstretched hands and nervous smiles for her, simply nervous looks for her tall companions.

"The governor's expecting you," one advised her, showing her the way to offices she remembered very well without. She went, and the kel'ein walked after her.

Stavros dead; and more than Stavros. The uniforms were different, the official emblems were subtly changed. There was a moment's feeling of madness, to have come back to the wrong world, the wrong age. There was a new constitution, so they had said at station: civilian government, a dismantling of the powers that had been AlSec and a reorganization of the bureaus; a restoration of institutions abandoned in the war, as if there was any going back. Kesrith had become a major world, an administrative headquarters for wide regions.

For a moment she yearned for Luiz, for his comfort: and that was gone. He had died by a world of a yellow star, whose name humans did not know, and probably the kel'ein did not . . . died in jump, still lost in the vertigo of no-time, in a place where human flesh did not belong, between phases. Luiz had always leaned on the drugs. She had, until the last, that she and some few of the crew risked what the mri did, to take jump without them: she played at shon'ai with the kel'ein, as the sen played, with wands, and not with weapons.

Your hands are not apt to weapons, they told her.

She blinked, offered a handshake to the middle-aged man who was introduced to her. Governor Lee.

And uncertainly Lee offered his hand to the kel'ein. She opened her mouth to warn, sensed laughter behind the veils, a slight crinkling of Hlil's amber eyes as he touched the offered hand with his fingertips. So Tuas touched. Ras would not, but stood with hands behind her; that was courtesy enough.

"Mri representatives," Lee said. "And the report is—a mishap overtook the other ships; and the regul."

"A mishap, yes," she said. "I understand regul are scarce here."

Lee's eyes slid from hers. He offered her and the mri chairs, seated himself behind his desk. Boaz sat down in the chair, but the kel'ein sat down on the carpet, against the wall where they might see the governor, which was for them more comfort.

"It is open knowledge," Lee said, "that the regul have—detached themselves. We don't know why, or in what interest. They've gone from Kesrith, abandoned worlds nearby, left every human vicinity. They explore in their own directions, perhaps. You can't answer . . . from your own viewpoint . . . or from events where you come from—*why,* can you?"

"They don't like us," Boaz said.

"No. Clearly they don't. Many who stayed here . . . many who were closest in contact with us . . . suicided." He shifted uncomfortably. "The mri envoys . . . do they understand?"

"Every word."

"They agree to peace?"

Boaz shook her head slightly. "To contact. Across an expanse wider than you imagine, sir. And regul are mightily afraid of them. A virtue—as anxious as I've heard the colonies are, out here. But the mri are explorers . . . from here to the rim."

"And mercenaries," Lee said. "On *our* side? Is that the proposal?"

"We have been mercenaries," Hlil said, "if that is the use of the hire we offer."

"But there is cost," Lee said.

"Always," Ras answered.

"What cost? In what—do you expect payment?"

"A place to stand," Ras's quiet voice pursued. "For that, the Kel is at your bidding, so long as you maintain us a world where only your feet and ours touch. And supplies, of course. We are not farmers. And ships; we shall need them."

Lee gnawed at his lip. "So you offered the regul. What benefit did they have of the bargain?"

"Ask," Boaz said, her palms sweating. "You are on the wrong track, governor. Ask *why;* ask why, and you will get a different answer."

"Why?" Lee asked after a moment. "Why do you make such a bargain?"

"For the going," said Ras very softly. "The going itself is our hire. Use us wisely, human sen'en, for we are a sharp sword, to part the Dark for you. So we did for the regul, I have heard, giving them many worlds. And when we have gone far enough, and the tether strains . . . bid us good-bye, and be wiser than the regul. We are the Face that Looks Outward. We are makers of paths, walkers on the wind; and the going itself . . . is the hire for which we have always served."

Boaz pressed her lips together, thinking for one cold moment on the dead worlds, about which human councils would have to know, the course of mri homeworlds, destroyed beneath the mri in fear, fears which had to come to former wielders of the Sword: dread that mri might serve others, one's near neighbors. Fear. Fear had killed the worlds between.

To use the mri, one had to play the Game, to cast them from the hand and let them go.

The belief that it would be different . . . this, she cherished, as she believed in humankind.

She played the Game.

It was a quiet place, the morning on the heights of the carven rocks, looking down on the plain of statues and on the Edun of the People, the heights where there was only the wind for company, the wind and the hope of dusei, which sometimes ventured in for the good hunting, to the terror of the elee.

Merai Niun-Tais hunted here many a morning, and many a morning wasted moments, in this place of the best view of all, from which one could survey all the land from the northern flats to the hazy depths of the basins westward, out of which the great winds came.

He was a dreamer of dreams, was Merai. Patience, the she'pan counseled him; he had yet to win his scars . . . save one that his truefather had dealt him in the Game, to mind him of discipline, and the vice of rashness, to venture the blades with a Master.

But each night he listened to the songs in Kel; and the songs were true. He knew that they were, for Duncan was with them, and talked sometimes, when they could persuade kel Duncan to tell them the tales; the tales made all their hearts burn to hear them, and made them look at the stars with hope.

From the days that he had been in Kath until he took the black robes of Kel he had climbed this height to hunt, and to think of far worlds . . . and secretly, to tease the dusei which came—sometimes—maddeningly close. Forlorn hope: they did not come to kel'ein now; they were all wild, all the dusei born of the great pair of the ja'anom Kel, and the one belonging to old Rhian of the hao'nath—even it had gone wild, in Rhian's passing.

There was one which came most persistently. He had hoped for it this morning, secretly, shamefully, had concealed a tidbit of meat to take to it; but it failed him. He set about his hunting, moving carefully among the rocks, skin out the creatures which sheltered at the deep places, near the watering of Ele'et.

And in hunting, he looked up. There was a star, a star in daylight, that burned.

He stood staring while the brightness became a glare, and the glare a shape.

Then he began to run, racing toward the edun, his heart pounding against his ribs. He was late to bear the news, for all the Kel had come out to see. He slowed his step in the sight of his trueparents and of Duncan; and of the she'pan, for even the Mother had come down out of her tower; and the sen, theirs of the ja'anom and the visitors of other tribes.

The ship settled, obscured in sand, crouched low and waited still for a time, until the sand had settled. Then a hatch opened, and a ramp came down to them.

Kel'ein; they were kel'ein foremost of the strangers, black-robes with dusei at their sides, three of them, striding out across the sands in haste toward the Kel.

He knew their names; they had been sung all his life. And the Kel stood still only for a moment more, then walked faster and faster to meet them, with the kel'anth and Duncan far in the lead.

PRECURSOR

by *C.J. Cherryh*

The Riveting Sequel to the *Foreigner* Series